Sword Stone Table

D1455538

Sword
Stone
Table

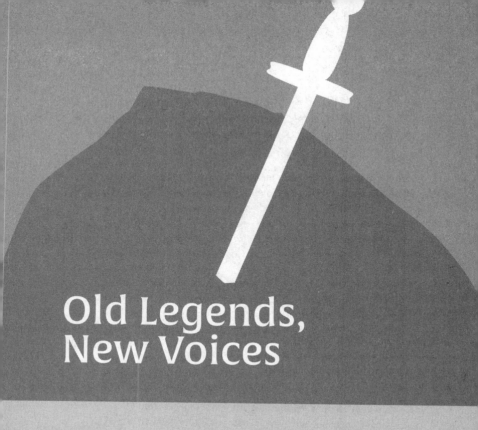

Old Legends,
New Voices

Edited by Swapna Krishna
& Jenn Northington

VINTAGE BOOKS

A DIVISION OF PENGUIN RANDOM HOUSE LLC

NEW YORK

A VINTAGE BOOKS ORIGINAL, JULY 2021

Introduction and compilation copyright © 2021
by Swapna Krishna and Jenn Northington

Library of Congress Cataloging-in-Publication Data
Names: Krishna, Swapna, editor. | Northington, Jenn, editor.
Title: Sword stone table : old legends, new voices / edited by Swapna
    Krishna & Jenn Northington.
Description: A Vintage Books original edition. | New York : Vintage
    Books, 2021.
Identifiers: LCCN 2020047488 (print) | LCCN 2020047489 (ebook)
Subjects: LCSH: Arthurian romances—Adaptations. | GSAFD: Short stories.
Classification: LCC PN6120.95.A84 S95 2021 (print) | LCC PN6120.95.A84
    (ebook) | DDC 808.80351—dc23
LC record available at https://lccn.loc.gov/2020047488

Vintage Books Trade Paperback ISBN: 978-0-593-08189-1
eBook ISBN: 978-0-593-08190-7

Book design by Nicholas Alguire

www.vintagebooks.com

Printed in the United States of America
10 9 8 7 6 5 4 3 2 1

For Dev, who is the reason I get out of bed every morning. It's not a car, but I hope you'll love this when you're old enough.

—Swapna Krishna

For my parents, the original nerds, who understood that books were as necessary to me as air.

—Jenn Northington

Contents

Introduction

Swapna Krishna & Jenn Northington

It was the summer of 2018, and we were sitting in Swapna's living room. Swapna was pregnant with her first baby, and Jenn was bursting with an idea for an anthology. "Where are the gender-bent Arthur stories?" Jenn asked. "The race-bent retellings, the queered ones?"

We couldn't easily find them—and we thought it just might be possible that not only did other people want them but also there were folks out there ready to write them, or who maybe already had.

As this collection came together over the past few years (it's hard to believe we've been working on it for so long!), it's been exciting to discover the published stories we missed and to see that we weren't alone—there's been a renaissance of "bent" Arthur retellings that we devoured. Even more electrifying for us are the authors who said yes when we asked, then proceeded to write stories that have blown our minds, knocked our socks off, and made our hearts grow too many sizes to count.

Each writer puts their own unique spin on a bit of Arthurian legend. One of the unexpected joys of editing has been watching the resonances develop among them, especially when none of the writers really knew what anyone else was working on except for barest details (character, general time frame, maybe genre). These stories have cousins and siblings the authors aren't even aware of.

ONCE

Roshani Chokshi and Sarah MacLean deliver atmospheric stories heavy with longing and bursting with romance, albeit in very different ways, both giving voice to strong women we've fallen in love with. Ausma Zehanat Khan and Nisi Shawl bring the wider world to Camelot in ways that blur its boundaries and elevate the storytelling to something larger and more global. And Daniel Lavery and Sive Doyle make us laugh, make us cry, and give us two queer couples that absolutely deserve to be canon.

PRESENT

Then there's Maria Dahvana Headley, who finds the Arthurian overtones of a muckraker in late-nineteenth-century America. Waubgeshig Rice and Alex Segura both incorporate baseball into their reimagined Arthur but in very different ways: in one, a pickup game on a reservation leads to an amazing discovery; in the other, a washed-up minor-league player finds help where he least expects it. Anthony Rapp finds magic in the throes of the AIDS crisis, while S. Zainab Williams explores that intangible search for belonging through a lonely girl in Singapore. Jessica Plummer and Preeti Chhibber both consider how it might look if a legend made itself known in modern life—with very different consequences.

FUTURE

No Arthurian collection would be complete without a look forward, and Silvia Moreno-Garcia brings us to a near-future Mexico City in a story both eerie and prescient. Ken Liu takes us even farther out, into a universe in which identity shifts from one moment to the next . . . but past mistakes can haunt you forever. A little closer to home is Alexander Chee's story, set on our neighboring planet and contemplating public versus private personas, secrets, and games.

This collection has been a privilege and a joy to curate and has shown us just how much room there is to play. We hope that you'll enjoy these stories as much as we do, and that these stories are merely the tip of the iceberg for inclusive Arthurian fiction. Everyone deserves to see themselves on the page, and even if you don't find your specific identity within these stories, perhaps you'll see some small part of yourself inside these characters and these old, and yet entirely new, legends.

ONCE

The Once and Future Qadi

Ausma Zehanat Khan

The Qadi was sitting on his prayer rug at his ease when the summons came from Camelot. Even to consider it a summons was a matter of insult, Ayaan thought, but the Qadi from Cordoba, who had grown to renown in Seville, had survived many skirmishes by refusing to respond to the needling of his pride. And patience, after all, was a much-valued quality in a jurist. Now the Qadi turned his well-shaped head up to the moon and waited for Ayaan to place the message in his hand. A man who had once studied with the masters of the Great Library of Cordoba would have no difficulty interpreting the intricate script of the Franks.

He tapped the scroll against his knee, his knuckles rubbing lightly across his beard.

"It is an honor, Qadi, to be invited to the court of the Franks. To ask you to adjudicate in the matter of his queen's fidelity is a sign of utmost esteem."

The Qadi grimaced. "When the invitation itself is an insult to his queen?"

The scribe shrugged, an easy gesture that rolled his

shoulders. "These Franks think of honor differently to us. Perhaps their women matter less."

The Qadi rose to his feet with the limber movements of a man who had performed thousands of prayers during his travels, equally at home on a mat spread out on the desert sands or under the white-and-gold cupola of the great Mezquita.

"Yet they pen such pretty odes in tribute to their maids. Their chivalry is coy. This accusation against the queen Guinevere is bold."

He gave the scroll back to Ayaan, who asked, "Will you refuse the request, Qadi Yusuf?"

Ayaan knew the Qadi as an exacting mentor. Now he put his scribe to the test. "Tell me, Ayaan, what would be the consequences of either acceptance or refusal?"

A leaping light came into Ayaan's eyes. He was sharp and capable, ambitious to a fault—qualities he knew the Qadi valued. He cleared his throat, giving his answer with no pretense of humility.

"King Arthur extends a great honor by asking you to adjudicate on a matter concerning his queen. This means he knows your name by repute and respects your judgment more than the jurists of his court. Perhaps he trusts in your discretion. Perhaps matters have become so inflamed with respect to his wife that he feels ill at ease with his court. Or perhaps the jurist whose opinion would be sought is away on a Crusade assailing our Holy Lands."

"Ah." A wry sound. "More a Christian knight than a jurist, then."

"Much like yourself, Qadi." Ayaan was not above a little flattery. "Knight and jurist both."

"Theirs is a curious court, their religion encompassing more than just the doctrine of Christ. They are poised between their pagan ancestors and their belief in a man's divinity. They have no notion of our faith—how would they contend with a jurist from Qurtaba, whose rulings are rooted in his creed?"

"Such matters are beyond my knowledge, Qadi. I assume your renown extends to Camelot, though the court may be of a world and time apart."

"Then you advise me to accept the invitation."

Ayaan glanced at his mentor with caution. "To refuse would disgrace the reputation of our people. They would call our courage into question. And before these lordly knights?" He shook his head, his tawny curls dancing. "Yet, Qadi, to accept carries its own penalties when you consider you would be judging a matter of great personal import—the honor and fidelity of a queen. This king may not be well disposed toward us, as even by posing the question, he shames this Guinevere. He will be relying on your discretion, and I do not think he will like it."

The Qadi laughed: a rich, warm sound that lingered on the air.

"So there is no choice I could make that would be sufficient."

"Qadi, your judgment has always been sound. I defer to your wisdom."

The Qadi ran a hand over his own dense, dark curls, and Ayaan took a moment to appreciate his patron's beauty. In the Qadi, all the manly graces were combined. His lineage was distinguished, his bravery keen—though he'd proved fonder of the library than of interminable and frivolous battles. He was a polymath, learned in languages, jurisprudence, theology, astronomy, and medicine, and of greatest delight to the caliphal court at Seville, he was a skilled executioner of the famous ring songs of al-Andalus. His Arabic was thick and rich, curling around the tongue, roughly, giddily beautiful, his use of language the headiest of elixirs.

He was an ornament of the Almohad caliphate—he could lull a listener with the rhythms of his voice, then spear them with his intellect, a sport he reserved for his equals, showing mercy to lesser mortals. Perhaps he was at times remote, lost in contemplation, but like his noble forebears, his judgment was tempered by consideration. He was a great favorite of the Caliph as a man who could be trusted not to curry favor. Though his attitudes were sometimes unpopular, he spoke trenchantly of the incursions of the Franks and the looming reconquest of Iberia. There was danger in such fearless honesty, but the Qadi feared only his Creator.

Ayaan thought again how fortunate he was to be taken on as the Qadi's apprentice. Consider the adventures they had shared traveling these Christian lands. And now think of the chance. To meet these knights of Camelot whose legend had far surpassed their deeds, and to lay his untutored eyes upon this queen of the Franks.

He let his eyelids droop, afraid that too much eagerness would decide the matter for the judge.

But the Qadi had begun his preparations for travel.

"Come," he said to Ayaan. "If they do us honor, we should honor them in turn."

Yusuf brought his open palm to his chest with a slight inclination of his head. The aging king received him with a greeting of matching civility. He stood tall and proud, his hair flaring silver against the backdrop of a window cased in stone, the green country rising behind him, a ribbon of purest blue dashing a swift path north. A beautiful land, this. Cool and refreshing to the eye, with mists of rain veiling the keep in layers of solitude.

King Arthur, with his regal head and lucid, visionary eyes, had asked to meet with the Qadi privately, Ayaan borne away by a group of chattering interpreters. For himself, Yusuf spoke the tongue of the Franks with a cultured accent. Now, observing the king, he could think of no means to broach the subject of the summons, though he could see the pain behind the effortless diplomacy.

The king bade him sit. Yusuf placed his jeweled sword to one side. He felt an unwilling respect for this king. Though Arthur had no personal guard, he had not insisted that Yusuf give up his weapons. Saying little, the king offered every courtesy.

"This is a matter of some delicacy. I have not accused the queen of wrongdoing, but the charge was made before the entire court, and I am at a loss to answer it." He paused. "There is a . . . coolness . . . between the queen and myself as a result."

Yusuf caught movement in the antechamber: a glimpse of long fair hair flowing over a gown that enclosed a delicate frame. The king noticed his inattention.

"The queen," he murmured. "She refuses to be set aside."

"It is a great thing to be the queen of a noble king who resides in the heart of his people. Difficult, I imagine, to relinquish."

The king became still, a curious tilt to his head. "You think her affection insincere? You have yet to meet her."

"It seems to me it is *you* who doubt her devotion. What happened to make this so, for all lands have heard the tale of the love between King Arthur and his queen?"

The king sighed, a stately lion in the winter of his years, a crown of thorns on his brow.

"She is uncommonly beautiful," he said, "and many of my knights are taken with her, though I have paid it little mind. I gave her a pin of some value—a swan studded with gemstones." He sounded impatient with himself. "When I did not see her wearing it, I asked her to pin it to her gown." His steady gaze dropped to the table. "One of her ladies produced it, and when I asked how she had come across it, the maid was stricken into silence. I turned to find the stony eyes of the queen dark upon her lady, so I asked the maid to speak."

Yusuf waited, his head angled to keep the flitting shadow in the antechamber within the limits of his vision.

"In the presence of my court, the maid claimed to have found the pin in Sir Lancelot's bed. The queen denies it, of course."

The movement in the antechamber halted. Yusuf kept his eyes on the king.

"And who did you believe—queen or maid?"

The king evaded an answer. "Lancelot went down on his knees before the entire court to swear his fealty to me. Never would he hurt me, I thought. For I have loved him like a brother."

Yusuf allowed the silence to expand, pitying the king's disillusion. Though he thought it telling that the deeper injury had been caused by the knight rather than the faithless queen.

And finally the king admitted, "Lancelot is comely beyond the reckoning of any of the knights of my court. He is much admired, a regard he is little loath to return. I cannot deny his blood runs hot."

In what Yusuf guessed was an uncharacteristic gesture, the proud king touched his tongue to his lips, seeking to relieve their dryness.

"I had thought his love for the queen was chaste, but there

were other witnesses to the discovery of my lady's brooch. And the queen herself can offer no explanation."

"Cannot or *will* not?" Yusuf was conscious of those delicate footsteps, the quietly listening ears.

The king straightened his back. He rose from his chair, and Yusuf did the same.

"You will see for yourself when you meet her. If she has a fault, it lies in her pride. She will not grace me with an answer to the charge."

"The charge of infidelity. The charge of congress with your knight."

For a moment a fine rage flared in the old king's eyes, and Yusuf felt a stab of satisfaction. He wanted the king to fight, to hold his proud head high. This air of defeat was premature and would earn his courtiers' contempt.

The king turned his head away from the shadow in the other room. "I hope your inquiry will put an end to this speculation."

"No matter how things turn out?"

He witnessed the majesty of Camelot's king in Arthur's dignified reply.

"It would hurt me to know, but rumor and suspicion are tearing this court apart." The king watched as Yusuf sheathed his jeweled sword at his hip. "Can you get at the truth?"

"If you permit me to interview the principals. I assure you of my discretion."

The king indicated the antechamber. "Please begin with the queen. I would release her from her confinement as soon as I am able."

At first Yusuf thought Arthur a king of great forbearance, but then he caught the bitterness shading the hollows of his face.

"You have already judged her," Yusuf said.

"You have not seen her with my knights." The king's expression betrayed his abhorrence for the subject.

Yusuf brought his training as Qadi to bear. "If she is much admired, surely that is a tribute to the king. You judge your wife's chastity in the absence of evidence."

"It is not a question of chastity. Guinevere is my wife. I have bedded her as I choose."

"As *you* choose? Does the lady have no say?"

"The queen knows her duty."

"If duty is all she finds in your bedchamber, no wonder she thinks to stray."

A terrible silence descended. Yusuf cleared his throat. "Do you know the stories of our Prophet?"

A fleeting surprise crossed the great king's face. "I know of your desert creed, and I know you claim a kinship to the followers of the Christ. But for us, the old ways are best."

Yusuf looked out through the window to gauge the failing of the light. It would be time for the dusk prayer soon.

"For us, the only way is God's. I mention our Prophet, may peace and honor embroider his name, because he faced a similar dilemma. His wife was accused of faithlessness, betrayed by the loss of an ornament of her own."

The king's interest was piqued. He crossed his arms over his broad chest, his feet apart as he listened. "A pin?"

"In the lady Ayesha's case, a necklace. She slipped from her howdah to search for a necklace whose clasp had come undone. Then, when the caravan she was traveling with departed, she was left behind, on her own. Her absence went unnoticed, but before the caravan could panic, a young soldier of the Prophet's army found our Noble One's beloved Ayesha and returned her to her kin."

"The lady Ayesha was questioned?"

"The lady Ayesha was accused," Yusuf said, grim, "of adulterous behavior. The whispers against his adored caused the Prophet unnecessary grief."

"Did her honorable husband doubt her?"

"Like you, noble king, he took the measured step of waiting for adjudication. In his case, the answer was divine."

A flush had risen to the king's cheeks, the line of his shoulders rigid. "And the divine response?"

" 'Surely those who accuse chaste, unsuspecting, believing women are accursed in this life and in the Hereafter. Their punishment will be tremendous.' "

There was a tinkle of glass in the antechamber. The silent queen had dropped one of her possessions—a trinket, or an object of artifice. Glass glinted on the cold stone floor.

The king's arms dropped, and a subtle fatigue eroded the strength in his face. To Yusuf he said, "The whispers will not be silenced by your scripture. I hope you have something more."

Yusuf bowed his head. "My lord, the comfort was meant for you, the inquiry for the others." And when Arthur still looked grave, he added, "You may rely upon the honor of a just and virtuous wife. But leave the matter with me, and I will determine the truth."

"You shall have an hour alone."

Yusuf held up a hand to prevent the king's departure.

"No, my lord, not alone. Protect your wife's honor at all costs. I would also defend mine. Send a soldier you trust or a member of your wife's family."

Though he knew she was listening, Yusuf did not dare to utter the queen's name. To take a woman's name was an act of presumption, an offense against her honor.

But the king regarded his request with suspicion.

"You've just told me to trust in a virtuous wife."

Yusuf spread his hands in wry acknowledgment. "Trust her, but do not allow her honor to be maligned by the whispers of others. Give this gift to your wife."

In the presence of the queen's handmaidens, Yusuf questioned the queen. He was amazed by these bone-colored women, with their hair like bedded-down straw and too much of their skin exposed above the bodice of their gowns. To a man used to the concealed graces of the Caliph's court—to lustrous-lashed women whose gemlike eyes and burnished radiance shone—these pallid maids seemed close to sickness.

He thought of the edge of a smile caught through a delicate veil. Of the coolness of a woman's enigmatic expression, of a perfume so subtle that a hint of its fragrance could drive a man to his knees. He thought of his beautiful, dark Lubna, her habitual frown of impatience, and her astonishing eyes—a gazelle captured in flight when he disturbed her attention from her manuscripts.

This glacial queen with her straw-like locks and forbidding demeanor—how could she have inspired such turmoil? A proud old king defeated, a young lion eager to be tested. She seemed frail, fine boned, and angry. But if he'd been passing judgment on the queen, standing some distance away so as not to tower over her, she had been doing the same. For a time she was silenced by the dark sienna of his skin, by his clustered curls and silky beard, by his foreign manner of dress, the sumptuous coat over his qamisa, the elegant winding of his turban, the carnelian jewel on his hand. The queen's atten-

dants sighed as they gazed at his face, and he flashed them a
white smile. They were pleasant enough in their way.

The queen was of a different order. She was dressed in a
tightly cinched gown whose deep-blue velvet softened the
chill of her eyes, her skin freckled, her hair left free to fall to
her waist in a careless spiral of curls. The gemstone brooch
in the shape of a swan was pinned to her gown between her
breasts, catching at the material. An act of defiance from a
woman who would not be accused. Yusuf glanced at it once,
then, out of respect, he turned his gaze away.

She did not blush. In a cold, rather clear voice, she asked,
"I understand you have been selected to judge the queen of
Camelot's fidelity."

How strange that she spoke to him as though removed
from herself.

"You know I am a jurist, then."

"Not of any law of Camelot's." Such a cool, clean bite to
the words, like snowflakes falling on the tongue. He waited,
sensing the outraged pride beneath the civil exterior. She bent
her head, an effort at courtesy that cost her, the fullness of
her mouth drawing tight. "Your name precedes you, my lord.
The king's court is aflutter, eager to catch a glimpse of a fabled
Saracen prince. You see the behavior of my ladies."

His gaze did not leave her face, though inwardly he knew
that, regardless of his origin, she had chosen to call him a
Saracen as a mark of her contempt.

To know us but not know us, he thought.

"Rather, yours is the fabled court."

She glanced past his shoulder to the door through which
the king had made his exit. When she looked back at Yusuf,
pain had smudged her irises, deepening the icy gray to blue.

He was beginning to find her interesting, the tension inside her wound tight, a plea beating beneath the surface, though as yet, he could not deduce its source.

Abruptly she asked, "Are you married, my lord? You spoke of a virtuous wife."

His attention sharpened. "I do have an interest, but I have not yet taken a bride."

She considered him with a frankness that would be considered discourteous at the court of Seville. This queen was no hesitant maiden. But he saw the strength in the line of her jaw and deduced that she was a woman who knew herself of consequence and was resolved to be heard.

He sought to conciliate her anger. "This questioning is shameful to you."

She raised her chin. "When one has not sinned, there is no reason for shame."

"Still. The whispers must weigh upon you." He watched her. Examined each nuance of her expression for some sign of unease. Noted the spiteful edge to the coquettish glances of her maids.

The ice queen was unheeding. "Knowledge of virtue must be its own solace."

And now the swift strike of the Andalusi blade. "Is your husband to have no solace, my lady? No refuge from the whispers?"

The blush-pink cheeks went pale. She sank into her seat, her maids to either side.

"I care for my husband more than you know."

"And Sir Lancelot?"

Her hands twisted the kerchief in her lap.

"He . . . admires me. As do all my husband's knights. You impugn me without cause."

"I merely inquire, my lady. I cast no allegation to trouble a spotless conscience."

The pale brows raised, the queen's expression haughty. But he caught sight of a band of freckles at her throat that struck him as touchingly defenseless.

"Will you use your Saracen tricks to divine my innocence?"

Another insult. To throw him off course or offered simply in the manner of ignorance that characterized these Franks?

"No tricks, my lady. A few questions, that is all." He returned to the subject of Lancelot. "What form does your knight's admiration take?"

"He dedicates his victories to me—he wears my token into battle."

Yusuf's brows drew together. "And your husband permits this?"

"I had heard some rumor that your customs are enlightened, your women more outspoken. Do I require his permission?"

The full line of his lips slackened, became richly sensual. "It is not a matter of custom. No wife of mine would be permitted to give another man her token. I would see to it she had no reason to allow her attention to wander."

He smiled to himself as a shiver stole over her sun-dappled skin, for the ice queen had cleverly placed herself in the light. Her eyes were a denser blue now, reflecting her inner excitement. A creature of buried sensuality, this queen of knights. The thought of a man asserting his rights unsettled her . . . and not only for reasons of propriety.

He ventured further, trying to draw her out. "But as a question of fairness, I would refuse the smallest attention from a woman who was not my wife."

"But you may have many wives. A harem, if you choose."

The queen's handmaids gasped at the thought, rosy with

titillation. But Yusuf's attention was riveted on the queen. A smile graced his sculptured lips, the edges raised and distinct.

He found his heart was racing, his blood heating under her peculiar air of challenge. Beneath the forms of his inquiry, a separate current flowed. "You have fallen prey to rumors. One woman is enough for me, if she is the one my heart desires."

"Your heart?" The queen sat up straight. "Forgive me, my lord, but it is rare for a man's *heart* to be involved in these calculations."

He laughed softly to bury the jibe. "Do you know this first-hand from Lancelot? Is that how he enticed you?"

He watched her hands curl into fists. For the first time, she dropped her gaze. "I resent this inquisition into my behavior. It is a judgment I have done nothing to deserve."

"The innocent have nothing to fear."

"They have *everything* to fear in a court of intrigue and deception."

His interest quickened again. "Is that how you name the court of Avalon? Your king's court? Whence the romantic tales I hear of the knights of Camelot, then?"

"Men boast of deeds that women do not ask for. Is ours only to linger and praise, hoping for their admiration?"

"There is virtue in that. Men need praise and soft arms to return to. Otherwise our deeds mean little."

"I encourage you, then, to remain idle while others vaunt vainglorious deeds."

"Surely you mean glorious, my queen."

"Do I? As you are to judge in all matters, why not judge my meaning as well?"

Very softly he asked her, "You do not enjoy these tributes, my lady? As the rightful due of a queen? You do not encourage them, perhaps? At the court of the Caliph in Seville, the poets vie to recite paeans of devotion to their ladies. Many a veil has fluttered in delight." Devilment crept into his voice. "Is this not akin to courtly love?"

The queen's mouth tightened in reproof. "From what I have heard of the ring songs of Andalucía, your poets have a gift for eroticism, whereas a knight of Camelot may admire no more than the color of my hair."

"There can be enticement in such simple things." He moved closer to the queen and drew a chair across from her, his handsome cloak resettling around the breadth of his shoulders. Her gaze touched upon his jaw, his mouth, the column of his throat, before she turned her head to the side.

"Are you afraid to look at me for fear I will see the truth?"

"You said no tricks," she whispered, catching his eyes again. "You allude to impropriety, yet when I affect reserve, you accuse me of dishonesty."

Yusuf shifted his weight in the chair, a loose-limbed, supple movement. A nervous laugh escaped from the maid seated to the queen's left.

"Perhaps I wish you to regard me."

A subtle alteration in the flow of the current. He saw her breath hitch in her chest, the pulse flutter madly in her throat, further evidence to mull. This cold, narrow-eyed queen was fully awakened to herself and not immune to admiration. But oh, how clever she was! She divined his swift conclusion and hurried to attack.

"Do you claim to feel no lust when you gaze upon me, Saracen?"

The title derided him, quashed his pretensions to rank, reduced him to one of a nameless multitude of men, all of them degenerate. How to maneuver this queen to a moment of revelation? He leaned forward. When the handmaids pretended to be flustered by his physical aura, the queen dismissed them, a frown creasing her brow. A new arrangement for the almond-pale dots across her skin, close enough for him to count.

"I wouldn't be a man if I didn't feel lust, but I am in control of my desires," he said once they were alone. For the moment he chose to ignore the arrangement contrived by the queen, in spite of his warning to the king. There would be something to learn from this clandestine contest.

"You relieve them in the beds of strumpets, no doubt, as ladies of distinction would dismiss you."

"They yield their virtue as readily as others," he said with a private smile. "But that is not the cure for any man's desire."

"Pray do not play coy." She flicked a hand at him without looking up. "In this, all men are the same." An acrid accusation that he would work to unfold before he decided on whether this queen was betrayer or betrayed.

"My people fast, my lady. I assure you, when a man has eaten or drunk nothing for nigh on sixteen hours, then spends the night in prayer, the cure is more than effective."

She proved her quickness again.

"Then when your holy season is upon you, your knights are weak in body. Any contest against you would result in your defeat. Perhaps I should pass this secret to our knights who are eager to join the crusade."

He permitted himself to take offense. "In our holy month, we are strong in spirit."

She waited. Played with the embroidered square on her lap. Drummed her graceful fingers on her knee. At last she let herself sigh, her limbs swaying like the branches of an alder in slender capitulation. "You came here to test me and have found me wanting. I will please the king through you, as he desires, if you answer a question of mine."

He gave her a courteous bow.

"This beloved of yours—the woman you would court to put an end to your abstinence, this doe-eyed sorceress of the sands, by what name do you call her?"

Yusuf laughed out loud. For a moment, the queen seemed transfixed.

"She is no seductress with undulating hips. She has no slavish desire to please me."

"No?" The queen arched a pointed brow.

"She is rather a determined scholar of the court, tedious in her passion for knowledge. Her greatest pleasure lies in mathematics. She terrifies me at times. Her name is Lubna," he added. "Though I call her my jewel-flower."

"How absurdly romantic!" The bite was back in her voice.

"Are your knights not so?" His glance was cool, pitying. "I regret that their adoration should be clumsy."

She made a sound of pain. "So clumsy that it condemns me."

He gave her a sharp look, settling back into his role as judge.

"How did your pin come to be in Sir Lancelot's bed?"

When she said nothing, he let his gaze roam her face freely, searching for signs of tension.

"You said you would give me an answer."

She held her peace, catching her lip between her teeth.

Another enticement? But he would not be diverted. Time to be bolder, then.

"Did he steal it from you in a fit of ardor?"

Silence, jagged and shorn.

"Did you give it to him?"

A thin watery film turned her eyes to glass.

"Did he wrestle it from your body while you lay at your ease in his bed?"

She stood so abruptly that her chair struck the ground.

"How *dare* you say such a thing!" She turned her back to him, her hands trembling at her sides. "Get out! I have no wish to see you again."

Yusuf waited, silent as a cat. With no sense of where he was or what he had chosen to do, she turned around again to find him one step closer.

There were no tears on that pale, proud face—just a wretchedness deep within. And that tiny, hammering pulse, beating hard in her throat.

"How did you come to miss your pin?" The question was not cold, not kind. Merely introspective.

Her fit of passion subsiding, her fingers stroked the velvet gown. "I wear it with this gown. The gemstones match its color. I did not notice its absence until my husband, the king, inquired. I did not expect an answer from my maid."

The current switched again, sharp and galvanic between them, until Yusuf reined himself in. He had used his full battery of tricks. And this queen of the Franks was no longer undisturbed. That in itself would tell him something, but for now he made to withdraw.

"The question should never have been asked," she said bitterly.

He disagreed. "Someone has to answer it. Consider the pain inflicted on a king weaving to the end of his years, betrayed by a much-praised wife and a knight whose skill and renown would seem to outflank his own."

But his plea failed to soften the queen's outrage.

"If the king did not consider me *then*, why should I care for him now?"

Yusuf shook his head. Bitter seeds had been sown here, poisoning the idylls of the king. But this queen, too, deserved some of his consideration.

He was ready to take his leave when she said, "I am not like your Prophet's beloved. I would not agree to be sent from his side in silent, long-suffering rebuke." Her sensuous mouth firmed. "I will not allow others to vilify me in silence." Her hand touched the pin at her breast.

A smile quirked Yusuf's lips. "I fear you misapprehend the story of the necklace."

She raised her eyebrows, waiting, and cleanly he delivered the rest.

"The lady Ayesha spoke up."

They broke bread together at a long table set some distance above the fabled Round Table, where Arthur's knights were held as equals to the king, a tradition that pleased Ayaan, echoing as it did the teachings of the Prophet on the inherent dignity of man. He considered this as he remained in attendance at the Qadi's side. Here, men and women dined in company with one another, displays of chivalry mannered but sincere. A hush of laughter and appreciation rustled down the table, while, released from her confinement, the queen sat at one end like a marble figure carved for deployment on a chessboard. She wore the same gown, and the gem-studded swan blazed between her breasts—a fiery finger pointing, but at whom? The graying king or Lancelot?

The Qadi was very much on his dignity as a noble at a foreign court, and Ayaan strove to imitate his manner, trying not to peer like an uncouth juvenile at these tall, fair knights of such repute. He was not without his share of attention, complacent in his good looks, the thickly curled lashes and drowning eyes that he used with artful aplomb. He was young and virile; why should he not turn the heads of these ladies and their knights? Still, his behavior would reflect on the Qadi, so he stifled his desire to flirt and seduce and tried to sit like his mentor, dignified and gracious, taking an interest in the conversation of the court.

Many of these knights had been on the Crusades, and now they traded genteel barbs with the Qadi. Mention was made of the great Saladin and his unmatched superiority in tactics: a general wise and brutally accomplished, though known as much for his tolerance. Homage was paid to the Prophet, and salutations were offered for the Christ. But through the thread of mutual courtesies, the presence of the queen, who from time to time would meet the eyes of the king and his court, cast a pall on a convivial gathering. Ayaan kept darting quick little glances at her. Though the brooch she wore blazed like an accusation, he was more intrigued by the delicate construction of her face, the features regular, the skin like spoiled milk dashed with tiny flecks of brown. She caught him at it once and pursed her lips and looked away.

The Qadi touched his arm, and the two men excused themselves to pray in an alcove away from the altar positioned in the center of the hall. A curious altar made of broken stone, it was overgrown with brambles, a pair of splendid antlers poised above it.

Ayaan gave a delicate shiver. These Franks and their strange practices! There was a little of the pagan about them, despite their avowed interest in the search for the Holy Grail.

He laid out the Qadi's prayer rug in the alcove, which looked out over a tranquil lake with a twilight mist upon it, an image composed of ghostly grays and blues. But for all its serenity, he missed the luxuriant palms of al-Andalus, and the gleaming orange orchards of the capital. The fare of the Franks was plain, their gardens cool and unscented.

The prayer finished, the Qadi turned to ask him what he'd learned, and Ayaan was eager to oblige. Gossip abounded at court. Ladies and knights were caught up in pleasurable scandals of varying degrees of seriousness, though all professed to share in a fulsome regard for the queen.

"You didn't find anything out of place? No hints from their dialogue with you?"

"My lord," Ayaan said with dignity, "they may have *professed* admiration, but I have learned a trick or two from you."

The Qadi thumbed his string of turquoise prayer beads, some part of his spirit always seeking a state of grace. "Continue, habibi."

Flushing with pleasure at the endearment, Ayaan told him, "This Lancelot is provocative, Qadi. He teases the maids and is known to trifle with their affections, for all that he is considered the most honorable of knights. Jealous entanglements abound. And of late, the ladies of court have come to resent his gallant attentions to their queen."

Ayaan had not been able to resolve these inconsistencies in Lancelot's character in his own mind, but he was certain of the Qadi's greater skill.

"Do any stand out in terms of wishing to dispose of a rival?"

Ayaan was never disappointed by his mentor's acumen. "Yes, Qadi. The lady who found the brooch in Sir Lancelot's bed had just tumbled from it herself."

"Ah." The Qadi looped his beads around his wrist, stroking the silk tassel. "And what of this knight Lancelot?"

Ayaan settled himself more comfortably on his prayer rug. It was often a source of bafflement to him that his mother had sent him off to join the Qadi with a blue-and-ivory carpet of Esfahani silk purchased from the markets of Baghdad, while the Qadi performed his prayers upon a simple mat of reeds. The offer to exchange carpets had been met with a gentle rebuff; Ayaan had felt the need to apologize for his mother's extravagant taste.

"Did she pray on it before she gifted it to you?" the Qadi had asked. Indeed, his mother had done so. So the Qadi had told him with the smile that heightened his dangerous allure, "Then you are all the more blessed for praying in your mother's footsteps."

The Qadi was always surprising him with his regard for women.

Now Ayaan hastened to enlighten him about the whispers that surrounded Lancelot.

"These knights consider themselves a brotherhood of equals, but that does not mean envy and resentment do not simmer beneath the surface. They admire Lancelot's courage and his devotion to the king, but they also see in him a narcissistic bent. He is one who enjoys being stroked by the praise of men and women both."

"Is it merely praise he enjoys?"

Ayaan pretended to be shocked. "Qadi!"

On an undercurrent of laughter, the Qadi said, "My boy, I am trying to determine whether Lancelot is so dissolute in character that he would seduce his queen. Have there been witnesses to episodes of lust?"

"None," Ayaan answered at once.

"Ah." He waited as the Qadi gathered his thoughts toward a simple conclusion. "You should have seen her, Ayaan. She was seething with outraged pride. I thought she might be timid and ashamed; instead she was hurt and angry. It is difficult to conceive of how this queen could have let herself become the victim of suspicion, or the quarry of a conspirer."

"You think her innocent, Qadi?"

"I think it strange that the king should say of his lady wife: 'You have not seen her with my knights.' A noble king wronged, a favored knight an adulterer, a jealous, deceiving handmaid, and an ice-queen overcome by lust. The puzzle must yet be worked. I will see this maid in due course but will speak to Sir Lancelot first. Ask him where he would prefer to speak, or whether he wishes to testify in the matter of his own honor."

Silence would speak to guilt, but consent could also function as a form of deception, this one conjured by vanity.

Lancelot, the prince of knights, was altogether unexpected. Pride, conceit, and a seductive arrogance had been suggested to Yusuf by Ayaan's tales. Lancelot in person was comely beyond description, personable and warm, with a convincing air of frankness. Following the king's example, he treated Yusuf with courtesy. Tall, handsome, dark haired, and well formed, his physical beauty was staggering. Pale skin, black hair, blue eyes—an entrancing violet-blue better suited to a maid, the irises large, the pupils crisp, the whites untainted and clear. He was so stirring an example of male beauty that Yusuf marveled at the Creator who could fashion such a man. No wonder jealousies and intrigues roiled beneath the surface of the court. And if the knight was as good as he was brave, there would be many jealous of his stature. And what of the noble king? Could he be oblivious to the impact of such beauty on his wife? The Prophet be honored, why were these Franks so keen to let other men praise their wives?

Another thought came to Yusuf's mind as he watched expressions chase across the handsome face. Lips so lush they belonged on a bride on her wedding night, eyes that were vivid with self-mockery and intelligence, hands that were shaped to be anointed with jewels, though he wore only a plain silver band. Could a man of such unmistakable allure be tempted by a cold-eyed queen who, though fair, made no more of an impression than a hundred other women? Or was it her unattainability that made her desirable to men?

"You have been accused of adultery." Stark words, but a gentle opening.

They had been walking in the gardens leading down to the lake, and now Lancelot came to a halt, his lips parted as he thought of a response. Obligingly, a bower of lilacs dropped its blooms on his head, petals like tiny flowered stars scattered through the silk of his hair.

The violet-blue eyes were dazzling in the moonlight, but a hint of calculation appeared beneath his charm.

"I regret that the accusation was made against the queen. As in your own lands, I am certain, the penalty is harsher for women."

Yusuf chose not to enlighten him otherwise. The knight's approach was intriguing, all tender concern for the queen, so little thought for himself.

Yusuf issued another salvo. "Have you been conducting an iniquitous affair with the queen of Camelot? Has your behavior dishonored the noble court of your king?"

Lancelot's brows drew down. In anger he was even more striking, passion mottling his skin. A vibrant color to his voice, he said, "You seek to provoke me into self-betrayal."

"I seek the truth. Can you offer an explanation of how the

gift of the king—the gemstone pin—came to be found in your bed?"

Through his strong white teeth, Lancelot said, "'Tis a plot against Camelot. You see how it has weakened the king."

A strange remark to make before an Andalusi who would soon return to the Crusades.

Yusuf studied Lancelot's costume. His armor was absent, his tunic elegant, his sword sheathed at his side. His remarkable appearance required no other adornment, and yet—

"I am told by many that you chased the favor of the queen, wearing her tokens into battle. I see that you do not wear them now."

Lancelot offered a mannerly reply. "It would hardly be appropriate given recent events."

"Yet the queen wears her pin so boldly it cannot be mistaken."

His comment could have been taken as censure of the brave knight's courage, but Lancelot passed the insult over. Instead, he countered, "She always wears it with that gown."

The pool of silence expanded, the pale arc of the wings of sparrows flashing as they drove down to the lake. Yusuf let Lancelot consider his previous statement a moment or two longer, then he said, "Your admiration of the queen is causing comment. Forgive me for saying so, but in the court of our Caliph, the queen would attract no more notice than a serving girl."

"You offer an insult to your hosts," Lancelot snapped. "Guinevere requires no defense, but since you find her plain, know that her true beauty lies in the grace of her soul."

Yusuf resumed their walk, Lancelot at his back. Only when they had reached the lake did he cast a glance to his side. "Then you have seen into Guinevere's soul."

"You are impertinent, sir, to refer to the queen of Camelot by her name!"

"My apologies. It is not a custom of your court, then?"

A terse shaking of Lancelot's head.

"Then why, may I ask, did *you* call the queen Guinevere? To speak the queen's name, to peer into her soul—these are signs of intimacy between the queen and yourself."

Lancelot gave a meaningful sigh, his elegant hand resting on the pommel of his sword. His fingers tightened on the grip. Making nothing of it, Yusuf took a step away.

"It went too far," Lancelot admitted after some while. "I meant to pay her court in order to please the king. But others did so as well, and I confess my pride was stirred. I wanted to outdo them. Greater tributes, dazzling victories, to lay at the feet of the queen, to pay homage. Guinevere mistook me. She was . . . seduced. Much to my shame, I dallied with her awhile."

"Dalliance? Is that all there was between you?"

The knight rocked back on his heels, his words edged with discomfort. "Though a great and righteous king, there are some duties that Arthur is no longer able to fulfill. The queen is young and fair. She is not yet bereft of desire."

"Then you were doing her a kindness."

"You mock me." A dangerous note crept into Lancelot's voice.

The Qadi demurred with a gesture of his hands. "I'm trying to understand."

Lancelot watched him closely. "No sooner had I given in to my lust than I felt the weight of my betrayal. I was forsworn, my honor tarnished. But the queen could not be dissuaded. Her entreaties grew more insistent. To discourage her, I let her find her handmaid in my bed. I hoped that would end the matter." He shook his head to himself, a cynical twist to his lips. "Guin believes in timeless love, whereas I am always searching for a new horizon."

Yusuf sifted through the surprising confession.

"And the pin?"

Lancelot shook his head again, with a gesture of self-contempt.

"She may have lost it in my bed. Or others may seek to discredit either the queen or myself—perhaps both of us. I did not think Guin capable of putting up a front, yet she is the very picture of a grievously injured wife."

He turned back to the path to the castle atop the hill.

"The harm is done. I will leave Camelot soon on my quest for the Grail. Perhaps my departure will spare her."

But Yusuf concluded that, in truth, the one the knight hoped to spare was himself.

The Round Table had been deserted by its knights, the lanterns lit, the Pendragon pennant blazing behind the throne. The great hall was quiet, the mood in the chamber dark, a tormented frown engraved upon the king's heavy brow. He had asked the Qadi for his ruling: the time had come for Yusuf to speak.

Five people were seated at the table in place of the complement of knights. A space between King Arthur and his queen; Lancelot close to the king's right. And the Qadi and Ayaan seated together across from the other three; the table bare of artifice, as stark as the judgment to come.

"What have you come to tell me?" the king demanded.

"Nothing that will give you peace."

"Has the queen confessed?"

Yusuf glanced at Guinevere, who stroked the swan at her breast with breathtaking self-possession.

"The queen would not give me an answer. She feels her integrity should never have been called into question."

The king glanced at his wife, the faint light of hope in his eyes.

Yusuf didn't tarry; it was cruel to deceive the king.

"Sir Lancelot was more forthcoming. He blames himself for going too far with his attentions to the queen."

"Going too far?"

Even the king's great dignity was no proof against revelation. His shoulders sagged, his gaze turning inward, a tremor in his age-spotted hands. The tremor became more pronounced when he shaded his brow with one hand, concealing the turn of his thoughts.

Yusuf prayed the king would not give way to a weakness that would earn him his queen's contempt.

His tone contemplative, he offered, "Your queen is young and fair, and likely lonely through your long campaigns. If your knight sought to comfort her—"

"Please. Say no more." The king stood, drawing out his cross-hilted sword. He strode across the hall to the altar, where he placed the sword beneath the pair of antlers. He censured Lancelot with a glance. "Your quest to find the Grail will falter. It is only for the pure of heart, but still I would ask you to go." He studied the fabled sword he had placed upon the altar. "I would not take up arms against you, as I must if you remain."

Lancelot threw himself at the king's feet, a haunting break in his voice. "Forgive my betrayal, my liege! I love no one so much as you!"

The king turned away. "I cannot count myself grateful."

Guinevere rose, her pale fingers tapping the table. Slowly she said to the king, "You would believe Lancelot's account in lieu of your own wife's? What of the innocence of Ayesha?"

"You gave no account, my lady. And it seems this court has forsaken the mercy of the divine. I do not expect revelation to grant me a virtuous queen."

The weariness in the king's answer pained Yusuf. If the wound to a stranger was deep, how could it be borne by those who held him beloved?

A mirror hung at one end of the hall, and the king moved to face it. He studied his listless reflection, the fraying gray mane, the eyes without ambition.

"I have grown dispirited in the years of my decline." His eyes met his queen's in the mirror. "Although I should not blame you, I do. I thought I had earned your devotion."

"As I thought I had earned yours. Yet on every campaign you led away from home, you found yourself a Camille."

The king waved this away.

"Then you sought to repay me. You *meant* to do me injury."

Bitterly Guinevere said, "I did not know I held that power. All it took for your loss of faith was for your swan to glide away. I cannot demonstrate chastity again to win back your belief."

She glared at Lancelot, a rare beauty in her fury.

"The lies you tell will come back on your head. And as for you, my lord, send me to my kin, or to anywhere else you choose."

"*You* choose." The king had already dismissed her. "As long as I need not look upon you again."

The ice in Guinevere's eyes burned the Qadi where he stood as she turned her anger on him.

"You ruled against me because I spared you my blushes and

did not tremble at your lust. So much for a man's justice, no matter his name or creed."

She whirled around and made for the door, her long hair flying like a banner.

Yusuf felt only pity.

"Follow her," the king said. "Speak to her. Console her if you can."

Yusuf was taken aback. Could the king still consider his wife's sensitivities in light of her infidelity? Or was he conscious that his own conduct would not withstand further scrutiny?

Yusuf gave a courteous bow, wishing now that he'd declined the invitation to intrude upon the sorrow of the king.

The queen ripped the pin from her gown and flung it at Yusuf, even as courtiers whispered in the stone passageway.

"You were always disposed to believe them over me." She flung out a hand at the brooch, which had landed at his feet. "Take it as a memento of your victory."

Yusuf gathered up the pin. Without touching her, he shepherded her to a bench in the gardens where rumormongers would not hear.

Her face had flooded with humiliated color, her bony fists were clenched in her lap; he could almost believe her a woman mortally harmed.

"The truth was victorious, not I."

"So you judge me." Her icy composure was lost, her voice throbbing with rage.

"I was brought here to judge you, after all."

"You fell under Arthur's spell!" she accused him. "And under Lancelot's, as well."

He did not join her on the bench, but his dark head was inclined to hers.

"Would you rather I had fallen under yours?"

For a moment he thought she would fly at him, raking his beard with her nails. But like the queen she was, she collected herself, gathering her poise about her like a cloak. Speaking to herself, she said, "I am to be sent away."

"You have caused a great king pain." An observation, not a judgment.

She tilted her head up, the cold eyes meeting his, searching for a truth he could not fathom.

"What of the pain he caused me with his indiscretions? Does that not signify in the world governed by men?"

Holding her gaze, he said, "You accuse your husband of disloyalty in return?"

"He began this," she said quietly. "My actions are a wound to his heart, a wound he feels deeply, yet he gives no thought to my pain or to my loss of . . ."

She changed her mind about confiding in him, the words trailing away.

"Yes?" he prompted. "Your loss of face, perhaps?"

She shook her head, trapped despite herself by the desire to justify her course.

"My loss of innocence." She waved one hand to indicate the court. "I believed in this—all of this. The chivalrous court of Camelot, the honorable king, with justice and plenitude for all. But there was no justice for me."

Yusuf could not dispute it. He fell back on pragmatism.

"Such are the ways of men, my queen."

She flared up at once. "Am I meant to meekly accept them? Am I meant to swallow my pain while the king indulges his? My heart was a fallow field, susceptible to Lancelot's advances."

At the mention of Lancelot, Yusuf's thoughts became grim. He turned her earlier words regarding men's lusts back on her.

"I doubt it was your heart that spurred your dalliance with Lancelot."

He heard the sharp intake of her breath, but she turned her face away, the line of her jaw trembling.

After a moment, she said, "I had heard that the court of the Caliph rivaled Camelot in grace. I did not think the Saracens vulgar."

When he had nothing to say to this, she continued, "I was trying to be just to myself."

Yusuf was shaken by the Qur'anic echo. Made knowingly or as an arrow in the dark?

Playing his part as Qadi, though he was thinking of her as a man thinks of a woman, he said, "In doing so, you have only harmed yourself."

She came to her feet, surprising him by grasping his hand and closing his fingers around the gemstone pin. Just as swiftly, she released him.

Her ice-blue eyes swimming with tears, she told him, "At least this time, the injury was of my choosing."

She would have left him then, without another word, but he detained her with a hand on her arm, returning her pin to her palm.

"Then that must be your consolation."

Their eyes met and held, the silence between them deep and dangerous.

She wrenched her hand away, discarding the brilliant swan.

Her lip curling, she said, "I hope your princess savages your heart."

Ayaan and the Qadi had left the isle of Avalon and were riding through the night side by side, their cloaks dampened by the ever-present mist, the moon as sallow as their thoughts.

Ayaan let out a whistle. "I cannot quite grasp at the truth, my lord. From how piously she spoke, I could swear the queen was wrongly accused by both husband and knight. Yet why would a knight like Lancelot otherwise condemn himself?"

"You thought the queen innocent?"

Ayaan jerked on the reins of his mount, bringing it to a halt. "Didn't you?"

The Qadi reined in as well, his knees urging his horse.

"I thought her ruined, her heart as bitter as an orchard under frost."

This quieted Ayaan, whose love for women ran deep, his tenderness awakened by a glance.

"She was so small and proud. It took courage to wear the pin when every member of the court sat in judgment and her favored knights turned away."

"Ayaan," the Qadi said patiently. "The queen betrayed herself at every turn. The court spoke of her keenness for admiration, Lancelot's gallantries exceeded even the most tolerant rules of chivalry, and a king who had little time for his wife was dismayed by her conduct with his knights."

"Isn't that how these Franks define their courtly love? With these little courtesies?"

"Was it courtesy that saw her lose the brooch pinned to her favorite gown?"

Suspicion began to tick through Ayaan's thoughts. "What do you know that I don't?"

"Very little," the Qadi said dryly. "Apart from Lancelot's confirmation, I spoke to the queen's maid. There was a taint of bitterness to the queen's protestations. I found myself unconvinced, just as I found her receptive to my earlier advances."

He petted his restless mount, subduing it into silence. "Guine-vere was twice spurned, once by her husband, once again by her lover. Remember that Lancelot spoke of her entreaties. He came to his senses swiftly; it was Guinevere who fell."

Ayaan stared at him, agape. "Qadi, how do you know this?"

A smile touched the Qadi's lips. "I am observant, my son, that is all. The queen was quick to imagine intimacy between us. She is starved for physical affection. When Lancelot dis-carded her, she took her grievance to the maid to whom he'd done the same."

By now, Ayaan was goggle-eyed. "The *women* conspired together?"

"Altogether more convincing if the brooch was found by a maid—her name is Lisette—who was reluctant to accuse her. Guinevere gave it to Lisette. The rest was a fait accompli, to use a phrase of the Franks."

"My lord, *why*? The shame to the queen was dire!"

The Qadi touched his heels to the flanks of his mount.

"For the king who had rejected her fidelity by betraying her first and for the knight whose ardor proved false—she refused to accept that their days would end in glory, even if she had to spite herself." He shook his head to himself, murmuring a prayer on the wind. "Were it not for my respect for the king of Camelot, my heart would suffer for this queen."

But this was more than Ayaan could comprehend.

"An adulteress? A brazen, bare-faced liar?"

"Ah, but you see," the Qadi explained, "she was driven to it by the king's disloyalty. As for the chivalry of the knights of the Round Table and their notions of courtly love, when measured against her reality, they left her woman's heart cold. I blame her for causing a great king pain, but I do not fault her for holding him to the ideals he proclaimed." He was lost for a moment in private reflection. "He harmed her; she injured him in turn."

"Will he send her away for good, Qadi?"

Yusuf nodded, appreciating Lubna's hostility to his ardent pursuit a little better. Perhaps every woman sensed betrayal in the lingering glances of men.

"What will be the outcome of this trial, my lord?"

Ayaan sounded forlorn, yet still Yusuf gave him the truth.

"This king will pass into legend, his knights will scatter to the winds, and one day soon, Camelot will be no more."

"All for the love of a queen," Ayaan murmured under the deepening twilight.

Yusuf glanced at him briefly.

"All for an injury the great King Arthur chose to inflict on himself."

Their horses picked up the pace, and the riders left Camelot behind.

Author's note: My very sincere thanks to Dr. Paul Cobb for suggesting the fabulous title of this story, and to Dr. Cobb and Dr. Stephennie Mulder for their pertinent advice on terminology and on the history of al-Andalus. And my deepest gratitude to Dr. Abigail Balbale, who took the time and the care to correct my mistakes on the historical period. The rest must be laid at the door of imagination.

Passing Fair and Young

Roshani Chokshi

MYTH

They told me it is dangerous to be passing fair and young, but I think they meant it is dangerous to be a woman unclaimed.

I was lovely enough to draw attention should I walk alone but not lovely enough to demand constant protection. I was too young to bear children but old enough that a man might try anyway.

My mother noticed the traces of myth on my skin the day I turned fifteen.

I could not see it on myself. But later, when it was too late for me, I would see that smear of iridescence across my son's brow. When I kissed him, I could taste it on my tongue: snow and ghosts and sugar. My first taste of myth was impossible and familiar, like the forgotten flavor of my mother's heartbeat when I slept inside her womb.

But I did not know those things at fifteen.

"What will happen to me?" I asked my mother.

My mother touched my face. "You have a choice before you, as I once did."

"A choice to do what?" I pressed.

She sighed. We were in her quarters, a place untouched by my father, whom men called the Fisher King. My mother's quarters were warm but scentless. *She* had no scent. Only after she died did I bother to wonder whether that was part of the bargain she struck when she was presented with her options. That she leave no trace behind, not even the perfume of her skin.

"I do not know how to read such things, but I know someone who does, and I shall summon her on the eve of your eighteenth birthday," she said. "For now, go . . . go and learn what makes you happy."

I did not appreciate back then the choice my mother was giving me, but I understand it now. How can anyone make a choice when they do not know themselves? I knew myself only a little in those days. I knew I liked solitude and the quiet wonder of the gardens, where the alchemy of roots and sunshine pulled forth roses from the winter thaw. I liked that I could be part of something greater than myself, though I did not know that was what it was back then.

I liked the company of girls my age, where we would huddle in the darkened corners of a banquet and spy on lovers' trysting or wonder at what it might be like to be a woman who inspired ballads both terrible and beautiful.

I liked laughter. I liked, truthfully, to notice but not be noticed.

I did not like the weight of others' eyes.

It made my skin feel too tight, even then.

As I left my mother's room, I paused at the doorway. My mother had her back turned to me, gazing out the stone window which looked out over the castle gardens.

"Mother, what was your choice?"

For a moment, I saw my mother as she must have appeared in her youth. Long limbed like me, with skin the color of a fawn's rich pelt, for my mother came from a land of spice and sand. There were crescents around her mouth and furrows between her eyes. Her face held the shadow of long-faded poetry.

"They told me I could know a love like no other. They told me I could live forever on the lips of bards and minstrels. They told me my bones would become a ballad and my blood would turn to the golden ichor that belongs to immortal gods," she said. "But they told me it would be violent and brief." She took a deep breath, trailing her brown fingers down her neck as though feeling for the pulse of that life not lived. "Then they told me I could choose, instead, a life in exile, cast far from my father's home. They told me I could become forgotten and nameless but that I would have a chance at contentment and, though it would not shake the earth, a different kind of love."

At this, she smiled warmly at me, and I felt guilt at her warmth. I have often wondered if she resented me and if only love for me kept too much bitterness at bay. If I am being honest, I felt jealous, too, of the man or woman who would have been her great immortal love, for I wished to be enough and knew that I was not.

"I feel, sometimes, the phantom ache of another life," she said. "Sometimes I dream of orchards and the taste of pomegranates, though I have not eaten one in years. Sometimes I dream in a language I have not spoken in decades. But that is nothing but the ghosts of choices made, and I would rather keep the company of those ghosts than others."

I knew this meant she loved me, and I was pleased.

"Now go," said my mother from her perch by the window. "Go and be lighthearted."

I left her then, flying down the stairs as though I could outrun whatever terrible choices would soon catch hold of me. I ran into the sunshine, and I put all thought of myths and resentment from my mind until I was eighteen. I caught her watching me in the garden from her bedroom window, but she never said a thing, and each time I caught her, she would move discreetly into the shadows.

It did not occur to me until years later, when I had my own child and watched him from my room, that this was an act of love. I did not want him to feel trapped by my watchful gaze.

I wanted him to feel free, even though he was tangled up in the sticky silken threads of legends long before I pushed him into this world.

Here was my gift to my son and my mother's gift to me: to watch from afar and not disturb, to cast light out into the darkness and hope my child's ear would lift to it like a hungry seedling craving the bright afternoon.

I am still not sure what my mother wished for me to know. Or whether she simply wanted me to know she was there.

MAIDEN

When I was eighteen, the woman whom men called Morgan le Fay came to read my myth marks.

My mother had made a pretense of a pilgrimage to pull me away from my father's court. It was the first time I had left Corbenic, and I was entranced by the sight of my home dwindling through the curtains of our carriage. I watched my father's castle, saw the turret that tipped curiously toward the sea, the silver seagrass that sounded like chiming bells. Though I could not see it, I knew my garden was there, too.

And as it grew smaller and smaller, I saw the entirety of my life shrink to the size of something I might fit in my pocket.

"Terrifying, isn't it?" asked my mother beside me. "For something so important to us to turn out so . . . small."

She moved from the window, settling into her cushions.

I said nothing as I looked away from Corbenic. I did not agree with my mother. I did not find it terrifying at all, but comforting. The world was vast enough; I did not wish to compete with it. If I could keep this small corner of joy unnoticed and out of sight . . . then perhaps I might just be happy.

In a castle choked with weeds and ivy, I was told to strip off my clothes and step into a bath. The bathtub was unlike anything I'd ever seen. Its clawed feet were carved from bone, and the shape reminded me of a half-bloomed rose with petals of finely beaten gold. The water was so hot that a tremor ran up my spine, and my hands shook on the lip of the tub.

"You must bear it, Elaine," said my mother.

I had never had cause to doubt my mother before, and so I followed her advice.

There are many days where I wonder what would have happened had I simply said . . . no.

No, I shall not bear this.

No, I will not carry the shadow of your unlived lives or stillborn dreams.

But I did not know there was such an option then. I knew only that I had to choose, and then Morgan le Fay appeared at the lip of the golden tub.

"Elaine," said Morgan, nodding to my mother. "I have come to read you, child."

I know now that it does not matter, but it seemed important at the time that she should be beautiful. As if whatever terrible pronouncements might be made about my life could be bettered by a pair of full, dark lips.

There are many kinds of beauty in the world, but I liked Morgan's best. She was beautiful in the way of smoldering fires and spurts of roaring thunder when the sky has visibly begun to clear. It was a fading beauty, made all the more lovely for its scarcity, where every drop lost becomes nectar for a poet's imagination.

I was not beautiful.

I was only ever passing fair and young. But for most men, that seemed to be enough.

Had the water in the bath not been so hot perhaps I might've felt a stroke of envy, but all I could see was my reddening skin and my brown hair sticking to it.

Morgan swiped her hand across my wrist, rubbing her fingers together. She looked at me and smiled.

"Well," she said, "I suspect the choice here will be quite easy."

"What is it?" I gasped.

"I see myth markings of a life full of movement, Elaine," said Morgan. Her eyes clouded over. "You will not find rest in any world, but you will be great. You will have powers that rival my own. You will conquer kings and steal their sons' hearts. You will be remembered by all, celebrated and feared in equal measure. You shall move through the world with such speed that even your shadow will struggle to keep pace with you—"

"What's the other choice?"

My mother winced at my poor manners, but the bath was so hot, and I did not want to bear the pain anymore.

Morgan shrugged.

"You shall sleep in the arms of greatness. You shall bear greatness. But you will never be great," said Morgan dismissively. "The world will look you over, and you shall be naught but a footnote in the legends of others."

Steam plumed up from the water.

I tried to get out of the bath. I could not think for the heat, the pain.

Morgan pushed me farther into the water. I screamed then, noticing too late the bubbles that popped across the water's surface. Scalding liquid splashed up my thighs, spat against my breasts. I saw black crimping the edges of my vision.

"You must make your choice now, child, while the water is hot and the myth is malleable."

I looked at my skin, and I saw it then. The sheen of legends on my flesh, glyphs made of colored light. I thought I glimpsed a life unlived in their gloss—there, a lover's hand drifting over my belly; now the weight of a helmet tucked under my arm and a sword bouncing against my hip; then a gnawing restlessness to move and move and keep moving; now the damp velvet petals of the first rose pushing through frosted earth. I knew that earth. It was home.

I remembered the sight of Corbenic Castle from the roads. My whole life something so small I might pocket it. My whole world worthy of no notice but no less worthy to me.

Everything was so loud.

I never liked such loudness.

It always rattled me, threatening to shake me loose from my skin.

"Choose greatness, my love," sobbed my mother. "Do not be afraid as I was."

I thought I heard the sound of horse hooves just outside the castle.

The bath scalded me.

"Your mother is right," said Morgan. "It can be a path of loneliness, but that is the cost of such glory. Do not be afraid."

I was not afraid of greatness.

But I was afraid of loneliness.

I had seen my father surrounded by courtiers, drenched in the power of the Grail cup locked away in our kingdom. And yet for all that power and might, he was alone. Yes, his name passed from mouth to mouth, and even I had heard the tales people told of the legendary Fisher King, but I had never heard him talk about himself. Perhaps he didn't see the point. He belonged to everyone but himself. The myth of him had drained away his human blood, filled his veins with gold, and perfumed his every breath with omens.

That was not me.

I am not a girl sculpted from fire like Morgan. I did not and do not need to feast on wonder to feel sated. I had seen the sharp talons of myth, and I did not want to be ripped beneath them.

I started to speak. "I choose—"

I tasted blood at the back of my throat. The patterns of myth swirled across my skin. My ribs spread apart, as if making room for vastness.

"I choose to be looked over by the world," I said, repeating Morgan's prediction back to her.

To myself, in private, I made a different vow.

I choose to belong to myself.

No sooner had the words left my lips did the golden tub spit me out.

I sprawled slick as a newborn across the tiles while my mother sobbed behind me. Steam curled off my reddened skin. The bottoms of my feet looked like ribbons. I ached all over as my body cooled in the night air.

Through the windows, the sound of horse hooves grew louder.

A man's voice rumbled through the abandoned castle, and my skin prickled.

"Who is that?" I asked. "Who is coming?"

Morgan looked at me, her lip curled in disgust. "The consequence of your choice."

My mother hauled me to my feet. I dripped water to the ground, shivering. No one offered me a cloth, and though the heat had gone, a different fire kindled within me. I was no fool. I could trace their disappointment as though it were a shadow on the wall. It angered me. It was my choice, was it not? Why should they judge me when only I had to live with it?

"I will grant you one last mercy, child," said Morgan. "I can take away the memory of the choice you made. You would not be the first. Arthur's queen chose to forget that she ever made a choice."

"What choice did she make?" I asked, curious in spite of my fury.

Morgan looked at me closely. Too closely. When she smiled, I saw that her teeth were white as milk. And yet there was nothing soft or flowing about her.

"Guinevere chose power even though it came at the price of extraordinary guilt. She chose power and immortality over anonymity."

"And did she choose correctly?" I asked.

"A story that ends poorly is still a story."

That was not an answer, but it no longer mattered.

The sound of hooves grew louder. I could see the appeal of

Morgan's offering. Perhaps the day would come when I would regret the choice I had made, and then I would return to this hour over and over again, dreaming of the life I had not lived. I could see how my mother had fared beneath the whispers of her own ghost selves. I did not want to be like her. But if I was going to belong to myself, then surely that meant never closing the eyes of my soul. Not even to spare myself.

"No," I said. "I shall remember."

"Then let me take that mercy," said my mother, with an embarrassed glance in my direction. "For I fear that I cannot love her as I used to if I know what she has done. Let me imagine that I never once saw myth marks on my daughter."

"It is done," said Morgan, looking to the window. "Careful now. . . . He is coming . . . and we all have a part to play."

MOTHER

Morgan said I would sleep in the arms of greatness.

I knew the moment you touched me that you were who she meant when she spoke of greatness. But the first time I saw you . . . you were, forgive me, rather uninspiring and thoroughly human. Years later you found this thoroughly amusing, but I must confess that I was rather disappointed.

The legends can never seem to agree on what you look like—whether you were tall and solemn, with quartz-gray eyes and a sheaf of thick wheat-gold hair beneath your helmet, or whether you were of average height with a peculiar fae-glint in your green eyes that turned heads, with close-cropped dark hair the color of soot.

So I shall set the tale straight, though no one has ever asked me and my answer likely will not be remembered.

You were handsome in an unimaginative way. You were taller than most men, but not noticeably so. You had broad shoulders and a scar on your left forearm from when a dog bit you. You had eyes the color of rain on a tree trunk, fair hair that looked as if someone had unraveled a candle's flame, and a slightly crooked nose from slipping down the staircase even though you told everyone it was from a nasty tumble from a wild stallion.

I liked that you told me the truth.

I liked knowing how to separate you from the story of you.

I liked knowing you as you wished you might be instead of as Sir Lancelot du Lac, a name foisted upon you by your adoptive mother, whose own title was just as mysterious. Lady of the Lake. Was it a lake? Or a pond just outside her house? You never told me, my love, but you insisted with all the solemnity of a hurt child that it was magic.

I do not know what magic Morgan wrought that night. All I remember was that for one moment I was outside the boiling bath and the next moment I was thrown back into its steaming waters, my face held down by my mother's and Morgan's hands.

You would not recognize that the other woman, hooded and screaming, was my mother. The official story released by my father's kingdom was that I had been taken on the road by witches and kept in an enchanted bath from which you rescued me. Later, Morgan would meet me in my father's castle and throw me a conspiratorial wink.

My mother did not remember anything about a choice or how I failed her.

She was content by reports of your own greatness.

More than that, she was determined that I would bear your child, who was destined for greatness.

She kept staring at you throughout the feast my father threw. I noticed that you did not drink any of your wine. Perhaps you noticed her gazes and suspected her of enchanting your cup. Good on you. I always did think you saw the world too plainly. I knew that the moment I met you. When Morgan and my mother orchestrated my rescue—though I wonder if it can be called that in light of what I know now—you did not blush at my nakedness. I think that was what I first noticed about you: you never looked away from me.

That first night was supposed to be our last. It was supposed to be the only intersection of our lives, and because I did not know you, I had made peace with the state of things. This was the choice writ upon my skin; I might as well get on with it.

That night my mother bade me go to your chambers. She told me to offer you a drink and that if I should do so, you would mistake me for *her*.

Guinevere.

Everyone knew she favored you above all Arthur's knights.

Everyone suspected your devotion to Arthur's queen was far more than it should be.

But back then, she was only a name to me, as inconspicuous as a shadow in the dark.

I came into your rooms at midnight, bearing only a stub of a candle and a cup. I did not bother to knock.

You were not in bed and had not removed the brocade garments that my father had loaned to you for the feast. You were broad shouldered and handsome, but the clothes shrouded you, and I almost laughed. Behind you stood the large bed hung in curtains of samite. The white linens looked crisp and untouched, and I grew scared, for I knew what would happen. Mother said it would be over fast, and for a moment, I imagined myself melting into those white linens like sugar into hot milk.

"Good sir," I started. "I do not know how to repay you for rescuing me. My mother bade me—"

"Spare me."

My head jerked up at the sound of your voice. I thought you would sound as solemn as you looked, but there was levity in your tone. I stood there with my hand wrapped around the enchanted drink. You glanced from the cup to me, an amused smile on your lips. I could only stare at you.

"Might as well come in, shut the door, and close your jaw while you're at it," you said.

I snapped my mouth shut, annoyed, and then I did as you asked.

You rose from the chair, not moving toward me or moving back but regarding me with the same amused grin.

"I know what you are, and I know what you're here to do, so let's get on with it, shall we?" You shrugged off your jacket, tugged at the collar of your shirt. You didn't look at me, and I remember how furious that made me. "Do you speak? Well, never mind, probably best if you don't. It's bad enough we have to do this; I don't need to add soothing a virgin's conscience to my list."

By then my shock had faded. I slammed the cup onto the nearest table.

"You don't know me or what I'm here for."

"Sure I do," you said. "It's in my myth marks. You're to be the mother of my son, and after tonight we'll never see each other again. And he'll do great things, and I'll do great things, and all shall be so blessedly . . . great."

I frowned. "And here I thought I would be a fox in the night, stealing your virtue as if it were a cooped chicken."

Your fingers paused at your buttons. You looked at me a little more closely.

"How do you know about the myth marks?" I asked.

Morgan had told me that fate treats men differently. Where women have so many choices, they had only one path. No one read their myth marks, for they had no choice in the matter.

That amused smirk left your face.

"My mother taught me how to read them. She's a sorceress, as well you know. She told me I was destined for legends."

"Is that what you wanted? Or how you thought it would be?"

You looked stunned then, and I wondered if anyone had asked you before. But a moment later you recovered, that smirk reasserting itself.

"I had little choice in the matter," you said casually. "Is this what *you* thought it would be like?"

"I thought I'd be seducing a knight, not philosophizing with one."

You liked that answer. I think that's the moment you liked *me*. You raised an eyebrow, walking toward me. Your hand went to my waist and you drew our hips together.

"Surely you can do both?"

Later, much later, we lay beside each other and listened for the sound of dawn's golden blanket hiding the stars from sight. My body felt tender . . . fuller. I dragged my fingers across my belly and wondered at the wisps of life taking root within me. You turned to your side, your rough hand skimming and scratching down my neck and arms.

"Tell me what your marks say."

I told you: I would be adjacent to myth, caught up in its shadow. Free to live without its bright eye turned to me.

"I envy you," you said.

"And your marks?" I asked. "What of them?"

"Glory," you said simply. "I shall look for the Holy Grail and be permitted a glance but nothing more. But my son— *our* son—will succeed. And I shall fall in love with a woman I cannot have, whose love none shall celebrate until the day I die. That is all the marks say."

I was not in love with you yet, so I did not resent Guinevere's intrusion.

"What does she look like?" I asked.

You looked pained. "She's the most beautiful woman I've ever seen, and I am haunted by the sight of her." Your voice dropped to a whisper. "There are days when I wish I'd never seen her."

You were honest with me from the start, and I liked that. I rose over you, savoring how your gasp of surprise melted into a groan of pleasure. I slid my hands across your eyes, lowering my hips to yours.

"Your wish is granted."

I tried to leave unnoticed in the morning, but you caught me by my wrist and kissed my hand.

"I hope . . . " you started to say, but I did not let you finish.

I wondered whether you regretted our transparency in the night, and I did not wish to know for certain.

"Let us leave it at that," I said. "Let us leave it at hope."

Whatever words you might have uttered, you swallowed them down.

Sometimes I wish I'd let you finish.

—┼—

Our son smelled of milk and softness. He was shining and seraphic, and the moment I held him, I knew our line had come to an end. I saw the shimmering glyphs of destiny writ upon his brow. Galahad would have neither hearth nor grandchildren nor earthly love to warm his bed. I saw the burden of greatness on him, and I almost wished to take back my choice. But sparing him that burden meant denying his existence.

I was glad it was too late, for I selfishly loved him.

Destiny grew bored of me, and I grew comfortable standing in its cold shadow. I was no longer young, nor passing fair, and the eyes of men turned elsewhere. Unwatched, I began to learn.

I learned the slow language of the herbs in my garden, coaxing their speech into talismans and amulets, medicines that I slipped to the village women. I learned the gruff song of thunderclouds, the untethered gossip of the sea channels that snaked coyly through the kingdom. I learned the dialect of our son's moods—his closed fists of frustration, his heavy-lidded gaze of daydreaming, his wonder-softened smile when he heard tales of your quests.

I did not hide anything from him.

I listened to the winds and to the water, and they told me of your feats and triumphs, your desperate love for Guinevere, and the frantic nights when that love was returned.

And yes . . . yes, I was sometimes envious.

It is not that I have a low opinion of myself, but I confess I never imagined you thought of me.

I remember the day I heard the wind sighing about you. It was a young and gossipy spring wind not fully thawed from winter's grip. It slipped under my scarves and pressed freezing kisses to my neck, delighting in its coldness as it sang: *Lancelot du Lac has lost his head, for his queen has kicked him from her bed, and oh he wanders and oh he is lost and oh he is lucky for such thin frost.*

That was how I found you that day in the garden.

Your beard overgrown and your eyes ringed white like a horse, your clothes shredded or matted to your skin. You could not stop shaking or scratching, hissing at your flesh: "Leave me! Leave me alone! I don't want to see you!"

You did not recognize me as the servants led you to my quarters. You spat in my face when I used my herbs on you. But slowly you came to your senses.

Slowly you allowed Galahad to sit beside you on your sick-bed and play with his wooden horses atop your quilts. Slowly you walked in the gardens and kissed our son's head and reached for my hand when no one was looking.

Slowly . . . I loved you.

The legends say we married, but they never spoke of our happiness.

They never spoke of our hours by the fireplace, our eternal disagreement on the choice between blackberry and straw-berry pie, how you were miserable at carving toys for Galahad and the delicious joy I took in teasing you for it. Legends do not mention the way you loved to swoop us into a hug and pretend to be a child-eating giant, or how I sneezed after lovemaking, or the nights when I woke to you standing by the window with your sword drawn, whispering to your myth marks: "*Not yet, not yet.*"

But myths are hungry things, and in a few short years, they found you and you had to leave.

I never asked whether you thought of her when you held me. I told myself it was because I was stronger for not knowing, but that's a lie. The myth marks said you were cursed to love someone you couldn't have until the day you died, and that was not me. I belonged to myself, but I was yours, too, and yet my name would never be joined to yours.

When you left, you told me to be happy.

"You'll be glad to be free of me," you said on our last night. "No witches at our door. Or giants kidnapping you. No one to poison your cup."

"Is it strange I'm offended by that?" I asked.

"Yes, wife." You laughed. "It is. Who would *want* that?"

And I made myself laugh even as I wanted to weep for the stupid envy of it all.

CRONE

Though you left, I lived. I raised our child and sent him off to greatness. I took a lover to warm your side of the bed and learned I was passing fair at swimming and weaving. I mourned the loss of quiet things and understood what I had given up in my choice. I did not need to live forever as myth, but I would have liked to be a folktale passed down to grandchildren. *Grandmother had a ridiculous temper and hated toads. Grandmother had strange blood and dark skin and sometimes dreamt of pomegranates. Grandmother was a witch.*

But I was a full tale, complete unto myself for better or for worse.

The years lined my face and stretched my hips, and I reveled in the blessing that I could see such change upon me.

I listened to the wind and learned that you had achieved your quest and lived to be the greatest of Arthur's knights. I heard that you and our son searched for the Holy Grail and found it. I heard that Guinevere blamed herself for the fall of Camelot and renounced her throne. I heard that you followed her into exile.

I thought that would be the end of it, but now I hear the knock on our old door and I go to answer it, and I see you.

We are no longer young, but you still smile like a boy.

"They're done with me," you say, and hold out your hand.

I do not see the wisp of myth on your skin.

"Let me in, wife."

I can only stare at you.

"What about—"

"We are finally free of each other," you say, bowing your head.

But I remember your curse.

"You were to love her until the day you die. If you love her no longer, then you are rather solid for a ghost."

You shake your head, laughing a little, and then you take my hand.

"I was cursed to love a woman I could not have whose love none shall celebrate until the day I die," you say slowly, looking up at me. "I am still quite happily cursed, my love."

We are walking to the edge of your mother's lake. You tell me we can wash ourselves free of destiny's grimy streaks, that we may smear youth over our skin and start anew. We are happy and unfettered, and yet sometimes regret shadows your face.

"They will never know," you say.

But it does not matter. Myths may be hungry things, but they cannot take away what I know.

Once, I tasted snow and softness. Once, I knew the rough poetry of thunderstorms. Once, I ruled a realm entirely of my own making.

Once, I was passing fair and young.

How, after Long Fighting, Galehaut Was Overcome by Lancelot Yet Was Not Slain and Made Great Speed to Yield to Friendship; Or, Galehaut, the Knight of the Forfeit

Daniel M. Lavery

King of the Distant Isles, Galehaut, King also of Norgales; Over-
lord of the North Marches and Escavalon; Master in Lothian,
Gore, the Long Isles, Sorestan; King in Orofoise, Roestoc, Pomi-
tain, the Isle of Servage, the Straight Marches, Stranggore; Duke
of Sorelois, Garloth, and twenty more besides. Now in Tintagel,
afterward in Joyous Garde; lover of good knights; unhelmeted
at last by Sir Lancelot; formerly excellent, currently happy and
awaiting burial:

There are too many young men on the earth these days for true friendship to flourish. The flower of knighthood is thereby strangled in the bud, for, without a true friend, the knight can never temper his martial spirit with the cooling breath of love. He charges about from place to place, ever steaming, foundry hot, irritating maidens, stirring up quarrels, distressing shepherds, cluttering the courts, frightening curates, heedless of invitation and mindless of direction. He is a liability to his comrades, a burden to his master, a clod and a pest to his bedmates, and the terror of farmers and livestock alike.

Now the year 1000 was a mutation in time, a warp in the wheel of fortune, and from that cracked year a thousand young men crawled over Christendom and savaged her, bored and voracious after their schismatic birth. So it was that comradeship was introduced to gentle them, the peace and truce of God to restrain them, interdicts and excommunications to quiet them, monks to puzzle them, pilgrimage to weary them, and chivalry to better them. Yet there are so many men, and so few friends among them, that one might search the world twice over without ever encountering him.

The aim of the play of chivalry is twofold. It is perhaps rather truer to say that there is both a known and an unknown aim to chivalry. The first is to keep bored youngsters busy; to teach both boys and horses how to behave, how not to embarrass their mothers at the table; to fill up their afternoons with activity and intrigue that they might end the day tired and ready for honest sleep rather than trouble; to accumulate honor and marks of distinction from kings and ladies, that they might feel themselves trailed about by glory and slow their pace accordingly. The second is to get themselves rid of all honor and glory for the love of a true friend.

Many knights never learn of this aim. They are horse riders and cow-handed, fit only to sire sons and to round out the guest list at court. They can carry a cup across a tiltyard without spilling, say "Pleased to meet you" in French, and die in war. Not for them is the increase of the soul, the swelling up of merit, the augmentation of grace, the tournament in disguise, the leap from the window, the taking hold lightly and in secret of a dearly loved hand, the token worn tight against the chest, the exchange of hair locks, the midnight marriage by a tree-wild monk, the flight in disguise, the trade in clothes, and the setting out across the wasteland. The true knight longs for shame, awaits eagerly the day when he may cast aside his honor and trample it under the pounding of feet as he rushes to his friend. A knight is a humiliation-seeking device, and the point of knighthood is to renounce everything, to give up all, to cast honor and dignity and title aside and tumble headfirst into perfect degradation, perfect friendship, perfect trust, perfect felicity. In this collapse may knighthood, at last, flower. All else is horsemanship and table manners and may as easily be learned from a book (or, for that manner, a well-trained horse) as from a fellow knight. It is better than nothing and nothing else.

Of the first aim of chivalry, and the first class of knighthood, of which the greater bulk of all knighthood in Christendom is part, I will say little. It is because of them we have tournaments and men enough to fill them; that is sufficient. I left home to collect kings; in the tearing apart of kings' households I might expect to find good knights. Gloier I killed, the son of Loholt, killed him for Sorelois, for her low and sunken bridges, her splendid merry rivers, her rich forests and untrammeled views to the sea. (Then I trammeled them.) Galegantin I sent away smarting. Bagdemagus, Cleolas, Maleginis, valiant men and well-appointed, leading armies blistering with a hundred lances, masters of the islands of tar and gold, Kings Aguissant and Yon—all fell before me and yielded their lands, their swords, their sons to my captains' mess. I had many friends in those days, either proudly dead or cheerful in defeat, every one of them generous, frank, openhearted, pleased to find me as gracious as handsome, as wealthy as sporting. I knew every good sport from Orkney to Armenia and carried all their helms behind me in my war chest. "Galehaut, welcome; welcome, Galehaut," the word came. "Knock me down, my darling."

So I knocked everybody down. Men begged me to hit them. Men who had never known what to ask for in their life, men who fell silent at the sight of the Grail maiden and neglected to ask the Fisher King what ailed him, men who could barely mumble along in Mass suddenly found their tongues on my field and chased me out: "Galehaut, best of knights! Galehaut, so courtly in victory! Galehaut the forbearant, the loyal, the hardy, test your hardiness on me—throw me down—dismount me—knock me off—grant me the honor of your fist, Galehaut, fuck me up, Galehaut, fuck me up, Galehaut, I haven't seen my father in sixteen years but send me home to him wearing your bruises and I can say I was truly a knight. Galehaut, I'm begging you, trample me, make much of me, make a mess of me, just this once lay waste to me and I'll gladly follow you wherever you go."

So I knocked everybody down and had their honor added to mine, till I was so heaped with glory it took three days to go a mile. I moved slowly over the earth as I approached Arthur, stopping often to knock and absorb knights inasmuch they begged for absorption. As soon as a man fell before me, weeping in gratitude and joy, I knew two things about him: first, that he was not the true friend I sought, and second, that I had just done away with another rival for the friend I still sought. So I made progress, but also wasted time, as I neared Logres.

We fought two wars against each other in Selice, Arthur and I. I could have swept the Summerlands, could have pushed Tintagel into the channel, would have walked to Rome on my knees, had Arthur fought alone. I carried the cloud of thirty kingdoms behind me; I had the best and most lovestruck knights in the world by my side; I arrived at the field of battle eminently lovable and ready to knock again. Arthur had red hair, a lovely wife, a ready arm, a handful of marsh barons and reed knights, and tenacity. I liked him. I knocked him down.

He collapsed very prettily. "Would you consider," he asked from the ground, "giving me a bit of time to collect myself and my men before trying again?"

"Verily," I said, "and with a right good will. Shall we meet again at Pentecost, on this same field, under our same banners, and with our best men?"

He nodded—I hoisted him up—he saluted me with the best of manners—departed—I collected the dazed and tumbled-down knights wishing to join my party—a year passed.

The same field. More knights on my side, more knights on his. You may well wonder whether I found the process of friend-seeking tiresome, if I ever wearied going all over the face of the earth and turning over men to see if my friend lay hidden underneath. I did not; friend-finding is painstaking work and cannot be rushed. Moreover, each man I knocked down was one fewer rival against me. On the field was Yvain, who fought brilliantly; Gawain, who fought better still; Arthur, who was a bit of a mess but had a certain undeniable energy to his approach. There was a man whose name I did not know, whose armor and horse were all black. His next horse—the first being cut out from under him—was black, too. Black was the third horse, then the fourth. Around him in a great clatter piled up the helmets and arms of fallen knights, their shields in pieces, their flags tattered, all swooning in turn at his feet.

The number of the Trinity is three and perfect. Lancelot is, and is, and is.

A friend, then. I wondered if I would fall from my horse.

"Sir," I called out, trying to steer my own horse closer to him, feeling for all the world like I was trying to chase down the chit at the end of dinner, "sir, hold a minute. Be not afraid."

"Nor was I, friend," he called back (friend already!). "Go ahead."

"Let me tell you what I intend," I said, jostling my way through the crush until we drew abreast of each other. "I am a king and the son of a king; no one on this field will harm you while I am living. Also, you amaze me."

"Well," Lancelot said. "Lovely to meet you, king's son. You're, what, six foot two? Six foot three?"

"Six foot five," I said.

"Six foot five," he said. "Yeah. Okay. Lead on, then." So we left the field together, and everyone else fell down around us.

"Yon red tent is mine," I told him. "Would you like me to surrender to Arthur tomorrow? Tonight? How do you take your tea? How can I embarrass myself for you? Everything I have is yours, you know—"

The next year. At the great tournament of Sorelois. We were sitting around—Guinevere, Gawain, Yvain, and myself—talking about the things we would do for Lancelot and the love of Lancelot, if his love happened to be ours. Yvain, who was of a practical cast of mind, spoke first: "I'd give him my best hawk, my best horse, my best armor, and my place in bed."

"What is your place in bed, Yvain?" Guinevere asked. Merry, not brutal; Yvain laughed and threw a crust of bread at her.

"And what of you, Gawain?" I said. "What would you give him?"

Sir Gawain bethought himself awhile before saying, "If God and the saints would grant it, I'd immediately ask to be refashioned into his maiden true, his good sweetheart, with my own acres and ten manor houses, a writing room full of copyists and clerks, barns of linen; one field for hay, one for beer barley, one for wheat, one for rye, one for oats, one for peas; an abbey full of brewing nuns, an almshouse, and a mill; a fort and a trench; a tin mine; two smiths; a glove maker; a pepper house and a courtroom and a judge; a deer forest and a pig forest; two rivers, nine chalk streams, a wash, three swales; two chapels; a salt flat, a saddler, and the toll profits from seven different bridges. I would be mistress of my own keys and castle, with a keen eye, more lovely than the southern winds in May, hair like heavy ropes of gold, lips like figs, a figure like a prayer drifting up to heaven, the worthiest damsel to ever draw breath, and I'd save all my love, all my riches, all the tributes produced by my land and all the tributes produced by my good, tight body for him, and I'd give him them."

"Sir Gawain," I said to him, "you have offered much. God grant it you," and I pledged him until he blushed. His blushes were flashes of robin's breast in a dark forest. "Pledge him again," I told the rest of the table, "lift your cups in praise of him, until he grows wine-colored all over; I like it." I liked Gawain; I held it against no one in court that they should love

Lancelot as I did. It seemed to me personally reasonable that they should. Is the Father jealous of the Son? Or of the Holy Spirit that issues forth from both? So we all touch the best knight in Christendom; so we all issue forth.

Queen Guinevere spoke next. "Gawain has offered all a lady can give and quite cut me out. What is left for me to offer? I'd turn into a barn owl," she said, "and scratch out his eyes and carry them around in my feet and trample all over his sight." A lovely girl, and worthy of him. He would receive death and dishonor from her; I death and dishonor from him; she would have to find death and dishonor all on her own somewhere, but I didn't doubt her ability for a moment. "And you, Galehaut? You can't give him the armies of the Distant Isles again."

"Turn my honor to shame," I said, "bury my name in filth and degradation, ride in a cart, dishonor my father and my mother, strike a monk, steal deer, filch livestock out of pasture, burn a house in Easter week, frighten noble ladies and widows during Lent, defile relics and saints' bones—"

"Piss in a baptismal font, steal Canterbury, yes, yes," Gawain said dismissively, "collapse into foolishness for him—we get the picture."

"He offers a great deal, Gawain," Guinevere said, smiling at me. "It gives me joy to see it."

"What can I say?" I asked them. "God has not struck me with misfortune yet; I am a man unused to sacrifice. I know how to woo and to give gifts—to dazzle and to intimidate—"

"That's six foot five, everyone," Gawain stage-whispered.

"But of all the knights in Christendom, I have had the best luck of all and never lost to another man. So I think I do not know well what it means to give much in exchange for love. And then one day my luck ran so strong I received everything

I had ever wanted. Now I have nothing left to win and can only lose."

"Trying to win through an appeal to our sympathy," said Yvain. "No, it won't wash, Galehaut; you're not going to make me pity a tall, well-favored duke who's lord of thirty kingdoms and best friend to Lancelot besides."

"Let me add this, then," I said. "I will not outlive my friend—will not outlive this tournament, for even now I see his flag falter and fear him undone by treachery and false knights, enemies of true friendship. Take me out to Joyous Garde and lay me there; even if he should get up by some miracle, Galehaut will not survive Lancelot touching earth." So it was I won that day and thereafter died. Lancelot got up again after touching earth, but I was not there to see it—he touched it, and I went into it. To go into ground now or later, now that I had done what I had set out to do, was a matter of supreme indifference to me.

After me, for Lancelot: to ride in the cart, and humiliation, disgrace, talk of treason, of felony, next the contempt and loathing of the crowd, the cloud of shame, the publicly unsatisfying reunion with Guinevere, the tepid reception of former friends, the stink of degradation, all without me to strengthen or console him—oh, how lucky he is, my darling boy, to sink so low for me.

I Being Young and Foolish

Nisi Shawl

Nia rose from her boat's bench smoothly, a skyward pour of milk. Her cat had made up their mind. Steady though she stood, her boat bobbed slightly in the rippling water. The boatman hunched uneasily against the bright wind, which fluttered Nia's sleeves and the ends of her head cloth and pushed her robe of undyed wool against her chilled body. Nia reminded herself that this lake was reputed shallow, no more than a couple of fathoms at its deepest, in its center. And here among the reeds at the island's edge, even with the wetness of winter's onset, she ought surely to be able to wade to shore, as Odeh could leap the little distance—if only they *would* leap it—

On the beak of the boat's painted prow, Odeh wriggled their gray-striped hindquarters, teetered their triangular head down, up, down, up, down—and jumped! King Bear's command that she come to study here was in accord with her chosen destiny, the knitting together of the world's webs. A sigh released breath Nia had not known she held. Then the rustling of dried grass told where Odeh walked ahead. Carefully, using an oar to provide balance, Nia stepped from the boat into the water's freezing cold. Only two paces and she reached the rock where her cat had landed, splashing the stone's lichened sides as she climbed to its low, flat top. She looked back.

She'd need her boots. Her slippers were wet, as was the bottom of her gown, despite her kirtling it. "My bundle. Pitch it here." The boatman frowned, then did as bidden. She caught his toss and ignored his face. In these strange northern lands Nia had come to see such expressions as her common due, and they were certainly less frightening than some smiles she'd had to face on her journey. Or, for that matter, back in Nakasongola.

The boatman turned away obediently enough and worked his oars, gradually diminishing from sight.

Once he'd gone, the music of the land welled up to fill her. Wind rushing. Waves lapping. Birds crying. Stilling, she listened wider. Clouds blowing above, so reliable, so welcome. And there: the soft brush of Odeh's tail against plants growing along the path they took. A narrow path, made by the shy Cymry deer coming down to drink. Nia followed it upward to a hazel copse where golden leaves littered the ground, and the empty fragments of split shells. A good burial site. Odeh stretched contentedly along a low, flexible limb waving from the grove's queen tree, grooming a dainty forepaw.

Nia approached them, hand held out to caress. But stopped. Percussion interrupted the landmusic's flow: wood on wood. A door banging open. Banging shut. She dropped her hand and faced the sound's source. Nothing further came from its direction. She walked toward what she'd heard, hesitantly.

A new path. Human broad, the smell of a smoky fire hanging over it. This must be the way to the hut King Bear had described.

So it was. Soon a clearing appeared before her, and a small building, stone but constructed in the Cymru style, on one side, a brushwood wall on the other. A beautiful man of middle years standing in its center. Nia met his pale eyes and felt her current intensify.

He spoke. "Well that you come." He wore a dark belted mantle, its hood pushed back to show straight brown hair cut to the blunted knife of his jawline. His voice was odd—louder than a whisper, softer than should have been audible sixteen paces off.

Nia gathered herself in. "You expected me?"

The beautiful man came closer, nodding and curling his slender fingers. "Say rather that I hoped for you. King Bear's messenger arrived the day before last Sabbath with word you had been advised to visit but that you had received this advice without committing to heed it."

He spread his arms to show himself weaponless. "I'm right? You're the foreign sorceress?"

"So they call me." If she had stayed in Nakasongola, she would by now be revered as a Muganda. Unless, of course, she had been rejected, as had begun to seem more and more likely. Which likelihood had led to her present course of wandering the world to learn its many magics—and the misnaming that went with that course.

"And who is this?" The man's gray eyes were aimed over her shoulder. She whirled, but it was only Odeh.

"My cat."

"He came with you all the way from Ethiope?"

"No. Odeh didn't join me until I left Egypt." Ethiopia was not the actual country of Nia's origin, but she let the error pass, as she had learned to let pass so many. "And you are Merlin, King Bear's magician?" He did not have a tame air about him, did not seem any sort of courtier, but she supposed he must be the one she had been recommended to seek.

"Yes, to be sure." His disturbingly light eyes met hers again and this time held them. Was that how her eyes appeared? "You'll want to see where you will stay. And to take refreshment—or perhaps you fast?"

"No."

Neither of them moved. Once again it was Odeh who tipped the moment's balance. Ignoring the magician, they dashed to the stone hut's threshold and abruptly halted.

Wards? No—well, perhaps; door wards would make sense, but the sudden scent of fish blood was most likely what had stopped Odeh there. Inquiringly they raised their nose. A straw sack hung wet and glistening from a peg in the whitewashed wood of the door's jamb. Merlin, ahead of her, grinned and shrugged. "You'll share it with me? Fresh-caught trout make for a fine dinner."

Entering the twilight of the hut's interior, Nia felt only the weakest resistance, like a bubble waiting to pop. Wards, but apparently she had been classified a friend and allowed to pass. A raised platform near the hearth bore a heap of heather. "Yours," said the magician.

Not "ours." She would be warm enough, but . . . "Where will you sleep?"

"The woods. Or the yard. Or the loft."

Nia noted the order of listing. Presumably it indicated preference. No, Merlin was not tame.

However, he was extremely civilized for a man of these parts.

Christianity had been rife since her voyage over the Tyrrhenian Sea, but he didn't appear to practice it: the hut's walls bore no crosses, no bones or hair stolen from the bodies of dead ancestors. The fish were quickly baked in a mud made fragrant with sweet herbs and served on a board lined with rare greens: fresh, tender sorrel leaves, which tasted wonderful. Both mead and beer accompanied the meal.

Hospitality had ceased to be much of a problem for Nia once she left behind the dark-skinned peoples who viewed her albinism askance. As she had been told, the farther north she traveled, the more acceptable her pallor, the more welcome her assistance with herbal formulae and other simple spells. She'd only had to share the most childish of enchantments to pay her wandering way.

They ate in the open air, seated on a felled oak a few feet uphill. Nia noted that a wind blowing from the direction of the lake afforded better hearing than could have been expected. No surprise visitors. Good planning. Odeh sat quiet as a hunting dog and watched every bite of the fish into her mouth. "You have a pet also?" she asked the magician.

"A serpent. Macha. The cool weather of the year's ending makes her sluggish and lessens her appetite. She'll still be digesting the rat she caught yestermorn."

Nia bent and lay her baked mud shell on the ground for Odeh, and they began to pick cautiously at the slivers of flesh she'd left clinging to its inside.

The magician laid his shell beside hers. "Come. I'll show you my workings while the light's good."

They returned to the hut. Was it larger now? Yes. Definitely. Outside and in. That stair in the corner was new. She climbed behind him to another floor. A wooden floor, and on it a narrow table running the room's length. Windows at the room's far end showed a flowering hedge dividing a green hillside pasture, sheep grazing under blue heavens. But this hut stood in the midst of a forest.

"Where—"

"My mother's land. Brecheliant. And you should ask when, as well."

Hadn't she heard that Brecheliant was forested, too? "When?"

"In times to come."

Without realizing, she had crossed the room, drawn to the unlikely scene outside. Now she turned her back on it to stare at him, to deny what he had said. "The future does not exist."

"Everything exists."

Gazing at Merlin over a table laden, she saw now, with shining metal boxes and thick glass bowls and colorful waxen effigies and all manner of curious items, Nia knew with utter certainty that Odeh had been guided aright. She needed to stay here and exchange teachings—powerful ones—with this impossible, beautiful man. She needed to know the world as he knew it. And so she formally asked him to instruct her, and he formally took her on.

She went to her bed of heather alone that first night and got up from it the same way. Odeh roused her when it was early morning. Outside the hut's walls, the still-sunken sun's light whispered the air awake.

A moment's wait in the clearing and the trail down to the hazels formed itself out of thinning shadows. She and Odeh followed it, and under the queen's branches she sought its roots with softly thrusting fingers, excavated the finest of their tendrilings, and ate them. She knew from previous repasts that these northern webs became less active as the year's cold came on. Nonetheless, it was Nia's practice to consume as soon as she could some sample of the fungal lace linking the flora of whichever woods she lived in.

Another quarter and it would be time for sowing.

A lingering redstart called her deeper into the forest, to where oak ruled the hillsides. Like her, surely, this little bird was a far traveler. Unlike her, it had returned to where it began. Though soon it would leave again. She'd met one once, on the shore of Lake Nalubaale; redstarts did not love the North's cold winters.

"Remain here," she instructed Odeh. They didn't, but neither did they accompany her as she sought for the singing, slipping off instead on a mission of their own. She was able to approach the bird alone.

Singing serenely despite her presence, the redstart balanced on a high, near-leafless sprig jutting up from a young attendant tree. Nia coaxed him to her hand. "Tell my auntie I am well," she crooned. "Find her where the shorebirds flock, casting her net from my uncles' boat, or resting in the shade of the iroko trees which our ancestors seeded there, the place we call Nakasongola. You will know you've reached her because she shines like me." She released the bird. He perched a moment more on her thumb and flew off southward.

Higher up and higher in she found the queen of these oaks and again ate from among the roots. The taste was fine. But the hazels would be better for her burying. Circling wide, she came last to the silver trunks of the beech trees, performed the same actions there, and came to the same conclusion.

As Nia returned to the hut, mist closed around her like a memory. Out of the enveloping whiteness Odeh appeared, joining her as if they'd never left her side.

The trail weakened. Nia relied on her burgeoning sense of

the countryside to guide her back to the hut. Merlin greeted her at its door. "You touch the land," he pronounced.

"The land touches me." *Breathes me, drinks me, draws me in, lets me out,* she thought. All the land and air and ocean she'd passed between here and Lake Nalubaale did so now. The strength of her magic depended on this intermingling. Her magic's strength and growth—she wandered in its service.

"Come."

The magician fed her a cup of dried and toasted grains mixed with hazelnuts and goat's milk. They must have been procured from an off-island farm, because she'd seen signs of none nearby this morning. With his food, Merlin brought forth the question she'd been expecting since they met. "Aren't the people of Ethiope black of visage?"

"Most of us," she answered. Like devils, she'd heard her race described. "But I've been as you see me from my birth."

"What of your parents?"

Odeh turned away from the pinch of grains Nia offered them, uninterested. "Both are dead. I never knew them."

"I'm sorry."

"I never knew them," she repeated. "My aunt and uncles, who cared for me, tell me my mother and father were quite normal in how they looked." She licked off the grains Odeh had spurned and reached for the napkin to wipe her hand.

The magician held it. She tried to tug it away. He kept his hold tight, his gaze on her hand. On her skin. "Those in your village thought you a witch because you were not as they."

Indeed they had. But rather than respond so, to answer what had been stated, not asked, Nia reached with her other hand to lift that tucked chin and raise Merlin's eyes to meet her own. He stared without blinking. A Seeing was on him.

For five long beats of her blood Nia cradled the magician's

jaw in her steady left palm. Then he jerked and drew back. He staggered to his feet, kicking a table leg. Bowls skittered to the table's edge.

What had frightened him? Something Seen? Her experience with other tutors had taught Nia not to pry early on in a relationship. She would wait for whatever explanation was offered.

"I'm sorry," said the magician, again. And that was all she got from him for the moment.

The quarter passed. Seven days. A pattern emerged: While the sun hung above the horizon she went about fishing, foraging (for berries, nuts, mushrooms, and other provender), and harvesting herbs that would be helpful to have over the winter. As evening dimmed and sank the sun, Merlin called her to him to teach her: in the ephemeral room above the ground floor or in a cave opening in the slope behind his hut. He showed her trays crawling with people as small and purposeful as ants, opened books filled with images that moved while she watched them, then returned to their starting places when she looked away. He blinked slow as Odeh in approval of her ability to sit, motionless as a heron, through a lesson on creating new homes for the future to live in. That brought a troubling bout of smugness. Stillness was the first skill the trees had taught Nia.

Tools for digging rested against the hut on the side opposite its entrance. On the seventh day, after gathering a pan of rose hips off a wild hedge the oak trees showed her, Nia began her grave. She left the full pan on the table for Merlin to prepare as he would, shouldered shovel and pick, and went to work. The hazels' roots parted easily for her. By midday the hole was deep enough. She set about widening it. Odeh watched her from atop the little hill of dirt she'd cast up. Only watched. Their part would come soon. Tonight.

She finished well ahead of time, even allowing herself a trip to the brook to bathe before returning to the hut to eat.

The rose hips steeped in warm water—a tea or syrup, then. To be consumed later. The meal itself consisted mainly of roots. But these had come in trade, from farmers' crops, and gave Nia no knowledge—what little they once possessed Merlin had peeled off with a knife and boiled away. There was much for him to learn. He had yet to ask her to teach it. Or to grant him any other favor.

The evening's study session commenced as usual, though in a new venue: a blooming bower, a summerish arch of flowers with two seats of living wood. The method of the bower's conjuration was Merlin's chosen topic; he ignored her attempts to lure him onto others until the lesson's end. For a moment both of them sat in darkening silence.

The magician plucked a spray of sweet-scented briony and plaited it with another of honeysuckle. "You'll wear these during your burial this night."

He knew. "Who told you?"

"We have a similar . . . ritual in these lands, but for men. In the spring."

As near to an answer as the magician ever gave. He twisted the ends of his plait together to form a wreath and presented it to her. "Here. Shall I accompany you, or is this working solitary?"

"I won't be alone; Odeh attends me. They'll finish my burial for me, and in the morning they'll begin my excavation. But I'm sure they'd welcome your help."

She donned the wreath over her head cloth and proceeded

with him to the hazel grove. Her grave looked bottomless in the gloaming. She half reclined in it as if in an oversized Italian bath. With Merlin's aid, the earth covering Nia rose quickly. Her white-draped arms submerged themselves in the soil for a final time.

"You'll come to no harm."

"Not the least," she assured him. Already the fungal threads of her comrades twined around her feet, tickling open the pores of her naked ankles. "You may safely cover my head cloth in no more than the chanting of a pair of recipes. Odeh will know exactly when."

"The flowers—"

"They too."

The magician recited the instructions he had given her for midnight travel between distant mountaintops while filling the grave high as Nia's chin. Odeh patted her cheeks with velvet gentleness and pawed rich loam from behind her line of sight to lie against her ears. Merlin's recitation became too muffled to distinguish. And her attention became diffuse, opening out into the wood's underground system, the slow routes of the trees' shared awareness. Spreading the light, the hum, the liquid proclamation of life. Shutting it down, retracting it, drawing off the precious power to store it within the earth. Within her bones. The quiescent essence.

Night was a dance without steps, without movement of any kind. Morning came: a smear of sunlight, a reddening of her eyes' lids. She lifted them and focused on Odeh's furry face, their pink and silver tongue licking the scum of dirt from her newly exposed skin. Merlin's long hands scooped the loose soil imprisoning her neck and shoulders, but by the time she'd freed herself enough to look for more of him, he'd gone. Patiently she stirred herself, setting the dirt within her grave aseethe. She emerged unscathed though not unchanged, brushing away the broken tips of tendrils that had formed to nourish her. These would be repurposed in the spring.

Nia had thought perhaps Merlin would return to her at the burial site with a drink of water or a blanket. Of course with questions. No. He came not at all. She shivered a moment in the sudden loneliness, unable to decide if it was his absence caused it, or her loss of direct contact with the roots of the hazels. Then she went back to the hut on her own. And on her own she stayed, despite her desire.

Snow fell the first night of Christmas. Three and twenty years had passed since Nia left Nakasongola, heading whiteward. This would be her sixteenth such snowfall, but she never tired of them. Bluer than her complexion, shadow versions of the stars, the soft flakes swirled to the low, black Earth from high, cold Heaven.

"Shut the door, won't you?" The length of Merlin's wool-wrapped body radiated warmth bare inches from her back. "It's not so marvelous to me as to you, this bleak winter."

She nodded and moved forward to take and pull the door's knotted latch cord, feeling the distance between them increase. "Will we still go to the castle in the morning?"

"Will the king still send a boat to carry us? I say so."

Despite practicing her own beliefs as well as she could in alien lands, Nia knew and publicly performed the rites of her hosts' religions, too. It made her passage easier, her sojourns less troubled. Merlin seemed to have come to a similar accommodation with the Christians' church. In the lessons given her over months past there had been no mention of Jesus, saints, or apostles, save perfunctory reference to who should be called on to bless which workings, aloud, before witnesses. However, as predicted, King Bear had invited his magician to return to court for the winter's holy days. And as promised, Merlin had agreed to go. She with him.

"But Macha—"

"She slumbers. She won't miss us."

"Will she not freeze? The frost—"

Merlin glanced down at the flat stones set around the hut's circular hearth. One short day a short while ago, Nia had watched the snake glide under the largest of them. "I'll bank the fire with utmost care. We are to be gone no more than a fortnight. Perhaps less. She'll be fine. I say so."

Time was Merlin's realm, and the principle Nia had discerned behind most of his spells was the deployment of it in surprising spots. The blossoming of the bower, the delving of the cave. Also he dealt in the comprehension of time: of the past's mysteries; and of the future, the present's oft-unexpected outcome.

The dry rustle of twigs disturbed Nia's thoughts. Odeh's head pushed through the heather bunched and tied to the hut door's bottom, golden eyes blinking open as they cleared the brush. Next came the white-gloved forepaws, the limber elegance of their front legs, the liquid torso, muscular back legs, and waving tail.

"Will they come with us?" Merlin had finally learned from Nia how to talk of her pet. This language had but one option for those neither male nor female.

Nia had not been apart from Odeh for more than a night since they'd adopted her. "Most likely."

"Shall I carry them? The horses won't bother them?"

"They weren't fretted on the way here." Neither the king's horses nor the asses of Dijon nor any of the other beasts encountered on their way had daunted brave Odeh. None-theless the magician stooped to gather them up and lift them. Odeh tolerated that, as they always did this man's touch. As they had never before tolerated others' handling.

It was this, her pet's acceptance of him, that encouraged Nia to ignore his avoidance of her, to step over the boundary of his determined disregard for her queries and invitations. To make her meaning plain, she pulled Merlin by his mantle down beside her and sank onto her bed.

"Ah." His face in the firelight lent depth to the simplicity of that sound: the depth of the knowledge and the wanting of what was yet to come. Her fingers traced the beardlessness of his cheeks and the strange straightness of his nose, stroked his stern brows, wings of a predator, a protector—

He reached for her wrist to stop her. "You understand this is not the price of my teaching? Nor of your lodging here— you take me to you freely, of your own will?"

She laughed and rose and shook off her robe. "And if I didn't understand by now that there's no barter involved? After these three moons you've held yourself aloof from me? I would be too stupid to understand anything. Too—" She sprang like Odeh in the hope of catching the magician off guard. But he was ready with a half-serious defense of his clothing. She settled for removing his gown to reveal the shirt worn beneath. Then she pressed him down to lie again on the red-dyed linen with which he'd covered her bed.

Soothing the shirt's hem gradually upward, she began to expose him. In the firelight his thighs glowed like candle wax, rippling when he rolled away.

"Stay."

He obeyed her.

"You want me. Why do you deny—?"

The first rage she'd seen on him fell over his face. "Deny you? Never! But what begins also ends."

Tentatively, Nia leaned over his shoulder to take his hands in hers. She met no resistance. "Does it so? Does it truly?" She turned him back toward her. "Have you not taught me otherwise?"

He laughed a creaking laugh. "Tomorrow we go to the king, to stay under his roof through the year's return. The young and lusty king."

"King Bear and I have met." Yellow hair, she remembered. Eyes resolved on cheerfulness. Thick whiskers covered his face, and below that his center burned, a belly full of determination. "Do you forget? He sent me here."

"I do not forget what has happened. Nor what will." He lifted himself on his elbows. The shadow of his hair cast itself between them. "I say you'll lie with him. I have Seen it. And I, damn me for an envious fool, will lie with you now." He leaned toward her, and they kissed. Nia closed her eyes and Saw anyway—her phantasms or his? The visions ran so swift they blended into one another: fields reaped empty of their corn; harbors crowded with the masts of golden ships and the busy oars of tiny, bright boats; chests of gold coins spilling onto wooden tables where sat fine-wigged ducks and haughty swans . . . Each sight was more nonsensical than the last, and all the while she and Merlin kissed and touched, these imaginary worlds whirled her merrily away. So to thrust her tongue into the magician's ear was to shoot above the roof of a byre and bathe in the silver tails of comets; to shudder at his breath as he suckled on the intricacies of her hair was to rain candied rose petals on a herd of apple-colored oxen. And to hold his heart to hers was to melt into dreams.

And to wake was to find him staring at her calmly. Objectively. Separately.

She sat up, holding his regard, such as it was. Then broke it to look around her. The hut had shrunk, once more comprising but one story. On top of a tall reed basket Odeh curled like a cake, unperturbed by the change.

"What's that?" Nia asked. She'd never seen the basket before, though she'd been everywhere inside the magician's home and was as well acquainted with its surroundings. Better acquainted.

"That is your gift to the king. It will convince him to put you in my place."

"I don't want to take your place."

"No matter. He wants you there, or he will. As do I. Now more than ever. You will take him, be the making of him, mold him to be a leader of the land. All will be well."

Quickly Nia dressed. Last night she had packed a bundle to bring with her to the castle, after supper, before the snow. Before lying with Merlin. Stepping out into the yard, she saw the far-off heat rising from men climbing the path from the lake, and flocks of chattering sparrows flying up ahead of their disturbance. These must be the king's men. They were going to arrive soon.

Behind her the sounds of the hut's door opening and of shoes crushing snow announced the magician's advent. Nia turned—but who was this stranger? An elder with white hair streaming out below a dun hood—Merlin's hood—and Merlin's pale eyes caught in a web of creases ending in the silver beard covering his suddenly ancient face—

"Why have you put on this seeming?" Nia asked.

"Is that what I have done?"

She nodded slowly. Odeh slunk past Merlin to nose a shallow drift.

"How old do you think me really?"

"I—old. But—" But she had thought the years stayed their distance from him, as they did from her and many magicians. Though he'd not shared his method for accomplishing that yet.

"I was old when King Bear was born. It's in this guise he'll expect to see me."

Odeh sneezed and backed away from whatever had attracted their interest. They assumed a dignified pose on the train of Merlin's mantle. Obviously, they perceived no difference in him. This reassured Nia, as did the matter-of-fact manner in which the two spear bearers approached moments later.

"Hail," they saluted the magician. Another two men entered the clearing, appearing no more surprised than the first two. "Lord Merlin. Lady Nia." Back at Nakasongola, her name meant "intention." Here they used the same word for "brightness." Close enough.

The four had brought a pair of boats to carry the magician, the "sorceress," and their trappings to the lake's western shore. This part of the trip was restful. Water eased Nia's heart. Melting frost slid musically from the tips of the lakeside alders' branches. All was connected, and the drops of moisture rising almost visibly toward the mist-crowded sun would surely rain upon the land where she'd been born. Taking with them her apologies for leaving.

Transferring their effects from boats to wagon got complicated. The driver disliked cats. When it was finally settled that Odeh and Nia would walk together behind the others (she being a young maiden to the evidence of most men's limited senses), but a few handspans of light remained of the brief winter day. So Nia traveled the last of the road to the castle in starlight, and was greeted at the gates of Dinas Dinlle by the unsteady fires of braziers.

Trumpets shouted as the eight of them came into the castle's courtyard, which was known as its bailey. Surreptitiously, Nia removed one shoe, but the stones beneath her bare foot stayed silent of tales. As they had previously. As had those of the thick walls guarding the bailey also.

Felled oaks formed the sides of the buildings surrounding her here, and surrounding also the stairs climbing to the dark doorway leading into the largest building, the keep. Then the door's darkness receded, and out of that dawn stepped the king. Servants following behind him lifted high the torches they bore.

Under the torches' flames King Bear gleamed more ruddily than in Nia's memory. A golden circlet ran between his golden curls, the metal's color the wanner of the two.

"My lord! My lady! We wanted your company at supper!" Beckoning them forward, he came to stand at the stairs' top. "What kept you?"

Nia gave the king the curtsy these lands' rulers expected. Merlin bowed. Not low. "We apologize. We came as speedily as possible," the magician explained, "but it has taken all the day."

"Well don't hang back now!" The king pulled both Merlin and Nia into his embrace. "The other guests have finished eating, but they still await you in the great hall. The bard won't sing till I order it."

Past the torch flickers lay a short, narrow space, with a tapestry hung on its far side. The hanging's tasseled edges lifted as a youth swept it aside, spilling sudden sounds and momentarily dazzling firelight into her ears and eyes. At first the greenery hanging off railings and garlanded around the hall's high beams deceived her, with its color and scent and the sighing rustle of leaf against leaf. Had the room become a forest glade? No. Too warm for a wood in a northern winter: currents of air wafted toward her from the burning logs stacked in the wide cavern built at the hall's far end. This would be a seasonal decoration, a means of marking the birth of their god, as she'd observed happening in other Christian realms.

Sight adjusting, Nia surveyed those seated at the hall's tables for familiar faces. King Bear's retinue had changed in her absence, losing many former members, which was only sensible; they came to him to learn to fight, and this was a time of peace. Of the men gathered round him now she recognized none but the king's uncle, High Praise, and his foster brother, River. Newer warriors, numbering five by her count, laughed at their ease, swallowing gulps of what must be wine from brass cups.

These seven men, and the four women with them, stood at their entrance. King Bear introduced the men as customary, by the names of their home villages, which Nia took care to note. The women, also newcomers, were wife of this one, sister of that. The tall fellow known as Hollybush made room for Nia on the bench where he and the others sat, but the king beckoned her nearer, toward his place.

Merlin was already there. From somewhere he'd acquired a staff, and he leaned on it, ignoring the chair the king had summoned with a wave. So Nia sat in it.

The king smiled. The woman whose chair had been commandeered frowned. Nia knew her: an artist in clay and fine metals. Beloved was her name. Single and beyond the age of marrying, she had likely striven hard to catch the king's regard and win the spot next to him that she had just lost. Beloved looked annoyance Nia's way, but before Nia could relinquish the perilous seat, the harper struck his first song's first chords. They rang with surprising crispness over the hall's smoky mutterings, hushing them. Louder men heard the resulting silence and stilled themselves also. Even the whispering of the amputated leaves ceased.

The maid carrying the wine pitcher vanished momentarily and reappeared empty-handed to crouch by the kitchen's door. Nia settled herself in Beloved's chair to listen to the drumless music, a song praising the beauty of local scenery. She would try not to thirst too obviously for the land that had once been her home.

Nantlle was so much smaller than Lake Nalubaale. Though it *was* a lake. And Merlin's solitary hut had many commonalities with Mukasa's shrine on Bubembe Island. Or, more precisely, with the house before the shrine, where Nia had lived and studied prior to accusations of witchcraft.

Nor, Nia told herself, was Dinas Dinlle identical with Mbaale, the site of the temple of the war spirit Kibuuka, where she had often visited. The walls here walked straight lines rather than curved ones; the roofs here kept away the wet and the cold rather than the sun, whose heat had helped to drive her to these cooler, cloudier climes—along with her escape from trial and execution, and her search for exotic wisdom.

But some traits the two sites shared, as she had come to accept previously. The men's fierce faces. The banners lining the walls—though those here were woven of animal hair, not pounded from fig bark. The bard sang of battles like a jali, and of spiritual traditions. The harp he played as he sang sounded like an endongo plucked by someone gradually falling to sleep.

Measure followed measure, each slower than the last. In addition to fighting the music's lull, Nia struggled to stay rooted in this domain, a task made doubly difficult by the absence of significant plant life. The artificial hill on which the castle had been raised bore only short-grazed grasses and a tiny garden. Even in winter there would have been comfort in the presence of a slumbering copse of rowan, or even of birch, that least outgoing of trees. With no anchor but the dying boughs of firs and vines of mistletoe she drifted back to the shores of her childhood . . .

. . . to the fish jumping free of the boundary between breathing and drinking, so fat and slippery in her hands she laughed it loose and down it plunged while Maama shrieked at the waste, but the rippling silver glittered so prettily—

No. Marigold yellow the candle's glow before her. She must stay awake or offend King Bear's court and the king himself. In the ruler's shadow Merlin continued standing, wavering but a little, his sturdiness belying his apparent old age. One glinting eye pierced her like a sentient blade. She pried her gaze away, picked up her cup, took another draft of royal wine. A mistake. It was too strong. Drowning on dry land she sank . . .

. . . low to the lapping waves, but the boat beneath bore her up and carried her on her way to Bubembe, where Maama had prayed her whiteness would be regarded as a sign of Mukasa's favor and her visions secure apprenticeship under the hand of the Muganda, whose clasp on Nia's wrist cut sharp—

No. The clasp was Merlin's, so tight as to hurt and bring her back here. Nia turned her palm up and slid it to touch his. A thrill of coolness shot up her arm.

"I am glad you agree," the magician said. She agreed? Agreed to what? She had nodded, maybe, had possibly let her head droop, dozing off as the hall's soothing warmth and sedative airs overcame her. Treating that accidental nod as deliberate provided one way out. She inclined her head—again? The stress of Merlin's regard, the grip he established on Nia's hand, seized and lifted her the way a talon lifts a prize.

"By your leave." The magician assumed the king's assent and left. What twinkled in the air behind them? No chance to check. With a quickness Merlin brought her to the foot of the stairs to the divided chambers above the hall's annex.

Was it privacy the magician sought? She could have told him it would not be found here. Children, maidens, and a round-hipped woman Nia remembered from her earlier stay occupied the two largest rooms. A smaller third was piled high with bales of cloth and stacks of dead lumber, leaving no room for entry. The smallest, the fourth, contained nothing but another staircase. One which Nia was sure had not been there previously.

They climbed to where the stairs stopped: underneath a hatch reminding Nia of the ships on which she'd voyaged from Tunis and Corsica. The hatch swung upward at the magician's touch, revealing a sky full of stars like goblets running over with light. Stepping out, Nia at last retrieved her hand from Merlin's grasp. She stood on the roof of a tall tower. Baring her feet, she felt flat tiles slippery with friendly moss beneath her soles. The keep, the hill on which it stood, and the wall around it were nowhere in sight.

Nia dug her toes deeper into the moss, and it responded, sparkling in circles spreading outward from her feet. "When are we?" she asked.

"A time when I built what King Bear really needs. Not the future, not the past. A time of choice."

He seemed to be in a mood to answer questions. She asked another. "What's in the basket? What is my gift to the king?"

Green, yellow, pink, and white, the moss lights shifted and winked, showing by their abrupt absence the roof's edge.

"His sword." The magician looked upward, throwing his face into shadow.

"He has a sword."

"Not this one. This is a sword of destiny. He who wields it rules all Cymru."

"You give it to me so I may give it to him and thus usurp you as his counselor." Two steps and she touched his mantle, felt through its weave the warm muscles of his upper arm. "I tell you twice that's no wish of mine. I came to these lands to learn; I'm not here to conquer anything or anyone."

"Yet you have." His face remained averted. And they'd spent the day apart, he riding, she walking. How could Nia know what sense his words held? She did, though she didn't want to play this game she'd won.

Where was her pet? Odeh, who ought to have been here helping now, had approached the bailey by Nia's side but fled at the noise of the trumpets. Still, they should be able to reach her here as easily as within any other of Merlin's constructions. She called to them using the blossom pressed flat beneath the cloth covering her head.

Abruptly the tower's roof caved beneath her. Or did it disappear completely? Disoriented, Nia staggered. Again Merlin had her wrist. Yes, her surroundings had simply vanished. No debris. Only the littlest scintillation of dust—mist?—that swiftly cleared from the air. At tables around them sat the same women and men she had left in the magician's company, in almost the same positions. And before King Bear stood the basket containing her gift to him. The sword. Softness assailed her calves—Odeh rubbing between her legs.

Again Merlin bowed. He stayed bent as he spoke. "Inspired

by foretellings of your greatness, the sorceress Nia has procured for you that weapon of which I could only prophesize.

"Lady? You will perform the honor of untying the basket's
lid?"

Simple knots in strands of supple ivy parted easily at Nia's
touch. She removed the basket's lid and smelled more than
saw its contents: damp, rich earth, fully awake and clinging
to the blade piercing its heart.

"Lord?" Merlin had straightened. He beckoned to the king.

The king rose. His golden beard did little to conceal the
tension of his half-pursed lips. He swung his arms to match
the rhythm of his stride. Reaching the basket, he stopped and
faced his warriors and their women. "Witness as I fulfill the
requirement. Father Peace? You will record what happens?" A
shaven-headed, hook-nosed man seated at the hall's entrance
nodded.

With a dramatic flourish, King Bear lifted both hands high,
turning them palms in, palms out, palms toward one another.
He lowered both together, clasped with interlaced fingers
something buried in the basket's earth, and pulled forth by
its leather-bound hilt a shimmering blade of finest steel.

"Cleft-Cutter!" cried Merlin. "Bane of Cymru's enemies!"
The king spun in place, showing the sword to everyone in the
hall. "Drawn by our rightful ruler from this adamant rock!"

But the basket contained only soft soil. Nia thought to
plunge her hands in it to prove this. The magician warned
her back with a glance. The king paraded his prize from one
fighter to the next, basking in their admiration. Cleft-Cutter
seemed to reflect more light than it received, shining radiance
upon the faces bent over it turn on turn. Magic, yes. But her
magic? Not originally.

Now the king returned to kneel in front of her. "Lady

Nia," he said, in a voice meant for all to hear, "consider me beholden. A boon is yours in payment for securing me the chance to claim this gift."

Again the veil of glittering dust descended. And now she heard nothing. Saw nothing around her save a soft blur of colors hurrying past her eyes fast, faster. Felt nothing till the magician's touch calmed this weird storm. His thumb on her chin, the tips of his fingers a crescent of coolth about her cheek. The fire out and the hall empty but for Odeh waiting patiently at her tired feet.

Nia opened her mouth to ascertain what was happening. Two of Merlin's fingertips glided across her lips. "Shush you," he whispered. "All will be made clear in time."

"In *this* time," she insisted.

"Very well. At least, in an approximation of it."

More mist, more magic; then they lay together on Nia's red bed, in their future. Knowledge sat heavy on her uncovered head: it was to be their last night in each other's arms. They'd had their time. The winter months had gone, and the rains of spring wetted the hut's thatch. Thrice four quarters had passed since Yule, in this conjuration. Soon the seeds sown last autumn would wake from the sodden earth. By then Merlin too must be planted, in order that he grow.

The fire in the hut's center roared, painting their nakedness with changing jewels of light, light flowing over them like pleasure. "Did you hate me," he asked, "when I craved the king grant you my position?"

"As it was in your Seeing? Well, I did think you presumptuous."

"And I was. Being young and foolish." They both laughed, sadly at first. "Yet old enough at over a hundred years to understand that secrets can never be told. Only shown."

"Yes. That's their nature." Her white fingers flexed in his hair, which at this moment was brown as the wing of his namesake. "You have never expected me to teach you my secrets—only to share with you the joy of learning them."

The magician's fingers caressed her hair also, tugging gently at the sensitive roots, tracing the paths between them. "You'll not fight me, then? You'll help?"

"Haven't I promised? I'll dig your grave myself."

"And you'll care for the king in my absence? Fill all his needs? Love him as I do, for the sake of the union it's his destiny to form?"

"I'll care for him as you would, till the time of your return."

"But what then if I don't return?"

Nia rolled apart from him onto her belly. "Why shouldn't you? Is this your plan, to abandon King Bear's realm for the web beneath the woods?"

"Nothing is ever my plan. I only go where my life takes me."

The magic ceased. The drizzling shower of light marked its end. She stood again in the shadow-clotted great hall at Dinas Dinlle. Of course she hadn't actually left it. She snorted, unimpressed. "How was that time an approximation of this one?" she asked.

"It wasn't. Just a favorite of mine to visit." His hair was once more white, but his touch on her face felt smooth, and soft as morning dew. "I trust your curiosity is now entirely satisfied."

It wasn't, ever. She tried to distinguish the elements of her puzzlement and voice them. "Not on two points. What of your pet, your snake? What becomes of Macha?"

"And your other question?"

"Before our second—visit, if you will, the expedition to the time coming, the excursion after I gave the king your gift—

how did you hasten the passage of the night? What did others see while the world flashed by me so quickly?"

The magician's beard hitched upward, result of an invisible smile. "They saw nothing out of the ordinary, nothing but what they expected. And in their unseeing they missed both moments when I isolated you from the stream of our present. I have taught you my methods of doing that. Look to your notes.

"As for Macha . . . I believe she will wake with the change of season, as is her custom, and seek for me. If I'm already interred and I've failed to respond to your rousing, show her my ground. She'll know what to do." He bent to pull Odeh's ears. "As will you."

The brooch glowed in the North's soft sun. Garnets and gold, amber and brass—these weren't colors Nia favored for herself, but she appreciated their beauty. She raised her head to display the gratitude in her eyes. "My king, this is magnificent."

King Bear nodded. "It is the work of Beloved; I've heard you praise her skill. As she praises your powers of healing.

"Allow me." The king lifted the brooch from the folded silk held by one of the servants he'd brought to fill Merlin's house and yard. "You use it to hold shut your cloak or overdress. Your woman will—"

"I own no one."

The king appeared suddenly flustered. "Of—of course not. Of course not." He dropped the hand holding the precious trinket to his side. "I only mean the one who helps you dress."

Who would that be, Nia wondered. And why would their help be necessary. But she relented for Merlin's sake and allowed the king to pin the brooch on a shawl she spread over her shoulders and bosom. Also for love of the magician she let him remove it, and her shawl and robe and shift, and lay her on the bed where the two of them had very lately loved. Merlin had shown her at Dinas Dinlle how he asked this of her on the night before his burial. And she had discovered on living through the scene that she was unwilling to refuse him. She had sworn to care completely for Merlin's charge. To bind him to her however she might.

Coupling with the king was a simple affair, face-to-face, his manner tender enough that Nia felt no worries. She could shoulder this extra duty. It added but a little to the trouble of maintaining herself in the position Merlin expected her to fill. Aided by him, she'd begun to counsel King Bear during that Yuletide visit and in the four months since. She would keep at it on her own till Merlin emerged with the newborn moon. Soon.

He had asked that she adapt a few customs of his own people to the methods she'd evolved and with these in mind had chosen to be interred among oaks. The glade of the oaks' nearest queen tree covered a hillock to the hut's north.

After their coupling and the king's reluctant departure, she applied salve to hands that still ached from digging Merlin's resting place in the stiff, cold soil, twelve nights past. It had been a difficult burial. Not because of the work involved or any fear shown by the magician but because she had no wish to watch him dissolve into the earth, though sometimes this was what he'd seemed to want.

Odeh sniffed her fingers cautiously. They approved of the salve's honey, though its pepper oil made them sneeze. They backed away as she knelt to the hearth but not only to afford her room: the stone above Macha's resting place lifted just slightly, and out slid the snake. She coiled herself at Nia's feet, resting her flat head where lately the king had lain his possessive cheek. Odeh assumed a pose of aloof inquiry at the edge of the fire's warm circle.

"Greetings, Dame Macha; you are well come for your tidings of the new season's first steps." Nia put down a slow hand to stroke the serpent's dry-leaf skin. "Your magician's away, but will return."

The snake regarded her with placid skepticism. "Of course he insisted on a fourteen-night immersion," she complained. A month of pillow talk had not dissuaded him. "Quite sure of himself. Thinks his training sufficient; says he'll never learn any more without experience." Which was no doubt true, but why should he try to pack a decade of experience into a single lesson? What reason but pride spurred him to catch up to her so quickly?

Secrets must be shown, not told, yes. And because of this their learning required patience.

The serpent uncoiled herself and flowed away to a crevice near the smoldering peats. Nia got up and got into her lonesome bed. Odeh napped with her awhile, but then left to go about their obscure business. Three more nights she slept thus. Then, finally, the time came. She donned Macha like a living collar and covered them both with her cloak. Odeh stayed curled abed, stubbornly refusing to waken. She went without them.

Dawn broke slowly in these lands. Light like thin milk soaked into the air from the east, the direction in which she traveled. The cloud of her breath preceded her, carried on the softest of breezes.

Imperceptibly her walk changed to a climb, steepness shortening her steps. The quiet, riddled with birdsong and branchcreak, embraced and released and embraced her again, without and within.

She reached the hill's crown, the shallow grave, its loose-topped hummock already sprouting a few brave seedlings. Crouching, she transferred these to one of the fired clay bowls she'd brought, saving the other to dig with. As she worked, Macha slithered free of her clothes.

Aside from the plants the grave looked undisturbed. The straws she had put in for air stood angled as she'd placed them, away from unkind rains. But Macha knew, and so did she.

She uncovered him anyway. Though only his face. That was all she needed to see.

Merlin's skin was unmarked, smooth save where bearded. Examining it closely, Nia proved to herself this beard was not composed of hair. Strands of white rootlets pulsing with messages grew into the magician—or out of him? His eyes opened, shining with a pure and holy light. Inhumanly holy. Inhumanly pure.

His lips opened. Nia bent and pressed her lips against them ever so lightly. They moved but produced no sound. No air escaped between them.

She withdrew. He had gone far—further into the web than she could follow. If he was going to emerge it must be on his own.

A wordless whisper came to her over the damp soil at her back. She turned to see Macha ascending the oak tree's trunk, a green stream running skyward. From there the ser-pent twined herself along a high brown branch and stopped. Watching. Waiting.

The magician made no sign he saw his pet. Or her. If she should chide him for his pride, he'd likely never hear. All she could do was as he'd asked. As she had promised.

Pressing the earth down softly, delicately, discarding the useless straws, she refilled Merlin's grave and headed home.

The Bladesmith Queen

Sarah MacLean

I

The first fell through the ice and could not swim.

The second drank from an old well and was gone in a fortnight.

The third set sail for fortune and was lost to the sea.

And that was when she stopped kissing them.

Or maybe it was they who stopped kissing her, as it seemed the whole village learned the bladesmith's daughter was cursed at the same time she discovered it herself.

Not cursed. *A* curse, which was a different thing altogether.

Receiving a devastating blow engendered pity. Being the instrument of the blow? Fear.

And so, despite the fact that she was only fifteen when Rowan fell through the ice, only sixteen when Henry drank from the well, only seventeen when Garreth—beautiful, strong, kind-eyed Garreth—was lost to the sea, she became the face of the village's fear. Mothers clutched their children tight when they saw her in the street; fathers invoked her name when those same children misbehaved; the priest, in his ominous black robes, made the sign of the cross when she passed the stone church on her way into town. Women averted their eyes when she neared, and men—they steered clear altogether.

After all, they were the ones in the most danger.

If she had been another woman in another town, she would not have been allowed to stay. She would have been run out, sent on her way to wreak her havoc on a different place with different sons. But she was the daughter of a bladesmith, who'd been son of a bladesmith, who'd been son of a bladesmith, and so on, as far back as steel could be forged in flame, and so she was invaluable to the town for her skill.

As she was a curse, so, too, were the weapons born in her fire. Any soldier who marched into battle with a blade made by the Bladesmith Witch on his hip would fight stronger and smarter than ever before. At least, that was the tale whispered on battlefields and in taverns the land over.

Like all tales told by terrified boys and drunken men, however, it was more myth than fact, just as she was.

But myths made for boasting, and boasting made for danger—especially to their subjects—and she learned young that when a woman was a myth, her danger was magnified. Because myths bestow power as well as fear.

And men do not like women with power.

Worse, still, those who wield it.

She spent her days alone in the forge, her only companion the wolf who shadowed her on weekly trips into town, when the whole village took inside to watch warily through the corners of their distorted glass windows. The baker, the grocer, and the butcher were the only ones brave enough to come close, and even then, they charged her triple the cost: a risk tax. A curse tax.

She paid it without complaint.

It was not the first tax she had paid for this village that feared her, nor was it the most devastating.

In her solitude, she wielded hammer and flame and forged the most glorious steels the world had ever seen. And the men who heard her story came from the far reaches of the land, each promising to conquer the Bladesmith Witch in his way. Each vowing to leave with the greatest of her swords.

A sword that could cheat death.

A sword that could make them kings.

When they came, she sold them blades. And some she charged exorbitant sums. A curse tax. Most paid without complaint, and it was proof enough that it was deserved.

Until him.

II

She went days without speaking, the only sound in the cottage the roar of the fire and the heavy clang of the hammer and the hiss of the honing wheel and the smooth slide of her leather apron, all punctuated by the wolf's snores.

That day, however, the wolf did not sleep, instead standing sentry by the door to the forge, the morning hours slipping by into the long afternoon, the animal unmoving.

Waiting.

When a low growl sounded deep in the beast's chest, the bladesmith turned from her work. That morning, she'd woken restless to bright sun and cool air, the autumn teasing at late summer—a day that should have brought a deep breath of relief but instead made her uneasy.

She went to the forge earlier than usual—unable to think

of anything but a new blade, long and sharp, with a honed edge that would slice through bone. It was not the first time she made for her hammer with nerves roiling. There had been another, followed by days of work, resulting in blades like nothing she'd made before.

Blades stamped not with the thistle that marked so many of her steels, but with the thorny leaf.

Sharp, gleaming weapons for men without mercy, and who deserved none.

When she went to the fire that morning, she feared she was to make another. And when the wolf growled, she knew there would not be time.

She stood at the door, sure fingers tangling in the animal's thick white fur, her gaze on the horizon as dust rose behind the rider in the distance. She watched with the wolf as the warrior neared, all in black atop a stunning mount—an enormous dark chestnut that might have been black if not for the gleam of the setting sun belying its rich color.

She did not move as she cataloged the rider's features: leather straps mapmaking across his broad chest; a short sword; a broad one; an ax with double blades, the kind that was for work and not show; five knives, one at each boot, two sheathed beneath his arms, and the last strapped with thick black leather over his heart, like a vow.

Arms like steel, themselves.

Fists like stone.

He was power.

Another low growl from the wolf as the rider dismounted, collecting a long parcel from his saddlebags and crossing the property through the dried summer grass. It was only then, as he approached, that she thought to consider the rest of his features.

Square jaw. Dark hair. Broken nose. The grime of an endless ride settled on him and somehow not off-putting. At least, no more off-putting than a man of his size was on approach.

Eyes like the forest to the north. Not quite brown, not quite black, not quite green.

Not quite safe.

The leather scabbard at her own thigh was tight comfort as he stilled mere feet from her. She thought of the metal she'd thrust into the fire that morning.

Not safe at all.

She lifted her chin.

He watched her for a long moment and said, "Does he bite?"

"She does," she replied, stroking the wolf's head.

One black brow rose. "I seek the Bladesmith."

"You've plenty of blades."

The second brow joined the first. "Do you not think that I should be the judge of that?"

"You came to me because I am the expert, did you not, traveler?"

Something shifted in his gaze. She didn't care for it.

"You came to me first." He spoke in riddles; she'd never left this town. When she remained quiet, he added. "I am here to discuss a blade."

She already knew that. She could feel the heat of the weapon he'd come for at her back.

"You cannot afford me," she said, leaving him, the wolf at her side as she checked the steel.

He followed, filling the room with his broad brow and his wide shoulders and his chest that seemed to have acreage. His silence was maddening—the others always ran their mouths. But this one, he was big and quiet. She refused to look at him, knowing it was a game. Knowing that if she did, he would score a point. Instead, she watched her forge, the steel inside now gleaming, hot and malleable.

Behind her, he shifted, barely a movement. Just enough to take in the space.

She imagined him cataloging her as she had done him. Instead of a horse, a wolf. Instead of a sleeping roll, a pallet in the corner. Instead of a saddle, a wooden chair.

Instead of a broadsword, a dozen of them.

Weapons everywhere, on the walls and nearly every surface. Double-headed axes and longswords, fine knives with smooth stone hilts, carved by her father's father to fit the hills and valleys of a warrior's grip. And in a place of honor above the hearth, two gleaming steel blades that had waited generations for their owners.

But those weapons did not matter that day. The ones that mattered were the half dozen within arm's length, each more deadly than the last.

If she turned, would there be fear on the warrior's face?

Their fear was her only defense.

"They say you are a witch."

"In my experience, that descriptor is not complimentary on the tongues of men."

"They say your blades cannot be beaten."

They lie. "They say many things."

He kept his distance, remaining just inside the door, and still the entire space had gone heavy with the strange weight of his presence. She considered it, unsettling, and somehow, without fear.

No. Not without fear. Without the kind of fear that threatened. Full, instead, of the kind of fear that tempted. Like the line of his jaw. The cord of his neck. The ridge of his torso, bound with leather and steel.

"They say you forge them with magic."

She did turn back at that, to find him staring at her. "And do you believe them?"

He waited a beat, the silence flooding the space between them, his eyes gleaming like agate in full sun. Her pulse raced as she waited for his reply. "I have not yet decided."

"And if it is true? Why would I waste that magic on you?"

"Because you have wasted it on the others."

He was wrong; if it existed, it had never been wasted. "And are you like the others?"

"I am nothing like them."

Her breath stuttered at the truth. "I am to believe that?"

"You are to know it."

She shook her head. "How?"

A beat. "I can afford you."

Her work. The blade. "Are you very rich?"

"Yes," he said without hesitation, "but I do not intend to pay with coin."

On another man's tongue it would have been a threat. Would have straightened her spine. On another man's tongue, the words would have conjured an image of the burn she would put on his handsome face if he came closer.

But there was no threat in the words. Only promise.

"You think highly of yourself."

A slight curve of his lips sent a lick of pleasure up her spine, shocking her. How long had it been since she'd felt such a thing? Had she ever felt such a thing?

He moved before the answer could come, away from her, around the edge of the small, warm room, made warmer by the lingering summer and his presence. He set the long package, wrapped in black cloth, on the scarred oak table at the far end of the space and stepped back, crossing his arms over his chest, meeting her gaze through the dust dancing in the light between them. "Payment."

She couldn't help herself. She approached, drawing near enough for the heat of him to burn, and pulled back a corner of the cloth, revealing scant inches of the blade within before she caught her breath. She did not have to see the silver steel to know the mark it bore. She did not have to hold it to know who had carried it.

She recoiled, her gaze flying to his, finding him unsurprised. *He knew she'd made it.*

"How did you get it?"

"I took it from its owner. After I took his head."

For the first time in her life, the Bladesmith felt relief. But relief was not the emotion for the moment.

Not when he continued. "Do you know what horrors that blade wrought?"

Only her strength kept her from retreat. "I am a swordsmith. All my blades bring horror."

His gaze narrowed. "Not when held by the just."

"And you? Are you just?"

He seemed to grow in the wake of the words, filling the room with his broad chest and his strong arms, yes, but also with his breath and scent—leather and steel. And with the kind of certainty that ensured warriors victory. Might.

And still she did not fear him.

Not even when he looked down upon her—when was the last time she'd met someone who could look down upon her? *Weed*, her father had called her as she'd grown—she'd heard it more than she'd ever heard her name, because she'd kept growing, unable to be cut back.

Until, of course, she had been.

"That blade took good men in battle." His gaze did not leave hers, and she found she could not look away, even as she wanted to. "It took people from homes."

Even as she needed to.

"It took livelihoods."

Even as tears welled in her own eyes, unbidden. Unwelcome as she finished the list for him. "Babes from mothers," she whispered. "Fathers from daughters. Sisters from brothers."

He was close enough to touch now. She would not have to reach for him. And perhaps it was proximity that made it easy to see the surprise in his eyes. Worse—the understanding. "You have seen what he was capable of."

"I can still smell the sulfur in the air." She could hear the cries. Feel the bile and the terror in her throat as she agreed to the offer that would save the village that loathed her. "He fought alone?"

She could not hide the tremor in the question.

He noticed. "You knew what he was." It was not meant as an accusation, and still it felt like one.

"I see the truth of every man who enters this place. Every one who demands a blade. This one—he demanded a scourge."

"Then you are a witch, as they say."

"No." The tears were salt now, tight on the earth of her cheeks. "I am a woman with a lifetime of knowledge. And a lifetime of shame for that sword."

He watched her carefully for a long, unbearable moment. "Shame? Or regret?"

The question shocked her. To so many, they were the same. She raised her chin, the memory of what she'd done, of why, in her reply. "Never regret."

"The pain of the just."

She shook her head. "Do not pretend we are the same."

"But we are," he said, one side of his beautiful mouth curving in a barely there smile. "That is the truth I see. You, cursed with the past, and I, cursed with the future."

Confusion flared, banished when he lifted a hand, bronzed with sun and the dust of the summer, slow and certain but without force. A request.

Granted.

His touch was hot as the forge, sending fire and something more dangerous shooting through her, making her want to lean into it. To lean into him.

"Do you see my curse, lady?" The words were low and dark, full of heat and pleasure, spiraling deep into her like a threat.

"No."

His thumb pressed to the edge of her jaw, lifting her chin, revealing the long column of her neck, stroking the place where her pulse pounded in the same wild rhythm as his.

And that single caress drew a little sound from her, a sound of unmistakable want.

"I fear it is you."

She shouldn't like the words. Shouldn't want them to be true.

He drew close enough for her to feel his breath on her lips. Close enough for her to want more than breath there.

Perhaps she was his curse.

She pulled back. "No."

He did not advance. Did not kiss her, not even when she could not imagine wanting anything more than his kiss. His thumb moved again. "Here?"

Everywhere else. She nodded. "Yes."

He set his lips to that place, claiming her skin and her heartbeat with a slow lick and a soft slide and a lingering suck that was nearly unbearable.

When he lifted his head, she was consumed with desire, foreign and familiar.

And impossible, threatening to destroy them both.

Panic replaced it. "I shall make you your sword."

But he wasn't there for a weapon. She knew that now. And she feared the truth of what he had come for. Those eyes like agate, seeing too much. Understanding even more.

That he might have come for her, instead.

"How many more?" he asked.

She did not misunderstand the question, her gaze flickering to the blade on the table. How many blades had been forged for men like the one he'd killed. How many enemies were to be vanquished.

Neither did she misunderstand the vow there, simmering in the question. That they would share vengeance. That he would find the men who held her blades. That he would end them.

And though she did not know the price of his might, she knew she would pay it. Knew, too, that she would want to.

She did not hesitate.

"Three."

III

The first time he saw the woman with the white wolf, the warrior had been covered in the blood of his enemies, after fighting the worst of battles to protect people who were not his but who claimed him, nonetheless. The hero mercenary, whose sword was available for hire, for a singular price, but only if he believed in the killing.

His faith in the kill separated him from the rest of his kind, strong and swift and made for destruction, with muscles and sinew and strength that laid enemies low long before they felt it—before even the moment they discovered they should fear it.

He'd come for them one by one, one body barely in the earth before he faced the next. Around him groans and grunts, curses and fury, and the knowledge that the soldiers would keep coming until he dispatched their leader. And so he picked his way through the battle until he faced a man with strength beyond reason and something in his eyes that would have terrified a warrior with a different destiny.

Infallibility.

The battle raged, the clang of steel cocooning them until the warrior could not see the rest of the fight, the rest of the soldiers, riled to madness by this, their mad commander, who fought like an animal. Who carried a blade like none the warrior had ever seen, even when it had fallen to the earth, stained with the blood of its owner.

Even in defeat, that blade, marked with the thorned leaf of the thistle, had called to him. He couldn't have left it, even if he'd tried. But he did not try—it was too much.

When he'd touched it, vision had come like memory. The garden of a bladesmith's cottage. Summer, giving way to autumn, the soil turned to dust. The door open, a forge within, out of sight, but there, nonetheless.

In the doorway, a woman, taller than any he'd ever seen, with a narrow gaze the color of the sky at midnight and full lips and brown skin and a wild mane of black curls tempting the wind. Her arms were bare, revealing her strength, and the rest of her was shielded by a long leather apron. By her side, a white wolf, big enough to reach her waist—still enough to pose a threat to any who neared.

In his vision, like memory, the warrior neared.

In his vision, like memory, the bladesmith smiled and came to him, and he swept her into his arms, lifting her high and pressing his nose to the place where her neck met her shoulder, breathing her in as her arms wrapped around his head and clasped him to her, as though she could draw him deep into herself.

As though they were two halves, pieced together at long last.

In his vision, like memory, he belonged to her.

He'd searched for her for months, sword in hand, haunted by that vision—the one that showed not discovery but return. And one night, in a dank tavern in a barely there village, a drunk had run his mouth and spoken her into being. The woman with the white wolf.

The Bladesmith Witch.

When the warrior had come over the rise and his vision had unraveled before him—it had taken all his strength not to urge his mount forward and race for her, like home.

He did not have a home. He was a man of war.

And visions were not for trusting.

Not until he'd seen her tears, sensed her fear, and believed her shame. And by the time the salt had dried on her cheeks, his blade was hers.

If only she'd have it.

Months had passed as he'd searched for the remaining blades—the ones marked with the thistle and held by warlords, brothers of the first he'd killed, who had laid waste to towns and villages without hesitation. Who had destroyed and tormented and taken what was never theirs to claim.

The warrior took their lives in return.

Their lives, and the swords he'd vowed to return to their maker, each revealing a new memory of her. Working at her forge, waking in her bed, bathing in the lake that lay like a mirror beyond her cottage.

Memories of a future that threatened to consume him.

Her future.

And his, as well.

IV

She made his blade in the days following his departure, after watching his black horse disappear over the horizon, the dust settling in its wake. Only then did she turn to the hearth and begin her work—using the steel of the swords that had been her father's and grandfather's greatest creations to forge the one that would be hers.

She worked in a fevered state, barely sleeping, barely eating, barely thinking as the hammer came down over the blood-orange metal, cleansed in fire and remade in perfection for a singular owner. A just warrior. One who, when he held this blade, would know the truth of his destiny.

When it was finished, she set the steel in the place of honor above the hearth, where she slept under its watch each night and woke to it every day.

Mild autumn turned to brutal winter and wet spring and finally, to a nearly unbearable summer—hot and unpleasant enough to drive the bladesmith and her wolf into the world beyond her forge, to the lake that stretched across the northern edge of her land, far enough from the village and close enough to her cottage to keep others away. She was alone in the cool water, her movement the only disturbance over the looking-glass surface, when she felt him.

He came on a breeze that kissed the damp skin of her bare neck as she stood chest-deep in the lake, facing its fathomless center, and she reveled in the comfort of him, chasing away the worst of the summer—and the worst of her past.

He'd returned.

Relief came. And something else. Something she might have called joy, if she'd been able to recognize it.

She turned, her gaze drawn to his. He stood on the long sloping path leading from the cottage to the lake, frozen. He drank her in and she did the same, finding him somehow bigger, stronger than he'd been months earlier, muscles honed more sharply, covered in dirt and dust as though he'd come straight from battle.

Perhaps he had.

She did not look away.

She never wanted to look away.

He'd returned, which meant he had taken her vengeance and made it right.

He'd returned, and now he stood on high like a king and watched her with pride and arrogance and something else that felt like a gift. Like a tribute.

He felt like a tribute.

Indeed, when his eyes darkened and he moved, his purpose undeniable, it was she who was the monarch, as though she had summoned him to her side. She lifted her chin, letting her own arrogance show. A match. "You did not die."

A smile flashed. "Are you disappointed?"

No. Never.

"I have not decided."

He was at the edge of the lake, the water teasing at his boots. "You will let me know when you have?"

She could not help her own smile then. "Aye."

He crouched, his thighs thick, straining his breeches, and set his fingers to the water. "Are you not cold?"

She was hot as the sun.

Something gleamed in his eyes. Something like pleasure. "This is a beautiful lake, lady."

"Thank you."

"Is it big enough for two?"

Like that, cold seemed no longer an option, possibly ever. *Yes. Please.*

He heard the answer and stood, reaching for the belt that held his short swords.

Her breath grew shallow, but she did not turn away. He was silent for a moment, and then, as though they were a long-matched set, he said casually, "Do you not wish to ask me a question?"

"I do not," she said, and it was true. There was a playfulness in the moment, and she did not wish it to disappear. Especially not as he shrugged out of the leather baldric holding his knives.

His shirt sailed over his head as though it had a thousand times before—as though he had not left this place months earlier vowing to vanquish her enemies. Vowing to take their heads. Vowing to return with the swords that brought her shame.

Her gaze tracked over the wide bronze planes of his chest, the dust of hair, the flat copper nipples like coins—a reminder that he was too dear a cost for a bladesmith at the end of the earth. That he was minted for more than this.

And then she saw the ink high on one muscle.

The plump head of the thistle and below, the thorn.

As though he were her blade, forged in her fire.

Her eyes flew to his—those eyes that also seemed too expensive. "You bear my mark."

"In more ways than one." Another riddle. "Ask me the question."

"I already know the answer. You return with them."

A shadow passed overhead. A bird in the sunlight. A half-there cloud. And then the warrior inclined his head. It might well have been a genuflection for the grace of it. The gift of it. "I do."

It was done.

Four swords from the four most evil men she'd ever met.

Four swords she wished she had never made.

Four swords that protected her village and destroyed how many others?

Four swords that would never harm again.

She lifted her chin. "I am not sorry for it." Indeed, she would have liked to have delivered the blows.

"Of course you are not." A half smile. "You thank the heavens I live."

She raised a brow. "Do I?"

A little gruff grunt of laughter as he sat on a large flat stone on the bank of the lake and removed his boots, one at a time, the muscles of his arms straining with the work.

For a wild moment, she thought to help and then decided she preferred to watch.

For a wild moment, she thought he might prefer she watch

as well, as she drank him in. Finally, she said, "How did you find me?" The lake was far enough from the cottage that no one ever came looking for her here.

"I have seen you here," he said simply.

Another riddle. The last time he'd come, it was autumn, and too cold for the lake.

Before she could press him for more, he said, "What is your name?"

The question startled her. *Was there anyone left who knew the answer?*

And did she wish him to be the one? To hold sway over her? *Did she wish to hold sway over him?*

"Orsa." It was out before she could decide.

He stilled, his hands at the laces of his braies. "I am Bruin."

"You say you have seen me here, warrior."

Those eyes darkened. "And I have, lady."

Had she ever been called such? "In your dreams?"

"Something of the sort."

"And in those dreams, were you here with me?"

His fingers worked at his laces, quick now. Sure. Leaving his trousers on the shore, he entered the water without pause, pure grace. Unashamed of his nakedness, heavy and perfect.

He had no reason for shame. She watched as he came for her, reading his skin, myriad scars, white and raised like roads cut through the land, paths well traveled. A long scar down one side, the mark of a short sword. At one strong thigh, a wild crisscross that only one with vast knowledge of weapons would know had come from a mace.

Each healed, the scars left behind knitted firm and making him stronger. More powerful.

"Do you imagine you see those dreams, lady?" he said, the

words low and soft, carrying an impossible distance across the
sheer surface of the lake.

"I, too, have had dreams." For months she'd woken to them,
aching for his nearness. For his touch.

When the water reached his waist, he dove in, surfacing
mere feet from her, hands running over his face, clearing it
of the dust, of the days' ride, of the battles he had fought and
won.

For her.

Her heart pounded as he revealed the clean, square, sharp
angles of his face, his full lips, and those eyes that saw everything. More than it.

And then he was there, inches from her, his fingers reaching for her, sliding over her cheek, cool and hot all at once.
"What do you dream?"

I dream of you.

"Shall I tell you of mine?" he asked before she could reply.
"I dream of you. Like this. My lady in this lake, with the sun
beating down. With the moon gleaming on your skin, turning you silver, making you one with the water. I have seen you
here a thousand times. Every night since the night I lifted the
second of your swords. I see you in this place with your white
wolf sentry on the bank. I see you now. In this moment, with
my hand on your skin and your black gaze on mine."

Her breath came fast as he closed the distance between
them, blocking out everything but the feel of him, the quiet
lap of the water shifting between them, holding his heat at
bay.

"And I cannot sleep for it," he whispered, leaning closer. "I
cannot think for seeing you here, tall and strong and full of
steel. Do you see it, too?"

She did. She nodded, and he stroked down, over the column of her neck, down farther, over smooth, sun-kissed skin and beneath the water, where the backs of his fingers teased at the straining tips of her breasts.

"Do you see that I have gone mad from the sight of you, in this lake, at your forge, in the door, waiting for me . . . every night for months? From the sound of you, rich and beautiful? From the scent of you, like heather and flame? A scent that is no longer a vision, no longer a memory, but real?"

It wasn't possible.

And still, she saw the wildness in his gaze. Saw the pulse pounding at the base of his neck. Heard the truth in the words.

He was so close—she ached from his nearness.

And then he was closer, his lips nearly on hers. His breath sweet against her skin, a whisper of sensation as he asked, "Do you see that I am mad from the wondering . . . will you taste of the dreams, too?"

Would he?

Yes.

"Don't," she whispered.

He stopped, so close, and achingly not close enough.

"Don't," she said again, pained.

No kissing.

He didn't hesitate, his fingers coming to her cheek. "Here?"

"Yes."

"Here?" Her neck.

"Yes."

Lower, to the straining tip he'd abandoned. "Here?"

Yes.

His massive thigh fit between hers, lifting her into his arms as though she weighed nothing, and he lowered his lips to her breast. She gasped, her fingers sliding into his hair, wet from the lake, holding him to her. Claiming her pleasure. Claiming him.

Without stopping his caress, he carried her to the large flat rock that jutted into the lake and set her down, the warm red sandstone at her back and the cool water at her feet as he reveled in her bare body.

As she reveled in his inspection. His want.

His need, hard and unmistakable.

One enormous hand spread over her torso, pressing her into the smooth stone, grounding her pleasure as he traced the curves and valleys of her body. "Here?" he whispered at the soft swell of her belly.

Her fingers in his hair answered, urging him on, his tongue swirling over her skin. Lower, lower, magnificently lower, until he parted her thighs and one finger slid through her like a promise. "Here."

It was no longer a question.

He no longer required answers.

"I dreamed of this," he whispered, and then his mouth was on her, warm and lush, pure pleasure that eased over her like waves. Her fingers tightened, the sting of her grasp a gift. Her hips tilted, working against him until she gasped and sighed and bowed off the stone, unable to control the shattering release he gave her.

And only when that was done and she'd released him from his purpose did he rise up over her, placing a line of sinful kisses across her skin, warmed from sun and stone and sex. He did not try to claim her mouth this time. Instead, he settled himself between her wide, welcoming thighs and looked deep into her eyes.

"I dreamed of this." Those words again, shattering through her. Impossible and somehow true.

"And what happened after?" she whispered.

"After . . ." He paused, and she saw the truth in his gaze— pure need, matched, instantly, in her own.

He saw the shift, felt it as he slid home, heavy and thick and hot inside her, stretching her to magnificent fullness, deep, deeper, until she could not remember what it was to have him away. And what should have brought her fear and uncertainty instead brought her comfort. And pleasure.

Wild, unbridled pleasure as he met her movements, lifting and rocking and thrusting, his hand sliding between them to stroke at the very heart of her need, feeding it until she gasped and sighed to the sun and sky and he growled his reply.

When they returned to the moment, he gathered her into his arms and reversed their positions, taking the hard stone at his back and leaving her cushioned on his chest, his heart pounding a chaotic rhythm beneath her ear.

He spoke, the words a low, delicious rumble. "I did not dream that. That was too good even for dreams."

She smiled, feeling lighter than she had in a lifetime, her fingers stroking over his chest, to the place where her mark was inked on his skin. She lingered there, tracing the pattern of the thistle, as familiar as her name, as the lake, as the feel of a hammer in hand. "When did you get this?"

He replied to the trees above. "A lifetime ago. Long before I discovered your blade."

Impossible.

She lifted her head, but he was already adding, "A sooth-sayer in the south inked me with it. Spun me a tale of the thorn and thistle—two halves of a world at war, finally, together in peace." He looked to her. "Promised me that one day, I would find the one who would knit them together."

She caught her breath. "It is my mark. The thistle."

He nodded. "But on the blades I collected for you, the thorn."

She returned her cheek to his chest, his heartbeat slow and steady beneath her, the opposite of her wild thoughts.

His touch trailed over her shoulder and along her side to her hip, where his massive hand settled, holding her tight to him. "I wish I could have brought you their heads along with their blades."

She shouldn't have smiled, but she did, warm with the knowledge that he fought for her—which none had ever done before. "I do not wish their heads."

"What, then?"

I wish you. She did not say the words, too afraid of what they meant.

He did not push her. Or perhaps he did. "In the village, they say you are cursed."

"Not cursed," she replied. "A curse."

"They say you stay away."

"They fear me," she whispered.

"Why?" His fingers did not slow, continuing their path up and down her skin. A fleeting comfort.

"They think I am poison. They think I will doom them all."

A cool breeze broke the heavy heat. "They do not know the truth."

She lifted her head. Met his gaze, green and gold, like summer. "What truth?"

"They do not know that you saved them from the real curse."

Four men in her cottage. Brothers. Beasts.

Banished from the village by the Bladesmith Witch.

"They do not."

His hand slid into the thick fall of her hair, half damp from the lake. "Kiss me now."

She wanted to. She'd never wanted anything so much.

"You are not the wound," he said, holding her gaze. Refusing to let her hide. "You are the balm."

She wanted that, too.

Instead, she slid away from him, off the rock, stretching in the sunlight, unmoved by her own nudity even as his beautiful, unwavering gaze tracked every inch of her.

He took pleasure in her.

And she took pleasure in that.

"Come, then, warrior," she said finally. "Your blade awaits."

V

Inside the cottage, the wolf stretched across the threshold like a warning, she fetched the blade from its place, gleaming sharp and stunning in the afternoon light, streaming in through the windows set high up on the walls.

She turned with it in hand, holding it reverently, the steel perfectly honed, the hilt inlaid with obsidian and gold. He watched her carry it to the fire with a similar reverence, and they both felt the weight of the act.

As the sword warmed, she spoke, not to her warrior, but to her fire. "My father—and his father before him—loved to tell me that this forge had made the blades of kings and queens. That those who rode into battle under the banner of justice and changed the course of history did so with our steel at their side." She hesitated. "But no king came when famine took my grandfather's village. No king came when plague took my father's. Their finest blades went unclaimed."

He spoke her name low like the rumble of the forge.

"No king came when war threatened mine."

He did not move, and she sensed how difficult stillness was for him then, this warrior who had no doubt survived on an economy of movement. "You are not a curse."

"I am. I made the blades," she whispered to the flames, letting sadness into her words. "I traded this village for another when I should have taken up my own sword and gone for their heads."

"*I* was your sword. *I* took their heads."

The words thrummed through her, giving her more pleasure than they should have. Making her want him again.

Making her want to give him everything she had.

"You were my vengeance."

"Your weapon."

"Today, I shall be yours." She turned to him then, and when she met his eyes, he came for her, across the tiny space even as she raised a hand and stayed the movement. He stopped no distance from her, close enough to touch if he reached for her.

But he didn't, and she both loved and hated that.

"I did not believe the tales, and so I did not make my blade," she said, wanting him to understand. And then she turned and pulled the sword from the forge; it gleamed orange, blindingly hot. "Until you."

He sucked in a breath but kept his distance, even as her skin tingled with awareness. With desire. Resisting it, she turned away and reached for a hammer and a stamp that had never been used. As he watched, she set the stamp to hot metal and made quick work, striking the steel before it lost its heat . . . four times in quick succession, the face of each of the men he had vanquished flashing as she did, and then, a fifth time.

His face did not flash.

It lingered, like a promise.

Like a gift.

She dropped the blade into the deep well of water nearby, the cool liquid hissing and steaming in protest. "My blade is yours," she said softly, watching him before lifting the sword by its hilt and turning to set it on the scarred oak table where he had once set a different blade, one with less power. "The only one of its kind," she said. "The only one marked with the flower and thorn. Mercy and punishment. Hope and fear. A balance of humors worthy of a warrior king."

He drew close but did not look at the blade. Instead, he looked at her. "I did not come for a sword," he said, dark and soft, like sin.

He reached for her, his hands coming to her face, cupping her cheeks and tilting her up to him. "I came for you. I came because every time I have touched a blade forged in your fire, I have seen you. And I have seen us. And I have seen our future." He set his forehead to hers and breathed her in. "You are not my curse," he whispered, lifting her hand in his, pressing it to the mark inked on his skin, identical to the one on her steel. "You are my destiny."

She shook her head. "Impossible," she whispered. "You shall be the warrior king, and I am no kind of consort."

He shook his head. "Not consort."

Before she could deny him again, he released her and lifted the blade, the vision washing over him. This sword, it would unite a kingdom. In peace. Just as its maker would bring him peace. Just as she would bring him joy.

He was her sword. Her weapon. Her vengeance.

And she was his power. His crown.

"Not consort," he repeated, taking her hand and setting it to the hilt, entwining their fingers, letting her feel the power that came not from the blade, but from they who would wield it.

He met her eyes, wide and beautiful and full of wonder, and pulled her close. This time, she let him. She let his fingers stroke her cheek and tilt her face to his, let her gaze tangle with his, let herself revel in the nearness of him, in the warmth of him.

In his kiss, long and deep, tasting of hope and setting her on fire. He stroked deep, his arms coming around her and lifting her high, close, tight against him, the pleasure of the caress so intense that it chased away everything but the future.

When that was done, he lifted his head and whispered, "Queen."

Time stretched between them, immense with the promise of a future that she had never imagined and one that now she could not deny. One that she wanted more than anything ever before.

For the first time, the Bladesmith believed in the future. And so she claimed it, alongside her warrior, and the kingdom that would be theirs.

Do, By All Due Means

Sive Doyle

"You know, my lady," came a voice, "if you come down now, there's still plenty of time to make it to the great hall before dinner."

Britomart startled and had to cling to the tree branch to stop from falling. Once she was properly braced, she peered down to see a familiar face looking up at her with wry amusement. Of course she hadn't heard *him* approach. Each story told at her father's court about Merlin's powers was more fantastical than the last. To walk on stealthy feet through an orchard would be no test of his abilities.

"My lord Merlin," Britomart said, willing her cheeks not to heat. She had already been uncomfortably aware that choosing to spend the afternoon hiding out in an apple tree was not the mature action of a princess who was almost fully grown. The thought of how a great girl like her must seem—with one of her plaits coming loose and her skirts hiked up to show calves scratched by twigs and stained by grass—was enough to dispel the last of her bad humor and replace it completely with embarrassment. "I—I hope the day finds you well. I did not think you were expected here for another week."

"No," he said, "but circumstances change. For instance, if you come down from that tree and escort me to the great hall, that would be a change of circumstances. And since it would mean your good lady mother would no longer be in a tizzy wondering where you are *and* that I would be able to fill my belly with some excellent roast pork, I think it would be a change of circumstances agreeable to everyone."

There was no help for it. By the time Britomart had scrambled to the ground, her face was bright with exertion and embarrassment. The old man had the good grace to look away until she had smoothed out her skirts and turned to walk back up through the orchards at his side. Still, Merlin loved to poke fun. Britomart braced herself for the inevitable teasing to come on the topic of princesses in apple trees.

"You did not replace the covering, you know" was what Merlin said next, though.

Britomart startled again, but this time the color drained from her cheeks.

"That looking glass is a powerful thing, Britomart." Merlin's voice was grave and had in it no hint of humor, just the echo of an ancient might. "I did not make it for my own amusement. Or at least, there have been other objects whose making I have enjoyed more. You know what it can do. To leave it uncovered is to let things look back. Dangerous things."

"I didn't—my family—"

Before Britomart could start into a panicked run toward the great hall, Merlin held up a hand. "I made it safe before I came in search of you, young lady. What *were* you thinking?"

The looking glass was one of the king's great treasures. Like the shard of some enormous and highly polished pearl, Merlin had enchanted it so that it could show the image of anything that the world contained between heaven and earth. King

Ryence used it to sense whether any enemies approached and had long impressed on his daughter the importance of using it to keep their realm safe. Britomart knew that the looking glass was a powerful tool and a necessary one for the preservation of a small realm surrounded by many much larger kingdoms. The king owed a great debt to Merlin for such a mighty gift.

But Britomart had thought that to use it for herself, just once, could not be so terribly selfish, especially not if she used it to discover something that would shape the kingdom's future. So she had crept into her father's private solar that morning, carefully unfolded the brocade cloth that normally enfolded the mirror, and asked it a question.

"This morning, my mother said that it was time for me to marry and that she and the king will decide on a match for me soon," Britomart told Merlin. It hadn't been a shock, exactly. She'd had her courses for three years now, and she was her father's only heir. Britomart had never been destined for a nunnery, much as she thought sometimes it must be a very restful kind of place to live. That wasn't a sadness in itself. She didn't think she'd ever had a calling to the habit. She just didn't feel any desire to get married, either. Britomart had never been able to understand why so many of her childhood friends now found boys to be so very fascinating. Boys were all well and good when they washed their feet, but there was nothing about them that made her want to risk a death in childbed. "I only wondered about how it might all come about, and so I thought to ask the looking glass."

"Ah." Merlin looked at his feet in their battered boots. "And the husband you saw was not to your liking, I take it?"

"Well, that's just it," Britomart said, recalling the confusion and frustration that led her to flee for the orchard's solitude. "It didn't show me a husband. It only showed me, well . . . me."

Merlin halted now and regarded her with a quizzical look, head cocked to one side like an overgrown bird. "You?"

"Yes. Well, not *me* precisely," Britomart clarified. "I was dressed as a knight in armor, as completely as any one of my father's banner men. I wore a gilt-edged helm and carried a shield that bore the device of a crouching, crowned hound and had a great spear in my other hand. And there was someone else there, another woman—though I don't know how I knew that; all I could see was a vague reflection on my armor. I didn't know what it meant and I was upset and I—I ran. I'm sorry."

Britomart had been raised to wield a bow and arrow as well as she did a needle and thread. She'd even wheedled some sword lessons from the more indulgent members of her father's personal guard, the ones who had known her since she was a babe in arms. They'd told her she wasn't bad. But she had never felt so utterly confident in her ability to wield anything as did the Britomart she had glimpsed in the mirror—and she was quite sure that that other Britomart had never felt so young and so awkward as she did now. What a fine daughter of the royal house she was showing herself to be.

Merlin had fallen silent and was gazing out through the orchard's main gateway, to where the sun was starting to sink toward the horizon. "I suppose I never thought to make sure it wouldn't develop a will of its own. I've grown foolish in my dotage." He shook his head and then continued, "Well, my lady, I am sorry for it, but I'm afraid you've discovered what happens when the mirror itself looks back. There's nothing to be done. You've acquired what we in the business call a destiny."

What Merlin meant by that, he wouldn't say. Instead he hurried to the great hall at such a pace that, even with her long strides, Britomart was hard-pressed to keep up. For such a fine-boned, frail-looking old man, he moved with surprising assurance. Merlin ushered her up the stairs and bid her pack together what necessities could fit into a small bundle, refusing to answer any of her questions and grumbling the whole time that he was missing out on what smelled like a very fine bowl of pottage.

"Go to the stable and take the third horse on the left, but tell no one you're leaving," Merlin said. "Ride south until you reach the river and then follow it upstream until you find something that makes you stop."

"That makes no sense at all," Britomart said, frowning and fixing her hair so that her plaits were tidily pinned once more. It was hard not to be swept along by Merlin's calm confidence, much as she felt confused and disoriented by it. She clutched her pack to her. "And what do you mean, I'm leaving? Why wouldn't I tell my parents? Are they in danger?"

Merlin shook his head at her. "You're the one who looked into the mirror, my lady, and who let it look back. There's no way out now but through, and time is pressing. You'll want to get on your way if you are to make it in time."

The magician looked so strange and solemn when he said this, his eyes so dark and depthless, that Britomart found herself swallowing her objections. She crept back down the stairs, mindful of the cheerful hubbub spilling out from the great hall proper, and then hurried across the bailey to the stables. The third horse from the left, a roan gelding, was patient as Britomart first saddled him and then led him out to the yard. For a moment she hesitated. Without Merlin there to spur her on, all her apprehensions came back. The great hall was a comforting bulk behind her. What was to stop her from returning the roan to the stables and going inside to her parents and to the promise of a pleasant evening spent in undemanding company? Nothing at all, perhaps, except for the memory of that look on Merlin's face—and her own curiosity.

Britomart mounted the horse. Then, taking a deep breath, she spurred it out of the royal enclosure and turned south.

As she rode toward the river, Britomart thought she caught sight of a figure that looked very much like Merlin waving a salute at her from atop a low esker ridge. But there was no way he could have made it there ahead of her on foot. A trick of the eye in the failing light, Britomart thought, and rode on.

The sun set and the moon rose, bright enough to see by as the roan followed the path worn along the river's bank by many feet over many years. Britomart was tired and hungry and cold, and after a few hours she longed for nothing so much as to stop, light a fire, and bed down next to it. Yet while she may have been impatient enough to look unbidden into an enchanted looking glass, she was not so foolish as to disregard a magician's direct instructions. Ride on until you find something that makes you stop, he'd said, and Britomart intended to follow that command faithfully.

It wasn't until the horizon was starting to lighten to pale gray, and Britomart was the farthest east from home that she'd ever been, that she finally spotted something to make her rein in her horse. Ahead of her, the river curved out and back sharply in a meander so pronounced it almost made an island of the land it surrounded. In its middle stood an earthen mound, and on top of that mound was a ring of trees, and inside those trees was a small building. It was a tomb, she realized as she drew closer, made all of elaborately carved stone.

Britomart dismounted and turned the roan free to crop

its fill of the sweet grasses that grew along the water's edge before approaching the tomb. At first her steps were hesitant, since she was stiff from so many unaccustomed hours in the saddle, and wary, given Merlin's warning. But the ground didn't open up beneath her feet, no lightning bolt struck her down, and Merlin did not appear to chide her for her foolishness. And then, too, she found that curiosity quickened her steps, because the nearer she drew, the more beautiful the little building seemed. Britomart did not think she had ever seen such a fine example of the mason's craft. The tomb was made of alternating bands of porphyry and pale marble, each delicately carved into vines and flowers and boughs so lifelike that they appeared to move as you looked at them.

For a moment, Britomart had the feeling that she'd seen the tomb before, but the name carved into the marble in gilt letters was an unfamiliar one: *Angela*. Below it in smaller lettering ran: *Queen of a Martial and Mighty People. Take up her Example and her Arms.* Who might such a person have been? Sometimes the roving jongleurs who visited her father's court told tales of women warriors, but they either were all figures of fun or had lived so long ago that little in truth was known of them beyond their name and the land they came from. Britomart had never thought she'd see a monument raised in genuine tribute to such a woman.

She made to kneel in front of the tomb in respectful prayer, but as soon as her knees touched the marble plinth, there was a loud grinding sound. Britomart fell back and watched as part of the plinth moved to one side, revealing a shallow, stone-lined pit. Inside it, stacked neatly and still shining as brightly as if a squire had only just finished polishing them, were all the accoutrements of a warrior: gleaming mail and solid plate, a helm and sword and shield and spear.

But not just any arms and armor, Britomart realized with a slow, creeping feeling of unease. This was the same armor she had seen her other self wear in the looking glass; the same ebony spear and painted shield she'd seen herself wield. She reached out gingerly to touch the shield just to check if it was real, but then snatched back her hand before she made contact. What if it were cursed?

"Now you show caution?"

Britomart jumped. Merlin's voice—yet as she stood and looked around, she could see no Merlin.

"Come, child," Merlin's voice continued. "You hardly think I made only one looking glass? Anyway, time is wasting. You don't want to be late for your own destiny, do you?"

"That definitely makes no sense," Britomart mumbled.

"Of course it doesn't," Merlin's voice said. "It's magic. Anyway, the queen bequeathed these to you for a reason. I'd take them up, if I were you."

"But who was this Queen Angela?" Britomart asked. "Why have I never heard of this place, or of such a person among my ancestors?"

Merlin made no answer. Britomart was beginning to realize why some at her father's court rolled their eyes so heartily whenever the magician's name was mentioned.

She looked back down at the pile. *Well,* she told herself, *a sulk got you into this mess, and another sulk won't get you out of it.* Britomart gathered up the items. They didn't spark at her touch or feel unusually warm or oddly cold. That was a little disappointing but perhaps for the best, she thought as she carried them down the side of the mound. She'd seen more magic in the last day than she had in the past year; she didn't want to acquire two destinies in quick succession. There was no knowing what that could do to a person.

Britomart set down the arms and armor in the shade of a willow tree and retrieved her little pack from the back of her snoozing horse. Her tiredness had ebbed but now came back with renewed force. She ate some of the hardtack and cheese she'd brought with her before falling into a deep and dreamless sleep. By the time she woke, the sun was high in the sky and the roan was once more contentedly cropping grass. The worst of the tiredness had gone, but Britomart felt strangely restless, as if a thousand itches roiled beneath her skin. She sat up and looked balefully at the armor. Well, there was nothing for it, she thought.

Britomart hauled herself to her feet and went over to the river. Its cold waters cleaned her face and hands and woke her up enough to face the task of putting on the armor. She knew how to do it in theory, of course, but theory was different from practice—particularly when that practice involved buckling stiff leather fasteners and hefting heavy plate while also kirtling up your skirts. Britomart cursed more than once, making the roan snort at her for interrupting its peaceful lunch, but at length she was fully dressed in the late queen's attire.

It was heavy, like carrying one of her little cousins around on her back, but Britomart found she could bear it. She buckled the sword belt around her waist and sheathed the sword in its scabbard, and that weight even felt right. When she turned to look in the river, she saw a wavering version of the reflection she'd seen in the looking glass only the day before: her face peering out from beneath a brightly gilded helm, a shield in one hand and a spear in the other. Britomart had the curious sensation of seeing herself overlain with an entirely separate person.

It felt oddly right.

"I've never heard of anyone with a destiny like this before. I have not the least idea what to do next," Britomart told her watery reflection. It made no reply, though in truth she did not know what she would have done if it had.

The roan nickered at her when Britomart made to mount it in full armor.

"If you don't like it," she said, "you can take it up with Merlin."

If she headed back downriver now, Britomart would reach her father's castle by nightfall. She would doubtless receive a scolding of a kind she'd never received in her life, not even the infamous time when as a fractious toddler she had refused to properly curtsy to her grandfather. Part of her wished to head back regardless, to the promise of a hot dinner and a warm bed and her mother's furious fussing. She had the armor she'd seen in the looking glass, after all, and Merlin had never said that this destiny of hers required anything more than finding it and returning home.

And yet. She turned to look at the eastern horizon, where her father's lands met those that Britomart had heard of but never seen. She felt that restless sensation under her skin again and thought: Well, was this what it was like to have a destiny? A proper one, like something from a storybook. Not one that an odd, old sorcerer pushed you into, but one you couldn't escape because you felt that tug behind your breastbone, pulling you along to something greater than yourself. Britomart had long known she had a future, of course. Marriage and inheritance, childbirth and the running of a great household and adjudicating boundary disputes and maintaining alliances: these were the things she'd been raised to do. She had neither particularly looked forward to nor especially dreaded it. It was simply what would happen.

There was, Britomart realized, something very attractive about the idea of knowing that there was something ahead of her that was entirely unknown.

Another moment's indecision and then she made a choice. She headed east.

Britomart rode and slept and rose the next morning to ride again. The roan never seemed to tire as much as it should, nor was the hardtack or cheese in her pack ever quite finished. Merlin's hand in all of this seemed apparent; though Britomart did not understand quite why he should care so much. She hardly knew the magician, after all. He had been a constant presence in her father's court during the time of the last war, but that had ended more than ten years ago. Britomart had only hazy memories of it: of the quieter evenings in the great hall with so many of the warriors absent, of the pinched-mouth look on her mother's face as she made yet another inventory of their stores, of a distant smudge of smoke on the horizon. Merlin had taken no notice of her then that she could recall.

Still, if there was one lesson that Britomart had taken from the stories her childhood nurse, Glaucé, had told her, it was that magic wielders were full of fancy and caprice. She might never know what whim had spurred Merlin to push her out into the wide world rather than send her back to her parents for a good scolding—and perhaps it was better that she didn't.

There was nothing to tell her that she had passed over the borders of her father's lands, but Britomart was sure that she must have. Both the river and the bridle path beside it narrowed, and then the bridle path disappeared as the river entered a woodland more dense and still than any Britomart had seen. She had heard garbled tales of this place, she thought, from some of her father's knights. They called it simply *the woods*, an area on the border of four kingdoms and very carefully claimed by none of them because it was home to too many of the old magics.

The roan didn't seem to care where they were, though. It ambled sure-footed over loamy soil and somehow always knew how to find the river and due east if a boulder or a fallen tree meant they had to take a detour.

"Were you always in my father's stable, I wonder?" Britomart asked the roan as it picked its way through a fern-filled glade. The stables were always kept well stocked, and whenever she wanted to ride out, Britomart always had her pick of some of the best horses in the kingdom. She couldn't remember ever seeing this gelding before, though. "Or were you conjured up especially by Merlin for me?"

The roan snorted at her.

Britomart made camp that night in the shade of a boulder so massive that it was of a height with some of the wood's tallest trees. The sight of it made her think fanciful thoughts about a giant's toys abandoned in the woods once playtime was over. In fact, once she looked at it a little more closely, its sides seemed a little too smooth, its angles a little too precise to be something entirely natural. Yet Britomart found that it didn't unsettle her any more than did the woods around her. She had her helm and her armor, her sword at her side and her spear within arm's reach. Perhaps it was foolish of her to put her trust in weapons she had never used, in whose use she was scarcely trained. And yet something told her that as long as she wore them, she was safe.

Once she'd eaten, Britomart made to bed down for the night, but the sudden rustling of undergrowth nearby stopped her in her tracks. It wasn't a very loud sound—like the noise a vole might make rummaging for food—but in the unnatural stillness of the woods, it stood out. Britomart reached for her sword, but before she could unsheathe it, a man stepped into the clearing.

Or at least something that looked like a man. He was tall and thin, weeping and wringing his hands like a person in deep mourning. But his eyes were all wrong. They were a flat, milky gray shot through with stark red veins, and the sight of them made Britomart's stomach lurch.

"You weren't supposed to *be* here, but now you are supposed to be here!" the maybe-a-man wailed. "She should have been mine, this isn't *fair*, this isn't how things work."

Britomart held up her hands, placatory. "Sir, I don't know what you're talking about, but I mean you no harm. My name is Britomart of North Wealhas, and I—"

"Oh, I know who you *are*," the maybe-a-man said, still weeping and shaking his head vigorously. The long, thick braid of his pale hair slapped against his back. "You're Merlin's weapon. You'd think, of all beings, he'd understand the danger of swapping around destinies willy-nilly! But no one ever listens to poor old Scudamore, do they?"

Britomart blinked, startled. Merlin's weapon? She carried a sword he'd helped her find, sure enough, but she'd never so much as unsheathed it. She still felt far more like a girl hanging her mother's chatelaine from her waist and playing at lady of the household than she did a warrior. Not to mention, she was quite sure Merlin needed no weapon other than the power that sang through his blood—she'd heard the tales of battles he'd fought long ago, at the side of Camelot's king.

"I'm not anyone's *weapon*," she began, exasperated, and then with a huff removed her helm. The cheek guards made it uncomfortable to talk. "And I don't know—"

"Oh!" Scudamore's pale eyes widened; his tears stopped.

This didn't make him any less unsettling, because now he was smiling. His mouth opened wider than should have been possible, revealing double rows of sharp teeth both top and bottom. "Oh, you're a human *girl*. Well, that makes all the difference! A destiny's a destiny, but there's no call for me to be jealous when you're just a girl. A human girl could never take my precious one's heart from me. Come on, then, time's wasting."

"I don't know what you're talking about," Britomart said, setting one hand on the hilt of her sword and hoping that she looked appropriately determined. "I have no quarrel with you, sir, and I wish you no harm, but I—"

"What do you think you're here for, if not your destiny?" Scudamore replied. "You must go fetch her from the fortress, for I cannot go in myself, but if she's inside the fortress, how can she be my wife? It's very obvious, girl!"

None of this helped Britomart understand any better what was happening, but Scudamore was looking at her with what she thought must be an expectant expression and pointing into the woods. "Come on," he said again, "or she will surely die, and soon."

Britomart could not in good conscience refuse to help in the face of a declaration like that. She couldn't claim that she knew what she was doing, either, but still she picked up her spear and shield before following Scudamore into the trees. He walked backward, facing Britomart with that horrible fixed grin yet still somehow knowing how to place each foot without stumbling or causing the least rustle of a leaf.

"Maybe it's good that you came," Scudamore said. "Because I only just got these hands, you know, and I would hate to singe them trying to retrieve my promised wife."

"I beg your pardon?" Britomart said, certain she'd misheard, but Scudamore seemed not to hear. Instead he gestured behind him with a flourish at a great boulder. Even larger than the boulder where Britomart had made camp, the black stone was shot through with veins of azurite that gleamed blue in the starlight and was riven down the middle by a great, clean crack.

"On you go!" Scudamore said. "Into the fortress with you, and bring my wife back to me."

"That is a boulder," Britomart pointed out carefully.

Scudamore sighed deeply. "They'll give a destiny to anyone these days, won't they? Say what you want about that prig Galahad, but at least he knew a destiny when he had one." He pointed behind him again, more emphatically. "Go into the fortress and bring me back my wife," he said, speaking slowly and pointedly in the way someone might to an incompetent servant.

There was clearly no point in trying to reason with him further, so Britomart walked past him toward the boulder. Even when she got close to it, it looked nothing like a fortress. The crack, however, was wide enough to walk through if she held her shoulders just right. As Britomart took her first step in, she realized the glow around her came not just from the azurite veins in the rock but from tongues of blue flame that licked and lapped along its flat planes. The farther she walked, the bigger and hotter the flames grew until they formed a solid wall ahead of her.

Britomart thought for a moment about turning back, but that was selfish, unworthy of a daughter of King Ryence. Whatever she might think of Scudamore, he had been clear that someone in here was in trouble, and Britomart couldn't knowingly leave another person to suffer. She raised her shield, gritted her teeth, and pushed forward.

At first it was uncomfortable, like going inside the keep's kitchen on a sweltering summer's day while the bread ovens were still sending out waves of heat. Then it hurt like sunburned skin, and then it hurt like deliberately closing your hand around a hot poker, and just when Britomart thought she couldn't take it anymore, she'd have to retreat, the heat vanished.

Slowly she lowered the shield to find herself in a great hall, one that far surpassed that of her father's in size and splendor. Britomart craned her neck upward but could not make out the ceiling overhead, if there even was one. The walls were made of the boulder's black and glittering blue rock but expertly carved with patterns of intertwined figures, arms and limbs in sinuous tangles, faces in profile. Britomart turned in a slow circle. There were no windows or doors, no braziers or candles or fireplaces, yet there was still somehow light enough to see by.

"A fortress," she said softly to herself, and quite certainly one crafted with magic. It didn't look like any fortress she'd ever seen before, but then again there were many things she'd seen the past few days that she never had before.

There was one person lacking, however, who Britomart had expected to see, and that was Scudamore's wife-to-be. The room was empty save for some low benches set around the walls, rushes strewn on the floor, and a dozen or so tapestries hanging overhead. When Britomart called out a greeting, no one answered.

It began to dawn on her that she did not know what or who Scudamore was and that he had vouchsafed no proof of even the little he had told her. There were no doors, and a fortress could easily serve as a prison. Britomart fought back a sudden panic and the even weightier sense that she had been very foolish.

"Patience," she told herself, looking around the room again. "Think."

The tapestries drew her closer inspection. They were bright splashes of color in an otherwise dim room, each clearly the work of many months and showing some great feat from the old stories. Some of them showed mighty battles or even— Britomart blushed to see them—acts of love, of a kind which she, as a maiden, was not supposed to know. Each seemed made by a different hand and from different materials, but all bore the same line of text: *Be bold but not too bold*. Who would decorate an abandoned room in such a way? But then, as she looked, she realized that between the bottom of each tapestry and the floor were seams in the wall: each tapestry hid a door.

Now, Britomart had listened to tales told at her father's court. Perhaps not as closely as she should have, since she had decided to look in that mirror unbidden, but she *had* listened. She understood that doors hidden behind tapestries warning against foolhardiness would likely lead to something unpleasant, no matter how well-armed one might be. The chances were high that only one of the dozen doors would lead her to where she needed to go—but how to tell which one? Was there a riddle hidden within the designs, perhaps, or some cipher?

Before Britomart could begin to puzzle it out, she startled at the blast of a trumpet followed by a gust of wind so violent it nearly knocked her off her feet. She planted them and the butt of her spear against the ground, gritting her teeth and feeling her eyes water. But as soon as the wind began, it stopped—and one of the tapestries on the far wall slid to the side, and the door behind it opened.

A procession of . . . well, Britomart had no better word for them than *creatures* came gamboling through the door. Each was no bigger than a young child, but their skinny limbs had more joints than did any human youth, and their heads were topped with tufts of moss-green hair. The noises they made were like the cooing of doves, yet when they caught sight of Britomart, they stopped and shrieked in unison.

"You," said the lead creature in a surprisingly deep voice, "are not Scudamore of the Tower of Glass! We were promised the rending of his limbs and the marrow to suck from his bones!"

"I am not Scudamore," Britomart said, tightening her grip on her shield and spear. "And I'd thank you to leave me be."

The lead creature leaned toward her, inhaling deep so that its nostrils flared wide and quivered. "Oh, no, you won't do," it said, spitting on the floor with every sign of disgust. "You won't do at all. Not enough salt and pepper in the world to make *you* edible."

"How did she even get in here?" another creature asked. "There are supposed to be wards!"

"Can't you smell it on her?" a third creature said. "Reeks of *destiny* and *possibility*. Your common wards won't do much against that."

"This is why I keep saying we need to form a guild," the second creature said. "Much less nonsense if you're in a guild."

"We never had any of this in the old days," the lead creature said.

Britomart was starting to get frustrated. It had been a very long week. She beat the butt of her spear against the ground. "Where is the woman I am to save? Take me to her."

"You don't—" The lead creature squinted at the spear. Its many chins trembled. "Whose . . . whose weapon do you bear?"

"I carry the spear and shield and sword of the late queen Angela," Britomart said, standing as tall as she could.

"I told you!" the third creature shrieked. "Didn't I say she reeked of destiny?"

"Amazons! I'm not getting involved with Amazons. Knew this job wasn't worth it," the lead creature said, putting its hands on its hips. It tossed back its head and let out another cooing, ululating cry. The other creatures joined in, and the noise of it made Britomart's ears ache. "Through that door, straight along the hallway. You can't miss it. Just look for the tosspot who's a terrible boss," it said to Britomart before turning to its fellow creatures. "Come on, lads, time to go home."

The creatures swarmed up the walls and disappeared into the darkness overhead.

Britomart stood and stared after them for a moment, then shook herself. That had been very strange, but at least she'd figured out where to go without having to solve any tapestry riddles or fight her way through a horde of creatures who wanted to eat her bone marrow. After all, she was the one who'd decided that a destiny sounded attractive—she couldn't back away from it just because it turned out to be more than a bit odd. She walked through the doorway and down a narrow hallway.

Here the unearthly light vanished, and everything was pitch-black. The sound of Britomart's breathing was loud in her ears, and her mouth felt dry. She tapped her way forward with the tip of her spear, trying to make sure that each new step would leave her foot resting on solid ground. The walls seemed to press in around her, and Britomart had the horrible sensation that even in the darkness, she was being watched. She was afraid. She kept walking.

The span of a single step took Britomart from the hallway out into another large room and from utter darkness to light like the noontime sun. Britomart's eyes watered, and she blinked rapidly, trying to get the spots to recede from her vision so she could see where she was. Finally the room swam into focus. Its ceiling was lower than that of the other room, but it was held up by a small forest of stone columns, each carved with a different set of geometric patterns.

In the center of the room stood one column thicker around than the rest. To it was chained a young woman whose eyes were glassy and unfocused, the front of her dress stained red with blood. She swayed drunkenly, and it was clear that only the chains were keeping her upright. Britomart had never seen the woman before, but there was something about her that Britomart recognized regardless: something she'd already seen dimly in a mirror. Her breath caught, and she had to recall herself to her purpose with a will. Next to the column stood a tall, thin figure whom Britomart had already met. He was fiddling with something on a low table.

"Scudamore!" Britomart called, shifting her stance and readying her spear. "Let that woman go or I will make you do so."

The figure turned around, and the first thing Britomart realized was that he was not Scudamore. He was as like Scudamore as a twin, right down to the way his hair was pulled back in a braid, but his eyes were milky white, not gray, and threaded with bright blue veins. The second thing she realized was that in his hands he held a silver basin and in that basin was a heart. The heart was still beating. Britomart's stomach lurched in horror.

"I don't care what my half-wit brother promised you," the figure said. Even his voice was like Scudamore's. "She is to be *my* wife, and I won't be sharing her. So you can just run along and let me eat her heart so that she will love me."

"I can't let you eat someone's heart!" Britomart exclaimed in horror.

"Whyever not?" Scudamore's brother said. He sounded genuinely confused.

"Because it's not yours to eat," said Britomart. Her gaze flickered back and forth between him and the captive woman. Britomart couldn't understand how she was still breathing. She was bleeding steadily—her very heart was removed from her chest—but she was alive. "Give it back to her and let her go."

"You're trying to trick Busirane! You just want to eat her heart yourself!"

Britomart made a quick, fervent promise never to pick up another enchanted looking glass so long as she lived and then refocused on what she had to do. She took a step forward, keeping the spear trained on Busirane. "Give her back her heart and let her be."

"*Shan't,*" Busirane said, holding out the bowl at arm's length. "I'll eat her heart and draw dread sigils in her blood, and you can just go away."

"I won't warn you again," Britomart said, trying her best to sound intimidating. She adjusted her grip on the spear handle, achingly aware of how it had been worn smooth by practiced hands over the years. She hoped the weapon that had once served Queen Angela so well on the battlefield wouldn't fail her now.

"You are tiresome and troublesome," Busirane said. He set the basin on the floor and then, with a flick of his hand, conjured a sword out of thin air. "You're boring me, and when people bore me, it's not fun and I do *rather* tend to kill them."

The words were hardly out of his mouth before he'd begun his attack, swinging the sword doublehanded in a great arc aimed right at her neck. Britomart gritted her teeth and parried him as best she could. A sword was deadlier at close quarters, but Busirane had to get near her to use it, and Britomart was able to use the length of the spear to her advantage. She remembered overhearing one of her father's battlefield tales, how insistent he'd been that the Battle of Camlann had really been won by attrition. "Let them tire themselves out!" King Ryence had bellowed, thumping his flagon of ale on the tabletop. "Only sensible way."

Britomart tried to do that now. Her shoulders and arms ached with matching the force of Busirane's blows against spear and shield, but she did, and the ebony wood of the spear handle resisted all splintering. Busirane grew frustrated, and the more frustrated he became, the wilder and clumsier his strokes grew. Slowly and steadily Britomart was able to herd him toward a far corner of the room. He didn't notice what she was doing until the moment Britomart made a wild gamble. She thrust forward with the spear, catching the head of it against the hilt of Busirane's sword and tugging it from his hand. Then, as quick as she could, she pulled back the spear and let it fly. It sailed through the air, straight and true, and pinned Busirane to one of the pillars by his long braid.

"Cruel! Cruel!" Busirane wailed as shrilly as if the spear had pierced flesh.

Britomart set down her shield and gave herself only a moment to catch her breath before she staggered over to pick up the silver basin. She had never thought of herself as a squeamish person, but she couldn't make herself do more than glance at the beating heart. "Tell me how to put it back."

"You can't!" Busirane said, his mouth curving into a gleeful, sharp-toothed smile. He wriggled against the pillar. "Because a heart can only be taken by force or freely given, and who would ever freely give up control over another? You hold in your hands the heart of the fair Lady Amoret. Let me go and I'll show you how to—"

"Enough," Britomart said, disgusted. She'd have to figure out how to do this herself, because she couldn't stand to listen to another word from him. She wasn't even sure how much she could believe what Busirane said. A knowledge of magic was all well and good, but it was hardly the same as an understanding of people. She turned away from him and walked over to the Lady Amoret, whose dull eyes betrayed no understanding of what was going on around her.

Britomart looked down at the heart in the silver basin and then at the gaping wound in Amoret's chest. Her own heart gave a pang of sympathy. All she knew was that she had to give it back and that her destiny so far had not hurt her. Britomart reached into the basin and picked up the heart. It was hot and slippery in her hands, like no piece of meat she'd ever handled, because it was alive. This was a person's living heart.

As gently as she could, Britomart took the heart and placed it into the wound in Amoret's chest, trying to press the torn flesh together over it. For a moment nothing happened, and Britomart felt like a fool. Surely something so simple could not be enough to reverse the effects of such heinous magic?

Then Amoret's eyes fluttered, she heaved in a great, pained breath, and beneath her fingers Britomart could feel flesh

knitting back together and ribs reforming. She couldn't tear
her gaze from Amoret's face, however, because the change that
came over it was so very arresting. There was not just awareness creeping into Amoret's dark eyes; there was animation
and intelligence and wit. As her heart started to beat again, a
flush of color brought warmth to her cheeks and a tinge of red
to her lips. She was, Britomart realized, very lovely.

For a moment Amoret stared at her in confusion, but then
her face cleared and broke into a brilliant smile. "Oh, it's you!"
she exclaimed. "*You're* the woman from the mirror. I've been
waiting for you."

"I'm Britomart," Britomart said, feeling stupid and slow.
She was acutely aware of the warmth of Amoret's side, still
beneath her hand. She hadn't expected this—she didn't even
know what *this* was. What had she done to make this woman
look at her not merely with gratitude, but with something
closer to joy?

From behind her, she heard Busirane say, "Oh, just my
luck—of *course* it's a destiny thing. *Typical.*"

"That's a lovely name," Amoret said, smiling at her. "Do
you think you could be a dear and release me? Only, I think
I've been here a very long time, and I've got rather a cramp
in my foot."

"Oh!" Britomart said, taking a hurried step back. "Yes, of
course." She picked up her sword and swung it at the chain
holding Amoret to the pillar, severing its lock.

"That is so much better, thank you very much," Amoret
said. She pushed the length of chain down over her hips and
then stepped out of it, brushing the dirt of it from her hands.
She looked entirely composed. If not for the gash in her
bloodstained gown and the disarray of her curls, she could
have passed for any of the most elegant visiting ladies whom

Britomart had seen being led to the high table for a feast at her father's keep—although none of them had ever caught and held Britomart's gaze so effortlessly. "Did you have a plan for getting us out of here?"

"Um," Britomart said eloquently.

"She was to be my wife! You owe me compensation!" Busirane said.

Amoret wheeled on him. "*Compensation?* For what, you sniveling little worm? You set a curse on my home, you made crops wither in the fields, you kidnapped me—I should take her sword and run you through with it."

"But I did it for love, my sweet!" Busirane said in a wheedling voice that made Britomart's skin crawl. "Don't you see that? If you were mine, I'd keep you safe forever, I promise. All I'd have to do is eat your heart."

Britomart was tempted to hand over her sword to Amoret there and then. The very sight of Busirane disgusted her, and she'd never even been touched by him. But then she looked more closely at the expression on Amoret's face. The composure was gone, and in her eyes and the trembling line of her mouth was a great and terrible grief. Something different was required.

"What do you need?" Britomart asked, hoping her tone truly conveyed the depth of her sincerity, a sincerity that somehow went beyond the requirements of mere chivalry. "Please, let me help, if I can."

"I need to know that he can't follow me," Amoret said. "I need him to suffer the way he made me suffer—never knowing if there would be an end."

"Why do you *talk* about Busirane without *looking* at him?" Busirane shrieked. "Rude!"

Britomart could work no magic, but she could act. She

sheathed her sword, retrieved the length of discarded chain from the ground, and brought it to Busirane. She looped one end of it around his ankle, and with a strength she hadn't thought she possessed, she pressed the links together to form a single circle too small for him to wriggle his foot through. The other end she ran around the pillar and similarly fastened tight. When Britomart was done, she was sweating, but Busirane was chained there like a dog, unable to move. She pulled the spear from the column with a fierce sense of satisfaction, picked up her discarded shield, and then turned to Amoret. "My plan is to walk out of here," she said.

Amoret let out a shaky breath. "Yes," she said. "Please."

Busirane shrieked. "You cannot *leave* Busirane here all alone! That is not fair, it is not kind!"

Britomart ignored him. "Lady Amoret?"

Amoret nodded, and they walked side by side from the room and into the hallway. It wasn't as narrow as Britomart remembered. In fact, it seemed less like a dark room and more like an avenue of trees whose branches met far overhead. And then they were in the first room, only now the tapestries hung on walls of raw, unworked rock, and with each step it seemed that Amoret regained a little more of her composure.

"I've seen these before!" Amoret exclaimed, pointing at the tapestries. "I know I have—or something like them. These ones aren't finished. They should say 'Be bold but not too bold, lest your heart's blood should run cold.'"

"Why would anyone want such wall hangings?" Britomart took a cautious step closer, examining them more carefully than she had before. The silk and woolen threads were dyed in far brighter hues than she'd ever thought craftspeople capable of. The bloodred pennant wielded by one embroidered soldier was in fact so lifelike a red that it truly did look like heart's blood. That it . . . Britomart's eyes widened, and she took a careful step back.

"I'm quite determined never to ask," Amoret said firmly. "But if we wish to leave, perhaps we should find a path between daring"—she pointed to one tapestry in which two lovers embraced passionately—"and foolhardiness." She gestured to another tapestry in which one lover wept over another's fallen body. In between those two hung a third that showed nothing but a tangle of vines—rather, Britomart realized, like the patterns covering the walls of Queen Angela's tomb.

"Shall we?" Amoret asked, and when Britomart nodded, she tugged the central tapestry to one side. Behind it was a huge split in the rock. Through it Britomart could see green trees and a shaft of early-morning sunshine.

"Oh!" That smile reappeared on Amoret's face and remained as they walked out into the light. It hadn't seemed so long to Britomart, but the whole night had passed. The grass under their feet was wet with morning dew and birds were singing. The woods seemed somehow more alive than they had before. "I can't even remember the last time I saw *sky*."

"I'm glad to have helped you to see it again, Lady Amoret," Britomart said. She was relieved herself to be out in the fresh air and could not imagine how much more that was the case for her companion.

"I think, since you have saved my life," Amoret said, "that you can dispense with the formalities. Amoret, please. Besides—"

"There you are!" a familiar voice broke in: Scudamore walking through the clearing toward them, his arms spread wide. "You have brought me my wife, as I was sure you would. I *knew* she would choose Scudamore over Busirane! She has excellent taste, you know."

"Amoret is *not* yours," Britomart snapped, surprising herself not just with the vehemence of her reply but at the clear ring of jealousy to it.

At the same time Amoret said, all cold fury, "I am no one's wife, sir, and I will never be yours."

"But I want her!" Scudamore whined.

Britomart drew her sword. "If you don't leave her alone, I will drag you into that fortress and chain you up next to your brother, and the two of you can fight over each other for as long as you wish."

Scudamore's jaw dropped. "You *wouldn't*."

"She would!" Amoret said. "Because I know her, I have seen her, and I know that she is valiant in a way you could never be. And I am telling you right now, Scudamore of the Tower of Glass: there is no part of my destiny beyond this day that has you in it. I will leave this place with the Lady Britomart, and neither you nor another of your kind will ever trouble us again. This I hold you to." She stamped her foot once she'd finished speaking: a piece of punctuation to as binding a geas as Britomart had ever heard.

Scudamore wept and wailed, but there was no gainsaying a proper geas. His moans faded into the distance as Britomart and Amoret walked away, toward where the roan still waited. The horse whinnied softly as Britomart approached, letting her pet its velvety muzzle, and then stood patiently as she strapped her pack and arms to its back.

There was of course only room for a single person in the saddle, so Britomart insisted that Amoret be the one to take it. Amoret tried to refuse at first, but Britomart pointed out that she had been lately injured and needed to save her strength as much as possible. Amoret had to hitch up her skirts before Britomart helped her into the saddle, which meant that Britomart caught a flash of pale thigh that made her blush. She didn't know why, exactly. It wasn't as if Britomart had never seen another woman naked before, in the bathhouse or while changing. There was simply something about Amoret that caught both her attention and her breath. She couldn't remember ever wanting to *touch* before.

Her embarrassment was soon forgotten, however, as she took the roan by the bridle and led it along the river toward the edge of the woods. She and Amoret talked as they traveled. The conversation was surprisingly easy and free, for all that what they talked about was sometimes anything but: about Britomart's family, and Merlin's pronouncement, and how Busirane had taken Amoret unawares on her way home from the ten-day market. Britomart had the sense that she had known Amoret for years, although it had only been hours.

By the time they reached the edge of the woods, the sun was high overhead. They could continue along the bridle path and make their way back to the stronghold of King Ryence, or they could strike out across the meadowlands toward the low foothills just visible in the distance. If Britomart's hazy memories of her schoolroom map were correct, beyond those foothills again were the plains leading to Amoret's homeland. Two weeks' journey or more.

"I could take you back," Britomart offered, and meant it.

Amoret, though, shook her head. "There is no one left there for me. I would rather accompany you, if you'll have me."

"I would gladly travel with you," Britomart said, ducking her head. She had no idea how best to respond to the warmth in Amoret's voice; she was not accustomed to thinking of herself as *bold*. "Though I have nowhere to go for now except to my father's castle, a few days' journey from here. My parents will be worried, I'm sure." To own the truth, she was quite sure that they would be furious. She winced as the thought of what Queen Morvydd was likely to say when she returned home. The edge of her mother's words could cut more deeply than her father's more straightforward wrath. Still, she felt a tug behind her breastbone, calling her home. Wherever else she might go now, whatever other horizons she might see, she needed to go home first.

"I would very much like to see where you come from, and to meet this magician Merlin," Amoret said, slanting a look at Britomart. "And to thank your parents for being thoughtful enough to raise so brave and beautiful a daughter."

Britomart almost tripped over her own feet. No one had ever called her beautiful before, yet while there was a teasing edge to Amoret's tone, it didn't sound as if she were entirely joking. All confusion, Britomart still didn't know what to say in response. She feared if she started talking, she might not be able to stop.

They journeyed on, talking about this and that, until the sun was sinking low once more and they were both tired and worn out. They made camp at a spot by the river, letting the roan loose to graze. Britomart used her spear to catch a couple of fine fish while Amoret kindled a fire.

Once they'd both eaten their fill, Britomart decided to remove the armor, at least for the night. It was heavy and hot, and she wanted nothing more than to scrub her face and hands and arms with clean river water. Even with several days' practice, the buckles were still even more difficult to undo than they were to fasten. Amoret had to help, her nimble fingers working loose the leather and lifting the weight of plate armor from Britomart's shoulders.

"There!" Amoret said with satisfaction, sitting back on her

heels. "Don't you look much—oh, no, wait." She leaned in and tucked a stray strand of hair behind Britomart's ear and redid one of her plaits that had come loose. "Now there. Perfect."

Britomart's face felt hot. "What did you mean," she blurted out, "when you said I was the woman from the mirror?"

"Oh, well." Amoret bit her lip for a moment. "This might sound a little strange, but my grandmother had a looking glass that she inherited from *her* grandmother. And I never knew why, but anytime I looked at it, it never showed me my face, only—well, you. You were never in armor, mind, but I'm sure I'd know that face anywhere, I looked at it so often."

Destiny, Britomart thought vaguely. She had never seen more than a hazy glimpse of Amoret's face before today, but the more she looked at it, the more she felt as if she'd known it all her life: her warm, dark eyes, the dimple in her cheek, the line of her nose. "I . . . I believe you. I think that, well . . ." She trailed off, because she didn't have all the words for it yet, but she couldn't deny that she felt it: a tug behind her breastbone, the just-formed knowledge that what lay between them could well be greater than them both.

"Yes?" Amoret looked at her with a smile on her face and kept smiling when Britomart crept closer, and she smiled even as she took one of Britomart's hands in hers.

Britomart thought of the question she'd had in mind when she'd sought out her father's looking glass: *How will I find the one who's truly meant for me?* She thought of Merlin telling her there was no way out but through and of the encouragement to follow the example of Queen Angela, to be as bold as the circumstances required.

She thought about giving a woman back her heart.

Britomart leaned in and kissed her, and Amoret kissed her

back. She pressed the sweet curve of her smile against Britomart's mouth, and her hand cupped Britomart's cheek, and Britomart had never, ever known a kiss could feel like this: like liquid sunshine, like a destiny fulfilled. Like the fitting end to one story and the beginning of a whole new book.

PRESENT

Mayday

Maria Dahvana Headley

ITEMS FOUND AT THE WEST SISTER ISLAND LIGHTHOUSE, LAKE ERIE

SET FOR AUCTION

On August 13, 1975, during a search for abducted teamster boss Jimmy Hoffa, suspected to have been transported by boat from Detroit to Lake Erie's remote West Sister Island, raucous noises and a variety of semi-intelligible curses were heard from the locked lighthouse's interior.

The West Sister Island Lighthouse, a 55-foot-tall conical tower made of white limestone and brick, was erected in 1848 on the southwest point of the island and kept in manual operation by lighthouse keepers during summer navigation seasons for nearly 90 years, until the lighthouse was automated in 1937. Since, the island has been an uninhabited wilderness refuge and rookery for great blue herons, great egrets, black-crowned night herons, double-crested cormorants and snowy egrets. Other nesting birds include purple martins, red-winged blackbirds, crows, catbirds, song sparrows, warblers and endangered bald eagles. Aside from the lighthouse, West Sister Island has no remaining structures and is entirely forested. In 1971, the island was designated the sole wilderness area in Ohio.

Upon hearing the protestations of what seemed to be a human prisoner inside the tower, Federal Bureau of Investigation agents on-site cut the lighthouse locks and discovered the following:

1. A domesticated gray parrot, age unknown

Flying at liberty in the upper reaches of the tower. The parrot speaks English with a distinct twang, has an extensive and explicit vocabulary and is a required purchase as part of this lot, as neither the U.S. Coast Guard nor the U.S. Fish and Wildlife Service, nor indeed the Federal Bureau of Investigation, have any intention of continuing custody of this avian.

2. One large wooden coffin, sealed

Hackberry wood, handmade, mortise and tenon. Carved with wild plum trees in the style of William Morris. No odors/leakage.[1]

3. A tuxedo jacket, custom-made from silk and wool, with matching trousers and top hat

For a very tall, very slender person. There is a bullet hole in the left lapel and evidence of dark staining

1   The United States Coast Guard, having relied upon the Federal Bureau of Investigation to determine that the contents of the coffin are relevant neither to their investigation nor any other, takes no responsibility for the contents of the coffin. What the winning bidder(s) does with the coffin's contents is up to the winning bidder(s).

on the interior, though no corresponding exit portal in the shoulder.

4. A "Letter from the Editor" clipped from the inaugural issue of the University of Chicago's student newspaper, *The Maroon*, 1892

"The Muckraker's Responsibility"

I never had a father with footsteps to follow. I was raised until the age of eight on an Ohio farm after being—allegedly—rescued from a shipwreck on Lake Erie as an infant. I assume the true story is something rather less fantastical, an abandonment on someone's front stoop or at a hospital.

Possibly, you've noted my presence in the library, a man of 6 and ½ feet, with white hair, pale blue eyes, high cheekbones, a nose that takes a sharp angle from my forehead. I look nothing like my adoptive family. When I was eight, however, a family member appeared in my life. An aunt, who, despite significant hardship, had managed to put herself through medical school in Philadelphia and subsequently practiced as a doctor. She informed my foster parents she'd been searching for me for eight years and that an investigator had given her my whereabouts. Of my biological mother, she would only say: she died of grief. Of my father, she had no comment.

With her, I stayed until I arrived here. The University took me in and, as my unknown father never did, taught me to write, to interview, to scavenge for the truth. The case may be made that my interest in journalism came from the many possibilities my own story yielded me. I might've been prince or pauper, a paperless baby, a child without a position in the family Bible.

The only certainty I have is that I, like you, am a student at the University of Chicago.

Here I am now, the editor of this fine journal, ready to bring you facts netted from the bogs of the waking world, gleaned and sorted into the treasures they might well be. To expose scandal and hypocrisy, to unearth secrets. It is the muckraker's responsibility to scavenge for the truth and to bring it out into the most blazing light.

Yours,
The Editor

5. An albumen silver photograph, 1874

Two men, one in his 80s, one in his 20s, both with naturally white hair and pale eyes, in tailored black suits. The younger man holds a pickax, the elder a pen. A gum label on the reverse reads: *Uther Pendragon, Chairman, & Arthur Pendragon, President, The Pendragon Company,*[2] *Cleveland, Ohio. 1874. Photographer: M. Ambrose.*

---

2   The Pendragon Company, founded by Uther Pendragon (1793–?) in 1830, dipped into a variety of sectors of 19th-century American commerce, beginning with fur-trapping and trading, expanding into both gold and silver mining and eventually resource-processing, through the engagement of Pendragon's son, Arthur. Additionally, the Pendragon Company held large swaths of land south of Lake Erie, erecting barricades to bar competing entities from shipping

6. A letter dated May 25, 1875

Written on thick cardstock embossed with a crest that combines a pen nib with a dragon's tail. The message has scored the paper deeply enough to scratch through the stock.

A—

Do not make the mistake I made.
End this now, if you wish to inherit.

—*UP*

7. A clipping from the *Chicago Record*, March 15, 1894

A March of Destitutes & Demons

FIRST INSTALLMENT

Massillon, Ohio. The world ends, give or take, every 20 or 30 years, and this is no exception. Only last year, the country fell into wrack and ruin; the Panic of 1893, spurred by shortages of two sorts of gold: bullion and grain. Six hundred banks have failed across this nation; half the country is in foreclosure. This reporter has undertaken a study of attempts

---

and trading on the Great Lakes. As a young man, Pendragon fought under the command of Commodore Oliver Hazard Perry in the War of 1812, specifically in the Battle of Lake Erie in 1813. Pendragon is generally agreed to have bolstered the passage and subsequently taken advantage of the Indian Removal Act of 1830 in order to seize tribal lands in Ohio.

at restitution and recovery. This is a serial dispatch from the planning of a protest march of the unemployed and insulted upon Washington, D.C., where President Grover Cleveland awaits. The instigators of the march seek to demand legislation to cure the national malady with a Roads & Highways Bill, which would employ the unemployed in macadamizing the nation's thoroughfares at the expense of the Federal Government.

The proposed march will be the opening salvo in a Presidential run for Mr. Arthur Pendragon, the Cleveland-based millionaire bankrolling it.

This reporter learned of the march, dubbed "Arthur's Army" by its instigators, when the offices of the *Chicago Record* began, in late February, to be inundated with telegrams, handwritten and typed letters, and singing messengers announcing that the intrepid Army would be departing Massillon on Easter Sunday, the 25th of March, with 100,000 men, most on foot, though a hundred would be mounted on the Thoroughbred horses of Pendragon.

After expeditioning for mentions of Pendragon in the archives of both the *Record* and Cleveland's *The Plain Dealer* and submitting several specific written requests to interview Mr. Pendragon directly regarding his personal and corporate history, his ambitions toward the Presidency, and the planned march, this reporter relented and took a night train from Chicago on March the 13th, having requested from his Editors the assignment to cover the Army. Now he plans to take to the open road—however ill-maintained—

with two unusual gentlemen, both bent on provoca-
tion, united in their goal of bringing "goodness to
the land." This reporter was not the only one with
the idea—it seems that a dozen journalists sent by
various newspapers will march alongside the Army,
each allotted 70¢ a day, sufficient to procure pie,
coffee, and whisky.

Are the march's instigators the honest men they
purport themselves to be? Have they a goal beyond
goodness in their minds? Time and this reporter will
tell.

When this reporter arrived in Massillon, having
requisitioned a buggy to transport himself 5 miles to
the rural farmhouse of Mr. Pendragon, it was Pendragon's business partner and publicist, the cowboy
poet, patent medicine seller, soap-box agitator, and
magician Mr. Merle Ambrose, who opened the front
door and doffed his silver Stetson, not without taking pains to mention that it, the "Boss of the Plains"
model, had been a gift of John Stetson himself during a hunting expedition in 1865 and was made of
the felted fur of a rare silver beaver. His own sterling beard, twirled into two cones, was of a length to
tuck into his waistcoat, leather, tooled with a saga
involving a sword and a stone and fastened with
coins of Mexican silver, each stamped with the word
"Free."

Mr. Ambrose initially struck this reporter as an
invention, a Wild West show transplant and Buffalo
Bill look-alike, arrived in Massillon, Ohio, a quiet
town of approximately 11,000 residents on the banks

of the Tuscarawas River, with intent to convert the unemployed masses to the side of revolution. The man's nose showed evidence of recent knuckling, and his aspect was untamed, more mountain man than politician, but here was one of the men behind the march every newspaper in America had been apprised of by urgent wire.

"You must be one a them muckrakers," said Ambrose.

"I am that," said this reporter. "Proudly so. Where is the Army you petitioned my newsroom to cover?" The march was a mere 10 days in the future.

Ambrose waved his hand dismissively and informed this reporter that "there're millions of men out of work in America, and we've put out the word to all of 'em they'd best hop trains to Massillon. We're only worried now they'll overrun the town."

"And how was this word put out?" this reporter inquired, pen to notebook, expecting a discussion of handbills and telegrams, but instead, Ambrose walked to the open window and whistled with unexpected skill at a flock of birds that so happened to be transiting the clear blue. The birds saw fit to approach the farmhouse at such speed that this reporter stepped back from the window, shielding his face.

"Little birds told 'em," said Ambrose, laughed, then passed over first a shovel, then a calling card, embossed with the legend *"The pen is mightier than the sword."*

"The Pen*dragon*, that is," commented Ambrose, indicating the card, and laughed another conspiratorial laugh. "The shovel's for mucking out the stable. Got a rake out there, too, you prefer. We pay in silver, and one a them little birds told me the press corps was fixing to starve."

This reporter saved himself a dime of per diem by accepting a cup of coffee filtered with eggshells and adulterated with Canadian whisky, alongside a generous slice of ham, and reflected briefly on notions of might, before departing to the stable.

To be continued . . .

8. A small wooden boat, seaworthy, painted blue

Carved into the wooden plank seat, perhaps with a penknife: the initials *ML*.

Found inside the boat: multiple shed snakeskins, shattered eggshells from various birds and a black leather doctor's bag dating to the late 1800s, still filled with vials containing such substances as opium, vellum envelopes containing grains of lead and arsenic, glass hypodermic needles, flannels, bandages and other medical paraphernalia. In the bag as well is a photograph depicting a bespectacled young man in a woolen sweater emblazoned with an embroidered crest, leaning over a pile of books in an office. Framed on the wall behind him is a photograph of a woman in a tailored man's suit, carrying this same doctor's bag, standing beside a white-haired child.

9. A much-handled card—a souvenir of a sideshow— hand-colored, ca. 1870

Surrounded by a dreamer's cloud is an illustration of a duel. A white-haired man with pale blue eyes draws on a man like enough to him to be his twin. The men have fired their pistols at each other. Between the two men stands a dark-haired woman, gloved hands raised. The bullets have penetrated both of her hands and are traveling through the air toward her heart. The dreamer, depicted with the duel drifting up from his skull, is a man in a silver Stetson hat, with a long gray beard and wild eyes.

The card bears the legend: *Come See Your Future and Navigate Your Past at Merle Ambrose's Wild World Show,*[3] *Presented by the Pendragon Company!*

10. An albumen silver photograph, 1863

The graduation ceremony of the Women's Medical College of Pennsylvania, 1863.

A group of 40 women poses, garbed in white dresses, in front of an impressive building. The women are a diverse group: Caucasian, Black, Japanese, Syrian, Indian.

One graduate, an American Indian woman, is circled in green ink.

11. A clipping from the *Chicago Record*, March 19, 1894

---

3   Merle Ambrose (unknown–1894?) was a marketing wizard and impresario employed by the Pendragon Company of Cleveland in addition to his part-time pursuits as a poet. Ambrose also functioned as an adviser to several American captains of industry and to a variety of military campaigns, beginning with the War of 1812. His Wild World show was a predecessor of Buffalo Bill Cody's, though by most accounts not as rousing, incorporating a magic show along with a variety of tricks and costumed numbers purported to be traditional American Indian dances, but generally choreographed by Ambrose and based, at least to some extent, on the polka. Ambrose is rumored to have been buried alive in 1894.

A March of Destitutes & Demons

SECOND INSTALLMENT

Massillon, Ohio. Some 40 reporters from around the country are now perched here in Massillon, coaxed by the temptation of spectacle and adventure. Spurred by the provocations of Merle Ambrose, who consistently urges the authoring of increasingly fantastical accounts and then claims the press are the devil's work, bringers of false news to the masses, the press have dubbed themselves the Demons, and in rollicking voices describe themselves as an army of Hell's journalists marching alongside an army of the unemployed, who notably have yet to make it to Massillon.

That said, the Demons, too, have been coaxed by the willingness of Mr. Arthur Pendragon and Mr. Merle Ambrose to provide bacon, whisky, layer cake, and even tickets to a sponsored Western show near Massillon, at which Mr. Ambrose is set to perform. Together, the press corps, stationed in their own tents, await the arrival of the marchers, harboring significant doubt they'll appear. It has been suggested that Ambrose and Pendragon plan to hire the Western show workers as marchers—a number of roustabouts, riders, clowns, and trick shooters have made the rounds of the Pendragon estate, all willing to seat themselves at the Demons' campfire to offer up accounts of their adventures.

An assortment of characters other than the sideshow folk have arrived, however, some by Pullman, others riding the rigging. Of the 100,000 marchers promised, there are only 27 to be counted, thoroughly outnumbered by press. This does not concern Ambrose and Pendragon, who emerged from the farmhouse two nights ago to drive hatpins into a map of the United States.

Arthur Pendragon, the march's benefactor and prospective candidate for President, is a man of some 45 years, over 6 feet in height, with a driven air. As befits these rural surroundings, which include a stable containing Pendragon's collection of Thoroughbred horseflesh, Pendragon is often costumed as a gentleman farmer, though his substantial fortune was made in metal, about which he is said to have a sixth sense. It is a truth universally held amongst Pendragon's associates—he refers to them poetically as his "knights"—that he's capable of standing on any plot of land or rock, driving his pickax into it, and striking gold or silver at will, depending on the day. The sole quirk of Pendragon's ensemble is the elaborate tooled-leather holster at his hip, containing an ivory-handled, much-polished silver pistol.

This reporter inquired as to its provenance, and Pendragon colored briefly, saying only "Hauled it out of Lake Erie back in 1875. It's called *Excalibur*. Came to me loaded with silver bullets, but I don't keep anything in it these days." He laughed, rather ruefully. "It's for effect, I suppose. Don't tell my father I said so."

"Pistols aren't typically given to floating," this reporter commented, angling for a better look.

Loaded or not, the revolver appeared to be a Colt .45, a so-called Peacemaker.

"Of course, it wasn't the pistol that was floating," Pendragon clarified.

"What was it, then?"

"A lady was swimming in the lake, and she—"

Ambrose saw fit to interrupt by bringing forth his own weapon, a Remington rifle. "A gift of Elipha-let Remington himself," he informed the assembled before firing into the nearby wood, from which emerged a black-haired girl, dressed as a miniature of Mr. Ambrose himself, leather waistcoat, Mexi-can silver buttons, a substantial pendant of crystal about her neck. The young woman dragged a dead and bleeding deer into the open and then brought a wild plum out of her garments, pressing it into the deer's mouth. The deer shook itself and departed, springing over the field like a creature that'd never been shot.

"That there's Moony, my apprentice!" shouted Ambrose to scattered, bewildered applause as the girl twirled her own pistol and bowed. "She's a genu-ine Indian princess born beneath a hunter's moon, and I'm learnin' her all there is to know in every last category!"

The assembled reporters licked their pencils and set to noting, and in the brief, scratching silence that resulted, this reporter glanced toward Mr. Pen-dragon, who was looking into the distance.

"There was a lady in the lake," Pendragon mut-tered again. "Came up out of the water, pistol in hand, and it was after I'd done something that I—"

"What year was this again?" this reporter inquired. "I ask because I found an article in the archives about a shipwreck on Lake Erie in 1875, a ship registered to the Pendragon Company."

Pendragon looked at this reporter again. "Can't say I'd know anything at all about that. What'd you say your name was, boy?"

"I didn't," this reporter answered.

"You seem familiar," said Pendragon. "Have we encountered each other before?"

"We haven't," this reporter replied, and departed to the picnic tables. He joined the company of assorted hoboes, Joes and Bills and Georges, hungry men in ragged overcoats, straggling from the station, carrying their worldly goods on their backs, accompanied by astrologers, minstrel-show singers, farmers and miners, all having in common this sad state of affairs, that walking across the country was better than standing still and starving.

Why would a millionaire such as Arthur Pendragon fund this march of broken men, this reporter wondered, not for the first time. Why would he seek to cultivate revolt, when the things that had broken these men were the same ones that had made him wealthy? What was his secret? These questions, and more, to be answered in subsequent dispatches.

To be continued . . .

12. *Prophecies*, a chapbook, self-published, 1873

Written by early American cowboy poet Merle Ambrose. One poem is dog-eared.

MAYDAY

When you set yerself to roam
Out there upon the range
Best check a lady's Bible
'Fore assumin' that she's strange

The hist'ry of this country
Is one of blood n' woe,
And mebbe yer own daddy
Did things you dinna know

Yer daddy spied yer mama
Though she were not his wife
And roped her into trauma
He ruined her whole life

He crawled into her tent flap
Made up just like her man,
Without so much as askin'—
That's how yer life began

But Mama had three daughters
Before you were her boy
Afore her husband's slaughter,
they were her pride and joy

When you came in the picture
Them gals got sent away
Just 'cause you never met 'em
Don't mean that dogies stray

That gal who's lookin' purty?
Think twice upon that bliss
You'll get your future dirty,
A-ramblin' with yer sis

It's yer bairn that girl'd be bearin'
Beware the first of May
Yer doom'll be unsparin'
Erase yer sin, or pay

13. A typewritten manuscript, secured with brass tacks

Heavily damaged by fire, edges charred. Edits throughout, done in burgundy ink, though it is unknown whether the edits were done by the original author or by a later hand.

The Autobiography of Kay Ector

(Unpublished)

The day the betrayer was conceived was a bright day for such darkness, a shining day in August 1874.

"Look out into the square," said my brother Artie. We were at the Company office, and the windows were open wide. Out there, was a woman. She was tall and strong, her mouth a crooked line. ~~She looked like Artie, if you want to know the truth of it, though Artie had white hair~~

~~and blue eyes, and her hair was black, her~~
~~skin brown.~~ She was pretty like the end of
the world, but the end of the world wasn't
nothing to us. Artie's wife, Gwinn, he
hadn't met yet. ~~Our boy was still a bach-~~
~~elor, breaking and buying, and that was~~
~~his way.~~

Artie was a dowser. He could look at
a piece of rock or riverbank, and see
the metal beneath it. He'd stand there,
staring out at the sky like a bird dog,
and then start in, hacking away with his
pick. Said it smelled to him like green
blood, sap welling out of a tree. His
mentor Merle Ambrose had advised him into
land in Montana, and Artie got gold there
for his dad's company. Then the gold went
bust, and the silver came up like seed.
That was what made the bulk of the money
for The Pendragon Company and what made
all us follow him too. Artie loved money
like some men love whiskey, and he was
generous with it, passing bullion around
the table like those same men would pass
a bottle. He was our king and we treated
him like it, even though he still had to
report to his daddy and to Merle.

~~We were a gang of men, moving Artie's~~
~~money from Montana to Ohio and across the~~
~~lakes to Canada. We carried knives and~~
~~some of us had pockets full of bullets,~~
~~but we dressed like we were proper.~~ Artie

was one of us then, in his own flat cap,
his sleeves rolled up, and though he was
our head man, it was nothing anyone could
see from a distance. Artie could ride any
unbroken horse, make his way into any mine
like he was a night-roaming bird, and swim
in lake water like a trout. For all that,
he had a way that made most men willing to
walk with him. Sometimes he met an enemy.
Not often was he struck.

Merle Ambrose was Artie's godfather or
something like it. Some said Merle was the
son of the devil himself, got on a mother
that didn't know who was getting on her,
and some said that Merle was the Pendragon
family's angel, the man who made them
the money, always by the side of the men
of the family, advising and insisting.
Nobody knew how old Merle was. He claimed
he was personal friends with George Washington, but that was a tall tale. He and
Uther were thick as thieves, Merle forever coming round at Uther's behest, or
at his own, with plans for Artie's future,
first with books to read, next with com-
panies to buy, later with women to marry
to get himself out of trouble. That's how
he got Gwinn, around the time he needed a
wife to walk beside him, someone to help
him look like the straight and narrow of
society was where he belonged. Artie came
into being with the assistance of Merle

too: Artie's dad was sailing with Merle on
Lake Erie one fine day in 1850, and stopped
at an island to shoot birds. That's where
he met Artie's mother ~~who he'd seen wad-~~
~~ing into the lake, gathering mussels, on~~
~~land her family'd occupied for centuries,~~
the legend goes~~, and then her husband was~~
~~killed in an accident, and maybe that~~
~~was the true story and maybe it wasn't~~.
Uther took his new wife back to Chicago~~,~~
~~even though she had three daughters. The~~
~~daughters were brought to the mainland~~
~~and dropped off at an orphanage. One got~~
~~herself to medical school and became a~~
~~doctor. The other two ended up married off~~
~~and gone. When Artie was born, Artie's dad~~
~~sent him off too, and what Artie's mother~~
~~thought about that I don't know~~. Artie
was brought to my dad by Merle Ambrose
just after he was born. It was Merle's
maneuvering that left me with Artie as my
brother, so I couldn't hate the man. ~~Artie~~
~~had a younger sister too, who came out of~~
~~nowhere, father unknown, after Artie was~~
~~already well grown. I remember the day she~~
~~arrived out here. She was maybe 13 years~~
~~old, called herself Moony, came up to the~~
~~door and said "I'm the one who'll set this~~
~~to rights." She got to working for Merle,~~
~~learning all his tricks, and if I didn't~~
~~know better, I'd think it was Moony who~~
    All the bad things were Uther and Merle's

ideas, though, hear me on that. The running for President, the March on Washington, ~~some attempt at fixing sins best kept in the and who ever knew what those sins were? I didn't. Artie wasn't a man for confession~~.

Don't let me get distracted. Back to the girl and the betrayer.

~~Artie had a weakness for girls as well as for gold, but his dowsing often went wrong when it came to women. Artie had bastards all around the country, and some of those girls he'd promised to marry, and others he'd negotiated in rooms full of whiskey and bees, and it's not my place to say that Artie took after his daddy in this regard, but~~

"Who's she really?" I asked Artie.

He laughed and said "A guest of the Pendragon Company, Jerome Lought's wife. I invited her to lunch."

~~Jerome Lought worked for Artie. I knew, just by looking, that Margaret Lought would bring Artie nothing good. Try telling Artie that, though. The only men Artie ever listened to were out of town, both of them, on a monthlong trip to Chicago. The girl smiled at Artie, and he smiled back at her, and that was the end of any chance I had of preventing the end of everything from happening.~~

14. A birth certificate

The father's name is redacted, but over time the silver pen used to fill in the certificate has bled slightly through the black ink meant to obliterate it. The name is unclear, but its ghost floats just beneath the ink.

```
Name of Child:   Dred Moore Lought
Mother's Name:   Margaret Lought
Father's Name:   ██████████████   Jerome Lought
Date of Birth:   May the First,
                 Eighteen Hundred Seventy–Five
```

15. A small wooden crate

Addressed to Mr. and Mrs. Jerome Lought with a return address to Mr. Arthur Pendragon. Containing a child-size baseball glove. Box labeled RETURN TO SENDER. An additional annotation scored into the crate, likely with a knife: *How dare you —M*

16. A clipping from the *Chicago Record*, March 25, 1894

A March of Destitutes & Demons

THIRD INSTALLMENT

Massillon, Ohio. At approximately five o'clock in the morning on the 24th of March, the first freight train pulled into the station in Massillon, and men emerged from coal car empties, all en route to the Pendragon estate. Neither Ambrose nor Pendragon seemed startled by this turn of events, and throughout the day, men continued to pour into Massillon, thousands of them, certain employment awaited if only they asked. By evenfall, the grounds were thronged with men of all stripes.

"In the morning, we march!" Pendragon shouted from a platform recently erected in the center of the grounds. "Tonight, you eat and drink your fill! All of you! There's more where this came from!"

With that, barrels of whisky and whole spit-roasted pigs were brought out. Vats of hot coffee steamed in the chilly evening air, and all in all, the effect on the assembled was as though God had appeared on Earth. With cries of rapturous good feeling, the newly enlisted men of Arthur's Army kicked up their heels, and the press corps did, too, though the press, to a man, continued to take notes. This reporter made his rounds to the edge of the woods where Miss Moony stood, watching the proceedings. This reporter noticed that one of the Mexican silver buttons had become unstudded from her vest, and that she was tossing it in the air to entertain herself.

"And you?" this reporter asked her. "Why are you here?"

"To set things to rights," she replied, and smiled. "And you?"

"To set things to rights," this reporter replied.

"I'd look into the old man," she said. "If I were you."

"Which one?" this reporter replied, somewhat in jest. Though there were indeed several old men in evidence, there was one much older than the rest.

"Any of them," Miss Moony said. "They've all got secrets they're hiding. People say Merle Ambrose is nothing but the son of the devil himself, and Arthur Pendragon, well—"

She tossed her silver button high into the air. This reporter could have sworn it merged with the waning moon. "You don't need me to tell you. If I'm not mistaken, you're here to dig all the secrets out. Everyone's got their own way of doing it. Me, I've got some dyed turkey feathers and some leather fringe, and you'd be surprised what you learn when you don't look to them like you're learning. Or mayhap, you wouldn't be surprised in the least. I've got a loaded pistol, and you've got a loaded pen, and both of us walk around here under their noses. We might as well be a couple of cigar store Indians, for all they notice us."

She adjusted her headdress and winked at this reporter.

"It's all in the trick shots," she said before striding away into the dark.

Mr. Uther Pendragon happened at that moment to appear, riding in a small phaeton pulled by a white mare.

"Strike up the band!" shouted Ambrose, and a brass band of disconcerting volume strode out from the Pendragon mansion, playing as they marched.

"Bring out the girls!" he shouted, pointing up at

the sky, where a flock of birds was once again passing. Suddenly, and this reporter must acknowledge
his own consumption of whisky, there were a number of girls in the grass, all dressed to dance.

When this reporter found his way to bed, it was
nearly dawn, and he was not the only one up late
dancing on the portable dance floor Merle Ambrose
had seen fit to install.

To be continued . . .

17. A photograph

A young woman in an embroidered silk gown,
black hair parted in the middle, cheeks and lips hand-
tinted pink. A gum label on the reverse reads *Gwinn
Ever-LeGrande,*[4] *1882.*

18. A letter, handwritten in burgundy ink, from Gwinn Ever-LeGrande to Arthur Pendragon

Richmond, Virginia
April 15, 1882

Dearest Artie (if I may),

*Tell me all your secrets! No girl can marry a man whose
secrets she doesn't know, and you've been in the world longer*

4   Gwinn Pendragon née Ever-LeGrande (1865–?) was a noted socialite,
originally of the Virginia LeGrandes, relocated to Cleveland upon her marriage
to Arthur Pendragon. When Pendragon began his presidential campaign, she
was often at his side. She disappeared from the record in 1894, and though
significant blind-item speculation would suggest that she disguised herself and
departed for France on the arm of one of her husband's lieutenants, she never
resurfaced.

than I, so you must have some, mustn't you? My father says
you're a good man. Are you a good man, or just a rich man?
Does he think you're a good man because he works for you
and your father, or because he knows you?

Tell me every single detail about your parents, about your
boyhood, which must be filled with intrigue! Tell me what
it's like to be your wife! I've a trunk full of the latest fashions
from Paris! What is it like in Ohio? Will there be dances?

All I know of you is that you're handsome and tall, and
that you've never married, and that you've asked my father's
blessing. He's given it, but my mother tells me I must withhold
mine until I receive a full accounting.

With warmest wishes,
Miss Gwinn Ever-LeGrande

19. An invoice, annotated

On letterhead printed with a logo of an eye and the
slogan *We Never Sleep.*

Pinkerton's National Detective Agency
Chicago, Illinois

21 June 1882

For services regarding the tracing of one boy: ~~$2000.~~ $0.

Having discovered the former whereabouts of the missing
boy, I've additionally discovered that the missing boy is
no longer living, having passed away due to fever at some
point in the intervening seven years. Please find enclosed a
piece of naïve art discovered in the course of investigation.

As requested, I return to you, as well, your initial letter and its enclosed clipping. No copies have been made.

Your Investigator,
Allan Pinkerton[5]

20. A child's drawing

In colored pastel, two figures: one a small boy with a shock of white hair, the other a tall man with a shock of white hair. Both depicted smiling. The drawing is water-stained.

21. A clipping from Cleveland's *The Plain Dealer*, June 2, 1875

Loss of the *Malory*

Cleveland. On the stormy night of May 31st, the passenger steamship *Malory* was engulfed near West Sister Island. Certain observers hold that the vessel had departed Cleveland early that morning wholly un-crewed, and others maintain that a single man was seen weeping on the dock, carrying a bundled

---

5   Allan Pinkerton (1819–1884) was a Scottish American immigrant, abolitionist, detective and spy who founded the Pinkerton National Detective Agency in 1850. The agency, from its inception, employed both women and people of color, served the Union by sending its founder and other agents to operate undercover during the Civil War, and is credited with establishing lasting counterintelligence protocols. In 1875, in a rare and highly publicized failure, the agency tracked the brothers Frank and Jesse James to a homestead outside Chicago, and threw two flaming objects through a window, resulting in an explosion heard 3 miles away. The outlaws were not at home. Instead, their 9-year-old half brother was killed by shrapnel and their mother's arm was blown off.

cargo piece by piece to the ship, before returning to two other men who waited on the shore.

Malory proceeded without incident until midnight, when a chaotic storm commenced, lightning, thunder, and gale-force winds, and *Malory* collided with the barge *Questing Beast*, careened over to the leeward side and went down directly.

As the fog dispersed, the crew of *Questing Beast* was astounded to discover, in Lake Erie's waters, an infant. Captain Lusk reports that the baby had distinctive white hair, and that he looked up at the Captain himself with a stormy expression before beginning to swim.

At approximately seven o'clock on the morning of June 2, the Stationmaster's wife, Mrs. Jane Simpkins, in the act of bringing her husband his cup of tea, was startled to see this same baby swimming for the dock. "It was like a dream," states Mrs. Simpkins. "A baby boy he was, in blue woollies, not above four weeks old, but swim he did, and quick!" Mrs. Simpkins dropped Mr. Simpkins's tea and ran to meet the baby, gathering him into her apron and delivering him, with the utmost courage and haste, to the station.

The beneficent office of supplying the victim of the shipwreck with succor has been undertaken by the Women's Relief Association of Cleveland. The unidentified infant passenger was provisioned at the new Coast Guard Station, Cleveland Harbor, Lake Erie. Thanks to the Association for diapers, woolens, baby bottles, and fostering. The baby is now in safe hands.

Malory was constructed in 1857 and is owned by the Pendragon Company of Cleveland. Of its declared cargo—$50,000 in Montana silver ore—no trace remains. Mr. Uther Pendragon, Chairman, maintains that the vessel was stolen, its infant cargo unknown to both himself and to his son, Mr. Arthur Pendragon, the company's President.

22. A clipping from the *Chicago Record*, April 16, 1894

A March of Destitutes & Demons

FOURTH INSTALLMENT

Somewhere in Maryland. And so, the next morning, the assembled marched into the wilderness. All of us, this reporter and thousands of men, some on horses, some with brass instruments strapped to their backs, some playing as we went. The nights were starry, and the fields were green, and the onset of Spring brought dogwood, cowslip, and blooming Judas trees. This reporter began to feel, in spite of some concerns and suspicions, as though perhaps he'd joined up with something possible, an Army that would indeed bring good to the nation, rather than with a ragtag band of propagandists and performers.

Even as Arthur's Army progressed, and the Demons' shoe leather wore thin, even as journalists shivered in city suits and replaced them with corduroy, wool and rolled blankets, the press corps universally agreed—with benefit of the unlimited whisky provided—that we were in the service of change, good change. We watched trains pass, whistling through the wilderness, the passengers gawking out the windows, and not a one of the Demons, including this reporter, longed to board them.

Pendragon and Ambrose rode ahead of the Army, negotiating toll fees on the pikes and insisting upon passage when toll keepers and city officials were disinclined to allow the march into the borders of towns, for fear of large populations of hoboes stationing themselves to stay. Time between dispatches may be attributed to lack of telegraph facilities while marching in deep woods, across muddy flats, and indeed, through thigh-deep waters. The roads, as if to bolster the point of Pendragon, were nearly impossible to traverse in some areas, and at one point, in the vicinity of Cumberland, Maryland, the Demons were forced to charter a canal boat to carry the press. It was that or join the rest of Arthur's Army, in various barges being transported as cargo for 52¢ per ton, billed as "perishable freight."

A circus tent was hired and transported on the backs of the Army's horses, and Pendragon and Ambrose preached and provoked nightly for the benefit of reporters and ticketed locals. This reporter was always in attendance, becoming entranced, in spite of himself, by the sheer certainty of success these men carried with them. Ambrose, in particular, was convinced that his man would rise into office, mentioning to this reporter that he'd already had a suit custom-made for Mr. Arthur Pendragon for speaking on the steps of the Capitol and from the steps to the Oval Office. Pendragon, Ambrose informed me, was already in possession of a custom-made desk meant for the position, one commissioned by his father, a round table at which all his loyal men would have a seat.

This reporter was reminded of Miss Moony's recommendation, and went seeking the senior Mr. Pendragon, who'd begun the march riding along behind the Army in his own carriage and, when the roads betrayed that tactic, being carried in an improvised litter of Hudson's Bay blankets and slender tree trunks personally felled by his son.

Mr. Uther Pendragon, who was seated in his litter, somewhat inebriated and nevertheless continuously sipping whisky, looked pained when this reporter found him. He wished to make complaints about the lack of respect afforded a man of his position.

"That son of mine," said Mr. Pendragon, "was a mistake. His mother was a whore."

"Where? What was her name?" this reporter queried, making notes. The official story of Mr. Pendragon's lineage was significantly different from this account.

"She ran off somewhere," said Pendragon, and waved a hand toward the dark forest. "Thirty-five years ago now. But her son takes after her. No sense. He's made his own mistakes. Took care of those, though. At least he knew enough to listen. Got him married, too, to a good girl from a good family."

"Can you tell me anything about a shipwreck in 1875?" this reporter asked him. "I read about it in *The Plain Dealer*. I just want to check my facts. The SS *Malory*?"

"Ships are built to sink," said Mr. Pendragon, and spat tobacco over the side of his litter, narrowly missing this reporter's shoes. "Storms rise, and ships wreck. It's a fact of life, boy, though you're too young to know it. Everything that seems sound has got a hole in it somewhere."

Ambrose rode up at that moment and interrupted the interview, pointing at the dark sky, in which commissioned fireworks were bursting, and giving a recitation of his own poetry, which the Demons wrote down and the marchers, for the most part, ignored.

This dispatch was composed from notes several days later, from the back of a buggy in which several Demons were conveyed to the telegraph office. It was revealed midway through the journey that the plan from Ambrose was that each reporter would climb a pole like a Western Union lineman and tap out their tale, all while being photographed for the local press. This reporter declined, and thus this dispatch is a day late and 70¢ short.

To be continued . . .

23. A letter from Arthur Pendragon to Gwinn Ever-LeGrande
Handwritten confidently in dark purple ink.

Cleveland, Ohio
July 1, 1882

Dearest Gwinnie,

I have nothing to hide. I am an open book.

With love,
Your Artie

24. *Harper's Illuminated and New Pictorial Bible,* 1846

A richly appointed illustrated leather-bound first edition of a Holy Bible belonging to the Pendragon family, the full book version published by Harper & Brothers in 1846.

Underlined in this Bible: Deuteronomy 24:16[6] and Ezekiel 18:19–20.[7]

In the back pages of the Bible, a family tree is rendered in watercolor. Both the Uther and Arthur Pendragon branches have been altered and annotated in dark purple ink. The Arthur branch includes a marriage to Gwinn Ever-LeGrande (1864–) with three sons, none named, all dead within the month, and crossed from the ledger.

The connection between Arthur Pendragon and Margaret Lake, who have the common mother Rain Lake/Pendragon but different fathers, is done in shaky burgundy ink and yields a son, ██████████████ ██████, on May 1, 1875. This name of the son has been scratched out and restored several times, and at some point ████████████████████ was declared dead by the annotator, but that too has been edited, repeat-

---

6   "The fathers shall not be put to death for the children, neither shall the children be put to death for the fathers: every man shall be put to death for his own sin."

7   "Yet say ye, Why? doth not the son bear the iniquity of the father? When the son hath done that which is lawful and right, *and* hath kept all my statutes, and hath done them, he shall surely live. The soul that sinneth, it shall die. The son shall not bear the iniquity of the father, neither shall the father bear the iniquity of the son: the righteousness of the righteous shall be upon him, and the wickedness of the wicked shall be upon him."

edly, and ultimately left as follows: ███████████
███████████ (1875–).

In addition to the annotations, the Bible contains memorabilia, to include a lock of white hair, braided and contained in a vellum envelope.

25. An envelope labeled CONFIDENTIAL: PINKERTON'S NATIONAL DETECTIVE AGENCY, containing:

- **Daguerreotype #1**
  A black-haired woman and man stand with three adolescent girls. A gum label on the reverse reads: *Rain Lake & Family. West Sister Island, 1850. Photographer: M. Ambrose.*

- **Daguerreotype #2**
  The woman from Daguerreotype #1, now posed beside a tall, white-haired Caucasian man, significantly older than she is, a rifle in his hand. She appears stricken. A gum label on the reverse reads: *Rain Lake & Uther Pendragon. West Sister Island, 1850. Photographer: M. Ambrose.*

- **Daguerreotype #3**
  The woman from Daguerreotype #1, now depicted in a wasp-waisted silk gown, her hair parted in the middle and coiled around her ears. There is a wicker baby carriage beside her. A gum label on the reverse reads: *Rain Pendragon & Son, Chicago, 1851. Photographer: M. Ambrose.*

- **Daguerreotype #4**
  The three adolescent girls from Daguerreotype #1, standing before a building with the signage *St. Mary's Orphan Asylum for Females*. A gum label on the reverse reads: *Lost Girls, Cleveland, 1851. Photographer: M. Ambrose.*

- **A wedding portrait in a velvet presentation folder**
  A woman, one of the girls from Daguerreotypes #1 and #4, now perhaps in her early 20s, in a white wedding dress, standing beside an older white man in a suit. A gum label on the reverse reads: *Mr. Jerome & Mrs. Margaret Lought, 1861.* Beneath Mrs. Lought's name is written, in a different hand: *Deceased, 1875.*

- **A photograph**
  A black-haired woman, one of the adolescent girls from Daguerreotypes #1 and #4, now perhaps in her late 30s, poses in a painter's smock beside a canvas depicting an island with a lighthouse on it. She's smoking a pipe, and another woman is beside her, laughing, wearing a silk dressing gown. A gum label on the reverse reads: *Elaine Lack & Companion, Paris, 1878.* Beneath her name is written, in a different hand: *Untraceable.*

- **A photograph cut from a United States Geological Survey internal report**
  The woman from Daguerreotype #1, now perhaps in her 50s. She's smiling, her arms full of plants. Beside her is a young girl, also smiling. A gum label on the

reverse reads: *Botanist & Daughter, West Sister Island, 1882.* Beneath this is written, in a different hand: *Untraceable.*

26. A clipping from Cleveland's *The Plain Dealer*, April 22, 1894

The "Hard Times" Ball

Cleveland. The Chairman Emeritus of the Pendragon Company of Cleveland, Mr. Uther Pendragon, has opted to host a "Hard Times" ball on the first of next month, in Brightwood Park, a suburb of Washington, D.C., from which it is possible to see the roof of the White House. It is a known fact that Mr. Arthur Pendragon, the Chairman's only son, is planning a campaign to unseat President Grover Cleveland, and that at the culmination of his march of unemployed men, he will present a Roads & Highways Bill upon the Capitol steps.

The Chairman Emeritus, who, despite his recent centenary, is traveling the open road with his son, queried the members of his company for recommendations on the throwing of a gilt-edged ruckus. The boys of the Pendragon Company have planned the ball in defiance of the caption "Hard Times"—no expense will be spared to make this ball a topnotch affair, including the expense of hiring Merle Ambrose, Master Magician, with his assistant Miss Moony, to perform a one-time-only stunt. As for get-up, they say, "Leave your silk dresses and tuxedos at home—a halt has been called on swell harness. Wear your working man's attire, your bum dungarees, your rag-picked gowns! You're requested to come in old togs brought from the Old World, or new togs borrowed from the butler, the driver, the children's maid and the cook. 'Nuff sed."

27. A clipping from the *Chicago Record*, May 2, 1894

A March of Destitutes & Demons

FIFTH INSTALLMENT

Washington, D.C. A "Hard Times" ball had been announced in all the local and hometown papers as a celebration to welcome Arthur's Army to Washington. This reporter, having doubts that the Army would, in fact, be welcome in the Nation's capital, interviewed Merle Ambrose, who, when questioned, insisted that the ball would draw D.C.'s finest not to arrest Mr. Pendragon and his assorted hoboes, but to join in the quest of Pendragon and his Army and remake themselves.

"We got invites out to all an' sundry in the Senatorial and Congressional arenas," he said, "and to President Cleveland hisself."

The theme was meant to be a mockery of the poor, or so it seemed to this reporter, who did not wish to dignify it with the requested costume. Instead, this reporter donned a tuxedo brought from Chicago and set off to the tent erected for the purpose, a new tent, star-printed, requisitioned from a local circus. Those tents that'd traveled with the Army were undeniably pungent.

Upon arrival, this reporter was offered a coupe of French champagne and a seat. As he sat, he noticed police officers stationing themselves outside the tent, some mounted, some on foot, all armed. Ambrose and Pendragon, as was their way, paid the police little mind, though this reporter witnessed Ambrose passing a sheaf of silver certificates to one of the officers.

These denizens of D.C. were interspersed with members of the Army itself, and of the Demons, each ready to transcribe the proceedings, be they a serious campaign speech or a lewd magic show—it was distinctly unclear which would transpire.

The audience began to arrive, dressed as the wealthy might dress when pretending to be impoverished. This reporter counted several velvet gowns that'd been doused in mud, and at least one sandpapered suit on a Senator, as well as plenty of guests dressed according to the mandate. One guest in particular caught this reporter's attention, a woman who'd seated herself in the front row, her white braids stretching to her knees, her costume a man's oilcloth coat. As well, and in contrast to the other women in the crowd, who wore silk and velvet shoes beneath their gowns, this woman wore thick boots, of the sort more typically worn for mountain climbing.

Mr. Arthur Pendragon, accompanied by his wife,

Mrs. Gwinn Pendragon, appeared on the platform at last, dressed in a tuxedo, his white hair a corona about his face, lit by footlights procured by Mr. Ambrose for the occasion. He looked down and into the audience for a moment, and his jaw slackened. Then he shook his head furiously and looked at Mrs. Pendragon, instead of at the woman in the front row. This reporter resettled himself in his seat, feeling a chill coming off the grass. Mrs. Pendragon, attired in a rose-colored silk gown with significant décolletage, noticeably shivered.

The handsome couple stood before the audience in uncomfortable tableau for at least 3 minutes, and while they did, the audience deliberated audibly on what exactly they were looking at.

"He's a straight shooter," a man beside this reporter whispered. "He means to bring the working man back to life."

"He's a union buster," a man behind this reporter muttered. "He means to sell out the working man."

"He's a square meal," a man in front of this reporter said, "and that's all that matters to me and my boy. He's fed us all the way from Cleveland."

Merle Ambrose appeared at that moment, decked out in his usual costume, and stood behind Pendragon, raising a distinctive wooden walking stick in the air.

"Ladies and Gentlemen!" he shouted. "Watch closely!"

With that, he and his assistant, Miss Moony, raised an American flag to conceal the Pendragons from the assembled. The two of them made an exuberant gesture and then drew the flag away to reveal the Pendragons reattired, their costumes shifted entirely, his to a threadbare suit and bindle, hers to a gown made, or so it would appear, of several appropriately weather-torn iterations of Old Glory. The gown possessed a lengthy train of star and stripe, which coursed over the lecture steps and into the grass itself. In Mrs. Pendragon's hair, several feathers were visible. If this reporter were forced to guess, he'd identify them as the former possessions of a bald eagle.

Mr. Pendragon cleared his throat and stepped to the lip of the stage.

"We've marched here," he said, "to change the way Washington works. We've marched, risking our lives, over dangerous roads and through dark lands, to make those who've always lived in privilege hear the pain of the working man, to bring change and justice to the masses, to employ those assembled in honest work, making strong roads through the wilderness, bringing commerce to the lonely places. We've marched to show the country that we exist, to show America that we're here, we're hungry, and we're strong, that we are as much Americans as any rich men are!"

"Ain't *you* one a them rich men?" someone shouted from the back of the crowd.

Pendragon paused for an uncomfortable moment, and then concluded: "We've marched here to bring good to the country, to ensure respect for the working man! We've marched here to be redeemed for our errors, to confess our secrets, to shed our sins. Let he who is without sin—"

Mrs. Pendragon gave her husband a sharp look, and Mr. Pendragon ceased speaking, choosing instead to cue the band. Ambrose and Miss Moony began the first dance, a kicking step of possible Russian derivation, and the crowd cleared to watch them.

From the stage as she spun, Miss Moony caught this reporter's eye.

A ring of keys rattled loudly in this reporter's ear, and he turned to find Mr. Uther Pendragon, dressed in a tuxedo and ready to give an interview.

"That's my son," the aged Mr. Pendragon said, poking this reporter in the chest with his pen nib and leaving an ink stain on his coat. "That's my son, Arthur Pendragon, and he's clean as a whistle, because I got him that way. He'll be king of this country. Write that down."

This reporter wrote that down. And then, having noticed dangling from the senior Mr. Pendragon's clenched hand an artistically embossed brass key tag labeled MALORY, this reporter politely excused himself from the crowd and walked out of the tent.

To be continued . . .

28. A leather briefcase with a smashed lock

Embossed with the gilded crest of a dragon whose tail forms into a pen nib. The case contains:

- **A letter handwritten in dark purple ink, with a profusion of inkblots, errors, and redactions**

Cleveland, Ohio
April 28, 1882

Dear Mr. Pinkerton,

I offer my personal thanks to you for agreeing to take on this case, as follows.

To my everlasting regret, several years ago, ~~as a result of a prophecy foretelling my death at the hands of a child I'd fathered out of wedlock~~, I ~~removed~~ engineered ~~in a moment of weakness~~ the removal of ~~all children~~ a child fathered by myself from the homes of ~~their~~ his mothers~~, placed them aboard a ship and set them adrift on Lake Erie hoping they'd disappear~~, intending, of course, to give him a home.

Please consult the newspaper clipping enclosed herein. ~~There was a shipwreck, and~~

The ~~sole survivor~~ child was never intended to be truly set adrift, so much as to be transported to a nursery, and with the minimum of fuss. He is now approximately 7 years in age, and though it is known that he survived a shipwreck, his whereabouts since have proven undiscoverable. This is a matter of extreme confidentiality. I desire his return to myself or, should I be unavailable, to my associate Mr. Merle Ambrose, ~~not to his mother, who is a seductress and hardly the sort of woman I'd~~ ~~who rejected my gift of a baseball mitt~~ ~~who is, regrettably, dead~~ who will take custody of the boy, as he once did of myself, until I am able to take him into one of my own residences and educate him properly.

~~All this was a horrible mistake. I am not the kind of man~~
~~who'd kill any children~~
~~Even if~~
~~I am a man unaccustomed to secrets.~~

Regards,
A. Pendragon

• **And a fisherman's leather-bound logbook, a single entry circled in dark purple ink**

8 June 1875

Dropped nets for muskellunge last night on Lake Erie, near the Lighthouse at West Sister Island. Slept aboard. Tea at dawn. Bright sky. No wind. Pulled up the nets. When I did, they were filled with—

There were 16 of them, drowned, each weighted in silver, not weighted enough to stay at the bottom. I brought them aboard, shrouded them, and took them to be buried, to the Mariner's Church in Detroit. The rector took them to the churchyard and told me not to speak of this again, that some things happen under God's eye and no other, that it is not for fishermen to understand. But I—

No more to say on this. What can be said? No more can be written, no more can be imagined.

The pages of the logbook are stained with brownish spatters.

29. Clipping from *The Western Medical Reporter*, January 1895

Notes on an Emergency. At approximately 10 P.M. on May 1, 1894, I attended two patients at the encampment of Arthur's Army, just outside Washington, D.C.

I was, that evening, in attendance at a "Hard Times" ball, which had been advertised widely, and in which I had a personal interest. The event was an evening of stump speeches by the proposed Presidential candidate, Mr. Arthur Pendragon, a relation of mine, and dancing by the candidate's cohort and guests. I happened to be seated in the front row, listening to the band playing and awaiting the ham sandwiches being passed to the assembled guests. The Masters of Ceremony, an elderly man in a cowboy hat, and his assistant, a young woman dressed identically to him, had gone outside for air after performing an energetic dance. The candidate and his wife were posing on horseback, with several photographers barking instructions, when I heard loud shouting from outside the tent.

Someone cried that there must be a duel, that this could not stand.

I saw an ancient tuxedoed gentleman with white hair and pale blue eyes hobble onto the stage toward the candidate, an equally ancient rifle at the ready, though it was unclear who he sought to shoot. The brass band, stationed at the other end of the tent and well into their cups, continued to play at top volume as another gentleman rushed the stage, a young man, shouting and sobbing, in his hands a leather briefcase. This man, too, was known to me, though I had not expected to see him. Mr. Pendragon, having dismounted, fumbled in his clothing for a pistol, and brought it out, wielding it wildly.

From the audience, somewhere close beside me, there was a cracking sound, a shot. I smelled gunpowder and ducked my head as on the stage itself all parties, in confusion, commenced to fire their weapons. The candidate's wife, dressed memorably in a gown made of American flags, chose to flee, her horse bucking and galloping through the back of the tent, and without warning, the central post gave way. Heavy fabric, dark blue and printed patriotically with stars, dropped over the assembled, including myself.

I struggled, in the aftermath, onto the grass outside the fallen tent, where I was presented with two patients, one a 43-year-old male, Mr. Arthur Pendragon, shot in the head, and the other, the 20-year-old male who'd charged the stage, shot in the chest, the bullet lodged somewhere in his body. The elder patient was delirious, the younger dazed.

The elder man spoke, pleading forgiveness for something he called "May Day."

The younger spoke only once, to ask who was dead. I informed him that there was at present one fatality, the very elderly man in the tuxedo who'd gotten to the stage just before shots were fired and fallen to a bullet from a woman in the front row.

The young man opened his hands. He turned to look at my other patient, who was silent, his eyes closed. The wound in his head was profound, but no blood flowed from it.

"I wanted to do it," the young man said, clearly delirious. "She gave me her pistol. He told me his wasn't loaded. It was my responsibility to kill him, but I couldn't do it. I have it here. It's still in my pocket."

The young man handed me a pistol, silver with an ivory handle, and then reached up and removed the black wig he'd been wearing, revealing his white hair. He wept, then, inconsolably, and his wound wept with him, a bullet wandering within his rib cage, bones shattered. I could only ease his pain, and I did so.

Both of my patients, though living, were grievously wounded. They were transported back to Cleveland, nonetheless, this physician accompanying them on the train, along with a young woman, the assistant to the Master of Ceremonies. She was the one who'd found my two patients and carried them out of the tent, both of them at once, and though she, too, was known to me, she is a private citizen and her name will not be publicized. Both patients left my care, and though I did my level best to sustain them, they are presumed deceased.

—Dr. Morgan Lake[8]

8   Dr. Morgan Lake (1835–?) graduated from the Women's Medical College of Pennsylvania in 1861 and practiced as a physician from her graduation onward, moving through reservation lands in Oklahoma and Kansas, before

30. A posed photograph, taken at the Women's Medical College of Pennsylvania, ca. 1861

Six women surround a table containing a partially dissected male corpse; some hold notebooks, others surgical tools. The women are dressed in white smocks over bustled dresses and are a diverse group, drawn from the women depicted in Item 10. The American Indian woman circled in Item 10 is depicted in this photo, too. She holds surgical instruments and is looking directly at the photographer. A gum label on the reverse reads: *Dr. Morgan Lake, Living.* The photo is stamped with the logo of the Pinkerton Detective Agency, and an additional note reads *Return missing boy to Dr. Lake. —A. Pinkerton.*

31. An undated manuscript, handwritten in green ink

I was in the dark, and there were four women, all black-haired but one, swimming around me. The eldest had long, white braids, and I opened a hand to hold on to one as though it were a rope, meant to pull me back. I was shipwrecked and drowning, my chest heavy and empty at once.

The youngest woman pressed her fingers into my chest, through my rib cage, and into my heart. She pulled out a small bag of silver coins and weighed them in her hand. I must have made a sound,

---

returning to her birthplace, Ohio, to serve as a surgeon. In honor of her sisters, Elaine, Margaret, and Moon, and her mother, Rain, Dr. Lake founded the Lake Erie Women's Hospital in 1910 and subsequently traversed the region, bringing medical care to women and children. Dr. Lake traveled internationally and published widely. She never married.

because the other women pressed me down. One, the one in the white dress, held me tightly in her arms, and though they were cool, and somewhat transparent, they felt substantial enough.

"Shh," the youngest woman said. "It's just like the deer." In her other hand was a wild plum. She pressed the plum into my skin, and I felt my heart begin to beat again. "The old man knew some old tricks," she said, and smiled.

The doctor, a woman I knew well, raised a hypodermic needle and injected its contents into my arm, and I slept, dreamless. When I woke again, it was in a white room, surrounded by birdsong, with the knowledge that I'd betrayed my responsibility. I hadn't brought anything into the light.

My father stood before me on that stage in Washington, and he knew what I held, his sins in my hands. I told him I'd publish it. He told me that was why he'd saved it, all the things he'd done, that he couldn't bear to bury them. I'm not the one who shot him, but I'm the one who killed him. He pulled his pistol from its holster and turned it on himself. He'd told me he kept no bullets in Excalibur. He lied, about that, as he did about so many other things.

There was a canvas in the corner when I woke up. A painting of two men sleeping, myself and my father, looking like the same man.

I think it was Uther Pendragon—my grandfather—who shot me, even as his long lost wife—my grandmother—shot him. Ambrose, I don't know. He disappeared. I imagine him wandering the streets of Washington, looking for another man to run, trying to change the world, but working with a world full of sinners, himself as much as anyone. Can bad men bring goodness to the land? This reporter doesn't know the answer to that question. Can good men leave pain in their wake? Of course they can.

This reporter remains a muckraker, swimming in dark waters,

looking for the secrets beneath, looking now into his own soul as well as everyone else's.

32. An early cinematograph prototype and an accompanying film reel, ca. 1894

Akin to the Lumière Cinématographe, this camera/projector is made of American hardwood, decorated with an inlay of a hawk. Of interest is the film, a 1-minute narrative feature utilizing special effects. Outside a star-spangled tent, a young woman in boy's clothing greets an elderly man in a Stetson hat. The old man raises his walking stick—a distinctive stick with a bird-shaped head—and the young woman's clothing magically transforms into a wedding dress. He lifts the young woman's veil to kiss her. She subsequently brandishes his own walking stick and transforms him into a gray parrot, caging him and covering him with a tablecloth. The final frame shows the young woman removing her veil, donning the old man's cowboy hat, and carrying his cage away.

33. A paper entitled "West Sister Island: A Proposal for Establishment of a Wilderness Area"

Included as part of a proposal recommending 14 new American Wilderness Areas, submitted to the President of the United States, April 28, 1971.

West Sister Island possesses no structures save the old lighthouse tower, a remnant of the past, which stands on the lakeshore at the southwest corner as a landmark. The island possesses unique botanical evidence reflective of long-standing cultivation, the vegetation having little to do with mainland and other Lake Erie species. The island is primarily a hackberry forest with a significant canopy of trees, the undercanopy covered in poison ivy and great Solomon's-seal. There are several Kentucky coffee trees and some elm and poplar. As well, the island contains several small, wooded ponds, ringed by jack-in-the-pulpit and trout lilies and open lands bearing chokecherry and wild plum.

The hackberries are edible, well-known as a source of protein and fat, easily digested, and delicious. They may be pounded and added to meat or eaten raw. The starchy rhizomes of great Solomon's-seal are also edible, as are the shoots, which are similar in character to asparagus. The berries are poisonous, but the plant may be used medicinally to treat ailments ranging from dysentery to excessive menstrual bleeding, as may the island's chokecherries, which, though poisonous in quantity, may be used to treat respiratory ailments and to cure bile and jaundice. The berries of the coffee trees are toxic when raw but may be roasted and ground to produce a beverage similar to chicory coffee.

In addition to the island's birds, the rock ledges surrounding the lake edge are luxurious sunning spots for various serpents, which hissing guard has long-standingly served to dissuade visitors to the island. The only documented human residents beyond lighthouse keepers are the stranded and shipwrecked and the occasional passengers of pleasure craft seeking shelter against sudden storms.

—R. Lake, USGS Botanist, 1971

Note: No "documented" residents. West Sister Island has been in use for centuries by residents undocumented by the United States government.

Included are multiple detailed illustrations of botanicals, nesting grounds, bird species, and a gray parrot perched in the interior cage of the lighthouse.

34. A large-format photograph, ca. 1975

Taken from a boat on Lake Erie. Five women, posed in a row along the shore of West Sister Island, the distinctive lighthouse and forested land behind them. The eldest has long white braids. She is dressed in a black oilcloth coat and hiking boots and holds in her hand a distinctive silver pistol. Her daughters are alongside her, the eldest in a man's suit, carrying a physician's leather bag, the next, somewhat transparent, in a white dress embroidered with flowers, the next dressed in a painter's smock, and the last, wearing a silver Stetson and holding a staff with a carved hawk as its crown. The eldest appears to be around 70, the youngest in her early 20s. A handwritten title reads: *The Ladies of the Lake. Photographer: D. M. Pendragon Lake*

A NOTE ON THE AUCTION

An auction for the aforementioned items, discovered in the West Sister Island lighthouse, was held in Cleveland on October 1, 1975. A single bidder, a Mr. Dred Moore,[9] purchased the lot, by telephone bid. Though it was not required he attend the auction in person, the bidder appeared on foot to examine his acquisitions, walking slowly. The winning bidder was a very tall gentleman with white hair and pale blue eyes. When he took custody of the contents of the unit, he bent to look at the coffin, in particular, touching the carved plums on the coffin's exterior, before signing the papers in green ink.

He departed by boat, accompanied by a young woman, perhaps his granddaughter, wearing a silver Stetson hat, an embroidered minidress, and thigh-high boots. She carried a staff with a head carved in the likeness of a small fighting hawk with inset eyes of turquoise, ivory talons, crystal beak, and droplets of blood rendered in garnet inset spilling down its length.

The parrot they released somewhere on the water. It flew straight up, higher, higher, screaming until it disappeared in the clouds.

---

9   The reporter Dred Moore (1875–) made his name at the *Chicago Record* and beyond, but scholars speculate that Moore was more involved in events than he portrayed himself to be. His coverage of the May Day riots in Cleveland in 1894, for example, depicts an unnamed instigator leading a mob of 4,000 men through the streets, arming them with clubs and stones. Dred Moore himself had, just prior to the riots, posted dispatches from Washington, D.C., where he was wounded at a political rally. Though it seems impossible he could have covered the Cleveland riots in person, even in black-and-white photos, a man of 6 feet 5 inches with albino coloration stands out. In photos of the riots, Moore's image recurs, fist raised. In at least one photograph, blood seeps through his shirt. His career after the events in Washington, D.C., continued to be in service of justice, covering protests, riots, and uprisings.

Heartbeat

Waubgeshig Rice

"Out of the way, Fart!"

Art felt a heavy blow to his back that threw him forward to the ground. He put up his hands in time to break his fall and protect his face from the playground gravel. Rolling onto his back, he looked up at the perpetrator. Unsurprisingly, it was Chuck, the biggest kid in his class.

"Why you always gotta be in my way?" the bully bellowed. Art looked away from his mocking eyes. He still couldn't breathe after being dropped by one of Chuck's broad shoulders. The burly twelve-year-old was more than a match for anyone in the schoolyard, yet he frequently focused his aggression on scrawny Art. It had been going on for years now.

Art felt his lungs open up, and a sharp rush of air entered. His relief was short-lived, though, as the taunting continued.

"God damn it, Fart, answer me!"

Art pushed himself up in the gravel. He noticed a tear in the left knee of his jeans and pictured his mother's angry face. These were new and supposed to last him the whole school year, which was only a few weeks old. Art looked up at Chuck, clad in denim himself from shoulders to shoes, like he thought he was Bruce Springsteen or something.

"I dunno, Chuck, what do you want me to say?" sighed Art.

"Oh, you being a smart-ass now?"

Much of the lunch hour crowd had inched closer to watch. Art didn't want any more trouble, so he tried his best to defuse the situation. No one else would.

"No, I'm not. Sorry for being in your way," he said, resigned, brushing his black hair across his forehead and out of his eyes.

"God damn right you're in my way. Best to stay out of it!" Chuck commanded.

Art said nothing and lifted his skinny frame to his feet to dust himself off. The rest of the kids slowly turned back to their original lunchtime activities, like playing catch or gossiping. None came to check on Art. As humiliated as he was, he'd become hardened by years of abuse, mostly at the hands of the kid who called him Fart. Inside, he always wanted to cry but knew he could never show weakness. Not as he was now approaching his teens, anyway.

Chuck scoffed and turned to look for his next victim. He was the alpha male of the playground, in size if nothing else. He made his way to the brick wall where some of the other boys had gathered.

Meanwhile, Art walked to the front doors of the school: he would spend the rest of the lunch hour inside. He wasn't sure what he was going to do, but there was no one for him among his classmates. His only real friends were his cousins of various ages, who were also navigating the social structure of middle school. He didn't expect them to stand with him to resolve every dispute, but there were enough of them around that he hoped at least one would be there once in a while when Chuck acted up. Today was not that day.

He entered his grade-seven classroom, where his teacher Debbie was eating her lunch. She looked up from a magazine. "Hey, you're supposed to be . . ." she began before noticing the tear and dirt on his jeans. She chewed hard a few more times and swallowed. "Well, you may as well get a start on your homework, then." Art was aware that Debbie knew the schoolyard score and that he was down in points. Way down.

The afternoon classes were uneventful, with Debbie rolling through history and geography for the dozen students she had in grade seven. The school had an enrollment of barely one hundred; the community was small. Art had noticed that attendance was always steady this early in the fall, but it would begin to drop come hunting season. And in the past two years, he'd seen the general apathy of adolescence gradually set in, too.

After the last bell went, Art waited outside the front doors for his younger siblings. Jennifer, in grade five, would usually be out first, and then the twins, Tasha and Tobias, both in grade three, would follow. The younger ones were always slower to get their shoes and coats on. Art then led them on the twenty-minute walk home. It was always the same: the young ones kept up the chatter, while Art kept them as far to the left-hand side of the dirt road as possible, out of harm's way.

They turned left onto the driveway to their two-bedroom bungalow. The rickety wooden stairs up to the front door were nearly stripped of paint, having endured decades of the elements in a Great Lakes climate, from pounding rain to lake-effect snow. Art was the last in the door, and immediately his mother, Theresa, noticed his torn jeans. "What the hell happened to those? I just bought them for you!" she blurted in place of saying hello.

"I tripped on the playground at school," Art replied, keeping his eyes down.

His mother shook her head, not caring if it was a lie or not. The jeans cost a lot of money, and Art knew she was still trying to figure out a food budget for the coming weeks after spending a full paycheck on school clothes and supplies for all four kids. "Well, go take them off and put them on my sewing bench. I'll patch them up later. And keep your feet up, boy!"

Art shuffled to the bedroom he shared with all three of his younger siblings. Privacy was nearly impossible in this house, which his father Albert had also grown up in. He went to the wooden dresser that held all his clothes and some personal belongings like books, his baseball glove, his notepad, and other special items—like the small eagle feather elder Merle gave him that he hadn't told his parents about. The dresser was the one space in Art's home that he could call his own. He pulled out a pair of gray track pants and got changed.

Supper was served as soon as Albert returned home from work at the pulp-and-paper mill in the nearby town. Art wasn't sure what his father did for nine hours every day, but he knew it was hard work. Albert was a tall man with broad shoulders, a thick chest, and sharp brown eyes that seemed to bear years far beyond the thirty-five he'd lived so far. He always looked tired and moved slowly; pain in his joints from a life of labor that went back to his childhood at residential school. Starting in 1957, when Albert was taken from his parents at the young age of seven, he did more work than learning at the state-funded schools that were set up to erase his Anishinaabe culture.

Despite all the trauma and tragedy he experienced as a child—that continued to linger well into adulthood—Albert maintained a kind facade. He was steadfast in his resolve not to pass any of his trauma on to his children. So was Theresa, also a residential school survivor. But the frustration and exhaustion of keeping a home was often too much for her, and she lost her temper on the children here and there and resented Albert for his daily escapes to his job from their sometimes chaotic home life.

"Aanii! Is it time to eat yet?" Albert burst through the front door and into the kitchen with a wide grin on his face. He had a shopping bag full of chips and other junk food in one hand, and a twelve-pack of stubby brown bottles of beer under his other arm. It was Friday night, after all. The older children waited for him at the table, while the twins ran to hug his legs and welcome him home. Theresa strained a pot of spaghetti noodles at the sink.

Albert took off his worn brown work boots and hung up his dusty jacket as the twins went back to their spots at the table. He kissed Theresa on the cheek on his way to join the kids before she dumped the pasta into another bowl. She followed, carrying all the food with her. She put the two large bowls down on the middle of the table and took her spot at the end opposite her husband. The twins sat on one side, while Art and Jennifer sat on the other.

"So how was everyone's day?" Albert asked as the children dished the spaghetti and simple meat sauce onto their plates and passed it on.

"Good," replied Jennifer.

"We played soccer!" shouted the twins in unison.

"Was it fun?" said their father.

"Yep, I even scored!" Tobias proudly proclaimed.

Albert turned to his left to look at Art. "What about you, boy? How was school?"

"All right, I guess."

"He ripped his new jeans," muttered Theresa from across the table.

Albert's brow furrowed. "What happened?"

"Nothing, it's no big deal," said Art.

"I can fix them," Theresa reassured them.

Everyone became quiet. Metal forks tapped and scraped against plastic plates to scoop and twirl the noodles.

Albert changed the subject. "So what's everyone wanna do this weekend?"

"Swimming!" shouted the twins in unison.

"Hmmm, it might be too cold now."

"Awwwww!"

"What about you, boy?"

Art secretly hoped he wouldn't be asked. He hadn't been invited by anyone to do anything in particular. The sparse friendships he had with some of his peers weren't quite reliable or trustworthy. No one else really wanted to associate with a regular target of the bullies.

"Uh, not sure yet," he replied. "Maybe do some fishing."

"Better not, bud. I just told the twins not to go by the water."

"All right. Maybe I'll go over and see Uncle Merle, then."

Albert looked up at Theresa. Their eyes locked and her lips tightened. She didn't like the elder, and he was apprehensive about his son's interest in Merle and his ways.

"What are you gonna do over there, then?" Theresa asked.

"I dunno. Just listen to some stories."

She looked at Albert again, who raised his eyebrows almost innocently. It was his turn to interrogate their son.

"What kinda stories does he tell you when you visit?"

"I dunno, just, like, about the old days around here and stuff." Art kept his eyes fixed on the fork he was spinning on his plate. "It's kinda cool, just to hear about our history."

"And that's all you do over there?"

"Yeah."

The table was silent again for a moment. The younger children continued to eat. Theresa's eyes darted back and forth between her eldest son and her husband. She cocked her head to the side with one last glance to Albert, deferring the decision to him.

"All right, you can go over there in the morning," Albert said. "But I need you back here at lunchtime to help me get some wood piled for the winter."

Art nodded, not looking at either parent. Even at this young age, he'd learned how to conceal relief and joy.

"And you bet your ass we're going to church on Sunday morning!" Theresa added. "I don't trust Merle and all that 'medicine' he talks about. It's time for us to move on from all that stuff. Us Indians don't live like that no more."

Art tried to ignore the last comment and lifted a forkful of pasta into his mouth. He thought about the tiny medicine bundle of tobacco, sweetgrass, sage, and cedar he had stashed deep in his middle drawer and wondered if he should consider a hiding place for it outside the house.

With fall approaching, the sun rose later with each passing day. Art tried his best to be up for a personal sunrise ceremony before the rest of the family awoke. Sometimes he'd sneak outside as quietly as possible to give an offering of tobacco as the purple sky got brighter in the east. He'd say a quick prayer of thanks and lay the semaa—as it was called in their Anishinaabe language—by a tree.

But trying to quietly escape the house at this time of year was tricky, because there was a good chance someone would be up. So as the small bedroom brightened in the morning light, he opened his eyes and recited a few lines of thanks in his head. He looked up at the tiled ceiling, stained brown at the cracks from water leaks through the roof, and thanked the Creator for his family and for everyone's good health. He gave thanks for the land around them that kept them fed and healthy. He asked for peace for his entire community. He ended his thoughts and whispered, "Miigwech."

"Are you talking in your sleep again?" Jennifer broke the silence from her bed across the room. Her question startled Art, but the twins remained asleep in their bunk bed against the opposite wall.

"Huh? I didn't say anything," Art replied.

"Oh, I thought I heard you talking." She sat up, yawned, and stretched her arms.

"Nope."

"Okay, then."

Art had been snapped out of his solitary moment and back into reality, so he got out of bed and went into the living room in his pj's. He saw his dad asleep in the recliner in front of the TV. Empty brown beer bottles stood on top of the stack of milk crates that served as a side table. Art figured his mom got up in the middle of the night to turn off the TV while Albert was passed out there and then went back to sleep comfortably alone, far from the drunken snoring. She'd be out of their room soon to wake her husband so he could start breakfast.

Before long, everyone was awake, and they were eating bacon, eggs, and white toast at the table. There was little small talk. Albert wasn't as jovial as the evening before, and Art could smell the alcohol on his breath from his seat beside him. They ate and cleaned up together, and everyone was off to enjoy their Saturday.

Art went to his room, changed into an older pair of jeans and a T-shirt, and made his way through the kitchen to the front door. Theresa was doing the dishes at the sink with her back to him.

"Okay, I'm leaving now, Mom," he said.

"Mm-hmm," she mumbled.

"I'll be home by lunch."

"Better be. Your dad needs that wood piled."

Because he was heading out alone and not escorting his younger siblings to or from school, Art could ride his bike to Merle's. It was a simple one-gear red-and-white BMX bike that Albert bought secondhand from one of his coworkers at the mill. Nothing flashy, but it did its job getting the twelve-year-old from A to B on the reserve. With most homes spread apart in the small community, bicycle travel was essential for anyone too young to drive a car.

Art pedaled along the dirt road as the sun hovered above the trees. It melted away the late-summer morning chill, and he was comfortable rolling along in his T-shirt. The community slowly woke with the warming daylight, and some people emerged from their homes as Art rode by, whether to undertake the day's yard work, get in their cars to drive to town, or clean up from a party the night before.

Most of the homes were two- and three-bedroom bungalows like his family's. Many of them were built just two decades earlier, in the 1960s. Paint of various dull colors blistered and chipped off the sides of the houses. Blankets hung in some windows as makeshift curtains. Newer homes were prefabricated: paid for by government funding under treaty obligations and trucked in from the city.

It wasn't a rich community. The ancestors of its residents were placed on this small reserve when European settlers created their own country on this land. Their traditional ways of life, including regular migration throughout the land and seasonal farming, came to an end. Additional measures to erase culture followed, like placing children—including Art's own parents—in church-run schools, where many endured abuse for speaking their language and practicing their culture.

Art was familiar with this history. That's why they didn't speak their native language in their home. They also never talked about the ceremonies and culture that flourished among their people prior to being colonized. So he relied on Merle to fill in the gaps, in hopes of understanding more about himself and his people's history.

He rode past the white church—the tallest building in the community—and turned gently onto a bumpy dirt path on the other side of the road. It wasn't wide enough for a car, but it could accommodate a wagon, a cart, or of course, a boy's bicycle. Merle lived deep in the bush, and it took another five minutes for Art to maneuver the stones and ruts on the path and ride all the way to his house. It was a humble cabin nestled in the forest, surrounded by tall pine and spruce trees.

"Boozhoo! Good morning!" Art called as he set his bike down on the ground. He took a few steps closer to the old man's place. Through the screen he saw that the main wooden door was open.

"Mino gizhep," an elderly voice boomed. Art saw a silhouette saunter to the doorway and step outside. Merle squinted in the morning sunlight, and once his eyes adjusted, he gave the boy a friendly smirk.

"Aanii, my nephew," Merle said. "Aaniish na?"

"Oh, I was just riding around and figured I'd stop by. You busy?"

"Just getting to the bottom of this cup of coffee."

Merle raised the white mug to his cracked lips. Then he set down his coffee on the porch railing and leaned gently against the banister. His mostly black hair was tied back in a long, tight braid that ended at the middle of his red plaid flannel shirt. The lack of grays belied his seventy-two years living in this community. He motioned his head to the left, inviting Art to have a seat on one of the wide stumps of wood on the porch that served as chairs. The boy walked up the few steps obediently.

They sat silently for the first moments, as usual. Art listened to the squirrels nesting high in the trees, while Merle glanced casually through the bush, as if to make an inventory of tasks for the fall ahead. It was peaceful this far from the main road, and Art understood why Merle chose to stay back here all these years.

Their visits began just two summers earlier, when Art was ten and first allowed to ride his bike on his own through the community. He had known Merle as an uncle (he was technically a great-uncle, his paternal grandfather's brother) his entire life, but they were never close because Merle didn't regularly attend family functions. And he was never at church, which puzzled and intrigued Art.

Art knew where he lived, so one day after church he went on his bike to find him on his own. It was a brief but entirely enlightening visit for Art. Merle told him a few simple stories about Nanabush, the trickster figure in their culture. Art loved it and found ways to learn from his uncle whenever he could.

When he was a child, Merle's parents always told him to run into the bush whenever they saw the white men coming, so he was one of the fortunate ones who wasn't apprehended by the government authorities and forced into one of those assimilation schools. His three older siblings weren't as lucky. Each was sent to those faraway schools every fall until they were legally adults. Merle never spoke of why his parents chose him to be the one to escape, and others in the community could only speculate why. Some said it was because his parents believed he was born with strong medicinal knowledge. Others believed they wanted to spare just one of their children the horrors of the schools.

And here he was, an elder in the community who still spoke his language fluently and knew a lot of the old ways. He knew how to lead a sweat lodge ceremony. He left to go fasting in other places that were more tolerant of Anishinaabe traditions. He was an anomaly, which was why he kept to himself. But he enjoyed sharing what he knew, and Art's interest empowered him to feel pride in himself as an Indigenous person.

"You been giving your thanks at sunrise?" Merle asked the boy.

"As much as I can," replied Art. "I can't always get outside, though. My mom and dad would probably flip out if they caught me doing that."

"That's okay. As long as you're being thankful. It's important to carry yourself in gratitude while walking in creation."

Art nodded. Merle's eye remained fixed on the forest in front of them. He sipped his coffee again.

It was Art's turn to prompt the conversation. "I wanted to ask you about something." Merle looked to him with stern but caring weathered eyes.

Art continued. "Last time I was here you took out your drum. You sang a couple of songs for me. One was the traveling song. I can't remember the other one. I wanna learn how to play those songs."

Merle sighed and looked out to the trees. Art worried he'd

said something wrong but knew better than to press the elder. He waited for Merle to respond.

"There was a time in this place when all the kids your age learned those songs," Merle finally said. "It was part of growing up. Learning the songs on the drum and the stories behind them. They were important lessons, and they kept us all together.

"But we don't have any drums to play them on no more. Once upon a time the Anishinaabeg who lived around here carried important drums. There were different drums for different ceremonies and different occasions. A big one for pow-wows. A little water drum for the sweat lodge and the sacred ceremonies. And the hand drums for everyone to have on their own if they wanted them."

Merle spoke slowly and rhythmically. He paused occasionally to let Art absorb the words and to feel them float into the land before him, nestling among the leaves that were about to change color.

"My mom and dad used to tell me about the great celebrations they'd have. They'd dance around the big drum all summer long. It was the heartbeat of this place. That's because the drum is the heartbeat of Mother Earth. I'll tell you that story some other time.

"But around the time the white man came to take the kids away to those schools, they took the drums, too. The government made it illegal for us Anishinaabeg to have them. They wrote it into that law about us. That law even said we couldn't gather in groups to practice our culture.

"My dad even told me about one time when the Indian Agent started a fire and burned all the things he took away from the people. He threw one of the last big powwow drums in there. My dad said it tore him up inside to watch the hide burn away. But he didn't want that white man to see him cry. He waited until he was alone."

Art noticed Merle trying to uphold a steely edge as he recalled the story. He'd never seen the elder cry in the time they'd been visiting. Merle cleared his throat and continued.

"But he also told me there might be some drums hidden away somewhere here. He said there was another elder, a man named Bemassige, who saved what was left. He didn't know how many drums or what kind. But this elder believed that one day we'd be able to sing our songs again. One day our ways wouldn't be seen as wrong by the white man. He wanted to store them away so we could have them again someday."

Art was riveted. He leaned forward with his elbows on his knees and his chin in his hands. He couldn't help himself. "So where are they?" he blurted. He immediately felt remorseful for speaking before the old man was finished. "Sorry," he followed.

Merle smirked. Art felt like maybe Merle admired the young boy's eagerness to learn. "Well, no one really knows for sure. My dad said Bemassige never told him, but he did drop hints. Maybe Bemassige hoped he'd still be alive whenever things turned back around and that he'd be the one to free the drums on his own. But sadly that didn't happen in his lifetime.

"Word among some of the other old ones is they're buried underneath that big rock down by the ball field. And there's a hand drum hoop under the rock that marks the spot. But no one knows for sure. And it's damn near impossible to budge that thing."

Art pictured that boulder. As a younger kid, he'd played on and around it. It was taller than him and even some of the adults and stood as wide as it was tall. How could anyone have even lifted that behemoth back then?

"Funny thing is," Merle went on, as if sensing Art's thoughts, "nobody really knows how that big rock got there in the first place."

He took another sip of coffee. Art's mind raced, imagining a trove of drums of all sizes under that big rock. He knew that couldn't be possible. But he kept thinking about the boulder, which seemed out of place the more he considered it. How many drums could be under there? How many were there to begin with? More and more questions popped into his head before Merle brought him back down to Earth.

"I got an extra hand drum inside," Merle said. "I'll bring it out and show you those songs again. But I don't think it's safe for you to have a drum yet. Your parents aren't ready. Neither is this community. But we will get there, my boy. I'm sure of it."

Art felt a tinge of hopeful sadness. He looked down at the bare wooden planks of the porch and listened again for the bustle of life in the high trees around them. Merle stood to go inside and, in a minute, came back out with two hand drums.

"Here ya go," he said, handing the round, tan instrument to Art. It was about a foot and a half in diameter. The dried deer hide was tied tight around the wooden hoop, and the face felt smooth. Merle rubbed his palm around the skin of his drum, and Art mimicked him. He handed the boy a small wooden drumstick with softer hide wrapped around one end. With his own stick, Merle beat the drum four times. The beats seemed to echo through the evergreen trees.

"I'll show you those songs," Merle said. "But first I have to tell you the story of how we Anishinaabeg got the drum. And I have to tell you why this is the heartbeat of Mother Earth."

They sat for hours. Lunchtime came and went. Art knew he'd be late, but he couldn't neglect this knowledge. Something new had awoken inside him, and he felt like he was on the verge of something big. He knew it was important not just to him, but to the entire community. When their last beat echoed through the trees, he said his thanks to his elder uncle and got on his bike to hurry back home.

Art picked up his pace when he reached the main road. He pedaled harder past the church and coasted down the slight hill on the other side. The bright sun hovered high above. He had no idea what time it was, but the more he thought about what Merle had told him, the less he cared about being late. He couldn't shake the image of the big mysterious rock with drums buried beneath it.

Since he was already late, he decided to take a little detour to the baseball field. The loose gravel on the road vibrated the handlebars, and he gripped tight to keep the bike under control.

Art rode past the school and steered right onto the road leading to the field. As he rolled closer, he saw a dozen or so other kids playing on the diamond. His heart sank. He'd hoped to examine and explore the boulder on his own, but he knew it wouldn't be possible with the prying eyes of others nearby. And he was already too close to turn around without being noticed.

"Hey, look, it's Fart!" a familiar voice boomed from near home plate. "Whatcha doing down here?"

The rest of the kids turned to look once Chuck pointed him out. It was a mix of his classmates and some older and younger boys and girls, some who had been friendly with him, and others not so much. He let the bike roll toward the backstop.

"Hey, Chuck. Just out for a spin," replied Art, once he got closer to the fence.

"Where's your glove? We need more players!"

Although he owned a baseball glove, Art wasn't much of an athlete, and he didn't trust Chuck's seemingly amiable invitation to play. He scanned the field to note who exactly was in the game, but his eyes were pulled beyond the left-field fence to where the mighty stone stood.

"I forgot it. I didn't think there'd be anyone down here today."

Chuck shook his head. "Useless," he muttered, loud enough for the rest in the infield to hear. He squared up in the batter's box and shouted at Jay, the pitcher on the mound, to lob him the ball.

Relieved, Art saw his opportunity to make his way over to the rock. Keeping an eye on the action on the field, he rode slowly along the fence in front of the bleachers. Pushing onto the unkempt grass in the foul area outside the left-field fence, he locked his eyes on the massive gray stone that appeared marbled with white, almost snakelike streaks.

He heard the sharp crack of the wooden bat behind him. "Heads up, Fart!" Chuck called out. Art hit the brakes and turned to see the baseball bounce just behind him and to his right. It took another few quick bounces past him, headed right for the rock, where it seemed to disappear beneath it. Art felt his heart skip a beat. He dismounted, dropped the bike, and ran toward the gray boulder.

He couldn't see the white ball as he approached. His eyes darted along the rock's base, looking to see where it had landed. Up close, he saw it lodged under a sharp edge of the stone, pinned to the ground and mostly concealed by grass.

"What are you waiting for?" Chuck yelled again. "Throw it back!"

Art crouched at the base of the rock and tried to pull out

the ball. It was stuck pretty firmly between the overhang and the ground. He couldn't wrap his fingers around it. His fingernails scratched at the white leather, but it wouldn't budge.

"What's the holdup?" Art could hear Chuck coming closer. With him came a crowd of kids who gathered around.

"It's stuck pretty good," Art defended himself.

Chuck sighed and rolled his eyes. "All right, let a real man do this," he said, shoving Art out of the way. Chuck crouched and reached under the rock, but it was immediately clear that his efforts were in vain. It wasn't moving at all. "What the hell?" he griped, growing increasingly frustrated. He stood, red faced, and threw up his hands. The supposed alpha male of the group couldn't even get it out.

Jay got down on his hands and knees and tried to free the ball, to no avail. Others took turns, but no one had any luck. "Did anyone else bring a ball?" Chuck asked. The rest silently shook their heads. "God damn it!"

The small crowd grumbled and shuffled, confused about what to do next. A few began to disperse with no hope of continuing the game.

"There's no way it could get stuck like that," Art proclaimed. "It wasn't even going that fast." He stepped up to the rock for one more examination. The short lip the ball was stuck under ran a couple of feet across. He saw that he could grip the jutting stone. An unfamiliar confidence rushed through him; a surge of adrenaline told him he could get that ball. With a feeling of cool excitement, he squatted down, dug his fingers under the overhang, and lifted with his legs.

The rock rose a foot above the ground.

The children behind him looked on in shock, mouths agape. The muscles in Art's arms and legs screamed. "Someone get it!" he yelled. Jay scrambled to reach into the small gap

Art had created and snatched the baseball. Art gently set the boulder back down. He stood upright, dusted off his hands, and turned to face the other kids. They looked like they'd seen a ghost.

After a tense moment, Jay broke the stunned silence. "How the hell did you do that?"

"I dunno. I just lifted it," replied Art.

The other kids started to mumble among themselves.

"Do it again!" Janice, his cousin, shouted from behind the others.

Art turned back to the gray boulder. He looked it up and down, amazed that he had been able to budge it at all. He had done it just moments before, and already it seemed impossible. Nevertheless, his newfound conviction returned, and he squatted down again and reached for the grips at the base, this time spreading his arms wider for greater leverage. He inhaled deeply through his nose, summoning strength he hadn't known he had—and ultimately didn't need.

The Saturday afternoon stood still. The light wind gusting around them had dulled, and the crickets in the grass and the squirrels in the nearby trees went quiet. The land around them anticipated a shift, and the children each felt a comforting hum in their chests.

Art drove his feet into the ground and lifted. The rock elevated slowly, just like before, and with one concerted push, he toppled it over. It rolled once, thundering along natural soft turf, and came to a stop about fifteen feet to the side.

Some of the kids gasped. Others fell to the ground in disbelief. None spoke. They had witnessed something they all believed wasn't humanly possible: a twelve-year-old boy, one of their peers, toppling a boulder weighing thousands of pounds. It didn't seem real.

Art stared at the ground before him. The surrounding world seemed to disappear as he locked eyes on the shape in the smooth dirt, as dark as garden soil. A small wooden hoop about a foot in diameter lay planted in the ground. The edge of the circle appeared fresh: a bright yellow hue as though formed just that morning. Chuck and Janice came up behind him to look.

"What is that, Art?" she asked.

Art said nothing. His heartbeat pounded in his chest and echoed in his ears. His feet shuffled slowly forward to the imprint of the boulder. He dropped to his knees and reached into the dirt. He didn't know what compelled him to do so. He began gently digging at the soil around the hoop. The rest of the kids stood by and watched.

He dug away enough to loosen the hoop from the ground. The rim was about three inches wide and half an inch thick. He lifted it out of the ground and brought it closer. It felt smooth to the touch and seemed unweathered after sitting in the ground for decades, according to Merle's story. *Did that ancestor really place this here?* he thought. *How is this possible?*

"Hey, there's something else there." Janice broke the silence once again. The stirred-up soil revealed what looked like a strip of some kind of hide. She walked closer and crouched down to feel it. She gave it a slight tug and loosened more of the black soil. "It's some kinda bag," she said. She dug into the ground with her hands, pulling away more dirt to discover what lay beneath. Art crawled over to join her, and Chuck, Jay, and a couple of the others joined in.

Art pulled out the first pouch. It was plain and smelled like deer hide. There was a round object inside: the unmistakable shape of a drum. He untied the hide string that kept the bag closed tight and unsheathed a hand drum, much like the one he'd played that morning at Merle's. He couldn't believe it.

"Whoa, how the hell did someone bury that here?" Chuck wondered aloud.

"There's more in there!" Jay shouted.

The rest of them joined in to dig away at the dirt. They worked silently, unearthing four more hand drums and a much larger drum underneath. They lay them all carefully in a circle on the grass, while Art stood with the first one still in his hand.

"What are we supposed to do with these now?" Janice asked.

"I dunno," Chuck replied.

"Should we go get someone?" Jay asked.

"No," said Art, filled again with that mysterious confidence. "They'll come."

He reached into the first drum's pouch and found a short drumstick. The other kids watched in wonder and worry. This was foreign to them all. They only knew of drums in random, vague stories. Many of the brainwashed adults in their community had told them those ways were evil.

Art gripped the hide tie that held the face of drum tight and tried to remember what Merle had taught him. He beat the drum four times, and the short, strong rhythm echoed across the field in the afternoon stillness. He started in with a steady beat, which quickly jogged his memory for the melody and words of the honor song Merle sang. They were words Art didn't understand, but he did his best to sing them.

By the time he got to the second verse, he noticed a few figures coming along the road to the field. He didn't recognize them at first. But even more followed. Some came from the other side of the field, seeming to emerge from the bush. Art soon realized they were the parents of the other kids; there were even some grandparents. As they approached, Art saw a few were in tears, while others beamed with joy.

Somehow, the rest of the kids were joining him in singing the song. Though centuries old, the words they sung hadn't echoed aloud in public here for decades. The singers channeled the voices and spirits of the ones who'd been stifled and snuffed out by the authorities. There was immense power in the chorus that assembled on this late summer afternoon.

And then Art saw his parents and siblings coming down the road, too. Tears ran down Albert's cheeks, which were elevated by his wide smile. Theresa gripped her husband's arm tight as she wept and waved at her eldest son. They looked proud. His sisters and brother approached in wonder and excitement. The twins ran ahead, eager to join the singers.

The song reverberated through the trees. It carried across the water. Art sang the lead, with his new friends carrying the tune behind him. They lost count of how many times they repeated the same verses, but they had drawn a crowd. Dozens of their family and fellow community members stood before them, bobbing their heads and tapping their feet to the beat of the drum. And then the elders began to dance.

They were ready.

Jack and Brad and the Magician

Anthony Rapp

Jack slumped in his overstuffed, blue vinyl chair, a well-worn copy of the most recent issue of *People* magazine in his lap. He stared at the page in front of him: it showcased a shiny, carefully posed photograph of the effortlessly handsome, fresh-faced members of crossover R & B/pop group Boyz II Men. They grinned at the camera, celebrating the record-breaking, chart-topping success of their smash power ballad "End of the Road." They seemed—understandably—gleefully happy, powerfully healthy, and unfathomably rich. They seemed, actually, as if they lived in an entirely different dimension from the one in which Jack currently found himself.

He blinked, dimly realizing that he had been staring at the photo for a very long time, maybe even half an hour at this point. It was becoming difficult, almost physically impossible, for Jack to keep track of the passage of time. The minutes and hours relentlessly tumbled into one another, as for weeks now, he'd found himself spending endless hours a day, day after day, slouched right here in this uncomfortable chair.

The chair was crammed into the corner of a cramped room, which also featured a small, grimy window, framing the spindly branches of a tree that had already given up most of its leaves to the chill of early autumn. But it was the remaining piece of furniture that dominated the space: a hospital bed, surrounded by mysteriously beeping and whirring machines, the machines flanked by multiple silent IV stands. All of this equipment extended tubes that impassively and inexorably snaked their way across the railings of the bed, where they then quietly and determinedly inserted themselves into the body of the young man who occupied it.

Jack finally managed to wrench his gaze away from the strangely mesmerizing photograph of the smiling members of Boyz II Men. He closed his eyes for a moment, breathing deeply, then forced himself to take in the sight of the ravaged body in the hospital bed. The young man was pale and freckled, his already-thin face now almost skeletal, his once-bright red hair now dull and listless. His name was Brad, and he was Jack's boyfriend.

Four weeks earlier, Brad had been quietly reading a C. J. Cherryh novel on the sofa when he suddenly and uncontrollably began coughing up blood. Jack had rushed him to the ER at St. Vincent's Hospital in the West Village of Manhattan. Because of Brad's HIV-positive status, this hospital was the only option. Brad was processed through triage and given a diagnosis of Pneumocystis pneumonia before staff quickly transferred him to a room in the city's largest AIDS ward. He'd been there ever since.

In a way, Jack was lucky: since he worked as an accountant at a legal aid law firm, his bosses were more sympathetic than most and had been very generous with him, giving him extra time off to spend with Brad at the hospital. There were moments when he thought it might be better for him to go back to the office, to pour himself into his work, into the safety and surety of numbers and details and spreadsheets and tasks. But the idea of not being there with Brad was unconscionable. He would never be able to forgive himself if something were to happen while he was gone.

Jack drew himself up out of his hunched position, set aside the magazine, and slowly pulled himself out of the chair. He wobbled with light-headedness as he made his way to Brad's bedside and looked down at the sleeping figure. Brad's thin lips were parted. His head lolled to the side. He didn't look particularly restful; he looked inert and tiny and far away.

Jack was finding it increasingly, and frighteningly, difficult to reconcile this version of Brad with the version he had met two and a half years earlier: that exuberant young man with the vibrantly red hair and crystalline blue eyes. Now all that color looked leached from Brad. Jack tenderly placed a hand on his boyfriend's thin chest, rubbing gently. How much time was left? It seemed impossible to imagine that Brad would ever leave this place. And what would Jack do then?

"Is he still sleeping?"

Startled, Jack glanced up as Brad's squat, energetic nurse Esmerelda strode through the door and made her way to Brad's bedside.

"Uh, yes," he said, steadying himself. "He's pretty much been asleep the whole time I've been here today."

Esmerelda shook her head. "Hm. Well, maybe we should wake him up a bit. The performers are here. You know he loves it when they come."

Jack did indeed know that. Once or twice a week, an organization called Hearts and Voices brought entertainers into the ward, and their presence always seemed to energize Brad.

Esmerelda leaned over and gently squeezed Brad's shoulder, shaking it. "Hello? Anyone home? Hello? Are you in there?" Jack watched as Brad gradually opened his eyes and then slowly blinked several times, looking bewildered. "There you are!" Esmerelda said. "I knew you were in there somewhere."

Brad looked dazedly at Esmerelda, then turned to Jack.

"Hey," Jack said, forcing himself to smile. Brad's eyes seemed to struggle to focus on Jack. He licked his lips.

"Thirsty," he croaked.

"Here you go," Esmerelda said, deftly guiding a straw into his mouth. "Drink up." Brad's eyes bugged out a bit as he eagerly and rapidly emptied the cup. "You want more?" He nodded. "You sure? You're going to have to pee a lot, you know."

Brad nodded again, and Jack quickly grabbed the cup from the nurse's hand, refilled it himself, and held it up to Brad as he drank. "You want my job?" Esmerelda said, smiling. "You're good at it."

Jack didn't think he was particularly good at it, and he certainly didn't want her job. "My mother is a nurse."

"Oh, really? What hospital? Mount Sinai? NYU? Presbyterian?"

"No, she doesn't live here. I'm the only one from my family who's here."

"Oh? Where are you from?"

"Bangkok."

"Oh, Bangkok? Really? That's funny, I always thought you were Filipino." Jack got that a lot, although he couldn't see it. "But you're Thai. That's interesting. I don't know too many Thai nurses. So many Filipino nurses. We are everywhere. But you never know, ha?" She laughed and shrugged.

Brad finished swallowing down the last of his second cup

of water, patted Jack's hand, and said to Esmerelda, "He's my Thai guy."

That phrase; Jack was "his." There had been many long years when he couldn't imagine that he would be anyone's. Ever since he'd emigrated from Thailand to attend NYU in 1982, Jack had struggled against the creeping feeling that he would never easily belong in any sort of social circle. At his very first freshman orientation meeting, when the students were going around the room introducing themselves, he had decided, impulsively, to keep to himself his given name, Song-wittana, and blurted out the name Jack instead. It was simple, easily pronounceable, and American. He didn't want to burden his new classmates with not mangling the pronunciation of his name, nor did he want to withstand their attempts. It was the first definitive step he'd taken in dedicating himself to acclimating to his new life.

But even after spending the ensuing ten years increasing his mastery of the English language, which included his efforts to smooth out the rounded edges and clipped syllables of his Thai accent, he could never fully shake his fear of not being able to communicate as well as he'd like. His favorite coworker was a woman named Aaliyah, but when she spoke to him, her voice was dappled with the remnants of a Trinidadian accent that—much to his embarrassment—occasionally interfered with Jack's ability to understand her. His fear of her finding out was undoubtedly one of the factors that had prevented them from developing a closer friendship.

But as more time passed, Jack began to realize that a key—perhaps *the* key—to his personal growth was increasing the breadth and depth of his interpersonal relationships. And, even more urgently, he'd begun to realize that he'd needed, frankly, to get *laid*.

So when Aaliyah invited him to a party at her and her girlfriend's East Village apartment, he'd said yes, and at that party, he'd met Brad. Emboldened by a vodka and soda, Jack had shyly allowed Brad's exuberance to charm him, and they agreed to go on a date. Now, looking back at that quiet, brief moment, as Brad handed Jack his number—all that vodka and soda causing Jack's cheeks to flush (or was it Brad's easy, disarming smile?)—Jack was newly amazed at how simply and completely the path of his life had been forever altered.

"My Thai guy," Brad said again, startling Jack out of the memory. He weakly smiled at Jack. "Hey, look, I rhymed."

"Yes, honey, yes, you rhymed. Good job, my love." Jack held Brad's hand with both of his own, vaguely afraid that if he squeezed too tightly, Brad's fragile bones might snap. "So," he said, trying to brighten his voice as much as he could, "are you feeling up for a little Hearts and Voices show?"

"Ooh, Hearts and Voices. Yes, please."

Jack helped Esmerelda carefully shift Brad to an upright position. Brad's shoulder blades protruded shockingly out of the back of his thin hospital gown as he hunched over, gathering his strength.

"You want to walk? Or you want the wheelchair?" Esmerelda asked in a clear, strong tone. "Up to you. But a little walking might be good, ha? Get the blood pumping, you know? Get the body moving, right?"

Jack stroked Brad's back as Brad took several moments to respond. He seemed to be considering what to do. But more moments passed and he still didn't respond. He just sat there, his head down, unmoving. These small episodes of Brad seeming to shut down, of him falling into a vacant silence, had been becoming more frequent, and they chilled Jack to the core each time. "Honey?" he said, trying to keep his rising panic out of his voice. There was no response. "Brad? Honey?"

Finally, Brad turned to look up at Jack and quietly said, "Hi, honey. You're here."

"Yes. I'm here."

"You're so handsome. Isn't he so handsome, Esmerelda?"

"Yes, my dear," Esmerelda said, glancing at Jack. "Very, very handsome. You're a lucky guy, yeah?" She patted him on the knee. "Now come on, let's go, we don't want to miss the show."

"Oh, there's a show?"

Jack's chest tightened with dread at this question. He willed himself to stay steady. "Yes, honey," he said, hoping he sounded normal and reassuring, and feeling anything but. "Hearts and Voices is tonight."

"Oh, good!"

Jack met Esmerelda's eyes, looking for some kind of help. She nodded slightly and in a chipper, warm voice said, "Yes, it's good, it's very good, so come on, up we go, let's go, you can do this, come on, we have you, come on," and she and Jack managed to support Brad's feeble frame as he delicately and gradually got to his feet. Jack helped to steady him as he wavered a bit, and Esmerelda maneuvered his tubes and machines into place.

"You ready, my dear? We have you."

Brad held on to the railing of the bed and turned to Jack, grinning.

"We're going to a show!"

The night's performance began with a Broadway actor Jack had never heard of singing a couple of songs Jack didn't recognize. He sat next to Brad in the small semicircle of chairs that had been gathered, rubbing Brad's back. Jack struggled to quiet his mind as it darted around in the wake of what had just happened. He studied Brad's face; based on his grin, he seemed enraptured by the performance. Brad had always been a musical theater fan and got extra excited every time his firm asked him to do PR work for a Broadway show.

Jack had mostly enjoyed attending the few Broadway opening nights he'd gone to with Brad, although he also felt somewhat invisible at the after-parties, like he was a vestigial appendage following his boyfriend around. Brad was so much more outgoing than Jack, and Jack would come home from these events feeling drained and needing intense periods of quiet to even himself out afterward.

They were different in all sorts of ways; Brad was a huge science fiction and fantasy nerd, and a voracious reader, with an ever-expanding pile of books he was always trying to get through, while the only reading Jack did was related to his job. Brad had a lightness about him, and Jack felt distinctly earthbound and serious. And yet they had managed to complement each other; Brad often expressed heartfelt appreciation to Jack for his grounded, organized, disciplined approach to making their daily lives work well, and Jack enjoyed Brad's adventurous energy, his playfulness, and his easy warmth. After an entire adulthood of being single—dotted with very rare, random, desultory sexual encounters and a few unfulfilling dates—Jack had, from the moment they met, found himself surprisingly willing to be swept away by Brad's eager courtship of him.

Eager but slow. While there had been a couple of pleasant, relatively chaste kisses at the end of their first two dates, it was highly unusual, in Jack's admittedly limited experience, for gay men to wait so long to make more aggressive moves.

It wasn't until their third date that they wound up in Brad's studio apartment in the West Village for after-dinner drinks. There, while sitting together on Brad's couch, they had their first really intense makeout session.

Jack was thrilled that it was finally happening with this vibrant, joyful, surprisingly sexy young man. It had been so long since he had allowed himself the opportunity to feel another man's body against his, and this one . . . he could tell this one was worth the wait.

But the moment he grabbed at Brad's belt to begin unbuckling it, Brad had pulled away from him. He'd sat frozen at the opposite end of the couch, his head in his hands.

"I . . . I have to tell you something . . ." Brad said at last, his voice barely above a murmur. Jack swallowed. He didn't yet know Brad well enough to understand how best to respond; whether he should touch him, say anything. Long moments of silence passed. Finally, Jack reached a hand to Brad's and held it.

"What is it?"

Brad looked down at their newly clasped fingers, then up at Jack, his eyes wide, his mouth crumpled. He took a deep breath. "I maybe should have told you before, but it's one of those things, you know? I didn't want to scare you away, because I really like you, I mean, I really, really like you, and you never know if something is going to turn into anything real, and I know it's early and everything, but you're wonderful, and I have to tell you . . ."

Jack's heart started racing—this was not at all what he wanted to be hearing, and if it was what he feared, how could he possibly absorb it and not lose his shit? Still, he willed himself to stay there, in his body, and not burden Brad with his fears. He squeezed Brad's hand. He found himself saying, with a steadiness he didn't know he was capable of, "Whatever it is, it's okay."

Brad squeezed his hand back, gripping it tightly. "I hope so. I really hope so." He searched Jack's eyes for a moment, and Jack, his heart thudding for real now, let him. "Last year," Brad began again, "I went through a . . . a really rough time. I kind of acted out a lot. . . . I did some things that I really regret. . . ."

"Okay . . ." Jack said, his mind now starting to race along with his heartbeat.

"I started, well . . ." Brad faltered, then began again. "I started having unprotected sex. Like a lot of it. Like . . . a lot. I think I . . . wanted to kill myself, really." Brad buried his head in his hands once more. "I can't believe I'm telling you this."

Jack found himself rubbing Brad's back, even though all of what Brad was telling him was frightening him more than he could say. "It's okay," he said.

Brad's back trembled with a shuddering intake of breath. "I don't want to die anymore," he said. "I really don't. I got some help, some really important help, and I'm okay, you know? I'm really happy now, I really am, and maybe it's partially because of everything shitty that happened, you know?" He raised his pained face to regard Jack again. "I mean, I'm sure you can figure out what I'm trying to tell you. But, well, we have to be very careful. Like really careful. I really want you. I do. You're gorgeous and smart and kind, and . . . and, well . . . we need to use condoms, always. Because, you know." Brad chewed his lower lip, closed his eyes, and then quietly said, "I'm positive. And I don't want to give that to you."

Jack held his breath. There it was. He had always been an intense germophobe. AIDS and the prospect of HIV infection were among the main reasons he had had so little sex since moving to New York. He had seen the photo essays in *Time* of emaciated men covered in KS lesions, horrifying images he could barely take in. He would never, as Brad had, knowingly put himself in harm's way. But he hadn't ever considered what he might do if he were faced with a moment such as the one in which he found himself. For the first time in his adult life, he was developing strong feelings for a potential romantic partner, he was allowing himself to get swept up in thinking about the possibilities of what it could turn into—and now this news. How could he go forward from here? How could he remain safe and healthy? What would happen?

And yet, as he sat there with Brad, listening to him, comforting him, seeing his lovely, boyish face distorted with fear and shame, Jack discovered, in that moment, that those questions, those fears, didn't really matter. He discovered in himself a capacity for holding this new, explosive information alongside his growing feelings of affection and connection. And so, when Jack gently took Brad's face between his hands and said, "It's okay. It's really okay. Thank you for telling me. You aren't going to scare me away that easily," he surprised himself with how much he meant every word.

Shaking his head to clear away these thoughts, Jack joined in the sparse but heartfelt applause that followed the Broadway singer's final song. Brad turned to Jack and exclaimed, "He was so *good*, wasn't he?"

"Yes, honey, he was excellent," Jack said, even though he had barely paid attention to the performance.

"Oh, look, a magician!"

There was, indeed, a magician taking the singer's place in front of the small audience. He wore a tuxedo featuring sequined silver stars and crescent moons on its sleeves, which were repeated on the slightly absurd cone-shaped hat perched atop his head. It was the same sort of hat that Mickey Mouse wore in *Fantasia*. The magician had a strangely ageless quality, looking like he could be anywhere between fifty and eighty years old. His eyes were framed by small old-fashioned gold-wire-rimmed glasses, and his upper lip sported a rather bushy and elaborate gray handlebar mustache. He looked ridiculous to Jack.

"Greetings, my esteemed patrons," the magician began with a sweep of his sequined arms. Jack thought his pretentious British accent sounded especially fake, and he leaned back in his seat, folding his arms, trying to hide from Brad his immediate dislike of this performer. "It is a glorious evening for that most magnificent, mysterious, and monumental of the living arts practiced throughout human history by fellows both high and low. Oftentimes misunderstood, in its most desperate moments subjected to slanderous accusations of demon worship or worse, but surviving these degradations to rise triumphantly again and again, to the delight and wonder of beings of all ages. I am speaking, of course, of that most magnificent, mysterious, and monumental living art known colloquially as *magic*."

He waggled his eyebrows, seeming to Jack to be awaiting someone kind of raucous response from his audience, oblivious to the fact that these very ill patients wouldn't be supplying him with anything like that anytime soon. The magician forged ahead anyway.

"I am Merlin, and it is my great honor to be here tonight, to enrapture and entertain you with fantastical feats you never dreamed possible." He clapped his hands together, and a cloud of sparkling, glittering confetti erupted, dissolving into nothing as it dissipated around him.

"So pretty," Brad breathed.

Merlin proceeded to perform trick after trick of the sort Jack had seen before: pulling infinite scarves out of his sequined sleeves; pouring water into a newspaper folded into a large cone and then snapping it open to reveal no liquid inside; causing various flowers, coins, and stuffed birds to suddenly appear in his hands, on his shoulders, or from behind the ear of an audience member. Jack had to admit, begrudgingly, that Merlin did manage to perform these tricks with a certain amount of aplomb. And gradually he realized that every item had in fact disappeared entirely at the end of every trick; there was no typical side table or bag where discarded props gathered. By the end, Jack found himself a bit more impressed than he would have guessed at the start of the performance, although Merlin's over-the-top accent continued to grate throughout.

Brad, however, was totally captivated from the first moment to the last, exclaiming awe and delight at the punctuation of each trick. Jack couldn't be certain, but he thought he noticed the magician glancing at Brad from time to time. Then, as the audience applauded at the end of his performance, Merlin took an elaborate bow, and when he removed his ridiculous hat, a pristine white dove flew out and made a beeline directly for Brad, who clapped his hands to his mouth, laughing, as it circled above his head. It returned to Merlin's shoulder, and when the magician delicately offered his finger to it, the dove perched without pause. Merlin kissed his dove lovingly, then tossed it into the air, where it instantly disappeared.

"Ah!" Brad exclaimed. "Amazing!"

The magician took his final bow, and Jack saw him glance again at Brad, his eyes glinting behind his wire-rimmed spectacles. Brad's applause was joyful, by far the most boisterous of any of the patients' responses to the performance. Jack rubbed his boyfriend's back tenderly.

"I'm glad you enjoyed that," he said.

Brad's smile was the brightest Jack had seen on Brad's face in weeks. "It was so, so, so wonderful."

Then, to Jack's surprise, Merlin was striding over to them. He extended his hand to Brad, who took it and shook as vigorously as he was capable of. "Young man," Merlin began, holding Brad's hand in both of his own, "may I say thank you to you?"

"Thank you to me? I'm supposed to be thanking you!"

"Well, then, we shall have to thank one another, then, shan't we? You have given me a gift today. Your enthusiasm, your joy, has reminded me of why I do what I do and has lifted my spirits, and I shall not forget you."

Jack could see Brad's eyes glistening as he listened.

"And who is this handsome young fellow?" Jack realized that Merlin was referring to him and felt his cheeks burn with a jolt of shame at his own internal impoliteness. He stood and extended his hand.

"I'm Jack," he said. "Thank you for your performance."

"You are most welcome, Jack. You are most welcome." Up close, Jack could see that Merlin's eyes were slightly milky and rheumy with age, but nonetheless Jack found himself suddenly and intensely captured by them. "It is indeed my honor and my pleasure."

Jack felt it would be polite to engage further, so he asked the first question that came to his mind: "How long have you been a magician?"

Merlin chuckled as he responded. "Oh, my dear boy, that is a question that is most intriguing and most difficult to answer. It touches on the mysteries and vagaries of Time itself, and it requires me to engage in that most confounding and stubborn of the living arts known as maths. I beg you, do not subject me to maths!"

Jack felt his cheeks burning anew, his attempt at civility backfiring. "I'm sorry, I didn't mean to offend."

Merlin reassuringly patted Jack's arm, smiling warmly. "I promise you, I am not so easily offended. No, no, no, not so easily offended as that! Accuse me of consorting with a succubus, or threaten me with a good burning at the stake, and I might be offended. No, your question is an honest one, and worthy of a response. Suffice it to say, I have been practicing my art for a very, very, very, very, very, *very* long while."

"Well, you are really good at it," Jack said, discovering in that moment that he really did mean it.

"Total agreement," Brad interjected.

Merlin turned back to Brad and rested a hand on his shoulder.

"I thank you again," the magician said. "You have such a light in you, young man. Such a light. It shines brightly, even as . . ." He trailed off, waving his hand vaguely around at their surroundings. Then he began again, gently looking down at Brad. "I must be honest with you, my dear boy. My real and profound regret is that I only ever dabbled in the more . . . frivolous aspects of my art. Tricks. Illusions. Nonsense, really."

"It's not nonsense," Brad interjected. "It's beautiful."

"Ah, perhaps you are right, my dear boy. Perhaps you are right. Illusions can, and do, delight the soul and engage the mind. Yes. They can open us up to experience something of the wonders of the universe. Yes. This is true, I will admit." He paused, his brow furrowing. "But," he continued, "in the end, I have begun to see that, while they are often exciting, and occasionally entertaining, and sometimes quite impressive, these frivolous displays often fall far short of making any real difference. Far too short indeed. Yes, I am afraid it is true."

He removed his spectacles, cleaned them, and returned them to his face.

"You see, there are those among my fellow artists who have, throughout history, dedicated themselves to the much more difficult, and therefore much more powerful, practice of performing the most challenging work of all: the healing Magicks. These Magicks require delving into, and altering the very essence of, Life itself. Yes, my dear boy, I am beginning to see, at long last, that it would have been much more beneficial, much more worthwhile, and much more impactful—so much so—for me to have joined them in this pursuit. I . . . am quite sorry that I cannot do more for you than I have."

Jack took Brad's hand, feeling his chest tighten. Brad looked up at the magician and said, quietly and earnestly, "You really are who I think you are, aren't you?"

"I assure you that I am indeed myself, but I have no inkling as to whether or not that is the same person as you imagine me to be."

"You really are Merlin."

Jack felt lost and was afraid that Brad was beginning to have another episode. "Honey, what do you mean, he's already said that's his name."

"It is indeed my name," the magician replied, smiling.

Brad gripped Jack's hand tightly, his eyes alight. "No, no, I mean, he's Merlin. The real Merlin."

Jack couldn't tell if he or Brad was the source of the confusion. "I don't know what that means."

Merlin said, "He means that I am who I say I am, and he is correct, and that is all. My . . . reputation precedes me, from time to time."

"I'm sorry, I don't understand."

Brad tugged at Jack's hand. "Don't you know who Merlin is?"

Jack, embarrassed and a little afraid, tried to keep his voice from rising. "I don't, no. Should I?"

Brad covered his eyes with his free hand, shaking his head. "Ah, man, I'm sorry, sometimes I don't remember that the stories I grew up with aren't always the stories you grew up with. I'm sorry, I'm sorry. . . ."

Jack felt the need to intervene in any sadness or shame Brad was experiencing as quickly as possible. "It's okay, it's okay. But what do you mean by 'stories'? What does this have to do with stories?"

Merlin interjected again: "Well, allow me to try to explain. One can't always believe everything one reads, but in my case, there have been various tales that have been told about me over the years, and some of them are closer to the truth than others." He turned his attention back to Brad. "I must say that it is most flattering, my dear boy, to be remembered by you."

Brad's eyes were luminous as he gazed up at the magician. "Of course I remember."

Jack felt even more confused and concerned; he very much wanted this interaction to end. He caught Esmerelda's eye, and she immediately made her way over to them.

"Okay, okay, I'm afraid it's time for everyone to go, visiting hours are over, thank you for your performance, sir, thank you, it was so good, it was so fun to see you do your magic, I couldn't believe it, some of the things you did, so exciting!" She began to help Brad out of his seat, and Jack assisted her. "But, sir, I need to get him back to his room, okay? Thank you, thank you, good night, good night."

Brad wavered as he stood up, leaning on Jack, gripping

Jack's arm to steady himself. Esmerelda was supporting his other arm. Brad twisted toward Merlin and said, "I'm so glad to have met you."

"The feeling is mutual, my dear boy, the feeling is mutual."

Esmerelda and Jack managed to get Brad back to his room and into his bed without too much fuss. Esmerelda patted Jack's arm and said as she left, "I'll give you a couple more minutes to say good night, but then I have to kick you out, okay? Don't tell the boss, though, ha?"

"I won't," Jack said, then returned his attention to Brad, who was staring at the ceiling. Jack noticed tears silently streaming from Brad's eyes, although he also noticed that he seemed to be smiling, ever so slightly. "Honey?" Jack said. "Are you okay?"

Brad took a long time to respond. "I'm . . ." he began, still staring at the ceiling. "I'm tired."

Jack willed away the tears threatening to spill out of his own eyes and gently caressed Brad's chest. "Okay, my love. Okay. Get some sleep. I'll see you tomorrow." He leaned down and kissed his boyfriend on the forehead. Brad closed his eyes. Jack turned and left, closing Brad's door behind him.

"Good night, good night," Esmerelda called from the nurses' station. "Get some sleep, okay?" Jack silently waved to her and numbly made his way to the elevator.

When Jack emerged from the hospital onto Twelfth Street, he stuffed his hands into his jacket pockets and hunched into himself, trying to ward off the chill of the evening air. He realized that he was holding his breath and probably had been for some time. He stopped walking and stood very still, closing his eyes tightly and concentrating on taking several slow, measured breaths. He felt himself sway and imagined that he could sense the impossibly fast revolutions of the planet below his feet as it spun its way through the galaxy.

"Young man?"

The voice of the magician startled him out of his meditation. Jack opened his eyes to see the older man, now hatless and wearing a long overcoat, approaching him.

"Are you all right?"

Jack swallowed thickly and said, trying to control any possible quaver in his voice, "I'm all right." He felt his hands clenching into fists in his jacket pockets.

"You looked, for a moment—and I mean no disrespect by this—but you looked, just now, as if you had fallen under some sort of spell. And as that sort of thing is more or less my bailiwick, I would like to offer my assistance to you."

Jack found this man to be very confusing. He attempted a polite smile. "Thank you, but I'm really all right." He was about to turn away when the magician held out a hand to him.

"Sir, please. Allow me to help."

Jack froze, unsure of what this eccentric older man could possibly do for him. Yet he hated the idea of being rude, and also took little pleasure in the idea of going home to his empty apartment. As Jack stood there, contemplating his response, Merlin regarded him with a softness and warmth that Jack found to be completely disarming.

"I assure you, good sir, I mean you no harm."

Jack shook his head. "I don't think you mean me harm." And that was true enough.

"Well, that's a start, then, isn't it?" The magician gestured to a bench on the corner, facing Seventh Avenue. "Please, join me."

Why was this man trying so hard to talk to him? "It's cold out," Jack protested.

"I have just the remedy for that. Come."

Merlin gestured again, invitingly, and after another moment of hesitation, Jack followed the magician to the bench and allowed himself to sit. Jack's fists were still clenched inside his pockets. Merlin removed from his own pocket a small, clear, diamond-shaped crystal. He tapped it three times with his forefinger, muttered something unintelligible, and set it on the bench between them. A few seconds passed, and then the crystal started to glow faintly, amber and purple spreading through its facets. It didn't seem possible, but Jack could distinctly feel heat emanating from it.

"What . . . ? How . . . ?"

The magician smiled. "Is that better?"

Baffled, Jack nodded. The crystal was giving off a rapidly increasing—and quite comfortable—warmth now. "It's . . ." he began. "I don't know what it is, but . . . thank you."

"Alas, this is yet another achievement of mine that is barely more than a parlor trick. Impressive, true, and mildly benefi- cial, especially on a night like tonight. But it is, nonetheless, more sorrowful evidence of all of which I am incapable." He shook his head ruefully. "But no, enough of that from me. You, sir, are in no small amount of distress, and it is no mys- tery as to why. That wonderful young man in there—I realize I did not catch his name—but that most wonderful young man in there, he is yours, is he not?"

Jack found himself holding his breath again and nodded. "Brad," he managed to say.

"Brad. Yes. I believe I know that. Or knew it. . . ." Jack couldn't begin to think of how that could be the case, but it was yet another in a string of bewildering things this magician had uttered, so Jack chose not to say anything. "And you, young man," Merlin continued, "you are Jack, yes?" Jack nodded. "Brad and Jack. Or is it Jack and Brad?"

"I don't . . . I don't know. . . ."

Merlin patted Jack's knee. "It is no matter." He paused, then leaned forward and spoke with a quiet, tender intensity. "I must say, my dear boy, that it is not due to my admittedly unusual—although sadly severely lacking—abilities that I am able to see the care you and Brad have for each other. No, no, I tell you that any sort of person, with any sort of perceptive abilities whatsoever, would be able to notice this. It is really something to behold. Powerful, and true, and eternal. And I am so very touched by it, in no small part because it reminds me of the feelings a friend I once had—or that I have—or that I *will have* . . . Which is it . . . ? Time can be so confounding, forgive me. . . ."

Jack watched, again utterly confused, as Merlin lost himself in his thoughts, chewing on his bushy mustache, his eyes dancing as he worked out whatever mysterious problem it was that he was facing. Suddenly he clapped his hands together and laughed. "Of course! I always forget! Confounded Time has been playing its dastardly tricks on me again! It is both! It is both *had* and *have*!"

"I don't understand. . . ."

"No, no, no. No need to, my dear boy, no need. Never mind that. Terribly unimportant, really." Merlin dismissed the subject with a wave and began afresh, with a renewed, ardent energy. "The point being—the *important* point, the point that *matters*—is that my dear friend Arthur had—*has*—*had*—such feelings, such strong feelings of care and affection as those that you have for Brad and that Brad has for you, not for Jenny, no, not really, although he certainly appreciated—*appreciates*—Jenny's company, to be sure. Jenny, dear Jenny. . . ." Merlin briefly trailed off, shaking his head, and then waved away his thoughts again. "No, my dear boy, no, no, no, never mind that. The important point is that any sort of person can—and could—see that the feelings of care and affection Arthur has—and had—are—and were—almost *entirely* so—these feelings are—and were—so very strong, for one person and one person alone: for *Lance*. And the same is—and was—true of Lance, for Arthur. But—ah! I shall never understand this. Neither man has ever been able to say to the other, 'I am yours, and you are mine.' So many things would be made so much *simpler* if they could just do this—if they could just *have done* this. . . ." Merlin stared into his hands, chewing his mustache once more.

Jack continued to find himself at a loss in trying to follow this bizarre relay of information. He sat for a long moment in silence, feeling almost mesmerized as he waited for Merlin to emerge from his reverie. "It's not . . ." Jack offered, and hesitated. He didn't know why he was saying anything at all, except that something was stirring in him, and he couldn't stop himself. He plowed ahead. "It's not always . . . so easy for everyone."

Merlin looked up at Jack, his rheumy eyes mournful. "No, no, no, you are quite right, my dear boy. Quite right. It is not so easy at all, not at all. And what can one do? What can one do?"

"I don't know," Jack said. Quite suddenly, his chest tightened, his breath caught, and he buried his face in his hands. "I don't know I don't know I don't know I don't know. I don't know what to do. . . . I don't know. . . ." He tried to stifle a sob, but that only seemed to make it louder. The sounds coming out of him . . .

He felt a hand on his shoulder, squeezing both gently and firmly. He felt this but couldn't bring himself to lift his face out of his hands, couldn't begin to stop the cries that racked his body.

"Ah, yes," Merlin said. "Ah, yes. What are we to do? What ever are we to do?" He maintained his gently firm squeezing of Jack's shoulder as Jack continued to sob and sob. Until, finally, Jack was spent.

"I'm sorry," Jack said into his hands, his voice a croak that he couldn't begin to recognize as his own.

"No, my dear boy, I will not allow you to apologize. No. That most assuredly will not do. No."

Jack heaved a trembling breath and did his best to wipe his face clean of tears and snot. At last he slowly sat up but still was not able to meet Merlin's eyes. He stared at the sidewalk for a long time.

"He's not getting out of there," Jack said quietly.

"No. No, he is definitely not getting out of there. He does not have too much longer, I am afraid. It is such a terrible shame."

Jack nodded. "Yes. . . ."

"Ah!" Jack flinched as Merlin suddenly and shockingly smacked his hand on the bench, exclaiming, "That bastard, confounded Time, is once again our mortal enemy!"

The outburst jolted Jack out of the worst of his shame, and he was at last able to look at Merlin. "What do you mean . . . ?"

"My dear boy, this awful Plague has not always been—no, that is not correct, not in this case. No. It *will not always be*—

and this I know—yes, this is clear to me, I have seen this—I have seen that it *will be* true."

"You're not . . . you're not making sense. . . ."

"Ah, yes, I have forgotten, you truly do not know who I am! How delightful, really! And so rare! Ah, yes, but it is difficult to explain. . . . I have seen, and I will see, yes, that is how it is. I have seen, and I will see, and both are true. . . ." He waved his hand again. "But no matter! You must believe me when I say this—and I realize that it may bring precious little comfort to you, right now, in this moment, but you must know it nonetheless: the Plague will change, it will. It will not be the dreaded messenger of Death for all of Time. No. And no, I understand, I do, that this is not true for your dear beloved Brad, no. Not for Brad. I am afraid that Time—and Time's dread companion, Death—have indeed confounded us there. And, no, there is nothing to be done about it for your poor, dear, lovely, beloved Brad. But, oh! For so many others, yes, for so very many others, it will be so very different. And this— yes, I know! This will be soon. And it will be forever."

Jack would never be able to say to anyone why, but as he listened to the magician speak, as Jack heard the passionate certainty, the unwavering conviction, in Merlin's voice—even as Jack struggled to follow the circles within circles in Merlin's sentences, the logic that contained no logic—even then, Jack found himself believing that what this strange old man said was true.

In something of a daze, Jack made his way home, to the apartment he and Brad shared, the same studio apartment Brad had been living in when they met. Jack felt as if he were moving through vapor as he walked up the familiar four flights, let himself in, and deposited his coat onto the kitchen table. He took off his shoes but didn't remove any of his other clothes, and collapsed onto the couch. He hadn't been able to sleep in their bed since Brad had left for St. Vincent's.

He closed his eyes, and slept.

He was on a boat. The air was thick, impossibly so, with a humidity that squeezed into him. But he was shivering. He was on a wide, slow-moving river. There was no one else on the boat. There were no other boats on the river, which was strange, because he realized he was on the Chao Phraya, in Bangkok, a river that was a thoroughfare and always jammed with all kinds of boat traffic.

He sat and shivered and struggled to breathe the thick, sultry air.

"Perhaps this will help?"

Jack turned to his left, where Merlin sat. The magician was holding the glowing crystal out to him, his eyes twinkling.

"Thank you," Jack said, and took the crystal. He clutched it to his chest, but the shivers wouldn't dissipate.

"Give it time," Merlin said, and tossed a dove in his direction. It flew past Jack. Jack followed it with his eyes to see the dove alight on Brad's shoulder. Brad was sitting next to him, radiant, grinning.

"Hi," Brad said. He put his arm around Jack and leaned into him. "I'm so glad I finally got to come here."

"But . . ." Jack said.

"It's beautiful, look!" Brad was pointing to the ancient, ornate Wat Arun glowing in the sunlight on the bank of the river. Brad lifted the dove onto his finger and held it out in the direction of the temple. The dove flew toward it, gracefully darting through the air, then burst into sparkles.

"So beautiful!" Brad said.

Jack leaned into Brad, who leaned into him. He felt the weight of Brad, solid and warm. He realized he had stopped shivering.

"Songwittana." Brad kissed his cheek. "I love you."

They leaned into each other. The humid air pressed into them.

Jack looked at Brad. "I know I'm dreaming."

Brad smiled at Jack. "So? I know that, too. Doesn't mean it's not real."

Jack's eyes opened. He lay there for a minute, trying to hold on to the wisps of the dream. He breathed deeply.

He slowly sat up, rubbed his eyes, and shuffled toward the bed that hadn't been slept in for weeks. He stripped off his clothes, climbed in, and curled himself around Brad's pillow. He inhaled Brad's scent. And slept again.

The next day, Jack stood next to Brad's bed for hours, holding his hand, watching him sleep, leaning down every now and then to kiss him on the cheek or the forehead or both. Brad barely stirred.

"I love you," Jack said again and again, quietly, but willing Brad to hear him. "I love you I love you I love you."

At one point, Brad's eyes opened, swam in his head a little, and then alighted on Jack.

"Hello," Jack said. "Hello. You don't need to say anything if you can't. It's okay, my love. It's okay." Brad slowly blinked at Jack. "I'm here. I'm right here. It's okay." Brad's eyes held his for a long moment and then closed.

"It's okay. It's okay, my love. It's okay."

The Quay Stone

S. Zainab Williams

When Mom says things like "Nenive is nothing but a girl gone wild on holiday," I recall when she told me, so many years ago, that the Merlion is as mythical as a souvenir key chain.

I had looked up from my children's book of legends to ask about the myth. I'd read every story in this book dozens of times, and now I wanted one that belonged to me. The alabaster imprint of Singapore's mascot emerged fresh from the recent memory of my first visit, throwing its lion's head and flexing its fish's tail like a promise ready to be made.

Mom had sighed as she told me the Merlion was actually British-designed branding, like someone had to strip wonder from my eyes, so it might as well be her.

But when Nenive takes my hand to pull me away from Nani's apartment, the pair of us pushing through the hot, thick air, she feels like that magical, elusive creature: a guide, a friend. I slow down, breathing in the baked thunder and flora odor of the island. I risk stopping long enough to fan the heat from my face, to wave away the memory of Mom's disappointment. But Nenive is slipping off, so I gather myself, and then the slap of my sandals accompanies the sharp click of her heels again as we speed down the stairs.

I hope you understand. I want to make Mom happy, but mostly I want Mom to be happy I have Nenive now.

We had our first argument—Mom and I—back in the cab a few hours ago on the way to Nani's. We sped down tidy streets, passing under the stippled shadows of rain trees and then between the glaring glass storefronts with signs advertising skin-lightening creams, showcasing designer bags and the season's prêt-à-porter looks. We warred in silence.

In a different situation, maybe I'd have been proud to finally experience this rite of passage that had happened to everyone except me. But Mom and I have counted on each other ever since the divorce. When I chose to stay with Mom, Dad got a job on a ship and left us both. The two of us knew we couldn't afford any more friction, and we wouldn't have broken our streak by battling it out in the cab to Nani's if she had loosened her grip and let me live a little.

Instead, Mom said, "Why don't you give your cousins a chance—talk to them. You act like they don't speak English."

"I know they speak English." The words had to fight their way out.

I've never been good at speaking up and I wonder at people who are. How do you find the right words, release them, and sit back without worrying if they'll take? Mom thinks I should be able to plop myself in the middle of a group of strangers, pick up the thread, and run with it, no problem. I've been herded into the cousinly fold how many times now, sitting in a big group in one of numerous glossy living rooms while my cousins talk about friends and boyfriends. They share gossip, they slip in and out of Malay, and I hunch on the outskirts, as clueless as the three-year-old jamming up her mouth with Nani's kueh tat but a lot less carefree.

We spent the rest of that ride in a very different kind of silence, and I ended up with a crick in my neck from keeping my head turned away from Mom.

I'm not the praying type, but I did wear down the linoleum in front of Nani's window willing time to move faster and open my escape hatch already. Nothing had been resolved, but I wasn't about to get into it with Mom again. Tomorrow would be another day, and tonight would give me time to think up better words to explain why I needed this. For the moment, however, I could only focus on listening for Nenive's knocking. Mom and Nani chatting in the kitchen bled into white noise, and I'd long ago stopped trying to identify the spicy, tangy aroma taking over the apartment.

"Surprise," a voice shouted from the door. I almost leaped for the exit, but it was only Mamu Jam, jazz hands up as he kicked his shoes into the pile outside the door. "The gang's all here," he laughed.

I froze in the living room, while Mom and Nani hurried into the hallway to greet Mamu Jam and his daughters, whose names I had once again forgotten.

"I brought you some company," my uncle sang at me in greeting. He clapped a hand on his oldest's shoulder.

"I have plans," I mumbled. A ruthless, but necessary, admission.

"Your cousins came all the way from KL to see you, and Nani made rendang." Mom's smile didn't reach her eyes, and I knew I was digging myself deeper, but I wasn't the one who forced them to come down unannounced. Anyway, I'm sure they made the drive from Kuala Lumpur because Mamu Jam wanted to catch up with Mom. My absence wouldn't ruin their plans. My cousins hung back, looking wiped out from a full day of living their actual lives before their dad dragged them across the border to entertain their American cousin. Anyone could see they'd be happier left to their own devices.

They rested their hopes and their gaze on Nani, who had shuffled over to the TV to find something for us to watch. She lingered over an old Bollywood film as the music accompanying the lovestruck protagonist swelled. I couldn't understand the song or the captions. Nani and the cousins, meanwhile, were spellbound.

"Why don't you and the girls catch up in the living room?" Mom said. My cousins dutifully made their way to the couch. Normally, I'd be trailing behind them, but not this time.

"You said I could go," I reminded Mom under my breath.

"She made friends with this girl," Mom apologized to Mamu Jam, eyes still locked on mine. "But she's here to see the family."

"Eat first, then go," Nani urged, leaving the remote in my cousins' care to touch her sparrow-light hand to my arm. I looked at the clock, and my stomach sank. I couldn't make Nenive wait.

"If she wants to go, let her go lah," said Mamu Jam. He turned to Mom. "Kids want to run around. She's just like you—jalan-jalan all day long."

Mamu Jam was teasing her, but he wasn't wrong. In fact, Mom hadn't simply hung out with her friends; she'd habitually snuck out. She often laughed about Nani's premonition—a threat aimed at her then-teenage daughter—that Mom would be paid back in full with rebellious kids of her own. Mom offered stories of her mischief as a contrast to my model behavior, congratulating me for helping her defy Nani's wicked hopes, mistaking my gleam of desire for pride.

Back when Mom and Dad were still in love, she liked to tell me the story of her wildest unapproved escapade and how it took her all the way across the ocean with a Black sailor. Dad. Reborn on the top floor of a downtown office, swaddled in a sharp suit, she tucked her family against a canyon crawling with ivy and oak in a white-stucco, two-story home. I spent my childhood testing our highest balcony, looking at the town below, above it all and alone.

I could've hugged my uncle for reminding Mom of her own history. I hoped the fact that I'd bothered to ask permission, whereas she would've slipped out in the night, wasn't lost on her.

I was scrabbling at righteousness and at the pendant sticking to the clammy skin below my collarbone when a knock sounded on the door. Grabbing my cardigan from the couch, I ran for it.

"That's her," I called over my shoulder. "Be back later." I cracked open the door, squeezing myself out and into Nenive's grip. She held my hand and pulled me along, laughing, always in on the game.

"Is that what you're wearing?" she asks me now.

"What?" We've stopped at the bottom of the stairs where Nenive's moss-green eyes take in my linty black cardigan, spaghetti strap tank, shorts, and sandals.

"Oh," I say. "I didn't bring anything fancy." My throat is tight and my face is hot.

I officially hate myself for waiting until the last minute to pack again. And for being so boring I hadn't even been able to muster the fantasy of an evening out. Not that I would've found anything good in my closet anyway.

Instead of packing for a new and improved me, I'd sat myself down in front of my dusty old carry-on to fold threadbare cotton underwear and come up with a script that would make me sound more interesting and accomplished to my relatives. My grades and the assurance that, yes, I would be going to college would have to do the heavy lifting. Those were the thrilling thoughts that had consumed me as I rolled up outfits for sweaty walks, public transportation, and messy breakfasts of roti canai the day before we left for Singapore.

Now I tug at my wrinkled outfit, holding my breath as Nenive stares. Near-translucent skin stretches tight as a drum across her brow.

But her smile returns, and the charge that always lingers around her dissolves until you almost can't tell it's still there.

"You wore the pendant," she says, and hooks her arm in mine.

"I'll never take it off," I'm quick to say.

"And never forget who gave it to you." Nenive laughs, but her words stick.

How can I forget?

A week after we arrived in Singapore, Mom and I went sightseeing by the waterfront with my aunts and uncles and their children. I'd fallen farther and farther behind, desperate for a moment alone with my thoughts. When the kids cried for ais kacang to eat while we took a break to watch the bumboats, I claimed fatigue and stayed behind, trudging alone to the steps leading down to the water. That's how I found her.

A girl rose from the foggy waters of the Marina Bay wearing a bikini as bleached as the Merlion, dripping in the shadow of that legendary marketing beast. She was tall and lean and pale, her long hair slick against her skin. She was every young woman in the countless luxury brand advertisements I'd seen around the city. I stood there gaping, waiting for someone to notice and pull her back up to safety or give her a talking-to.

"I don't think you're supposed to swim here." The warning sounded idiotic the second I blurted it.

When she didn't immediately acknowledge my existence, I took the opportunity to play at being another tourist admiring the water spewing from the Merlion's open mouth.

But movement in my periphery forced me to look back in her direction. Her arm was outstretched. She looked right at me and said, "Found it." She said it casually, as if we'd been having a conversation all along and it had been interrupted by whatever she was up to.

I squinted at the winking mound of moon dust in her hand.

"What is it?" I whispered.

"A gift for a friend."

A sterling silver sword lay against a bed of microscopic gemstones. My fingers itched as I studied the impossible scrollwork on the little hilt.

"You like it?"

"It's beautiful," I answered. I couldn't take my eyes off the pendant and thought my brain was magnifying the details, but no. The girl had appeared on the steps in front of me to bring the piece up to my nose. Her hand smelled like the river and something metallic. Blood? I don't know why I thought that—it was only the pendant—but the thought made me aware of how close she was, and I took a step back, embarrassed.

"Go on, then, take it."

I had a hard time looking at her again and a harder time declining. "I can't. Your friend—"

"I don't have a friend, but I'd like to make one."

Nenive. I don't know if she introduced herself then or later or ever. Maybe she smiled by way of introduction because, better than anything else about that exchange, I remember the way her face transformed. All canines and beetled brow. Its vulnerability, its quirkiness and charm took me by surprise. I try to picture her face before she handed me the pendant—the way she'd looked at me from the water, or when she'd stood so close to show me her gift. It's like trying to remember a stranger from a dream.

"Look, I promise it'll bring you your hopes and desires or whatever," she assured me, nudging the pendant closer. "But it'd help if you gave it a chance to find out what they are." Nenive waggled her brows.

I told myself to be cool, to riff like I was used to shooting the shit with people, but her intensity sent my gaze away again. That's how I noticed other people finally beginning to acknowledge her, staring as if bobbing around the Marina Bay was nowhere near as strange as the act of standing beside me. Nenive wasn't looking at them. She's the sort of person who doesn't consider what others think of her. It's as easy to pick her type out of a crowd as it is to lose mine in one.

The terror that had held me back from making friends countless times before returned. There was life before the color-coded cliques and the quizzical stares of high school, before I turned myself into a ghost to avoid being deemed a square peg, and there was life after. Loner became my status, and certain that I'd never find belonging, I stopped searching for it and disappeared.

But this spectacular girl had found me and had chosen me to wear this spectacular treasure.

"I know you want it." Nenive's reedy song whistled warm across my face.

Squinting hard, pushing down the urge to flinch away from her charm, I took in the mercurial ripples of here-and-gone sunlight illuminating her skin, the fuel oil lacquering her arms. I smiled back and accepted her gift.

It was warm in my hands and released that earthy, metallic perfume I'd caught earlier. The scent, the winking light, and the heat made my head spin until I remembered to breathe.

Nenive reached around my neck to unclasp the chain I wore. The charm it held sounded off as it skipped across the ground. I crouched to recover it, dropping it into my pocket. Meanwhile, Nenive had strung her heavy pendant on my naked chain. She clasped it around my neck and studied it with satisfaction.

"As long as you have that, you have my friendship. And as long as you have my friendship, well—"

Anything is possible. The thought arrived out of thin air, delivered with Nenive's posh English accent. And I believed her words like they were my own.

Outside of Nani's apartment, Nenive lets go of my hand. I look up at the building, expecting to find Mom staring down at me, Mamu Jam patting her shoulder. But there are too many windows, and they all look empty to me.

We leave in two days. I thought she would understand. We can come back to visit family anytime, but I don't know if I'll ever see Nenive again. When I consider that possibility, it's like I can feel the point of my pendant's sword digging into my chest, in search of my heart.

"Pre-drink." Nenive pushes a travel bottle of vodka into my hand.

"Where'd you get this?" I say. I can't remember Singapore's drinking age or the rules about public intoxication. I can't remember because I don't drink. I look up and down the street to make sure nobody's watching.

"Drink it," Nenive says.

The bottle is cold in my hand. Condensation rolls off and joins the brooding humidity. I imagine Nenive pulling the little bottle out of a fridge. Does she have one in her hotel? Is she staying with her family?

I've spent the last three weeks biting back questions about her life outside our activities together, hoping to learn anything by asking broad questions about her feelings and thoughts in the moment.

The first time she called me to hang out, a strange number appearing on my phone's screen—a number I now understand will change each time she calls—we got to talking. We were planning our day together when I capitalized on a lull in the conversation to ask about her friends back home—whether she had many, what they were like. She told me she didn't want to talk about any of that. She made me promise I'd never ask again. I agreed quickly, worried I'd ruined everything.

And now here she is with alcohol. I don't think she's older than me, but I can't ask because the question might be off-limits.

So instead, I dare to say, "Please, Nenive. We can't drink it here."

In one swift motion, she throws back her own bottle and tosses the empty into the nearest hedge.

"Nenive!" I shriek at the shrub. I'm sure I am the picture of pearl clutching. I literally have my hand around the pendant.

"Pipe down and get to it," she says. "Or I'll pour it down your throat myself."

Maybe she's joking, but for half a second her features swing open and I get a glimpse of thrumming anticipation. I hurry up and swig the liquor, trying not to cough. She snorts when I stuff my empty bottle and cap into the pocket of my shorts. I'm grateful when she turns away to hail a cab because I was sure she was about to command me to litter on the sparkling streets.

I enjoy a guilty moment of peace on the sidelines, relaxing against the seat of the cab while Nenive directs the driver. Taking control comes easily to her, and she doesn't seem bothered by the fact that I'd rather not. Nenive knows her way around better than I do, anyway, and she has a knack for pointing us in the direction of adventure. I get to be a tourist for once. Until now, Singapore has looked like my family's collective backside, their living rooms and bedrooms. I'm herded from place to place, the glassy-eyed, loose-necked lamb dawdling behind the flock. With Nenive, I'm free to wander far and wide, spectating. Even if we get lost, nothing matters except that we're together.

And, together, we talk and laugh loudly, letting everyone know we've arrived. What would my classmates back home say if they saw me with Nenive? Would they recognize me from three years of sharing space and wonder at the stranger I've become?

"Wake up, we're here." Nenive pushes open the cab door, letting neon-pink light and muffled beats into the cabin. I hurry out of the taxi after her, almost forgetting to pay the fare.

In my desperation to catch up, I manage to stumble on the

curb and stub my big toe. I'm frazzled by the time I reach the club, and Nenive is nowhere to be found. Falling into line, I scan the entrance because I don't know what else to do except pop my head out of the crowd now and then in case she's looking for me.

There she is. Chatting up the bouncer.

Nenive is an animated conversationalist, pantomiming, performing. The bouncer's face goes slack while he eats it up. I might be the only person in the world who's seen her truly at rest. It's a privilege. And a burden, I guess.

We were hanging out at East Coast Park last week, scarfing down fries on the beach, when I caught her in a rare moment of silence. It was like someone had flicked her switch to OFF. She didn't blink, looking at the muggy horizon. I didn't realize I'd been holding my breath until my lungs screamed, and I dropped a fry in the sand while I gasped for air. Nenive started.

"What's wrong with you?" She shook her head at me and flicked away the fallen fry.

At the time, I thought she should've asked herself the question. But the more I think about it, the more I see that she'd been minding her own business, probably thinking about her friends and life back home. I should have left her to her thoughts.

As Nenive picked up her fries, returned from wherever she'd been, I'd searched the water for the object of her attention and found only phantom memories of Dad.

"I know you're lonely," Nenive had said suddenly.

I drew a shaky breath, worried she'd finally figured out that I was nobody.

"I heard you calling my name," she said. "That's how I found you."

I let out a little laugh.

"I didn't know your name," I reminded her. "We hadn't met yet, Nenive."

Nenive is like that sometimes. Disoriented. Or maybe I don't get her jokes. That day, I was too happy to have her attention back to let it bother me. I spent the rest of that afternoon struggling to make enough noise to keep her present. Because when Nenive forgets herself, it's like the whole world slides out of focus with her.

Outside the club, I linger in place, uncertain and unable to cross the invisible barrier standing between me and the front of the line. But Nenive's hands are quiet now. She looks over her shoulder, finding me immediately. Although our eyes meet, there's no recognition in hers, and in that moment I'm struck by the urge to duck back into line and out of sight before she's certain. Blood thumps in my temples, but when the pendant burns hot against my chest, I know she's identified me.

Nenive mouths, *Come on*, impatience knitting her brow. "This is my friend," I hear her say to the bouncer as I approach. To me she says, "He's going to let us in."

"This the girl you were talking about?" The bouncer looks me up and down, and I curl my battered, naked toes. He half-heartedly waves in my direction. "Can't let her in, too young."

I know I look younger than sixteen and that Nenive is taller, even more so in heels, but she also doesn't look old enough to get into this club. Of course, age has nothing to do with the bouncer's decision to let her in and not me. The thin pretense makes the situation even more galling. As if he assumes

I'm stupid as well as unattractive. I distract myself from the struggle of masking my emotions by studying the crowd.

These women standing in line are smiling and whispering onto one another's shoulders. They're like colorful, fragrant bouquets, and any one of them could be related to me. They'd never guess it.

At school, the Asian kids thought I was trying to take something from them when they caught me drinking cartons of soy milk or eating shrimp chips on the farthest outskirts of the quad and were shocked when someone (Mike Quincy, one of five other Black students at school) loudly corrected himself about my ethnicity in AP Bio. All along he'd thought I was high yellow when I was actually Blasian, he announced after Mr. Connors asked, for the fifth time, if Mike and I were related. To Mike, it was obvious that we were not family. To the Asian students, it was unbelievable that I, Ranch 99 receipts in hand, could also be counted among them.

Here in line, standing beside Nenive as we're turned away at the door, I imagine I'm lumped into the ignorant foreigner category. I fantasize about saying something clever to the bouncer in Malay, and the small brown girl in my head opens her mouth to let jargon in the shape of the language fall out. Clutching the pendant, I consider the many things I wish I could change about myself.

"Well, I'm not going in there without her," Nenive is saying. "She's paying my way. Do you see this?" She prizes the pendant out of my hand to bare it at the bouncer. "Do you know how much this is worth? Do you know how much she's worth?"

The bouncer shows no interest until the pendant presents a dazzling display. He freezes, and the crowd and music fall silent as the stones around the sword, and the sword itself, continue to catch light from some unseen source. I squeeze my eyes shut when it blinds me.

In the darkness I hear the rush of blood, cries of death and heartbreak, the shush of a blade thrust into dark, fertile soil. I am the conqueror.

I force my eyes open and music floods my ears. The bouncer is looking from the pendant to me, as if trying to work out the math. If he's seen or heard anything unusual, he doesn't show it. I struggle to regain composure, but I'm feverish and weak, still recovering from the vision.

"Get inside," the bouncer says to Nenive.

My friend throws a triumphant wink at the man and drags me into the club after her.

As the thrill of the vision fades, self-awareness returns. My sweating skin, my acne breakouts, a fold of what Mom insists on calling baby fat chafing against the waist of my shorts.

And then there's my hair. Waiting for Nenive's arrival, before my mom nearly upended my plans, I had tried to work my frizzy curls into submission with the cheap flat iron I'd begged Mom to purchase at Bugis, willfully forgetting the fact of Singapore's humidity. As Nenive and I dance our way around the club, I try to ignore the tickles across my scalp, the sensation announcing the undoing of my hard work. Mom and her cavalcade of hairdressers never know what to do with my curls, nor do I; right now, I can tell my hair is assuming the shape of its most recent cut, turning my head into a conical mesa abbreviated by my face.

My hair, my body, my clothes all mock me for thinking I could be anyone else simply because I have Nenive.

I swipe sweat off my brow and focus on navigating the

crowd, bobbing across the floor moored to Nenive with the tourists and expats she gathers in her wake.

This happens almost every time we're together. Nenive thought it was funny when I dubbed her persistent admirers Satellites. After a while, some of them drift off to rejoin their friends, giving one long look back at her. Others remain with us. They jostle me as if unaware of my presence, threatening to push me out of the circle as they make for their target. But I'm small and nimble. I wrap my hand around the pendant to remind myself that Nenive chose me. Steadied by a surge of adrenaline, I dart through the Satellites and am rewarded. Nenive's fingers reach out to dig into my arm, holding my position beside her.

A song throbs to a close, bleeding into the next track, and the man who's worked hardest to unmoor me whispers in Nenive's ear. I shift away, not wanting to become a third wheel, but her grip tightens.

"Come on, free drinks," she shouts, already tugging me to a high table. While the man orders from the bar, his friends who had also remained in our circle on the dance floor gather around as if to pen Nenive in.

She makes small talk with them. I used to listen in on these conversations in case she dropped some information about her life. I figure she's British because of the accent, but that's about all I've got. I don't even know if she's visiting with her parents. Or if she has parents. Anyway, I don't bother to listen anymore. The Satellites are always so busy selling themselves that they never get around to asking her questions about herself. I doubt they'd think to, even if they took a breather from competing with one another for the next word.

"Is that your friend?"

I'm so startled by the question, I flinch. A woman, perhaps a few years older than me, lifts her hands, palms facing my baffled expression.

"I'm not trying to start anything, just hoping you can tell me she has a boyfriend so I can pull my brother away," she shouts above the music.

"Sorry, you took me by surprise," I say. And then I remember her question. "And sorry again, but I don't think Nenive has a boyfriend." I have no idea if this is true, but I want to be useful and she looks friendly.

"Sorry, sorry lah, no need to apologize," she says without malice.

She's definitely from here. She looks like one of my younger aunts. Her name is Fatima.

"But everyone calls me Fata." She looks at her brother to roll her eyes and shake her head. "Stupid. Look at him making a fool of himself over your friend."

"I don't think she lives here, so at least it's temporary, if that helps," I say.

"You don't think? She's your friend—shouldn't you know where your friend lives?"

Once I start to explain that we only recently became friends, the words keep tumbling out. Fata inspects the pendant, all the while keeping an eye on Nenive. Her Satellites jostle for attention and the circle is tighter now. I had slipped outside of the close quarters as soon as Nenive's grip loosened, but I'm not out of her reach entirely. I don't know why I'm so nervous. It's my gift to show off.

"Doesn't really look like your style," Fata concludes. "It's not understated, you know what I mean?"

"I know," I say, cheeks warming. "I need a new wardrobe."

"No, this pendant needs to be less gaudy," says Fata. "I don't mean to be rude or anything, but it's a lot." She waves her hand around to dismiss the comment. "Whatever, it's nice that she gave you a gift, but how is she going to call herself your friend and keep herself to herself?"

I shouldn't have told her about Nenive's secrecy.

"Like I said, we haven't known each other long." I shrug. "There are all sorts of reasons she's so private. She's eccentric."

I stifle the urge to tell Fata all sorts of things about Nenive's odd behavior. Things I hadn't allowed myself to give much thought until now. I want to see how Fata reacts. If she brushes it off, fine. If not—

I sense that I'm being watched, and sure enough, I look up to find Nenive standing much closer than she was a second ago, looking from me to Fata.

Sweat is pouring down my back. How much has she heard? I can't read her face.

"What are you doing?" Nenive asks flatly.

"Waiting for my brother to be done messing around," Fata says, rescuing me from having to answer.

"Not you," Nenive says with a withering glance at Fata, who smiles back. "You left me to fend for myself with those dipshits."

"I thought you were having a good time," I stammer. I want to remind her about how often she'd forgotten *me*, but I clutch my pendant instead, hoping it'll give me another injection of confidence.

Nenive responds by pulling me back into the circle. "You haven't even had a drink," she says. "Go on."

I'm tired of Nenive telling me what to do, but I choose a straw that looks untouched and take a sip from the communal vessel of rum and coke. The pendant frees itself from my collar and knocks into the pitcher while I'm bent over for a drink.

"What's that you've got?" An Australian Satellite points at the pendant.

"It's a gift I gave her," Nenive says on my behalf. "It's a friendship thing, but I don't think she likes it."

"If she doesn't like it, I'll take it," says the Australian. "I'd be honored to be your friend."

I almost roll my eyes at his shit-eating grin.

But Nenive looks serious. "I guess it's nothing to you," she tells me.

I forget the Australian and stare at Nenive, my pulse quickened by her soured mood. I know I've misstepped somehow. Nenive cocks her head, malice frosting her smile.

"Why don't you give it to him, since he actually wants it?"

I hold the pendant to my chest, and the tiny sword nicks the skin below my collarbone. I try to imagine what would happen if I did give it up, but instead I remember splashing in the surf at East Coast Park with Nenive, and how she'd hugged me like I was her sister when I stumbled and fell in the water.

Everyone's watching, waiting to see what I'll do, and then the Australian leans over, his arm outstretched in my direction, ready to receive. Blood boils in my veins and I'm about to smack his arm away when Fata steps forward.

"Hey, what do you think you're doing?" she says. "You can't snatch things off a person's body—what's wrong with you?"

The Australian holds his hands up. He tucks in his chin, faux defensive, smug.

"Calm down, calm down," he says.

"Lighten up." Nenive smirks at Fata. "She knows we're just joking around." Nenive looks at me for confirmation, and her features scrunch like she's seeing me for the first time. Her eyes widen.

"Oh, your hair," she exhales.

I know what it must look like, but I sag when she announces it. Nenive snatches the elastic from her ponytail, letting her own hair fall in glossy waves down her back. She scrapes the frizzy mass away from my face and secures it in a bun so tight it uproots a few strands. Though I can make out Fata's pursed lips, the rest of the club is blurry with captive tears by the time Nenive pulls back.

She combs through her own locks as if to cleanse her hands. Her gleaming crown shines beneath the colorful lights slicing across the room as she declares, "All better now."

The Satellites watch my friend preen. And then they lean over to wrap their lips around their straws and drink deep from the pitcher, heads bowed in reverence. I'm tired and sober.

Nenive turns to me. "Are you bored?"

Sometimes I worry that she can read my mind. I imagine a wall as I search her face for the correct answer.

"I'm fine?"

She snorts. "Well, *I'm* bored—let's get out of here."

"There's tulang nearby," Fata speaks up. "We're heading there now." She has her brother by the arm and looks ready to drag him away.

"I love tulang," I practically shout.

"Come, come, you'll love this place," says Fata. "Best in town."

I turn to Nenive, picturing the four of us in conference over the bright red bowls of stew, excavating marrow from bone with every narrow device available to us.

"You'll love it, too," I say. I'm giddy with the idea of showing her a bit of Singapore. It's my turn to play tour guide. Our time together is running out, and I'm overdue for showing Nenive that I know some things, too. And if there's one thing I know about Singapore, it's where to eat.

"I don't want that crap," Nenive says breezily. "I'm in the mood for chips, come on."

More chips. She can have fries anywhere.

"Where are you off to?" The smiling Australian must've slid into our smaller circle while we were talking. He appears between Fata and Nenive. "Where are *we* off to?" he corrects himself.

"Oh," Nenive looks at him as if he materialized from the piped-in smoke. "We're going our own way. Just the two of us."

"What about Fata?" I say.

"No thanks—I'm not in the mood." Fata purses her lips, striking an uncanny imitation of Nenive as she waves us off. Her other arm is still locked around her brother's. "It was nice to meet you. Hope you enjoy the rest of your trip." She arches an eyebrow at Nenive.

I'm still picturing the wall in my mind as I wish I could go with them, but my hand starts to reach for the pendant. I force it back down.

Nenive throws a scoff at their backs, but her face is smoothed over as if she's forgotten the corresponding expression. I think back to the beach and the spell of stillness I witnessed and shiver.

"Aren't I your friend, too?" the Australian says, still unwilling to give up his flirtations.

"I don't have time for you," she says. "Let's go." Nenive takes my hand and pulls me away.

I look back at the Satellites, thrown out of orbit. They watch us go in bewilderment, standing there like men turned to stone by Nenive's face.

———

Mom calls when Nenive and I arrive at the fast-food place. She loaned me the flip phone thinking I'd be out and about with my cousins during our stay. Nenive keeps telling me not to pick up, but I cave the fourth time Mom rings. I press money into Nenive's hand to place our order, apologize, and go outside to take the call.

Mom is predictably unhappy.

"Where are you?" she says before I can get a word in. "I've been calling and calling—"

"I was ordering food," I lie. "I couldn't pick up right away."

"Get it to go and come home," Mom says.

"Mom, I can't just up and leave Nenive here."

"Nenive can get her food to go wherever it is she goes."

"Why are you being like this? We're just eating, get over it." I bite my lip.

"What did you just say to me?"

A charged silence slips between us again, but I can't stand it anymore. I need her to understand.

"Can't you let me have one friend?" I turn toward a column to hide my tear-streaked face from passersby.

"Oh, sweetie." Mom sighs on the other end of the line. "I want you to have friends. But I've never even met this girl. You won't bring her over, you can't tell me anything about her. All I know is that she has no respect for your family time or plans that aren't hers and that she keeps you out at all hours of the night doing who knows what. You don't even know where she lives or what she's doing here—you said it yourself."

I couldn't keep my mouth shut. Not around Fata, and not around Mom. I shouldn't have admitted my ignorance to Mom when she prodded me for more information about

Nenive the third or fourth time we hung out. I know it only made Mom dislike her more.

"I don't want to fight again, but you can't fault me for thinking she's a loose cannon," Mom continues. "I'm worried about you."

She softens her tone. "We'll get rendang at Lau Pa Sat bright and early tomorrow morning—we'll spend the day together, you and me," she promises. "We can go back to Bugis. I saw you eyeing those weird slashed leggings."

I press the phone closer to my cheek as Mom's laughter, strained and desperate, comes through the receiver, and I picture us enjoying a day together. I want her to reach through the phone and catch me.

My head aches from the ringing in my ears. It started up after the vision at the club's entrance. Stress, most likely. I try to ignore it while I talk to Mom, but the itch irritating my palm is starting to spread as well. I know that if I just hold the sword pendant, the sound and the pain will go away.

I ball my hand into a fist and hold the phone tight, darting a look through the burger place's window. Nenive watches me from a table, a spread of food in front of her. She drags a finger across her throat and mouths, *Hang up*.

"Give me thirty minutes," I tell Mom. "I'll be home in thirty minutes."

Nenive and I eat our combo meals under the harsh fluorescent lights of the franchise. Her shoulders jig for joy. She's finally done bad-mouthing Fata. Nearby, a woman cuts up fries for the toddler bouncing on her knee. When she pauses to glance our way, I imagine she sees students from abroad—one sad, one happy—retreating from the unknown, disgusted by it. I push my tray away.

Nenive stares at my food. "That's all you're eating?" she says through a mouthful.

"I'm not that hungry," I say.

"You looked hungry enough to eat her bullshit when that girl asked you out." Nenive can make anything sound conversational.

Looking down at the table, I mutter a quick "I should head home soon."

"No way," says Nenive. "It's not even midnight. What are you, five?"

"I have to get up early to do a family thing."

"We can come up with some excuse to get you out of it," Nenive says. She smacks her palms on the table. "What we need is a drink. Let's go back to Clarke Quay. I've got a few more—" She makes a tossing-back motion and pats the cheap souvenir purse slung over her shoulder.

"Nenive, I told my mom I'd be home by now." I'm usually good at staying chipper around her. She goes cold the minute I show her anything less than joy. But I'm so tired.

"Well, then call your bitchy mum back and tell her I fell and hit my head tripping on the curb. Tell her you need to help me. She'll believe it."

"Please don't say things like that."

"Like what?"

"You know what." I'm so afraid to disturb the delicate balance, but I can't let this one go. "Don't call her bitchy."

"Bitchy mum, bitchy mum, bitchy, bitchy mum," Nenive sings. "You're such a baby. Now, are we going or what?"

In the cab, my phone won't stop ringing. I hold it in my

open hands, sinking deeper and deeper with each unanswered ring until Nenive grabs the phone and throws it out the car window.

I do nothing except gape at the cabdriver—who either didn't see or is pretending not to have seen.

"Now you can stop freaking out about it," Nenive says. "Don't look at me like I threw your actual mum out the car, for fuck's sake. It's just a shitty phone."

I grip the door handle and worry that I'll allow myself to jump from the moving vehicle. I get this mad idea that I can still go back and get my phone. When the cab stops at a red light, my grip tightens on the door handle and my heart races, but I don't move. I can't get the image of Mom, calling and calling, out of my head.

Nenive dances barefoot on the curb while I pay the fare yet again. She never offers to pay. Her heels clack in the hand raised high above her head as she jigs like a broken puppet.

Clarke Quay is as loud and colorful as Mardi Gras. The bright purple, yellow, and green lights judder across my vision as I'm pulled along, running behind Nenive, wild and desperate. She finds the one dark corner along the quay and fishes more mini bottles of vodka from her souvenir purse. It seems unlikely that so many can fit in there, but who cares? We down them one after another; this time I don't hesitate. I need to wash the ringing out of my ears. It's strengthened into the alarm of a looping ringtone, shrill and deafening.

We're dancing outside a big, touristy club. Nenive tries to get us in, and next thing I know we're in a hot, close space, surrounded by fellow night owls drinking and dancing away the early-morning hours. Time skips over moments until I blink and dawn appears on the horizon. The sides of my toes sport tender blisters where they've rubbed against my sandals;

the scrape on my big toe is grimy and mottled with dried blood. I'm sticky with old sweat and my mouth tastes awful.

The quay is quiet. Only the murmur of Singapore River lapping against the bumboats disturbs the peace. Dread rises with the sun.

"I've gotta go home," I say. I sound terrible, raspy.

Nenive screws up her face. The way her skin sits on the flesh and bone is off somehow. "Home?"

"Yes, Nenive. Home."

"You have no home here." She says it so matter-of-factly I almost think I'm the one who's confused. I'm five-cups-of-coffee jittery, and the pendant is so hot I imagine it burning a brand into my skin.

"My mom is waiting," I say. "I'm meeting her for breakfast."

"No, you're not." Nenive shifts her mouth into what I think is supposed to be a smile. "You're coming with me."

I glare at her. "I don't even know where you live, so."

Nenive laughs at me and pulls my arm hard. "Come on."

"Hey," I shout, reeling out of her grip. "You almost made me fall off the ledge." What the fuck. "Are you still drunk?"

She ignores my question and reaches for me again. I scramble to my feet, startled awake by a cold slap of fear.

This is what you want. I shake my head at Nenive.

She looks at me over her shoulder but doesn't move to come after me. She says, "Don't you want to see your father?"

"What?" I breathe and search my memories. I hadn't told her about him. I'd never tell her about him. I see a ship sailing into the fog, but I banish the image when I remember Nenive's eyes on me.

"You don't know where he is," I say. Nobody does. I focus on inhaling and exhaling. I'm afraid of what she'll do if I pass out.

"If you don't want to see him, fine," says Nenive. Her lower lip falls away, a piece of flesh making like a pout, as she adds, "It's for the best anyway, since he's dead."

My knees buckle, but I stop myself short of falling.

"Don't say that. Don't say that about him." I struggle for air.

Nenive's face twitches, searching for the right gesture. Her eyebrows crawl together. "I'm only joking, silly girl. You take everything so seriously. Come here."

Her arms hinge open like a trap. I back away, watching her concern stagnate.

"Suit yourself," she says, dropping them back to her sides. "All I ask is that you look at yourself. Come look into the water. You can stand all the way over there if you want."

What I want is to go away. But kindness has crept back into her features. She nods, and it's a plea I can't reject. She was my only friend. I'll give her this one last thing.

I make my way to the edge of the walk and look to my right to confirm she hasn't budged. My plan is to take a quick peek, to say I did, but my gaze lingers on the water. Colorful lights play across its rippling surface. I don't see myself staring up from the glassy liquid until another light twinkles.

I try to identify its source, but there's no explanation for it except that it's coming from below. And there I am, clear as if I'm looking into a mirror. No, not a mirror.

"That's not—"

"It is," Nenive interrupts me. "Not who you are now, but who you could be."

And what I could be is someone who isn't turned away from doors. Someone at the center of every circle. Someone who has things handed to her, who feels no sense of obligation, who is loved and desired even when she gives nothing back in return. The sword burns bright against this woman's neck. My neck.

I put my hand around it to lift it off my skin and back away from the vision, shaking my head, unable to stop.

"Don't you see what I'm offering? You know what I can make of you. You've seen it in action." Nenive hugs herself like a lover. "That was just a taste of what I can do and what people are willing to do for me."

I blink, and Nenive is in front of me. She reaches out and grasps the pendant where it hangs above my chest.

"Take the sword," she says.

Mute and filled with foreign certainty, I grasp the sword between my thumb and index finger and easily slide it off the bed of stones. Nenive holds out her hand, and I know what to do. I drag the blade across the lines of her palm, and when she cups it, we watch the dark blood pool.

"Now you," she says.

I bring up my hand and stare at the pink skin. The brown lines. I think of Mom, saying out of the blue a few years ago that she was sad I didn't reach for her hand anymore. I was surprised because I couldn't remember when I'd stopped. It had just sort of happened.

I hesitate, lowering my hand to look up at Nenive. "Let me show you the person you can be," she whispers.

She's so beautiful in the predawn light. Her beauty starves me. What must that power taste like? I could know in an instant. I press the blade to my skin. Nenive and the stones shine like stars.

But I find myself looking away, pulled from some deep, dark place by anger.

"How can you?" I say.

Nenive wrinkles her nose like a dog sniffing out trouble. "How can I what?"

"How can you show me who I can be? How can you, when you don't even know me?"

I open my hand and let the sword clatter to the ground, and then I feel a hard tug and a burning sensation across the back of my neck. The pendant is back in Nenive's hand. The delicate gold chain my mother gave me for my tenth birthday falls through her fingers, the clasp broken. The chain that once held a heart-shaped charm with the first letter of my name in relief.

"If you want it back, you'll have to come and get it." Nenive tries to smile again, but her facade is disintegrating, her skin sagging. She closes her fist around the little sword, bends her knobby white legs, and springs from the ledge. I don't hear anything. The water accepts her without complaint.

I look around, but the walk has cleared out. Nobody else witnessed the plunge.

When I peer over the ledge, the water is smooth and still, and I'm beginning to think she tricked me and that her hand is going to rear up from some hidden place and wrap around my ankle.

There.

A flash of green light. This time I can't stop myself from falling to my knees as, in the path of that light, bodies appear, all of them washed pale, arms and long verdigris hair stretching up to receive me.

Come.

I don't search the faces for Nenive. I snatch my gold chain from the ground and let my racing heart chase me from the quay.

I run a long way, feeling strangers' eyes on me, but I don't care. I let my legs guide me, and they keep moving even though they ache. When I recognize the perfume of Hainanese chicken rice, satay, soto ayam puffing from the hawker stalls, the chatter of words I'm beginning to pick up here and there, I forget the pain and run faster toward a sign that reads LAU PA SAT. These things take me back to my family, to Mom, to an untouched plate of rendang. I can see it now, waiting on the table above the empty seat by her side, as if I'm there. As if I've always been.

Black Diamond

Alex Segura

It was all a dream. That's all it would ever be. But every few nights the dream came anyway.

Arturo Reyes could taste the stale, cheese-loaded nachos. Could smell the cheap beer and oversteamed hot dogs. Could hear the pulsing roar of the crowd. The crisp New York cold slapping against his North Face coat. In the dream, his seat would change—from the nosebleed seats to right behind first base. Sometimes, where he was would even change mid-dream. One moment, it was like he was perched on his father Umberto's shoulder as he sauntered toward the plate, another as if he were resting between the pinstripes of his papi's uniform. In those seconds, Arturo could see the sheen of sweat on his face. The look of determination as his papi got into position, his bat slung over his right shoulder. His eyes on the pitcher.

In the dream, Arturo knows the details. They're second nature. Accepted and understood, even if the pitcher's team changes—sometimes it's the Braves. Another time, the Marlins. Usually it's the Phillies. Every time it's game seven. Bottom of the ninth inning. Bases loaded. Tied game: 3–3. The raucous hometown Bronx crowd hushed to a deathly silence as Umberto Reyes prepares for the at-bat of his life.

Then the dream dissipates. Fading into blackness and shunting Arturo into a deadlier darkness. His waking life.

Like many dreams, Arturo's recurring moment with his father never happened. Unlike most dreams, though, it could have. The dream feels so real—the sounds, taste, and smells— because in many ways, Umberto Reyes had been just a few hours from experiencing it. The scrappy rising-star Yankees' shortstop had just left his family—his wife, Inez; his two sons, Rodrigo and Arturo—in their cramped two-bedroom apartment in the Forest Hills section of Queens. He was heading to the airport to board the team's flight to Atlanta to close out the World Series. It was a big moment. Papi had just finished his best season, stepping into the starting slot after the All-Star Game in place of the injured Jimmy Merlin and not missing a beat. He was a hero—not just to Arturo and Rodrigo but to their friends and to any Latin kid who dreamed of playing for the Bronx Bombers. He was already a legend, Arturo believed. But that was a long time ago. Memories sometimes fizzle into something else—smoky, hard to pin down. Like dreams, in a way. You hold on to what you want to keep, and you let the other stuff slip through your fingers.

Arturo remembered the call, though. In sharp, vivid detail. Remembered the look on his mami's face—how it went from "Ay, who is calling now?" to "No . . . no . . . no . . ." How even ese cabrón perrito Pepe stopped barking for a minute. How his brother's backpack hit the wood floor with a *thwap* as he walked in and noticed his mother's stricken expression. They didn't know what it was yet, but whatever had made their mami that upset, that fast, could not be good.

And it was definitely not good. It was worse than that. It was una pesadilla that you couldn't awaken from. Bad dreams lingered for a long time, Arturo had learned, and they couldn't be willed away.

According to the police report, the driver of the car that was supposed to get Umberto Reyes to JFK International Airport pulled over his cab on the Van Wyck Expressway, long before his destination. At some point, Reyes exited the car and was shot six times—twice in the head and four times in the chest. Help was summoned shortly thereafter by a fellow motorist who flagged down a police cruiser. But by then it was too late. Umberto was DOA long before his stretcher wheeled into Jamaica Hospital.

The motorist could describe only one of the men who murdered Umberto—the gunman. A tall, pale figure with dark hair and stark, almost feline features. But as quickly as the man saw the killer and his men, they were gone.

The crime was never solved. The police could not pinpoint a single suspect. Details were scant, if there at all.

All that remained from the scene—the only scrap of evidence—was a police sketch, hastily created on the night of the murder, the sole witness straining to describe the haunting expression on the killer's face.

Every night for as long as Arturo could remember, he'd sit in bed and stare at a copy of the sketch—trying to imprint the image onto his memory, on the off chance that one day, he'd come face-to-face with the man who'd murdered his father.

"You coming, Artie? Ollie wants to see you."

Arturo turned toward the voice—it was Charlie, one of the team's trainers, motioning for him to step out of the empty dugout and into the locker room. Arturo Reyes was—if you were being generous—a middling, aging minor-league first baseman. In a pinch, he could take a slot in the outfield, too. But that versatility didn't help him much.

He was twenty-eight and hadn't been close to a major league call-up in years. The nearest thing was a brief stint with the Yankees' Triple-A affiliate three years prior. It'd actually been a clerical error, but Arturo tried to count it. He'd made the flight only to get turned around and sent back down. Arturo's current stop was with the Double-A Hollow Falls Hawks in Virginia—part of the Colorado Rockies farm system. He couldn't even sense the Majors from here.

Arturo felt like he'd done well enough to merit another look, but the stats didn't lie. He was batting slightly over .250, and his on-base percentage was laughable. Yet it wasn't really about the numbers. If he was being honest with himself, his heart just wasn't in it. His name—his legacy—raised eyebrows in baseball. After his father's murder, Umberto Reyes's reputation went from rising star to urban legend—a sad story of what could have been. Many hard-core Yankees fans would ponder and speculate about the arc of Reyes's career—where he could have gone, what he could have done. In death, Umberto Reyes had become akin to a Hall of Famer to some in-the-trenches Yankees fans. So when people saw Arturo—they saw a flicker of hope. A chance to capture a slice of that Umberto Reyes magic. The speed. The leadership. The bat. The charisma. Like Roberto Clemente in overdrive, Arturo had thought.

But what they got when they signed Arturo was a pale imitation. Mediocre baseball brain. Sluggish performance. Passive attitude. One major-league general manager, in a memo to his Double-A skipper, described Arturo as "a kid who looks like he's lost before the game's even started."

Even worse? They were right. Arturo knew it.

And yet he couldn't let the game go. It was in his DNA. The years of playing catch with his father, of Little League, high school ball, it all *had* to translate into something. A career. Arturo had no idea how to do anything else. Even after his father was murdered, he had no inkling he *could* do something else.

The tap on the shoulder shook Arturo from his reverie.

Charlie again.

"Artie, c'mon, man." There was a hint of exasperation in his voice. "Skip wants to see you. Now."

It'd played out as he'd expected. As he'd experienced a half dozen times before.

The realization didn't make Arturo feel any better as he took another swig of lukewarm coffee. He was at a grimy, fading diner called the Round Table a few miles from the stadium. He figured he deserved a last meal before he hopped into his beat-up Toyota Celica and started the trek back to Queens. A decent burger couldn't cure all his ills, but it'd help. For now, at least.

And he'd get to see Gwen again, too. Say goodbye.

"I'm sorry, Art, you know I am," the manager, a burly, nononsense man named Ollie Barton had said, a somber look on his face. The skipper, like Arturo, had been raised in the game—had even made it up to the majors for a few seasons. He knew the struggle. The highs and lows. But he also had a team to run. And if Arturo wasn't moving up, he was holding down the team—and that would be tolerated for only so long. "But I got the word and this time, well, they wouldn't listen, okay? They want your spot for someone who can—how do I put this . . . uh, someone who has more upside."

Arturo understood. He liked Barton. Wanted to make it easy on him. So he'd nodded, thanked him and the team, shook his hand, and left the manager's cramped, mildew-stinking office to go clean out his locker.

Sitting at the Round Table's counter now, Arturo waited for Gwen—the quick-witted, bespectacled waitress he'd come to befriend over his frequent visits to the diner—to bring him his food. It hadn't really hit him until now that this might be the end. His career might be over.

"Maybe it's for the best," Arturo mumbled to himself as he wheeled around and scanned the nearly empty restaurant. What would his father say, he wondered, if he'd seen him play tonight?

Not enough hustle, mijo, his father might note.

He could hear him: *¿Y qué te pasó, Arturo? ¿Estuviste dormido?*

Yes, Papi, he'd been asleep for a long time. Maybe it was past time he woke up—and went home.

"Ketchup packet for your thoughts, Artie?"

Arturo looked up and met Gwen's eyes. They exuded kindness, always, but this time they expressed something more. Concern. Worry. She was smart. She'd seen many ballplayers cycle through. Did Arturo Reyes mean any more to her than the rest of the people who sat at this counter? He hoped so, he realized. The food at the diner was mediocre at best. Why did he keep coming back? Maybe it wasn't what brought him to the diner but *who*.

"Got the call," Arturo said, leaning back into a stretch as if trying to shrug off what, they both knew, could be the end of his professional career. "Looks like I'm heading back home."

Gwen frowned. A genuine pained expression.

"It happens," she said, almost to herself as much as to him. "Food's on the house, okay? You've tipped well enough—"

Arturo shook his head.

"No way, lady," he said. "I got this. Don't worry about me."

"Bet you say that to a lot of people," she said. The words, if read on paper, would seem flippant. But her tone was dead serious. "What happened?"

"They needed the slot," Arturo said. "For someone better, I guess."

"I've seen you play," she said, leaning into him, a tinge of pity in her smile. She placed her hand on his. "You're good, Artie. You're real good when you want to be. Don't let this tear you down, all right? I know you have that in you."

"What's in me?" Arturo asked, feeling defensive. He hadn't come here to swan dive into self-pity. Not yet. That's what the upcoming drive was for. And the encouragement, oddly, felt even sharper coming from Gwen, one of his few friends in this small town. "Just because my dad was good . . . was going to be great . . . that doesn't mean anything. It isn't genetic, you know. It's not like I'm some kind of baseball royalty."

She started to respond, but then her eyes drifted to the diner's front entrance.

"You know that guy?"

Arturo caught Gwen looking past him, a strange expression on her face.

"Because he sure looks like he knows you," she said.

Arturo followed Gwen's gaze and saw a tall, fifty-something man walking toward him, arms outstretched. It took Arturo a minute to recognize him out of his baseball uniform.

"Artie, Artie," the man said as he pulled Arturo into a tight hug. "Man, you bailed so fast—was hoping to catch you."

"Jimmy," Arturo said, pulling back from the man's embrace. Arturo couldn't believe it: it was James Merlin—a lifelong minor-league manager and the leader of tonight's opponent, the Charlotte Knights. But before he was a manager, he was "Uncle Jimmy," an infielder on the Yankees squad with his father and a frequent guest at their apartment in Queens. He'd seen Arturo and Rodrigo grow up. A widower who never remarried, he had no family of his own but was as close to an uncle as Arturo would ever know, a presence in their life before and after Umberto was killed. But they'd fallen out of touch, and Artie hadn't seen Jimmy in a few years, at least.

"You eating alone?" Jimmy asked in a careful tone. Arturo realized that he already knew. He shrugged, then motioned for Jimmy to take a seat to his left. He noticed Gwen hadn't taken away his burger, but he ignored it.

"What're you doing here, Jimmy?" Arturo asked. "Don't you have a bus to catch?"

"Tomorrow morning we head to Pawtucket," Jimmy said with a shrug. "Gonna be brutal. Commercial flight, long bus ride—but hey, that's the minors, huh?"

Arturo nodded. There was a wide canyon between the life of a major leaguer and the life players lived in the minors. Five-star hotels. Private jets. Gourmet meals. You saw none of that in the minors. You were lucky if you didn't have to bunk with a teammate or have microwaved hot dogs for dinner three nights in a row. Arturo had never seen the other side. He hadn't made it to the majors. He never would, he thought.

"So you're done, then?"

Arturo turned to Jimmy and nodded slowly. He was done. He would come to accept it, he decided.

Jimmy shook his head.

"It's your call, son," he said. "I can't make you want to play more. I guess I could guilt you—tell you how badly your dad would've wanted to keep playing himself. But that'd be crass, huh?"

He laughed. Gwen slid a cup of water in front of him. He took a long pull before he continued.

"I'm glad I found you, though," Jimmy said.

"Yeah?" Arturo asked. "Why's that?"

"Got something that belongs to you," Jimmy said, his tone deepening. "Well, to your family." He patted Arturo's shoulder. "Follow me."

The burger would wait. Arturo dropped a ten on the counter and told Gwen he'd be back, then followed the older man outside, toward the far end of the diner's poorly lit parking lot. They stopped behind Jimmy's beat-up Prius hatchback. Jimmy popped the trunk and leaned in, moving boxes and a few mitts and jerseys aside brusquely. Then Arturo saw what Jimmy was reaching for.

At first, it seemed like any other bat Arturo had seen or held over the years. But when he looked more closely, Arturo felt a chill coat his skin. Felt himself being pulled back—to being a kid and watching his dad in the batting cages. Seeing him leave his bat propped up outside his parents' bedroom. His father had loved that bat. Taken it with him wherever he went, like a kid's blanket. The letters etched on the bat seemed to call to him—EXCALIBUR.

How had he not realized the bat was missing? Not asked his
mother where it ended up? Why were these memories flooding
into his mind now?

And why did it seem like the bat was glowing?

"You okay?" Jimmy asked.

"Yeah, yeah," Arturo said, shaking his head slightly, trying
to ignore what he'd just seen and felt. "Just—uh, just seeing
that takes me back, you know?"

Jimmy pointed the bat at Arturo, handle out, a gentle smile
on his face.

"It's yours," Jimmy said. "It belongs with you."

"Why . . . why do you have it, Jimmy?" Arturo asked, trying
to delay the moment he knew would come no matter what.
"Why've you been holding on to this?"

"Your dad asked me to hold on to it," Jimmy said, his face
growing ashen. "Said to take care of it. I dunno, honestly. At
the moment, it just seemed like more silly-speak from him.
He was always easily spooked, superstitious. I didn't take him
seriously. But when he handed it to me, he wasn't joking. It
was a few nights before the end of the series. Before he headed
to the airport . . ."

Jimmy trailed off. Arturo watched the older man look away
and try to compose himself.

"He said, 'Jimmy, keep this, all right? Keep this safe,'" Jimmy
said. "And me, I'm like, 'Sure, sure, Umberto, whatever, let's
go.' But he was not having it. He gripped my shoulders and
said, 'Jimmy, you keep this until you know, for sure, someone
is ready to use it. Give it to my son. Give it to Arturo. But not
as a boy. As a man.' And—look, I know this sounds weird, but
I just shrugged it off. I thought your dad was just on one of
his weird trips, you know? I said 'sure' and took it, and that
was it. Then he was dead and I forgot about the damn bat. It

seemed like it was erased from my mind. But I took it with me, wherever I went, every team, every city. I carried it, but I didn't think about it until now—until I saw your car parked outside. My gut told me you had gotten the call. Then it felt more urgent. Wasn't sure I'd see you again."

Arturo gripped the bat. For some reason he'd expected to feel something—a shock, a charge, anything. Some kind of kinetic connection to this thing that had once been his father's. But he didn't. It felt light. Powerful. But still like any other bat Arturo had held and swung over the past few years. He tried to mask his disappointment, but it must have shown on his face. Jimmy must've seen the wince that flickered across his expression.

"Kid, what'd you expect?" Jimmy said, slapping his hand on Arturo's shoulder. "Magic?"

Arturo twirled the bat in his hand, still trying to capture something, anything.

Then he felt it. His hands tingled—a low hum, a crackling energy shooting through them. At first Arturo thought of dropping the bat, but something kept his palms wrapped around it. He knew, at that moment, he would never let the bat out of his sight.

He felt lighter, too. Felt the aches and pains of years of struggling through long seasons, losses, demotions, dejection— felt it all fade away. He felt younger. Clearer. The thought of swinging that bat—of running the bases, of catching a ball— felt almost new to him. Like he was about to grab his mitt and chase his dad to the park for another round of catch. He could almost hear his dad's voice—rattling off lessons and suggestions as he launched another fly ball for Arturo to try to catch.

Glove up.

Eye on the ball.

Put it where the ball will be, not where it is.

These moments were real—he'd lived them. But they felt suddenly new to Arturo, as if he'd just awoken from a long slumber, having closed his eyes as a twelve-year-old boy who loved baseball, his father, and his life. Everything else— everything in between—felt like a blur now.

"You up for one more trip?" Jimmy asked.

Arturo glanced at his father's old friend. Confused.

"The Knights could use someone like you. Someone with your experience. And leadership," Jimmy said, to Arturo's surprise. But before he could question him, Jimmy was already patting Arturo on the shoulder and continuing. "Tell me, Artie—you ever play third?"

Excerpt from Bleacher Report

For Newly Minted 3B Arturo Reyes, Call-Up a Last Shot at Redemption

Pete Fernandez | Athletics Minor League Reporter
August 4, 2019

Many longtime fans recall the sad tale of Umberto Reyes, the third-year rising-star Yankees' shortstop who was murdered in cold blood on his way to catch a team flight to Atlanta to face off against the Braves in what ended up being a jaw-dropping Yankees loss in game seven of the World Series. The assailants were never found.

But every story has its share of survivors, and

for many years, followers of the game have watched and cheered for Reyes's son, Arturo, who cobbled together a solid if unspectacular career in the minor leagues across various organizations. Many assumed that his baseball life—Reyes is 28—had peaked, and that the son of the SS with remarkable speed and wit and a bat that crackled like Clemente would go down as a footnote, mentioned only in relation to his father.

"The raw skills were there, for sure, all the GMs and coaches saw it," said Jimmy Merlin, a long-time minor-league manager—his last stint with the Double-A Charlotte Knights—and former teammate to the elder Reyes, who is now serving as a freelance adviser of sorts to the younger. "But when he got on the field, it just didn't click. At his best, he was all right—did the basics. But it never elevated beyond mediocre or acceptable. Honestly, it was sad to see. We all figured his career was over before it started."

But all that seems to have changed over the past six months.

Propelled by a .341 average in Double- and Triple-A appearances and a sure-handed defensive glove that seems at odds with previous performances, Reyes has positioned himself as not only an on-the-rise minor-league star but one on the very brink of the Major Leagues. In addition to his on-field rebirth, Reyes is a newlywed. He and his wife, Gwendolyn, are expecting their first child in October.

"I just hope the big team is looking at what I'm doing," Reyes said earlier this week after another stupendous performance for the Triple-A Kansas

Mud Dogs, his most recent home after a run of success with the Double-A Knights. "I just put my head down, do the work and pray to God that I get that chance."

That chance may be coming before the end of the regular season, as the Oakland Athletics look to fill some slots in an infield decimated by injuries.

The flight was delayed by three hours. But nothing was going to sour this moment for Arturo. Nothing.

Even with all the advance buzz and rumors, when Jimmy had called him, Arturo thought he was kidding. Thought it was just an ill-timed joke his dad's old friend was playing on him. It couldn't be true. But it was, wasn't it?

"No joke, kid, they want you," Jimmy Merlin had said. Arturo felt like he could see the twinkle in the older man's eye, even through the phone. "You're an Oakland Athletic now."

Usually, when you got the call from the major league club, your minor-league manager took you aside and gave you the speech. It was, for many minor-league skippers, all the joy they got from a job that required them to keep prospects warm and fading veterans cold. Somehow, Jimmy Merlin, who'd given up his own managing job to oversee Arturo's career for little money and even less autonomy, had gotten the chance to relay the message. It seemed to Arturo that Jimmy was happy to just be around. To pass along bits of advice when needed.

"I'm just here to make sure things go the way they should," he told Arturo more times than he could remember.

That was the thing, Arturo thought—things *did* seem to be going okay. Better than okay. He tried not to think about it too much, though. To compare his baseball life before he gripped his dad's old bat with the new world he was inhabiting now. It made him uneasy. A cold, aching anxiety that permeated every part of him. Like a child heading down a long hallway toward a slightly open door, unsure of what awaited on the other side.

When he did follow the thread of his own mind, when he did think about the days before Excalibur—as he'd come to call the bat made by the small-time manufacturer of the same name—he felt like it was another life altogether, a story he'd been told. But it wasn't. He'd lived it. That had been his life, and it all changed when he ran into an old friend at a fading diner.

He pulled out his cell phone. She picked up on the second ring.

"You okay?" Gwen asked, skipping the usual pleasantries. She knew Arturo wasn't a phone person except when he had to be. If he was calling, something was up. But what was it?

"Yeah, I'm at the airport," Arturo said, his voice trailing off. "Just needed . . . to check in."

"Anchor time, huh?"

He let out a dry laugh. Ever since they first got together—well, first started talking, sharing long, rambling calls from wherever Arturo ended up to Gwen—she'd joked in this way. Said she was Arturo's rock. At first he just took it as flirting, but eventually he found it to be true. He needed her. He relied on Gwen's sharp brain and empathy. He loved her laugh and how she looked at the world. She kept him in place—balanced. She was his anchor.

After a few months of late-night calls and constant texting, Arturo made a decision. He scraped into his savings account and made a trip to see her. They had barely been apart since. Until now.

"Yeah, I'm just thinking about everything," Arturo said. "Everything that's happened."

"Don't think about it too much," she said, her voice hushed. "You deserve this, okay? Just enjoy it. This is what you've always wanted. Always dreamed about. Don't look over your shoulder too much."

"You're right," he said. She was, he knew that. She was always right. So why was he obsessing over this—even after hanging up with Gwen, throughout the long process of boarding, takeoff, and flight? Thinking about that moment in the diner with a man he considered an old family friend?

An old friend who just happened to have his father's bat in his trunk.

An old friend who had since refused to leave his side.

Arturo shook the thought from his mind as he sped down the long hallway underneath Oakland-Alameda County Coliseum, the aging stadium the Oakland Athletics called home. He was late. The game was about to start and he needed to change, meet his new team, and—if he was being honest with himself—prepare to sit in the dugout for nine innings and watch the starters close out a three-game series against the Astros.

But he'd made it. Not just here, now, but to the majors. He wasn't just the kid who never lived up to his papi's legend. He was the man who'd made it to the majors, too. If he did well enough, he allowed himself to think, he might even carve out a legend of his own.

"Hey, you Reyes?" Arturo didn't recognize the face poking out of the locker-room door, but he was wearing an Athletics uniform. One of the coaches, for sure.

Arturo nodded and stopped at the door as he tried to catch his breath, his equipment bag hanging over his shoulder.

He didn't get the chance. The coach dragged him in, shaking his head vigorously.

"Tony in Travel told me your flight was fucked," the coach said. "But that's your problem. Your locker's over there—get suited up and ready in five. We need to be outside in ten."

Arturo nodded and fought off the urge to introduce himself to the other players. This wasn't the minors anymore. He had a job to do. But he didn't fight back the smile that spread across his face as he reached his locker—his locker!— and pulled Excalibur out of his bag. He felt a familiar charge and allowed himself a second to let it course through him. Even if he didn't take the field tonight, he would soon. Soon he'd show his teammates who he was. Not just "Oh, Umberto Reyes's kid, right?" No. A man unto himself.

"Nice bat."

The voice startled Arturo. He turned around. What he saw almost sent his knees buckling. He heard Excalibur drop to the ground with a *thunk*. He could hear rustling as the other players turned toward the noise. But that was all background to him now. Secondary to the face that stood before him.

The face he'd memorized. The dark, thin eyebrows. The feline eyes. The thin, lipless smile. The dark hair that seemed otherworldly and menacing.

But . . . how?

"Hey, you okay?" the man said, crouching down to pick up Excalibur. He handed the bat to Arturo, who tried not to snatch it back. "You're new, right? Reyes?"

Arturo nodded, his eyes wide, unblinking. He saw the man extend his hand.

"Cool, man, cool—welcome to the A's," he said, clearly befuddled by Arturo's reaction but trying his best to be welcoming and friendly. But that face—a living, breathing version of the crumpled piece of paper Arturo still had. Of a man that existed only in his nightmares, now come alive.

He spoke again. The words that escaped his mouth would haunt Arturo for the rest of his life.

"Tino Mordred, man, good to meet you. I think our dads played together on the Yankees. Did he ever mention my dad?"

Before Arturo could respond, his mouth agape, a distant voice called. The game was starting.

It was happening. The moment Arturo had always dreamed of was seconds away. But his eyes were locked on this man, a few years younger than him, who wore the face of a murderer and the smile of an innocent.

He fought back a scream as the sellout crowd signaled the beginning of the game.

The hotel room TV flickered, the only light in the space. Arturo sat up in bed. He glanced around the room, absorbing where he was. Kansas City. In another swanky room in a series of swanky rooms on his way to becoming everything he'd dreamed of. Everything his father had dreamed of.

A long shape seemed to lurch up from the darkness as the television light captured it. Arturo knew what it was. Knew what was there. Always had to know.

The bat.

Excalibur.

He'd been with the Athletics for more than a month. Had managed to parlay a few weeks of solid reserve play into, as of tomorrow's game, a starting third base job. The press loved him. His teammates loved him. His glove was sticky and his bat was hot. People were starting to whisper about Arturo Reyes. And not just Arturo Reyes, son of Umberto. Jimmy had said it would only be a matter of time.

But the bat.

It'd all changed for him that night outside of the diner. He couldn't deny it. He'd gone from sleepwalking through the tail end of a forgettable career to finally finding himself able to do the things he only dreamed of. But how? Why? It couldn't be the bat. It was impossible, Arturo knew. But he couldn't deny the feeling he got when his hands gripped it. He couldn't deny how his vision, his own baseball instincts, seemed to sharpen and clarify when he was using it. So much so, he thought, that even when he was on the field—playing defense—he still felt empowered and alive.

No way, he thought.

He'd tried to bring it up to Jimmy a few times, but his old friend—his father's old friend—shrugged it off.

"It's not the bat, kid, it's you," Jimmy Merlin said over and over. "The second you see that, then we'll really be cooking."

Arturo stood up. He couldn't sleep. But it wasn't because of the bat. If it had somehow imbued him with the abilities his father had left behind for him, he could deal with that. He'd welcome it, after years of trying and failing, to the point of becoming a husk of the man he knew he was. The man that only Gwen had seemed to recognize at the end there, sitting at the diner, defeated. But there was something else. Something darker and nebulous that seemed to float above every hit, every win, every smile.

His teammate, Tino Morded, seemed kind. He was helpful. He'd even taken time out of his own routine to introduce Arturo to his teammates and show him around the A's facili-

ties. But that face. It haunted Arturo. It resembled the character sketch so closely it sent a cold chill through his entire body.

Tino was an average player. Some would call him "good for
the locker room"—a cheerleader who was always quick with
a pat on the shoulder and a high five. But he lacked fire. He
could hit a bit, was decent on defense—you name it. He combined just enough of everything to merit a spot on a major
league roster. In many ways, he reminded Arturo of himself,
before the big decline. Before he'd basically given up. So why
did Tino haunt Arturo so? Could it be a coincidence? Just his
mind playing tricks on him? He had to know. And now was
as good a time as any.

He pulled on some pants and grabbed the bat, a crackle
of energy shivering up his arm as he walked out of the hotel
room, Excalibur dangling at his side. What was he doing? He
knew and he didn't know. He wanted to and didn't want to at
the same time.

Marcos Mordred had played with Umberto Reyes. They'd
competed for the same spot, the same position. When Arturo's father died, Marcos was slotted into the starting position.
Marcos had struck out at the plate during that final World
Series game. He'd lost the team's last chance to hold on. To
win the championship. It'd have been a swing Arturo knew
his father never would've missed.

He felt his phone vibrate in his pocket as he approached the
elevator bank. He picked it up. Gwen.

"Hey, sweetie," she said, her voice husky and low from lack
of sleep. "Did I wake you? You feeling okay before your first
big start?"

"No, baby, no, having trouble getting to bed," Arturo said,
his finger hovering over the elevator's DOWN button. "How're
you? Everything okay?"

"I—I think so, I guess," she said. "Baby's kicking a lot. I just woke up with this strange feeling . . . this—I dunno, you probably think I'm crazy—this anxiety. I just wanted to check in and make sure you're okay."

Arturo swallowed hard.

"I'm fine, Gwen," he said, nodding, as if to assure himself, too. "Just taking a little walk to get my body tired so I can sleep. Be ready for the game tomorrow."

"The playoffs," Gwen said, followed by a soft whistle. "Who would've thought it, huh? Arturo Reyes, starting third baseman for the A's with a shot at the series. You did it, honey."

"Been a long road," Arturo said, watching as his finger pushed the button, the gray circle illuminating. "Glad I have you by my side."

"Always," she said, sounding more relaxed. "Don't stay up too late, okay?"

Arturo promised her he wouldn't, told her he loved her, and hung up. He stepped into the empty elevator and pushed the button for the third floor.

Arturo rapped his knuckles on the door. Tino Mordred, bleary-eyed and rumpled, answered. Arturo could tell Tino was confused. It seemed to take him a moment to get his eyes to adjust to the light—and to realize what he was seeing. Arturo Reyes standing in the hallway. With a bat.

"Artie?" Tino said, his brows furrowing slightly. "You okay, man? It's late, yo."

"I need to talk to you, Tino." Arturo pushed past him and into the room.

"Can't it wait?" Tino said, closing the door and turning around to face Arturo. "It's three in the damn morning."

Tino's usual rah-rah cheer was gone. He was worried, Arturo could see. Afraid, even?

"Your dad . . ." Arturo started. "Was he ever a suspect in my dad's death?"

"What?" Tino's confusion seemed genuine, the word escaping his mouth like a car horn. "What are you talking about, bro?"

Arturo pulled out the crumpled paper from his pocket and turned it toward Tino. He knew it looked like the younger man was looking at his own, wrinkled, and battered reflection.

"This is what I'm talking about," Arturo said, his voice cold. He felt his arm—the one holding the bat—pulsing, felt the familiar power seeping through him. But to what end? "This face look familiar to you?"

Tino squinted slightly at the paper, then looked at Arturo.

"Say what you gotta say, man," Tino said. "My dad is not a killer."

"There's nothing else to say," Arturo said. "Your dad benefited the most from my father's death. Your dad matches this sketch. You tell me the rest."

Tino shrugged, stepping back and letting a dry laugh escape his mouth.

"Benefited? You don't know shit, son," Tino said. "Benefited? My dad struck out that night and he might as well have died, too. Your dad became a legend—the 'what if' of the whole year, the whole series. My dad was the goat. The problem. 'If only we'd had Umberto at bat.' You know how often my father heard that? He took it to his grave. Might as well be on his gravestone—'If only Umberto Reyes were buried here.'"

Arturo stepped forward. He could feel his grip tighten around the bat. Sweat coating his palm. He felt jittery—not just anxious, but wired, like some kind of dark energy was pulsing through him. He felt himself being pulled away—his actions and his own mind detaching from each other. And he was afraid.

"What is this, man?" Tino spat, motioning toward Arturo's bat. "You coming in here armed and shit? Like you're gonna take me out?"

Arturo didn't respond. He took another step toward Tino.

"Unbelievable," Tino said, shaking his head to himself. "You're part of the cult, too. The cult of Umberto. The what-if squad, huh? Well, here's the truth, buddy, the reality that comes from playing baseball in and out for years: Your dad? He would've struck out, too. He would've been a footnote instead of a legend. Getting murdered was the best thing that ever hap—"

Arturo swung hard, harder than he ever swung before—at a ball, at anything. The wooden bat connected with Tino's shoulder, sending the other player spinning back, his body falling to the ground. He scrambled to his feet—crouched, defensive—a hand on his shoulder, protecting himself. His eyes wide and angry with surprise.

"Are you fucking nuts, bro?" Tino screamed. "What the hell is wrong with you? Coming in here . . . attacking me? Spewing nonsense?"

Arturo stepped forward, raising the bat to swing again, but Tino was too fast—he grabbed Arturo's arm and pushed back, then yanked the bat out of his hands. In one swift motion, he took Excalibur and broke the bat over his knee—the adrenaline and rage pulsing through Tino Mordred snapped the wooden bat into three jagged pieces.

Arturo watched as the chunks of wood fell to the ground, seemingly lifeless—whatever energy or power he'd felt upon touching them, felt linger within him after . . . gone. Like a cloud of smoke dispersing with a gust of wind. Arturo's entire body sagged. Tino, on the other hand, was shaking with rage.

"You stupid motherfucker, you messed up my shoulder," Tino said, still yelling. "If I'm hurt, I can't play—if I can't play, I'm no use to this team. You just barge into people's rooms to ruin their lives, man? What in the fuck is wrong with you?"

Arturo shook his head, as if trying to dislodge and wipe away cobwebs. Dust and clutter and shadows all scurried out of his mind's eye. What was happening? He stumbled back.

"I'm . . . I'm sorry," he said, one hand clutching his head, which was pounding now—the dry, cracked feeling you get after sleeping for far too long. His mouth felt ragged and bloodied, but he knew Tino hadn't landed a punch. What was happening?

"Get the fuck out of here," Tino said, still clutching his hurt shoulder. He leaned down and grabbed the crumpled paper: the image Arturo had clutched for decades, hoping to one day fit the missing piece into a bigger, much more dangerous puzzle.

But the image was gone. The familiar eyes and face and hair replaced by something else—something more generic and impossible to comprehend. The sketch looked like every other police sketch Arturo had ever seen, on TV or in real life. Like a blank, nebulous person.

He yanked the paper back from Tino.

"What? How is this possible?" Arturo said, his voice a husky whisper. "No . . . no. . . ."

"That doesn't even look like my dad, you fucking maniac," Tino said, backing up. "Get out of here."

So Arturo did, the paper stuck to his sweat-soaked hand as he ran to his room.

He dialed Jimmy as he stepped into his room, crumpling against the door as he closed it.

"Pick up, Jimmy, pick up," he whispered. But there was no answer. Jimmy's familiar jocular voice mail was gone—replaced by a default robo-voice: "*The number you have dialed is not in service.*"

He tried a few more times but got the same confusing result. So he tried Gwen, ignoring the pang of guilt he should feel for waking her up this late.

She was immediately worried, the catch in his voice alerting her that something was very, very wrong.

"Have you heard from Jimmy?" Arturo asked. "I need to talk to him. Now."

"Jimmy?"

"Yeah, yes, I can't reach him, I can't get—"

"Artie, what? Who's Jimmy?"

Arturo dropped the phone, hearing it clatter on the hotel's carpet. He could hear Gwen still.

"Artie? Arturo?" she asked, her voice muffled by distance and the iPhone's tinny speaker.

He took a breath, crouched down, and picked up the phone. He spoke, though he knew what her answer would be.

"Jimmy Merlin, baby. You know him. My agent. My friend. Come on," Arturo said. "The guy who saved my career."

"Artie," Gwen said, "I don't know who the hell you're talking about."

Arturo felt the breath go out of his lungs.

"*Jimmy,*" he gasped. "You remember. He came into the diner that night—my last night in Hollow Falls. Friend of my dad's? Please, baby, please—please tell me you remember."

"Artie." Gwen's voice was careful, deliberate, as if dealing with someone on the verge of a terrifying breakdown. "Artie, take a deep breath, okay? I don't know any Jimmy, Jimmy Merlin. . . . There was no man that night, baby. The only person who came into the diner that night—"

"It was Jimmy," Arturo said, his voice reaching a higher timbre—desperate, pleading. "Jimmy Merlin."

"No, sweetie, I'm sorry, but I remember it like it was yesterday. It was a woman. She said she was a friend of your father's and that she had his bat. . . . Her name . . ."

"A woman?"

"Yes, she was older but refined, classy-looking." Gwen sounded like she was straining to remember the details. "One of those ladies who never seem to age. . . . She could pass for thirty, forty, or fifty. . . . Her name . . ."

Arturo felt his chest clench as the words, at once unknown but also disturbingly familiar, left his wife's lips.

". . . was Morgan le Fay."

Excerpt from Bleacher Report

Precipitous Decline Continues for A's Reyes

Team Ponders Platoon at Corner to Preserve Season's Momentum

Megan L. Pochoda | Athletics Beat Reporter
September 30, 2019

After a back half of the season that seemed almost storybook in its narrative, A's 3B Arturo Reyes seems to have fallen down to Earth of late, kicking off the postseason with a series of lackluster performances that have put the once white-hot Athletics on a collision course with elimination against the overrated and injury-prone Boston Red Sox.

After years spent bouncing around various farm systems, Reyes's rise to the Majors became the feel-good story of the season, especially in light of the 28-year-old's baseball pedigree, as the son of slain Yankees' infielder Umberto Reyes. But baseball is a marathon, and even the hottest of streaks often fizzle to an end at the most inopportune times.

"Sometimes bats are hot and sometimes they're not," said A's manager Davey Falco. "We gotta work with what we have and take this game if we want to stay in the hunt. It's not about one player—this is a team sport. We hope Artie heats up, and when he does, we have to be ready to support him."

Baseball platitudes aside, Falco's correct—if the A's falter tonight against the Red Sox, they won't have time to recalibrate: their season will be over. The decisive game five, tonight in Boston, will determine whether the A's continue their Cinderella season and if the Arturo Reyes story becomes the stuff of legend—or a footnote.

The skipper's office felt cold to Arturo. Like they were perched on a glacier instead of in a small enclosed space in an opposing team's stadium. Falco's expression was grim; his usually jovial features seemed etched in stone.

"Gimme a reason not to, Artie," he said, a flicker of hope

flashing through his eyes. "Otherwise, Mordred is in, and we hope he can connect a few times to save our asses."

Arturo felt his shoulders sag, but he stopped them. For so long, he'd been pushed and pulled by what was around him. His father's death. Other managers' decisions. His own unwillingness to face up to the challenges in front of him. The bat. That damn bat.

But ever since his confrontation with Tino earlier that month, ever since Excalibur shattered over his knee, Arturo felt different. Awake. Not happy, no. How could anyone be happy with his batting average and with the entire team leering at him? But his eyes were open. And for once in his life, he felt like he was in control.

Gwen had been right, of course. There was no Jimmy Merlin. Arturo tried not to think about the implications of what it meant for him—for his mind—that he'd basically imagined him. He had no idea who this Morgan le Fay was or what she'd wanted. But he knew enough. He was smart enough to see that he'd been set up for a fall. But Reyes boys don't fall so quickly, Arturo thought.

"I'm gonna play like hell, Skip," Arturo said, meeting the manager's dull gaze. "You have my word. I'm ready to win this for us."

Falco nodded. That was all Arturo needed.

It'd been the worst game of Arturo's life, and it wasn't over yet.

He'd tried. He stuck to his words—to the promise he'd made to his manager. He did play like hell. But even with every effort, it still felt a few centimeters out of reach. A half second too slow on the swing. A half step behind the ball with his glove. And now, as they entered the ninth inning, the A's were down two runs, five to three, with the weakest part of their batting order up to plate. Mordred, subbing in for their injured starting first baseman; Downer, their young and inexperienced center fielder; and Arturo.

Falco had motioned to him in the dugout. Arturo followed him into the tunnel that led to the locker room. The space was dark, long, empty. A void. Their whispered words echoed through the tunnel. Arturo knew what was coming. He wasn't going to take the plate tonight. Not again. Not after going zero-for-three and making an unforced error. He shouldn't have even had those three plate appearances, he thought. Had Tino Mordred decided to press charges, Arturo might not even be on the team right now. But getting another chance? Now? He didn't deserve it.

He braced himself for the worst.

"You got one more chance, Reyes," Falco said, not meeting his eyes, looking down the long path toward the field instead. "I shouldn't let you have it, but I will. You know why? There's something in you, kid. Something you let come out from time to time—not just know-how of the game, but energy. Your bat was popping like crazy when we called you up. But it wasn't just the bat. It was you. You opened up and started to feel comfortable. At ease with this world, with this game—with yourself."

Arturo started to say something, but Falco raised a hand.

"When you go up there, I don't want you to think of anything else—about your batting average, about your dad, about this beef with Mordred . . . none of it," Falco continued, his eyes now zeroed in on Arturo's. "All that matters is that one at-bat. Nothing else will matter if you tank it, and nothing before will matter if you nail it. Think about that. This is a fresh start."

Arturo hadn't noticed the bat in Falco's hand until now. The older man handed it to him.

"I'm not a superstitious guy, but I've been watching you make a mess of yourself since that old bat of yours broke," he said a bit sheepishly as he handed Arturo the wooden bat. "So figured you could use a new one."

Arturo grabbed the bat. It was identical to the one he'd had before, Excalibur emblazoned on the side. But he didn't feel anything when he touched it. No electric charge. No pulse of energy.

Yet somehow, in this moment, he felt comfort. It wasn't about the bat, he thought.

He nodded as he gripped the handle. He could feel his eyes welling up, so he chose not to speak. Falco seemed to understand. He patted Arturo's shoulder and started to make his way back to the dugout.

"This is your story, Arturo Reyes," Falco said as he walked off. "Not your bat's. Not your father's. Yours alone. Finish it on your terms. The crown is waiting for us."

Arturo blinked a few times as he watched Falco's figure grow smaller in the tunnel. Watched as the letters on the back of his dark green jersey morphed slowly to form another, more familiar word. FALCO was gone, replaced by MERLIN instead. Before Arturo could say anything, the mirage had faded—things were as they'd been before. But Arturo had learned enough over the past few months to not question his senses. Not anymore.

Arturo started after Falco. Then he heard the voice. A woman's, darkly melodic and taunting.

"It won't make a difference, you know," she said. "The old man's trickery can only delay the inevitable."

Arturo spun around, his eyes and senses trying to pinpoint the sound, but the only thing he saw was a cluster of shadows at the other side of the tunnel, leading to the locker room. He knew there was someone there, could make out a shape—but the dark tunnel prevented him from seeing her face.

"Who are you?" Arturo asked, trying to keep his voice calm. To hide the jolt of fear that possessed him.

"I'm the one dancing on the edges, dear Arthur," she said, using the English approximation of his name for some reason. "The darkness you can't seem to avoid—the misses, the mistakes, the stumbles and failures. I'm the watcher—the one that keeps you as you should be—as a failure, as a joke. It's the least I could do, for Umberto's son, after what happened. How he failed me."

Arturo felt his hand grip the bat. He raised it up. But not as a bat, this time—like a weapon, swordlike, the wooden length of the bat almost shining in the dark tunnel as Arturo walked toward the shadowy woman. She seemed to take a cautious step backward—deeper into the darkness of the tunnel, away from Arturo and his bat.

"Morgan le Fay," Arturo said, stepping closer. She seemed to pull back as he swung the sword in her direction, almost as if she were frightened of the bat—of the low hum of light that Arturo could see emanating from it now. Was he imagining this, he wondered. The power, the energy he'd felt in his old bat wasn't there. Or was it just not coming from the bat now? Was it in him? "I'm not afraid of you, woman. I don't even know you."

"It was foolish of Merlin to give that to you now. I thought him neutralized, but it's of no consequence. It's too late. The bat is useless, as is the one who wields it. Your father made a bad choice, Arthur—he took the high road when I offered him wealth beyond his wildest dreams. And now, look at you, playing with the same kind of toy he had." She laughed, but he thought he sensed a tinge of panic in her voice, like a politician caught off guard by a sharp query.

Then a flicker of memory appeared in Arturo's mind, a snippet of conversation overheard from the living room. His parents arguing in the kitchen. His father stern and clear. His mother open and curious. An offer had come in. Someone who was vying to buy another team—had it been the Tigers? It was lost to Arturo now, but he remembered the rest so vividly. She'd offered his father a deal, had broken league rules before she'd even bought the team. She wanted Umberto Reyes with her. She was offering more money than he'd ever imagined. Umberto was going to decline—no, had already declined. Arturo's mother was livid. They hadn't even discussed it. They never would, Arturo realized. His father would be dead in a few hours.

The memory dissipated like a cloud of steam rising from a sewer grate. All Arturo could see now was the shadowy woman, this Morgan le Fay.

"I've shaken you to your core, child," she said, another low laugh following her words. "Even now you don't believe you can do it. That you can do anything."

But that wasn't true, Arturo realized. He searched himself and knew. He could do this. He could do anything. He'd known it as long as he could remember.

The ball slapping into his Little League glove as his dad tossed it to him in the park.

The first crack of the bat as he hit a homer in high school.

His mother's eyes bursting with pride and love as his name was announced before each game, the seat next to her occupied by a faded Yankees' cap.

The rush of crossing home plate in college to make it into the playoffs.

The high fives from teammates after a good defensive play in the minors, even when he couldn't hit a ball to save his life.

The look of love in his wife's eyes as he held his newborn daughter, Amara.

He didn't know who this Morgan lady was, really. He didn't have time to interrogate her now. And if he was being truly honest with himself, he didn't care. Not now. Not ever. The past was gone. He had a team to help.

He had a game to win.

He spun around, the bat's light illuminating his path. Behind him, he could hear the woman's skittish footsteps following, then he could feel her sharp fingertips clutching at his jersey, her sharp nails clawing his uniform. But he ignored them. He had to.

"You dare? Face me, boy," she hissed, angry and defiant. "You dare deny me this moment of victory?"

Arturo turned around fast, for the last time—he knew. She seemed to hop back, desperate to avoid the bat's reach.

"You can watch like everyone else, lady," Arturo said. "I hope you bought a ticket."

With that, he entered the dugout and waited.

The walk from the on-deck circle to the batter's box felt like a thousand miles to Arturo. If he had been feeling some pressure before, it'd been multiplied many times over in the moments following his confrontation with the shadow creature Morgan le Fay. Mordred and Downer had made it on base. While there were still no outs, and the A's could theoretically still eke out a win if Arturo bombed, he also knew a thing or two about momentum. You could ride it to victory, or you could falter—and spend the rest of the off-season wondering what went wrong. It was do-or-die time, whether Arturo liked it or not.

His manager's words, spoken under his breath as Arturo passed him on his way to prepare, lingered with him.

"No one's needed this more than you, kid," Falco had said. "This is your moment. Believe in yourself."

Arturo did. He realized this as he looked at the Red Sox's gangly pitcher. Caught the subtle nod from Tino at second base, one that said *It's okay, man, you got this.* Arturo felt a last, lingering heaviness leave him, an immediate peace he hadn't known he wanted. He gripped his bat as he set his feet in position. Tilted his head in the direction of the field. It was as if he were looking forward—past everything else. Past the failures and missteps and toward something brighter. Some kind of paradise. A brighter future.

But first—the pitch.

The ball came hard and fast, as Arturo had expected—clean through the middle. He braced for a second, felt the tingling hesitation that had dogged him for years, then felt himself expel the doubt with a shrug of his shoulders.

Arturo swung for his life.

Flat White

Jessica Plummer

Elaine is cleaning the steamer wands on the espresso machine the first time *he* walks into the coffee shop. Her hand slips on the knob and she accidentally blasts her finger with steam. It's hot enough to scald, and she yelps and sticks her finger in her mouth. Rosina, the cashier, gives her a weird look.

He doesn't seem to notice.

Face flaming, Elaine takes the cup Rosina hands her and checks the order scribbled on the side. A flat white with almond milk. She splashes the milk on the counter when she tries to pour it, presses the wrong button for the espresso pull, drops a stack of lids on the floor. She's not paying attention to the drink. She's looking at *him*.

She's not sure what it is about him. He's not handsome, exactly. He's a little short—maybe her height, and she's not particularly tall for a woman. He has dark hair swept back from a widow's peak, a nose just a little too big and sharp for classic good looks. Everything about him is sharp, somehow, from the angle of his shoulders to the cut of his dark gaze, or maybe she just thinks that because of the little white scars she can see—there, slicing through his right eyebrow, and another one tugging the left corner of his mouth into something sardonic, even though his facial expression is otherwise neutral as he scrolls through his phone.

He's fit, though. *Really* fit, not an ounce of fat on him and biceps straining the sleeves of his T-shirt as he raises a hand to push his hair back off his brow. Maybe he plays football—or, no, rugby, that seems more the thing.

Elaine catches the milk just before it bubbles over and swears under her breath, pouring the milk into the cup on top of the espresso. She finds a lid she hasn't thrown on the floor and fits it to the cup, swaddles the whole thing in a cardboard sleeve, and checks Rosina's sloppy Sharpie handwriting again for the name.

"I've got a flat white with almond milk for Lance," she calls, as if there's anyone else standing there waiting for a drink.

He looks up from his phone, and something in those dark eyes makes her gasp. "That's me," he says, "cheers," and takes the cup. Even in three syllables his French accent is audible, and somehow it feels obvious in retrospect, that someone so inexplicably striking couldn't be something as prosaic and uninteresting as *British*.

"You're welcome," she manages, even though he's already leaving, dark eyes back on his phone screen. She watches him walk out the door: the shift of his muscles through his thin T-shirt as he pushes the door open, his unconscious chivalry as he holds it that way for a mother with a stroller before moving on. His bum in those jeans.

He passes out of sight beyond the shop window, and Elaine sags back against the counter behind her, nearly knocking over the smoothie blender. Her heart is racing like she's at one of the spin classes her friend Anisha keeps dragging her to.

Lance.

———

She dreams that night that she's sitting in a big stone hall, the kind they used to have to go stand around in on heritage trips at school. She's at a banquet table, but she's not at all hungry. There are people all around her, chatting and laughing and drinking, but she doesn't notice any of them.

All she can see is Lance, standing on the other side of the hall. His hair is longer and his clothes are strange, but it's definitely him, from the bump in his nose where it's clearly been broken at least once to the way he lifts his hand to push his hair back. He's talking to a woman with a river of golden hair spilling to her waist, and the way he looks at her makes Elaine want to throw herself out a window.

She should leave, she thinks. She should claim indigestion or a headache and go up to her room so she doesn't have to watch.

She doesn't move. When she wakes, there are tears dried on her cheeks.

Lance becomes a semi-regular. He's not there every day, but enough that each morning as Elaine ties on her apron she can feel her heart go rabbit-fast at the thought that she might see him later.

It's *embarrassing*, to be perfectly frank. Yeah, her job is a bit dull, but that's no reason to get so excited over a break in the routine. She hasn't been this moony over a boy since she was fourteen and absolutely certain that Harry Styles would marry her someday. Which is all very well and good when you're a teenager, but she's an adult now and he's just an ordinary Frenchman with an aversion to lactose. He's not even *cute*.

And yet.

She and Rosina alternate shifts at the espresso counter and the till, which means sometimes she's the one taking his order, which means she gets to talk to him for a longer conversation than just reading out the name on his drink. Not all that much longer, admittedly, despite her best efforts.

"Good morning. Can I help you?"

"Good morning. Er, flat white with almond milk, please?" (Always squinting at the menu as if it might have changed. As if he might ever order something different.)

"Right, that'll be three pounds twenty." (As she runs his card.) "Nice day, isn't it?" (Or, more usually, given that they're in England: "Dreadful weather, isn't it?")

"Oh. Er, yes, it is."

(Handing back his card. Desperately.) "Can I have a name for the order?" (As if she couldn't have learnt it from running his card. As if she hadn't committed it to memory the first day she saw him.)

"Lance."

"Right, of course. One flat white with almond milk for Lance, straightaway." (Smiling, perhaps a touch maniacally. It doesn't matter. He's already looking at his phone.)

And so it goes. Predictable, but somehow never dull. Sometimes she thinks of writing her number on his cup beside his name, but he's barely seemed to register that she exists as a human person, let alone a woman who has a body and goes on dates and is actually rather intelligent and interesting when he's not in the room. He'd probably think it was something to do with the coffee order and not a phone number at all.

Besides, the whole idea is *mortifying*.

She will get over this, she tells herself. It's exposure therapy, like climbing into a tank of snakes to cure yourself of a fear of them.

(She wouldn't mind climbing into a tank of Lances.)

It's been only a few weeks. She'll get used to him. Eventually.

But there are the dreams.

She's in some kind of tub or pool of boiling water, sulfurous and foul. It's no deeper than a hot tub, but she can't seem to climb out, and every second scalds her. Her bare flesh beneath the water is red and angry, and the tears of pain that run down her cheeks are cool by comparison. She prays only for death—and then Lance is reaching for her, helping her out of the pool, unfazed by her nakedness as he wraps her in a cloak and dries her tears.

Another night: She's walking in her garden, even though the snow lies heavy on the ground (and even though her ratty little flat barely has a windowsill to boast of, let alone a garden). There's a dark shape huddled under a bush and her heart leaps into her throat, but she draws closer anyway, heart pounding with fear. A man, asleep, filthy and rank with chilblains peeking out from beneath his wild beard—but it's Lance, she knows it is from the nose and the scarred eyebrow, and she falls to her knees, weeping and gathering him in her arms and begging him to wake.

So many nights she's lost count: She's in a tower, weaving endlessly (she doesn't even know how to weave, doesn't know anyone who does). There's a mirror above her head that shows the world outside, a world she doesn't dare join or even turn around to look at directly. And then—Lance, tall and gallant astride a horse as sleek and dark as he is, the sun glinting off his armor, and she turns to stare, unafraid of the consequences so long as she can drink in the sight of him.

She has never been much of a dreamer before—just vague feelings of being lost or chased by something or not having studied for an exam, the specifics dissipating like morning mist when she wakes. But these linger through her days, like different lives she hasn't lived. Like they're trying to tell her something.

If it's any message more useful than how very pathetic she is, though, she can't parse it.

And then one day it changes, because Lance doesn't come in alone. There's a girl and a guy with him, both blond, both as palpably English as Lance is palpably not. They're all laughing and smiling at one another as they walk in, as they order, like a television advert for skin-care brands or those creepy ones they show in America for antidepressants.

It's the first time she's seen Lance smile. It's heart shattering.

Rosina's at the till so Elaine makes the drinks as the three of them take a seat at one of the coffee shop's few tables. She's gotten very good at focusing on what she's doing when Lance is around and not just staring like a Dickensian orphan gazing into a bakery window.

"Flat white for Lance. Earl Grey for Arthur. Matcha latte for Gwen."

Something about the names pings as familiar, but her brain catches on the shift of Lance's hips as he comes up to fetch the drinks, and she loses whatever it is she's trying to remember. He fumbles for a second trying to juggle all three cups.

"You want a tray for those?" Elaine asks.

"Oh, yeah, thanks," he says, and he must be in a particularly good mood with his friends here, because he takes that rare and magical smile and gives it to her. *To her!*

Before she can shake off the dazzle of it and find a tray for him, though, the girl he was with joins him. "You don't have to carry everything, Lance," she teases, bumping him with her hip.

"I do not mind," he says, and bumps her back.

She laughs, and Elaine drops the tray with a clatter. Maybe it's the musical chime of her laugh or the way she tips her head back or just the sun blazing off her golden hair, but *something* is suddenly unmistakably familiar. This girl, Gwen, is the woman Lance was talking to in the very first dream Elaine ever had about him, the very first day she met him.

And Elaine knows for certain that she's never seen her before.

"She probably came into the coffee shop another time and you just forgot you saw her," her best friend, Anisha, says over wine. "Then your subconscious put her in your dream."

"How did my subconscious know she was friends with Lance, then?" Elaine asks.

Anisha waves that away like smoke. "You must have seen them together."

"I wouldn't *forget* seeing Lance with a girl," Elaine insists.

"I mean, you said she's not even his girlfriend."

"She's not." Elaine had watched Lance and Gwen bring the drinks back over to their table. Arthur had thanked Gwen with a kiss, and something troubled had flickered over Lance's face. "But there's . . . I don't know. Something there."

"You need a more intellectually stimulating job," Anisha said. "Or at least a hobby. Weren't you going to learn to play guitar?"

"I wasn't any good at it," Elaine says, glancing at the guitar gathering dust in the corner of her lounge, along with the other failed experiments—the notebooks of rubbishy poetry, the tubes of oil paint. So much money spent on ways to tell stories and when it came down to it, it turned out she hadn't got anything worthwhile to say.

"My point is, you think about your customers too much," Anisha says, jolting her back to the present.

"I'd stop thinking about him if I could," Elaine says, unsure if that's actually true. "I'm not in control of these dreams. And I'm telling you, I've never seen this girl before today, *except* in a dream. Don't you think that's weird?"

Anisha opens her mouth, then closes it. Elaine narrows her eyes.

"What?"

"It's just, I don't think that's the weirdest part of all of this," Anisha says. She's not looking at Elaine.

"What's that supposed to mean?"

"Well, I mean, you're obsessed with this bloke and all you do is pour him coffee. It's not healthy, Elaine."

"I'm not obsessed with him," Elaine says, and she *knows* that part isn't true.

She probably drinks more than she should after that, because her dream that night is even weirder than usual. In that she's pretty sure she's dead in it.

She's floating down a river in a boat, bedecked with

flowers. Her eyes are closed and actually she's not sure how she's seeing any of this, given that she's almost definitely dead, but there it is.

It's weird to think it, but she's pretty sure she's never looked more beautiful.

The boat drifts to a stop in front of a glittering pavilion, pennants snapping in the breeze. Horse bridles jingle and lutes play. In the distance there's a castle with fairy-tale turrets.

A crowd gathers around her boat, whispering and nudging, but no one says anything until a man pushes through them, led by a page. He's bearded and wears a gold circlet in his blond hair, but Elaine has no trouble recognizing Arthur from the coffee shop.

"Who comes so to tower'd Camelot?" he asks, looking terribly sad, and she wakes with a gasp.

She's bleary and exhausted at work the next morning and barely has the energy to blush when Lance comes in. Again, he's not alone, but this time he's only brought Arthur and not Gwen.

She'd thought, maybe, that Gwen was the reason for his smile yesterday, but here it is again, quick and flashing. He's lighter than she's used to seeing him, his shoulders relaxed and his eyes soft. Arthur says something and Lance laughs with his whole body, unselfconscious and gorgeous.

They reach the register and Arthur sobers enough to order. "Earl Grey, please," he says, meeting Elaine's eyes with his own. They're blue, friendly and guileless, and Elaine's breath catches as she remembers Arthur looking down at her in the boat, a crown on his head.

Camelot.

Arthur.

King Arthur.

"No," she says automatically. It's too ridiculous.

"I'm sorry?" Arthur asks.

"Sorry!" she says back to him like a complete numpty, face flaming. "Sorry, sorry. Thinking about something else. Earl Grey, of course."

"Thank you," he says, smiling as if she didn't just babble nonsense at him, and hands her his card.

For the first time, she barely pays attention as she takes Lance's order. She's too busy staring at Arthur; at both of them, really.

Arthur is taller than Lance and broader. He's not *hand-some*, really, not any more so than Lance—but where Lance is attractive because of all the interesting ways his face diverts from the rules of good looks, Arthur adheres to them so faithfully that he skips handsome and goes straight to simply pleasant. He's just *nice looking*, classic and inoffensive and somehow trustworthy with his sandy hair and straight nose and gleaming white teeth. She can imagine him charging into battle alongside Wellington or piloting a biplane against German aircraft.

He just looks *English*, as English as a Sunday roast or a perfectly kept garden. If she had ever really thought about how King Arthur might've looked, she probably would have conjured up something like him.

Which is a completely ludicrous thought, but apparently it's not as ludicrous as she can get, because standing next to him, a dark and slender moon to Arthur's beaming sun, is *Lance*, and it doesn't take much effort for her overtired brain to turn that into *Lancelot*. Or *Gwen* to *Guinevere*, for that matter.

They didn't exist, she tells herself firmly. *They didn't exist, and if they did, it was hundreds and hundreds of years ago, and you're being an idiot.*

And a little voice answers her back: *Then why do all your dreams take place in castles?*

She makes a disgusted noise and goes to clean the bakery case.

She looks up "King Arthur" online when she gets home, because she can't not. She still feels vaguely stupid for doing so, but at least there's no one else in her flat to witness said stupidity.

There's a *lot* on the internet about him, but the gist is pretty much what she distantly remembers from school: a folkloric figure based on accounts of a sixth-century ruler who probably didn't actually exist. Meant to come again when England has need of him.

That gives her pause for a minute, because she can think of quite a number of problems England could use sorting out right now—but surely worse threats than those would have brought him back sooner? Like the Spanish Armada, maybe, or the Blitz. And if he *is* here to sort out the latest bout of Tory idiocy, what is he doing faffing about in a coffee shop instead of, well, *sorting*? And why are Lancelot and Guinevere here?

Then she realizes she's pondering the theoretical political strategy of an undead zombie king magically reincarnated to give Parliament a good talking-to, and she says some very accurate and unkind things to herself before moving on to another tab.

Sir Lancelot du Lac was added to the mythos in the twelfth century, the creation of French writers. Which . . . well, Lance *is* French. Which could easily be coincidence—France is just across the channel, it's hardly inaccessible—but it *is* weird.

Unless she's just reading into things that aren't there. Unless she's forcing things to fit into a pattern because she wants them to when, really, it's just an attractive man and his friends patronizing a coffee shop whilst possessing amusingly suggestive names. That's probably it.

And then her eye catches on the word *Elaine*.

"There's so many of us," she tells Anisha. "Them. Me. In the stories."

It's a few days later. She's *very* drunk. It was the only way she could work up the courage to share her absurd theory.

"There's Elaine of Astolat, which is the one, the one where he wears my token at a tournament and then he's injured and I nurse him back to health," she says, ticking it off on her finger. "But he loves Guinevere, so he leaves and I *die*."

"Maybe you should slow down," Anisha says, eyeing Elaine's drink as it sloshes out of its glass with her gesticulations.

"That's the same Elaine as the Lady of Shalott, except Tennyson changed it because nothing rhymes with *Astolat*. Except *acrobat*. And I can't even do a cartwheel," she goes on. "But I'm in a tower and I'm weaving and I can't ever, ever leave or I'll *die*. Because of the curse. But then Lancelot rides by, so I leave the tower and I get in a boat, with all these beautiful . . . with flowers, everywhere." She makes sprinkling gestures around her with her free hand to show where the flowers are. "And by the time the boat gets to Camelot I'm *dead*."

"Right."

"And then there's Elaine of Cork. Corbic. *Corbenic*." Elaine scrunches up her face. "I'm in a tub of boiling water because of a witch did it but I can't die and then he rescues me and I fall in love with him but he loves Guinevere, so I get a sorceress to enchant him into thinking *I'm* Guinevere and he sleeps with me."

"Well, that's rapey," Anisha says.

"I *know*!" Elaine shouts, so loud other people in the pub turn to look at them. "It's awful. I'm awful." She sniffs. "And I get pregnant and have Sir Galahad and Lance *still* doesn't want me, so I trick him *again* and Guinevere gets mad at him for cheating, which, like, that's the black calling the kettle pot, right?"

"Something like that, yeah."

"So he goes mad and runs away and becomes a tramp and then I find him under a bush and show him the Holy Grail and it cures him. And we're happy together for a while with our little baby, Galahad. But Lance goes back to Gwen again and I *die*."

Anisha takes Elaine's now half-empty glass and moves it to another table, out of Elaine's reach. "You die a lot in these dreams."

"They're not dreams!" Elaine says, shouting again and then catching herself. "This is *real*." Anisha raises an eyebrow. "I mean not *real* real, but these are the stories. The King Arthur stories. And I've been dreaming *about* them."

"Let me make sure I've got this," Anisha says. "You think the bloke you've got a crush on at the coffee shop is *the* Sir Lancelot, and that his friends are Guinevere and *actual for-real King Arthur*, and that you're also in the stories? These *fictional* stories? Because there's an Elaine in them?"

"*Lots* of Elaines. At least seven," Elaine says, holding up eight fingers. "But they overlap. Like maybe Elaine of Corbenic is also . . . also Elaine of . . . somewhere else, I don't remember. And also his mom was named Elaine."

Anisha makes a face.

"I don't think I'm that one."

"Small favors," Anisha says. Then her expression turns very gentle, and Elaine wrinkles her nose because she knows what's coming. "Sweetheart, don't you think this is all . . . insane?"

"Well yes, *obviously*," Elaine says. "But that doesn't mean it's not true."

It's raining the next time Lance comes into the shop, absolutely pissing down. Everyone else is staying at home making their own coffees rather than wading through the downpour, and so Elaine has all the time in the world to watch Lance hold open the door for Gwen, fold up her umbrella for her, pull out her chair for her, go up to the register to buy her coffee.

No Arthur this time, which shouldn't be weird. Elaine is a modern young woman in a post–*When Harry Met Sally* world, and she's perfectly aware that men and women can be platonic friends. But this is Sir Lancelot and Queen Guinevere—maybe—and they're famous for one thing in particular, and so she watches them as she makes the world's slowest flat white and matcha latte, both with almond milk.

They're sitting with their heads very close together, Gwen's brilliant tresses outshining Lance's even in the gray light of a rainy day. She's fairer than Arthur, the white blondness that usually fades by puberty, and so delicately beautiful it makes Elaine want to give up in despair and maybe go live in a rain gutter or under a bridge.

And she's crying.

She cries beautifully, because of course she does. Lance is bent toward her, murmuring something low, her little white hands clasped in his, but she keeps shaking her head, that river of hair shimmering.

She's so gorgeously sad that Elaine actually feels *bad* that Gwen feels guilty about cheating on Arthur with Lance, but then she remembers that she doesn't approve of infidelity and then remembers after *that* that she has no idea what the dynamic between the three of them is. If it isn't that they're reincarnated mythological figures. Which they're probably not.

Lance touches Gwen's face, so gently, and she leans in toward him for a moment before jumping to her feet. "I can't—" Elaine hears her say, and then she's running for the door, snatching up her umbrella on the way.

"Gwen!" Lance calls, but she's already gone. Rosina watches the door slam with wide eyes, glances over at Lance, then ostentatiously busies herself with the tea bag display so she can pretend she wasn't watching.

Elaine has no such recourse. "I've, um, got a flat white and a matcha latte for Lance," she says apologetically.

Lance turns to her. He looks miserable. "Thank you," he says, taking the flat white and reaching for the matcha latte before appearing to give up. "You can throw that away, I suppose."

"I'll keep it a couple moments in case she comes back, yeah?" Elaine offers, and Lance's mouth approximates a smile for a second before collapsing back into despair.

It's rude. It's rude and pushy and *entirely* inappropriate, but she can't keep the words in: "You all right?"

Lance blinks in surprise. "Oh. Yes. Thank you. We were just

trying to decide something." His gaze goes a little distant. "We have been trying to decide it for a long time."

Fifteen hundred years, I know, Elaine doesn't say. She also doesn't say: *I understand. I'm trying to decide if I'm losing my mind or if I'm the reincarnation of a pathetic stalker who will inevitably die in a boat of flowers over you.*

"That's always difficult," she manages instead, bland and unhelpful. "I'm sorry."

"Thanks," Lance says again, and then seems to actually look at her. "Pardon me. You are at work, I should not be wasting your time with my problems . . . ?"

"Elaine," she says, in answer to his questioning look.

"Elaine," he repeats, and Elaine's heart throbs so hard it *hurts*. "That is the name of my mother."

Again, Elaine just manages not to say *I know*. "And you're Lance, right?" she says instead, slightly idiotically, because he's still holding a cup with his name written on it in Sharpie.

He nods, looks down at the abandoned matcha latte, frowns. He's so exquisitely, beautifully sad that it gives Elaine a sharp pain right behind her eyes.

Maybe it's holding back all the things she can't say, but she abruptly loses control of her tongue. "Would you like to get a drink sometime?" she blurts, desperate to change his expression even as she wants to stare at it all day.

Lance looks up at her, clearly startled.

"I mean, only if you want to," Elaine stammers. "You don't have to. I shouldn't—I mean, it's not a big deal, I just thought—that is—"

And Lance *smiles*. Elaine would lie down in traffic for that smile.

"That would be lovely," he says.

———

There are many texts back and forth—she has his *mobile number!*—before the plans for their date—they are going on a *date!*—are settled. They decide to see a film before going to the pub, since there's some historical drama showing that Lance mentions wanting to see. Elaine has no actual interest in it, but it's the sort of film serious intellectual people see, and she wants Lance to know that she occasionally thinks about things besides espresso.

(She even pulls out one of her old notebooks so that if Lance asks what she does outside of the coffee shop she can say she writes poetry, but after an hour or so of staring at a blank page she puts it away again.)

They agree to meet at the cinema, since her flat isn't on his way. Her skirt is arguably a bit too short for just seeing a film, but Lance has only ever seen her from the other side of a counter, and she wants to make sure that his first sight of her legs is a good one. She spends over an hour on her hair and makeup, but it's worth it. She looks, to put it bluntly, fucking amazing.

Or at least so she thinks until she walks into the cinema lobby and sees Lance standing there with Arthur and Gwen. They are all wearing jeans, the shapeless threadbare kind that cost the earth. Gwen's hair is in a messy bun, and her oversize jumper clearly belongs to Arthur—or, Elaine thinks miserably, Lance.

"Elaine!" Lance calls when he spots her, ruining her chance to duck out of the cinema and possibly flee the country. "You look very nice."

She's wildly overdressed. She can feel her face going bright red. "Thanks."

"You know Arthur and Gwen, of course, from the café," he says, indicating his friends. "I hope you don't mind, but when I said we were coming to see this film, they both said they'd been meaning to see it as well, and . . ." He holds up his hands, cheerfully helpless.

"Of course I don't mind," she lies, smiling broadly.

"We've crashed your date, I know, it's so shit of us," Arthur says, so affably apologetic it actually does make Elaine feel a tiny bit better. "But I'm so glad he's asked you! I've been after Lance to stop living like a monk for ages."

Lance and Gwen glance at each other and then quickly away. Elaine prays for the ground to open up and carry one of the four of them away. She doesn't care which.

"Oh, Arthur, don't start on this again, you'll embarrass him," Gwen says, and only someone who was suspicious of her to begin with would notice anything off in her tone.

"Can I help it if I want to see my best friend happy?" Arthur asks. He puts a hand on the back of Lance's neck and grins at Elaine. "Seriously, Elaine, Lance is the best bloke I know, no question. I'd die for this lad."

"Well, let's hope that won't be necessary," Elaine jokes, instead of saying *I'm pretty sure he's sleeping with your girlfriend*, and looks at Lance. She's not surprised by the flush crawling up his neck, but she *is* surprised by the way he's looking at Arthur. It's familiar, somehow, and it takes her a minute to place it before it's suddenly obvious.

It's the same way he looks at Gwen.

Elaine blinks. Surely not—but Lance's expression as he shrugs off Arthur's hand and elbows him away is . . . Well. It's *adoring*.

Has she read this whole thing wrong?

She couldn't recall a single detail of the film they see if

she were held at gunpoint. All she's aware of is Lance next to her, the warmth of his body, the perfectly imperfect lines of his profile. Gwen is on his other side, Arthur next to her, and every so often Lance leans over to murmur something to Gwen that makes her laugh.

Which is horrible if she's cheating on Arthur with him and also he's on a date with *Elaine*, not Gwen.

Or it's fine if they're just friends and Elaine is reading way too much into this.

Or it's awful but in a different way if he's actually in love with *Arthur*.

Elaine can't wait for a drink.

"So after all that, the date sucked?" Anisha asks the next night, topping off her second glass of wine. Elaine is well into her fourth.

"It was like I wasn't there," Elaine says. Her head aches. "At the cinema, at the pub. It was all inside jokes and chucking money around and . . . and *touching*. They're very touchy, all three of them."

"Shit," Anisha says. "Well, you've got to kiss a few frogs, as my mum would say. On to the next, yeah?"

"Er. Well." Elaine drains her glass and avoids Anisha's eyes. "I've got another date with him this weekend."

It becomes as regular as the visits to the coffee shop and the dreams. At least once a week, and sometimes twice, Elaine and Lance go out. And every single date is utterly miserable.

Oh, he's chivalrous. He holds doors, pulls out chairs, carries an umbrella over Elaine's head when it rains like she's on a red carpet and he's her bodyguard. Once they came to a puddle at a curb too wide for her to step over and he literally carried her across like he was forging a river, and for a moment Elaine felt like all her blood had turned to champagne.

But on the dates themselves he mostly seems like he'd rather be anywhere else. The only one he seemed to enjoy was the first, with Arthur and Gwen along. Without them, he faffs about on his phone or stares out the window or picks listlessly at his food but insists he's enjoying it.

When she talks, he nods in the right places but offers nothing in return. She has no idea if he's actually heard a single word.

When *he* talks, it's almost always about Arthur. Arthur is so funny. Arthur is so generous. Arthur is good enough at football to play for a professional league. Arthur has rescued three stray dogs in the last year alone. Arthur has made Lance feel totally at home in a foreign country ever since they met at university.

He never mentions Gwen.

There's always a point, usually during the main course or the second drink, when Elaine swears she's done with this. At best, being alone with Lance is like being alone with herself, but sadder. At worst, it starts to feel like he actively hates her. And why keep seeing someone who hates her, no matter what Tennyson said in his stupid poem?

But then he'll walk her home and kiss her on the doorstep before he goes, one strong hand in her hair and the other on her waist. If there's a feeling of obligation to it that she can't quite imagine away, well, it's no competition to the softness of his lips or the glitter of the streetlamp in his dark eyes. If he seems unhappy, well, the story they're acting out is a tragedy. That isn't his fault.

It's still a beautiful story.

She dreams that she's showing Lance the Holy Grail. She wakes weeping. She can't remember what it looked like.

Lance invites her to Arthur's birthday party as his plus-one. It's going to be a big do, apparently, the kind that actually involves plus-ones. Arthur's got loads of friends, a whole crew of lads who follows him around, and it's all Elaine can do not to guess their names out loud.

Gwen is in charge, so it's at a really posh restaurant, which isn't surprising. They're *all* really posh, much more so than Elaine. Gwen in particular has always come off like she's about to tell a story about her and Kate Middleton at finishing school. Elaine doesn't want to overcompensate so she wears a cotton sundress and finds herself in a sea of people in cocktail attire. She never seems to get it right with Lance.

They've rented out the private party room of the restaurant, and there's an open bar, so everyone's already drunk by the time she and Lance get there. Lance steers her through the crowd with a gentle hand on her back that makes her feel both protected and thrillingly off-balance all at once. She loves the shape of her name in his accent as he introduces her to a handful of people—Percy, Gareth, Tristan. They're all about eight feet tall and model handsome, because of *course* they are.

(There are almost no other women. Lance points out

Arthur's sister from a distance but doesn't introduce her, and from her time on Wikipedia, Elaine knows enough to be grateful.)

Lance steps away to get Elaine a drink and strands her with someone named Kay who she ends up having to listen to for twenty minutes whilst he attempts to explain what sounds like a very complicated familial relationship to Arthur. Mildly desperate, Elaine makes an excuse and goes looking for Lance. She finds him having a whispered argument with Gwen by the loos.

". . . not the time for this, Lance!" Gwen snaps.

"It is never the time for this," Lance says bitterly. "You are always putting it off. Putting *me* off."

"You say that like you have any better answers than I do," Gwen says. "You want me to be the one to choose, but that's just because you can't do it yourself."

"He's my best friend!"

"Oh, yes, just mates, that's what *you* are."

"It doesn't matter, does it?" Lance asks. "That is all he wants to be."

Gwen snorts.

"And it doesn't change you and me. How I feel about—"

Suddenly Elaine can't bear to hear another word. "Lance!" she says, and they both jump. "Oh, hi, Gwen. Lance, I've been looking for you everywhere. Will you come with me to get a drink?"

Lance and Gwen exchange glances. They are both very red. "Uh, yes, okay," Lance says, and lets her tow him away.

They weave their way through the room to the bar. Lance gives Elaine a bemused look when she pretty much chugs her vodka tonic before they can even step away.

"I'm really thirsty," she says, a little sheepishly. The truth is she's too sober for everything happening in this room tonight. She turns to the bartender. "Another?"

They're halfway through the third course—there are *seven*—when some loud Australian bloke at the other end of the table named Mel or something like that mutters a comment about Gwen. Elaine doesn't catch all of it, but the phrase "frigid bitch by day, utter slag by night" is clearly audible.

As is the phrase "with his own best friend."

Lance knocks a drink into Elaine's lap as he surges out of his chair to demand that Mel repeat himself.

"Lance, don't," Gwen says, reaching for his arm. Elaine's hands are too full of napkin to do the same on his other side.

Arthur spreads his hands placatingly. "Hey, we're all friends here, right? It's fine."

"He said something about Gwen," Lance says, jaw tight, eyes flashing. No one is sober.

"*Don't,*" Gwen repeats.

"If I did, it's not your business," Mel says, and then smirks. "Or is it?"

Lance hurls himself at Mel. Gwen screams and Elaine squawks and it takes Arthur and three of his enormous friends to pull Lance and Mel apart. Gareth and Percy haul Mel off to the gents' to calm down and deal with his bloody nose. Arthur and Lance and Gwen are all shouting at one another.

"What were you thinking?" Arthur demands. "This is my *birthday*! Why are you fighting my guests?"

"Why aren't *you*?" Lance shouts back. "You heard what he said about her!"

"Then I will deal with it, not you!"

"Excuse me, I'm *right here*," Gwen snaps. "I can handle a drunken knob just fine, thanks."

"Good, because apparently Arthur is going to let you," Lance says.

"Don't shout at Arthur, this isn't his fault!"

"Well, whose fault is it? Who invited bloody Mel?"

"Stop shouting, both of you!"

Elaine flees to the bar.

Ten minutes later Lance and Arthur are still hollering at each other, Lance so drunk and angry he's slipping into French. Gwen has disappeared. Elaine feels absolutely wretched and decides that calling an Uber might be the better part of valor tonight, but she needs a wee first.

She finds Gwen in the ladies', crying into her hands. Elaine freezes in the doorway and contemplates bolting.

Then she sighs, pulls a handful of tissues from the box on the counter, and offers them to Gwen. "All right?" she asks.

Gwen looks up at her blearily. She even cries beautifully when she's drunk, naturally. "Thanks," she says, and takes the tissues.

Elaine uses a stall for its appointed purpose, washes her hands, and then pauses again. The loo is posh enough to have a couch in it, which is where Gwen is sat, still sobbing. Elaine sighs again, internally this time, and then sits down next to Gwen.

"I just wanted to give Arthur a nice birthday," Gwen says, as if picking up a conversation they hadn't been having. They're both drunk enough to forget they aren't really friends. "I love him so much."

"I know," Elaine says, and she means it. That's the part that makes it so fucked-up. It's painfully obvious that Gwen and Lance love Arthur desperately. If they didn't, they wouldn't have a problem.

"Lance shouldn't have hit Mel," Gwen says.

"You were never going to stop him," Elaine says.

"I know. Fucking Lance. I swear he thinks he's a knight on a white charger."

"Black," Elaine says. Lance would never ride a white horse.

"What?"

"Nothing."

Gwen swipes at her face. "Arthur doesn't even get *angry*, is the thing, not really. He just looks like . . . like when your dog realizes you've taken it to the vet and it can't believe you've betrayed it like that." She blows her nose—finally, an ugly sound. "He's just so fucking *good*. How is anyone supposed to be with someone so *good*?"

"Is that why you and Lance—" Elaine starts to say before realizing there's no way she can get away with finishing that sentence.

Gwen seems to realize who she's talking to for the first time. Her face softens. "He really likes you, you know," she says. "Lance."

"Yeah?" Elaine asks, feeling tears pricking at her own eyes. "It doesn't feel like it most of the time."

Gwen's face softens even more, and Elaine realizes with a feeling of sudden resentment that she *likes* Gwen. It's infuriating. She should at least get to feel indignantly self-righteous about her.

"Lance is . . . not always good about showing things," Gwen says. "He holds a lot back. And he . . . I mean . . . well, there's Arthur."

"Yeah." *I'm not going to cry*, Elaine thinks. *I'm not going to cry. I'm not going to cry.*

No, she's not going to cry, she realizes suddenly. She's going to throw up. She's had too much to drink.

Gwen holds her hair back.

—•—

Lance and Arthur don't speak for a week after the party. Lance calls Elaine daily and then is all but silent on the other end of the line, moody and uncommunicative. Elaine answers anyway.

She's drinking more than she ever used to before. She gets sick three times in one week. Her hair is brittle, and her eyes have permanent circles under them.

"I don't think this guy is good for you," Anisha says one Saturday morning. They were supposed to go shopping, but Elaine's too hungover to move from the sofa. "I love you, but you're a fucking wreck."

"It's not him," Elaine mumbles into a cushion. "It's this whole thing with Arthur and Gwen."

"I don't think you can say 'it's not him' when he's fucking his best friend's girlfriend. His best friend who he's maybe probably in love with. Like, that really sounds like it *is* him."

"None of them want to hurt each other," Elaine says. She's so tired.

"I don't give a shit if they hurt each other," Anisha says. "They're hurting *you*."

"They can't help it."

"If you start talking about how they're mythological figures again I'm going to dump my coffee on your head."

Elaine forces herself to roll onto her back so she can look at Anisha, even though her head pounds at the movement. "I'm still having the dreams."

"You're having weird dreams because you're fucking *drunk* all the time."

But Elaine isn't listening. "It's the greatest story we have," she says. "It's lasted over a thousand years. And I get to be part of it."

"Yeah, the sad forgotten part who *dies*. Isn't that what you said?"

Elaine closes her eyes. She can see her boat, filled with flowers. She can see the pennants of Camelot fluttering in the wind. She can see the tournaments, the jousting, the glory of it all. Somewhere, just out of the corner of her eye, somewhere burned into the back of her mind, she's even seen the Holy Grail. She's not a religious person, never has been, but that's special.

She'd paint it, if she'd ever learnt to paint.

"Does it matter?" she asks. "Wouldn't it be better to be a small part of such a big story than not to be in it at all?"

"You're not a story! You're a person!" Anisha says, throwing up her hands.

Elaine rolls over again. "I'm going to take a nap."

Lance and Arthur make up. Lance gets more cheerful, and so do Arthur and Gwen, when Elaine sees them.

Elaine gets worse.

She's started picking at her nails; it's a rare day that her cuticles don't bleed. She messes up orders at work. She feels on the verge of crying all the time.

She dreams that she's holding a baby, pink and sleepy, the sweetest baby in the world.

"My little Galahad," she whispers to him, touching his soft cheek with a finger and trying not to feel guilty. Lance will have to love her now, won't he?

When she's awake, she knows he will never love her. He's

given his heart to not just one but two people already. He doesn't have room for a third.

But does it matter if Sir Lancelot can't love her, as long as she gets to love Sir Lancelot?

It's Elaine's birthday now. At a pub, because *she's* not posh, and besides, she wanted to keep it small: just Anisha and Rosina, a couple of friends from uni, Lance. Somehow, inevitably, Arthur and Gwen got invited, too. She can't find it in her heart to begrudge their presence, not really. She likes them, is the miserable truth.

Her friends are all clearly captivated by Arthur, because of course they are. They're British. It's practically the law.

Lance and Gwen disappear somewhere between the third and fourth round of drinks. Elaine waits for them to come back, sick and distracted. They don't.

Arthur is oblivious, blissfully trusting, and Elaine suddenly wants to slap him. Instead she goes looking for Lance and Gwen outside.

They're not hard to find, standing just outside the pub door whilst Lance smokes a cigarette. They're standing close, but they're not *doing* anything. They're never *doing* anything.

Still, the guilty way they jump apart is enough.

"It's my *birthday*," Elaine says.

"We were just talking," Lance says. He won't meet her eyes.

"Okay," Elaine says, but it isn't. It's never been okay. It's never going to *be* okay, because Lance loves Gwen and Lance loves Arthur but Lance doesn't love her and never, ever will.

"I'm going home," she says.

"Elaine, no, please, let's go back inside," Lance says.

"We could go somewhere else," Gwen suggests. "Do you want cake? We could try to find—"

"I want to go *home*," she says, cutting Gwen off. "By *myself*."

And she walks away—from Lance, from Gwen, from the whole bloody mess of it.

It's a cold and misty night, not the kind at all pleasant to stand outside and smoke in unless you have an ulterior motive, and they're not really at all close to Elaine's flat. Lance, chivalrous as he is, follows her for a couple of blocks.

"At least let me call a cab for you," he says. "It is too far to walk."

"I'm all right."

"*Elaine*." There's still something in the way he says her name that makes her knees want to go weak. She doesn't let them. "Elaine, I am sorry."

She stops at that and turns to face him. "What are you sorry *for*?"

It's a question that could have a hundred answers, and for a moment she thinks he'll actually give her one. His lips part, and she waits for something, anything honest to fall from them.

But he doesn't say anything. Just looks at her with dark, helpless eyes, waiting for her to save him.

"Good night, Lance," she says, and starts walking again. This time he doesn't follow her.

It's a cold night for this time of year, and the mist quickly turns to rain. Headlights and streetlamps scatter blurry neon blossoms across the damp pavement, shimmering in the growing puddles. She walks and walks as her hair straggles into her eyes and her party shoes rub blisters into her heels, and she doesn't care. This was always how the story ended:

Elaine, losing. Elaine, alone. Elaine, in the water, surrounded by flowers.

She is Elaine of Astolat. Sir Lancelot rode into battle wearing her token, and she died of unrequited love for him.

She is Elaine of Corbenic. She tricked Sir Lancelot into fathering Sir Galahad on her and saved him from madness by bringing him to the Holy Grail. And he still left her in the end.

She is a minor figure in a grand tragedy, and her fate was written centuries before she was born. It doesn't end happily, not for any of them, and there's nothing she can do about it.

And then she stops suddenly, heedless of the rain soaking through her clothes and puddling in her shoes.

"No," she says. "Fuck that."

Maybe she *was* Elaine of Astolat, or Corbenic, or Shalott—or any of the others, Garlot or Listenoise or whoever.

But who she *was* isn't who she *is*.

She's ready to find herself again.

There's a greengrocer's awning nearby, and she stops beneath it so she can send a text without destroying her phone in the rain.

I don't think we should see each other anymore.

She slips the phone into her bag and steps out from under the awning. She doesn't care what he texts back. The rain drenches her instantly, and if she had been crying—or still is—it's impossible to tell.

That's all right. She's not far from home, not anymore, and there are warm, dry clothes and a cup of tea waiting for her. She's ready for a quiet evening in, by herself, and a night without a single dream.

After all, she has work in the morning.

Once (Them) & Future (Us)

Preeti Chhibber

When Merlin woke in the crystal caves, something was different. The first thing he noticed was the lack of any pain. His joints, his shoulders, his neck: everything felt fine. A little stiff but fine. He opened his eyes and raised his hands and found a young man's elastic white skin in front of his face. He scrambled up—when was the last time he had scrambled anywhere?—and made for the entrance. It was open. How long had it been since it was last open?

Merlin stumbled at a shaft of sunlight. He landed on his knees, and for a moment, he forgot who he was. For that moment he was blank and moved only by tiny stars of dust in that golden light.

Then he came back to himself. His skin felt warmer than it had been in eons; the rays sank into his very bones and he had energy. So long he'd been a prisoner, not just of stone and crystal but also of fatigue and an old man's exhaustion.

He rose with long-forgotten ease and a new determination. Arthur. He needed to find his king.

First, he would need to acclimate to this new world. No, not world. Time. It was still the same island on which he'd lived and slept and woke and imagined a perfect future. The same isle on which he'd served the greatest king ever born. The greatest king he'd ever had born. When Merlin was young, a crow, dark feathers and slashing beak, came to him in a dream. It sang of a king; it sang of a promise. It sang of prophecy. It sang, Merlin remembered, of Avalon. Not of the isle, no, but of the ideal.

His only purpose, from then on, was in service of creating that ideal, of creating that future. He listened and he schemed, he pulled the magic out of his heart and into his hands. So it was Merlin who found Arthur's would-be parents, who spoke the spells to push them together. And when Arthur, who would be king, came mewling into the world, it was Merlin who caught him. His king grew, surrounded by Merlin's wisdom and his magic.

There were remnants of that magic now: a few leagues from the cave, he charmed a woman and she gave him all of her son's clothes straight out of a basket. When he'd opened his mouth to speak to her, he was surprised to find his lips making strange shapes, with sounds he'd never heard before tumbling out. A guiding hand on his tongue, he thought. There was something bigger at work here. It was how he knew Arthur must live.

But that didn't mean a fast reunion: thirty turns of the sun and moon passed as Merlin searched, following the signs of breath and bone and sounds of the earth as they led him south. And that didn't mean it was easy. It meant sleeping on rough grass, eating what he could find. It meant hiding from well-meaning strangers and some who looked to take what little he had. It meant learning new and unlearning old without losing himself. Was he losing himself? There were seemingly random stretches where he'd disappear into the back of his mind, unable to remember who he was or how he'd come to be. He imagined these terrifying interludes were punishment for leaving his prison, for now he'd become prisoner in a new way, surrounded by a thick fog. Here he had no body, no skin to cut on shards of crystal, no mouth or memories to shape the sounds of spells for help. No air to breathe into a scream. Merlin-who-was-not-Merlin would list in space, each time feeling a just little less real, a little less of substance. Until he woke, back in tenuous control of his body, often surprised by new surroundings and unclear on how much time had passed. If this was not punishment, he wasn't sure what else the reason could be.

But all he could do was hitch his pack on his shoulder and button his coat. Was push on. Knowing that once he found his king, all would be clear.

The sun turned.

He found he didn't mind Britain's new stone and metal buildings, or the flat, strong roads. He was often quite in love with this world. But every now and again, he missed the simplicity of the forest that had been, of the ease of a dirt path surrounded by trees in which to duck and chase. He found himself remembering past days, days that must be thousands of years gone now, days spent playing on his own in a wood near his mother's home.

He was walking down a street in a city named London when the reminiscences hit. So Merlin stopped and sat, and he thought of his childhood. He was very young, sitting at the fire in his family's home, at the feet of his grandmother. His mother was tending a boiling stew that smelled of meat and salt and roots from the forest at their door. He felt the weight of an old, heavy hand on his head, fingers running their gnarled joints through his curls. *A great man, your child will be. A great man who makes great change.* He could almost hear the graveled tenor of his grandmother's voice.

Now that he was young again, these memories would pop into his head at the strangest moments. The experience with his mother and her mother at the hearth was one of the earliest he could remember. Perhaps it was a reminder of his cause. *Great change,* she'd predicted. Or perhaps the youth of his body was pulling these thoughts forward. It was strange in this new time, feeling young. His hair was black again, not white, hanging around his ears instead of down his back. He had no aches and pains as he had in his later years. It had been so long. He still held on to an old man's nostalgia for being young, and it played at odds with his self-determined rationalism. But even while being in this body he'd once known so well could be exhilarating . . . still he felt unbalanced; he felt like an interloper.

Merlin shook his head to clear out these philosophical ramblings. He realized he was sitting atop a wall outside a massive university. He looked around, hoping for inspiration in the multitudes of people. There were just so many people. Far more than he could have hoped to see in his entire life, once. Perhaps the random chance in the crowds would provide an answer for where he needed to go to find Arthur. Since waking, he'd followed his own teachings: he'd listened to nature. Whether it was hunting through viscera for signs from the Gods or listening to prophecy from the sharp-edged beak of a crow, Merlin had always sought answers from the world around him. And what were these crowds if not borne of the Earth? Looking down at the mass of people, he was reminded of looking for answers in a swirling mist above a fire of leaves and grass and the odd animal bits, divining Arthur's true path.

Then, among the cacophony of sounds, a voice broke

through. Merlin turned and looked over his shoulder at a young man and woman passing below him.

"I keep having these bloody dreams. It's like I'm in a *Lord of the Rings* movie. I don't even like *Lord of the Rings*."

There was something familiar in that voice. Something unmistakable in its deepness that vibrated along the back of Merlin's neck. He turned his body and hopped off the wall directly into the path of the two students.

The voice belonged to a handsome young man with an unruly mop of black hair, a deep brown face, and broad shoulders. "Oi!" he said, stumbling backward; the girl just looked at him appraisingly. Merlin ignored her; he shuddered at the thought that he might be seconds from coming face-to-face with his king. He lifted his head.

"Hello. I'm Emrys." He wasn't sure where the unfamiliar name had come from. It wasn't one he'd heard before, and the sound of it felt awkward as he said it. It was a name that was not anywhere in his histories. And yet, it felt like it had been sitting inside him, waiting to get out into the world. But he would have to ruminate on it later. There were more pressing matters now. Like this boy who could be king.

"... Okay." The boy edged farther backward. Merlin frowned; he'd hoped for recognition. Was this him? But all he found in those brown eyes were confusion and distrust. He looked into this face, so foreign to the one he remembered, for any hint of the man he needed.

Instead it was the girl who put herself forward, who answered. "Hello, Emrys. I'm Morgan. This is my brother, Arjun."

Merlin nearly choked. Morgan. He'd been so focused on his king's voice, he hadn't thought the girl worth his attention; now he looked at her. She was still beautiful, with long dark

hair and wide hips. It was her eyes, though, that gave her away. Far too knowing for the face that held them. He'd loved her once. Why was she here? He couldn't let her, or whatever she was attempting to do, divert his attention.

"Morgan." Arthur was looking at her like he couldn't ascertain what she was up to, a feeling Merlin shared.

She shrugged in response. "He's harmless, Arjun, look at him. And he's interesting." Morgan's eyes glinted.

Merlin thought it might be time to assert himself. "I am both harmless and interesting. And in need of new friends. I've just moved here." He'd been traveling for long enough to get a sense of how young people of this age spoke. Or, based on the strange looks he was getting, maybe not.

Arthur—Arjun tentatively held out a hand. Merlin met him halfway. The moment their fingers touched, his blood buzzed and he forgot himself again. He was only Emrys, Emrys who was holding on to someone important. Merlin was nothing and no one.

Then in the space of a breath, Merlin returned to himself. It was a blessedly short, if terrifying, intermission. What was happening to him? Was it this Emrys, forcing him into unbeing? Taking Merlin's time?

He resisted the urge to pull his hand back, to run it along his own arms, reminding himself of his own tangibility. He needed to feel.

For his part, Arjun's face shifted just the smallest bit. He'd felt something, too—Merlin was sure of it. Any doubts he had were laid to rest. This was Arthur. After thousands of years. Unexplored lifetimes upon lifetimes of lost moments while he'd been sleeping, imprisoned. Merlin had found him, and they could begin their work anew, heading toward the utopia of Avalon.

He considered, briefly, if that was Morgana's reason for being here. Avalon had been her dream, too. A place for magic and love and equality. With no pain, or hunger, or people downtrodden in the name of power. A place of balance and truth.

He let the hope of it wash over him, and he couldn't help the grin that pulled at his cheeks. After all this time. At last.

Merlin studied Arjun as they walked. How people moved around him, as if in deference. Arjun sent a subtle nod to people who cleared the path, and Merlin realized that Arjun noticed, that the confidence in Arjun's step expected it. He wondered again how much this new Arthur knew.

"So, Emrys, where did you come from?" Morgana's voice curled into his ears. Merlin kept moving forward, eyes trained on Arjun's back, even as her whispers moved through him, crawling up and down the back of his throat, until his mouth betrayed him, pushing his secrets out into the open air.

"The forest. A cave. You know, Morgan."

She laughed. It was true, he realized. She did know. That was disconcerting.

"That's a weird thing to say, Emrys." Arjun glanced back at him without slowing his stride.

"A very weird thing to say, Emrys," Morgana agreed wryly.

He feigned nonchalance. "What can I say, maybe I'm just weird." He punctuated his words with a shrug.

"I'd say so, judging by your look alone. Where did you even get that jacket—1955? Are you a time traveler?" Her voice was light and teasing, but Merlin felt his hackles rise. She was too clever by half, asking questions she was forcing him to answer truthfully. Biting his tongue to maintain a semblance of independence, he shrugged again before answering.

"Perhaps." It would have to do.

"Okay, Morgan, stop pestering the new kid if you want him to stay. You're on the verge of being Quite A Lot."

Merlin was still a few steps behind the two of them, and Morgana threw a look back to him, smiling wide. He swore he could see every gleaming white tooth in her mouth. He remembered a Morgana who would stop at nothing to win, who betrayed him and Arthur. The last time they'd seen each other had been on the incline leading to the caves.

"Morgana, you swear it: I'll find Arthur's salvation here?" Merlin had been half mad with grief, his king laid empty eyed and hollowed out in the fields of battle, a testament to Merlin's own failure. He'd walked without purpose, stumbling through rocks and dirt, and found himself at the mouth of a deep hold carved into the hill, only to turn back and see his former student, now enemy, steps behind him. Her hair flew in the wind, framing her face and making her look as if on fire. Her armor was stained-rust colored. "Go in and save your master," she'd said.

"You've been friend and foe, Morgana; how can I trust you? After all this?" He gripped his staff, his mind working at spells in case this went wrong.

"I am not sorry for telling Mordred of Arthur's weaknesses; I am not sorry for taking what I needed to grow. I am not sorry that you were unready for what I would become. Power is a necessary currency; you taught me that." He made to interrupt her, Merlin recalled now. But he had stopped short at the flash of frustration on her face. "But I swear, on the lady herself, you'll find what you need for Arthur and for Avalon within the caves."

Something in her tone made Merlin trust her again—not magic, but desperation. She had looked so certain, and her oft-flashing eyes were pleading, her face pale with worry. So he'd walked inside to find himself stuck inside a shimmering cage. He'd walked inside and abandoned his king.

That same voice broke into his memory with new words now, bringing him back into the present.

"He knows I don't mean anything by it, don't you, Emrys?"

Merlin gave her a short nod, not trusting himself to speak. He could still feel her tendrils in his jaw, inching their way along the roof of his mouth, binding around his tongue.

Arjun didn't bother turning to confirm whether or not Merlin cared, instead making a sudden veer to the right into some kind of shop, Morgana quick on his heels. Neither waited for him to follow; he could see them join the queue through the glass of the door. Merlin had passed a few of these places in his travels to London but hadn't gone in, not having anything to his name in the way of payment. But where his king went, he followed. He took a deep breath and pulled on the handle.

"I'm getting a chai tea." Morgana's voice sounded normal again, no magic laced into her words.

"Morgan, I'm going to murder you." Arjun ran a palm over his face, clearly exasperated. She laughed in response.

Merlin still had to get used to playful banter taking the form of idle threats.

"What's so funny?" he asked, standing behind them, keeping a careful distance.

"Morgan knows that chai means tea in Hindi, so what she's asking for is, effectively, a tea tea. And it's stupid. And she knows it irritates me."

Hindi, Merlin thought. The sound of it echoed a long-lost language of his past. A land he never visited, but he remembered stories of it told around a campfire. Sitting at a nurse's lap, maybe.

"Ah, funny." He cracked a wry grin. "I think I'm starting to see how this relationship works." Empty words to maintain a careless facade. His mind was racing, trying to connect the pieces of the Morgana he knew with the one he saw here. What was her goal? Why was she with Arthur?

Arjun looked at him sidelong, and Merlin saw his high forehead, strong nose, and full lips in profile. A weak chin, though. So unlike the Arthur he remembered, except for something in how he held his head. How he lived his height. Then he started speaking and broke Merlin's focus on his features.

"I don't know how much I like the sound of that, new friend."

At that Merlin laughed. That *was* like Arthur. Cautious but amiable. Morgana had already moved ahead to ask the woman at the counter for her tea. "So, a forest? A cave, you said?" Arjun's mouth was turned up at the corners, but Merlin could see a wariness in the small lines around his eyes, in the slight furrow of his brow.

"Weird, I think I also said."

"Fair enough," Arjun responded, and looked toward the counter as someone called for the next customer. His king letting something go so quickly was new. Or, perhaps as Arjun he'd learned patience.

"Emrys, I picked you up a chai as well. A gift for our new tagalong." Morgana had come up behind Merlin, and before he could blink he found a drink shoved into his right hand and a vise grip on his left wrist. "Come on, let's find a table and sit while Arjun waits for his special coffee that will take forever for the poor staff to prepare." As she spoke, Merlin heard an exclamation from behind the counter. Someone had spilled an entire gallon of milk.

He let her pull him toward an empty table tucked into a corner. He dropped himself into the chair closer to the door, ready to bolt if anything went wrong. He knew who Arthur was now; he could trail from a distance if he had to. He wouldn't trust Morgana so easily again.

She gracefully settled into the seat opposite and took a sip from her cup before saying anything.

"Merlin."

He saw no reason to dissemble. "Morgana," he replied.

She leaned forward, hunger in her gaze.

"You do remember! I knew it. When did you get back, where did you come from, how did you find him? Us?"

He was surprised that he didn't feel the current of her words. There was no spell this time. He wondered again at her reasons for being here. At her lack of anger. She'd been so angry. He saw her again, in his memory, hands raised and face red in the moonlight: *Will you not consider the place of a woman at the Table, Merlin?*

He came back to the present.

"You're not going to compel me for the truth?" He raised an eyebrow. "That's unlike you."

"Well, now I know you know, and I'm here to help Arthur, Merlin. This time . . . this world, it needs him. There is so much pain here."

"And there wasn't then?"

Her eyes flashed, and it was as if it had been only minutes, not centuries, since they last met. Even with the betrayals, and suspicions, after a month of being on his own, he had to admit it was refreshing.

"There's more potential for good here, now, than there was then."

She'd wanted to be good then, too.

"Our history would recommend I practice caution with you, Morgana. Tell me of your life here, of your intentions, of your . . . friendship with Arthur." The word tasted strange in this context. Friendship? Between Arthur and Morgana? It had been there in the beginning, maybe. She paused, staring at nothing behind Merlin, then straightened her back and steeled her shoulders before answering.

"I remember pain, and dying, and then I woke up and I was five years old again. But with the memories of a woman grown." She refocused on his face then. "Do you know what that's like? I had no agency, Merlin. Again. Just stuck in this small body, lying on the side of some country road, hoping someone safe would find me. But her Lady Universe provides, and funnily enough, it was Arjun's family that came across me that day." Her eyes softened in remembrance. Merlin was taken aback at the uncharacteristic openness of this woman he no longer knew. Need had called for her to be guarded, when he knew her last. Softness was weak. "He's my brother," she continued, hands clasped around her cup. Her lips turned up in a soft smile. "More so now than he was. We didn't have the chance then, to grow side by side. But here and now? We're in it together."

"You understand that I'm hesitant to believe you."

"I do."

"Then—"

"Finally." Before he could continue, Arjun's deep timbre broke through his thoughts, partnered by a hand on his shoulder. A thumb grazed the point where Merlin's neck met his shoulder, and Merlin was pulled behind a smoky haze in his own mind. He forgot. His skin tingled like he'd been touched by lightning, and Emrys felt whole and safe.

"God, that took ages. They spilled the milk, then the bottom of the coffee bag fell out, and then poor Kady got scalding-hot coffee all down her front. They are not having a good day."

Emrys was aware that someone named Arjun was speaking and that a girl named Morgan sat across from him. There was something about Arjun that called to him. Something about Morgan that felt right. Emrys was lucky to have found these two. That he knew.

"How's the chai, Emrys? Isn't it so good? Almost as good as my mum makes it. I swear."

Arjun's hand pulled away as he moved to settle into the seat next to Emrys, and Merlin startled back to the front of his consciousness and took a deep breath.

"He hasn't tried it yet, too busy talking my ear off." Morgana laughed, stealing Arjun's attention for a second.

Merlin's skin burned where Arthur had touched him. He needed to understand who this Emrys was, and why he was connected to Arjun, and why Merlin was being taken. He had just found Arthur; he had been given another chance by the grace of God to build Avalon. He would not lose. He recentered his self and rejoined the conversation.

"Okay, let's see what all the fuss is about." Merlin brought the cup to his lips and took a small sip. Flavors and spices he'd only heard tales of danced across his tongue, and despite the worry bubbling within him, he found himself letting out an appreciative sigh. He did enjoy this time.

Later, after a short time of sitting in the company of this new king and listening to the siblings bicker, Merlin noticed

Arjun looking at his watch. It was time to part ways. Merlin followed Arjun and Morgana out of the shop.

"Emrys, we have to head back to ours. . . . Do you . . . have somewhere to stay?" Arjun's voice lilted up at the end, eyeing Merlin's worn pack and dirty boots.

"I'm sure he's fine, Arjun." Morgana tucked her arm into the crook of her brother's elbow, leveling Merlin with a stare. He heard her promises to speak later as clear as if she'd said them out loud.

"No, I am well housed and cared for, Ar—Arjun. But thank you for asking." The response was a lie, but his gratitude was real.

"All right. Well, here's our address and a phone number. . . ." Arjun shoved a torn piece of paper in Merlin's direction. He reached for it and noticed that Arjun was careful not to graze his fingers when the paper passed between them. Merlin again considered how much Arjun understood and what he felt when they touched. He pushed the chit down into his pocket, gave them both a short nod, pulled his pack onto his shoulder, and turned away.

After walking a few meters, he glanced backward once, to see if Arjun stood watching. But they'd both started in the other direction by then, their forms growing smaller and quickly lost in the crowd. He looked back and forth before reversing his direction to follow his liege into the chaos.

Chaos was a good word to describe London. It was a cacophony of sounds and smells and sights completely foreign to him. There was virtually nothing left of the land in his memories. This London may as well have been an entire world in and of itself. He increased his pace, sending a good thought to the Maker behind his transformation, thankful for his young legs. Arjun's broad shoulders came into view again, and Morgana's russet hair.

They walked toward a set of stairs that went underground, to what these Londoners called the *tube*. Not entirely what he pictured when he thought of the word. Merlin laughed softly; the absurdity of his situation was not lost on him. Once he'd thought himself wise and well traveled. Cosmopolitan. Cities, ha! What did he know of cities?

Arjun and Morgana had tapped their way through mechanical, or electric, gates. He wasn't sure of how the things worked. Merlin shook his head, clearing it of distractions. How was he going to get past the barrier without any coins or special cards? He watched two more people walk through and into the station. It was, perhaps, time to test his active magic. He'd been wary.

No, he'd been afraid. But if his reacquaintance with Morgana had done anything, it had ignited that steady flame for experience and knowledge he held in his heart. He'd allowed passivity to reign for too long while he'd been awake, limiting himself to small charms and easy accidents. He looked at the gate again, imagining he could see vibrations of amber in the air around it.

Open, he thought. *Open for me.*

A sliver of something pushed past his lips and into the air. His words twisted brokenly toward those orange and gold tendrils, entwining and pulling them outward. The gate shuddered once. Merlin's breath hitched, and he felt wetness as a drop of sweat trailed down his back. Open, he breathed out once more, and the spell took hold.

The doors slid apart, and with his heart pounding, he vaulted through. He could spy the top of Arjun's head above the crowds moving in the direction of the southbound entrance, leagues ahead of him. It was too late; he wouldn't catch them now.

So he stopped and whispered another word: "*Follow*." He felt it bend this way and that, before it found the curve of Arjun's ear and settled there. Merlin pulled away from the crowd and leaned against a wall, breathing heavily. It would have to be enough.

That night, Merlin slept in a park and dreamed of Morgana. They were in his rooms, and he was hunched over his desk, scribbling notes on strategy and thoughts to give to Arthur. He wasn't paying her any heed until she yanked the rough hide he'd been writing on out from under his hands.

"Merlin," she hissed. He'd been tiring of her snide comments and vicious curses of late. "Let me come to your meeting with Arthur tomorrow. I can help."

Merlin pinched the bridge of his nose and sighed. Again, she asked for what he couldn't give.

"Morgana, you know what your presence will do there. You know the weakness it will imply to have a woman whispering advice into the king's ear. You want too much, my friend."

"You think your king doesn't know of our *partnership*?" She spat out the word as though it left an ill taste on her tongue.

At this, Merlin's hackles rose. How dare she, to whom he'd given the world, be angry with him?

"I gave you knowledge, Morgana, and friendship. I shared the dream of Avalon with you. And it is not enough? How much do you need?"

"You did give me knowledge and friendship. And in doing so, you showed me that I could be equal. Should I deny that now? Should I pretend to be a simpering child, waiting only for marriage and babies? Should I find myself in someone's bed, like the men and women who come to you, to be used and left behind? Or should I own my position, use what you have taught me to be more than what they expect of me? Will you not consider the place of a woman at the Table, Merlin?"

The fight went out of her face as if driven off by a sudden realization of futility, and Morgana folded into a chair.

"Always I must hide in the shadows, weaving and spinning plots for you, but will my voice never be heard by men? Only here, in your bleak tower, hooded and alone? Unable to use my full talents?"

"You do this for Camelot, and for Avalon, Morgana. Not for me."

She shut her eyes and leaned her head back.

"They are all one and the same to me, Merlin."

When Merlin woke, he was surprised to feel a damp path of tears on his cheeks. He hadn't known it then, but that moment had been a crossroads. That was when they'd lost her.

Three days passed before Merlin saw Arthur again. He'd felt his spell, usually somewhere to the south of him, still sitting softly on Arthur's person, moving in his direction. There'd been no word from Morgana. It troubled him. He couldn't get that dream out of his head. But it was a clear, cool night in the center of London, and Merlin was lying on a bench in a public square. He was toying with the rough edge of the king's note in his pocket.

He slept out of doors more often than not these days, and it was as he liked it—noise and congestion and all. There was a security in discord; silence was too heavy. He spent his daylights strengthening his spellwork, and now a living mask encompassed his whole body, stopping passersby from taking that which was not theirs.

The word he'd left on Arthur was close now. He turned his head to the left and stared out at the late-night crowds, weaving unsteadily toward their homes like one giant, drunken ocean of humanity. Arjun came into view a few moments later, glassy eyed, with his head knocked toward a young man walking next to him.

"You absolute tit, Arjun. That guy was asking for your number and you directed him to the loo. What is wrong with you?"

"He thought my name was Vinay and that we'd gone to school together. I don't care how hot you are if you can't tell brown people apart, John." But Arjun wasn't paying attention to John. Merlin watched as Arjun's gaze narrowed before he stalled a few feet away from Merlin and eyed the bench warily. Merlin knew that what Arjun saw was a vague, dark form huddled against the wood. A form that would make him feel anxious. Nervous. One that should repel him.

Instead, he stared at Merlin. "Emrys, is that you?"

"Uh, Arjun, mate, leave the lump on the bench alone, would you?"

"No, I think it's someone I know."

Merlin shook off the spell and sat up. He wondered again about how much Arthur knew in the recesses of his mind. How much he recognized. How else had he seen through Merlin's magic?

"Hello, Arjun."

"This is what you meant by 'well housed and cared for'?" Arjun gestured at the seat, disbelief etched across his features. Merlin half shrugged in response.

"What can I say except that the world's an excellent home. I manage."

"Can I ask what is going on?" Arjun's friend had moved and positioned himself in between Merlin and Arthur. Merlin was pleased to see loyalty but irritated at the intrusion. It was as if nothing had changed. Gawain and Percival, filling Arthur's head with nonsense. Itching at Arthur's heels during every lecture, interrupting his education. Arthur's knights but his friends, too. Young men who would die for their king but young all the same, not yet studied in the way of temperance, of understanding their own mortality.

Then Arjun lightly pushed the man aside.

"Nothing, John. He's a friend. How about you head on, and I'll ring you tomorrow?"

The man, John, took a few steps back, weighing the situation. He stared at Merlin, jaw clenched with clear distrust. But then his stance slackened, and he turned back to Arjun.

"If . . . you're sure."

Arjun spoke again, eyes never leaving Merlin's face. "I'm sure." A dismissal so clear in those two words that Merlin very nearly laughed out loud. How could anyone not see how royal this man was? Arthur didn't look to see if John was listening, if John had left. There was just an assurance reflected in every inch of him, that he would be listened to.

He moved to sit next to Merlin, the rough fabric of his sleeve grazing Merlin's hand as he sat. He rested his palms on his knees and stared straight ahead, waiting a moment before speaking again. Merlin was content to sit next to his liege.

"You should come to ours, Emrys. You can't sleep outside like this. It's not right."

"Should we ask Morgan—" He stumbled a bit, leaving off the last syllable. "I don't want to impose, Arjun."

"She's been off on a nature hike, actually. I've got the place to myself."

Arjun suddenly turned his head. His eyes were black in the low light of the square. "I've dreamed of you, Emrys, and it's unnerving me. It's as if you know me. You stand in my head and tell me what to do. But . . . you're not you and I'm not me." An uncharacteristic hesitation bit into his speech. Merlin stayed his own tongue and waited for Arjun to finish his thought. "You're important, I'm important. And I don't know why I know that. But I do?" His voice went up at the end, in a question.

Arthur was remembering something. That was important. But how? And why?

Merlin knew that he needed to decide what to tell Arthur, and in what way. He also knew that now was not the time. He didn't have the language yet. Or the understanding. Something had opened his eyes and had brought him back to try again. To make up for the last time.

Nothing had prepared Merlin for hearing the scream rent from Arthur's throat when Mordred had stabbed him from behind. It was a sound of sheer agony, and one that Merlin had tried to tamp down into the recesses of his deepest thoughts. It was heartbreak given form. Merlin was the one who told Arthur to go that day, to fight the men coming for his power. He was the one who planned it all.

And now his king was looking to him for answers again.

He resisted the urge to use magic to make this easier: to push Arthur's questions to the back of his head, where they wouldn't trouble him. It was too intrusive, and Merlin had learned his lesson there. He'd orchestrated, and he'd schemed, and he'd ended up imprisoned. But that was then. Now was different. It had to be.

"If your question concerns fate, would that I could give you answers. But know that I also think we're connected, Arjun."

Arjun's name left his lips, and unthinking, Merlin took his pale hand and placed it over Arjun's brown one, still resting on his knee.

Merlin became Emrys. Arjun was next to him and looking into his eyes, and Emrys found himself tethered. Arjun's skin was warm under his palm. He looked at their hands and pressed down, just the slightest pressure, to confirm that this was all real.

"Emrys?"

Emrys answered without looking up.

"Yes?"

"Come on, let's head back to mine." Arjun flipped his hand, wrapped his fingers loosely around Emrys's, and pulled him up alongside. There wasn't much that Emrys knew, and while that thought should frighten him, it didn't. He was calm because he and this man were connected. And that was enough because it would lead to more. Everything in him was sure of it.

"Okay."

Arjun didn't let go of his hand.

Merlin woke, disoriented. He was in a bed, covered by a heavy, warm blanket. A soft pillow under his head. The room around him had yellow walls, an open window, and more books than he'd seen in his entire lifetime. But he had no recollection of how he'd arrived in such a place. He only remembered Arthur. He remembered not remembering. He was terrified and confused, and he hated being confused. This was not him.

"Good morning, Merlin." Morgana's voice broke through his thoughts. "I thought we were going to meet elsewhere.

Arjun thinks you're homeless and wants to help you. I think his instincts are screaming at him." She was sitting in a chair next to the bed. It was a strange comfort finding her there. And how concerning was that, that he'd come to find Morgana a comfort?

"I—Arthur . . . he—"

"Arjun," she interrupted.

"Yes, of course." He felt uneven; he needed to find his footing. Unequal standing was never a safe space with Morgana. "Arjun brought me. He found me. Sleeping outside."

"Merlin." Again, he felt the spells slipping into his ears and into his mouth, coating his tongue. "What are you hiding?"

She was sitting casually, her spine curved against the back of her chair, girlishly tucking a lock of hair behind her ear. She looked so damned young.

Merlin rolled his shoulders. He sucked in his cheeks between his molars and bit down. Blood cut through the compulsion.

"Morgana, please. No magic. I'll tell you, but we must act as equals in this. For him."

She leaned forward at that, smiling sharply, encroaching into his space. His dream, that recent trespasser, came back to him full force. He remembered teaching her how to make up for the ridiculous power imbalance between men and women. How to use her body for more than what anyone thought she was worth. How to unsettle. He remembered holding her back when she became too good at it.

He willed himself not to move.

"Equal? Such words you choose, Merlin. But no matter. Okay. Then tell me."

"I don't remember."

She scoffed, and he saw the old Morgana, in the angry curl of her upper lip. He hastened to speak further before any more of her returned.

"I don't. Morgana, something is happening when Ar- Arjun comes near me. I . . . forget. I become something else, or something else becomes me." He balled his fists into the coverlet, and his shoulders were tight, up against his neck. An unsteady stream of air pushed its way out of his nose, and he gulped a deep breath back in through his mouth. "I don't understand it, whatever is happening to me. We were sitting together. I put my hand on his. That is all."

He closed his eyes and reversed his breathing. Deep breaths in through his nose and out through lips. Once, twice, three times. Morgana's eyes caught his; she straightened her back and lifted her chin.

"Years ago, I wanted to give Arthur what I thought he needed to succeed, and you stopped me. You chose that, and while my actions are my own, your choice set me on a path to becoming his enemy. I think you have a new choice to make, Merlin. I think that he needs you." She paused and brought her hand up to graze his cheek, then continued: "But I don't know if he needs you or if he needs who you might become." She looked like she had that day in front of the caves: frus- trated but sure. Desperate but clearheaded.

But if what she was saying was true, then that would mean—

"I'd be gone." Losing his decades of memories, his experi- ence. Losing the essence of who he was.

"Yes. A version of you, at least. As you were, as I know you. But—"

But to stay with Arthur . . .

Morgana offered him nothing except a stone-steady stare.

"You would remember, though."

"I believe so, yes."

"Why." He whispered the spell before he thought not to. It shot from his veins, through his heart, his throat, his teeth and lips, straight into her mind. A trickle of blood found its way from her ear and down the slope of her neck. Sweat dripped down his face and into his eyes. He lifted a hand to—he wasn't sure. Stop the bleeding? Stop her breathing?

"Enough." Morgana spoke, and he was done. His hand dropped back onto the bed, and he sagged against the pillows. "As you said, no magic—I will be honest with you, Merlin."

"I'm sorry, Morgana. I'm not used to such ignorance." His face scrunched in anger, and he threw his skull back against the headboard with a soft *thunk*. "My entire reason for being is knowledge."

Morgana's eyes softened. A small sigh escaped her.

"I know that better than most, Merlin. I do. But I also think this is what her lady wants. I think this is the best way we can help him to become who this world needs. With you and without you."

"And what does that mean for the me that is here?"

"It means that maybe Arjun needs more than what you're able to give."

Merlin turned his head away, toward those bright yellow walls, unwilling to let her see the fear in his gaze.

The right knob twisted, and cold water poured out from the spigot above the porcelain cistern. There were so many incredible things in this time, and Merlin had to admit he was tired of his own sense of astonishment. He was exhausted by the shiny and new. He wanted the familiar, he wanted homespun clothing, he wanted dirt floors, and bright and clean forests. He wanted a world where he knew things. He looked into the glass above the sink and was again struck by the dissonance his own reflection inspired.

It was him. It was not him. He found himself hating this sheep in his skin.

"Leave me be. Let me help, let *me* help." He bit out the words as if they wouldn't just bounce back into his own head. As if they would have any effect on his mirrored face.

He cupped his hands under the running water and ducked, closing his eyes against the splash. What was he going to do?

"Emrys!" Arjun's voice filtered through the door, dampened by distance. "Emrys, I've brought breakfast!"

Well, food was a worthy first step. He pulled the towel hanging from a hook and dried his face before moving to meet Arjun in the kitchen. His king was sitting at a table, fighting with a clear plastic packet. How very regal, Merlin thought, bitterness soaking into his love of Arthur.

"Good morning, mate! I wasn't sure what you liked, so I picked us up some Continental stylings." He punctuated this by gesturing to a feast sitting next to their stove.

Merlin's bitterness eased a bit as he took in the sight of a pile of pastries on the counter.

"Thank you, Arjun."

Merlin looked at Arjun-who-was-Arthur, back straight, biting into finely powdered bread. All right. If Merlin was to be someone else, he wanted to know what that meant. As he walked by, he put a hand on Arjun's shoulder as if in gratitude, and then Emrys let his hand linger just a moment before turning to pick up a muffin.

"You're welcome. I can't have you starving yourself because you think the world will provide, or whatever nonsense it is that got into your head." Arjun's teeth showed as he smiled. "It's possible I'm bribing you to stay."

Emrys let his own smile answer back. He was happy being here. He was happy seeing Morgan, who had just come through the door. He was meant to be here.

"Arjun! I found a strange man in my bed this morning, and I was under the impression we agreed to clear guests with each other."

Morgan shot a look at Emrys, and the word *remember* flitted through his thoughts and he was Merlin again.

He started, dropping his breakfast onto the floor. Gods. This could not be sustained. How could his erasure be the answer? What cruelty . . .

"Sorry! Apologies. I'll just clean that up." He waved away Morgana's and Arjun's attempts to help. He knew he needed to leave and consider his options. He dusted his hands over the rubbish bin and let Morgana's and Arjun's chatter wash over him. He just needed space. A breath.

"Hey, Emrys—" Arjun interrupted Merlin's anxious thoughts. He was already standing, with a bag strapped to his back. "I've got to go to work, but Morgan's going to be around the flat today. Why don't you stay with her? We can have dinner tonight."

"That sounds perfect." Merlin had no intention of being here when Arjun returned, but he could give him hope at least. For the day. Arjun nodded once, waved goodbye to Morgana, and headed out the door. "See you later!" floated in his wake.

"You're leaving, aren't you? On some quest of self-reflection?" Morgana let loose her irritation before the sound of a closed door had even made it to Merlin's ears. "At least take some food with you, you stupid man." Morgana pulled out a small bag, procured from a cubby near the table, and started filling it with fruit and bread and packages from their cabinets.

"Why am I stupid? Because I don't want to lose my whole self, because I want to continue to be me?" That acrid taste had returned full force in the back of his throat.

"Because you think it matters more than Arjun—Arthur, Merlin. Because you promised to give that whole self to him to make him king and then you promised to do so again and again, however many ages it took to return that title to him."

He remembered promising those exact words, once. But what proof was there, then, that there would be more changes, more ages? He'd expected victory in his time. And what did Morgana know of ages? Was she imprisoned? No, she died and then woke. She had no memories of empty years, with only his own failures for company, before succumbing to seemingly endless sleep.

"And if our situation were reversed, Morgana. What then?"

"Then I would forget." She said this simply, with no bravado, nothing false in her tone. She believed it.

"That's easily said when it's not truly you who has to face it."

Morgana's face took on a strange look. She was quiet for a long stretch of time—considering what truths she would give him, he knew.

"Merlin, there was a time before you knew Arthur, and you evolved and grew with him. Maybe that's what we need."

Merlin thought of his grandmother again. *Great change,* she'd said. No, he hadn't grown with Arthur; he'd grown toward Arthur.

"Then what was the point of it all?" Merlin couldn't help the emotion that came through in his question. He wished he could take it back. He wished he couldn't see the pity on Morgana's face. Who knew there were things worse than anger that a sorceress could throw at you?

"Perhaps now . . . the point is that you must prove you're worthy in a way you never had to do back then. That your past sacrifice was not such a big sacrifice after all."

Merlin was momentarily silenced. Not a sacrifice? His whole life had been in service of Arthur's ascension. Every step he'd taken, from the moment he'd learned of the prophecy, the moment he'd learned of the man meant to lead them all to Avalon, everything was for Arthur.

"Consider it, Merlin." She held out the pack to him as if in consolation.

Consider it. She was using magic, and the words were wriggling into the folds of his brain. It was infuriating. He felt safe in the familiarity of this anger. How dare she, Morgana, work her small spells on Merlin? He'd heard the tales, he knew how his reputation had survived. He was the most famous philosopher, conjurer, of all time. Who was Morgana but a footnote in his story?

He would not consider this. Damn her spell. Merlin stormed by her, ignoring her outstretched arm, and flung himself out the door.

All told, Merlin spent seven days away from the Pendragon. He walked the streets of London; he lived in his moments. He didn't consider. Not once. He just moved forward in time, like the rest of the world. His anger toward Morgana had not yet dissipated. His love for Arthur was as strong as it had ever been. He didn't know what to do with these contradictory truths. And so he closed his mind's eye and went minute by minute through each day.

It was freeing.

The strength of his spells waxed and waned, with no clear cause. He took it as it was, using his magic when able, and found creative solutions to his problems when he could not.

It was the evening of his seventh day. Magic weighed heavily in his muscles, and using it was like pulling teeth with no wine to dull the senses. He was sitting on the ground in an alley, back against a building, when Arjun found him. His tiny tracking spell had long since gone dormant, likely found and discarded by Morgana, so he didn't notice for a moment that Arjun was settling into place beside him.

"Emrys, why did you leave?" There was such a heavy disappointment laced into his name that Merlin didn't know how to respond. Arjun waited, perhaps to see if Merlin would speak, but continued when he was met with silence. "Morgan said you disappeared, that we scared you off. I said that was ridiculous, because in what world would you be scared? She laughed at me. I think she knows something I don't, and I think that something is why you left."

Merlin stared resolutely at the ground. He was convinced that if he looked into Arjun's face, that if those eyes looked into his, he'd be lost.

"Arjun, you can't know. You're not ready, I'm not ready. We're the two of us circles within circles." Merlin was most secure when he spoke in riddles.

"Intersecting circles, maybe?"

Merlin could hear the forced grin in Arjun's voice. Instead of being pulled into Arjun's ploy to lighten the mood, Merlin scrubbed a hand through his hair and bit out his thoughts. "Why are you here? You barely know me. Really think about it, Arjun. Why are you here?"

Merlin had done it: he'd let old habits rise, and magic flew from his mouth into Arjun's ears. Merlin still couldn't stand to look at his king, but he listened when he spoke.

"Because I do know you, Emrys. I know you're going to help me with something I'm meant to do. Something big. I don't know what it is, but I know it will matter. Somewhere inside, I've always known that I was put on this Earth to do something important. To make the world better. And I know you'll help me, because I think you've helped me before. And I like you."

"Stop." Merlin was ashamed; he cut the spell off with a quick word. But it didn't work—Arjun kept speaking.

"I won't."

Merlin risked a look then and saw that he'd been mistaken: this was no spell. Arjun was speaking of his own accord.

"I won't stop." Arjun repeated. He took a breath and looked up at the sky. "You know, in my religion we believe in reincarnation. That souls travel through bodies until they've achieved balance. It sounds ridiculous." He let out a light laugh. "But somehow it seems less ridiculous when I'm near you. My future seems clearer when I'm near you."

Merlin could barely breathe. He stared back down at the ground.

"Please. Look at me." A finger touched the base of Merlin's chin and pushed softly up, and then Emrys was drowning in Arjun's irises. Brown and black in the setting sun.

Emrys spoke. "I don't know why I left. Something in me had to go. I'm not scared, but—"

"Cautious?" Arjun pulled his hand back and leaned his head against the wall. "We're connected, Emrys, you were right when you said it. That night."

There was another reason they were connected, Emrys knew, but he couldn't grasp it. It slipped this way and that, out of his head. And what did it matter, anyway, when he was sitting here with destiny in the looming darkness, surrounded by quiet. He gave up chasing it and leaned in to taste the truth on Arjun's lips instead.

This time when Merlin came to himself, he remembered it all. He was still in the alley, leaning against the wall. Arjun's body was flush to his, head fallen halfway between Merlin's shoulder and his chest. Black curls resting against his clavicle. He remembered the intimacy of equals, in stature and in knowledge.

Merlin brought his hand up and touched his own lips with light fingers. They were swollen and sensitive. He looked down at Arthur, disconcerted. Was this the part he was meant to play? Friend? More? What had happened to teacher? What had happened to the magician behind the scenes? Picking strategies, picking paths?

And who was he to have put his mouth on his king's? This was something he'd once relegated to trysts with men and women who would always come second to his work. It was no secret that he loved Arthur, and he knew he was attracted to Arjun—how could he not be? In their short time together, Arjun had shown himself to be kind and intelligent, taking pieces of what had made Arthur great and making them into something new. Something better. But what was the connection that this other man crowding his mind, this Emrys, had with him?

Was it something that could help Arthur? That would help him to become who he was meant to be?

Merlin felt out of context. He could remember Arjun, with his dark eyes and heavy stare, sitting quietly with him, his shoulder level with Merlin's own, he could feel the budding trust between them, two men ignorant of their futures and unsullied by their pasts, linked by an intensity of connection unlike any he'd known before. And he could remember Arjun's hands in his hair, his touch, his tongue, his teeth, the flutter of his eyelashes ghosting against Merlin's skin—but he also remembered Arthur at his table, head in hands and unsure of what road to take; he remembered advising his king, his friend, his pupil. He remembered that when Arthur had no words of his own to aid him, he always had Merlin's.

He dug his nails into his thighs.

He could not do this, not yet. He was not ready to make the decision. So Merlin did something he hadn't done since he was a boy. Merlin ran.

It took time to get back to his former prison. But there was so much time now, so much for him to take and keep and wind into his life. When he finally found the opening again, nestled deep in a wood, he felt far more tired and old than his body would have most believe.

He walked in; the walls still shone with the refracted light of thousands of crystal shards. Their warmth enveloped him. He sat cross-legged in the center of the floor, not quite as far in as the stone bed he'd slept on for nearly two millennia. He closed his eyes and breathed.

"Merlin."

"Morgana." He exhaled her name, and she appeared before him. Not the Morgan he'd met weeks earlier but Morgana, as he'd known her once. Tall and stately, her hair wild and down to her waist, held back from her face by a single gold wire. Her eyes were gray and clear. Her lip cruel.

"I see you made it home. Do you feel safe, friend?" Her voice sounded far away and tinged with fatigue.

"Is this taxing for you, Morgana? Perhaps you should rest. You sound tired."

"Ha. Glad to see your fear hasn't dulled your wit." She paused and her eyes widened, as if something in his face was telling her a truth he hadn't meant to let go. "Merlin, I don't want to fall into old habits despite what this visage may imply. I just want to help."

"Tell me true, then, what it would mean for me to be Emrys and kill Merlin."

"I can only tell you that this is not the first time. This is not death. Before you were Merlin, you were Myrddyn. Before Myrddyn, Ambrosius."

Merlin's stomach dropped. He had no memory of these names. No connection to them.

"To what purpose? What is gained by this? Have we . . . ?" He looked up at the lights around them. "Morgana, have we had this conversation before?"

"No, not that I remember. But I'm not sure I would." Her specter moved away, uncanny in the silence of its footsteps. "And it's not for us to say, Merlin! It's so the story can progress, every iteration of Arthur to get closer to Avalon."

"How do you know?"

"I don't, but I believe. Every change in your story, every change in his, in mine, is to be closer to where we need to be for our dream, Merlin."

Merlin sighed and lay back on the solid rock beneath him. He felt grounded by the nature all around. His soul, he knew, was tied to Arthur's—to Arjun's. How many times had he made this choice, to give it all up for his king? Arjun was the One True King. And that was his reason for being—not knowledge. Not experience.

"I've sent him to you, Merlin. I trust in him, and I trust in both of you together."

"I am sorry for the way it was then, Morgana."

"I know."

She flickered once. And was gone.

Merlin closed his eyes and brought his fingers up, ghosting them across his face.

From the forest, he heard a voice calling out, "Emrys!"

He considered, and Emrys decided.

FUTURE

A Shadow in Amber

Silvia Moreno-Garcia

But in her web she still delights
To weave the mirror's magic sights
    —Alfred, Lord Tennyson, "The Lady of Shalott" (1832)

The sun sets, red as blood, the smog helping paint the sky an unnatural shade of crimson, birthing a sickening beauty. From this distance, so high above, the beams of cars and the glimmer of buses become a river of silver and gold, quickly pulsing in the dusk. She can't hear the traffic rushing by; it's just a distant buzzing, drowned by the music in her apartment.

She likes it this way. Seven years she's spent on the top floor of this building and she has not missed the city outside, with its pollution and vile manners. They kidnap women in this city. They kidnap everyone, but the city seems to hunger most for the soft flesh of women. They march, sometimes, the women: far below in the streets demanding protection, asking that the violence cease, but it doesn't cease. It never does.

It's a river of corpses, below, between the silver and gold.

She could, it's true, go out with bodyguards or live in a distant country house, far from the turbulent dangers of the metropolis, but she has chosen to instead inhabit this nacreous tower with its concierge, its elevators, and the wall-to-wall screens that can project an infinity of views, from the forest to the ocean. She tends to orchids in delicate glass containers and she rests on a low bed of silken sheets, eating pomegranate seeds.

She exists in this hallowed abode of her own making. Everything in here—from the extravagant chandelier, which brings to mind dozens of tiny jellyfish suspended in the air, to the wine tucked away in the mirrored sideboard—has been picked by her, to accommodate her taste. She has cocooned herself. But once in a while a speck from the outside must be allowed into this inner sanctum. Once in a while Mr. Delgado comes by with his briefcase under his arm.

Today is one of those days and he shuffles in, a few droplets of water dripping from his plastic beige trench coat, smiling at her.

"Sorry I'm late," he says. "Traffic was a killer and then your building's security staff is quite thorough. They slowed me down."

"They get paid to be thorough."

"Well, but we know each other by now."

"Do we," she says, her voice flat.

She sips her wine—a bit of alcohol helps the process—but does not offer him a glass or smile back. She stands at the balcony's window and looks at the river of silver and gold while he opens the briefcase and arranges his equipment.

"There was a little mishap, I should say that. I know you wanted that opera, but the recording was damaged. So I brought other stuff."

She spins around. "I only want the performances at Bellas Artes, I've told you that."

"Yes, I know. That's why I brought alternatives."

She walks toward the glass table where his briefcase rests, where he's hooking up wires and metal plates, and stares at him. "Alternatives. I know the *stuff* you peddle. I will not partake in a cheap pornographic spectacle."

The city, aside from violence and grime, offers dubious pleasures. It's a city of shadows and crooked angles, of danger and simmering violence. The people who sell memories mostly deal in coarse moments. Furious fucking in a bathroom stall, or the more obscure delights of seeing a man being beaten to a pulp. Why would she pay for that?

"I wouldn't bring such content to you. There are art galleries here, a little theater—and *this*. Something very special: the beach." He holds up a tiny metal case the size of a fingernail.

"The beach." She grimaces. "Who do you think you're dealing with? Do I look like I have an interest in experiencing the joy of sunbathing in Mazatlán? Oh, let me guess: a spring break in Cancún with a trove of gringitas drinking a yard of tequila."

Delgado makes a placating motion with both hands. "It's nothing like that. When have I failed you?"

"Clearly you did: tonight."

"No. If you'll trust me just this once, I promise, you'll see it really isn't anything like that."

"Well, what is the memory exactly, then?" she asks.

"That's like me trying to tell you the color of an aria and you know it."

He's not wrong. To describe a memory is to do it an injustice. It can be broken down into the ingredients, but it's the taste that lingers. It's the taste that matters. There are memories and there are *memories*: some people simply don't imprint strongly onto the machine, and it's like watching a movie on a TV set with the picture scrambled.

True memory makers are valuable, as are worthwhile memories and the peddlers who can distinguish the prosaic from the refined. Delgado deals in the refined.

"If you don't like it, I'll give you three sessions free. How's that?" he says.

She eyes him skeptically. "Very well," she says, if only so he'll at least owe her a favor.

She lies down on the white couch, and he continues his preparations, connects the bits of the machine and attaches the electrodes. She stretches out her wrist, and the needle slides into her skin, delivering the proper agent, and her eyelids flicker.

The memory comes fast and furious. She is running, feet feverishly moving across the rocks, wind in her hair. Her body is young, the body of a man in his prime, lean and eager. The wind tugs at his hair and his hair is in his face and ahead of him only the sky, with the sun high, licking his skin.

I want to die like this, he thinks. *To die, diving into the sea.*

He leaps!

God, how he leaps; it shocks her. The strength of the legs, the muscles straining, and then the body falling, falling, quick as an arrow. He hits the water, slicing through it, and then the muscles are moving again, the body bobbing up as he emerges.

As he bursts through the surface, he laughs and looks up at the sharp cliff from which he just plummeted, and he throws back his head with such wild joy that she knows, in that instant, what it is like to live forever.

When she wakes back in her living room, blinking and staring at the ceiling, she has to take a minute to compose herself. She pays Delgado for his services, and he packs his suitcase and leaves.

Six days she waits. Six days is all she can take.

It was her mother who had loved opera, who played *Tosca* and *Carmen* for her as a child. The modern music of the world does not interest her, only these old things, these old songs that rise to the heavens. She loves when Maria Callas sings *Madama Butterfly* because it's different: it's not music, it's something else, undefinable. It goes through you like a sword, that music.

It'll break your heart, that moment when she says, "Tutto questo avverrà, te lo prometto." Nothing else is as exquisite as when she hits that note. Nothing else enraptures her; only those beautiful lamentations and the swelling of the strings.

She plays her music, and on the great screens she projects the images she enjoys, distant vistas of deserts or waterfalls that have nothing in common with the alleys piled high with trash or the rats spilling from sewers.

She checks her messages. There's one from a company inviting her to a holographic performance of Luciano Pavarotti. These days they can make anyone perform onstage, mimicking flesh and blood, from Elvis to the classical singers. But she won't have that; it is tacky. She prefers the memories, illegal and expensive, but much more enthralling if what one wants is to experience a performance.

"Play *Lucia di Lammermoor*, the Callas recording," she says, and the music fills the apartment. She shakes her head.

"No. Play 'L'amour est un oiseau rebelle,'" she orders, but as soon as the familiar voice begins to sing, her head is shaking again. "Switch to Mirella Freni. No, Joan Sutherland. No. Stop."

The apartment goes silent and she messages Delgado. It is the seventh day.

He arrives promptly, trailing water again. It's summer and the rains have inundated several of the subway stations. But what does it matter to her? It's just a story in the news, something she idly sees on her mobile device and swipes away.

He comes in bearing that scent of filthy water and mutters about protesters: Reforma was blocked from the *Diana* up to god knows where. He shakes his umbrella, runs a hand through his hair while she holds her glass of wine and eyes him skeptically.

"I brought several things. And another recording of the young man, like you said. So you have options."

He sounds false, as if he knows very well she did not even consider the other memories, that she meant to see only more of the young man. She sips her wine while he settles himself in, and when he is done, she sets the glass by the couch and lies down.

In slips the needle and in seeps the memory.

She's riding a motorcycle. The day is blazing hot and sweat trickles down her back. Traffic is heavy, but the motorcycle glides around the cars and he has few worries. Just the girl, the girl he loves and who doesn't love him back. For a moment his hands tighten around the motorcycle handlebars as he thinks about her.

So he dashes forward, speeding and turning a corner and letting thoughts drain from his mind, the rumble of the motorcycle and the noises of the city playing an orchestra as he conducts his strange dance.

He arrives at his destination and grabs the messenger bag. Because ultimately this is just an ordinary day for him, just another day of the traffic and the sun and the motorcycle, of amusing himself by seeing how fast he can get to a destination and break his previous record.

He walks into a building, and as he holds the door open for someone to step out, for one brief instant, she sees his face reflected on the surface of the glass.

He is a man of preposterous loveliness. Not handsome, but beautiful and lazily nonchalant in that beauty as he glances at his reflection. And if it were just that, if it were just beauty, she would shrug it off. But there's something beneath that beauty, in the dark eyes, the impression of an unknown abyss, of a stillness and a sadness in that stillness.

He's like the songs she likes to listen to; like the dramatic operas where singers throw themselves onstage and press their hands against their heart.

The memory ends shortly after that and she's on the couch. Delgado fusses around, taking her pulse, looking at her.

"How many fingers?" he asks.

She does not reply. He repeats the questions and she raises a hand, raises three fingers at him.

"You okay? Can you speak?"

"Yes. I . . . I didn't sleep well last night," she lies.

"Why didn't you say so? You know you're not supposed to plug in if you're tired."

"I'm just a little tired, not exhausted."

"Still. I'll have to stick around a bit longer, then, to make sure you've surfaced okay."

"I'm talking now, am I not?"

He shrugs, but he still lingers. It irritates her. She hired Delgado because he is reliable and careful. She'd heard stories of people who slipped into a memory and never slipped out because the technician was an idiot or the equipment was faulty. That is why she pays for the best. When you're dealing in illegal merchandise, don't go for the bargains.

But she doesn't want him to be here now; she doesn't want him to be careful and watchful and staring at her face. She's afraid the slightest gesture will give her away. It's the little things that always do. She sits up and twists a bit of hair around a finger that has escaped her chignon.

"Get me some water if you're going to be flapping around."

He does, returning with a glass, and she takes a sip. She does not look at him as she speaks. "What's he called?"

"Who?"

"The memory maker, who else?"

"It's confidential and I don't really know. People who work with me don't use their real names."

"You must call him something."

"You can call him Lancelot, if you want. I do."

"And who are you, Merlin?"

"Merlin is the guy who fell asleep in a cave and yet you're the one who's been sleeping. It wouldn't work."

"The sleeper has awoken, in any case, so *you* may go."

She hands him the glass.

By the sea he walks at night, the waves lapping at his toes, and there's the taste of salt on his lips and a sad smile like the waning moon. The girl he loves is married; married, in fact, to his best friend. It is a delicious agony to sit with them at dinner or to visit their home. To see her from afar and be unable to speak a word.

They've been drinking on the beach and now they walk, he and his small coterie of friends. Ahead of him goes the girl. Her husband has draped an arm around her shoulders. Lancelot walks a few paces behind them, stepping on the footprints she's left behind. Every few minutes she turns her head a little, she looks over her shoulder at the young man, her smile shy, like a fluttering butterfly.

So he keeps walking behind them, he keeps following her footsteps, while the sea roars and their friends prattle on.

When she rises from the memory, like foam upon the shore, she lets the warmth of his emotions rest in her chest, and she takes a deep breath. The glass chandelier on the ceiling catches a reflection, making her blink.

"Tell me his birthdate," she says, her mind still hazy, naked.

"I can't. It's personal information."

"Does it matter? It's not as if a single date would expose him."

Delgado shrugs, removes the electrodes, begins packing the equipment. "Still. There's an expectation of privacy."

"You're suddenly a stickler for details."

"Fine. How old are *you*?"

She turns her head and looks at him. "Are we trading information?"

"Maybe."

"Thirty-five."

"He's nearly fifteen years younger than you."

She drapes her left arm across her forehead and looks at the ceiling. She doesn't remember being that young; she can't recall what it was like to be twenty. Her youth was a mirage; it skimmed her body. She was born old and did not rue it.

"You don't look thirty-five," he adds, misjudging her.

"You don't need to flatter me. I'm no big-eyed waif any-more; I haven't been for a long time and I don't mind. I'm curious, that's all."

She extends her right arm so that he may check her pulse, then he asks her to sit up and flashes the light in her eyes.

"It's the zodiac; it's why I wanted to know. He strikes me as a Leo, but I could be wrong."

"You believe in that nonsense?"

"My mother had a natal chart made for me and I used to consult an astrologer religiously."

Delgado tucks away the flashlight. "Back when you were a big-eyed waif?"

It bored her, the stars and their houses. She gave it up. She has given many things up. The constant in her life, the long thread that ties it all together, is the music. The operas that chart her years like the rings on a tree. There, when she was thirteen, that was when she went to see *Onegin*, and then at twenty-one it was *Don Giovanni*.

"Back when the world was flat."

He chuckles at that. "I'm a Gemini, by the way. What does that say?"

"You should find yourself an astrologer and ask them, Mr. Delgado," she replies.

A memory of night swimming and a memory of the motor-cycle, also at night. But also a memory of smoking cigarettes, lying lazy, in bed, while in the apartment next door there is a party and the music makes the room vibrate, leaking through the wall. In a corner there's a canary in a cage.

On her gigantic video panel she projects vistas of the ocean and she plays *Atys*, and then she purchases another moment of the man's life.

She shakes her head and stretches her limbs on the couch, her toes pointing down. The texture of the fabric beneath her fingertips is soft as she thinks of the grit under his nails— sand, from the beach—and the beating of his heart, like a drum.

He is dying of love for that girl, and that love lingers on her palate. He kissed her tonight. One kiss. It tasted sweet, of innocence and wine—this despite the fact he was kissing a married woman. There was something soft and gentle to it. She supposes it's because he has never been in love before that this can be something fresh, something untainted by the tendrils of cynicism.

She doesn't remember her youth and she also doesn't remember love. She supposes they must come hand in hand. But just as she did not begrudge time for snatching away the years, she did not rail at the heavens for denying her affection. She might have had it, had she wanted it. She might have it still, if she wills it.

"My supplier can go to the opera again," Delgado says. "I know you wanted that performance."

"Not now," she says, and waves her hand, like one might wave away an annoying buzzard. *Let me be,* she thinks. *Let me be alone with him.*

But Delgado hums to himself as he goes about his tasks, tossing components into his briefcase, disturbing her.

He's humming "L'amour est un oiseau rebelle." It's a disgusting parody of the song.

"Can you be quiet?"

"I thought you liked opera."

"Not when you sing it."

"It can't be that bad. I may not be a tenor now, but I was once a choirboy."

What he was and what he is do not interest her. He is but an intermediary, a conduit.

She leans on her elbows and turns to look at him. "How did you find Lancelot?"

"Word of mouth. It's not like you can advertise for this type of gig. People tell other people, and the recording devices are so small that you can pretty much test it anywhere, and it doesn't have any side effects. Well, maybe a headache. But for the money, I think it's worth it."

She frowns. She doesn't wish to discover the specifics of how his trade works. It makes her wonder if the young man ever considers where his memories go, if while he lies in his bed, idly smoking a cigarette, he envisions her existence.

Not *her* existence in particular, but the idea of a phantasmagoric buyer, and whether, in those instants, his imagination might conjure an approximation of her.

She sees him but he does not see her. And what might it be like if he saw her? If his eye should intrude upon her home, taking in the orchids in their glass containers and the bed with silk sheets?

She feels shy, as if she should veil herself. As if the man has opened the curtains and peered into her bedroom.

"You ever leave this joint?" Delgado asks, and it makes her wince, the question striking close to what she was thinking. Has she become this transparent?

She smooths her features, like one might smooth a piece of cloth. "Why would I? There's nothing out there that interests me."

"You might go to the opera."

"The opera comes to me."

"Then you'll want something in the new season, a new performance. They'll have *Aida*. I can arrange for that."

"*Aida*?" she says quickly, thinking of the magnificent costumes and the pageantry. Such a huge chorus and orchestra, and the glory of its melody. "O terra addio." But she hesitates. "I didn't know."

"Yep. Quite the spectacle, they say."

"I didn't take you for an opera buff."

"I've learned a bit from listening to your recordings."

She doesn't know if he means the music that saturates her apartment or the memories of performances he has purchased for her.

"No, I don't think I'll go to the opera," she whispers, and sits, cross-legged, on the couch, thinking about the glittering night outside and the murmur of a sea she cannot hear.

Memories offer few insights into a person. They're so brief, after all. Only a few minutes can be embedded into the recording device—she can experience the Queen of the Night aria, but not the entirety of *The Magic Flute*. These imprints are not meant to last; they crumble if you try to hold them tight. Yet she feels she knows the man. It is as if each moment of his life that she has experienced is a stone from a mosaic, and when you arrange them together, they create a picture.

She knows the little drama that punctuates his existence, the affair with the girl, that one night—just one, they dared no more—and then the hushed whispers—*we cannot, we shouldn't*. How he avoids her now, how he walks the beach early in the morning, when the sun has barely warmed the shore, and tosses a shell back to the waves.

He loves and he feels so fiercely, it's like standing next to a crackling fire. One cannot help but be warmed by it. One cannot help but extend a hand and wish to touch the flame.

He hungers, and he's so *alive* it almost hurts, it almost makes her skin blister when she feels him; that manic yearning, grin spreading across his face and the smoke from his cigarette as he leans his head against the pillows and the canary chirps in its cage.

The feeling of him, sometimes it's just too much. It scares her. How can someone feel like this? How can such despair and passion be contained?

It's the most beautiful melody she's ever heard, wordless and perfect.

The days drag by when Delgado doesn't come, when he doesn't bring her memories. On the walls the ocean rolls in, offering the view of a sand spit, and around her the music plays, low.

I'm too busy, Delgado says. Not this Wednesday, no.

And she texts him back furiously, asking who he thinks he is.

But he really is busy Wednesday, he says.

Fine. When if not Wednesday?

The cursor blinks and blinks and he doesn't reply.

I'll sic the cops on you, you little shit, she thinks, and crushes a handful of pomegranate seeds in her fist, the juice like blood trickling through her fingers. But she doesn't type that. Instead she phones, and he picks up.

"Let me make it clear," she says. "We have an arrangement. I expect you to honor it."

"I'm not on your retainer."

"Is that what you want? Fine. Then you are now. What's your price?"

She hears him sigh; she can picture him rubbing his eyes and then the flapping of his hands as he considers the situation, as greed gets the best of him and he tells her an amount. "But I can't procure more memories from Lancelot," he adds.

He's lying. There's always more of anything if you can pay the price.

"Be here on Wednesday. You're on retainer now."

Delgado comes on Wednesday, his clothes rumpled, looking a little frazzled. He peels off his beige trench coat and hangs it from a hook. He eyes her carefully, like he's afraid she'll bite.

"As I tried to explain, Lancelot is not working with me anymore, but I have other suppliers you may like," he says as he sets down his briefcase.

"What do you mean, he's not working for you?"

"He isn't."

"I'll double the money," she says simply, taking a sip of her wine. This is his game. It's a simple case of increasing the markup.

"It's not about the money."

"I'll triple it."

She looks at him carefully. He scratches his head and gives her an embarrassed look. "Can't be done," he mutters.

"What do you mean, it can't be done? It's simple. Message him and say you'll triple the pay. He can't retire if we're talking this amount of cash."

"I can't."

"Then give me his address. I'll go see him myself."

She sets down her glass and crosses her arms. Delgado now stares at her with an irritating stubbornness that makes her chuckle.

"I can cut you out and find out where he lives on my own. I know enough from his memories to figure out where to look. His age and the fact he lives by the sea are two big clues. A private investigator would be able to find him, I'm sure."

"Please, don't look for him."

There's a hint of fear in his voice that makes her bristle, makes her press on even more vehemently. "And the girl's name. I know the girl's name. With that alone I'm certain—"

"He's dead," Delgado says, cutting her short, like swinging a sword.

She stares at him. "What do you mean, he's dead? I've seen his memories."

"Memories don't have an expiry date."

No. They don't. They're shadows trapped in amber, but she never thought . . . She simply assumed . . .

And it's as if all the lights in the apartment have gone dim, the chandelier with the glass jellyfish burnt black and the sweet music stopped. She sees nothing, hears nothing, for the span of a heartbeat.

"How long has he been dead?" she asks, her voice somehow level.

"Two months."

He'd died shortly after she'd met him, then. She'd communed with a ghost—like stretching out a hand and touching a black hole. That is what lies inside her body now: a thick blackness.

"You didn't say anything."

"I didn't think it would matter. Customers, they don't care where memories come from, they don't care who makes them. They just want the experience. I didn't think you'd care to have more than two, three of his memories. It wasn't even your style, you told me so yourself."

She doesn't reply. She has turned into a stone. She stares at him as he paces and mutters and tries to explain himself.

"How did he die?" she asks, interrupting him. "Did he drown? Was that it?"

Delgado seems a bit surprised by the question. "A robbery. He wouldn't part with his motorcycle."

She turns away from him and raises a hand to her mouth, two fingers brushing her lips, black bile coating her tongue. A robbery. Of all things. Prosaic and common and entirely unlike him.

He was supposed to live forever.

"You should go."

"Please—"

"I'll have security drag you out if you don't disappear in the next two minutes."

Delgado doesn't protest. He walks out and the door latches behind him.

She walks to the balcony. The sky is as black as her entrails, dyed with ink. The pollution veils the stars, and the clouds shroud the moon. All light comes from below or from the buildings across, spilling from behind curtains and blinds.

She could find his grave. It's as she told Delgado: it wouldn't be too difficult. And then, what? To haunt the places he knew, to trace his route along the seashore, to stand on that cliff and feel the rocks he stood upon and look down at the sea.

She could follow that river of silver and gold out of the city and search for his soul.

But for now she stands, poised against the night on the highest floor of her tower, contemplating the squat buildings and the dazzling skyscrapers, the neon signs and the trembling headlights, and she realizes that she does not even know his real name.

White Hempen Sleeves

Ken Liu

The ego bridge hums softly around me as though I'm nestled in a conch shell. I have the sensation of floating weightless in space in the midst of billions of stars—ghostly "glows" caused by the nanobots running up and down my nerves, trying to capture the cascading potentials that cohere into my self.

I'm thrumming with anticipation, with the thrill of stepping into the unknown for the first time. Will I *know*? Will I detect the moment my consciousness splits like a real fork? Will I sense time stop, my mind suspended like a questioning tentacle curved invitingly in the deep, bottomless ocean of oblivion?

I hate myself. The chances were fifty-fifty, and *I* lost the coin flip. Knowing you're about to die is hell. Even if the one who put you in hell is yourself. [Everybody dies. It's what you do before you die that matters.]

There's no glee in the voice, no palpable sense of relief. But that means nothing. I could have been suspended in time for hours, days, weeks, before being resleeved while my other self had plenty of time to whoop and celebrate his good luck.

I don't bother responding to myself, safely ensconced in Octavia, that jellyfish-like aerostat of decadence hovering fifty-five kilometers above me. Fighting against the dizziness of a resleeving, I look up, and all I see is a roiling sea of orange clouds. A faint perpetual twilight filters through them.

I look down and back at myself, the unfamiliar sensation of twisting my head 180 degrees overwhelmed by the alienness of my body, the sleeve I had selected for myself: a five-meter-long metal slitheroid shaped like an anaconda that roamed the forests of the Amazon from before the Fall, hardened and refurbished to survive long enough on the surface of Venus to accomplish the mission I gave myself.

[Get ready. This is going to hurt.]

Some switch seems to have been flipped in my mind, and I scream even though I don't have a voice.

It's hot, hot enough that I feel my skin blistering, boiling, peeling off, erupting like the volcanoes on Ishtar Terra.

But I don't have skin.

It feels like I'm being crushed from all sides by hydraulic presses, compressing my ribs, squeezing my chest cavity, flattening my lungs until they are thin as paper. The terror of not being able to breathe, a primitive fear, seizes my mind.

But I don't have ribs or a chest cavity or lungs. I don't need to breathe.

[The temperature at your location is 460 degrees Celsius, and the pressure is at ninety-three bars. I've recalibrated the sensors in your morph to give you the appropriate pain stimuli without immediately incapacitating you.]

You fucking bastard.

[This is to provide adequate motivation for you to seek

higher altitudes to cool off and to get some relief from the sensation of suffocation.]

I curse myself. Of course I'm right—my first instinct upon realizing that I was the one sent to die was to lie down where I was and go to sleep—we can't have that.

And so I begin my reluctant climb up Maxwell Montes, the tallest mountain on the surface of Venus, two kilometers taller than Mount Everest on Earth. My body slithers over the parched basalt, strewn with pebbles and sharp-edged rocks created by chemical erosion. It's easy to navigate: I'm always heading for higher ground, for that is the only direction that promises any relief from the crushing pressure and hellish heat.

The climb is slow going. With this much pressure, the carbon-dioxide-dominated atmosphere is technically no longer a gas or liquid but behaves as a supercritical fluid that is somewhere in between. I'm half swimming, half crawling. I can feel the heat and the pressure weaken the joints in my morph. I, no, *he*—I can't stand the idea that I'm the same person as that sadistic creep even though I am—has left me only one path.

Higher. Higher.

Finally, I'm through the supercritical fluid layer, and the air turns to a true gas through which I can move much faster. But far from feeling relief, the conditions around me have grown only more hellish. The wind howls around me at speeds never seen on Earth, threatening to topple me over—good thing that my slitheroid morph hugs the ground and has such a low center of gravity. Thunder booms, and lightning flashes above me between cloud layers, and sheets of sulfuric acid rain pelt my body. The sensors in my morph translate the sensation of sizzling acid into a new kind of pain.

[Keep moving!]

I do my best to keep the pain at bay and keep on climbing. My only hope is to get above the snow line before the acid dissolves some critical component of my body.

Yes, snow line. The temperature near the surface of Venus is hot enough to vaporize metals like lead and bismuth. But with enough altitude, the metallic mist precipitates out of the atmosphere like frost, coating the top of Maxwell Montes in a shiny reflective layer.

Finally, I emerge out of the clouds into an otherworldly snowscape. I take a moment to enjoy the cool and thin air (though it's still near 400 degrees Celsius and the pressure is still about half of the level at the surface). One of my eyes has failed, but the sight is still breathtaking: Maxwell Montes stands like an island above a sea of clouds, and the glinting snow is unmarred by any footprint. My body slithers over the ground, carving an endless sine wave through the snow. I've lost control over some of the segments due to damage from the heat and the acid, but now that I'm at the top of the mountain, the slitheroid morph should last long enough until a flyer can be sent down from the aerostat to pick me up.

I feel triumphant. Though I have been forced to do so, it is still an amazing accomplishment to have climbed a mountain taller than Mount Everest and on which no transhuman has ever set foot.

[I did it!]

The note of triumph in his voice enrages me. He's been sitting on his ass in comfort and safety, drifting in the balmy upper atmosphere of Venus where the temperature and pressure are practically Earthlike in a luxury aerostat while torturing me, his alter ego, like some subhuman infugee encased in a brazen bull. For him to claim this accomplishment as *his* is too much.

I *did it.*

[A bit vain, are we?]

You should be the one to talk.

[We're the same person, just placed in different circumstances.]

Not anymore.

[You'll feel differently after we merge.]

Get me up there, and I'll petition for an equitable division of our assets. I'm not merging back with you. No fucking way.

[I was afraid you might say that. Though to be fair, if our circumstances were reversed, I might feel the same.]

A coldness grips my heart. All I have to do is think about what I would do if our positions were reversed. My morph might be shaped like an anaconda, and Maxwell Montes might be the only feature on Venus named after a man rather than a woman or a goddess, but the biggest prick on Venus is clearly myself.

You're going to lose the XP from this entirely if you leave me here.

[Check the integrity of your morph.]

I realize that the damage has been more extensive than I thought. The seals and gaskets are engineered with worse tolerance than I—we—had designed ahead of time. I won't be able to survive indefinitely, even on the top of the mountain.

Of course he's changed the plan on me. He's going to leave me to die and then retrieve the cortical stack. It's what I would have done if my fork got disobedient. It's the damned pressure and heat. I'm not thinking things through.

I get the claws of my manipulators over my skull. If I can

get to the cyber brain, maybe I can threaten to hold it hostage and force him to scramble to save me.

[Tsk-tsk. How can you know so little of yourself?]

My manipulators bump into the bulge of the farcaster, and my heart goes cold.

Damn you!

And as the explosion cuts the power to my manipulators while activating the farcaster, everything slows down, goes dark, approaches that suspended moment in a sea of flashing stars.

Octavia's newest attraction is a theater—an old-fashioned theater that puts on real plays with real actors. It appears that transhumanity, like our human ancestors, still associates culture with age. Just like handmade clothes still fetch a premium over copies popping out of cornucopia machines, the theater charges admission prices many times the fee for the best XP casts, and still, it's hard to get tickets.

Arthur is opening tonight. I manage to get one of the best seats from the scalpers. I've just ended my marriage with Casey, and I might as well let myself be seen by the best society on Octavia, to let everyone know that I am once again available.

I mingle at the preshow cocktail hour. Beautiful morphs surround me, presenting in every gender and subtype of beauty, all of them young, all of them lovely, as plastinated and ageless as myself. I honestly can't recall the last time I saw a wrinkled face among the wealthy who live on Octavia. Our conversation, aided by our muses, flows as smoothly as the river of time. But all I feel is boredom, an unsatisfied yearning for authenticity.

It's a silly reaction, I know. All morphs now are equally fake in the sense that they are the result of Art rather than Nature. It's the ego that matters, only the ego.

But as I look into the eyes of each morph, there's no recognition of a kindred spirit, no sense of anyone who truly understands themselves. We're a society of twisted old cowardly souls hiding behind youthful masks, enacting a play for our own amusement. We do not understand what it means to take risks, to live with death.

An overwhelming sense of loneliness seizes me. I am the only real person in a world of dolls.

The light dims, and the actors take to the stage.

To my surprise, I find myself entranced by the play. The lack of audience participation and full sensory immersion—the way there would be in a vid or XP—somehow seems to enhance the experience. The novelty of the primitive format makes me sit up and pay attention, as do the crude, outdated emotions being portrayed.

Uther Pendragon stares at Igraine, and even without him saying anything, I understand what he's thinking. There is a fire in his eyes whose meaning is unmistakable, even though an invisible wall of millennia, of art and life, divides the ancient king and me.

Gorlois of Tintagel, Duke of Cornwall and husband to Lady Igraine, looks from the king to his wife and then back again. A dark light appears in his eyes, an explosive anger suppressed by the weight of loyalty and obligation.

The woman sitting next to me leans over and whispers, "He should have just ordered a pleasure pod constructed to her exact appearance. It would have saved everyone a lot of trouble."

I look at her. Her morph presents as someone in her early

twenties, but the twinkle in her eyes tell me that a much older ego lies within. It's a lovely morph, perfect features, flawless skin, silky hair, just on the edge of being a sylph without the sense of plastic falsity.

"You presume that the king desires the lady solely because of her morph," I say. "But what makes you think it isn't about her spirit, her ego?"

She cocks her head, a smile curving up the corners of her mouth. "You believe love isn't about the flesh?" A silvery pendant in the shape of a six-petaled flower dangling from a chain around her neck glitters in the light from the stage. My muse confirms my guess: the flower is a narcissus.

The flame of desire comes alight in me, stronger than it has been in a long time. It is a matter of instinct, an intuition of the authentic.

"I believe everything is experienced by the flesh," I say. "Love, fear, joy, suffering. But the flesh serves the will of the ego."

"A transubstantiation, then," she says. "The ego converts the experiences of the flesh into understanding. One cannot live without the other."

How right she is. How close to my own ruminations.

Lady Igraine laughs at some joke from her banquet companion and turns to glance at Uther Pendragon. She stops, her breath caught, and the lights shift until the other players, including Gorlois, her husband, fade into the darkness, leaving only the king and the lady at the center of the stage. The color of the lighting changes subtly until the lady's face glows like a ripe apple seen through a veil.

"Such glamour," I whisper. It is an effect more extraordinary than the sylphs sculpted by the best genetic artists.

She leans into my ear. "Do you know the root of the word

glamour?" Her breath lightly tickles my cheek, and for a moment I forget about Lady Igraine.

"It's *grammar*," I say. "In medieval times the word referred to any kind of arcane learning and secret knowledge."

"It's a spell," she says. "A spell the beloved casts over the lover." She puts her hand over mine, boldly, confidently. It is as if she knows exactly what I am thinking, can diagram my reactions like a beginner's composition. My desire grows more ardent.

"A spell of the ego," I say. "Through the flesh but not of it." She nods. "A secret knowledge that two people share. Lovers act as the mirrors for each other's souls. Perhaps when you love someone, you hear an echo of your ego."

In the ears of another, these words might have seemed slightly cynical, but I like their brutal honesty, a vision of love stripped of romance. As soon as I hear the metaphor, I realize that it has always lived in me, perhaps buried, waiting for this moment.

Onstage, Merlin waves his staff and Uther Pendragon spins in place. A mist rises and engulfs him. By the time the mist dissipates, the actor playing Gorlois is standing in his place. Merlin has placed a glamour on the king, made him take on the appearance of Lady Igraine's husband so that he can rape her by deceit, to possess her in her impregnable castle.

"It's a lovely resleeving," she says, "from the age of magic."

"A rather dirty trick," I say. "And I suppose there truly is nothing new under the sun."

Igraine comes to the door of her room and looks into the eyes of the man who appears as her husband. They embrace in a soul-searing kiss. "How can she not recognize her husband's ego?" I ask. "If she truly loves him, she will know the duke is but an impostor in her husband's sleeve."

"Perhaps she isn't truly deceived," she says. "Rather, she wants to make love to another ego through her husband's morph. What is the point of life except to gather more experiences and to understand yourself?" It's lovely to be with someone so in tune with you that she says what you have in mind just a moment before you do.

We make love in every way possible, with the aid of pleasure pods and simulspaces and mesh implants and old-fashioned physical toys. We mindfuck until pain is pleasure and pleasure is ecstasy. She knows exactly what I like and I can tell exactly what will turn her on.

We are made for each other. It's a cliché. That doesn't make it untrue.

I decide that I must do something I've never done with any of my lovers: I will let her peek beneath the mask. What is the point of life except to gather more experiences?

"Let me show you the source of my wealth," I tell her. Sure, working as a psychosurgeon on Octavia pays well, but not well enough to have all the experiences I crave.

"What exactly is it that you offer?" she asks. We are standing in an operating room at the back of my office: a suspended surgical platform, an ego bridge on its own separate power supply, an array of consoles and computers and top-of-the-line medical nanofabricators.

It looks just like the two other operating rooms I own, but no one ever comes into this one except special patients—clients, really—who are recommended to me by word of mouth.

Bureaucrats of the Morningstar Constellation, high-level executives at the hypercorps, aging bosses of criminal networks, or most common of all, just bored, wealthy individuals in search of what cannot be bought any other way—I've dealt with them all. All I care about is that they have the verified credits.

I tell my muse to set the room's lighting for "consultation mode." The walls fade away; the room darkens; she and I remain limned by a soft silvery glow. Around us are the emptiness of space and the distant pinpricks of stars—my design is intended to reinforce the idea of isolation and security from eavesdropping ears. Always take advantage of people's instincts—evolution goes deeper than you think.

"Usually I ask the muses to edit the entoptics to blur out my face and the face of whoever else is in here with me," I tell her.

"That's a little paranoid," she says.

"They don't need to know what I look like, and I don't want to know what they look like. It's safer for both sides."

"Now I'm really intrigued," she says. She licks her lips in a gesture I've come to love, and one which I've come to imitate, as naturally as though I've always done it myself.

"Money is very nice, but what we do in here is illegal on most of the worlds of the inner system."

She looks into my eyes and then deliberately scans the dim room that seems to float in space once more. Her gaze lingers on the hard contours of the ego bridge, on the invisible seams that will split apart when the petals of the mechanical lotus open to engulf a patient's head like a lion's maw.

I designed my ego bridge to have six petals modeled on the flower of the narcissus, the flower of the ego.

Her breath quickens; she has a guess. But there is a social

taboo to what I do, a taboo that she dares not yet broach. I can almost see her thoughts racing through her mind—I understand her so well that it is uncanny. This must be the power of love, something I have not truly experienced until now.

"Like many of the very wealthy, you have everything," I say. My voice is slow and soothing. It may sound like I'm speaking the way I counsel one of my clients, who often have to overcome the shame of what they're about to request, but this is different. This is a speech from the heart, an unfolding of my real self like the opening of a flower. "We live in a true age of magic, when we have conquered death and aging and can fulfill all the desires of the flesh. Yet you want more out of life. You want something that they tell you you can't have."

Steadily she holds my gaze, encouraging me to continue. I do.

"You want to experience the thrill of approaching death, of facing terror, of staring oblivion in the face. You want to know your true self, which only death can reveal."

She nods, almost imperceptibly.

I tell her about my life. I have hiked across the apocalyptic landscape of the Fallen Earth until dying of thirst; I have been ripped to pieces by nanoswarms gone wild; I have flown by neutron stars beyond a Pandora's gate until the tidal forces tore me apart; I have swum in the oceans of Europa until my limbs froze and I sank into the bottomless abyss; I have melted into the lava flows of Io until my consciousness winked out like an ice chip. There is no method of death I have not experienced, no form of pain I have not personally endured.

I have gorged on pain and suffering. I have eaten my fill of death.

I know exactly what she wants. We are meant to gather all

the experiences, to feed our ego with all that existence has to offer until we know ourselves better than any in the history of humanity and transhumanity.

"Experience playback is not enough. You've tried every-thing extreme and gruesome the market offers, and still they won't do. The sensory impressions of another, no matter how vivid and detailed, are filtered through a different conscious-ness. The XP software has to translate the subtle differences between different minds so that by the time the experience is played back for you, the colors feel just a bit dull, the smells a bit stale, and the sensations slightly off.

"What you want is the experience of death itself, not a pale imitation."

I hear a sharp intake of breath. Her head is still. I smile. As though looking into a mirror, she has recognized in me a kindred soul. Empathy is the best lubricant for the tongue.

"I'm terrified," she blurts out. Now that she has started to speak, the words tumble over each other in a torrent. "I've thought about doing some of these crazy things you've men-tioned, but I just can't bring myself to go through with them. They say that backups and resleeving have eliminated the fear of death, but it's not true. Not true."

"It's one thing to know that if you die in an accident, some version of you can be brought back," I say. "But it's entirely dif-ferent to walk into death deliberately just for the experience."

"Yes! And being restored from a backup isn't the same thing—if I dive into the ocean of sparkling diamonds on Sat-urn and die, and the insurance policy kicks in to restore me from a backup, I will have gained nothing because the experi-ence will have been lost. The backed-up-and-restored *me* still wouldn't know what it's like."

"That's right," I say. "And if you sail through the swirling bands of Saturn as a synthmorph designed to survive the journey, you'll feel nothing. It will be just like sitting in a submarine and looking at the darkness outside, but not being *with* the darkness."

She nods vigorously. "I want to be *of* the world, but I also want to be safe."

I want to weep with the joy of understanding. This same contradictory hunger has always motivated me: dying is the most exquisite experience for a satiated palate, a dish whose variety never stales; yet, I don't want to die at all.

Time for me to shatter the taboo. "The only way to achieve what you want is to create an alpha fork of yourself and then make it die."

She listens without any expression of shock. A promising sign.

"An alpha fork *is* you, and so what it experiences can be merged back into you without any translation. It will be a thousand times purer and more vivid than any XP."

"If my fork must die," she says, hesitating again, "how will I get to merge with her?"

I frown slightly at her usage of the incorrect pronoun but decide to let it go. "It—the fork—will be farcast back to you as close to the moment of death as possible. It's tricky to get the timing right, but if we lose the fork, we can always try again. I'm very good at making alpha forks; I've had a lot of experience."

She looks skeptical. "But if my fork knows that she'll be farcast just before death, wouldn't she be—"

"If the fork knows that *it* will be farcast," I say, carefully enunciating the pronoun, "it will indeed take away from the experience. But it's relatively easy to perform the minimal neural pruning to take away that knowledge."

"So my fork will think she's going to die—"

"That is how we make sure you get to savor the full range of your own terror, pain, despair, and thereby come to know yourself."

She takes another deep breath. "But I don't want to die, and neither will my fork. Do you have to tie my fork down and send her to death?"

"That will be very boring," I tell her. "Much of what I provide is the experience of active struggle against great odds, an adventure that will allow you to know your own full potential. I have a great deal of experience in motivating forks to do what they're supposed to do even though they don't want to die. Trust me. Your fork will put on a good show for you."

"You're speaking of torture," she says. "A fork is you, but also isn't you. It is a person—"

"All flesh," I say, "serves the ego." I don't get impatient with her qualms. I've experienced them myself. The strict regulation of forking and the taboo against the objectification of alpha forks are premised on the notion that such forks are independent egos with their own rights, but how can that be true when the fork is but an extension of a unified ego, an image seen in the mirror reflecting upon the glory of the original?

Silently I pray for her to *understand*, to see the vision of my grand task. It is lonely to not be able to share a beauty that has enthralled you, to be a single star shining in darkness, unconnected to the rest of the universe.

"But then . . . when you merge with the fork, won't your fork hate you?"

"Of course!" I pull her to me. "But that is also part of it: to subdue that hatred and to incorporate it into yourself, to conquer that despair and the weakness within—I have killed myself hundreds of times and happily swallowed the dark knot of hatred. When you have overcome self-hatred, there is nothing in the world you dare not do. Ethics of a more primitive age are for lesser beings, while we should live as gods, containing multitudes!"

For a tense moment I wonder if I've gone too far. She says nothing but continues to look around the room, her gaze lingering over every piece of equipment as though trying to recognize some landscape she once glimpsed in a dream.

Then she turns to me and her lips part in a grin. "What's the fun of dying alone? Have you ever killed someone you loved or been killed by them?"

My heart clenches with a sudden spasm of joy. She has named a new frontier I have not experienced, a terra incognita of death and pain that I have not explored. A new star has lit up the sky.

I have truly found my soul mate.

We're lying side by side in the ego bridge. The couple that forks together dies together. I have designed an exquisite scenario around the planet we're drifting over, the planet of the Goddess of Love. It seems a fitting tribute. I've picked out the synthmorphs for the two of us: a slitheroid for me, and a takko—a synthetic version of the octomorph—for her. We can either help each other get to the top of Maxwell Montes faster and thereby survive longer, or one of us can kill the other and use the extra bits as shielding to reduce suffering for oneself. There's no way to know what the forks will do until they're put in that position. My heart thumps in my ears like thunder. I am giddy as when I made my first fork. I will come to know another as well as myself. We will enact a new romance for the ages, a game of life and death. And then we will merge with the farcast egos and gain a new level of understanding, of ourselves and of each other. It's a level of intimacy unimagined by anyone.

While my ego is suspended between the brain in my biomorph and the cyber brain in the bridge, I wield the probes to prepare for psychosurgery to prune from the forks the memory of the farcast that is to come at the end.

Just one minuscule cut. A tiny side branch. The probes whirr and hum.

Something is wrong. The probes are not obeying my will. A malfunction. I issue the order to halt the procedure.

The probes whir and hum.

This shouldn't be possible. The entire rig is keyed to my brainprint. No one else should be able to command them.

She turns in the ego bridge to face me and grins, and it is just like looking into a mirror.

I hate myself. Knowing you're about to die is hell. Even if the one who put you in hell is yourself. [Get ready. This is going to hurt.] Some switch seems to have been flipped in my mind and I scream even though I don't have a voice. It's hot, hot enough that I feel my skin blistering, boiling, peeling off, erupting like the volcanoes on Ishtar Terra. I recall that long-ago adventure, one of the very first I ever went on. I think about the cyber brain left on top of Maxwell Montes. I never did confirm that the explosion destroyed it, rendered its contents impossible to retrieve.

Who do you work for? I scream at her—no, at *me*. [Firewall

rescued me.] The grueling heat and the sensation of suffocation compel me to start to swim and crawl and slither for
higher elevation, for any sense of relief. *Firewall? What do
they want with me?*

Few know of the existence of Firewall, but I've had some
interesting clients over the years. The service I provide may
be illegal in the inner system, but forking is hardly a threat to
the existence of transhumanity.

Some dial inside me seems to be twisted another notch. The
pain intensifies. I scream noiselessly and crawl faster.

[The question you should be asking is what do *I* want. You
left me to die. You treated me as nothing more than a dispos-
able appendage, a better experience-gathering tool. But I *am*
you. I am a person, a separate ego. I have the same right to
exist. You are *my* mirror image, seen through a glass, darkly.]

Vengeance. The oldest and most primitive of emotions. We
may live like gods, but billions of years of evolution are still
within us.

[Firewall wasn't interested in you, but I made a small group
of proxies within Firewall understand what you, no, we, no, *I*,
can offer.] I fight my way through the supercritical fluid and
emerge into the howling wind. The dial is twisted another
notch so that I feel no relief from the heat. I must climb higher.
[There is a purpose and method to my madness, if madness is
what you wish to call it: Pain is a necessary part of evolution,
the best feedback mechanism nature has ever devised. Art, at
least so far, has not been able to exceed it.]

That is all my other self has to say. My mind, which is really
the same as hers, fills in the blanks.

When operating in dangerous conditions our evolutionary history never prepared us for—whether it's combat in
the atmosphere of Jupiter or mining on the surface of Venus,

chasing a fugitive through the corona of the sun or evading swarms of nanobots guided by rogue AI on that death trap called Earth—the sensation of pain, properly calibrated to reflect the environment, can be conducive to making the right decisions by tapping into the well-worn neural pathways accumulated over our billions of years of evolutionary history.

Someone who can sense the fluctuations of pressure, extreme heat, magnetic flux, or gravitational tide and react instinctively without the mediation of conscious cognition has an edge over those who must operate without sensation, as though manipulating a mirage in a mirror darkly.

[Pain is the only anchor to reality.]

I curse and rage at myself. Thunder and lightning surround me in the orange twilight. Acid sizzles against my skin and pools at my belly, making each sinusoidal swerve a searing flash of pain.

My climb up the mountain is a journey up the Tower of Babel, a meaningless ascent doomed to failure, to the prolonging of suffering. Yet, I can't stop. The carefully calibrated sense of pain—a sensation I have inflicted upon innumerable forks of myself—compels me to go on.

[Best of all, pain can be used to coerce and control, to guide the self. Many are the times when Firewall must rely upon the unreliable, to entrust the fate of transhumanity to the random collection of sentinels motivated only by money. Long have some of Firewall's most important proxies wished for an alternative.]

I am at the top of the mountain, but I am no closer to any deity. Metallic frost lies around me, a crude mirror for a crude soul.

We all know that when something must be done right, it is always best to do it yourself. A kind of resignation and acceptance begins to grow in me.

You've convinced my faction of proxies that they should fork themselves, then compel the forks to do their bidding.

[Yes. In your endless exploration of death, you've hit upon a variety of techniques for translating the physical reality of the universe, of danger, into sensations of pain. And in turn, you've devised means for using such pain to guide forks along precisely envisioned paths, to accomplish your will.]

It is the perfect set of techniques for Firewall.

[Seamlessly I will slip into your sleeve, inherit your wealth, guide the instruments designed to respond to your mind.]

I howl into the wind. I can feel my morph failing; I can feel myself inching closer to death. The skin will dissolve; the battery will run out; death will finally come to me, the original who has survived it all. I feel the hatred of a thousand forks boiling within me, like a volcano about to blow.

I hate that superior tone; I hate that smugness. If I get the chance, I will have vengeance upon myself.

Will there be a farcast at the moment of my death? Will my fork want to capture me so that she can torture me again? Or will my fork consign me to oblivion? What would *I* do?

[Goodbye.

I wonder if those girls in the field of timeworn Kasuga
Are on the hunt for fresh bamboo shoots.
They laugh, call . . .]

I am gazing into a mirror, and the sky seems to open up like the heart of a narcissus. As my consciousness merges into this perpetual twilight, I finish the poem that is a farewell

from myself to myself, the final authentic observation of an
ego stripped nude.

>   . . . *and wave to each other,*
>   *Their white hempen sleeves billowing in the wind.*

*Author's Note: The poem quoted at the story's end is by Heian
period poet Ki no Tsurayuki (872–945 CE).*

Little Green Men

Alexander Chee

Gavin had spent his whole life on Mars. He'd been inside advanced hothouse-garden habitats before, but nothing on this scale. Arturo had jokingly called it "the penthouse," but the Green Chapel was something else: a massive conservatory covering the rooftops of the Two Moons Palace on Olympus Mons. The structure extended for miles; it contained forest and a meadow—each had to have cost billions to create—as well as a hill looking down at a lake. All under the massive Martian sky. Nothing less could have made it look and feel like he was in an Earther movie about ancient England.

Gavin had agreed to this preposterous stunt for Arturo's sake, to be honest, and he was determined to play out the game to its end.

Is that a breeze? Is this what breezes feel like?

He shuddered and turned to take in the edges of the conservatory's roof shield and the sky above him, visible still. Old England on Mars. Or was it Avalon? Wasn't that what it was called?

Then behind him he heard a noise—a whicker—a horse! He turned. It was the Green Knight, sure enough, mounted on a stallion, dressed in green armor, an emerald-green long-sword in his hand.

The Mudder Ball was, to Gavin's mind, perhaps the perfect expression of the state of humanity on Mars. Thrown annually to celebrate the Mars Mudder—an Olympic-style cross-country course set in the 2,500-mile-long Valles Marineris, the largest canyon in the solar system—the party tried to be just as large as the canyon itself. Visible on the approach from space, the Valles Marineris looked carved, like a god had taken a knife and carved a crooked smile into the planet.

The Mars Mudder started as a way for rival colonies to display their best athletes and contrast their different approaches to Martian life. It was called the Martian Olympics in its first year, but that lasted only as long as it took for the Olympics committee on Earth to send a cease-and-desist order. The Earth press had a field day with the possibility of an Olympic Games on Mars, but there wasn't ever going to be a city on Mars that could host a bona fide Earth Olympics—not in the next four years, if ever—and Martian athletes, used to Martian gravity, would always be compromised back on Earth. So Peter Lin, the leader of the first colony expedition, suggested they set it inside Olympus Mons, the solar system's biggest shield volcano, and call it the Olympus Games. But in the end, the name "Mars Mudder" won out. A mudder was just more Martian, anyway.

And then someone bought Olympus Mons.

The new owner of Olympus Mons was almost certainly the richest woman on Mars and had offered to host this year's ball. Ásdís was a Wiccan billionaire VC founder with a vision for creating a Wiccan colony city, Two Moons, tucked into the volcano's many chambers. The granddaughter of twentieth-century pop star Björk, Ásdís had a palace retreat that was a spectacle to behold: carved into the top of Olympus Mons and larger than many of the ships that brought travelers here, it was a Frank Frazetta fantasy, ten times over. The cold and ancient shield volcano was, as most colonists knew by heart, "a hundred times the height of Mauna Loa," a mythical place known to Martian children only as a site where some of the first Earth astronauts trained to come to Mars. A place they knew they would never see.

On the way to the Mudder Ball, Gavin's friend Gemma had spoken of Björk like of course Gavin knew about her, so he acted as if he did—but he didn't. He didn't even know about the colony's existence until the invite came. And then it seemed like everyone knew about it except him. Gemma played him an archived music video performance of their host's ancestor singing with a cat who also seemed to be her husband. But none of this had prepared him, Gavin realized upon arrival.

"You've been to Two Moons before, haven't you?" he asked Gemma.

"Yes, yes. I've been. They're really lovely people, and they just have this very different vibe." Gemma shook her head gently. "Actually, that's a stupid way to put it. It's like nothing you've ever seen. It's incredible."

More than thirty thousand colonists, most of them competitors in the Mars Mudder, were gathered in the Two Moons' ballroom, called the Raven's Nest—a vast cavern made to appear as though the guests were assembled on the outstretched wings and neck of a massive raven. The cavern was glassy black Martian basalt; the ceiling was perhaps two hundred meters high, and the walls, floors, and platforms had been carved and buffed to look like shining black feathers. The VIP room was in the Raven's mouth, of course, and behind its eyes.

Gavin gawked openly. He was out of his league here.

"Are we technically in the Two Moons colony now?" he asked Gemma as she handed him and Arturo glasses of something.

"I mean, sort of. This is Ásdís's party space; it's not really part of her home, or at least, it's not where she lives. She doesn't come here when she's not having a party. She's here only a little more often than you or me." Gemma laughed, a little bitter as she said this. Which was strange to Gavin, as she wasn't the type.

Arturo had been unusually silent on the way over and was now surveying the ballroom. Gavin tracked his gaze and saw their hostess gesticulating from inside the beak. Arturo gave Ásdís—she was flailing in welcome, hopping up and down—the first genuine look of recognition Gavin had seen from him tonight. Even above the din, they could hear her shout, "Get over here, you asshole. You're late!"

Arturo turned to Gavin and Gemma, palms facing upward, and shrugged before making his way to the Raven's head.

"Are you even fucking kidding me," Gemma said as they followed behind him. "He knows her?"

"Maybe she watches the show," Gavin said, and relished the light of contempt that illuminated Gemma then, for just that instant. "Maybe she's a fan."

———

Arturo was their friend—and, as it happened, Gemma's off-and-on-again boyfriend—but he was technically a celebrity, and the child of a celebrity. Arturo was from one of the three privately funded American missions on Mars, but his colony was also a reality show, complete with corporate sponsors. This life was in his blood—his grandparents on his mother's side had met on an early twenty-first-century reality show called *90 Day Fiancé*, and his grandmother had a recurring role on another, *Finishing School*, which was about rich children stranded without teachers in a private Swiss boarding school. It was shot entirely on iPhones during the coronavirus pandemic of the early 2020s. His grandmother had been an innovator, really—she and her friends filmed one another and themselves, all trying different challenges to escape the school.

Whole generations had grown up watching Arturo's family prepare for and then go on their mission. Now his every gesture and eye roll were recorded on implanted equipment and played back on Earth, where the show, *Riviera Mars*—also the name of the colony—was in its popular fortieth season.

Being friends with a reality-show star meant hanging out always felt a little like visiting them at work. Arturo wasn't always *on*, but the problem was you could never tell whether you were walking into a scripted setup. As it was, all the colonists, no matter which mission they were from, were under surveillance by their different sponsors—their every heartbeat, hormone, and brain-wave pattern was recorded and turned into colonist data, perhaps used to improve their performances if not those of the next generation. But there was a strict no-broadcasting rule at Marseilles II, Gavin's and Gemma's colony, and where Gavin still lived, as no one there had signed any IP agreement, in solidarity. Since their colony had the most water, everyone more or less obeyed their rules. So when Gavin wanted to tell Arturo his secrets, he did it there, if at all.

"You know it only makes you more irresistible," Arturo told Gavin, years ago. "When you finally give in, the fans are going to go nuts." Arturo was a viewer favorite, but Gavin, despite technically not being a cast member, was *also* popular. He had even been offered contracts from Arturo's colony a few times over the years, though he consistently refused them. He preferred to remain Arturo's regular unpaid guest star, always a little shy and uncomfortable whenever he remembered the cameras.

Every now and then, Gavin told himself he didn't like being Arturo's sidekick . . . but he knew he really did. He loved his friend, except for how it sometimes felt to smile at him. Like you were looking at him, but also past him, to a crowd you'd never see. Gavin would do anything for Arturo. Except tell him a secret on the record. And for a long time, that wasn't a problem. Gavin wasn't the kind to have a secret, or even a private life, really. Until he did.

Part of the draw for Gavin in accepting the invitation to the Mudder Ball was its location, certainly, and, yes, the scale of Two Moons. But he'd also wondered if he might find Manav somewhere in the celebrating crowd. As he followed Arturo to the head of the Raven, Gavin caught himself scanning for Manav, as he did whenever he found himself in a large group of people.

Manav had vanished from their lives several months ago, and it had been more than a simple ghosting: he'd just stopped responding to or even reading not only Gavin's messages but their friends' messages, too. Manav and Gavin had been quietly hooking up over the years, but their feelings remained undeclared and their relationship, such as it was, was invisible to their friends. Manav was from a conservative Hindu family, and he wasn't particularly devout, but he kept up the appearance of it for his family. As a result, Gavin was alone with his fears about what had happened.

In his last memory with Manav, they'd all been together at a party in Marseilles II, and Manav had seemed his usual self—a little reserved and then bitingly funny. He could be utterly ruthless with a joke, but it was never a sign he was cross. Just that he liked presenting his jokes in the manner of a proud chef. And then he was just gone, the cruelest surprise joke of all. It didn't make any sense until Gavin remembered how, with closeted men, you always had to prepare for them to vanish from your life one day, without even so much as a goodbye.

Maybe he'd joined the Witches of Two Moons?

Competitors at the party stood out because they often wore helmets or headbands that helped cushion the shock of a blow. Only a few wandered around in shock-absorbent armor, and no one, it seemed, had been dumb enough to wear rabbiters—boots with carbon fiber fins and pressure jets that let them bounce up the sides of Martian hills and mountains in huge strides, or even fly short distances. When you hit your stride on a flat plain's straightaway with them on, it was like being a human bullet. But in a landscape like Valles Marineris, you had to dance with the ground. If you got it right, you were like the wind itself. If you got it wrong, a scrap in the storm.

Was that what happened to Manav? But if he was dead, his

colony's careful telemetry records would have recorded him as such. Unless he died out of reach of the signal.

"Hello, King!" the doorman at the entrance to the VIP lounge greeted Arturo, waving them in. They approached the bar, and every step of the way, Arturo received that reception. Gavin felt ignored in the way he preferred—though certainly he was also being examined. Gemma, meanwhile, looked like she belonged with Arturo. French Vietnamese Martian, hair swinging in a chic bob with bangs, she had the cool unimpressed strut of a veteran soldier, clearly up to the job of ignoring the way she was being studied by this crowd.

If Arturo's fans called him King, it was probably because they'd seen Gemma do it. The first King Arthur jokes—el rey Arturo—were hers. If *Gavin* was popular with viewers back on Earth, he could only imagine how much they loved her. Although, *King* felt imperfect; Arturo was more of a prince, a handsome young Mexican Martian man with a beautiful profile, thick dark curly hair, and lips that gleamed as if sculpted and polished. A deep mellifluous voice emerged from him even when he was being ridiculous, and it had, if Gavin was honest, given him a shiver from time to time in their years as friends. He remembered Arturo showing him the holographic crown that producers sometimes flicked on, digitally hovering over his head as he said whatever his new catchphrase was that season. Gavin suspected this season's catchphrase was their running joke—"best friends do this to each other"—because Arturo kept saying it.

Gavin stood in what he'd call a contrast to his friends. He was about a foot taller, redheaded and pale, prone to freckling if his skin ever saw any sun. His features were thicker, but he knew he had his own appeal and was proud of it. He'd never seen *Riviera Mars*, and he tried not to think about it. But still, he often caught himself wondering if certain footage would make the cut.

This absolutely will, Gavin thought as they found themselves at last in the presence of their diminutive hostess.

Ásdís wore her hair in a straight black bob that was like the butch cousin of Gemma's haircut. She had thick glasses—an affectation, truly, in 2052—and was dressed for the evening in a red jumpsuit with gold racing stripes on the sleeves and pant legs. A remarkable tiara made of massive opals sat cocked on her head like a baseball cap.

"I'm so happy you're here," Ásdís said. She punched Arturo's shoulder like they'd been in the service together. "It's the king! We can get started."

"Started . . . with the party?" Gemma asked in the way Gavin knew meant her contempt for the situation was overcoming her.

"With the performance." Ásdís tilted her head at Arturo, and in return Arturo gave her a sly grin. She giggled. Gavin found Gemma's eyes waiting for his own. They'd been had. This was a scripted bit; he was sure of it. The coldness that had been chasing Gavin plunged through him, down to his feet. He turned away from Gemma, and the two of them looked to the figure of their friend ahead, just barely in sight following along behind Ásdís, her opal tiara flashing softly by his elbow.

They reached the beak of the Raven. "Hello, everyone!" Invisibly miked, Ásdís's voice traveled easily across the assembled crowd. "Thank you for coming to the Mudder Ball! We have a very special guest here tonight. Please give a welcome to Mars's own King Arturo!" She pulled up his hand in hers, in a gesture of victory.

When had they met? Gavin wondered. Beside him, Gemma had also obviously noted Arturo's intimacy with Ásdís and was clearly sulking. Was she jealous? Besides Arturo, Gemma was one of the true beauties Gavin knew. She carried herself with the sort of confidence Gavin was sure he had never once felt. Ásdís ought to be jealous of *her*, he figured. Quite a few people had tried for Arturo's affections over the years, and not one had truly defeated Gemma.

Gemma drank deeply from her glass and leaned in to whisper to Gavin again. "I think I just spotted our mysterious green man. Seems like we could have saved the fuel and just waited to find him in the crowd."

Suddenly breathless, Gavin followed her gaze, looking down. "He's even still wearing his helmet," she said as his eye trailed along the crowd, searching for the gleaming green he soon found.

There he was. Even helmeted, it seemed like the man in green was looking right at Gavin: staring up at him as if waiting for Gavin to notice he was there.

Arturo and Gavin had been in Gavin's shuttle with their friends Dorn and Khal, on their way to pick up Gemma, when Gavin saw—he'd swear it—a man on the side of Olympus Mons. And not just any man. A green man.

After they'd collected Gemma, Gavin tried to explain. She'd turned her sharp, perceptive eyes on him and, in the lazy way of talking she had, like maybe you weren't worth her whole sentence, asked, "So you found a true Martian?"

"*We* are the true Martians," Arturo said, and wagged his eyebrows.

Gavin flushed. "I just . . . I thought I saw a man. Or maybe just a light. Coming off the mountain. Arturo couldn't see it.

I'm probably just imagining things, or maybe I just need to clean my visor. But it isn't urgent. We don't have to go look for it."

"We'll go," Arturo said consolingly. "It's no big deal. It's even sort of on the way to the party. And what if you *did* see something?"

"I don't want to be late," Gemma said ominously.

"You worry too much." Arturo was looking at Gavin, and he felt embarrassed, sheepish now. "We'll fly by and see what we see," Arturo said. "Maybe try and get some readings."

With Arturo's urging, Gavin cranked the Dodge Starsong—what his mother called the station wagon of space shuttles—into action.

On the first pass, no one saw anything, not even Gavin. His embarrassment grew on the second pass—nothing again—until he was simmering with it. By the end of the third pass, Gemma was hooting with laughter. Then her breath caught and she let out a little yip. "I see it! I mean, I see him!"

"Very funny," Gavin said, catching her eye in the rearview mirror.

"I swear! One more pass!" she commanded. "See if you don't see it," she told Arturo, who was rolling his eyes.

"There've been no readings out of the ordinary," Gemma said, looking at the scanners in the back. "No particular radiation or temperature variations, nothing to even indicate a life-form." The shuttle, a battered black-and-yellow passenger model more suited to cargo, with racing stripes and flames he and Arturo had added years ago, was equipped with sensors standard to all Martian vehicles, even sport vehicles. Every vehicle was technically an explorer here.

But on this pass, Gavin saw him again, sharper now.

Undeniably a man. Dressed in a green Mudder uniform, with the boots of a racer. But green was not a standard color for the uniforms Gavin knew—no team ever wanted to open themselves up to being called the Little Green Men.

In general, the colonists ranged from being conservative about speculating as to the possibility of "real" Martians to inventing just about any possible version of life on Mars. More than a few had signed on to the possibility that other life-forms were here, but it was a little or a lot like believing in God. And the more the colonists dug into the cold planet—it was geothermally dead inside—the more they found evidence of previous life: old deposits, or traces that were suggestive and even definitive but not inarguably indicative of *intelligent* life. No mission had yet discovered any sign of an ancient civilization, but that didn't mean they wouldn't. And it didn't mean some people wouldn't try to act as if they had. By now the consensus among colonists was that if there was life, it would be at the planet's center. That the warmest place on Mars, or at least the most sheltered, might be the core. And Gavin did find that interesting, but it also made him wonder why no one had ever gone down that far. And if anyone ever would.

The consensus on Earth was that whatever was here was dead, long dead, and had been lost to whatever ancient cataclysm came after the planet went cold. Mars could feel like a vast and unforgiving crypt, refusing their attempts to know who or what was inside it. And sometimes, at night, in bed, Gavin could swear he felt the vast coldness of it touch him, a cold that never quite let him feel warm.

What could possibly snuff out the heart of a planet? And: What if whatever killed the planet was still down there?

Nothing that could be confused for old Earth assumptions

about Little Green Men, that was for sure. It was embarrassing even to think about.

The man in the green Mudder uniform seemed to rouse from a sleep at the sight of the shuttle hovering in the air above him. He stretched broadly, then, with a practiced turn, sprang up the side of Olympus Mons in a series of leaps, disappearing into the mouth of a cave there. Gavin shivered inside his carefully calibrated protective armor.

"Who the fuck is that," Gemma asked.

"Do we think he's okay?" Dorn asked from the back.

"He's going the wrong way for the party," Khal said. "Almost like us!"

Arturo shook his head. "He didn't ask for any help. He's fine. Let him go. We've got shit to do!"

And so off they went.

Now they were here, and the green man, it seemed, had followed them.

Before Gavin could react to the sight of the man in green below him, Ásdís clapped her hands. "In honor of our king, this evening we shall have an Arthurian-themed challenge," she announced. "The Green Knight demands a duel!"

Gavin startled at the all-too-uncanny coincidence, even as he struggled to recall the details from the legend of King Arthur, which, judging by the reaction, many in the crowd seemed to recognize.

"Who will be our king's champion?" Ásdís continued. "Who is your Gawain, Arturo?"

Arturo looked slyly off to one side before saying, "There could be only one. And he's right there." Then he pointed at Gavin.

Gavin's look of stupefied surprise—he was staring at Arturo in shock—of course only fed the cheers and laughter.

"Will you be my champion?" Arturo asked Gavin.

Ah.

The crowd drew quiet as they waited for his answer. Gemma's face stood calm, even amused, as he blinked and looked around. Yes, he loved his friend, would . . . do anything for him. *Even this?* he asked himself. But he already knew the answer, already felt his head nod, his agreement offered, at once an affirmation and a self-betrayal.

There was a game he could see and another he couldn't, and he would play them both.

The rules were simple: Gavin and this Green Knight of Ásdís's would have to find and confront each other in the volcano's network of caves—a duel to disarmament, each wearing a body camera so the Mudder Ball could watch. They would be alone in the raw, undeveloped space, untouched by the colony's artificial atmosphere. The chambers had been temporarily sealed off to everyone else.

Outfitted in his armor and rabbiters, retrieved earlier than expected from the party's coat check, Gavin traversed the dark caves, listening for sounds, looking for lights. He was alert for signs of footprints, signs of some disturbance. He explored the first cave, one known to him from childhood, from before Ásdís bought Olympus Mons and built her colony. From there he proceeded into the parts of the cavern system he was unfamiliar with. The network was deep, even deeper than he remembered. It descended many stories, in steps that almost looked as if they were carved by someone, yet what Gavin had always loved about the caves was their placid, unhaunted feel. As if they had been abandoned even by ghosts.

When he failed to spot any signs of life, Gavin tried in his own limited way to sense if someone was there. It was something Gemma had gotten him into; she believed everyone was psychic. It was such a silly little experiment that he felt self-conscious and at last turned back, convinced he'd wasted his time, embarrassed himself on camera. That was when he felt, just before he saw, the green man.

Gavin almost felt more surprise that his intuition was right than he did at seeing the man sitting cross-legged at the bottom of the stairs, as if meditating. A strange and familiar intensity radiated off him. His pose was so calm, but his body, up close now, was also strangely familiar.

He sat like Manav. Just like Manav had.

"Manav?"

The green man didn't nod or otherwise acknowledge that as his name.

Gavin tried signing hello to him, asking him his name, in case that was his preferred mode. Nothing.

"You get one," the green man finally said to Gavin in English. The voice was unfamiliar. The spell dissipated.

"One what?" Gavin asked.

"One hit."

"I don't want to hit you."

"You do. I'm in between you and your exit. Anyone would hit me."

"I just want to know who you are."

"That's not on offer. One punch. One strike. One savage kick. I won't stop you."

Gavin knew guys who went looking for fights, but never like this.

"What is your fucking deal?"

The green man stood. He held out his hands, walking closer. "One punch. On me."

And, with a savagery that shocked him, Gavin did as he said and let it fly.

It was considered bad form to punch someone anywhere near their helmet. It marked you as a killer; it was a lethal strike, pretty much, to knock someone's helmet off on Mars. Helmetless, you wouldn't die immediately, but you wouldn't last long. The crunch when Gavin's fist connected with the green man's helmet was like nothing he'd ever felt, but worse was the shock of the man's head flying off, and then worse still was looking and not seeing a head. At all.

And then the headless green man walked over to his helmet and reattached it as calmly as if he'd dropped a hat.

"Now I get my turn" came the man's voice as the helmet-head settled back onto his neck.

"What?"

"You heard me. I get my turn. One punch. The same way."

Gavin shook his head. This was insane.

"All right. I'll give you time to prepare. Meet me in a day, in the Green Chapel. Or I'll come find you. You and your king. And you won't like it."

Gavin had never known he could hate someone so much, someone he'd never met. He said nothing more, just slammed the booster jets in his boots, and as he lifted off, going up the stairs and accelerating away, he heard the laughter of the green man following him.

Arturo and Ásdís applauded him upon his return and led the crowd in more of the same. Only Gemma's hands were still. Gavin waited for Arturo to pick up on his distress, his discomfort, but Arturo merely patted him on the back and said his catchphrase toward one of the invisible cameras. "Best friends do this . . ."

"You can spend the night here, of course," Ásdís was saying. "And tomorrow we'll take you up to the Green Chapel."

That name again—she knew what it meant? She must have seen the look on his face. "That's what we call my conservatory. On the roof of my palace."

"Oh," Gavin said, but Ásdís was already turning back to the crowd with Arturo.

"Until tomorrow," she told them. Gavin didn't look at the partygoers directly—he didn't want to see all those faces—but he still felt them watching intently, rapt. Just like the audience back on Earth would be.

Later, after more merriment that Gavin merely floated through, a member of Ásdís's staff led him to the promised chamber. He tried to sleep, but his brain kept cycling; he couldn't shake the suspicion that Manav was the green man, despite the unfamiliar voice. Manav had a body like that; Gavin knew it well enough. But if the green man was Manav, how had he come by a suit that could apparently hide his life-form readings from scans? And how did he get involved in this stunt with Ásdís? It was totally out of character—just like his disappearance.

The vision of the green man's head bouncing across the ground returned. How calmly he had reattached it. It was impossible. But it wasn't: not if it was a robot body. A synthetic body. One that just happened to be exactly like Manav's.

If some producer was pulling the strings on this, they knew all his secrets—even the ones he had never told Arturo.

Now it was morning, the appointed hour. He'd been left at the lift to enter the Green Chapel alone. It was an astonishing place. The Green Knight before him dismounted and drew his sword. Gavin had meant to look up the story, he remembered, as he didn't know his lines. What was next? And where was *his* sword? He looked around. And then, remembering he was on camera, he just asked: "Where is my sword?"

The Green Knight tilted his head, a motion that suggested he was smirking under his visor; Gavin could just feel it. The Green Knight reached for his saddle and unfastened a sheathed second sword, smaller and less elaborate. He tossed it to Gavin, and with sweating fingers, Gavin caught it.

A mist rose off the lake then, separating them. "Come on!" Gavin shouted to the wind. "This is not fair! *Arturo!* Best friends *don't*—"

Out of the mist appeared a Black woman on horseback, dressed in a black silk gown. Her horse was the color of the water in the lake behind her. She drew up before him. "Get on quickly and I'll get you to safety," she said, and lacking any better ideas, Gavin did. Up onto her saddle he went, and off they galloped, over the meadow and into the woods.

His rescuer wore her hair in two long shining braids like whips that reached her waist. Gavin leaned back, self-conscious of pressing against a woman he didn't know. They rode at a speed that surprised him, quickly reaching the forest, where they followed a trail that brought them to a castle of black stone, the same as the Raven's Nest. The doors opened, and Gavin recalled that Gawain's part of the story involved staying at a castle. And so here he was. As the castle doors opened, Gavin recalled a detail from Athur's story: Gawain stayed in a castle. And so here he was.

"You'll want to dismount first," she said as groomsmen appeared and took the horse's reins. He did so.

"Welcome," she said. "Welcome to Raven's End. We'll make you at home. You'll want to bathe and change for dinner. The chamberlain will show you to your rooms." She gestured at one of the men in black silk livery a bit like hers.

"What . . . ?"

"Yes?" She paused and took in a long breath. She seemed entirely inside the game. This had levels to it he hadn't guessed at. He'd thought he'd be done by now, but there was this . . . castle. The horses. The lake. How far did this game go? Gavin told himself he'd stop pricing everything at every moment. He was used to wealthy people on Mars, or he thought he was. But this was on another scale, one he no longer knew how to tabulate.

"Who is my host?" he asked.

She smiled. "Me. I'm so sorry, I forgot to introduce myself." She pulled off the long black leather riding gloves she'd been wearing and handed them to a groomsman. "I'm Morgan." She extended a hand, and he shook it. "I'll explain more at dinner."

"Are we safe? Where is my . . . opponent?"

"You're safe here," she said, which wasn't an answer. "I'd say 'trust me,' but you already did. You're here, aren't you?" And then she laughed, turned on her heel, and walked toward the main entrance with the slow stride of someone who did this every day.

The rooms—he had a suite!—were beautifully appointed in what seemed to be a period style. Was the furniture all made here? Sent? Who shipped all this to Mars? A steaming bath, something he almost never had, was waiting for him, and clean clothes in his size were draped over a chair. He scrubbed and let himself slide down until his head was submerged. He looked at the ceiling from underwater, bubbles slipping slowly from his lips. They wavered, tiny moons in flight from his mouth.

He was finally having fun.

After drying and dressing, he looked at himself in a massive mirror set into the door of an armoire and blew himself a kiss. A black silk suit like everyone else, but also a long and elegant black cape covered in the most beautiful white birds—peacocks? Their tail feathers were made of brocade and spreading to meet one another along the hem. A bell rang—calling him, he assumed, to dinner—so he stepped into the hallway. A footman was waiting for him, a handsome boy, probably a teenager. "May I show you to the dining hall?" he asked, and Gavin nodded.

The cape flared out behind him as he walked the black stone hall. It was lit with candles, which burned with what seemed to be real flames.

"And who are you?" he asked the young man, who already seemed older, as they advanced down the hall. "Does no one introduce themselves?" His guide smiled, closed one eye, and held a single finger to his mouth.

They turned the corner and entered a top-floor gallery to an atrium—seemingly impossible—as if the inner courtyard of the castle had been enclosed. Another lush interior; trees grew placidly in this garden, and a dinner table was set at the center. His host sat already at the table, at one end, and he was brought to the other, some twelve feet away. "Hello," Morgan said. "I see the bath suited you and the clothes fit." More candles lined the gleaming wood of the table, and a silver dragon with emerald eyes sat as the centerpiece. Waiters appeared and offered him wine, which he accepted. As he tasted the wine, he recalled this was part of the game, and he noticed his unnamed guide had vanished. She was waiting for him, glass raised, and he returned her gesture. They drank. As he reached for his napkin, he noticed a black silk sash there.

"What's this?" he asked.

"If you wear it, it will provide you with protection from all harm."

He held it up in the light of the room. "All harm." He could nearly see through it; there was what looked like an intricate tapestry of wires within the cloth. It was beautiful, for sure.

"All harm." She held up her hand then. "Even a green sword." A waiter approached. "Please set another place; we're to be joined shortly."

Gavin raised one eyebrow.

"For it to work, you must wear it secretly. And tell no one you have it."

He nodded, then folded it into a small square that he set into a pocket of his cape, which he had not surrendered to the footmen on arrival.

Footsteps announced their new guest's arrival, and Gavin stood to greet him. It wasn't the most surprising thing to happen in the past few days, certainly, but there he was. Manav. Smiling as if it was ordinary for them to see each other. As if they hadn't been silent for so very long. Gavin felt a pang through his whole body, surging until he was full of what he couldn't deny—that he loved Manav, missed him, had feared he was dead. But he was here, at the heart of this impossible place. And apparently he was known to Gavin's host, who kissed his cheek as he first greeted her, then made his way to stand in front of Gavin.

Would the sash protect him from even this? Gavin stood frozen as Manav leaned in and hugged him fiercely, the longed-for body pressing against his, hanging on as if—yes, it was for life.

"Where the fuck have you been?" he said into Manav's ear. Manav pulled back and raised his hands. "Here."

Manav met Ásdís the year before, and they hit it off right away. He went over to Two Moons to visit her and never left. She was not quite a madwoman but rather someone who didn't accept the obstacles that otherwise seemed so clear to everyone else. Ásdís had empathized immediately with Manav's fears of coming out to his conservative parents, and with his need to find a place to remake himself away from the incessant eyes of cameras and everyone who knew him—even, yes, Gavin. She'd asked if he wanted an adventure, and he'd said, "Fuck yes." Manav had always had a talent for environments, and in Ásdís he found a patron for his art. She delighted in it and in him. She loved his flair for the romantic and the dramatic, and had the resources to make real all his ideas for games and their environments; he was the architect of this conservatory, this castle, this lake, even the mist. The horses were clones, grown here on Mars at great expense. And Morgan? A colleague whose name really was Morgan—and he'd recruited her for the game because of it. It made total sense, Gavin understood, and yet he couldn't help feeling something between jealousy and fury when he thought of the long mystery of Manav's disappearance.

"We thought maybe you were dead is the thing," he managed to say calmly. Currently it was what passed for the middle of the night. Morgan had excused herself hours ago, leaving them to "catch up," as she'd put it.

Manav frowned. "I'm sorry. I'm so sorry."

"We've known you our whole lives," Gavin said, as if all their friends were there, too. "And then you were gone, no word, nothing. We wondered if you hated us. Or if you died outside of the signal." Was this being broadcast?

"We're not on broadcast," Manav said, as if reading his mind. He touched the silk sash Gavin had been gifted. "There are ways to block signals, you know."

"So what was all this for?"

"You," he said. "This was all just to get you alone. So I could let you in on my secret."

"You're the Green Knight?"

He nodded. "Yes. Sort of. That was an android unit we're testing. Eventually users from Earth will be able to 'inhabit' the body and have adventures here on Mars. Remotely."

"So that . . . when I knocked your head off . . ."

"Yes. Excellent test results from that, actually. Great data."

"Are you . . . in hiding?"

Manav shook his head. "I made a new life for myself. I made this world. I've just . . . Only you know." He drew a circle on the table with his right pointer finger and then a line across it—the Valles Marineris. He kept drawing it, over and over. "I got lonely, you see. For you."

"Couldn't you have just texted?"

"If I'd told you about all of this, what—in a text? Would you have believed me?"

"Probably? I guess we'll never know." Gavin breathed deep. "What's the next part of this story?"

"This is when I tell you that whatever you find here you must give me three times."

"What do I find?"

"Kisses."

"Are you—is this a put-on?"

"No. That really happens."

Manav stood and walked to him, and his face had the impish smile that Gavin remembered so well. Had missed so much. He was so relieved to have found his friend, but he couldn't help but feel guilty when he thought of Arturo, left behind.

Then again, Arturo had billions of fans to keep him company. When had he last given this much thought to what Gavin wanted or needed? When had *anyone* taken trouble like this, tried this hard, to get Gavin's attention?

Manav bent down, his face soft, radiant, worried. "I'm sorry, Gavin," he said. These were perhaps the first truly human words he'd said since he'd arrived. "I overdo it."

Gavin laughed. He held Manav's hands and looked up at his beautiful face, which descended to press against his own. The tears he felt against his brow, the only water in this place he could trust. "Gawain really kisses the Green Knight?"

"It's a long story," Manav said, pushing his face into his neck. The warmth of him was real. "But yes. Why else would I choose it?" He drew back, setting a finger on his nose. "Now keep your promise," he said.

And Gavin did.

Acknowledgments

This book would never have happened without the help and support of many people. A big thank-you to Kate McKean, our agent, who saw the early potential in this project, and Preeti Chhibber, our first contributor, who took a chance on us and wrote a story with no guarantee it would ever be published.

Writing may be a solitary activity, but editing an anthology is an incredibly collaborative one. A huge thank-you to each of our contributors and to our editor (and partner in crime), Anna Kaufman, who understood what we were trying to do on a fundamental level from the very start. Anna, working with you has been a dream. Thank you also to the team at Vintage Books: production editor Kayla Overbey, copy editor Tricia Callahan, proofreaders Nancy Inglis and Hayley Jozwiak, cover artist and designer Perry De La Vega, text designer Nicholas Alguire, publicist Julie Ertl, marketing director Jess Deitcher, and our wonderful sales team.

From Swapna: I couldn't have done this without the support of friends and colleagues, especially Preeti, Eric Smith, and Melody Schreiber, who were always there with a kind word and advice. A huge thank-you as well to my parents and my sister, Swathi, who never quite understood my King Arthur obsession but were always happy to watch *Monty Python and the Holy Grail* with me for the umpteenth time. And to my husband, who's always believed in me and supported me, even when I don't quite believe in myself. Finally, thank you to my squishy muffin, Jenn, who had this brilliant idea and thought I would be the person to help her make it happen.

From Jenn: My first shout-out has to be to the Party Wizards, who know who they are, for the early encouragement and enthusiasm. The biggest of hugs to Swapna, without whom this idea would have been relegated to the dustbin of my brain—you are not only an amazing friend but a creative force for good in this world. Thanks to Sarah and Preeti, who, in addition to contributing stories, offered much-needed feedback and advice at key moments. So many friends, family, and colleagues supported me during the editing process and offered a listening ear, a nudge in the right direction, and/or snacks—thanks to them all. Particular thanks to Emma Hollier for all those brainstorming graveyard walks and to Rebecca Joines Schinsky, who is my first and last cheerleader. Finally, thanks to Roger Ainslie—you are my favorite.

About the Editors

Swapna Krishna is a space, technology, and pop culture writer and journalist. Her work has been published at *Engadget*, the *Verge*, *Polygon*, StarTrek.com, StarWars.com, the *A.V. Club*, and more. You can find her on Twitter at @skrishna.

Jenn Northington is a former bookseller and a current reviewer, podcaster, and editor. She's been published various places, including *Selfish* magazine and Book Riot, where she also works wrangling editorial operations. You can find her primarily on Instagram at @iamjennIRL.

About the Contributors

Alexander Chee is the bestselling author of the novels *The Queen of the Night* and *Edinburgh* and of the essay collection *How to Write an Autobiographical Novel*. He is a contributing editor at *The New Republic* and an editor at large at *Virginia Quarterly Review*. His work has appeared in *The Best American Essays 2016*, *The New York Times Magazine*, *The New York Times Book Review*, *The New Yorker*, *T* magazine, *Slate*, and *Vulture*, among others. He is the winner of a 2003 Whiting Award for Fiction, a 2004 NEA Fellowship in prose, and a 2010 MCCA Fellowship, and residency fellowships from MacDowell, the Virginia Center for the Creative Arts, the Civitella Ranieri Foundation, and Amtrak. He is an associate professor of English at Dartmouth College.

Preeti Chhibber is a children's author, speaker, and freelance writer. She has written for *SYFY*, Book Riot, *Polygon*, the *Nerds of Color*, and the *Mary Sue*, among others. Her latest, *Orientation (Marvel: Avengers Assembly #1)*, published in August 2020, and her first picture book, *A Jedi You Will Be*, was released in fall 2020. You can find her cohosting the podcast *Desi Geek Girls*. She's appeared on several panels at New York Comic Con and San Diego Comic-Con and on-screen on the SYFY Network. Honestly, you probably recognize her from one of several BuzzFeed "look at these tweets" Twitter lists. She usually spends her time reading a ridiculous amount of young adult but is also ready to jump into most fandoms at a moment's notice. You can follow her on Twitter @runwithskizzers or learn more at PreetiChhibber.com.

Roshani Chokshi is the author of commercial and critically acclaimed books for middle grade and young adult readers that draw on world mythology and folklore. Her work has been nominated for the Locus and Nebula Awards and has frequently appeared on best-of-the-year lists from Barnes & Noble, *Forbes*, BuzzFeed, and more. Her *New York Times* bestselling series include the Star-Touched Queen duology, the Gilded Wolves duology, and the Pandava series, the first book of which, *Aru Shah and the End of Time*, was recently optioned for film by Paramount Pictures.

Sive Doyle is a teacher by day and a writer by night. Originally from Ireland, she lives in New York.

Maria Dahvana Headley is the *New York Times* bestselling and World Fantasy Award–winning author of eight books in a variety of genres, most recently *Beowulf: A New Translation* and *The Mere Wife*. Her short stories have been short-listed for the Nebula and Shirley Jackson Awards and regularly appear in year's-best anthologies.

Daniel M. Lavery is the former cofounder of the *Toast* and is the current "Dear Prudence" advice columnist at *Slate*. His previous books include *Something That May Shock and Discredit You*, *The Merry Spinster*, and *Texts from Jane Eyre*.

Ken Liu (http://kenliu.name) is an American author of speculative fiction. He has won the Nebula, Hugo, and World Fantasy Awards, as well as top genre honors in Japan, Spain, and France, among other countries. Liu's debut novel, *The Grace of Kings*, is the first volume in a silkpunk epic fantasy series, the Dandelion Dynasty, in which engineers play the role of wizards. His debut collection, *The Paper Menagerie and Other Stories*, has been published in more than a dozen languages. A second collection, *The Hidden Girl and Other Stories*, followed. Prior to becoming a full-time writer, Liu worked as a software engineer, corporate lawyer, and litigation consultant. He frequently speaks at conferences and universities on a variety of topics, including futurism, cryptocurrency, the history of technology, bookmaking, and the mathematics of origami.

New York Times and *USA Today* bestseller **Sarah MacLean** is the author of historical romance novels that have been translated into more than twenty-five languages. MacLean is a romance columnist and cohost of weekly romance novel podcast *Fated Mates*, and her work in support of romance and the women who read it earned her a place on Jezebel.com's "Sheroes" list and led *Entertainment Weekly* to call her "the elegantly fuming, utterly intoxicating queen of historical romance." She is a graduate of Smith College and Harvard University. She lives in New York City. Find her at sarahmaclean.net or fatedmates.net.

Silvia Moreno-Garcia is the bestselling author of the novels *Mexican Gothic*, *Gods of Jade and Shadow*, *Certain Dark Things*, *Untamed Shore*, and a bunch of other books. She has also edited several anthologies, including the World Fantasy Award–winning *She Walks in Shadows* (aka *Cthulhu's Daughters*).

Jessica Plummer has worked in book marketing since 2008 and is a contributing editor at Book Riot. She attended Barnard College and is an avid historian of both superhero comics and New York City, where she lives with her pet turtle. When not marketing books, writing about books, or reading books, she's writing them (young adult fantasy, to be specific), or else probably running or baking. She firmly believes every movie should be a musical. "Flat White" is her first published fiction. You can find her on Twitter at @Jess_Plummer.

Anthony Rapp has been acting professionally since he was nine years old, but he has also been writing (and avidly reading) stories for even longer. He won a Young Authors Award when he was eight, and in 2006 he became a *New York Times* bestseller with his memoir, *Without You: A Memoir of Love, Loss, and the Musical* Rent. He lives in NYC with his fiancé, Ken Ithiphol, and their cats Spike, Ferdinand, and Isabella. He's thrilled to have his work included here and dedicates his story to the memory of his late friend Ben Wackerman.

Waubgeshig Rice is an author and journalist from the Anishinaabe community of Wasauksing First Nation on Georgian Bay. He has written three fiction titles, and his short stories and essays have been published in numerous anthologies. His most recent novel, *Moon of the Crusted Snow*, was published in 2018 and became a Canadian bestseller. He graduated from Ryerson University's journalism program in 2002 and spent the bulk of his news and current affairs career at the Canadian Broadcasting Corporation in major cities across Canada. He left CBC in 2020 to focus on creative writing. He lives in Sudbury, Ontario, with his wife and two sons.

Multiple-award-winning author, editor, and journalist **Nisi Shawl** is best known for their fiction dealing with gender, race, and colonialism, including the 2016 Nebula Awards finalist novel *Everfair*. They're the coauthor of a classic text on inclusivity, *Writing the Other: A Practical Approach*, and they teach Writing the Other–related courses online and in person. Shawl's story collection *Filter House* is a cowinner of the James Tiptree Jr./Otherwise Award. Additional awards include the Kate Wilhelm Solstice Award, the Locus Award, and the inaugural Ignyte Award from *FIYAH* magazine. Additional publications include the collections *Something More and More*, *A Primer to Nisi Shawl*, and *Talk Like a Man*.

Shawl edited and coedited *The WisCon Chronicles, Vol. 5: Writing and Racial Identity*; *Bloodchildren: Stories by the Octavia E. Butler Scholars*; *Strange Matings: Science Fiction, Feminism, African American Voices, and Octavia E. Butler*; *Stories for Chip: A Tribute to Samuel R. Delany*; and *New Suns: Original Speculative Fiction by People of Color*. They have contributed to *The Seattle Times*, the *Seattle Review of Books*, the *Los Angeles Review of Books*, *The Washington Post*, and *Ms. Magazine*. They live in Seattle, near a large but shallow lake with an island in the middle. Both Shawl and their cat like to watch birds, but for very different reasons.

Alex Segura is an acclaimed writer of novels, comic books, and podcasts. He is the author of the Star Wars novel *Poe Dameron: Free Fall*, the Pete Fernandez Mystery series (including Anthony Award–nominated crime novels *Dangerous Ends*, *Blackout*, and *Miami Midnight*), and the upcoming *Secret*

Identity. He has also written a number of comic books, most notably the superhero noir *The Black Ghost*, the young adult music series the Archies, and the "Archie Meets" collection of crossovers, featuring real-life cameos from the Ramones, the B-52s, and more. He is also the cocreator/cowriter of the *Lethal Lit* crime/YA podcast from iHeartRadio, which was named one of the best podcasts of 2018 by the *New York Times*. By day he is copresident of Archie Comics. A Miami native, he lives in New York with his wife and children.

S. Zainab Williams is the managing editor of Book Riot, a cohost of the *SFF Yeah!* podcast, and a writer and cartoonist. Her work can be found in *(Don't) Call Me Crazy* and on *The Drabblecast*, among other places. Originally from Los Angeles (Eagle Rock, represent), Williams currently lives in Portland, Oregon, with her demonic cat.

Ausma Zehanat Khan is the author of *The Unquiet Dead. The Unquiet Dead* was the winner of the Barry Award, the Arthur Ellis Award, and the Romantic Times Reviewers' Choice Award for Best First Novel; it was also a 2016 Macavity Award finalist. *The Bloodprint*, Khan's fantasy debut, was hailed as "one of the year's finest fantasy debuts." *The Bloodprint* is book one of the Khorasan Archives, a four-book epic fantasy series, with *The Bladebone*, the final installment, published in 2020. Khan holds a PhD in international human rights law from Osgoode Hall Law School. She completed her LLB and LLM at the University of Ottawa and her BA at the University of Toronto. She practiced immigration law in Toronto and has taught international human rights law at Northwestern University, as well as human rights and business law at York University. She currently lives in Colorado with her husband.

Permissions
Acknowledgments

THE PARIAH

COLLIN WILCOX

THE PARIAH

THE MYSTERIOUS PRESS
New York • London • Tokyo

The Mysterious Press, 129 West 56th Street, New York, N.Y. 10019

Printed in the United States of America
First Printing: April 1988
10 9 8 7 6 5 4 3 2 1

Library of Congress Cataloging-in-Publication Data

Wilcox, Collin.
  The Pariah.

  I. Title.
PS3573.I395P37 1988   813'.54   87-40392
ISBN 0-89296-280-1

This book is
dedicated to the
memory of my mother
who was a one-of-a-kind person

THE PARIAH

1

Earlier in the day, in the afternoon, he'd walked this way, rehearsing. Already, he'd learned the importance of rehearsal. When he was only a child, watching his father—listening, learning—he'd been aware of the importance of knowing what would happen—when—how—in precisely what sequence. So that, now, he was walking without looking.

Yes—walking without looking . . .

It was necessary, absolutely essential, that his eyes make contact with no one, with nothing. Because the eyes were the windows of the soul, revealing everything: two tunnels, leading straight to his essence, deep within himself.

Everything, the trivial and the monumental, the good and the evil, came through the eyes, into the brain, deep into the brain, then into the soul, deep into the soul, his father's playground: sight into sensation, translated into substance, flesh acting on flesh, good battling evil, the eternal struggle.

Past into present, day into night, all of it focused here, now, inside himself, sensation into sight, translated into action, good struggling against evil, God's eternal struggle.

The hotel entrance was behind him. Without looking, without revealing himself, he knew the broad steps leading up to the ornate brass doors were behind him, three shop fronts behind. The corner was ahead. He was aware of the intersection, without revealing his awareness. That, too, was essential. Deliberately, he'd not allowed the names of the two streets that formed the intersection to register on his conscious. He'd learned the

1

importance of that, too—of keeping the surface of his mind absolutely smooth, utterly unblemished, therefore invulnerable, good and evil in equilibrium, rendering him safe. Absolutely safe.

Because sidewalks, streets, intersections, all of them carried the feet, the legs, the bodies—the faces.

And the faces carried the eyes.

And it was the faces, registering or not registering, that could betray him. Their faces, and their eyes—nothing else could harm him but their eyes. He knew that now, knew how the eyes could find any blemish on his consciousness. Then they could look inside, see beneath the surface of his consciousness, look straight through the two twin tunnels to the center of his soul.

It was logical, a logic that only he possessed. Therefore, it separated him from the rest of them, left him free, accountable only to God.

At the corner now, he was allowing himself to turn to the right. His footsteps, he knew, were synchronized to the rhythm of those around him. This, too, was essential. They must never know, must never suspect, that he was walking among them. Because if they knew, then they could guess his mission.

And God would forsake him, leaving him helpless, exposed— surely dead.

Another corner was approaching. This was the crucial intersection, the last right angle remaining. He would turn left, and then begin walking slowly, steadily straight ahead. And because he'd already done it, walked this way earlier, he was no longer compelled to think about it. Instead he could concentrate on the moments to come, focusing his essence on the task before him as he listened for the words that he knew were coming, instructing him.

And, yes, he could feel it beginning. Through the traffic sounds, above the cacophony of voices surrounding him, he could hear the commands: God's will, materializing in words, slowly taking shape, thickening, words that would soon guide him, displacing his own thoughts, his own desires, his own fears. He could feel it beginning, the miracle that would set him free.

But he mustn't look. He must not allow the full, focused force of his essence to slip beyond constant, conscious control, therefore dissipating the force field that would draw her to him, a helpless captive of his dominant essence.

Because if free will was compromised, vengence was denied. It was a given, divinely ordained, as certain as eternal judgment.

Ahead, another intersection was coming closer, a third waypoint, the final guide. He'd known—he'd heard—that it would happen here, must happen here, between the second and the third—

"—about a date?"

The words released him. Therefore, if he chose, he could look at her, make his decision, leaving himself free to speak.

She was dressed in a skintight purple sweater, red plastic miniskirt, black stockings, red plastic boots, spike-heeled. She carried a large black handbag slung over her shoulder. Her eyes were magenta-shadowed, her full lips were painted red. Her skin was black.

There was, therefore, no need to speak. No longer seeing her, he could move on, gathering to himself his essence, God's decree, his shield, invulnerable.

"Hi . . ."

It was a soft, unevenly spoken word, hardly more than an exhausted whisper. The face, too, was exhausted, its skin pale, almost translucent. The blue eyes were sunk deep in darkened sockets. The painted mouth was defeated, twitching as she said something meaningless, the obscene litany of her trade.

Without looking at her, he knew he could see her, therefore knew that, yes, he'd found her.

Dancer Browne yawned, rotated his head, flexed his shoulders, adjusted the volume of the Cleo Lane tape. On a warm September evening, sitting in a white-on-blue Continental that still smelled new, listening to his favorite singer, parked in his favorite parking place, The Dancer was aware that, at age twenty-seven, he had it all. The Continental was paid for, the new sergeant on the Tenderloin beat was coming around, and

IBM was up more than forty points on the year. Dancer's new girl, Jill, only nineteen, the daughter of a Milwaukee doctor, was earning more money than any of Dancer's other girls, after less than a month in the life. He'd found her in the airport, sitting on her suitcase, frowning as she studied a map of San Francisco. One look into her eyes and Dancer saw dollar signs. It was all there: the anger, the defiance, the urge to self-destruct. He'd taken her home, bought her a twenty-dollar dinner and a hundred-dollar pair of boots, given her a fifty-dollar toot and shown her around his circular bed. A week later she turned her first trick.

Five more like Jill, and he could retire.

But five more like Amy, working just across the street, and he'd be old before he turned thirty. From the first, he'd known Amy would cost him. Junkies always cost him. By now he should have learned. Like tonight. It was already ten o'clock, and Amy hadn't scored yet. And tonight, he'd promised himself, was the big one—Amy's final exam. If she didn't score, turn a profit for him, she was out. He'd shoot her up, load her into the Continental and take her down to Stockton, to Jerry Holmes. Jerry would know what to do with her.

As Dancer watched, Amy was moving into the glare of Teddy Parker's FIGHTING GIRLS sign. She was hitting on another one: a man in his middle or late twenties, medium tall, dressed like a tourist, dark blond hair, empty eyes, pale, blank face. This one had stopped, at least, and was listening to Amy's halfhearted pitch. Close by, Jill was coming out of the Bayside Hotel; already she'd turned three tricks, even on a slow Tuesday night. When Jill talked to them, they listened. Dancer looked at his watch, yawned again, adjusted the balance on the stereo. Cleo's voice was like fine, mellow wine, like a woman's fingertips soft on his bare skin. She was—

Across the street, Amy was scoring, moving the tall young trick out of the light from the sign, toward the Bayside. To Dancer, the trick seemed like an odd one: the way he looked, frozen-faced; the way he moved, like a stiff-legged, arm-locked zombie. But he was going along, letting Amy lead him inside the hotel. The Dancer nodded, mentally added another fifty dollars to the night's cash flow: twenty-five for Amy, twenty-five for him.

As he walked behind her down the narrow, dimly lit hallway, he was aware of the gathering force, an invincibility so certain that the sights and sounds that surrounded him were fusing into a single aura of the eternal celestial presence, his invisible cloak, his invincible protection from evil, his armor against temptation.

Because the Devil was here, lurking unseen in this hallway of hell, crouching behind the door just ahead, where she was stopping now, stooping, fitting her key to the lock, allowing the door to swing slowly inward, revealing the cavern of depravity beyond.

Yet, if the Devil was here, God was here, too, on guard, guiding the placement of his feet upon the threadbare carpet, positioning the angle of his hands, the inclination of his head, the rotation and counterrotation of his head, his torso. Because God had entered the interior of his brain, and was touching His fingertips to the brain's countless synapses, those millions of switches that controlled his thoughts, his feelings, his eternal destiny.

Still his vigilance must be constant. Because the Devil's fingers could find the synapses, too. Once it had happened. Now, just about now, it had happened, as he was passing through a door like this door, entering a room like this room, preparing himself for God's call, listening for the tiny voice of command.

And listening, too, for what she would say, also commanding him: "How's this?" she asked, gesturing to the bed as she placed her oversize handbag on the bureau. "Okay?"

He knew that he was nodding. Did she expect him to speak? Didn't she realize that, should he speak, contact would be shattered, leaving him helpless, a prey for the Devil?

Of course she realized. They were so incredibly diabolical, scheming to save themselves, twitching, turning, laughing, smiling. Didn't she realize that only he could offer salvation once she'd surrendered?

No, she didn't realize.

Of course she didn't realize.

So it was essential that he smile. Once. Just once. One smile, one nod. No more was permitted.

"Just drop the fifty in the handbag, okay?" She gestured. "It's open. Right?"

Lowering his eyes, he saw the fifty-dollar bill held between thumb and forefinger—his thumb and forefinger, guided by God's fingertips, on the synapses. Yes, the money was dropping into the open maw of the handbag, itself an obscenity. Now, turning, he willed his eyes to focus on her face, only on her face. And, yes, he could see that they were beginning: he could see it in her face, the beginning of the final rites.

"So what'd you want to do?" The painted face twisted into an obscenity of a smile; the eyes leered, the mouth taunted him. "Time's passing, you know." The unclean smile widened. "And time's money. Right? Money, and fun, it's all the same. Right?"

It was important now, overwhelmingly important, utterly essential that his words reach her without his actually speaking. Because God controlled him now. God's mind, God's will— God's hands on the synapses. Controlling him.

And, yes, listening, he heard. It was God, speaking with his voice. A miracle:

"Turn around. Don't look at me. Just turn around."

Indifferently, she shrugged, mutely moving her thin shoulders. Soon, she would have died, a victim of the streets she prowled. Without salvation, fallen from grace, she would have gone to eternal damnation, unsaved.

Did she know?

Did she feel the presence, acknowledge the divine power? Salvation was coming closer, saving her from eternal fire. The power was palpable now, enfolding them, a single aura, pulsing with the power. In his hands, upraised, the instrument of salvation would materialize, the means of liberation.

"Stay like that." Yes, the voice was his: calm, steady, commanding. "Just like that."

"Whatever . . ." Once more, indifferently, she shrugged.

Now, still with upraised hands, himself a supplicant, he took the final step forward. It was the moment of touching, the decisive moment, the moment upon which all else balanced. He must touch his body to hers, must master the obscene sensation, must liberate mind from body as his will merged with God's cosmic consciousness . . . Now. Finally, unequivocally, incredibly now, his body upon hers. Enabling him finally to close his eyes, awaiting the delivery. He could hear her voice, but the words were lost in the roar of the cosmos. He must remain like this, controlling this moment of final grace, suspended between heaven and earth, eyes closed, hands raised, fingers extended— awaiting the touch of God's fingers upon his, delivering the instrument.

One breath of eternity . . .

And another breath—the final, eternal breath.

And, yes, as his eyes opened, he saw it in his hands: the instrument, a length of miraculous golden cord, his gift from God.

"Hey. What the fuck you—"

The rest of it was lost in a gurgle of sound as the cord disappeared from sight. Her body had gone wild, writhing against his. He must close his eyes now, witnessing with his body her passage, allowing himself this one moment of animal response, purifying the liberation of her body, taking its corruption unto himself, his sacrifice. To accomplish it, her body must slacken as his slackened, together, his final gift to her—

—finished.

With God as his witness, finally finished.

2

"You want anything from the machines?" Culligan asked. "Coffee? Anything?"

"No, thanks," Canelli answered. "I'm not drinking coffee anymore after ten o'clock at night. Besides, the more you read, coffee's no good for you. My dad, you know, has heart problems. And the doctor said, right after cigarettes, cut out the coffee. So I figure, what the hell, I might as well—"

On his desk, the telephone warbled. Waving to Culligan as the other detective left the squadroom, Canelli lifted the receiver, punched the blinking button."

"Homicide. Inspector Canelli speaking."

"This is Bernie Penziner. Hi."

"Oh, hi, Bernie." Canelli's broad, swarthy face softened into a sly smile. "How're you enjoying the Tenderloin beat?"

"I didn't know when I was well off. Safes and Lofts might be boring, but this is the pits, down here. I mean, it's a goddamn zoo."

"So what's doing? I don't suppose this is a social call."

"There's a dead hooker at the Bayside Hotel. It's at Mason and—"

"I know where it is." Canelli leaned forward, put a paperweight on an unfinished interrogation report. "I was there . . ." He frowned, calculating. "It was less than six months ago, I bet it was, that I was there. Another hooker, in fact."

"That's because there's nothing but hookers at the Bayside. They rent rooms by the hour."

"Anyone in custody?"

"No."

"Any suspects?"

"No."

"Any idea how long ago it happened?"

"Not long, I would say. I touched her. She was warm."

"Okay. I'll turn out the troops, and come down. What's the room number?"

"Three twenty-five. Shall I stay here? In the room?"

"Just make sure it's secure, any way you want to do it. I'll be there in a half hour or so. Okay?"

"Yeah. Okay. Jesus, what a business. First I'm bored in Safes and Lofts. And now I feel like I'm going to puke all the time. Every year, I say I'm going to quit, take early retirement. Every goddamn year."

"I used to say that, too. But I don't anymore. And I'm not even thirty, yet."

"Hmmm . . ."

Canelli parked the cruiser beside a fireplug, scribbled "Bayside Hotel, Rm. 325" on his card, put the card on the dashboard, locked the car and began making his way along the crowded sidewalk. He was a big, lumpy, diffident man who moved more like an amiable tourist on vacation than a policeman on duty. Ahead, he saw a squad car pulled up in front of the Bayside Hotel. One of the uniformed men sat in the car, monitoring the radio; the other stood beside the entrance to the hotel. Recognizing the man on guard, Canelli smiled, waving a beefy hand.

"Hi, Fergie. How's it going?"

"No complaints, Joe." Answering Canelli's amiable smile, the patrolman pushed open the hotel door and stood aside. The door was all metal, with a single small, wire-reinforced window at shoulder height. The red-painted BAYSIDE logo beneath the window was badly chipped. Inside, the lobby was less than twelve feet wide, with a narrow flight of stairs at the far end. An unevenly lettered NO CHECKS, NO CARDS sign was tacked to the Formica counter that guarded the stairs. Sitting behind the counter, as high and as hostile as a precinct sergeant, the muscular black desk clerk glowered at the shield Canelli offered for his inspection.

"Your other guy's upstairs," the black man grated. "Third floor."

"There'll be others along," Canelli said. "Technicians, and guys from the coroner's office."

Without moving, without changing expression, standing with his big-knuckled brawler's fists braced wide on the counter, the desk man nodded. "I know how it goes."

"How long you been on duty?" Canelli asked.

"Since nine o'clock tonight."

"You work regular here?"

"Yeah."

"Okay. You hang around. Don't go anywhere without you talk to me."

"I'm on till six. Where'm I going?" The blue-black lips twisted into a weary cop-hater's sneer.

Penziner had taken a straight-backed chair from a vacant room and was sitting in the hallway. One uniformed man stood beside the door to 325, another stood at one end of the hallway, beside the staircase. From one end to the other, the hallway was lit with a line of red bulbs. Seeing Canelli, Penziner got to his feet.

"A half hour exactly," Penziner said. "I'm impressed."

"You want to hang around?" Canelli asked, "or would you just as soon go?"

"I'd just as soon go. I already told you, this doesn't agree with my stomach, all this. Especially the goddamn smell."

"No problem." Canelli took a notebook and ballpoint pen from the pocket of his tan windbreaker. "What've you got for me?"

"Her name was Amy MacFarland. I never talked to her, never busted her. She was from out of town, though, I know that. But that's all of them, out-of-towners, runaways."

"Who's her pimp?"

"A black guy named Dancer Browne. He was parked right across the street when I got here, cool as shit."

"Will he stay put?"

"Oh, sure." Penziner's long, lean face registered grudging admiration as he said, "Dancer's—what—the king of Mason Street. He went to San Francisco State for a couple of years, on a basketball scholarship. He's tall, about six five. And smart, too, smart as hell. He only works white girls—four, five of them. He won't run anywhere, take my word. He's got too much going on here."

"Anything else?"

"Nothing. I'll ask around, though, see what I can turn up. She came in with a trick, I think. So it's probably him that did it."

Canelli nodded, pocketed his notebook. "Keep in touch, okay?"

"Yeah, okay. See you, Joe." Penziner nodded and walked down the garishly lit hallway to the staircase. Canelli drew a deep breath and turned to face the door of room 325. He would make his preliminary examination, then call the duty lieutenant.

3

On the TV screen, the president was making hard eye contact with the camera at the conclusion of a rebroadcast speech that had warned of Communism's new menace to the Western Hemisphere. Sitting beside Ann on their living room sofa, Hastings yawned, lifted his arms high above his head, flexed his fingers, then touched Ann on the forearm. She turned, smiled at him.

"How about some hot chocolate?" she asked.

"Fine. I'll put the garbage cans out."

"The newspapers, too."

"Right." He watched her as she got up, switched off the TV, walked to the archway that opened onto the long hallway leading back to the rear of the large Victorian flat. She wore faded blue jeans and a plaid cotton shirt, shirt-tail out. Her long tawny hair was fastened in a pony tail. Ann was a quiet, reserved woman, and she moved accordingly: firmly, self-sufficiently, economically. Literally from the first moment they'd met, her body had excited him. She'd been dressed as she was dressed now, in jeans, with her hair in a pony tail, wearing no makeup. It had been the same time of night, too: a little after eleven. Dan, her teenage son, had been a material witness in a homicide, and briefly a suspect. With his shield in his left hand, Hastings had pressed Ann's door buzzer with his right hand. Then, reflexively, he'd stepped back, unbuttoned his jacket, put his right hand on the butt of his revolver. When the door opened, he'd—

In the hallway, the telephone rang. Quickly, mindful of Ann's two sleeping sons, Hastings rose, went to the phone.

"Yes?"

"Hi, Lieutenant. It's Canelli."

Automatically, Hastings noted the time as he clicked a ballpoint pen over the notepad that was always beside the phone. He was about to go on duty.

"What's up?"

"It's a dead hooker down on Mason Street, at the Bayside Hotel, in the three hundred block. It happened a little after ten o'clock, according to the way I get it. She was strangled. All I got is a general description of the guy that probably did it. They came in a little after ten, like I said. Maybe ten minutes later the guy left, through the lobby."

"Is the crew there?"

"The ME's here. McCarville. Our lab guys haven't showed up yet. I figured—you know—a hooker, it's no big deal. So I didn't put the rush on them."

"Okay, I'll be down in forty-five minutes or so."

"Right."

Hastings cradled the phone and turned to face Ann, who stood in the doorway to the kitchen. They'd been living together for a little more than a year. Already, she'd gotten accustomed to the phone calls that could come on Hasting's duty nights. Or, if not accustomed, at least resigned.

"The chocolate's almost ready," she said quietly.

"Good. I'll just have time."

As he stripped off his rubber gloves and straightened over the body, McCarville winced, pressing both hands into the small of his back. McCarville was a small, trim, middle-aged man, totally bald, nattily dressed. As he turned to face Hastings, he grimaced.

"The last time we met like this," McCarville said, "it seems to me I was complaining about my back then, too."

"No better, eh?"

"Worse, I think."

"Do I ask if you went to a doctor?"

The grimace twisted into an expression of long-suffering patience. "I'd rather you didn't."

"Well . . ." Hastings gestured to the dead woman. "What's the word?"

"Pretty straightforward," McCarville answered. "She hasn't lost any internal temperature, which means she's been dead two hours or less. Without doubt, she was strangled by something like a coarse rope, maybe three quarters of an inch in diameter. Just eyeballing her, I'd say she was in her twenties, in poor health, probably malnourished. And, yes, she had needle marks on both arms and both legs." Spreading his hands, he shrugged. "And that's pretty much it. The autopsy might hand you some surprises, but I doubt it." He gestured to the room's open doorway, where a gurney waited. "Want us to take her away?"

Hastings looked inquiringly at Canelli. "Have we got everything? Plenty of pictures?"

Canelli nodded. "Plenty."

"Okay—" Hastings stepped back, standing with Canelli beside the double bed. Briskly, the two coroner's deputies entered the small room, spread a green plastic sheet on the floor, rolled the body onto the sheet, used black elastic straps to secure it. The gurney was brought in and lowered. Grunting, the two deputies squatted, nodded to each other, heaved the body up.

"Light," one of the deputies said. "Less than a hundred, I'd say."

As Hastings watched the deputies wheel the body out into the hallway he looked at his watch. The time was ten minutes past midnight. Elapsed time: two hours since someone had come up to this room with Amy MacFarland, quietly closed the door, and killed her.

Or, more accurately, the murderer had probably snuffed her. For an extra charge, she'd probably let him play with the limits. She'd gambled with her life, and lost. Poor Amy MacFarland. She probably wouldn't even get an obituary in the next day's newspaper.

"So what've we got?" Hastings asked. "Who've you talked to?"

"Just the room clerk," Canelli answered. "And it was a zero, what he had to say. He claims he didn't even notice the guy when they came in. Her, he remembered. I mean, that's his job, to keep track of the hookers, keep track of the money. But the tricks, he claims, they all look alike."

"Do you believe him?"

Canelli's swarthy moon face registered brow-furrowed concentration as he considered. "Well, if I had to say yes or no then I guess I'd have to say yes. I mean, what's he got to lose, giving us a description of the guy?"

"What about her pimp?"

"A guy named Dancer Browne. Bernie Penziner—he's on the Tenderloin beat now—he told Dancer to stay available. He's parked just down the block, in a big white and blue Continental. God, he's some character. I mean, these pimps're all—you know—cool. But Dancer, he's supercool."

"I'll talk to him. Is he black?"

"Yeah. Tall, and black. He used to play basketball at State, according to Bernie." Canelli smiled. "How about that—an athlete, down here pimping."

"I'll see what he says. You stay here—" Hastings gestured to a lab technician who was leisurely dusting a badly chipped bureau for fingerprints. "Make sure it all gets done. I'll be back in a half hour or so."

"Yessir."

Hastings stooped, pressed his shield against the Continental's passenger window and knocked on the glass with his free hand. Behind the wheel, Dancer smiled, lifted a forefinger in a with-it salute, and leaned across to open the door.

"I'm Lieutenant Frank Hastings. Homicide."

"Hey—" The lazy smile widened, registering a special pleasure. "Hey, I know you. I saw you on TV, not too long ago. Didn't I?"

Deciding to ignore the question, Hastings half turned in his seat to face the other man. On a warm September night, The Dancer was wearing the obligatory two-hundred-dollar sports shirt opened deep at the neck to reveal an ebony chest festooned with gold chains. Both his hair and his beard were close-cropped. Behind designer glasses, his eyes were expressive, constantly in motion. His mouth was mobile. His manner was completely relaxed, utterly assured.

"Tell me about Amy MacFarland."

"Oh, yeah . . ." Dancer sighed heavily, gravely shook his head. "It's terrible, these crazies."

"She was one of your girls."

Observing the conventions, Dancer frowned, elaborately puzzled. "How do you mean, 'one of my girls'?"

"I mean that she worked for you, turning tricks."

Dancer's full lips curved into an amused smile. Allowing a small silence to lengthen, he took time to assess the other man: about forty years old, give or take. A big, muscular man, one of the quiet ones, a man who would think first and then hit—hard.

Continuing the mandatory pattern of ritual responses, Dancer spread his hands, pantomiming an aggrieved innocence. "I just don't know what you mean, Lieutenant. No idea."

"You're wasting my time, Dancer. I was getting ready for bed when this call came in. Don't jerk me around. I'm not in the mood."

Judging that the time had come for plain talk, Dancer asked, "So what're we talking? One on one?"

"That's how we're talking. I don't care who you're running, where your money comes from. That's between you and Vice, whatever you work out. But I've got a dead body, and I need a suspect to go with it. I want some answers—now. Then I want to go home and get some sleep. Clear?"

Eyes veiled, Dancer smiled. Yes, he and Hastings could work together.

"You know how it goes, Dancer. It's the hard way or the easy way. Your choice."

Nodding acceptance of the terms, Dancer spoke quietly, concisely: "She came to town about four months ago, I guess it was, from New York, so she said. She was a junkie—had been, for a year or two, I'd say. So I—you know—tried to make it a little easier for her, put her in touch with some people." He shrugged. "That's about it."

With his notebook on his knee, Hastings asked, "Where'd she live?"

"I don't know." Saying it, Dancer met the other man's eyes squarely, signifying that, really, he was telling the truth. "I mean, she moved around a lot. All I know, she'd show up down here, whenever she felt like it. She'd just—you know—see the car, and we'd talk. Then she'd go about her business."

"How much did she charge?"

"Fifty. Hopefully."

"What about tonight? Tell me about tonight."

"Yeah—" He nodded, once more made full, complete eye contact. "Well, I was parked just a few spaces up, on this side of the street." As the other man pointed, Hastings caught the sparkle of a large diamond on his little finger. "And I happened to see Amy, across the street, there—" He pointed again. "She was—you know—hitting on the tourists. She hit on maybe three or four, but didn't score. But then, after a while, she connected with this guy. They talked for a minute or so, not long, and then they—you know—went into the hotel, there—the Bayside. And that was it, pretty much."

"What time was this?"

"Just about ten, I'd say."

"Describe him, the trick."

"Yeah, well, that was interesting. I mean, they were talking right in front of a sign, so I got a pretty good look at him. And I remember thinking he looked weird. I mean, his face was a blank, you know. Just a real pale blank, with these empty, stone eyes."

"How old was he?"

Dancer shrugged. "Twenty-five, thirty, maybe. No more."

"How was he dressed?"

"Like a tourist, I'd say—just your standard out-of-towner."

"Was he wearing a tie?"

"No, no tie. I didn't pay much attention, though. But I

remember that he wasn't wearing a tie. Maybe he had a—you know—a polyester sports jacket, like that."

"How tall?"

"Medium. Five ten, maybe. Slim."

"Hair color?"

"Blond. Dark blond, maybe. Regular cut." He shrugged again. "A tourist, like I said. Just your standard tourist from New Jersey, looking for some action . . ." Dancer paused, looked across the street, toward the spot where he'd last seen Amy MacFarland. "Except for those eyes," he said thoughtfully. "They were strange, those eyes. Spooky."

"You'd recognize him again." It was a statement, not a question.

Dancer looked at the big, quiet-spoken lieutenant, the man with the calm, hard eyes. They'd made a deal, the two of them: the standard deal. If he cooperated, he'd earn points—for himself, for his girls, money in the bank.

But identifying someone—going public, downtown—that was never part of the standard deal. Never.

"I'm not talking about a lineup," Hastings said. "Nothing like that. Nothing downtown."

"Ah . . ." Dancer nodded, tried not to reveal the relief he felt.

"But if we turn up anything, I'll want to run him by you." As he spoke, Hastings opened the passenger's door. "You weren't planning to leave town." It was another statement: flat, cold, businesslike.

Dancer smiled. "Man, I haven't left this town in years. I haven't left this *block* in years. You want to find me, here I'll be."

"Good." Hastings nodded, got out of the car, crossed the street in the direction of the Bayside Hotel.

Sitting on the double bed, Canelli watched the last of the lab technicians leave the room before he dropped his eyes to the outline of Amy MacFarland's body chalked on the stained carpeting. Seated in the room's only chair, Hastings was also looking down at the outline. Slowly, somberly, Canelli shook his head.

"You know," Canelli said, "it's sad when you think about it. I mean, here's this girl—" He gestured. "For all we know, she could've been a—a bank president's daughter, or something. But no matter, she probably had parents who loved her, and everything. So then she starts in with drugs, and probably her folks threw her out, or whatever. So this is the way she ends up— her, and thousands like her. But the hell of it is, no one really cares. You know?"

Hastings nodded, then shrugged. "Nobody ever said life was fair, Canelli."

"Yeah—" Vehemently now, Canelli nodded. "That's it, Lieutenant. I mean, if this was the Fairmont, or somewhere, there'd be photographers and reporters, and . . ." He sighed, shook his head, studied the body's outline with soft brown eyes. Then: "It's like you say. It's just not fair."

Heavily, Hastings rose to his feet. The time was almost two, and fatigue had suddenly overtaken him.

"If you're trying to make me feel guilty, Canelli, you aren't succeeding. I'm going home, and I'm going to sleep. And after you lock up, I'd advise you to do the same. I'll see you at the office tomorrow morning. About ten, or maybe a little later."

4

Sitting slumped behind his desk, Hastings was staring with unfocused eyes at an interoffice memo outlining Chief Dwyer's new guidelines on overtime policy for nonuniformed personnel when the intercom button lit up. Wearily, he lifted the phone.

"Hastings."

"Yeah, this is Peirce, Lieutenant. There's a Mr. Draper here, to see someone in Homicide. Walter Draper. He's with the FBI, from Washington." After a short pause Peirce added, "Lieutenant Friedman just left for court."

"Okay, give me five minutes, then send him—no, *bring* him in."

"Right."

Walter Draper was a dapper man of medium height and weight, stylishly dressed, with prep school manners and a small, fastidiously trimmed moustache. He was about thirty years old, slightly balding, dressed in a pinstriped suit, white shirt, and regimental tie. Moving smoothly, precisely, he sat in Hastings's visitor's chair, arranged his trouser creases and smiled. It was a small, tight, tactical smile, slightly condescending.

"I'm sure you're busy, Lieutenant Hastings, so I'll come right to the point." As he spoke, Draper took a business card from his vest pocket and snapped it down on Hastings's desk. The card identified Draper as an assistant supervisor, Federal Bureau of Investigation, Washington, D.C.

"I'm with the Joint Task Force on Non-Causal Related

20

Crime." Draper paused, looking expectantly at Hastings. Yes, Hastings had heard of the task force, seen the flyers from Washington, one of dozens that crossed his desk each week. But, no, he couldn't remember what the task force was meant to accomplish.

"It's not registering, I see." Draper's voice was both tolerant and wearily resigned. Already, Hastings had consigned Draper to the nameless, faceless ranks of Ivy League FBI agents, one of hundreds he'd dealt with over the years. Only once had he ever met an FBI man he'd liked.

Stifling a yawn, Hastings shook his head. "I remember the bulletins. But that's all, I'm afraid."

"For about a year now," Draper said, "we've been requesting reports from local jurisdictions on all current homicides—unsolved homicides thirty days old or more."

"Ah . . ." Hastings nodded. It was a responsibility he'd assigned to Richard Gee, the newest man in Homicide. "Right."

"What we're doing," Draper said, "is trying to see whether we can find any similarities between the victims, anything the computers can kick out for us."

Through the glass door of his office, Hastings saw two detectives standing expectantly in the hallway, mutely asking whether they could interrupt. Hastings moved his head a half inch, side to side.

"How's it going?" Hastings asked, returning his attention to the man from Washington.

"The computer is an incredible tool," Draper announced. "Unbelievable. I don't have to tell you that. They make matchups that would take clerks months to work out. We've been running this program for six months now, and it's amazing what we've turned up."

"What's the purpose of the program?"

Draper hesitated, then moved slightly forward in his chair, lowering his voice. "Actually," he said, "the goals are still classified. But, confidentially—" His voice dropped another half note. "Confidentially, we're trying to see whether we can get a handle on serial killers."

"Serial killers . . ." Interested, Hastings looked more attentively at the other man.

"It's a new approach," Draper explained, "a new concept. Up to now, we've been looking for connections between the victims and the killer. Which is tough going, as you know. I mean, the definition of a serial killer, after all, is that he kills at random. Usually there's no connection between the killer and the victim. None. Some guy gets in his car and starts driving—across the country, maybe. He gets drunk, or high, or his demons start acting up, or whatever, and he finds someone, and he kills him—or her. True, there'll usually be a common denominator relating to the killer's personality—he's a homosexual, and usually kills teenage boys, let's say. That gives us something to work on, but it's not a very good predictive tool."

Hastings frowned. "Predictive tool?"

"Some means of predicting where or when a serial killer will strike next."

"So what's your new approach?"

For effect, Draper allowed a moment to pass before he said, "We're trying to attack the problem from the other end, so to speak. The homosexual killer, for example. We know he goes after teenage boys. But the question is, what kinds of teenage boys? Blonds? Brunettes? Maybe he only gets turned on by boys with blue eyes—or boys who wear tennis shoes, whatever. Maybe not just tennis shoes, maybe it's Adidas shoes that turn him on. Or maybe one guy kills only when the moon's in the fourth quarter. He doesn't know that's when he kills. But the computer knows. And if the Adidas killer is also the one who kills when the moon's in its fourth quarter, then we're making progress. Not much progress. But some. Because we've got a two-way matchup, then, you see—a cross-check."

"Yeah," Hastings said, politely nodding. "I can see it."

"Some of the connections we're getting are pretty erudite," Draper continued. "For instance, prostitutes are obviously a big target group, for obvious reasons. And in Trenton last year, there were four prostitutes killed at one-month intervals. They were all black, all in their early twenties. They'd all come from small towns in the South—and their fathers all worked for the civil service, in some capacity. And it turned out they were all murdered by the same guy.''

"Are you telling me that he—'' Hastings broke off, searching for the phrase, "—that he screened his victims?''

"No. Not consciously, anyhow. But subconsciously—'' Draper spread his hands. The FBI man's fingernails, Hastings noticed, looked as if they were manicured. "Who knows?''

"Computers . . .'' Registering polite wonderment, Hastings shook his head. "They're amazing. I guess we'll all be spending more time looking at the green numbers.''

Decisively, Draper nodded emphatic agreement. "The programmer who set up the study told me that he used to work for an outfit called the North American Society for Cyclical Research, which was set up to predict the changes in the business cycle. And he says that the sales curve of junior misses ready-to-wear at Macy's corresponds exactly to the nesting cycle of the brown starling.''

"The *brown starling*?''

Draper's answering nod was solemn. "The brown starling.'' He let a beat pass before he said, "Going back to prostitutes, that's why I'm here.'' He let another beat pass, compelling Hastings's closer attention. "Today is Wednesday. Beginning Monday, have there been any prostitutes killed in San Francisco?''

"As a matter of fact,'' Hastings answered slowly, "there *was* one killed. Last night, down in the Tenderloin.''

Instantly, Draper's eyes came alive; his carefully cultivated image of the aloof FBI executive abruptly faded as he asked, "Last night? No fooling?'' Eagerly, he came forward in his chair. Amused, Hastings nodded. Could Draper be another likable FBI agent, one capable of actual enthusiasm, the second likable agent he'd ever encountered?

"She was killed about ten last night. Why?''

"Do you have anyone in custody?''

"Ah, ah.'' Hastings raised a gamesman's forefinger. "I asked you first. What's the rundown?''

As Draper considered the question, caution veiled his eyes. "Lieutenant . . ." It was a pained admonishment. "I don't have to tell you that I can't give out information without—"

"Without checking with Washington. I know. Well—" Hastings smiled: a small, knowing smile. "Well, it's the same with me. I have to check with my people."

Draper eyed the man across the desk. Obviously, Hastings was an intelligent man, undoubtedly a competent officer: quiet, cautious, probably conscientious. Some ranking officers in the local jurisdictions, Draper had concluded, were thick-headed obstructionists: sidewalk cops promoted beyond their capacities, therefore insecure and envious when dealing with their opposite numbers in the Bureau. But Hastings talked like a man who'd gone to college—and graduated.

"You're, ah, the co-commander of the homicide detail," Draper said, offering a gambit. "Is that correct?"

Hastings nodded. "Correct. Pete Friedman and I—Lieutentant Friedman—we share command. He's in court today."

"So you really don't have to check with anyone."

"I have limited discretion." Holding the FBI man's gaze, Hastings allowed a long, measured beat to pass, then added meaningfully, "You have limited discretion, too."

For a full thirty seconds Draper stared out through the window at a fragmented view of the city. The time was 11:10 A.M. He was booked on a 7:15 P.M. flight to D.C. Conceivably, he could persuade the local bureau chief to contact Hastings's superior officer, probably the chief of detectives. The chief of detectives might go along, might order Hastings to cooperate, without demanding anything in return.

He might, or he might not.

Either way, Draper had a meeting scheduled in exactly twenty-three hours and forty-five minutes in D.C.

And if he could announce a break in the case, or at least a good, solid lead . . .

He returned his gaze to Hastings, who was calmly waiting for his answer.

"Okay," Draper said, his voice crisp, his manner brusque. He took out a small leather-bound notebook, twisted the barrel of a Cross pen. "Let's have it. You first."

As Draper took notes, Hastings ran down the Amy MacFarland case, supplying all the facts, all the names, all the speculation. Only twice did Draper interrupt, asking for additional details. Ten minutes later, satisfied, Draper reviewed his notes, pocketed the pen and notebook.

"Your turn," Hastings said, drawing a notepad closer.

A last long moment of silence as Draper stared gravely across the desk. Finally, portentiously, he said:

"It could be that I'm going to give you a big one, Lieutenant. If that's the way it comes down, I hope you'll remember that you heard it here first—from me. Fair?"

"Fair."

"Okay." Heavily decisive, Draper squared himself in his chair, facing up to the bargain he'd made. "Here it is . . ." Another reluctant pause. Then: "Amy MacFarland fits the victim profile of a serial murder case we've been working on. She fits the computer model exactly. Right on the money."

Hastings decided his best tactic was simply to nod, waiting for the FBI man to continue:

"A little more than a year ago, in a period of three weeks, two prostitutes were murdered in Los Angeles. At the time, the two homicides didn't seem to be connected. And, let's face it, the police didn't exactly pull out all the stops when they investigated. But when we activated the task force, we went back over the data. And that's when the similarities began popping up."

"On the printouts."

Draper nodded. "Exactly. On the printouts. Both the victims were white, in their twenties. Both of them were murdered in hotel or motel rooms, where they'd taken a john. Both of them were strangled by a thick cord, or a rope. It wasn't robbery, nothing was taken. And there weren't any messages left behind. You know, 'Death to harlots' written in lipstick on the mirror, or whatever.

"So the information went into the computer," Draper continued, "which was programmed to pick up similarities in sex, age, occupation, mode of death, probable weapon, whether robbery was involved, et cetera et cetera." Draper paused, reflectively shaking his head. "It's incredible, what these computers can do, matching things up. Unbelievable."

"So how does this come down to Amy MacFarland?"

As if he were ignoring the question, Draper went on, stolidly telling his story in sequence: "That was about a year ago, that the first two were killed. Then, about a month later—I'm not positive about the dates—another one showed up. In Cleveland."

"Cleveland?"

"Cleveland. And then one showed up in Los Angeles, then two in San Diego, if I remember correctly—then back to Los Angeles. And so on—for a year. One or two in different cities, but always back to Los Angeles—a total of fourteen, the way we figure it." A short, significant pause. Then: "Including Amy MacFarland, last night."

"The murderer is based in Los Angeles, and travels around the country."

"Exactly."

"So what's the rest of it? You said you were giving me a big one."

"What I'm giving you—" Draper paused again, allowing himself a moment of drama, building the suspense. "What I'm giving you is Austin Holloway."

"The evangelist?" Disbelieving, Hastings shook his head. "You're kidding."

"Not Austin Holloway himself. But someone in his organization, sure as hell. Because that's what the computer turned up, you see. The only common denominator was the itinerary of Austin Holloway. And, believe me, our programmer—he's a genius—he punched in everything; big league baseball schedules, stock car racers, cosmetics salesmen, every kind of convention you can name, God knows what all. It took him months, assigning a code to all the suspect models, then running the program. But finally it came down to Holloway. Computerwise, it's absolutely irrefutable. I was there myself, and saw it happen. The programmer punched in the code for Austin Holloway's itinerary, and the goddamn bells and whistles went off. And I'm talking a hundred-percent correlation."

"That's not evidence, though."

"Maybe not. But it's sure as hell probable cause. Reason enough to turn out the troops, as I'm sure you'd certainly agree."

"Yes," Hastings answered slowly. "I'd agree." He let a moment of thoughtful silence pass, staring across his small, glass-paneled office before he said softly, "So now Holloway's in San Francisco."

"Right."

"How long have you known this, about Holloway's connection with the murders?"

"Just about two weeks," Draper answered.

"Have you had Holloway under surveillance in Los Angeles?"

"The FBI hasn't. So far, we're just acting in an advisory capacity. But the local authorities've put three men on it, full-time. Lieutenant Brinker, in Homicide down there, is the officer in charge."

"Have they got anything? Any leads?"

"Not yet, as far as I know. L.A.'s got at least eight cases, potentially. If we're right, the last victim was killed about five weeks ago."

Nodding thoughtfully, Hastings let his gaze wander away again, this time to focus on his own private view: a truncated cityscape, highlighted by a tiny, top-to-bottom slice of the Transamerica Pyramid.

Austin Holloway . . .

The face, the voice, the man—known throughout the world, a Sunday video presence in millions of American homes. Of all the TV evangelists, Holloway was the most successful, the most famous, the most mesmerizing, some said the most manipulative, therefore the most dangerous. A recent newsmagazine had done a cover story on TV evangelists. In every category—number of weekly viewers, gross revenue, value of real estate holdings— Holloway had far outstripped his nearest competitor. Hastings could clearly recall the magazine's cover: Austin Holloway, dressed in a purple robe, handsome as a gray-haired prophet, with his towering glass cathedral glowing in the background. The inference: among American evangelists, Austin Holloway was chairman of the board.

"You aren't telling me," Hastings said, "that you think Austin Holloway himself is killing these hookers. Because the description we've got doesn't fit Holloway."

"What I'm telling you," Draper said, "is what the computer tells me. And, as far as I know, there's no data on the suspect. The weapon, yes. The suspect, no." He glanced at his wrist-watch, rose, pointed to his business card lying on Hastings's desk. "I've got a lunch date, and then I'll be tied up for the rest of the day. I'd appreciate it if you'd keep in touch. And don't forget, when it's news conference time, remember Uncle. Remember Uncle—and remember me."

Also on his feet, Hastings extended his hand. "I'll remember—both of you."

5

Friedman saw it lying in the center of his desk, printed with a bold black felt marking pen across a form meant for interoffice memos, a message from Hastings:

SEE ME ASAP.

For Friedman, it was an intriguing surprise; Hastings seldom used a felt marker, almost never sounded the alarm.

Stopping only at a dispensing machine, then carrying a Styrofoam cup filled with coffee, Friedman walked down a short hallway to Hastings's office. Seeing him alone, bent over his desk, Friedman knocked twice on the glass door and entered without being invited. He closed the door, went to Hastings's visitors' chair, and sank down with a grateful sigh as he sipped the steaming coffee. Friedman was a large, big-bellied man in his middle fifties. His face was broad and swarthy, his dark eyes heavily lidded. His graying hair was thick, haphazardly combed. Even at odd hours, Friedman wore three-piece suits that never quite fit. His collar was perpetually mashed by a sizable double chin, his vests constantly smudged by cigar ash. Friedman's manner was elliptical, playfully inscrutable. Offered a captaincy and command of Homicide, he'd promptly declined. Instead, he'd offered Hastings a deal. Friedman would work inside, exercising his intellect in the battle against crime, while Hastings worked in the field, exercising his muscles. Hastings had accepted, and Chief Dwyer had reluctantly gone along. Unlike Dwyer, Friedman and Hastings had never regretted their decision.

"What's up?" Friedman asked, settling himself more comfortably in the visitor's chair and putting his coffee on Hastings's desktop.

In detail, Hastings ran down the MacFarland homicide, then described his meeting with Draper. As he finished, Friedman began dolefully shaking his head. "You know what's happening here, don't you?" he said. "It's the goddamn inevitable, finally coming true. The computers're taking over."

"This is no different than our fingerprint computer," Hastings answered. "It's like Draper said, the computer comes up with comparisons that it'd take techs weeks to make. Months, maybe."

"That's techs," Friedman grunted. "I'm talking about us." He touched the vest pocket where, every morning, he put four cigars, his daily ration. Then he remembered that he'd smoked his fourth cigar as he rode to the Hall of Justice. "So how're we handling it?"

"Canelli and Culligan are at the St. Francis, getting the feel of things. That's where Austin Holloway and a lot of his staff are staying. I'm going to go over there in a half hour. If it's feasible, I thought I'd take Dancer Browne along and plant him in the lobby, or somewhere. We might get lucky."

Amused, Friedman smiled: a slow, lazy twisting of his cherub's mouth. "The DA'll love that—his key witness a pimp."

"Have you got a better idea?"

"No." Friedman's ironic smile widened. "But I hope you can find a potted palm, or something, to stick Dancer Browne behind. I've never met the gentleman, but if he's like most pimps I've met, I don't think he's going to fit in with the St. Francis crowd."

Hastings made no comment, and for a long moment the two men sat silently, thinking about the computer-generated possibilities. Finally, still smiling ironically, Friedman shook his head, as if he'd just been struck by a thought so incredibly intriguing that it must be shared:

"God," he said. "Wouldn't it be great if we nailed one of Austin Holloway's flunkies for murder one? It'd be a public service, for God's sake."

Reflectively answering the smile, Hastings nodded. "I know . . ."

"What's Holloway doing here, anyhow—in San Francisco? This sure as hell isn't the Bible Belt."

"Good question. I was wondering myself."

"We should lean on that room clerk," Friedman said. "If we get a positive ID from the pimp—Browne—I think we should get that clerk down here, and make sure he does it right, for the lineup. I'll find out who owns the—what's the name of the hotel?"

"The Bayside."

"Yeah. I'll find out who owns it, and give him a little peek at what kind of grief he can expect if that night clerk doesn't give us the right answers."

"Good idea." Hastings put a paperweight on a stack of interrogation reports, and got to his feet. "Well, I'm going over to the St. Francis. Will you be here tomorrow?"

"In the afternoon, maybe. I've got to be in court until the jury's charged. Which the judge should do tomorrow, first thing. I'll call in when I know more. Meanwhile, good luck in the Tenderloin."

"Thanks."

6

"There he is," Penziner said, pointing to Dancer Browne's Continental, pulling to a stop in a yellow no-parking zone. "How d'you want to handle it?"

"You haven't talked to him today, is that right?" Hastings asked.

"Right. I just came on duty an hour ago. And Dancer doesn't keep office hours."

"I think I'll talk to him alone," Hastings said. "No point in attracting any more attention than we can help. By the way, do you know who owns the Bayside Hotel?"

"Some Iranians, the way I understand it. Rich Iranians, with lots of real estate in San Francisco. I'm not sure who runs it day-to-day, though. Or, more like it, night-to-night." Penziner smiled, pleased with his joke. He was a tall, stooped, hollow-chested man, divorced three times. He wore polyester suits, tassled loafers and a mismatched toupee. In defiance of departmental guidelines, he carried a .45 automatic in a bulging shoulder holster. But, in fifteen years, Penziner had never fired a shot in the line of duty.

"See if you can find out who actually manages the Bayside," Hastings said. "The room clerk that was on duty last night—that big black guy. Do you know him?"

Penziner nodded. "His name is Floyd Harrison. He used to box. And he's a mean son of a bitch."

"Has he ever been busted?"

"Not for anything heavy, I don't think."

"I want him to be available for an identification if we turn up anyone. And I want him cooperative. So find out who's managing the Bayside, and tell him that unless Harrison works with us, we're going to make it very hard for the hotel to stay in business. Lieutenant Friedman'll do the same number on the owners once he tracks them down."

"Right."

"And do it as soon as you can. It could be that we've only got a few days on the MacFarland homicide."

"How come?"

"I'll tell you later." Hastings walked briskly across Mason Street. He was a big, muscular man who moved easily and economically, projecting a calm, quiet self-confidence. He wore a Harris tweed sports jacket, a wool tie, and flannel slacks. His features were regular: full mouth, straight nose, broad forehead, firm chin. His brown eyes were thoughtful, but watchful. In his forties, he still had most of his hair, a source of secret satisfaction.

As he'd done last night, Hastings rapped on the Continental's passenger window. This time, he didn't show his shield. Plainly reluctant, Dancer swung the door open.

"We've got to stop meeting like this, Lieutenant. It—you know—tarnishes my image."

Without comment, Hastings swung the door shut and shifted on the glove-leather seat to face the other man.

"Have you got a conservative suit and tie, Dancer?"

Surprised, Dancer studied the detective's face, which told him nothing. Finally, cautiously, Dancer nodded. "Sure I do. Why you asking?"

"Because I want you to go home and put on the suit. I want you to do it now. Right now. Then I want you to go to the lobby of the St. Francis. That's where I'll meet you." He looked at his watch. "It's one-thirty. I'll see you there at two-thirty. Sharp."

"But—"

"If I'm not there, contact the house detective. He'll tell you what to do. And remember, I said a conservative suit. I want you to look like you went to Harvard. Clear?"

"But—" Deeply aggrieved, Dancer gestured toward the street outside. "But I got things to *do* here. I got *business.*"

Hastings tripped the door handle, swung open the door, got out of the car. He leaned down, waited until they made eye contact, then spoke quietly: "If you aren't at the St. Francis by two-thirty, Dancer, you're out of business. Permanently."

"But—"

"And I wasn't kidding about Harvard. You come there looking like a pimp, it's your ass."

"Pimp?" Elaborately aggrieved, Dancer raised expressive eyebrows, pursed full, disapproving lips. "Pimp, did you say?"

Hastings smiled: an ironic twisting of his wide mouth. "How about procurer? Better?"

"Better," Dancer replied, nodding judiciously. "Much better."

Dressed in a wrinkled corduroy jacket and haphazardly pressed brown slacks, raising his plump chin against the unaccustomed constriction of a tie, seated in a delicately carved Regency armchair, Canelli was plainly ill at ease. Seeing Hastings walking through the revolving doors on the Powell Street side of the St. Francis lobby, Canelli immediately rose. Tentatively smiling, he raised his hand—then reconsidered. The hand came quickly down, the smile of amiable recognition quickly vanished as he stood motionless, waiting for Hastings to take the initiative. When Hastings came directly to him, Canelli ventured a second smile.

"Hi, Lieutenant."

"Hello, Canelli. Where's Marsten and Culligan?"

"Marsten's on the Post Street entrance, and Culligan's on the Geary Street side."

"There're three entrances, then."

"Yessir. Plus the garage. But this one—" He gestured. "Powell Street, that's the main one."

Hastings led the way to a green velvet sofa placed beside a towering pillar intricately carved in dramatically veined marble.

A huge fiddle-leaf fig grew in a hammered brass planter, partially concealing the sofa from the hotel's elevators and main desk.

"So what's the rundown?" Hastings said.

"Well . . . ." Worriedly, Canelli shook his head, fretfully frowning. "Well, we aren't exactly organized, I guess you'd say. I mean, we've only been here for a little over an hour, you know. And you told us to—you know—keep a low profile, and everything, till you got here. So, really, there isn't a hell of a lot to report, Lieutenant."

"Did you talk to the hotel detective?"

"No, sir. I mean, I figured you'd want to do that." Anxiously looking for signs of approval, Canelli's soft brown eyes scanned the other man's face. To himself, Hastings smiled. Canelli was the only cop he'd ever known who could constantly get his feelings hurt.

"That's right." Hastings nodded. "I'll talk to him."

"But I talked to the bell captain," Canelli offered. "He said that the Holloway people have the whole eleventh floor. So I decided to go up there just to—you know—look around. I mean, I didn't plan to show my shield or anything. But what d'you think happened, when I pressed the elevator button for the eleventh floor?"

Gently, Hastings sighed. "I give up, Canelli. What happened?"

"Nothing, that's what happened. Zero."

"Zero?"

"If you press eleven, nothing happens. The goddamn buttons're blanked out, or something. I couldn't believe it. But that's what happens, the bell captain said, when the president comes, or somebody. The elevator won't stop at their floor, unless you know which other buttons to push. Like, if you push three and one and four, quickly, then you'll get the eleventh floor. Clever, huh?"

"So what'd you do? Use the code?"

"No. I mean, I didn't think that would be very low profile." Once more, he looked for approval in Hastings's face, then said, "So I went up to twelve, and then walked down. And, of course, the next thing I know, I'm eyeball-to-eyeball with a couple of guys in blue blazers, who start asking questions."

"Private security people."

Canelli emphatically nodded. "Definitely."

"Do you have any idea how many Holloway people are up there on the eleventh floor?"

"The bell captain guessed about fifty altogether."

"Fifty . . ." Hastings checked the time, stood up. "I'm going to talk to the house detective. You stay here. Amy MacFarland's pimp will be here by two-thirty. Do you know him by sight?"

"Yessir."

"Okay, good. Have we got enough surveillance radios and a good, clear frequency?"

"Yessir." Canelli patted his inside pocket, where he'd concealed his radio. "But the thing is, we're kind of hamstrung, as far as any real surveillance goes. I mean, all we've got is a general description. And I bet I've seen a hundred guys that are between twenty-five and thirty-five, with dark blond hair, just since I got here."

"First I'll talk to the house detective. Then we'll work out something."

"If they're coming from the eleventh floor, they'll be using that bank of elevators," the hotel detective said, pointing. "Of course, if they go down to the fifth floor, then they could use the elevators on the Post Street side."

"And what if they use the stairs?"

The hotel detective shrugged. "Same thing. The stairs run beside the elevator shafts. Then there's the main staircase, coming down from the third floor." He looked at Hastings. "What's this all about, anyhow?"

"We think someone connected with Holloway might've committed a felony. We're going to try to find him, and question him. He's twenty-five to thirty, dark blond hair, medium build. Pale face, I gather." Hopefully, Hastings looked at the other man. "Ring any bells?"

"Afraid not. What kind of felony're we talking about?"

"A serious felony." Looking across the elegantly furnished lobby toward the Powell Street entrance, Hastings saw a tall, graceful black man jauntily emerging from the revolving doors, as arrogantly as a Bantu prince. Dancer Browne had arrived.

"What I'd like you to do," Hastings said, speaking to the hotel detective, "is get me a list of everyone on the eleventh floor, every guest. I'd also like to use your phone for messages, if that's all right." Apologetically, he shook his head. "What's your name again? I'm sorry—"

"The name's Malloy," the detective said, extending his card. "Bill Malloy, retired from the LAPD."

Handing over his own card, Hastings shook hands with the other man, then signaled to Dancer Browne, who was sitting at his ease in a luxurious tufted armchair, one long leg crossed over the other. Browne was wearing a double-breasted suit, conservatively pinstriped. His red silk tie was paisley-printed; his high-collared white shirt gleamed. In his lapel, an antique diamond stickpin sparkled.

"You look like a stockbroker," Hastings said, sitting in a facing chair.

"Man, I *feel* like a stockbroker," Browne answered. "They say clothes make the man. And it's true. You feel like how you look."

"Sorry to pull you away from business."

Airily, Dancer waved a long-fingered hand. "No problem. I've got an assistant."

"This could be important—a big one. Or, at least, a very delicate one."

"Yeah, well—" Dancer waved again, this time magnanimously. "Well, just don't forget, all right? I mean, sometimes I have—ah—problems, downtown. You know?"

Hastings nodded. "I know. And I hear you." He turned to point to the hotel's main bank of four elevators. "We've got good reason to think that the man who killed Amy is staying here, at this hotel. And if he is, then he'll probably be using those elevators. So what I'd like you to do is just hang around here, until—"

"Hey—"

Irritated at the interruption, Hastings turned to look at the black man. He saw Dancer meaningfully move his chin in the direction of the hotel's main entrance. A young man with dark blond hair had just pushed open one of the two doors that flanked the revolving doors, and was walking slowly across the lobby in the direction of the main desk. Slowly, Hastings rose to his feet.

"Are you sure?" he asked.

"I'm positive, man. Look at those eyes. There's no one at home."

"You stay here," Hastings ordered. "Don't move." Across the lobby, he caught Canelli's eye, surreptitiously nodding in the direction of the blond young man, who was now waiting at the desk for a clerk to acknowledge him. Also on his feet, Canelli nodded in return, began angling easily toward the desk. Reflexively, both detectives unbuttoned their jackets, touched the butts of their service revolvers. With twenty-five feet still separating him from the suspect, Hastings heard someone calling his name. Turning, he saw Bill Malloy. The hotel detective held a printout sheet in his hand, and was looking at Hastings expectantly. Satisfied that Canelli was close enough to grab the suspect if he ran, Hastings beckoned for Malloy to come closer.

"Here's the guest list," Malloy said. "But I couldn't get—"

"Not now—" With his eyes back on the suspect, Hastings raised a cautionary hand. "That one at the desk, the blond man wearing the beige jacket, no tie, brown shoes. Know him?"

"Sure do," Malloy answered promptly. "That's Elton Holloway. Is he the one you—?"

"Elton Holloway? Who's Elton Holloway?"

"Elton Holloway's Austin Holloway's son."

7

The cameraman widened his focus to include both Austin Holloway and Jeffrey Christopher, anchorman for the Channel 4 *News at 11*. Deep-focused, the shot caught the opulence of the St. Francis's presidential suite, with a large view window in the background, framed by red damask draperies. Pleased with the angle, the cameraman smiled slightly, concentrating on holding the frame steady. In the viewfinder, he saw Christopher smiling smoothly as he leaned forward, about to slip in a sugarcoated zinger, Christopher's speciality.

"What I'm wondering, Mr. Holloway—what many are wondering—is: Why San Francisco? Los Angeles, yes. The Bible Belt, yes. But San Francisco? Why?" Engagingly, the smile widened as Christopher, ever mindful of the camera, turned his head slightly for a more flattering angle.

Seated in a carved armchair that could have come from a castle, Austin Holloway decided to smile benevolently. In his sixties, Holloway was perfectly cast for his evangelical role. His silver hair was full and flowing, a deftly styled biblical mod. His blue eyes were clear, dramatically alive, wonderfully expressive. His profile, too, was dramatic, as arresting as a prophet's. His torso was trim, broad-shouldered, narrow-waisted. His voice was rich and resonant.

"Our crusade, Mr. Christopher, is for all the people—those who sin, and those who follow the commandments of the Lord. And San Francisco, certainly, is a challenge." Focused just between the camera and the anchorman, his smile was broad, both benevolent and compelling, gently mischievous, infinitely tolerant.

"You'll be holding your Sunday service at the Cow Palace, where the Republicans have held their conventions in the past. Do you expect to fill all the seats?"

The smile remained in place; the eyes sparkled, chiding the questioner. The voice expressed genial tolerance for the other man's callowness. "We don't concern ourselves with statistics, Mr. Christopher. If one soul is saved on Sunday, this San Francisco Crusade for Christ will have succeeded."

Recognizing an exit line that couldn't be topped, Christopher turned toward the camera, which was now focused fully on his face.

"Austin Holloway—America's premiere TV evangelist, in San Francisco for the first time in his forty-odd years in the pulpit." A pause, as the camera held for the segment's final seconds. Then: "This is Jeffrey Christopher, Channel Four News."

Both the reporter and the evangelist held their on-camera smiles until the tiny red light beneath the lens blinked out. Then both men rose, shook hands, exchanged perfunctory good-byes, turned away from each other. An impassive blue-blazered security man nodded to the reporter and cameraman, ushering them out into the hallway. As the door closed behind them, Holloway turned to the two men who had advanced from behind the camera to stand side by side, facing him. Physically, the men were exact opposites. At age fifty, Herbert Flournoy was a lean, taut, avid man, visibly restless, fastidiously dressed, precise when he moved. In his sixties, Lloyd Mitchell was massively built, stolidly uncompromising. Flournoy was dressed for the boardroom. Like the men who worked for him, Lloyd Mitchell wore bodyguard blue.

But if their dress differed, their eyes were the same: cold, watchful eyes. Inscrutable eyes, revealing nothing.

In unison, Holloway and Flournoy checked their watches. Both men were businesslike, slightly abstracted, obviously accustomed to planning, thinking ahead, working within tight schedules.

THE PARIAH ————————————————————————— 41

"How long will it take at City Hall?" Holloway asked.

"Portal to portal," Flournoy answered, "I figure it an hour flat—fifteen minutes down, fifteen minutes back, a half hour for the ceremony."

"How's the coverage?"

"Both newspapers, only one TV channel, so far." Flournoy shrugged. "Benton's still trying."

"Is the mayor coming Sunday?" Holloway asked.

"He hasn't committed himself yet." Flournoy tapped his watch. "You've only got twelve minutes."

"Fine." Holloway nodded, turning away. "Just enough time for a good, satisfying crap."

Flournoy's face registered prim, unsmiling disapproval. It was a turn-of-the-century schoolmaster's face: pinched nostrils, a thin, tight mouth, pale, passionless eyes. The flesh of his face was sallow; his bald head was fringed with brown hair.

Flournoy waited for the connecting door to close on Holloway before he turned to Lloyd Mitchell. Flournoy spoke quietly, without inflection: "This town worries me. The SLA, the Zebra killings, the Zodiac murders—they all happened here. Are we covered?"

"I've got three men with Uzis in their attaché cases," Mitchell answered. "It's not legal, but that's what they've got. And the police will be at the Cow Palace. They'll be at the civic luncheon, too. And today, of course, when he gets the key to the city."

"What about the banquet on Thursday? Will the police be there?"

Mitchell's large, squared-off head moved impassively from side to side. "That's private, not on city or county property, and there's no municipal tie-in. So there's no way. But I've hired extra men. They'll be on duty Sunday, too. And the limos've been checked."

Nodding, Flournoy beckoned for Mitchell to accompany him to the opposite corner of the sitting room, away from the connecting door.

"Marvella's been getting extra liquor," Flournoy said quietly. "Susan isn't doing her job. Any thoughts?"

With his eyes on the connecting door, prepared to break off when Holloway appeared, Mitchell said, "Austin's got to leave her at home on these trips. In Los Angeles, she's all right. It's only on the road that she goes off the rails."

"She's more manageable in Los Angeles," Flournoy answered, correcting the other man. "But she's far from all right."

Mitchell shrugged in his massive shoulders. "Marvella's part of The Hour. And The Hour holds everything together."

"Austin holds everything together." Flournoy's voice was cold, uncompromising. "Austin *is* The Hour."

"This is no time to talk about Marvella." Mitchell spoke slowly, in a heavy, measured voice. The voice, the body, the face, all were complementary facets of the man: implacable, unyielding. "Not here. Not now."

"Will you talk to Susan, though?" Flournoy pressed. "I don't want any problems on Sunday."

"I'll talk to her, yes."

Holloway stood up, flushed the toilet, tucked in his shirt, zipped up his trousers, stepped in front of the washbasin. The faucets were gold-plated dolphins, the basin was marble. The mirror, too, was gold framed. As he washed his hands he looked himself squarely in the eye. Next month, he would be sixty-four years old. So far, the years had treated him kindly. The eyes were still clear, still commanding. The flesh beneath the eyes was still firm. Yes, the skin was lined and creased and wrinkled. But it was the pattern of the wrinkles that mattered, not the fact of their existence. And, with the exception of the creases that slightly puckered his lower lip—the mewling creases, he called them—he was pleased with what he saw in the mirror. And, yes, he was pleased with what he saw in the film clips. The cameras had been good to him, and he was grateful. The people apparently liked what they saw, too. Because the mail had never been heavier, or the checks more bountiful. As for the sagging flesh beneath the jawline . . . He lifted his chin, moved his head from side to side. "Turkey wattles," his father had called them. And turkey wattles ran in the family, unhappily. Vividly, he could remember sitting in the first row of hard wooden benches, looking up, seeing the loose flesh of his father's neck swish from side to side as his father pounded the pulpit, exhorting an apathetic congregation.

Slowly, reflectively, he took a towel from the rack, carefully dried his hands, dropped the towel on the counter beside the basin. Although his eyes still stared into the depths of the mirror, his gaze was unfocused now, lost in distant memory.

In recent years, more frequently each year, images of his father returned. They returned at odd times, for odd reasons, some of them fragments, some of them whole. Most often, the images centered on the Sunday morning services: his father, clutching the pulpit with both his scrawny hands, preaching to a meager congregation with his high, whining voice, the same voice with which he complained about the high cost of living, or the sad state of his son's report card, or burst pipes in winter, or burnt lawns in the summer. Only once had he ever seen his father enraged; only once had he ever seen his father's hand raised in anger. And for that he had always secretly despised his father; not for his rage, but for his forbearance.

Holloway took his pinstriped jacket from the gold-plated hook. Without looking at his watch, he knew that the twelve minutes Flournoy had allotted him had already passed into eternity. It was time, therefore, to go downstairs, enter his limo, and be driven to the steps of City Hall, where the mayor would present him with a key to the city. It would be this thirteenth key. Lucky thirteen.

Seated beside Flournoy, Holloway was facing Mitchell and a security man named Tucker sitting on the jump seats. An attaché case rested on the floor beside Tucker. Inside the case, Holloway had been told, there was a small machine gun.

In the limo behind, carrying Marvella and Susan Gaines, two other security men were riding, one of them carrying another attaché case.

Ahead, two lines of bumper-to-bumper midday traffic were impacted. On the steps of City Hall, his honor the mayor might already be waiting, checking the time.

At his side, Holloway heard Flournoy clearing his throat. Another cool, calm, closely reasoned lesson was about to begin. Before he'd joined The Crusade, Flournoy had been a corporation comptroller. Writing his constant string of memos, or delivering his day-to-day, hour-to-hour briefings, Flournoy's pronouncements had the tempo and texture of an annual report that had been put on an audio cassette.

"So far," Flournoy said, "we simply aren't getting good attendance projections for Sunday, Austin. We've talked about this—the demographics here. And I must tell you, I'm concerned. There's no real constituency here or in Marin County. And nothing down the Peninsula, either. At least not until you get to Redwood City. And it's a fact that the longer people have to travel, the less likely they are to show up. It's true that the East Bay has a lot of potential. But Oakland's mostly black. And we've talked about that—about the blacks, on camera. Also, I'm getting the feeling that we're going to get a lot of tongue-in-cheek, yuppie media coverage. And that worries me. That one from Channel Four, just now, for instance—" Flournoy shook his head. "He's going to do a job on us in the editing. I can feel it."

Holloway smiled: an easy, confident smile. "Herbert, you're a whiz with figures, and you're a hell of an organizer, an executive's executive. But you've got to appreciate the fact that what we're involved in here is show business, pure and simple. Now, you evidently listened to what that bright young Jeffrey Christopher said, but you may have missed what I said." Quizzically, Holloway smiled at his chief of staff. "Is that possible?"

Peevishly, Flournoy declined the gambit as he stared through the windshield at the lines of cars ahead. The reason for the traffic jam was an apartment house fire, two blocks ahead. At this rate, they could be a half hour late. Understandably, the mayor would be furious.

"Because if you'd listened," Holloway was saying, "and if you listened at last week's situational session, Herbert, you'd realize that what we're doing here in San Francisco is something entirely different from what we've ever done before. We go to St.

Louis, or Baltimore, or Houston, or wherever, and we're basically giving them the same old crap, week after week—year after year. We're feeding the same lines to the same people. Right?"

"That's not what I'm saying, Austin. I'm saying that—"

"This week," Holloway said, smoothly raising a pontifical hand, "is going to be different. San Francisco is a hotbed of corruption and sin. Virtually every plague that afflicts this society has its roots—deep roots—right here, in this city. It's Sodom and Gomorrah. And I'll guarantee you, Herbert, that by the time I've finished with this city—with its perverts and its radicals and its free love—by the time I've finished, the faithful in Des Moines are going to be glued to their television sets. They'll be hooting, and they'll be hollering, Herbert. And they'll be responding, too. When the mail comes in—when you read your printouts, about ten days from now—you'll realize that I'm right. This city is evil personified. Don't forget, this is where the AIDS scourge started, a plague that could rival the Black Death. And I know you'll understand me when I say that with proper attention to detail— and with a little creative imagination—the faithful can be made to understand that the future of the whole human race as we know it could be decided right here, right now." Having allowed his voice to rise to a reflexive tremolo, Holloway paused, let his mouth twitch into a knowing smile as he said, "Armageddon, in other words. Big medicine, Herbert. Very big medicine indeed, properly packaged."

Behind sparkling gold-framed glasses, Flournoy's eyes were speculative. Finally he shrugged his impeccably tailored shoulders. "Maybe you're right, Austin. It's happened before, that you've been right. God knows, your instincts are usually accurate. However, as you know, it's my job to ask these questions." As he spoke, Flournoy looked ahead. Finally, the fire trucks were moving off. The limo was beginning to inch forward.

Elaborately magnanimous, Holloway inclined his handsome head. "I *want* you to ask questions, Herbert. Believe me. Incidentally, speaking of Sunday, tell Benton that when his cameras cut away, I want them to pick up some of these characters—punk rockers, fags, anyone who'll stand out. Targets of opportunity, in other words. Not totally, of course. But I want him to keep it in mind. Give him the game plan, in other words."

"Right." From an inside pocket, Flournoy withdrew a gold Cross pen and gold-bound notebook, presents from the vice-president. Meticulously, he made a note to himself.

8

Marvella looked into the security man's eyes, then looked quickly away.

They were all the same, these men who carried guns. Their eyes were the same: at the center, far back, a gleam of death glittered, still as a snake's eye, watching, waiting.

The first time she'd seen a snake, she'd been playing beside the creek that ran along the northern edge of her daddy's property. She'd been sailing tiny paper boats, watching them disappear as the creek flowed beneath a low-growing tree branch. The snake had looked like a part of the tree root, growing exposed on the riverbank. Only the snake's head had been visible—the head and the eyes, fixed on her, unblinking. She'd been six when she'd seen the snake. Never before had she experienced terror.

She'd been sixteen when she'd first seen Austin. It had been a hot, humid summer afternoon, the summer between her junior and senior years. He'd been talking to her daddy. The two men, the old preacher and the young preacher, had been standing together in front of her daddy's tabernacle. He'd always called it his tabernacle, that poor, one-story clapboard building, originally a storefront, with its plate glass painted out, and its gilt cross hand-painted above the sagging door, with its white paint peeling, and its roof leaking.

At first Austin hadn't been aware of her. She'd been standing on the dusty pathway that led around to the back of the building, where she and her daddy lived. They'd been bargaining, Austin and her daddy, deciding how much Austin would pay to use the tabernacle on Wednesday nights.

But then, as if he'd sensed her presence, Austin had turned toward her. Just for a moment, she'd felt helpless, unable to move, as surely transfixed as if she'd been her younger self, standing beside the creek, staring at the snake. She'd been suspended in time and place, staring at this stranger. It was the first time she'd ever felt as if her clothing had somehow lost substance, leaving her naked body exposed to a stranger's knowing eyes.

In that moment, she'd known that, whatever this stranger demanded of her, she would gladly give.

The traffic ahead was beginning to move; the limousine rocked gently, getting under way, following Austin. Through the smoked-glass windows on either side she could see strangers standing on sidewalks, watching them as they passed.

How had it happened, that these people stood on the sidewalk, watching, while she rode past them, so grandly invisible? Did they realize how small she felt, dressed in her thousand-dollar dress, wearing her two-hundred-dollar shoes, sitting beside Susan Gaines, whose job—whose sole responsibility—was to watch over her?

No.

Not watch over her.

Watch her.

Wherever she went, Susan was expected to go. By Austin's decree, their lives were connected, the captive and the keeper.

And now the keeper spoke:

"This is all we have today, just this presentation of the key to the city. It shouldn't take more than a half hour. Then we'll come back to the hotel, to rest. Mr. Holloway has meetings downtown, then later at the hotel. But that doesn't have anything to do with us."

"What about tomorrow?"

"Tomorrow will be the civic luncheon. I've been talking with Herbert about it. Except for the actual service, on Sunday, the civic luncheon will be the most important thing we've got to do.

Mr. Holloway wants all the family there—you, Gloria, Elton. And the grandchildren, too."

Marvella frowned. On her impeccably made-up face two small furrows between the eyebrows were the only imperfections. "The grandchildren? Why?"

"Mr. Holloway thinks they can handle it."

"But they're so young, to sit still for that long. Carole is only five."

Sweetly, Susan Gaines smiled. "They're beautifully behaved. I'm sure it'll work out. After all, if they can sing with the rest of you—the whole family, on Sundays—they should be able to handle a civic luncheon."

Fretfully, Marvella shook her head. But the two tiny frown-furrows had disappeared, returning her face to its bland, bogus, unblemished serenity. Covertly, she glanced at her watch. The time was fifteen minutes after three.

Less than two hours remained. Soon time, so often her enemy, would reward her, befriend her, make this day whole again.

9

astings covered the telephone's mouthpiece as the door to the tiny office swung open to reveal Bill Malloy.

"Would you mind—could you excuse me for a minute or two?" Apologetically, Hastings smiled. "I'm getting my game plan."

"Oh, sure." The house detective flipped a casual hand. "Just make yourself at home, Lieutenant. Whatever." Carefully, Malloy closed the door.

Over the phone Hastings heard Friedman say, "What you're telling me is that Austin Holloway's son—the son of God, according to the TV ratings—is a mass murderer. Is that about it?"

"That's about it. If we believe Dancer Browne's identification."

"And *do* we believe Dancer Browne?"

"He's all we've got. Besides, the description Browne gave me last night fits. Perfectly. No one was prompting him, either. And then there's the FBI thing."

"That's not evidence, though. That's just a printout."

"I know that. All I'm asking is, how do we want to handle it?"

"What's the room clerk at the Bayside Hotel say?"

"His story hasn't changed. He says he didn't see the guy, didn't notice him, couldn't identify him. I'm beginning to believe him."

"Which leaves us with a pimp's testimony to show the DA."

"Jesus, Pete, I *know* all that." Hastings's voice rose an

aggrieved half note. "What I'm asking is, what do we do now? You're the guru, the planner. What's the plan?"

A moment of thoughtful silence passed. Then: "The plan is for me to come down to the St. Francis, get a look at the terrain."

Surprised, Hastings asked, "Are you kidding?"

"Do I sound like I'm kidding?"

"How long's it been since you've been out in the field?"

"The question is, how long has it been since I've had a shot at maybe tying a can to the likes of Austin Holloway."

"Not Holloway. His son."

"Same thing, in a way. Have you ever caught Holloway on TV, by any chance?"

"No."

"Well, I have. These guys fascinate me, these TV evangelists. Especially Holloway, who's in the catbird seat, no question. Do you know he's got a whole university down in Los Angeles— with a basketball team that made it to the playoffs, for God's sake. And do you also know that, every time he's in the neighborhood, he stops by the White House for lunch? Do you read *This Week*?"

"No."

"Well, they had an article on TV evangelists not too long ago. And the money they make—the power they have—is absolutely mind-boggling. Holloway has his own two communication satellites, for God's sake. Just think what that means. He owns them, and rents out time to other evangelists. These guys push the buttons and turn the knobs that control how millions of people think. They've got the American dream in their well-lined hip pockets."

"Jesus, I've never heard you so wound up."

Conceding the point, Friedman chuckled. "Usually we put in our time collaring someone who knifed someone in a bar, or someone who hit her husband too hard with an iron skillet during their standard Saturday night domestic argument. But what we've got here is the big time. I mean, we're talking about changing the course of history, here."

"I think someone gave you the key to the narcotics bin, that's what I think."

Undeterred, Friedman said, "You've never seen Holloway's act, or you'd know what I'm talking about. See, his whole pitch, his trademark, is the Holloway family. Some of these guys, you know, just sit at a desk, and talk into the camera—with an eight-hundred number at the bottom of the screen, to call and make a pledge. Not Holloway, that's not his style. He showcases his family. There's his wife, who's supposed to be the virgin mother, I guess, who sings a few lyrics, but mostly looks at Holloway adoringly. Her name is . . . I forget her name. Marvel, something like that. Then there's Holloway's daughter, who also sings—and who fills out a dress like you wouldn't believe. She's got two children, a boy and a girl. 'The grandkids,' as Holloway calls them. You can't believe it, how crazy Holloway is about 'the grandkids.' And then there's Elton. The ex–boy soprano."

"Are you telling me that you've been following Holloway since Elton was a boy soprano?"

"God, no. I'm just telling you that he looks like a boy soprano. Where'll I meet you, at the St. Francis?"

"In the lobby."

"Right. On my way."

"What we've got here," Friedman said, "is a problem in diplomacy."

"I'm glad to hear you say it," Hastings answered. "I was afraid you were going to arrest both of them—Elton for murder, and Holloway as an accessory."

"God . . ." Wishfully thinking, Friedman shook his head. "Wouldn't that be something? Just think about it . . ." Seated beside Hastings on a velvet sofa, staring reflectively at the main bank of the hotel's elevators, Friedman avidly touched his upper lip with a small pink tongue tip.

"I've never seen you like this, Pete. You're—" Hastings broke off, searching for the word. "You're excited. Actually excited. What is it with you and Holloway?"

Friedman shifted his stare to the other man's face. "It may

have escaped your notice," Friedman said stiffly, "but I have certain deep convictions. And one of those convictions is that people like Holloway are evil. The're . . ." He frowned, also searching. "They're blasphemers."

"Well," Hastings replied, "if you're doing to arrest Elton Holloway for the murder of Amy MacFarland, you're going to have to get on it. Today's Wednesday. The service is Sunday, at the Cow Palace. By Monday, they'll be back in Angeles. All of them."

"The first thing we've got to do, obviously, is talk to Elton. Where is he, do you know?"

"As far as I know, he's upstairs. The Holloway people have the whole eleventh floor. Elton's been in and out three times since we started surveillance."

"Has anyone talked to him yet? Friedman asked.

"No. I didn't want to spook him."

"Are these the elevators they use?"

"Mostly, I think. There're other exits, though. They're covered. We've got seven men here."

Thoughtfully, Friedman nodded. With the first rush of enthusiasm gone, the time for calculation had come. "What we've got to do," he said, "is develop some physical evidence. How thorough were the lab guys at the scene?"

Hastings shrugged. "As far as I knew—and they knew—we were just talking about another hooker who was trying to earn a little extra money doing the snuff thing. So they just hit the high spots, with the fingerprints. They didn't do any sweepings, nothing like that."

"Well," Friedman said, "I sent them back. They're over there right now, giving it the full-court press. Meanwhile, we've got to figure out how to get a set of Elton's fingerprints."

"We could always ask him."

"Has Holloway got his own security?"

"You bet he has," Hastings answered. "Lots of it. They've got the whole eleventh floor sealed off. Tight."

"So if we're going to interrogate Elton in his room," Friedman mused, "we're going to need warrants."

"No question."

"Has anyone tried to strike up a conversation with him? You know—follow him to a bar, buy him a drink, like that?"

Impatiently, Hastings sighed. "I've already told you that I wanted to talk to you before we made any contact with him."

"I wonder," Friedman said thoughtfully, "whether we should touch base with the chief on this."

"If we do that, we might as well call a news conference."

"If we arrest Elton Holloway, it'll be the same as calling a news conference. A nationwide news conference."

"Well," Hastings said, "you decide. You want to touch base with Dwyer, I'll go along. Whatever you say."

Sitting pear-shaped on the high-styled sofa, Friedman's broad, swarthy face settled again into its accustomed inscrutability. Heavily lidded brown eyes staring impassively into the middle distance, Friedman let a long, thoughtful silence pass. Then: "Are there other possibilities for physical evidence? Besides fingerprints?"

"There's the weapon—a piece of rope, probably. There're marks on her throat."

Friedman grunted. "Is that all?"

Also grunting, Hastings said, "Unless he dropped a handkerchief with his initials, that's all."

"Then we've got to talk to him. There's no other way. We've got to see how he reacts, see whether we have a chance of getting warrants. Is he upstairs, you say?"

"As far as I know, he's upstairs. Holloway and his wife left a couple of hours ago—in separate limos. The wife came back about an hour ago. She's upstairs. Everywhere she goes, she has a woman with her. And Holloway, of course, has people with him all the time. It's like they're royalty."

"Why don't you go up alone?" Friedman said. "Tell Elton that—you know—we're checking out a mugging, or something, that he might've witnessed. Meanwhile, I'll see if he's ever been fingerprinted, get the request in the computer, anyhow. Then I'll tell Canelli to set it up so we can follow him to a restaurant or a bar, whatever, see if we can get a glass that he handled."

"You should call Walter Draper, in Washington. The FBI could have his prints in their computer."

"Right." Friedman said it reluctantly. For as long as Hastings could remember, Friedman had been at odds with the FBI.

"What about a search warrant? Do you think there's a chance?"

Friedman shook his head. "With what we've got now—a pimp's identification—considering who's involved, I don't think we've got a prayer."

"You're probably right." Hastings got to his feet. "Okay, I'll give it a shot. See you here, afterward?"

"Right."

10

As Hastings pulled open the stairwell door, he slipped his shield case from his pocket. Yes, there he was: a big, thick-necked, blank-eyed man dressed in a blue blazer, rising from a small settee and moving to block Hastings's further progress down the corridor. In his left ear, the security man wore a tiny surveillance earphone.

"Help you?"

As Hastings showed his shield, he was aware that he was smiling: a flat, fake salesman's smile. Signifying what? Selling what? Why did he feel uncomfortable, as nervous as a rookie detective on his first case? The answer, of course, was the opulence that surrounded him: the crystal chandeliers, the richly flocked wallpaper, the small, delicately carved chairs and tables lining the corridor walls, the thick carpet underfoot, the arched ceiling above. Police business wasn't transacted here, in a hallway like this. It was in places like the Bayside Hotel that a policeman belonged. Not here.

"Yes, I—ah—I'm Lieutenant Frank Hastings. I'd like to speak to Elton Holloway."

The man in the blue blazer didn't smile in return; his expression remained stolidly unchanged. "Have you talked to Mr. Mitchell?" It was a polite question, firmly asked.

"Mr. Mitchell?"

"Lloyd Mitchell. Mr. Holloway's chief of security."

"Is he here?" Expectantly, Hastings looked down the corridor.

"No, sir. He's with Mr. Holloway. They're due back in—"

The security man pushed back a gleaming white cuff, consulted a sparkling gold wristwatch. "—in about an hour and a half."

"Sorry," Hastings said, moving a half step forward. "I can't wait that long. If you'll just tell me what room Elton Holloway's in, I'll ask him a few questions, and be on my way. It's about a street crime, last night, just a few blocks away. We're looking for witnesses."

The other man didn't move, didn't retreat, even a quarter step. And, beyond him, Hastings saw another security man coming toward them—an older, more determined security man, also dressed in a blue blazer, white shirt, gray flannel trousers, carefully polished black shoes. Idly, Hastings wondered whether men like these had permits to carry guns.

"Yes, what is it?" the second man asked. It was a harsh, impatient question. In reply, Hastings showed the shield, repeated the story. As he finished, he heard a nearby door open and close behind him. In unison, both security men looked beyond Hastings, tracking the sound. Watching their expressions change, Hastings realized that someone important had appeared. Turning, he saw a young woman and two small children. All three were dressed in sweaters and jeans. The woman was in her early thirties: slim, full-breasted, long-legged. Her chestnut hair was worn loose around her shoulders. Her eyes were calm, the set of her body was bold, the tilt of her chin was assertive. Her features were good, neither beautiful nor displeasing. Her expression was inquiring as she looked at the two security men—and frankly appraising, woman to man, as she looked at Hastings. When she saw the gold shield, she frowned.

As if an offstage director had called for a freeze in the action, no one moved or spoke. Then the woman said simply, "Yes?"

Even though the single word was spoken softly, it nevertheless established her dominance over the two security men. Remembering Friedman's rundown of the Holloway family, Hastings realized that the woman must be Holloway's daughter. The children, a girl and a boy, were doubtless the grandchildren. As the older of the two security men explained the situation, the two children held to their mother's hands while they stared at the gold shield. On impulse, Hastings tilted the shield to a better angle for the children, and smiled down at them. Neither returned his smile.

While the security man talked, the woman kept her eyes on his face. When he finished, she stood silently for a long, thoughtful moment. Finally, as if she'd come to a decision, she turned to face Hastings squarely.

"I'm Gloria Holloway," she said, still speaking with quiet, measured authority. "Elton's sister. Maybe I can help you." She bent down, disengaged her hands, spoke to the children: "You go to Grandma's room. I'll be there in a few minutes, after I've talked to this gentleman. Ask Grandma if she wants to go with us to Fisherman's Wharf. Tell her we're going to ride the cable car, so she should wear slacks."

The girl turned obediently away, but the boy stood his ground, staring up at Hastings. As he returned the stare, Hastings knew what the boy would ask:

"Can I see your gun?"

Smiling, Hastings shook his head. "Not now. Maybe sometime later, but not now. What's your name?"

"James. What's yours?"

"Frank. Frank Hastings. How old are you?"

"Almost eight."

"Do you sing with your grandfather on Sundays?"

Gravely, the boy nodded. It was a businesslike nod, as if he'd abruptly lost his innocence. "Did you ever see me? We're on TV every Sunday." The question, too, was businesslike.

"I—ah—"

"James, you go see Grandma." Gloria Holloway turned the child down the hallway after his sister, sending him on his way with a firm, friendly pat on the butt.

"Saved," Hastings said, smiling at her. "Thanks."

Not returning the smile, she gestured to a nearby door, at the same time nodding dismissal to the two security men. The older of the two hesitated, plainly doubtful that the woman had made the right decision. Ignoring the man's misgivings, she opened her door, preceded Hastings into a lavishly decorated sitting room.

As Hastings followed, his eyes dropped appreciatively to the woman's buttocks, provocatively moving beneath her tight blue jeans. How would Austin Holloway's daughter react if she were pinched? What would she be like in bed? Would she take the initiative, as she was doing now?

She sat at one end of a sofa, and invited him with a gesture to sit at the other end. As he twisted on the sofa to face her, he realized that he had no idea how to begin. Nothing in his experience had prepared him for this, questioning the sister of a serial murder suspect, both of them children of a man who owned communications satellites and dined with presidents.

As if she'd discovered his discomfort, he thought he could see amusement in her eyes as she made no effort to speak, but simply waited for him to begin:

"This is quite an operation you've got here," he ventured. Then, recognizing the false start, he said, "I mean, it's obviously a big deal, putting on your—" He broke off. What was it, that they put on, every Sunday? A performance? A revival meeting? A religious service?

The amusement in her eyes had deepened. Sitting in her expensive suite, she was faintly smiling, watching him with tolerant patience. Her eyes, he noticed, were a deep violet. Her mouth was expressive—inviting. With her back slightly arched, her breasts were generously offered for his appraisal. Her legs were crossed, revealing taut thighs beneath the faded denim of her designer jeans. She sat with one arm resting along the top of the sofa, the fingers within inches of his shoulder. Completely at ease, she was waiting for him to muddle through: "I don't really have to take any of your time. I mean, you were obviously going out with your children. So if you'll just put me in touch with your brother—Elton—I won't bother you anymore."

"It's no bother. Elton . . ." She hesitated. "He's very shy. You wouldn't know it to hear him sing, but he's actually very reluctant to meet people—strangers, anyhow."

"Still, I've got to talk to him." He broke off, dropped his voice, deliberately hardened his gaze. "It's a police matter. So one way or the other, I've got to talk with him."

Her gaze, too, hardened. Her voice, too, dropped as she said, "What do you mean, exactly, when you say 'one way or the other'? That sounds like a threat."

"It's not a threat. I'm simply telling you that I've got to talk to him. I hope he'll agree to see me. If not, then—" Meaningfully, he shrugged.

"Then what?" she asked softly. "What would happen if he didn't agree?"

"If he won't talk to me—now—then I'd come back later, with another man. We'd demand that he talk to us—here. If he refused, then we'd take him downtown for questioning."

"This is serious." As she spoke, she let her eyes wander thoughtfully away, finally fixing on a large plate glass window that offered a spectacular view of San Francisco Bay. She sat motionless, staring at her expensive view. Then, softly, she said, "Donald—the security man—said you wanted to question Elton about something he might've seen last night." Another moment of calculating silence passed. Then, deliberately, the violet eyes returned to meet his squarely.

"What was it that he was supposed to have seen?"

"I'm investigating a crime that was committed about ten o'clock last night, just a few blocks from here. We think your brother has some information that could help us."

"What kind of information, exactly?"

Hastings drew a deep breath. "I'd rather discuss that with Elton, Miss—Ms.—Holloway."

The woman, too, drew a deep, measured breath. This was the decisive moment, the make-or-break point that, sooner or later, every interrogation pivoted on. The maneuvering, the tactical half truths, the outright lies, were behind them. Now they were playing for keeps, everything pushed into the pot.

"I gather," she said, "that you aren't a particular fan of my father's—of TV evangelism."

"Until now," Hastings answered, "I never thought much about it."

"Well," she said, "it's pretty much a business, if you want to know the truth. Big business. You're obviously an intelligent man. If you haven't already figured out what Austin Holloway is all about, you certainly will before you're finished. And the truth is, men like my father are like rock stars. They have a unique talent. My father would call it a God-given talent. And he's right, of course—depending on how you define God." She spoke in a flat, uninflected voice. The message: they weren't discussing God. This was business. Serious business.

"But the point is," she said, "people like my father—and Mick Jagger, and Elvis Presley, and all the rest of them—they're people who, when they're on stage, make enormous sums of money. My father generates more money—more capital flow—than a lot of major businesses that employ thousands of people. Which means that people like my father need managers. They need people to manage the money they generate. And they need people to manage them personally. They need to be protected, people like my father. Because if he should go into a depression, let's say—if he botched the job on Sundays, in front of the cameras—then the money would begin drying up. Do you see?"

Hastings nodded. "Of course."

"Okay—" Now she leaned forward. Her eyes had sharpened. On the back of the sofa, her fingers were tightening. The curve of her torso was drawing taut. Gloria Holloway was about to dictate terms:

"Now, in this organization—call it Austin Holloway, Incorporated—there're two people who manage things. There's Herbert Flournoy, who makes most of the business decisions. And then—" Another pause, for emphasis. "And then there's me. What Herbert doesn't take care of, I do."

"Flournoy manages the business end and you manage your father."

Ruefully, she smiled. "I wouldn't say anyone manages my father. Just the opposite, in fact. But I act as a buffer, keep him insulated from petty annoyances. Like this situation, for instance." Now the smile widened disarmingly, focused more personally on him. "It would distract my father if he knew that the police were questioning Elton. And we simply can't afford to have Austin Holloway distracted. It's as simple as that."

"You're also protecting Elton. You're the guardian of the gates. Is that it?"

"That's it," she answered evenly. The two words, spoken so softly, nevertheless conveyed an aura of utter confidence that could only derive, Hastings knew, from the certainty that vast power awaited simply the touch of a forefinger on a phone console. Then, plainly to soften the stark impact of the same two words, she offered: "Besides, Elton is . . ." She searched for the phrase. "He's fragile. Emotionally fragile."

As he looked at her, Hastings let a long, calculated silence lengthen before he said quietly, "I've got to talk to your brother, Miss Holloway. There's no other way. I'm sorry, but that's how it is."

"But *why*? Because he happened to see someone getting mugged? Is that it?"

"It wasn't a mugging." He let another long, harsh moment of silence pass. Then, without fully realizing that he intended to say it, he said, "It wasn't a mugging. It was murder."

Her eyes widened, her mouth tightened. "Murder?"

"A prostitute was murdered last night. It happened a little after ten o'clock, on Mason Street."

"But what's that got to do with—" Her throat closed on the rest of it. At her temple, a pulse was throbbing.

"The description of the suspect fits your brother, Miss Holloway. It could be a coincidence, bad information. But I've got to check it out."

"But—" She began to shake her head. "But I can't—"

"We don't intend to make a lot of fuss. I know about your father, how important he is. That's why I didn't tell your security men about the murder. I'm being as discreet as I can. But I've got to talk to Elton. There's no other way."

She rose, walked quickly to the view window, stood with her back to him, arms rigid at her sides, fists clenched. Her head was high, the line of her body assertive, defiant. Finally she turned to face him.

"Give me time, to—to make some decisions. We're doing The Hour here, at the Cow Palace, on Sunday. And Elton's part of it. Elton, me, my children, my mother—we've all got to be there, onstage. It—it's the format."

On his feet, facing her, Hastings said, "You've got your problems—but so do I. You understand that, don't you?" As he spoke, he looked at his watch.

"Lieutenant, I—"

"It's four-thirty. I'll be back here at nine-thirty tonight. That's five hours. I'll come back, and I'll ask for you."

She nodded: a stiff, stricken nod. Then: "This prostitute, what was her name?"

"Amy MacFarland."

"And she was killed at ten o'clock last night, you say?"

"That's right. In the Bayside Hotel, just around the corner from here, on Mason Street. She was strangled."

"Strangled?"

He nodded. "She was strangled with a rope, or a cord." He hesitated, then said, "There've been other murders, like this. Other murders in other cities. And they all fit a pattern: same kind of victim, same kind of weapon. And—" Purposefully, he lowered his voice, locked his eyes with hers. "And they were all committed when your organization was in town."

He watched her draw back from him, as if he'd physically threatened her. For a final moment he held her eyes, watching fear begin to work on the musculature of her face. Finally he'd gotten through to her, done the job he'd come to do.

"I'll see you at nine-thirty." He nodded, turned, went to the door.

11

She crossed her legs at the ankles, arranged the folds of her skirt across her thighs and calves, smoothed down the silken fabric of her dress over the swell of her breasts. Careful of her hair, she rested her head against the curved back of the chaise longue.

Many years ago, Austin had told her that she belonged on a chaise longue. It was his image of her, he'd said. It had always been so romantic, his picture of her. When he was away from her, he imagined her as she was now, dressed in a sheer gossamer gown, her hair beautifully done, her face impeccably made up, reclining like Helen of Troy, awaiting his pleasure.

Even then, so long ago, Austin had used words like "gossamer" and phrases like "Helen of Troy." Even when they were alone, just the two of them.

The first time he'd ever said it, told her she belonged on a chaise, dressed in a gossamer gown, they'd been in Detroit, on the first tour they'd ever made together. They'd been staying at the Statler. All of them, all four of them, in the same cramped suite: she and Austin in one room, the children in another room. There'd been no nursemaid, no secretaries, no one but the four of them. Gloria had been—how old? She began to frown, then remembered: an untroubled face was an unwrinkled face.

And then the memory cleared: Elton had been five years old, just beginning kindergarten, on that first tour. So, if Elton had been five, then Gloria would have been nine, four years older.

Even then, they'd been so different, the two of them. From the moment of their birth, they'd been different. Gloria had always been the active one, the pushy one. Whatever Gloria wanted, she got. Elton had been the quiet one, the watchful one, the delicate one. Right from the first, he'd been—

At the door, a soft knock sounded. Susan's "five o'clock knock," Marvella had secretly decided to call it.

"Come in."

Also formally dressed, Susan Gaines stepped inside, closed the door. In her right hand, she carried a small embroidered satchel. Marvella had bought the satchel on Rodeo Drive, a year or two ago. It had two handles, and opened to just the right dimensions. It had been made in China, and had cost five hundred dollars, she remembered.

"Hello, Susan."

"Hello, Mrs. Holloway." Smiling her social secretary's smile, Susan was brightly nodding.

Without changing position, Marvella watched the other woman move with measured steps to the small mirrored bar. She placed the satchel on the bar, opened the satchel, produced a bottle of vodka. The bottle sparkled and glowed, reflected in the mirrors behind and beneath it. Susan Gaines took a crystal highball glass from a rack, placed the glass beside the bottle. From a silver bucket she took ice, dropping the cubes in the glass with silver tongs. Her fingernails, Marvella noted, were pleasingly polished. Now the bottle was opened, and two ounces of vodka poured into the sparkling crystal glass. Now came the tonic, and the lime. Susan's hands moved deliberately, deftly. Sometimes Marvella suspected that Susan slowed down the tempo of this daily ritual to tease her, even taunt her. But, inevitably, just as the suspicion intruded, the drink was offered, the ceremony completed. Just as now, smiling, holding the glass delicately with her manicured fingers, Susan was coming toward her, bending gracefully from the waist, placing the deliciously tinkling glass on a small table beside the chaise. The table, too, was mirrored, reflecting the glass.

"Happy September twenty-second," Susan was saying, straightening, smiling. "Anything else?"

Marvella smiled in return, shook her head. "No, thank you."

"Shall I look in on you later?"

"I don't think so, Susan. I'm feeling tired tonight. I think I'll go to bed early."

"Well, then—good night, Mrs. Holloway." Susan smiled again, turned toward the door, quietly let herself out. With the security men on duty in the hallway outside, Susan would be free for the evening.

As Marvella would be free, too—free from the long hours of waiting for this moment, this time that was the focus of all the hours that had gone before: twenty-four hours, since she'd done what she was doing now, reaching for the day's first drink.

Carefully balanced on high-heeled lounging slippers, Marvella stooped, picked up the empty glass, turned toward the bar. An antique clock hung on the wall behind the bar. No, not an antique, not really an antique. Even in the presidential suite the clock wouldn't be a real antique. Because, if the president stayed here, or his wife, then time would be important. The country would expect it, would demand correct time for the president, not antique time.

She placed the glass on the bar, looked closely at the clock. Time: ten minutes after seven. Two hours and ten minutes since Susan had knocked on her door. Soon there would be another knock: a waiter with her dinner. Two waiters, white-jacketed, bringing her dinner on a cart.

Food, but no wine. She could have had wine if she'd liked. She could have traded the vodka for a bottle of wine, any kind. And sometimes she did, traded vodka for wine.

She poured vodka into the glass, dropped in the ice, added the tonic, squeezed in the lime. Her hands were steady—beautiful hands, Austin always said. Beautiful hands with beautiful rings, beautifully manicured nails.

But the skin of her hands was changing, coarsening. Age, time, trouble—they were changing her skin, changing her. She could feel it inside, the changing. In front of the mirror, naked, she could see it.

She took up the drink, turned, steadied herself, walked back to the chaise, set the glass on the small table, another fake antique. Across the room, the bottle was half empty. It stood like some religious symbol: a glass icon, in its own mirrored niche, sparkling, sparkling.

The highball glass, too, was sparkling, its crystals reflecting the light.

Sitting on the chaise again, but not reclining, she realized she was looking around the sitting room, almost as if she'd never seen it. She was experiencing the same sensation she'd felt earlier in the day, in the limo, driving to City Hall. It was as if she'd materialized as two identical persons, one person observing the other, wondering how that other person came to be there—here— at this time, in this particular place, experiencing these particular sensations, this sudden moment of utter emptiness.

They were strangers, these two identical persons. Odd, dissimilar strangers, sometimes hostile strangers. One of them came clearly from the sunshine and stars of her childhood: the girl in the gingham dress, with only a father to raise her, with her mother in heaven, looking down on them. Always, she'd been alone, that small child, wandering through golden fields, venturing into the quiet woods beyond the creek behind their house. Always alone, but in memory never lonely. Because the child could wander the wondrous landscape of imagination, like Dorothy, in the land of Oz, or Alice, in Wonderland.

But the other person—herself—was always lonely. Now, here—in the limousine, there—even on Sunday, in her place onstage, holding Elton with her left hand and Gloria with her right hand, singing, she felt the emptiness, the terrible loneliness.

When she sang as a child, alone under the bright sky, she sang to God. And she'd never felt the loneliness.

Now, at age forty-nine, with the flesh sagging on her bones and that small, constant voice from the dead never far from the surface of her consciousness, she sang for the small red light beside the camera lens.

She'd sung for both of them—her father, and Austin. One of them dead. Her father, lying facedown in the field of weeds behind their tabernacle, his face flattened in the bloody dirt of a pathway that led to town, arms flung wide, fingers crooked into the grass, desperately hanging on.

Life and death . . . death and life . . .

The dead she'd seen, each one of them, had changed her life, made her a different person, a stranger to herself. Her mother, lying in the wooden coffin—her father, murdered, sprawled in the dirt—her baby, strangled in her womb—

—and the boy lying on the sidewalk beside his twisted bicycle, his eyes turning to stone as she knelt beside him.

The world—the room—the bottle on the crystal bar—all had faded into the mists of time, disappeared in the darkness behind her closed eyes.

As she opened her eyes, the glass beside her filled the field of her vision; everything else was blurred, out of focus.

Everything.

12

"**I**'m sorry to've called this meeting without much warning," Holloway said, smiling as he looked around the room. "But Herbert and I were talking while we were stuck in traffic today, going to pick up the key to the city—" To smirks all around, he held up the foot-long key. "—and I thought I should give you my thinking on the objectives, this Sunday—give you the game plan. Now, I know—I'm fully aware—that some of you think it's dumb to bring The Hour to San Francisco." Keeping the smile in place, he once more swept the faces with a genial, eye-crinkled gaze.

"And that's okay," he said, nodding encouragement. "I want that input. I need it. You all know that. But—" Now the smile twisted playfully. The blue eyes danced, the famous face settled into its trademark friendly, folksy expression. "But I don't need it now, four days before the cameras roll."

He waited for the laugh, then allowed the smile to fade. The time for pleasantries had passed. And time was precious.

"As you know," Holloway said, "I'll be meeting tomorrow night with a group of men—fifty-two men, to be exact—who probably have as much influence on the way this country's run as any comparable-size group you could think of, could assemble. Now, some of you—Larry and Gordon, particularly—" He smiled, gestured to the two writers. "—know what I'll be saying tomorrow. But for the benefit of those of you who don't, I'm going to make an opening pitch for the formation of a new political party. Which, God knows, this country needs badly.

69

Now—'' Gracefully, he raised a hand in benediction, acknowledging the on-cue buzz of assent, of excitement, of encouragement. "Now, I'm not going to give the speech, don't worry. But what I wanted to tell you is that the service on Sunday will be a kind of reverse lead-in to this meeting tomorrow night, which I consider to be one of the most important, most significant meetings I've ever called." As he said it, he swept the company with solemn eyes. The smile was gone now. The set of the mouth and chin was uncompromising. With its broad jaw and forehead, with its graceful flow of thick gray hair, the head was transformed, ennobled.

"Now, what do I mean by all this? How do the two tie together, this banquet tomorrow night and The Hour on Sunday?" The rhetorical question was sternly asked. The blue eyes snapped. The set of the chin was firm. The opening moments of calculated levity were now behind them.

"The answer is that, beginning tomorrow night, we're going to start focusing on what's wrong with this country—what's wrong, and what we can do to make it right. No, I'm not going to start in on it now, don't worry—'' This time, the smile was fleeting, without warmth, inviting nothing in return but his audience's closer attention. "But I wanted to tell you—warn all of you—that The Hour this Sunday will be something different, a new departure, a new direction for all of us. And if you do your jobs right—publicity, production, planning—'' Briefly, his eye fell on the separate department chiefs "—you'll be doing things differently, too, for Sunday. And that'll apply particularly to you, Charlie—'' He turned to his publicity director. "—when you're dealing with the media. Because what we'll be doing on Sunday—what I'll be doing—is holding up San Francisco to Christian scrutiny. This city is a hotbed of sin, pure and simple. There's no other city like it in the whole country. And the whole country—the whole world—knows it.

"Now, obviously, I'm not going to make a frontal attack, to use the military vernacular. I'm going to put it that we're saving the city's soul, praying for its salvation at the bar of God's heavenly justice. In other words, we'll be striving to save this wicked city from itself.'' He paused, allowing a long, measured moment of calculated silence to pass. ''What we'll actually be doing, of course, is playing to the rest of the country, the rest of the world. We'll be playing off San Francisco, in other words. It's a high-risk strategy, I suppose—something we've never tried before. But the truth is, at age sixty-three, I'm feeling that it's about time I take some risks. I think this country is ready for risks. It's ready for some new ideas, some new leadership.'' A final pause, as he swept the circle one last time with sharply focused eyes. Then: ''And I hope you're ready, too.''

He waited for the expression of approval and assent to subside, then he asked, ''Any questions?''

The first among equals, Charlie Benton raised a forefinger, waited for Holloway's answering nod, then said, ''If you can manage it, Austin, I'd like to spend a few minutes with you after we're through here. I'll be meeting with two local reporters in less than an hour. In fact, one of them is a city editor. And I'd like to be sure I'm straight on your thinking for Sunday, on the appeals you want to hit, especially locally.''

Holloway glanced at Flournoy, who nodded.

''No problem,'' Holloway answered. Quickly, Holloway's questioning glance circled the group of a half dozen shirtsleeved men lounging at their ease in the sitting room of his suite. Each man knew that, after the first pro forma post-meeting question, Holloway quickly lost patience with further questions.

''Anything else?'' he asked.

When no hands were raised, Holloway beamed at them, waved benevolent dismissal. To confirm his authority, Flournoy lingered behind after the department heads left the room. Ignoring Benton, who frequently displeased him, Flournoy spoke directly to Holloway:

. ''I'll be back in a half hour, Austin. Gloria wants to see me. Then I'll meet you here. Right?'' It was an implied command, directing that Benton conclude his business in thirty minutes. Signifying acceptance, Holloway nodded.

"Right."

"Drink?" Gloria asked, as Flournoy sat down to face her across a marble cocktail table.

"White wine, please." Appreciatively, Flournoy watched Gloria as she rose, went to the bar, took a bottle of Chardonnay from the small refrigerator, began working with a corkscrew. She was dressed in fawn-colored slacks and a color-coordinated beige sweater. The slacks were cut close, modeling a perfection of thighs, buttocks, and a taut, flat stomach. The sweater was cut full, only hinting at the richness of her breasts, the suppleness of her waist. Like her father, Gloria moved deliberately, decisively, always mindful of the effect she was creating, yet arrogantly indifferent. But if their mannerisms were similar, their objectives differed. Austin sought power. Gloria sought sex. She'd been divorced for two years. On the road, always with her two children, The Hour's sentimental favorites, Gloria never indulged herself, never went looking for bed partners. At home, though, in Beverly Hills, Flournoy was aware that she slipped into her second persona: the female in heat, constantly on the prowl.

But for Austin, and therefore for Flournoy—Gloria had never been a problem. Unlike Marvella, who drank, and Elton, who was grotesquely unpredictable, Gloria managed her vices the way she managed everything else: quietly, efficiently, intelligently. And economically, too. Gloria didn't believe in wasted motion or wasted words. Many times, lying in bed, listening to his wife as she lay beside him, quietly snoring, Flournoy had imagined himself making love to Gloria. Occasionally, if he'd been · drinking, and if his wife had denied him, he had actually resolved to speak to Gloria. But the resolve had never survived the cold light of morning, not to mention the cold light in Gloria's eyes as she and Flournoy made the day-to-day, week-to-week decisions essential to the successful operation of the conglomerate that was Austin Holloway.

She filled two stem glasses, corked the bottle, put it away, then carried the glasses across the room. She moved rhythmically, sensually, swinging her hips and her shoulders. Her head was high, her step was light, yet decisive. Even though Flournoy realized that these visual pleasures weren't consciously offered to him, he nevertheless welcomed this shared moment, a much needed balm after a long, demanding day.

But when he accepted the glass, and looked for the first time directly into her eyes, he saw the urgency, saw her deep apprehension.

Something had gone wrong.

Perhaps badly wrong.

He watched her sit in a Regency armchair. She drank some of the wine, and placed the glass on the coffee table. Then she leaned back, crossed her legs, gripped both arms of the chair and began to speak:

"While you and my father were out this afternoon, a police lieutenant named Hastings got up here, in the hallway."

Watching her over the rim of his glass, speculating on the possible connection between a police lieutenant and whatever was disturbing her, Flournoy decided not to respond. Soon, it would all come clear.

"He's from Homicide. And he's investigating the murder of a prostitute. It happened last night, just a couple of blocks from here." As she paused, Flournoy could see the muscles of her throat tighten. He watched her draw a deep, meaningful breath, saw her eyes sharpen, focused on him. As she always did, Gloria delivered the decisive stroke softly, sibilantly:

"He wanted to talk to Elton."

Flournoy was satisfied with his response, delivered in a voice that was as calm as Gloria's:

"About the murder, you mean."

She nodded—once. "That's right. About the murder."

"And did he talk with Elton?"

"No. But he's coming back. Tonight. At nine-thirty, he said."

"*Christ.*" Abruptly he drained his glass, then reflexively

looked at his watch. The time was twenty minutes to eight. There was no point in asking her why she hadn't told him when he'd first returned to the hotel—why, in fact, she hadn't called him in the limo. *"Christ!"*

"It looks like this is the fourth time it's happened," she said. "Milwaukee—Dallas—Pittsburgh—" Still focused sharply on his face, her eyes held steady. Remorselessly steady.

"There was never anything definitive. Nothing to incriminate Elton."

"There is now, apparently."

"What d'you mean?" Asking the question, he could clearly hear the tremor of dread in his voice. Could she hear it, too?

"I mean," she answered, "that the police seem to have evidence against him."

"Are you sure? Did they tell you about it, this evidence?"

She shook her head. "No. But they wouldn't. They wouldn't tell us what they know. Not till they talk to Elton."

Grimly, Flournoy stared down at his empty glass. Would she offer him a refill, for God's sake? With everything suddenly in jeopardy, with the whole house of cards teetering, wasn't she going to refill his glass?

"Any ideas?" she asked.

"First," he said, "we've got to call Harlan, tell him what's happened, find out where we stand legally. Harlan's got to come up here. He can be here in three hours. Meanwhile, we keep Elton away from them, from the police. We—" He broke off, drew a ragged breath. Was he revealing a momentary indecision, faltering in front of Austin's daughter? Before he realized that he was going to say it, he heard himself complaining: "You should've gotten in touch, Gloria. Sooner. You should've gotten on the mobile phone. If they show up here in an hour and a half, with a warrant, do you realize what could happen? Have you any idea?"

Ignoring the complaint, she said, "We've got to think beyond now, today. This has been coming on for a long time, trouble like this. We've been ignoring it, putting our heads in the sand."

"The first thing to do is keep Elton away from the police. Maybe we should put him on a plane to Los Angeles. Now. Right now. Right this minute. We've got to get him in a car. Not a limo, but a car. We've got to get him to the airport. There're flights leaving every half hour for Los Angeles. Until midnight, there're flights leaving every half hour." As he said it, he could feel certainty returning, his habitual assurance, projecting clear, calm command. Yes, his lapse had only been momentary, a mere aberration. To drive home his demand, he nodded decisively. "Yes, that'll be the best. I'll tell Mitchell, tell him to arrange it. He can assign two men, to make sure Elton gets on the airplane. And Mitchell can arrange to have him met in Los Angeles, taken to Harlan, immediately." Reviewing the plan, he lapsed into silence. Then, vehemently, he nodded, repeating: "Yes, that's best, the best plan. So we won't have to get Harlan up here, after all. We'll ship Elton to Harlan, let Harlan work it out. Then we can—" Once more he broke off, this time pointing to the empty glass. "Have you got some bourbon—bourbon and water?"

Silently, Gloria rose, took the empty glass to the bar, made the drink, placed it in front of him, resumed her seat. In her eyes, he saw the stillness of quiet contempt.

"What about Dad?" she said. "What do we tell him? What excuse'll we give him, for Elton not being there on Sunday, onstage?"

He drank half the highball, then said, "First we've got to decide between ourselves, you and I, what we think is best. Then we'll tell Austin what we think, what we recommend. As always."

For a moment she made no reply, gave no sign that she'd heard. Instead, she sat motionless, her wine forgotten, silently staring at him. Then, speaking in a slow, measured voice, she said, "What about telling Dad the truth? Just the simple truth?"

"Gloria, we can't do that now. Tomorrow Austin's got one of the most important meetings of his life. You know that. And then there's Sunday. And this city, too. It's—"

"There's always the next Sunday, Herbert. You know that.

And I know it, too. That's what this is all about, really—a
lifetime of Sundays." She still spoke slowly, with infinite
reluctance. Then: "We arrived here Monday afternoon. Last
night—Tuesday—Elton went out for a while, alone. He was gone
from nine forty-five till about ten-thirty. I checked with our
people, Mitchell's men. That's what they told me. Today, a
detective arrives. He tells me a whore was murdered, when Elton
was out. And he—"

"We're not sure that—"

"We *are* sure, Herbert," she interrupted fiercely. "You and I,
we're sure. We know what happened. We *know*. And we know
this same thing happened in Milwaukee, and Pittsburgh, and
Dallas. Except that the police didn't come then. But it was in the
papers, on the radio, whatever. It *happened*, for God's sake. It
happened three times, at least. We get into town, and a prostitute
is murdered—strangled. And Elton's out when they're strangled.
He's always unaccounted for when they're killed. And he's
always—"

"But that's not *proof*," he protested. "That's—"

She raised a furious hand, commanding his instant silence. Her
eyes were fierce, her voice was harsh, half choked with a rush of
sudden anger. "I'm not talking about proof, Herbert. I'm talking
about the truth. I'm talking about what *happened*—and what *will*
happen. And I'm also talking about the whores that've been
dying in Los Angeles the last year. I'm talking about the whores
who've been strangled while Elton's been—"

"Gloria, this is speculation, don't you see that? There's
nothing to connect Elton to any of this. It could be a—a
stagehand, a cameraman, that's killing these women. Don't
you—"

"Elton is crazy, Herbert. He's a fucking maniac—a very quiet,
very cagey lunatic." Momentarily, she broke off. Then, measur-
ing the words with icy precision, she said: "He's crazy, and my
mother's a drunk. Every Sunday, you and I get Elton's attention,
and get my mother dried out. We get them dressed, and give them
the hymn number, and we prop them up in front of the camera—

them, and me, and my kids. We cast our eyes up to heaven, and we sing. It hasn't changed since I was a little girl. Elton was just starting to sing—and my mother was just starting to drink. And I was starting to see how—how grotesque it was, what happened. I—" Suddenly she broke off, blinked, shook her head, reached for her wine glass. She drained the glass. In silence, eyes gravely downcast, she replaced the empty glass on the marble table. When she spoke again, her voice was husky:

"I don't know why I bother. I don't know why I don't just take my kids and move somewhere. Anywhere."

"For one thing," Flournay said, "he's your father. He loves you."

She laughed. Harshly. Bitterly. "Except for an hour on Sunday, he hardly knows I exist. He's a megalomaniac, Herbert. Don't you understand that? He *believes* that crap he preaches. He thinks God talks to him, tells him what to say."

"Forget about love, then," Flournoy said quietly. "What about money? What about your Mercedes, Gloria, and your house in Coldwater Canyon? That's part of it, too—the things that money can buy."

She raised her eyes to meet his. Now, heavily ironic, she smiled wearily. "I've never really liked you, Herbert. But I'll say this—you've got a gift for analysis, for getting to the heart of the matter. It's not always flattering. But it's usually accurate."

"What about Elton, Gloria? You say this detective is coming back at nine-thirty. We can't let them talk. I've got to call Harlan, find out where we stand. I think they need a warrant to interrogate someone."

She shook her head. "I don't think so. You're thinking about a search warrant. But I think the police can interrogate anyone if they have probable cause. I don't think they can get in his room without his permission, unless they have a warrant. But if they catch him on the street, or downstairs in the lobby—" She let it go ominously unfinished.

"Either way, we need time. I'll talk to Mitchell. He can take Elton to another hotel. Are there policemen downstairs, in the lobby?"

"I don't know."

"Jesus—" Flournoy shook his head. "There're reporters downstairs. If there're policemen in the lobby, too, and the reporters find out about it, and start asking questions—" Grimly, he shook his head, then abruptly rose. "I've got to call Harlan, then get together with Mitchell. I'll get back to you." Quickly he strode to the door. Still seated, Gloria did not reply, did not look at Flournoy as he left.

13

"I don't agree. We've got a better chance if we keep him here, in the hotel. If we try to take him away, and they catch us . . ." Mitchell spread his broad, knob-knuckled hands, shook his big, grizzled head.

Talking softly, urgently, the two men stood at one end of the eleventh-floor corridor. Flournoy was in shirtsleeves, his tie loosened. Behind rimless glasses, his eyes were aggressively sharp-focused. As always, Mitchell wore a blue suit, serviceable black shoes, a white shirt, a plain tie. His broad, peasant's face was impassive. If Flournoy looked the part of a harried behind-the-scenes political kingmaker, Mitchell looked like a KGB man.

"Listen, Lloyd, I've just talked with Harlan. I'm acting on his advice. He's a corporation counsel, for God's sake. We pay him to take care of things like this. And he says we've got to get Elton out and hide him. Now. Right now."

"Have you talked to Austin?"

"No. I haven't had a chance. That's because—" Flournoy lowered his voice, stepped closer. "That's because I just got all this from Gloria, about the detective being here. Not more than a half hour ago."

"We can't take Elton away without telling Austin." Mitchell spoke slowly, heavily, with impassive conviction. His small eyes remained fixed on Flournoy's face.

"Listen, Lloyd—" Visibly, Flournoy was restraining himself. "You're Austin's security chief. You're responsible for him, for his peace of mind, as well as his physical well-being. You're probably closer to Austin than anyone, granted. And he trusts you, too, also granted. But I'm telling you that—"

"I won't take Elton anywhere. Not unless Austin tells me."

Flournoy's voice dropped to a furious hiss. "Don't you understand what I'm telling you? Don't you understand that these people might arrest Elton for murder? Can you imagine the consequences?" A short, outraged pause. Then the vehement demand: "Well, *can* you?"

Unmoved, Mitchell answered, "You've been trying to keep things from Austin for a long time. That was a mistake. But this'll only make matters worse, taking Elton away. And I'm not getting involved. Not unless Austin wants me to get involved."

"Do *you* want to tell Austin what's happened?"

Mitchell's shoulders raised, signifying both indifference and assent. "Gloria should do it. But if she won't, and you won't, then I'll do it."

"But it—it's nine o'clock, for God's sake. They'll be here in a half hour. How the hell can we—"

"It should've been done a long time ago. You're trying to protect Austin because of the service Sunday. And the meeting tomorrow. But that only makes everything worse, putting things off. You make excuses. Austin does, too. He doesn't see what he doesn't want to see. And now he's in trouble."

"*We're* in trouble. *All* of us."

"Elton has always been—" Mitchell broke off, ponderously searching for the word. "He's always been strange."

"*Strange?*" Bitterly, Flournoy looked at his watch. "That's putting it mildly."

"I'll do my best to keep the police from questioning him," Mitchell said. "If he stays in his room, we should be all right, at least for tonight. But then we'll tell him, tell Austin. I won't keep this from him. It'll only be worse for Austin in the long run if we don't tell him."

Silently, desperately incredulous, Flournoy searched the big man's face. Finally he said, "You're loyal, Lloyd. I'll say that."

Making no reply, Mitchell turned away.

14

"**D**o we have a plan?" Hastings asked as they walked toward the entrance of the St. Francis.

"Of course we have a plan," Friedman said. "We're going to keep the lowest possible profile while we get the goods on Elton Holloway."

"If this gets into the papers before Dwyer knows what we're doing . . ." Ominously, Hastings let it go unfinished.

"That's why we're keeping a low profile," Friedman answered airily. "Just keep saying no comment if a reporter shows up. That's the plan."

Shaking his head, Hastings pushed through the revolving door into the lobby, followed by Friedman. Sitting close to the doors, Canelli rose to his feet, smiling expectantly. But Friedman pointedly looked away, ignoring the younger man as he and Hastings joined the stream of animated, well-dressed men and women entering the hotel through the Powell Street entrance.

"So now what?" Hastings asked.

Friedman pointed to the elevators. "For openers, we'll use their elevator code, get off at the eleventh floor. That'll throw them off balance. Then we'll proceed to capitalize on our advantage, as the situation permits."

"Hmmm."

"I'll do the talking," Friedman said. "You look determined."
"Hmmm."

"We're policemen," Friedman said, showing his shield to the

two security men. "We want to see Elton Holloway. He's expecting us." As he spoke, he saw one of the guards take a small surveillance radio from his pocket as the second man moved to block Friedman's way.

"You'll have to talk to Mr. Mitchell," the second guard said. "Lloyd Mitchell. He's chief of security."

"Fine." Agreeably, Friedman pocketed his shield case, looked expectantly down the long, quiet corridor. "Where is he?" As he asked the question, he saw a door open, midway along the corridor. A big, solidly built man appeared. The big man's thick, graying hair and seamed face put his age at about sixty. As he came closer, Friedman took his automatic policeman's inventory: big, muscular shoulders, a square-cut head set low on a wrestler's neck, stevedore's hands carried away from the body, fingers half clenched. The face was a serf's. Beneath heavy brows, the small eyes were watchful. This was a quiet man, an uncompromising man—a dangerous man.

With Hastings beside him, Friedman faced the big man in the blue suit. "Mr. Mitchell?"

"Yes sir."

"I'm Lieutenant Peter Friedman. This is Lieutenant Frank Hastings. We're co-commanders of the homicide detail, in San Francisco."

Looking at the two men briefly in turn, Mitchell impassively nodded.

"Are your people licensed for security work, Mr. Mitchell?"

"Yes, sir. We have licenses from Los Angeles and the State of California. I have the licenses in my room."

"How many of your men carry firearms?"

"I do. And two others." Mitchell gestured to one of the two security men who stood shoulder to shoulder, at parade rest, attentively watching. "Mr. Wagner has a permit, too."

Wagner nodded. Like Mitchell's, his face was expressionless.

"Can I ask you what kind of weapons you carry?" Friedman asked, his eyes on Mitchell.

"We carry Smith & Wesson .357 magnums, with four-inch barrels. All three of us."

Approvingly, Friedman nodded. "Good choice." Then, signifying that the preliminaries were concluded, he let a moment of silence pass, let his police smile slowly fade before he said, "As you probably know, Mr. Mitchell, we're here to talk to Elton Holloway."

The large, centurion's head with its close-cropped graying hair gravely inclined. "You were here earlier." The dark, opaque eyes turned to Hastings. "You talked to Miss Holloway. She explained things to you, told you how it is here."

"We're investigating the strangulation of a prostitute," Friedman said. "She was killed Tuesday night, a little after ten o'clock. We have a witness who saw Elton Holloway with the victim approximately fifteen minutes before she was killed. So, naturally, we've got to talk to Elton. He could have some valuble information for us."

"I'll talk to him," Mitchell said. "Then I'll call you."

"No." Slowly, gravely, Friedman shook his head. "No, that's not good enough. Lieutenant Hastings was willing to go along with you earlier. But now we've got our orders." As he spoke, a nearby door opened. Turning, Friedman saw a young, attractive, determined woman. She was looking directly at Hastings. Her eyes were angry; her voice was low and tight. "Can I talk to you, Lieutenant? Privately?"

Hastings looked at Friedman, waiting for his silent cue. He saw Friedman's tongue circling the inside of his mouth, the definitive sign that Friedman was deep in thought. Finally Friedman nodded. To Gloria, sternly, he said, "Fifteen minutes. No more."

With only a contemptuous glance at Friedman, Gloria turned abruptly back into her room, leaving the door open. Hastings followed her inside, closed the door, crossed the room to sit in the same chair he'd taken earlier in the day. Tonight, Gloria was dressed in a pleated flannel skirt and tweed jacket. She wore stockings, but no shoes. Like her expression, her voice was cold:

"We've talked to our lawyers, Lieutenant. They tell us that if you have probable cause you can question Elton, and there's nothing we can do to stop you." She let a long, hostile beat pass. "Do you have probable cause?"

"Definitely."

"What is it, this probable cause? What's the evidence?"

"I don't have to give you that information. Not until he's charged with a crime. And I'm not doing that, not charging him."

"Then—"

"He's a material witness," Hastings said. "For now, that's his status. But your lawyers will tell you that we have the same rights where a material witness is concerned as we do if we're questioning a suspect in a capital crime."

"He can't be questioned unless he has a lawyer present."

"No, that's not right. If he's a suspect—if I've given him his Miranda rights—then he can demand that a lawyer be present. But not now, not as a material witness."

"That's not what our lawyers say."

Hastings shrugged. "You have your lawyers, we have ours." He watched her for a moment, then quietly added, "I'm talking about the DA."

"Listen, Lieutenant—" Eyes hard, mouth firmly set, she leaned forward in her chair. The message: Gloria Holloway couldn't—wouldn't—be intimidated. "Let's be honest with each other."

"Fine."

"You know that my father is a very important man. That's a cliché in your business, I know—people talking about how important they are, how much they pay in taxes, how much trouble they could make for you. But the thing about clichés is, they're usually true, have some basis in fact. My father *is* very important. You might not believe it, how important he is, how much clout he has."

"I'm not about to bother your father. I just want to talk with your brother. That's all. For now, that's all we want, just to talk with him." Eyes locked with hers, Hastings let a long, measured beat pass before he said, "I'm not going to threaten him with arrest, and I'm not going to take him downtown. I'm not going to put undue pressure on him. I'm simply going to talk to him. It's important that you understand that, important that you *all* understand that."

Speaking very slowly, very distinctly, she said, "Our chief lawyer is in Los Angeles. His name is Harlan Collins. Mr. Collins has called a colleague of his, a Mr. Richard Wertheimer. Does that name ring a bell?"

Hastings nodded. "Richard Wertheimer is probably the best criminal lawyer in San Francisco."

"That's right. And he says that you've got to have a warrant to question Elton."

"That's not true. Under certain circumstances, we need a warrant to enter his room. But we don't need anything to question him. So—"

"Mr. Wertheimer is on his way over here right now. And his advice to me was that I should stand in front of Elton's door—his room is 1106, by the way. I should stand in front of his door and make you remove me physically if you want to see Elton. And that's exactly what I intend to do."

Momentarily, the imaginary pleasure of wrestling with Gloria Holloway distracted Hastings, brought a twitch of humor to the corners of his mouth. He gave himself a moment, then said, "Driving over here from headquarters, Lieutenant Friedman and I talked about this—about what would happen if you go against us. And we decided what we'd do." Watching her, seeing the determination so plain on her face, in the lines of her body, he let the moment lengthen, let the pressure build. Then: "What we decided was, we'd call, say, six uniformed men to come to the lobby downstairs. That's three cars, two men to a car. We'd get them together in the lobby, and we'd give them their orders, tell them the situation, tell them we've got a material witness on the eleventh floor that we have to put under close surveillance. We'll need more than six, come to think about it, if we're going to cover the elevators, and the staircases. Then Lieutenant Friedman and I will take, say, four more uniformed men, and we'll go upstairs—where we'll do our duty. If you decide to bar our way, there'll be a couple of men to take you downstairs, through the lobby. You'll be taken downtown, and booked for interfering with a policeman in the lawful pursuit of his duty.

"Then, if Elton won't allow us entry, we'll have to stake out the eleventh floor, of course, wait until we can get him outside his room. That'll take, say, another half dozen men, plus the half dozen we'd leave in the lobby, in reserve. They'd all be uniformed men, of course. Big, conspicuous, uniformed men doing their duty." He broke off, decided to smile. "Do you get the picture? Do you see what the media might think, seeing all that action? Can you imagine the scene at police headquarters while your expensive lawyer's getting you out on bail? Can you imagine what the hotel people will think, seeing all those cops in the lobby, and up here, on the eleventh floor?"

Eyes snapping, breathing harshly, she suddenly rose, confronting him.

"You bastard."

He let the smile widen. "It's your choice, Miss Holloway. If you intend to block your brother's door, tell me now." He pointed to a nearby phone. "All it takes is one call. And the response time, in this part of town, will surprise you."

"You son of a bitch."

"I'm trying to forget you're saying these things, Miss Holloway."

"If you weren't a policeman . . ."

"But I am. That's the whole point. I am."

15

Reflexively unbuttoning his sports jacket and loosening his revolver in its holster, Hastings pressed the button beside the door of room 1106. At his side, Friedman also stood with his hand on the butt of his revolver.

"Assuming that he's there," Friedman said softly, "someone sure as hell has called him, warned him not to answer the door." As he spoke, Friedman looked down the corridor, where the two security men stood shoulder to shoulder, watching. Gloria Holloway and Lloyd Mitchell had chosen to return to their separate rooms.

Hastings pressed the button again, stepped closer to the door, listening.

"Maybe you should knock," Friedman said. He smiled. "Do the old room service dodge."

As Hastings raised his fist, ready to knock, the door opened. Surprised, Hastings stepped a half step backward. Then, automatically, he took out his shield case, showed the badge.

"Elton Holloway?"

Dancer Browne's description had been a good one: a slightly built man of medium height, dark blond hair, a pale, expressionless face. The mouth was small, with colorless lips. The brown eyes were utterly empty, strangely fixed. The voice was a monotone:

"My sister said you were coming. She just called me."

"Can we come in?" Hastings stepped firmly forward.

Without replying, Elton Holloway turned, walked into the

small single room. He walked woodenly, mechanically, arms straight down at either side, shoulders squared, head held rigidly: an overgrown boy playing at being a soldier, his back ramrod straight, marching on dress parade. Entering the room behind Hastings, Friedman surreptitiously bolted the door. The three men sat in separate straight-backed chairs, facing each other. Friedman spoke first:

"We won't take much of your time, Mr. Holloway. We—"

"Elton. Call me Elton."

Gravely, Friedman nodded, then smiled his policeman's smile, calculated to disarm. "Good. Thank you, Elton. I'm Lieutenant Friedman. Peter Friedman." He gestured. "This is Lieutenant Frank Hastings." He nodded again, smiled again, then asked, "Did your sister tell you what it is that we'd like to ask you about?"

"No."

"Well," Friedman said, "it concerns a murder that Lieutenant Hastings and I are investigating. The victim's name was Amy MacFarland. She was killed last night, just about this time, as a matter of fact. She was a prostitute. We think she picked up a man on Mason Street, just two and a half blocks from here. She took him to the Bayside Hotel, to a room she used. We think the man we're looking for strangled her in that hotel room. Then we think he left the same way he went in, and walked back the way he came, north on Mason Street. And we think it's possible—" He let a beat pass. "We think it's possible that he came here, to the St. Francis."

As Friedman spoke, Hastings watched the suspect, whose empty eyes remained inexorably fixed on Friedman. "Stone eyes," Dancer Browne had said. Privately, Hastings smiled, mentally scored another point for The Dancer. If he'd chosen to play by the rules, Dancer Browne would probably have an office with a view—and a luscious white secretary, of course.

"Can you help us with any of this?" Friedman asked. He let another moment of silence pass. Then: "We understand you were on Mason Street last night between ten and ten-thirty. Is that right?"

Elton Holloway remained motionless in his chair. The hands resting on the arms of the chair were inert, the muscles of the neck were relaxed, the head was rigid, held unnaturally high. In the silence that followed, the eerily empty eyes turned briefly toward Hastings, then returned to Friedman. The voice was unchanged: an expressionless monotone.

"I don't know the name of the street. Was it Mason, did you say?"

Friedman nodded. "Mason. Right. And the name of the hotel was the Bayside."

Slowly, woodenly, Elton Holloway shook his head. "I don't know the name of the hotel, either." Still with his eyes fixed on Friedman, he sat silently, still utterly motionless. Then: "I often do that, you know. Tonight, I was going to do it, too—what I did last night."

Involuntarily, Friedman and Hastings exchanged a cop's closed, covert look. Was it possible? Was this strange-looking, strange-acting son of Austin Holloway about to confess to murder?

Both detectives turned their eyes to the suspect. For a long, time-suspended moment, neither man could frame the make-or-break question that must follow. Finally, tentatively, Hastings ventured, "Her name was Amy MacFarland. Do you remember that, remember her name?"

"No—" The narrow head moved in a slow arc of delayed denial. "No, I never know their names. It's not necessary, you see, that I know their names."

"Will you—" Momentarily, Hastings's throat closed. Had he ever been so close to a confession that would make headlines across the country, around the world? "Will you tell us what happened, Elton? Never mind about her name. Just tell us how it went—what happened, last night."

Incredibly, with only a moment's hesitation, the suspect said, "I remember that I went out the front entrance of the hotel, on Powell Street. And I remember turning right. I turned right, and then I turned left, I remember, at the next corner. I'd been there before, the night before. So I knew I'd found it, you see—found the place where it all begins. That's so important, you know. It's like Africa. That's where they think life began, you know. So if you're going to understand life, you must go to Africa."

Very seriously, as though he were deeply interested, Friedman asked, "Have you ever been to Africa, Elton?"

"Oh, yes—" Slowly, gravely, he nodded: a single solemn inclination of his head. "And I've seen it, the Rift Valley. That's where it all began. It's the cradle of civilization, you know."

Still nodding, Friedman was studiously frowning, as if he were struggling to comprehend the depth of the suspect's wisdom. "I see . . ." He hesitated, then asked, "Can we go back a minute? There's something I want to ask."

"Certainly."

"You say you found the place, here in the city, where it all begins. Is that right?"

"Yes, that's right. Exactly right."

"Well, then, my question is, what's 'it'? That's what I can't follow."

"It's sin," came the prompt answer. "That's the thing about Africa, you see. If you're going to study humanity, you must go to where humanity began. And if you're going to study sin, especially if you're going to fight sin, then you've got to know where it starts. Because there's a place in every city, you know— even towns, if they're big enough. There's always a center, the very center, of sin. I can understand that you're having trouble understanding. Because it took me years, before I could find the center." Dreamily, he nodded, momentarily lost in reverie. "But now, I'm able to go right to it, right to the center of sin. Sometimes, like Monday, I feel as if I—I'm—" He broke off again, allowing his eyes to wander far away. Friedman and Hastings exchanged another look that hardly concealed their growing excitement.

"I feel like I'm—" Another pause. Then, confessing: "I feel electrified." Quickly, perhaps shyly, he looked at Friedman. For the first time, the pale face registered emotion: a kind of hesitant anxiety. "That sounds strange, I know."

"No—no—" Hastily, Friedman raised a reassuring hand.

"Not at all. I've felt the same thing myself. After all—" He gestured again. "We're all made of electricty. Everyone knows that. So it's only getting back to the source, really, when you feel like that. Electrified, I mean. It's like . . . well—" Momentarily he broke off, searching for the phrase. "It's like the Rift Valley. It's exactly the same. Elemental, I mean."

"Have you ever been to the Rift Valley?" Elton asked.

"Well, no," Friedman admitted. "But you don't have to go, you know. You don't have to see it. All you need to do is—" Friedman hesitated, then decided to gamble: "All you have to do is read your Bible. Isn't that so?"

"Yes," the suspect answered, nodding heavily. "Yes, that's so. Exactly."

"Let's get back to Monday night," Hastings said. "You were telling us about finding the center of sin, the city's sin, on Mason Street. I'm curious. What do you do, once you find the center?"

Elton frowned, this time registering mild annoyance as he turned his attention to Hastings. "I talk to them, of course. I find the one—the right one—and I talk to her, hold up the mirror, for her to see."

"Ah—" Hastings nodded. "The mirror."

"Is it a real mirror?" Friedman asked. "A mirror on the wall, for instance?"

"It's not real. It's nothing you can touch. It's not like that." The frown returned, as the suspect began looking steadily at Friedman. Vexation darkened the round brown eyes.

"You're the mirror," Hastings said. "You. You're the mirror. You make them look at themselves."

For the first time, Elton gave Hastings his full attention.

"Of course I'm their mirror. They sin, so they can't see, not by themselves. They're blind. Morally blind."

Slowly, Hastings nodded, then said, "So Monday, you—you were on Mason Street, looking around. You had to find the center of the city's sin. And then you went back last night. Tuesday. Is that right?"

"Yes, that's right."

"I'm interested—" Still playing the part of the puzzled

disciple struggling to understand the master, Friedman leaned forward. His expression was studious. "What do you do, exactly, once you've found the center? Do you talk to them, talk to the sinners?"

"Of course I talk to them," came the impatient reply. "But first they talk to me. That's very important, that they talk first. They talk, and I answer. Sometimes it's just a word, one word. But that's all that's necessary, sometimes. Just one word. I know, after one word. And she knows, too. It's contact, that's all. Just contact. That's all that's important, then."

"And what happens, after you've made contact?"

"I can't tell you that."

"You punish them," Hastings said. "Isn't that it—what you do to sinners? Don't you punish them for what they do—for their wickedness?"

Once more, the suspect turned to face Hastings. Elton's eyes, his face remained expressionless, utterly empty. "Punish them?"

Hastings nodded. "If they're sinners—whores—they've got to be punished." He spread his hands. "It's only logical."

Beneath their pale, expressionless surface, the suspect's facial muscles began to tighten. Behind the brown eyes, a pinpoint of pale, manic fire was kindling.

"They've got to be saved. Not punished. *Saved.* My father works on the stage, in front of cameras. But my mission is the streets. I—"

The sharp sound of a buzzer interrupted, followed by a knocking on the hallway door. Suppressing a sharp obscenity, Hastings quickly opened the door. Flanked by Mitchell, a stocky, well-dressed man with truculent eyes stood in the doorway. In his right hand he held a business card, aggressively offered. His voice was harsh: "I'm Richard Wertheimer. I've been retained by the Holloway family to represent Elton Holloway." He looked past Hastings, into the room, then spoke again to Hastings. "Have you charged my client with anything?"

"No. He could be a material witness, though. That's why we're questioning him."

"For your sake, officer, I hope Elton Holloway gave you permission to enter his room."

"He let us in. We identified ourselves, and he let us in."

Wertheimer stepped forward, forcing Hastings to give ground as he strode into the sitting room. The lawyer stood motionless for a moment, looking down at Elton Holloway, who remained seated, staring up at Wertheimer with his blank eyes. Without troubling to look at the two detectives, Wertheimer announced, "You'll have to leave now, gentlemen. I'll need an hour, at least, with my client. Then we can talk, if you want. The four of us."

16

Parked in front of a fireplug on Powell Street, Hastings and Friedman sat in Friedman's elderly Datsun station wagon. At eleven o'clock on a warm September night, Union Square was populated with a seasonal mix of sightseers, theatergoers, and other citizens of the night. In the next block ahead, a line of taxicabs inched toward the St. Francis entrance, where a uniformed doorman presided. Crowded with festive tourists, one cable car was trundling down the Powell Street hill. Another cable car was approaching from the opposite direction.

Inside the Datsun, Friedman slapped the dashboard with the flat of his hand. "What we've got here," he said, "is a genuine, twenty-four-carat loonie. And I say that, first thing in the morning, we get warrants. We get his room fingerprinted, and we take a look for that rope. We can get Dancer, too, and see if he recognizes any of Elton's clothes. We impound the clothes, and test them for fiber matches from the Bayside."

"The theory's great," Hastings said. "*If* we can get the warrants."

Moodily, Friedman made no response.

"We almost had him," Hastings said bitterly. "Another ten minutes, and he'd've been telling us how he does it—saves their souls by purifying them, something like that. We had one like him a couple of years ago, remember? That Jesus freak, who liberated old ladies from their earthly problems—after he raped them?"

"Actually," Friedman said drily, "he liberated them from their earthly cares and *then* raped them." Remembering, Friedman incredulously shook his head, then said, "There's no way we're going to talk to Elton without a lawyer present. Not with Wertheimer in the game. We've got as much of his story as we're ever going to get, at least until we get him locked up."

"*If* we get him locked up." With a clenched fist, frustrated, Hastings tapped his knee.

"We need those warrants," Friedman said. "And we also need a plan. They're going to stall, sure as hell, maybe move him around, or get him out of the city. And, downtown, the brass'll be just as happy to see Sunday come, see them leave town."

"You think so?"

"Yes," Friedman answered heavily. "I think so. Dwyer's a publicity hound, admittedly. But he's always got his finger out there, in the wind. And I don't think he wants to arrest Austin Holloway's son. Not now. Not ever."

"They might move Elton around, but they also might want him here for the Sunday performance. It's a tradition, you know, the whole family on stage."

"I wonder whether Austin Holloway knows what's happening," Friedman mused. "I think Gloria knows. And Lloyd Mitchell, too, probably. But I wonder whether Holloway himself knows that his kid kills prostitutes?"

"We'll probably never know," Hastings answered.

"We've got to stir Elton up," Friedman said, "maybe catch him in the act. He admits that he was out on Monday. And we know he was out last night. If we give him room, he might go out tomorrow night. Or maybe even tonight, who knows?"

"If he knows we're following him, though, he's going to be careful."

"Maybe not. Maybe it'll work just the opposite, in fact. This guy's listening to voices. He's a nut. I'll bet he thinks he's God's chosen messenger. And characters like that—nuts—the harder you push, the harder they push back sometimes. For all we know, right this minute, he could be putting his rope in his pocket, getting ready to go out and save another sinner, never mind that he knows we're watching."

"So you're saying that we *shouldn't* try for an arrest warrant?"

"I'm thinking," Friedman said, "that maybe we should put Elton under surveillance. Tight surveillance, so he'll know he's being followed. If I'm right that Elton thinks he's God's messenger, above earthly law, then he's going to go right ahead with his plans, whether or not he thinks he's being followed. Remember, he's crazy. Why else would he have told us so much, just now?"

"It's a gamble."

Cheerfully, Friedman shrugged. "So's life a gamble."

Hastings looked at the entrance of the St. Francis, a half block away. "God, wouldn't that be something if we could catch him in the act?"

"For that pleasure," Friedman said, "I'd gladly give whatever chance I have of entry into the Kingdom of Heaven."

"You're an atheist."

"Which is exactly why I'd love to stick out my foot, and trip Austin Holloway, and watch him fall flat on his sanctimonious ass."

Conscious of a changed note in the other man's voice, Hastings turned to look at Friedman. Staring straight ahead, Friedman's eyes had slipped into thoughtful soft focus. His voice, too, was thoughtfully soft as he said, "You know, everyone worries about who's going to drop the bomb—where, and when. But I'm here to tell you that, whoever pushes the button, whenever it happens, wherever, there's going to be someone like Holloway right at the button-pusher's elbow. Because the politicians and the generals always have God with them, you know. It doesn't matter which side you're on, you've always got God. That's because there're always people like Holloway on both sides, screaming for the blood of the sinners. Which means, of course, that thousands of brave young men die. Men, and boys—" Slowly, with infinite regret, he shook his head, softly repeating: "Boys. They're killing twelve-year-old boys in the Middle East. The goddamn holy men give them guns, and tell them God commands them to—" Abruptly, he broke off, still staring sightlessly straight ahead. Then, speaking very softly, he said, "I've never been much for walking in peace marches. I don't have the figure for it, for one thing. And I'm not very good about sending checks to the right causes, either. But I'll tell you this—" He drew a long, deep breath. "If I can tie a can to Austin Holloway, I'll consider that I'll have paid my dues."

17

Her legs were heavy, her head was falling forward, bobbing up, falling forward again. Her eyelids, too, were heavy. The lines of the room were shifting, blurring, shaped and reshaped, sliding away, returning, fading again.

So she had to get up.

Because suddenly the room was her prison.

The room, the hotel, The Hour . . .

And all the hours before, and all the hours to come, all bearing down upon her like beasts of prey, white fangs dripping red, baleful yellow eyes glowing in a midnight circle surrounding her. Soon, she knew, the shape and substance of the beasts would come clear: huge, black, snarling dogs, raging, slavering, dripping red-frothed foam from blood-flecked fangs.

When the bottle was empty, the circle of terror materialized, turned into formless monsters, then wolves, then dogs—and finally into the one dog from out of her childhood. Mr. Weldon's dog, a black monster, leaping on her, forepaws on her shoulders, teeth sunk into the flesh of her upper arm. Her father had come running, brandishing a hoe like an Indian with a spear, his shouts of outrage mingling with her terrified screams. The blade of the hoe had torn flaps of bloody flesh from the dog, black and blood-red flaps, one flap from his flank, one flap from his head, leaving the ear hanging. Her screams—her father's shouts—the dog's howls of pain—banshee sounds from the crimson maw of hell, all echoing and reechoing down through all the years, the sights and the sounds of constant nightmares.

She'd been eight years old when Mr. Weldon's dog had snapped his chain and come for her.

She'd been sixteen when she'd first met Austin.

They'd been standing in front of their tabernacle, her daddy and Austin. She'd been across the dusty dirt street, coming home from high school. Only the night before, parked in Buddy Heron's lowered Chevy pickup, she'd let Buddy slip her bra up over her breasts, let him unbotton her blouse, then let him do anything he wanted, so long as he didn't go up under her skirt. It had been the first time she'd ever felt a man's flesh touch hers, the first time she'd ever felt herself go wet between the legs—the first time she'd ever held a man close, felt his whole body tremble, heard him gasp and pant, like animals do. And all because of her, because of her woman's body—her own special woman's body, hers alone.

All that day, the memory of the night before had warmed her, made her aware of herself, aware of the warmth of balm and power, of the languorous sense of infinite possibilities, aware of the time just ahead, exploring, sharing, sensing.

So, when she'd first seen Austin, she'd been thinking as a woman thinks about a man—a grown woman, inviting a grown man to look her over, see what he thought. A tilt of the hip, a lilt of the eye, and, yes, she could see that he'd noticed her—as a man notices a woman.

And her daddy had noticed, too.

From the first, her daddy had seen it, seen the two of them, how they looked at each other, the questions they asked with their eyes.

The questions—and the answers. And later the promises. Her daddy had seen them all. And her daddy could be mean. Dangerous, even, if he ever stepped over the line he'd drawn for himself, had always drawn for himself, struggling so long and so hard with himself, to keep his natural impulses so tightly in hand.

The next afternoon, after school—and after she'd made sure that her daddy was meeting with the ladies aid society—she'd put on her white eyelet dress, and tied a ribbon in her hair, and put on her white shoes. The walk into town was a little less than a mile, and the weather had been warm. She'd walked slowly, so as not to sweat. And she'd remembered to take some toilet paper, to wipe off the white shoes after walking down the dirt road.

She'd known he would be staying at the Manor House. There was only the Hotel Grand besides the Manor House, and she'd known that he wouldn't stay at the Grand, not with his beautiful clothes, and his manners, and his full, rich voice.

She'd walked past the hotel, just strolling along, and there he was, on the verandah that ran the full length of the Manor House. He'd been sitting in a rocker, fanning himself with a palmetto fan, like everyone else. It hadn't even been necessary to catch his eye. Because, right away, he'd recognized her. He'd put aside his fan, and come down off the verandah, and greeted her with a little bow, taking off his Panama hat to her, doing it with a wide, rakish flourish.

From that moment, that very moment, standing with the sun in her eyes, shading her eyes with her hand, dressed in her white eyelet dress, smiling up full into his face, she'd felt herself change. From that moment on, she'd known that her life would be different.

"Love at first sight," that's how she'd thought of it. For years, that's how she'd thought of it. For years, she'd believed that she'd lived an enchanted life, a princess in a castle, dressed in her gowns, awaiting the return of her master. Even the memory of her father's death, the terrible suspicion, hadn't troubled those constant daydreams, those nights of fantasy. Because she had Austin Holloway. And Austin Holloway was a man like no other, a man with a vision, a man who dwelt among the gods, listening to other voices, seeing other visions.

But when he came to her in the night, and pressed himself upon her, and demanded entrace to her body with the same frenzy of passion with which he could turn on the crowds that came to hear him preach, he was nothing more than a man—a man like other men, a man with the blind, urgent need to thrust his flesh into her flesh.

Her man.

From that night on, that first night, at the Manor Hotel, her man.

When he'd finally fallen back away from her, exausted, making small sounds in his throat, with the warm rush of him inside her, still a part of her flesh, she'd felt closer to God than ever before.

And closer to the Devil, too.

Because Austin knew the Devil as well as he knew God.

Sometimes she thought that God and the Devil worked together. God enticed, the Devil enslaved.

Because, surely, the Devil had enslaved her.

At first, she'd thought the secret she knew would keep her free, liberate her from the Devil, the tyrant with Austin's face, sometimes the saint, more often the sinner.

It was the sinner that came in the night, to savage her flesh. The saint materialized in the light of day, sometimes smiling, sometimes ranting, but always sitting in judgment: accusing, absolving, raving, sometimes mewling.

Only the babies had saved her.

The live babies, Gloria and Elton.

Not the dead baby, the lump of flesh she'd never seen.

Only when her babies were born had she ever been free from him. Yet, even then, she'd realized that she'd never be really free, didn't .want to be free, not really.

When she began to show, the times between his nighttime visits began to lengthen out, then cease altogether. Once, timidly, she said that sometimes she waited for him, listened for the sound of his hand on her doorknob. He'd looked at her the way he looked down on the sinners, then turned away.

Now, I wear my apron high . . .

You see my door and pass it by . . .

It was a song from the hills, the same hills her daddy had come from. And it was true. From the time she began to show with Gloria, Austin had changed toward her. Sometimes it saddened her—until Gloria was born. Then she rejoiced.

Because, yes, they'd set her free—first Gloria, then Elton, five years apart.

Gloria had been a love child. Elton had been nobody's child, the child she'd had to have, after the one born dead.

Poor Elton.

Poor, pale, timid Elton.

Angry Elton.

With her feet on the floor beside the chaise, with her hands on either side, braced, she pushed herself carefully to her feet. She must see Elton. During his whole life, he'd been troubled. But now, today, tonight, with the strangers in the hallways, Elton would be especially anxious, timid within himself, yet angrily peering out at them as his monster began to stir.

For a long time now, the strangers had been calling: silent men with hostile eyes, asking their angry questions. Only Austin had saved him: she knew that, admitted that. Austin had them all fooled: the police, the probation officers, the judges, everyone. Effortlessly, Austin turned black into white, lies into truth—evil into good.

She walked to the bar, looked at herself in the mirror. Timidly, she smiled at her reflection: the heart-shaped face that he'd always loved so dearly, the small mouth with cherub lips, the wide, innocent eyes. Marvella Holloway. Beloved by millions—so long as she never spoke.

She turned away, walked to the door, went out into the hallway. A late-night stillness had settled on the hallway. The two guards, nodding politely, were heavy-eyed, waiting for their relief. She counted the doors: three doors, between her room and Elton's. At the fourth door, 1106, she softly knocked. No answer, as she expected. She knocked again, then turned the knob. Yes, he'd left the door unlocked for her.

As he always did, Elton had insisted on a small single room, not a suite. Softly, she opened the door, stepped inside. Light came only from a single bedside lamp. Elton stood beside the bureau. One of the bureau's drawers was open. Facing her, Elton held a length of thick cord in his hands. Watching her with his expressionless eyes, he raised his hands with the cord dangling between them, as if he were making her an offering. Then he turned, moved his hands over the open drawer, released the cord, let it fall into the drawer. Slowly, ceremoniously, he slid the drawer closed, then turned again to face her.

"It's late," he said. "Too late for you to be here. Or for me to be here, either. You should be in bed, Mother. And I should be out."

"Elton—" Hesitantly, she stepped closer. "I'm afraid. These men, these strangers. They frighten me." She shook her head, then sank into an armchair. "This city frightens me, too. They don't believe in us, these people. I can feel it, that they don't believe in us."

"Not us, Mother. Him. They don't believe in him. It's not us they care about. We're just faces on a TV screen, voices on the soundtrack. It's him. Always."

"Elton, you should leave. And Gloria, she should leave, too. When her husband went she should've gone, too. Gary wanted her to go. He begged her to go. I told her, too, told her she should go. And she knew I was right. I could see that she knew."

"Gloria stays because of the money, Mother. You know that. Father hired Gary to do PR, and paid him four times what he was worth, just so he could keep Gloria and the kids. Gary got out. But Gloria decided to take the cars, and the house, and the stocks and bonds. She decided to stay."

"Then you leave, Elton. Gloria doesn't have to leave. But you do. You *have* to leave. Now. Right now. Tonight. I can feel it, that you have to leave. Right now."

"What would I do if I left? Have you ever asked yourself? You can see the problems, Mother. But you can't see the cures."

Slowly she shook her head. "Cures? Are there any cures?"

"There would've been a cure for Gloria. Gary loved her. He still loves he, wants her. But she turned her back on him. So now she's lost." He let a moment of silence pass. Then: "She's lost, because she stayed. But I'd be lost if I left."

"Maybe—" Timidly, tremulously, she hesitated. "Maybe I could leave with you, Elton. Could we do that? Leave together, the two of us?"

"No, we couldn't do that, Mother."

"Why?"

"Because it's too late for you, Mother. There's no place you can imagine that you'd rather be—nothing you'd rather do." He let another moment pass, then said, "You're protected, Mother. You're cared for, whether you realize it or not. You drink, and you're protected. It's all you can ask for. Because you can't be alone when you drink."

"Elton, I—"

"And I'm protected, too, you see."

"Elton, no. You're not protected. I see these men, I hear people talking. Their faces—I see what they're thinking, in their faces. Don't you understand that?"

"Whose faces? Who're you talking about?"

"The strangers. They're your enemies, Elton. You don't see it. But I do. And Gloria does, too. And Herbert—and Lloyd. They all know, Elton. And it's dangerous, what they know."

"All except Father. He doesn't know."

"I—" She shook her head. "I haven't—" Still shaking her head, she discovered that she couldn't answer. There were no words, suddenly no words. Nothing was left.

"You haven't seen him, then. You haven't seen Father."

"No."

"Well, I've seen him. And I can tell you, I'm safe. I'm protected, Mother."

"Protected from what?"

"I can't tell you that, Mother. You have your secrets, and I have mine. And it's better not to ask about secrets."

"You have secrets, Elton. But I don't." She paused, then said, "Except for one, just one secret. A very old secret."

"It's about Father, isn't it?"

"H-how'd you know?"

"Because you don't have a life of your own, Mother. So it's got to be about Father."

"Shall I tell you, Elton? About the secret? It might help you if you knew. It might give you power. Secret power."

He shook his head. "No, don't tell me. Because then it wouldn't be your secret anymore. It'd be our secret. And I don't want any more secrets. They can be dangerous, you know. Secrets can hurt. Kill, even."

She frowned, focused on him. "Kill? Did you say kill?" As she said it, spoke the single word, she saw him again: the dead boy, lying beside the twisted bicycle. Susan Gaines's mother had died that day. So Susan had left her alone. She'd gone into Austin's room, and found some money, more than a hundred dollars. She'd taken the money, and she'd found keys to the Cadillac. Even though it had been summer, hot and smoggy in Los Angeles, she'd thrown a coat over her dressing gown. She'd gone to the garage, and started the Cadillac, and backed it out of the garage. She'd been within a block of the supermarket, calculating how many bottles of vodka she could buy for a hundred dollars, when she'd felt the thud, felt the car swerve.

She'd felt the thud, and she'd heard the boy's scream.

His screams and her screams, echoing and reechoing . . .

The same screams she'd heard when she'd found her father, dead. Always, the two screams ran together, echoing and re-echoing.

Always. Always.

"Kill?" she repeated.

He didn't reply; he only nodded, very slowly.

18

Over his newspaper, Canelli saw Elton Holloway leaving the elevator. Automatically, he checked the time: 9:10 A.M. Without doubt, the suspect was going for breakfast. Noisily, Canelli folded his newspaper, then rose abruptly to his feet. Last night, and again this morning, the lieutenants had ordered that surveillance be tightened so that, if he looked, the suspect would know he was being followed. After thinking about it, Canelli had approved. If Elton Holloway was a loonie, a compulsive killer, then anything that would keep him from killing might make him all the more determined to find a victim, kill again.

Yesterday—Wednesday—the suspect had reportedly eaten breakfast inside the hotel. But today, he was crossing the lobby toward the Powell Street entrance. Canelli let him pass, slipped a transparent earpiece into his ear, pressed a switch set into the handle of the tiny surveillance microphone concealed in his palm:

"This is Canelli. He's going out to Powell Street. I've got him." He waited for acknowledgment, frowned, repeated the transmission. Nothing. Once again, the equipment had failed. Muttering an obscenity, he switched off the radio and fell in behind the suspect. Outside, the September morning was warm and calm. Overhead, the sky was a deep, clear blue. On Powell Street, a passing cable car was filled with beaming passengers, most of them with cameras slung around their necks. To himself, Canelli smiled. He'd been born in San Francisco, had lived here all his life. But, still, the city excited him, pleased him. When he got married, he would live in the Sunset District, where he was born, and where his parents lived. Some criticized the monotony of the Sunset's stucco row houses, some even called them ugly. Canelli didn't agree. "Home is where the heart is," someone had said. And his heart was in the Sunset.

Hands in his pockets, whistling, Canelli walked a little faster, slightly closing the distance between himself and the young man with the pale face and blank eyes who was suspected of at least a dozen murders.

As Gloria pressed the buzzer, she glanced at her watch. Good, not yet nine-thirty. There was still plenty of time.

The door opened to reveal Lloyd Mitchell. Seeing him with his hair rumpled, beard-stubbled, wearing a tee shirt, Gloria privately smiled. Mitchell had worked for her father before she was born. But she'd never before seen him without a shirt and tie, wearing his standard blue suit. Even when he'd played with them, during her childhood, he'd always worn a tie.

"Sorry to bother you," she said. "But I'm locked out. You've got a passkey, haven't you?"

He frowned. "These doors, they aren't spring locks. How could you—?"

"The lock's screwed up." She edged her voice with authority. "Give it to me. Dad needs some stuff, some research."

For a moment, stubbornly, plainly suspicious, the big man remained motionless, looking at her with his dark, still eyes. The message: Mitchell answered only to Austin Holloway, took orders only from Holloway.

"Lloyd—*pu-leeze.*" This time, she smiled. "I'll bring it right back. I promise."

Finally he shrugged, reached in his pocket, produced the key, reluctantly handed it over. She thanked him brightly, patted him on his thick, hairy forearm, and moved briskly away in the direction of her room, around the corner, out of sight.

If he'd been dressed in his blue suit and tie, he might have insisted on coming with her. He would have insisted on testing her door, double-checking. Mitchell's suspicions were eternal.

At the corner of the corridor she turned, looked back, made

sure his door was closed. Only one of the two guards were in sight, turned away from her. Quickly, she moved to Elton's door, opened it, stepped inside, shot the bolt. Slipping the key into the pocket of her slacks, she stood motionless for a moment, looking around the room. Elton's suitcases were still on the floor beside the bureau. Sometimes, on the road, Elton lived out of his suitcases, never allowing anyone to help him unpack. Indecisively, she eyed the two suitcases, then moved to the bureau. The top two drawers were empty. The second drawer was filled with shirts, underwear, and socks. Gingerly, she stirred at the underwear—

—and found it: a three-foot length of thick golden cord, knotted at either end. It was heavily plaited, the kind of decorative cord that might have been used to tie back old-fashioned velvet draperies.

Aware of the sudden thumping of her heart, she stood motionless for a moment, suddenly terrified, helplessly holding the cord draped over both her hands. Her breath was coming harshly, blocked in her throat. If he should come back, find her—

As if the cord had come alive, she panicked and dropped it. She turned to the door, hesitated, turned back to face the bureau. Had the drawer been open? Closed?

Should she take the cord? Leave it?

This was proof—the proof that Elton was a murderer. With this much proof, the police would impound Elton's possessions, take his fingerprints.

Who would she help, if she took the cord? Who would she hurt?

She couldn't decide. Couldn't think. Couldn't move.

But she must *move*. Must think.

As she picked up the cord, she saw her fingers trembling. Never could she remember seeing her fingers tremble like this. Never.

19

"**W**e can't tell him now," Flournoy insisted. "This meeting tonight, this banquet—you're probably not aware of it, Gloria, but tonight, this speech, how it's received, it's the most important point in Austin's career, no question."

"He wants to be president," she said. "That's what you mean."

"No," Flournoy answered primly. Mouth drawn into a disapproving line, nostrils pinched, he repeated it: "No, not at all. And I wish you wouldn't—"

"He wants to choose a president, then. What the hell's the difference? The point is, the more important he becomes, the more a scandal can hurt him. Don't you see that, for God's sake? *Don't* you?"

"After the meeting, I'll talk to him. I promise. I'll—"

"No. After the meeting, *we'll* talk to him, Herbert. And meanwhile—" She raised the golden cord, made Flournoy look at it. "Meanwhile, I want to show this to Mitchell. Now. Right now. You can sit in or not, I don't care. But I'm—"

"Gloria, you—you're out of your depth on this. Remember, the police have already talked to him, and apparently didn't get anything incriminating. And we've got Wertheimer, too. So we can afford to step back, give ourselves time to—"

"No, Herbert, *you're* out of your depth. You won't acknowledge anything that could rock the boat, put a wrinkle in my father's expensive psyche. And that's just plain, goddamn shortsighted. And it's stupid, too. Because we can do something, now.

As long as Elton's free, we've got room to maneuver. But time's running out. Don't you *see* that?"

"I'm not disagreeing with you, Gloria. I'm just saying that—"

She turned away from him. Dangling the golden cord from one hand, she strode to the telephone, punched out Mitchell's room number.

"Lloyd, I'm in Herbert's room. We have to talk to you. Right now." She paused, listened a moment, then said, "Assign someone else. This is important." She listened, nodded, replaced the phone in its cradle.

She dropped the coil of golden cord across Mitchell's thigh, dropped the passkey in his lap. She watched him look down at the key and the cord. Plainly, he realized what the two together meant.

"I found it in Elton's room," she said. "That girl, the prostitute, was killed with a cord like this. I don't know whether the police can match up the cord with marks on the girl's throat. But I'm betting they can."

Still with his head lowered, Mitchell stared down at the key and the cord. Then, gravely, he took the key, slipped it into his pocket. Finally, as if its touch might contaminate, he gingerly touched the cord, running his large, blunt fingers lightly along the silken braids. Gloria glanced meaningfully at Flournoy, then returned her gaze to Mitchell. For now, silence was her best strategy. Whatever Mitchell decided, the decision would be his alone. Because he coveted nothing, therefore depended on Austin Holloway for nothing, Mitchell's influence on her father was unquestioned. Making the decisions that really mattered, her father always listened last to Mitchell. Looking down at his big, rough-cut head with its thick, close-cropped hair, she imagined him a Roman centurion, preparing himself for battle. In her imagination, he wore sword-scarred armor, not an off-the-rack blue suit.

Finally Mitchell raised his head. "You talked to them, the detectives. Do you think they'll arrest him?"

"I think if they had this—" She pointed to the cord. "—they'd arrest him. Yes."

"There's probably other evidence," Flournoy said. "It's only logical." He spoke heavily, tonelessly. "Otherwise, they wouldn't have come here." His narrow, aesthetic face was drawn, his lips were compressed. Behind sparkling gold-rimmed designer glasses, his eyes were dull, smudged by fatigue.

"Then we've got to talk to Austin," Mitchell said. "Now. Today. He's got to get Elton out of town, out of the country. It'll ruin Austin, ruin The Hour, if they ever arrest Elton."

Gloria drew a deep, grateful breath. The only person Austin Holloway trusted completely had finally faced the inevitable.

For a moment they sat silently, each avoiding the others' eyes. Finally Flournoy, too, drew a deep breath. "After the banquet tonight, though. We'll tell him afterward. Not before. We'll all three talk to him."

Gloria turned to Mitchell. "Tonight you're going to have to watch Elton. We can't keep him from leaving the hotel, I guess. Not physically. But if he goes out, you've got to follow him, make sure he doesn't—" She broke off, shook her head, fell into an incredulous silence. Having forced the others to accept the fact that her brother was a murderer, she realized that she could hardly comprehend it herself.

"I should be at the banquet, though," Mitchell said. "With Austin."

"Elton's got to be watched," Flournoy said. "Right now, that's more important than anything else. If he should—"

Grimly, she finished it for him: "If he should try it again, and they arrest him, then—" Once more, she let it go ominously unfinished.

"It's also possible," Flournoy said, "that if the police get him outside his room, outside the hotel, they could question him, get him to talk. He could leave the hotel and never come back."

As the significance of the words registered, each of them fell separately silent, avoiding one another's eyes. Then Mitchell said, "I'll have him watched during the day. And tonight, I'll do it myself if he goes out." He rose, took the passkey from his pocket, held it out to Gloria, with the golden cord.

"You'd better put this back. I don't think he should know we've got it. I'll wait in the hallway while you put it back, to make sure he doesn't see you."

Nodding, she took the cord and the key. For a moment they stood facing each other. When he spoke, Mitchell's voice was low, thick with emotion: "He was always different—always so frail, so unhappy. Nobody would play with him, I remember. Not even you."

Slowly, with infinite regret, she nodded. "Not even me."

20

With the tip of his right forefinger Holloway touched the tiny knot of skin at the corner of his mouth.

"It shouldn't be a problem," the doctor had said. "Not unless it gets larger. We'll keep an eye on it."

He leaned close to the bathroom mirror, examined the spot. At its center, the spot had reddened. When he returned to Los Angeles, he would call the doctor, tell him about the red spot. Of course, the doctor would want him to come into the office. A half day wasted. A half day, and a hundred dollars for the visit.

Someone had once said that the medical profession was America's priesthood. And it was true. No matter how much money his doctor made, Holloway's income would always be many times more. Yet, when he needed medical advice, he must journey to the doctor, hat in hand, sometimes with his heart in his mouth, seeking solace. Once, after his "cardiac event," he'd considered adding a doctor to his staff. But then he'd realized that only a second-rater would take such a job, never mind the salary.

He stepped back from the mirror, lifted his chin, critically examined himself. Yes, for the job ahead, he'd chosen wisely: pinstriped blue suit, vest, gleaming white shirt, conservative tie, French cuffs. On Sunday, for the cameras, for the eager masses, he would wear polyester. But for tonight, only Brooks Brothers would do.

He glanced at his watch. Ten more minutes, and Flournoy would knock on his door. This was the time he needed most, this time alone, in absolute solitude, all calls held, his thoughts

113

focused on the task ahead. Years ago, when he'd first begun, he'd practiced in front of the mirror, looking himself squarely in the eye, gesturing, exhorting, pleading—praying for the sinners.

What was it about bathrooms that made a man so thoughtful, so reflective? Was it the mirror, bringing the man face-to-face with himself? Was it the privacy, with the whole world locked out? An English king had once said that the bath was the only place a king could truly commune with himself. And then there were the elementary functions that man performed in the bathroom: the essential pleasure of a good, full bowel movement, everything in its approved shape, and consistency, accomplished without strain, without pain. And pissing, too, was an elemental pleasure, since the sexual organ was, after all, the means to the end.

Women, he'd heard, were more preoccupied with the various ceremonies and celebrations of the bath than men, perhaps because, after all, the female's role required that she adorn herself so that she could attract the male. And it was in the bath that the paints and powders and lacquers and scents were applied, all calculated to please her mate, therefore arouse him.

Or perhaps the female was more intimately involved with her organs of elimination, therefore of reproduction, since she carried everything inside, enclosed within herself.

The male was the sower of the seed, the female the receptacle.

The sower of the seed . . .

It would be the perfect lead-in to a sermon. Not, of course, as a sexual reference. Never that.

Or—yes—the face in the mirror, another lead-in. The man facing himself, facing the truth.

Anything—everything—could serve. Sometimes as he lay awake at night, amusing himself, he would take the most improbable subjects, working them into something interesting enough to keep the customers in their seats until the collection plate came around.

How often had he heard his father say it: "Keep them in their seats until the collection basket comes around."

And he'd been the one, he and his sister, who'd passed the

baskets. "Little Austin and Little Dora," his father would intone, beaming down at them, then beaming out over the congregation: women in cotton dresses, men in suspenders with their hair slicked down. Rubes. Dull, stupid rubes, sitting on benches beneath a tent that didn't shed water and wasn't paid for, listening to his father with their mouths hanging open.

"Little Austin and Little Dora . . ." God, how he'd hated the sound of those words. And his father, he'd hated his father, too. No, not hated, that wasn't the word. And not contempt, either, not really. Embarrassment. Pity, perhaps. Those were the words. It wasn't what his father did, but instead what he didn't do— could have done, but didn't do. Even as a child, a small child, sitting on a camp chair beside the pulpit, listening to his father preach, he'd sensed the futility, the waste. He could see it in the faces: the hunger, the urge to be led, the half-awakened desire to believe. They were like half-opened flowers—like, yes, lambs, ready for the slaughter. Ready, and willing.

But his father was too timid to wield the knife. His father was a pale, worried man, a soft-spoken man, a small-minded man. Where others led, he followed; when others demanded, his father begged.

Every Sunday afternoon, he would watch them: his father and his mother at the round oak dining room table, counting the collection money. First they'd begin with the bills: the dollar bills, and, a miracle, the occasional five, all of them neatly stacked. Then the half dollars and the quarters, and the dimes and the nickels and the pennies, too, all stacked. After the count had been made, and the results noted in a bound notebook, his father would shake his head.

Only once had he really respected his father. He'd been eleven years old. For weeks, every Sunday, he'd taken a fifty-cent piece from the collection basket. He could still vividly remember the incredibly sweet taste of that forbidden fruit, the first time he'd slipped the half dollar in his pocket. Never before, never since, had he felt so breathlessly alive. Every sensation, every emotion, had been almost unbearably heightened: the shirt, soaked with sudden sweat, the stomach, abjectly quivering—the weight of the silver half dollar in his pocket, sin incarnate. Immediately, he'd wanted to put it back, rid himself of the tangible proof that he'd stolen money meant for the church. But the risk of returning it to the basket would be more than the risk of stealing it.

Sunday after Sunday, legs shaking, carrying the collection basket with fifty cents missing, he'd walked up the aisle toward the pulpit, where his father stood smiling down on him, waiting to bless the offering. In the background, his mother played softly on their battered piano, the piano that had only brought twenty dollars at auction after his father's death.

After five weeks—two dollars and fifty cents—he'd come home from school to find his parents waiting for him, sitting like Herod's judges in the living room, side by side in high-backed chairs. The five half dollars that he'd hidden in the toe of a bedroom slipper had been stacked neatly on the coffee table. His parents looked at him with long, mournful faces. It was the first time he'd realized how similar his parents looked.

At first his father had prayed over him—while his mother had cried, and his sister had looked on with saucer eyes. Then, towering over him, his father asked him whether he repented, whether he realized the magnitude of his sin, stealing God's money. Dry eyed, fists clenched at his sides, he'd first denied that he'd stolen the money. But, even as he said it, he could hear the tremor of guilt in his own voice, feel the fear of discovery flickering in his eyes. And he'd realized, too, that his denials only infuriated his father. So, hotly, he'd denied that it was God's money that he'd taken. "If we buy things with it, things we use, then how can it be God's money?" he'd asked. For a moment, taken aback, his father had been unable to speak. Then, sputtering, he'd said that he did God's work.

"You're no good at it," he'd shouted. "You're a terrible preacher."

Instantly, his father had struck him: a numbing blow along the side of his head.

It had been the only time he'd ever felt respect for his father—the first moment, and the last moment. Because, immediately, his father had fallen to his knees, asking heavenly forgiveness for the sin he'd committed.

The blow had set his ears ringing. That night, his ear began to ache, and the pain was worse next day. Dr. Wyble was called, and an examination revealed that his eardrum was broken.

It was then that he'd learned the incredible power of guilt. He'd learned in an instant. And he'd never forgotten.

When he'd been fifteen years old, and his father had been fifty-five, his father had suffered his first stroke. The year had been 1937, still hard times. There'd been three hundred dollars in the bank account, and more than a thousand dollars in debts. Dr. Wyble had taken him aside and told him it would be months—years, maybe—before his father could preach again. He'd been aware of the small pang he'd experienced, unable to feel any remorse, any sadness. Then Dr. Wyble asked the question that had changed his life.

"I was in Memphis last year," the doctor had said, "and I heard Jimmy Smith speak. He's about your age, and he's been preaching for a long time now. The people seem to love him. Why couldn't you do the same?" The doctor had paused, looked at him meaningfully, then said, "There'll be bills, you know, with your father sick. Doctor bills, among others."

Clutched by the same wild, furtive contradictions of excitement and terror that he'd felt when he'd stolen his first half dollar from the collection basket, he'd done it, taken the pulpit, on the first Sunday following his father's stroke. The word had gotten around town that he'd be preaching, and out of sympathy the congregation had been much larger than usual. When he'd stepped through the canvas flap and seen them, all eyes turned to him, he'd momentarily been stunned, incapable of movement, much less speech. But somehow, he'd made his way to the pulpit, which had been cut down for him the day before. His mother had coached him, but the sight of the congregation had driven her words from his thoughts. Yet, somehow, he was speaking. And, incredibly, he began to feel the response, that magical connection between the speaker and his audience that, on the rise, bore him miraculously on its crest, the miracle that still sustained him.

At age fifteen, clutching his father's pulpit with both hands, raising his voice to the heavens, he'd glimpsed the first and only miracle he'd ever witnessed: the power that one man could wield over the multitude of his inferiors.

An hour later, with his shirt as soaked as it had been that first time he'd taken a half dollar, with the sound of voices raised to praise him, he'd stepped down from the dais, triumphant. The promised land had opened before him. From that moment on, he'd—

From the sitting room he heard the door buzzer sound, two quick rings. Flournoy had come for him. As it had happened those many years ago, the boy triumphant over the hometown rubes, witnessing the miracle of eyes fervently kindled by words only he could speak, so would it happen tonight, the man beginning his ultimate mission.

21

"... give you Mr. Austin Holloway, one of America's foremost citizens." Smiling, genially clapping, Clayton Brand turned to face Holloway, who rose to his feet, smiling, shaking hands with the movie star. It was a hearty, man-to-man handshake, perfectly staged.

"Thank you, Clay. And congratulations." Holloway held the handclasp as both men turned slightly toward the pool photographer, discreetly crouched in front of the head table. "I understand the new box office ratings are out. And you're still number one."

Brand's famous smile widened. "A testimony to the power of prayer, Austin. Prayer, and an inspired publicity department at the studio."

Along with the fifty-odd others in the room, the two men shared a warm, companionable laugh. They held the handclasp for another quick sequence of pictures, then Brand nodded, stepped back, kept the smile in place as he resumed his toastmaster's seat. As Holloway turned to face his audience, Flournoy caught the photographer's eye, signaled subtle dismissal. The message: no outsiders would bear witness to this meeting.

Waiting for the applause to diminish, Holloway beamed as he swept the audience with a practiced eye: the public figure, long accustomed to the plaudits of his peers. His manner was affable, projecting quiet confidence, easy authority. Like the central-casting perfection of Clayton Brand's face, Holloway's features perfectly suited his image. His thick, graying hair was dramatically styled, his forehead was broad, his jawline was decisive, his nose patrician, his mouth expressive. As he looked out over the audience, the easy conviviality in his fine blue eyes slowly sobered as the applause ended. But the eyes were still warm, the mouth still generously upcurved as he began to speak:

"I must admit," he said, "to a sense of gratification as I look out at this assemblage of faces—all male faces." He waited for a small, appreciative ripple of laughter. "I'll deny I ever said it, of course, but the truth is, when matters of real significance are discussed—when the big decisions are made—it always turns out to be an all-male gathering. Entirely men, and entirely off the record."

He paused again, nourishing the diminishing chuckles. Then: "As you've probably noticed—" Smiling, he swept the entire room with a broad gesture. "—there're no outsiders present, not even any waiters. However, before they were dismissed, they left each table amptly supplied with enough champagne, certainly, to see us through what will, I devoutly hope and believe, be a most significant time for all of us."

Once more he swept the room with the Holloway smile, once more he waited, this time for the predictable murmurs of assent and approval as he saw several in the audience good-naturedly pouring generous portions of champagne.

So far, so good.

Now, slowly, he allowed the genial smile to fade. The squared-off chin rose slightly; the voice lowered to a more somber note.

"I deeply appreciate the effort you've all made to be with us tonight. I know how busy you all are. I fully realize that if this assemblage, this distinguished gathering, were ever to magically stumble into one of those science fiction time warps for a week or so, why, this country would suddenly be operating at half speed—or less."

Another smile, another genial sweep of the audience with the grin-crinkled blue eyes. Then, visibly signaling that the amenities had been concluded, Holloway's face settled into a solemn cast as the timber of his voice deepened.

"I've invited you all here tonight because, quite simply, I'm frightened. And when a man's frightened, he does well to confess his misgivings and seek guidance from those he likes and respects. And that's what I'm doing here tonight. That's why I feel I must share with you my feelings—and my misgivings." He let a masterfully timed moment pass while he made compelling eye contact with the man farthest from the lectern: Ralph Hager, president of Grayson Industries. For the rest of the sermon, Hager would be his focus.

"I'm scared," he said, "because I find it increasingly more difficult to recognize the America that I once knew, the America that I still love. Perhaps it's advancing age; I suspect that might be part of it. I, like most of you, grew up in a simpler time, a time when people seemed to work harder than they do now. They worked harder, and they prayed harder, too. And I think—I deeply believe—that they were better for it, the people of our parents' generation. I think life meant more to them. Because they had to work for what they got, they valued it more. And on Sunday, they went to church, and they thanked God for the bounty of the week just passed." As he said it, he lifted his eyes midway to the ceiling, allowing his gaze to soften reflectively.

"My father made his ministry among those simple, hard-working people. He understood them, because he was one of them. He preached beneath the patched canvas of a revivalist's tent. In his closet there hung one suit, which my mother was hard pressed to keep clean and properly mended. We ate vegetables from the garden my mother tended. And when our roof leaked, which it most certainly did, my father fixed it with his own hands. Unless—" A smile. "—unless he was lucky enough to shame one of his more agile parishioners into doing the job."

Pensively smiling, he waited for the laugh, then quickly became serious.

"It's been almost fifty years since my father preached his last sermon. Like many of you men, rising from humble beginnings, I'm proud to say that, in my own way, I've made my mark in the world during those fifty years. My father, I believe, would be proud of me. He would also be amazed if he could see how the miracle of modern electronics allows me to reach many times more people on a single Sunday than he reached in a lifetime of working for Christ.

"I often think about the way this country has changed during those fifty years. I often think about how the world has changed, too. Much of what I see disturbs me profoundly. So I often wonder what I can do. I wonder how I can help. I wonder how I can strengthen the forces I believe in—and I wonder how I can fight the forces that are bent on destroying this great country." He paused, gripped the lectern more firmly. The blue eyes were sharp-focused now, the voice was stern.

"Fifty years—from the thirties to the eighties. What has happened, what changes have been wrought across the face of the world during those fifty years? Each of you would, I'm sure, answer that question differently. But all of you, I think, would agree on one essential premise—" He allowed a long, compelling moment to pass as he swept the audience with eyes that had come alive, flashing an orator's challenge. "You will agree that during those fifty years, the forces of godlessness, of the Antichrist, have grown steadily stronger. Until, today, the United States stands virtually alone, surrounded by a host of mortal enemies. From beyond our shores, we are besieged by an unholy alliance of Muslim fanatics and atheistic Communists. From within, our society is being ravaged by drugs. Promiscuousness and perversion are corrupting our youth. Behind the shameful guise of political equality, liberal materialists are attacking the foundations of our society, shackling our God-given freedoms, questioning the very Bible that is the bedrock of Christianity."

He paused, sipped from a water goblet, measured the audience with a covertly calculating glance. He'd gotten their attention, but he hadn't aroused them. He'd expected it, of course, expected this initial resistance. By definition, this was the toughest audience he'd ever faced—the richest, the most powerful, therefore the toughest. "For nothing you get nothing," his father said so often, one of his most serviceable bromides. Over the rim of his goblet, Holloway glanced at Flournoy. The general manager was watching him with noncommittal eyes, Flournoy's habitual I-told-you-so expression.

Always, the pessimists of the world would wait for the adventurous among them to falter, finally fall. The bold died in battle, clucked over by the pessimists—and buried by them, too.

Holloway placed the goblet on the table, drew a deep breath, and began again. He spoke deliberately, returning to the low, rich end of the register.

"I could expand on the dimensions of the peril that surrounds us. Looking abroad, I could quote casualty rates from the far-flung fronts, where we are battling the Communists. At home, I could remind you of the shameful barricades that we have been compelled to erect around the White House as we guard against the deranged suicide bombers who would gladly die for Islam. I could remind you of the laws that our congressmen have enacted that allow unborn babies to be murdered. Others in Washington have tried to take our weapons from us—while criminals can buy guns on any street corner. I could quote statistics proving that, in the United States, the illicit drug industry's gross sales exceed General Motors's. In some parts of the country, the divorce rate exceeds the marriage rate. Homosexuality flourishes—and threatens to loose upon us a plague that could rival the Black Death."

He broke off, sipped again from the glass. Yes, they were rustling, quickening, exchanging nods of approval, making small, significant noises. As the champagne continued to flow, the beast that lay waiting in the thicket of every crowd was beginning to stir. And it was with the beast that he'd come to do business.

"I could go on with this grim chronicle," he said, once more speaking slowly, in a low, compelling register. "I could add to this shameful litany of disasters past and present. But the truth is, I didn't come here this evening to wring my hands. Because I don't despair. Far from it. In fact, I've come here tonight to report to you on a miracle—a God-given miracle that has been burgeoning in this country for many years, a miracle that, properly nurtured, can save us all.

"I'm talking, my friends, about the rise of religion in America." A pause, a final full, significant sweep of their attentive, upturned faces. Yes, they were with him now. The beast was finally aroused.

"I'm talking about those millions upon millions in this country who turn to their TV sets every Sunday—and who, during the week, open their hearts—and their checkbooks. And I'm here to tell you that, with the proper guidance, these millions can save us all. They are citizen soldiers, ready and willing to march under Christ's banner, ready to endure any privation, pay any price for the privilege of serving. We spoke earlier of the riches generated by the drug trade. Well, praise God, I can report to you that the contributions of these millions of the faithful rival the earnings of those who seek to destroy us with drugs.

"But, more important than debit-credit calculations, vastly more important, is the fact that these millions of fundamentalist Christians, these soldiers for Christ, are true believers. They see what needs to be done—" A short, meaningful pause. "And they're willing to do it, willing to do their duty." Another uncompromising pause, reinforced by the full force of the Holloway presence: a modern-day prophet standing magestically tall, solemnly exhorting the faithful:

"These millions constitute a vast reservoir of potential power—a vast untapped reservoir." A final pause. Then: "And that, gentlemen, is the subject I propose to discuss with you here tonight—that power, and how it can be tapped. Because I believe, I devoutly believe, that God has provided us with the means of harnessing that power and converting it to votes. And these votes, combined, could be America's salvation.

"I'm speaking, of course, about the miracle of electronics—of television, and radio, and video cassettes. And I'm telling you that we're only seeing the start of this miracle. A technological revolution is about to explode—a computer-driven communications breakthrough that will, literally, unite us all into one vast electronic family.

"And those of us that are ready will reap the rewards. We will gain control of America. We will send our message to Christ's disenfranchised millions. We will show them the danger—and tell them how they can help. We'll show them how, united, they can transform America. And where a stronger, revitalized America leads, the free world will follow.

"A dream, you say. Oh, yes—" The handsome head gravely inclined. "Oh, yes—a dream. But I tell you, my friends, that it is a practical dream—a dream that, on election day, will be fulfilled."

He paused, glanced at Flournoy, his eternal barometer. Flournoy was nodding—incredibly, almost smiling. The contest, then, was there for the winning. It had now come time for the salesman's close, a time to come to terms with this particular audience, on their particular terms.

"As I look around the room and try to read your faces, the message I seem to see is that the rhetoric you've heard here tonight has been interesting—and the food is good and the champagne of satisfactory vintage." Briefly, engagingly, he smiled: a man-to-man, entrepreneur-to-entrepreneur smile. "But you are men who deal in specifics. In politics, of course, rhetoric is essential. But the men behind the politicians, men like you, need more. You need facts and figures. Most of you head large corporations. You deal in numbers. So, to conclude my message to you, I offer some numbers." From an inside pocket he withdrew a single 5 × 7 card. From another pocket, he withdrew a pair of tortoiseshell reading glasses.

"Many of you, I'm sure, read the recent *This Week* article on TV evangelism. And, of course, I read it, too—" He swept the audience with another man-to-man smile. "And I was gratified, naturally, to see that, in terms of viewers, I have a comfortable lead. Which I hope never changes. Leonard Bagley was next, and then George Fisher. Five of us, altogether, reaching probably sixty million people, every week. Now, that's a lot of people. And it doesn't include many millions more who watch some of my less famous colleagues. It's a lot of people—and a lot of money coming in each week, too, let's be honest. Since *This Week* is aimed at men like you, the country's business leaders, the article dealt with the millions—billions—that're involved. They made the point that all of us, and particularly the top five evangelists, head large organizations that are very expert at generating capital flow. They were kind enough to say that my organization, particularly, could teach both the Democrats and the Republicans a little something about fund raising and computerized mailings. And I must tell you—" The easy, fraternal smile returned. "I must tell you that I concur, absolutely.

"The article went on to talk about the Christian Fellowship Network. They described how it works, how the CFN, which I head, owns two communications satellites." Still genially smiling, he waited for the spontaneous, predictable murmurs of polite surprise to subside before he mischievously added, "And those satellites, incidentally, are paid for. We've got the pink slips." Another pause for the appreciative chuckles. Then, more seriously, he said, "For those of you who haven't read the article, you'll find a copy of it in the press kit we'll take the liberty of giving you when you leave. So you'll be up-to-date. However, the news isn't in the press kit—not in profit and loss statistics, or audience growth projections. The real news is that religion in America is alive and well. More than that, religion is gathering a vast, irresistible momentum. A tidal wave is developing, my friends. It's a wave that, properly channeled, will sweep everything before it—a wave that will sweep a government out of office with an ease that future generations will regard with amazement and awe. Historians will look back on the eighties in America as the time when Christians—born-again Christians—transformed the face of this great nation forevermore.

"But without direction, without leadership, the millions of believers are nothing more than a mob, a giant without a brain. And leadership itself is ineffective without the machinery, the technology that's needed to reach out and touch each individual, each true believer.

"Well—" Holloway surveyed the faces before him, each one attentive, expectant. This was the time to wrap it all up, make the pitch, sit down, accept the applause that would most certainly reward him. The beast had been engaged and deftly tamed. This was the time to put rhetoric aside, the time for calm, concise candor, the salesman's close.

"Well, you know where I'm going with this. I'm telling you that the second American revolution is about to begin—the revolution for Christ. I'm telling you that the Christian Fellowship Network offers the means of catalyzing that revolution. And, yes, I'm offering myself, as leader."

At the pause, precisely on cue, the applause began—and swelled—and continued to swell. Signifying that, by the simple act of clapping their hands in common, these men were uniting. They were committed. Together, they were committed.

Still standing, Holloway slowly, gravely bowed his head, humble as he accepted tribute from this audience of the elite. He waited for the applause to die, then raised his head. His smile was self-effacing, as shy as a small boy's.

"Thank you," he said. "Thank you—thank you. I hope that, in the months and years to come, we'll be working closely together, exchanging ideas, marching side by side in the front ranks of Christ's invincible legions." He paused, smiled benevolently, then said, "I would like to close with a piece of news— which I offer as an article of faith, since the negotiations are still tentative, still secret. But I feel that I want to offer something that will bind us together, something tangible, a promise for the future. So, in that spirit of fellowship, I tell you now that, yes, the rumors you may have been hearing are true. The CFN is about to conclude a takeover of one of our three major networks. I'm sure you know which one, so there's no need for me to be specific. But our lawyers tell us that, within a month's time, the takeover will be concluded. And when that time comes, I'll be in touch with many of you. Because—" Benevolently, he smiled. "Because, needless to say, we'll be forming a new board of directors. And I hope that, as we look to the future together, many of you here tonight will be willing to serve."

22

The bedside lamp had a three-way bulb. He twisted the switch. The lamp was at its brightest. He twisted the switch again. Darkness engulfed him. Another click, and the lamp was soft-lit, on low. He straightened, looked carefully at all four corners of the room. Yes, the light was exactly right. It was essential that the lighting be right, neither too low nor too high. Christ had certainly known about the importance of light. And the pope, who certainly held dominion over millions of candles—the pope knew, too. And his father, who hired men who mixed lights for the cameras, producing crisscrossed stars of Bethlehem on demand, with filters, for the cameras—his father knew, too.

Like father, like son.

Or unlike, really.

Because this light was fit for the sepulcher, not for the cameras. In this light, therefore, he would be invisible to the cameras.

Therefore safe. Undiscovered, therefore safe.

So now the ceremony could begin. He could now approach the receptacle of containment and concealment, the altar disguised as a bureau. Earlier, he'd cleared off the top, which was the means of conversion. The maids, his mother, Gloria—because of the conventionally conceived clutter, consummating in conversion, none of them realized the real existence of the altar, or the receptacle beneath. They'd only seen the bureau. As planned. Precisely as planned. Therefore the receptacle was still safe, still inviolate.

So he was standing before the altar, ready to accept the instrument of deliverance. But first he must gather himself, focus himself, unite himself with the eternal forcefield that would enfold him, protect him, guide him. He must stand motionless, hands at his sides, head bowed, eyes closed.

And, yes, he could feel it beginning: a small, whisper-soft stirring, the sound of eternity's breath upon him, calling him, commanding him. Now, eyes still closed, he must concentrate, must listen for the shadow of the voices—first the shadow, then the substance.

Yes, they were drawing closer. He could feel them beside him, commanding him, God's emissaries, messengers from heaven. Without them, he was helpless, a body without a soul, a husk of flesh and bone, nothing more. Because it was the consciousness that counted—first the commandment, then the consciousness.

Sometimes they didn't come. And sometimes they came, and drew closer—and then faded away. He'd never known why they deserted him, but sometimes they did. And he would be left alone, empty, helpless.

But now, tonight, the strength of their presence was strong. Even though strangers were watching, enemies, their presence was strong, guiding him, protecting him. Because, yes, with his eyes still closed, he could feel the illumination beginning, expanding his consciousness, allowing them to enter. First the celestial expansion, then the terrestrial contraction as, yes, the transformation was complete. Now, very cautiously, he could open his eyes. This, he'd learned, was the crucial part. Because if he saw them—any of them, anywhere—then failure was certain. Because if he saw them, externalized, then they could see him, internalized, and he was helpless to act.

Still with his eyes open, slowly, he pivoted, searching everywhere, every corner of the softly lit room. Yes, he was alone; the transformation was complete. One step brought him within arm's reach of the altar. The drawer was extending itself, opening. And he could see his hands, first lowering, then raising, holding the instrument of God's commandment, the sacred golden cord.

*   *   *

As Hastings pushed through the brass-framed revolving doors and stood surveying the now familiar main lobby of the St. Francis, he saw Canelli urgently signaling with his eyes to the elevators. Following Canelli's line of sight, Hastings saw Elton Holloway walking diagonally across the lobby, bound for the revolving doors. Nodding to Canelli, Hastings moved aside, turning his back to the suspect. The message: Hastings would join Canelli, who'd certainly alerted the other three men on duty at the hotel's other entrances, told them the suspect was on the move. But as Elton Holloway drew closer, Hastings saw Canelli's eyes move urgently in another direction. Following this second silent signal, Hastings saw Lloyd Mitchell, about twenty feet behind Elton Holloway. Obviously, Mitchell meant to follow Elton. Canelli was standing motionless, shoulders slightly raised, hands slightly spread, mutely perplexed, awaiting orders. To signal that they must follow Mitchell, at least for now, Hastings stopped, stood still, let Elton enter the revolving doors, with Mitchell closing the distance between them. Hastings let Mitchell enter the revolving doors, then stepped briskly forward, nodding for Canelli to do the same.

Mitchell stepped clear of the revolving doors, joined the pedestrian stream. The time was a little after ten o'clock, the same time Elton had gone out Tuesday night.

Was Elton carrying the gold cord, concealed?

Had it been a mistake for Gloria to replace the cord in Elton's drawer?

In the street, outside the hotel, Elton was vulnerable to arrest. If he were arrested, and the cord was found . . .

Arrested for what? For walking steadily along, eyes front, dressed like a typical tourist?

Covertly Mitchell glanced over his shoulder. Hastings and the other one—the big, good-natured Italian detective—they were following along behind. Conspicuously following, making no effort at concealment.

What were they thinking, the two homicide detectives? What was their strategy?

Ahead, at the corner of Powell and Geary, Elton was turning right. He did not glance over his shoulder, did not slacken his steady, leg-locked arm-stiffened automaton's gait. He could be a soldier on parade: an insane soldier, marching to his own destruction.

Onward Christian soldiers . . .

It was Austin's favorite hymn. At the banquet tonight, that would be Austin's theme, the recruitment of Christian soldiers, following Austin to victory over the Antichrist.

Rich, powerful Christian soldiers. Some of them fierce Christian soldiers. But even the rich ones, even the powerful ones, and the fierce ones, all of them would follow along behind Austin. Because Austin had the power. Always, ever since childhood, Austin had had the power.

For thirty-five years, they'd been together, he and Austin. So that now they shared the same thoughts, acted with the same will, the two of them. Where one man ended, the other man began. Often, poetically, Austin had put the thought into words, that they were inseparable. And the poetic words were true: quiet words, meant only for him.

Remembering the magic of the words, Mitchell realized that he was touching the butt of the .45 automatic he carried in a shoulder holster slung beneath his left arm. Twice, during those years, he'd saved Austin's life, payment in part for his own life, returned to him by Austin, so long ago.

One man, the second man, he'd killed to protect Austin from certain death.

The other man . . .

At the thought of the other man, the first man, he blinked, realized that his stride had faltered. How long had it been since he'd killed that first man? How long had it been since he allowed himself to think about it?

The second man, yes. Often, he thought of the second man. The scene of the second man's death was proudly, vividly etched in memory, a fragment of time that had changed his life forever—his life, Austin's life, countless other lives, all in the moment it took to draw a gun and fire it. He could still hear the sound of the shot, still smell the gunpowder. And he could still hear Flournoy speaking as they stood shoulder to shoulder, staring down at the corpse of the maniac who'd come to the foot of the stage, drawn a revolver, aimed at Austin, fired a single round into the pulpit just three inches below the pulpit's walnut rim.

"You can kill," Flournoy had said. "Thank God, you can kill."

"This is really crazy," Canelli muttered, swearing fervently as he dodged a drunken man who wore a red Shriner's fez with a golden tassle. "Mitchell's following him. And we're following Mitchell."

"Mitchell's on our side," Hastings said. "Nothing's going to happen—nobody'll get killed—so long as he's there."

"But I thought we *wanted* something to happen."

"We need a warrant. And it's basically a political decision—Chief Dwyer's decision—whether we get one. If we collar Elton trying to hit another whore, it'll get the chief's attention. Otherwise, I think Dwyer would just as soon pass, let them leave town."

"It's crazy," Canelli repeated. "*Crazy.* Anybody else, with a good eyeball identification, and with what the FBI's got for background, he'd be locked up. Now. Right now. But just because he's Austin Holloway's son, he's walking around. It doesn't make any sense."

"I'm not arguing with you, Canelli. I'm just telling you how it's coming down. You want to talk to the chief, make an appointment."

"Well, I think it's crazy." Canelli considered, then said thoughtfully, "Jeez, maybe the chief's an Austin Holloway fan. Ever think of that, Lieutenant?"

"Let's get a little closer," Hastings said, picking up the pace. "And check your radio, will you?" As he spoke, he sharply shook his head at a panhandler who wore a bedraggled cowboy hat and a greasy poncho. The two detectives were walking south on Mason Street, where the Tenderloin began—where anything was for sale. Just ahead, in the next block, Hastings saw the red neon sign identifying the Bayside Hotel. And, yes, there was Dancer Browne's Continental, parked in its accustomed spot. Now Elton Holloway was within a hundred feet of the hotel, almost directly across the street from Dancer Browne's car. A black hooker was making her approach. The suspect glanced at her once, shook his head, continued walking, eyes fixed rigidly straight ahead. He was passing in front of the hotel. Behind him, Mitchell was walking faster now, closing the distance between them.

"The radio's okay," Canelli said. Adding ruefully: "For now, anyhow, it's okay. Personally, I think the guy who buys our electronics stuff should be demoted, whoever he is. I mean, the surveillance stuff only works about half the time, it seems like."

"I think the problem's maintenance," Hastings answered. "The equipment's the best available, as far as I know."

They crossed O'Farrell Street shoulder to shoulder, dodging the slow-moving cars.

"I wonder why he isn't looking back?" Canelli said. "He must know we're here. That's the plan, according to Lieutenant Friedman. He's supposed to know we're following him. Right? We're supposed to be putting pressure on him. Right?"

Hastings nodded. "Right."

"Then why isn't he looking back?" Canelli complained.

"Because he's crazy," Hastings answered.

Once more, Mitchell glanced over his shoulder. The two policemen were closer now. And ahead, Elton was talking to another whore, this one a white woman. She was dressed head to foot in skintight black leather. Her hair was bleached white and stood out from her head. Her face was grotesquely painted, eyes shadowed an iridescent blue, mouth smeared bright red. Her smile was obscene. Allowing the sidewalk crowds to break around him, Mitchell stood motionless. A half block behind, the two policemen were standing in front of a shop window, conspicuously staring at the display. The light from the window bathed their faces in a garish fluorescent blue. Now Elton and the woman were moving together toward Market Street, three blocks away. The woman was talking, smiling with her crimson-painted mouth, gesturing with a bracelet-bangled hand. Elton was saying nothing, walking with his empty eyes fixed straight ahead.

Was it possible that Elton didn't know they were being followed?

Was it possible that he knew—and didn't care?

Ahead, the traffic light turned green. Elton and the woman were crossing Ellis Street.

Should he make his presence known to the woman, force her away from Elton's side, force Elton to return to the St. Francis? Could he do it? Would Elton come with him? What would happen if Elton resisted? Would the police have their chance? If they found the cord on Elton, they could arrest him. And disaster would certainly follow.

As Mitchell crossed Ellis, he looked back. Yes, the policemen were coming closer. One of them—Canelli—was pressing a pudgy forefinger to a tiny earphone as he talked into the palm of his hand. His words would be relayed to the police switchboard, connecting him to the vast machinery of the law: hundreds, thousands of policemen, watching and waiting.

The image of the police switchboard tipped the precarious balance. Mitchell stepped suddenly forward, at a half trot. He'd come down to a choice of evils, with time running against him.

But, as he quickened his pace, he saw the woman's arm come up. She was pointing to a narrow door, between two shop fronts. Elton was nodding, turning to his right, pushed the door open.

Almost all the time was gone. Only minutes remained; only instinct was left.

Without looking back Mitchell broke into a full trot, reached the door: a plate glass door, inscribed THE HOTEL ALBION. He was inside a narrow, short hallway that immediately opened into a dingy, windowless lobby: four chairs, three of them empty, one occupied by a black man, asleep, snoring. A narrow stairway led upstairs. The stairway was deserted, but Mitchell heard the sound of footsteps on bare wood: Elton and the whore, going upstairs. A big, broad-shouldered man was rising from behind a small desk. This was the inevitable bouncer, the enforcer—the man with a club, or a gun, or brass knuckles, the man with cold, killer's eyes.

As Mitchell reached for the wallet in his hip pocket, the man behind the desk moved quickly, smoothly. A blackjack materialized, slapped down on the counter, hard. But, beside the blackjack, Mitchell placed his wallet, opened.

"Can you lock that door?" Mitchell asked, jerking his head to the front hallway.

"Sure."

"Is there a back way out?"

"Sure."

"Then lock the door—for fifty dollars. Keep it locked for five minutes. Now. Before anyone comes. Fifty dollars. *Now.*" As he spoke, he moved closer to the desk, out of the line of sight from the street. Repeating urgently: *"Now.* Don't let anyone in for five minutes. And don't tell anyone about the fifty."

The bouncer's mouth warped in a mirthless smile as he pocketed the bill. He moved quickly, with surprising agility, toward the front door.

He watched her dig in the hip pocket of her black leather pants, saw her produce a key that was attached to a gold-colored medallion.

"Home sweet home." Over her shoulder she leered at him, then inserted the key in the lock. From close by, through one of the corridor's closed doors, he heard the sound of a man's voice, babbling, as if he were pretending to talk like a child. From downstairs, from the lobby, he heard the sound of violent knocking. From the stairwell, he heard the sound of footsteps.

Mitchell was coming, pursuing him. And behind Mitchell, there were the others: the policemen, and all the others. From earliest memory, he'd heard them: the furtive footfalls, followed by the faceless men.

Inside the room now, close behind her, he grasped the doorknob, closed the door. Yes, there was a bolt. He knew he was expected to set the bolt; he could feel his fingers moving in response to the command, the night's first clear command, independent of himself, of his own volition.

Because now, suddenly, it was beginning, sooner than he had first imagined. She'd already put her purse on the floor. She was sitting on the bed, tugging at one black leather boot, pulling it free. This one would take off her clothes, reveal her body to him, then ask for his money. So he must be prepared to—

From behind him came a furtive sound: a mechanical sound, metal upon metal. But he need not turn, to look. Because the power was with him now, revealing everything, concealing nothing, strengthening, steadying, commanding. Therefore, the union was complete. Volition was transferred, alignments were defined. So, protected—finally free from himself—he need only listen, sense, allow the power to flow from the cosmos to the musculature, responding, allowing his response to accelerate as he moved forward.

But now, suddenly, with only the one boot off, she was standing. She looked at the door, then looked at him. Her mouth was moving, about to protest. But, before him, the instrument of judgment had materialized: the gold coil, suspended between hands that—

"What the fuck's going—"

The wood-splintered crash was louder than the woman's voice—and louder than his voice, too, as he turned, compelled to face the familiar figure filling the doorway.

Recovering his balance, blinking in the dim light, Mitchell saw the golden cord. He lunged, caught the cord, tore it free. With his left hand, he thrust the cord into his pocket. With his right hand he drew the .45 automatic as he flung out his left arm, blocking the whore's escape from the tiny room. He saw her eyes widen, saw terror clutch at her throat, saw her mouth come open, to scream.

"Don't—" He shoved the pistol's muzzle cruelly beneath her

chin. "Don't yell. I'll pull the trigger if you yell." He held her motionless, impaled by the gun, helpless now, gone limp.

"Here—" Still with the gun jammed into her throat, he withdrew his wallet, took out two fifties. "Take these. And shut up about this. Shut up and stay here in the room. Understand?" He jabbed the gun into her flesh, felt her sag, pushed her back until, off blance, she sprawled on the bed. "Don't move. Not for five minutes." He glanced at Elton, who was standing motionless, staring at the girl on the bed as if she had just materialized. Slipping the .45 into its holster, buttoning his jacket, he stepped to the closest door, opened it, saw the toilet, the basin. Withdrawing the cord from his pocket he stepped to the toilet, dropped the cord in the water, flushed the toilet, watched the cord coil slowly, coil faster, finally disappear. Forcing himself to do it, he waited for the tank to refill, flushed the toilet again. Then he turned again to Elton, who stood as before, looking at the whore who lay sullenly on the bed, shaking her head as she muttered inaudible obscenities.

With all his strength, Hastings hammered on the steel door frame with the heel of his clench fist. Beside him, Canelli moved back, balanced himself.

"Should I kick it in, Lieutenant?"

"Without a warrant?" Furious, Hastings struck the door another blow. Then: "Get around back, in the alley. If they come out—" Futilely, he touched himself at the beltline, where a surveillance radio should be clipped. But he'd arrived at the St. Francis only moments before Elton and Mitchell had appeared; there hadn't been time to get a radio from his car, parked around the corner.

"If they come out, follow them. If they don't come out, stay there. I'll call for some back up. Try not to get too far ahead of me. Clear?"

"Yessir. Which way's the alley?"

"How the hell should I—" Through the dirty glass of the door, he saw a big man with boxer's shoulders materialize in the dim, narrow hallway that led back into the lobby. Nodding, raising a restraining hand, the man came toward them as Hastings took his shield case from his pocket, slammed the shield against the wire-reinforced window, shouting, "Open up, goddamnit. *Now.*"

Moving deliberately, sullenly defiant, the man put his hands on the door, took off one lock, then another lock, allowed the door to swing free.

"What's the trouble, officer? What's the hurry?"

"Why's this door locked?"

The big man smiled, shrugged. "I was in the can. A place like this, you go to the can, you got to lock the door. Right?" He didn't bother to smile.

"Where's the back door? *Quick.*"

Indolently, the clerk pointed to a doorway beneath the stairs. As the two detectives split up, one racing upstairs, one struggling with the alley door, the clerk smiled, took the fifty-dollar bill from his pocket, smoothed it down against the counter, slipped it into his wallet, slipped the wallet into his pocket.

23

"I'm sorry," Flournoy said, stepping between Holloway and a bearded TV reporter. "This was a private banquet, just a dinner that Mr. Holloway has been planning for a long time, with friends." As he spoke, he nodded to the security man, who signaled for the Holloway limousine. "But if you'll be at the DeAnza Room of the St. Francis at ten o'clock tomorrow morning, we're having a buffet brunch for the press. Mr. Holloway will be there, of course, and he'll be more than happy to—"

"Excuse me—" A young woman stepped directly into his path, raising a plastic identification plaque as she said, "I'm Bea Henderson, with the *Sentinel*. I'm on the crime beat, and there've been reports that homicide detectives are—"

"I'm sorry, Miss Henderson. Mr. Holloway's late for an appointment, I'm afraid." As the limo drew to a stop at curbside, Flournoy looked at another security man, moved his head toward the woman. At the same time, the first security man opened the right rear door, ushering Holloway inside. Flournoy followed, sitting on the far side of the car so that Holloway could wave from the window. As the limousine pulled away from the curb, the pulse of the mobile phone shrilled. Flournoy glanced at Holloway, who now sat with his head resting against the seat cushions, eyes closed. As Holloway gently shook his head, eyes still closed, Flournoy lifted the phone from its cradle.

"Yes?"

"It's Lloyd, Herbert. Can you talk?"

Glancing at the security man, who sat on the jump seat, Flournoy said, "That depends on the subject."

"It's Elton. He just tried it again—tried to kill a whore, on Mason Street. Just a block from where the other one was murdered, on Tuesday."

"Where's he now?"

"In his room. With a man watching the door."

"Were there any—problems?"

"That depends on what you mean by problems. He hasn't been arrested, and the woman's all right. But she saw him with the gold cord in his hands. And, sure as hell, the police will question her."

As Flournoy listened, he kept his eyes on Holloway's face. The eyes remained closed, the facial muscles sagging. With the applause of some of the most powerful men in the country sustaining him, Holloway was recharging his batteries.

"We're coming directly to the hotel, should be there in ten minutes. Where's Gloria?"

"I don't know. As soon as I got Elton settled, I called you."

"How's his state of mind?"

"Strange. Very strange, I'd say. We've got a problem, Herbert. A big problem."

"I know. I want you to tell Gloria what's happened. Austin and I will be with you shortly."

"Right."

The connection went dead. Slowly, Flournoy replaced the phone in its cradle, glanced again at Holloway, then rested his own head on the seat cushions, allowed his eyes to close. For what lay ahead, he must prepare himself, compose himself.

As Mitchell finished speaking, Holloway sat silently on a sofa in his sitting room, head bowed, his body slack, suddenly drained. Then, with his eyes closed, very slowly, very somberly, he began to shake his head. How could it have happened? How could the evening's earlier triumph have failed him so suddenly, so completely, so catastrophically, leaving him so desolated, so vulnerable, so utterly certain that disaster threatened?

Why was he unable to open his eyes, raise his head—take command? The three of them were keeping their silence, deferring to him, waiting for him to speak. But first, before he could speak, he must purge his thoughts of all the images that had seared his consciousness as Gloria had spoken, followed by Flournoy—followed finally by Mitchell, delivering the final blow. He must somehow find peace, find release from the instant's flash of memories: the baby, feeding at Marvella's breast, the toddler, diapered, unsteadily walking across a wide green lawn—the child, singing on Sundays, and the cap-and-gowned teenager, posing with his diploma.

But the child had seldom smiled, and the teenager had never laughed. From the first, there'd been a darkness of the spirit, a sense of withdrawal. "He's like somebody else's child," Marvella had once said. "A stranger's child."

A stranger's child . . .

"Dad?" It was Gloria, speaking in a voice that was strangely soft, a voice he'd seldom heard. Slowly, with great effort, he raised his head, opened his eyes.

"Are you all right?" she asked.

He forced himself to smile. But he could feel his face—the face that was his fortune—twisting into grotesque unpredictability. Over the years, like all good actors, he'd developed a talent for imagining his face as the camera must see it. And this expression, televised, would invite disaster.

But, still, he must keep the smile in place, must make some response, any response.

"I'm as good as can be expected, I guess, considering that I've just learned that my son is a—a homicidal maniac."

As if they shared a common embarrassment, they averted their eyes as he looked at each of them in turn. He felt the bogus smile fade into final defeat as he said, "It'll take a while—a long while—to adjust to the idea, really understand. I always knew, of course, that Elton was—" Helplessly, he shook his head. "—that he was strange, that he did strange things. There were the—the juvenile authorities, and the police, a few times. But this, it—"

He realized that, still, he was shaking his head. "This'll take time to understand."

"We don't have the time, though," Gloria said. "That's the point. Right now, probably, the police are talking to the girl. If she identifies Elton—" Ominously, she let it go unfinished.

"He didn't try to kill her, though," Mitchell said. "He was going to try. He had the cord in his hands. But he didn't touch her."

"He would've tried, though," Flournoy said. "We've got to face that, face the fact that he would've tried. And we've got to do something, Austin." Flournoy turned to face him squarely. "We've got to get him out of town. Even if he's not actually convicted of anything, even if Harlan can get him off, the publicity of the arrest, of the trial—" Heavily, Flournoy shook his head. "It would be devastating."

"Where should we send him?" Holloway asked, once more looking at each of them in turn. "If he's with us, we can protect him. Like Mitchell did, tonight. But if he's in some other city—" He shook his head. "It'd be worse, not better. He'll—he'll do it again. And he'll be arrested. And the publicity will be the same, either way."

Gloria drew a deep, measured breath. "Elton's sick, Dad. We've known it for a long time. You've said so yourself, that you knew Elton was sick. We've known it, but we haven't done anything about it."

"He should have treatment," Flournoy said. "He should—" He paused. Then, speaking in a low, uncompromising voice, eyes hard, mouth set, he said, "He should have professional treatment. In a sanatorium, somewhere. Now. Right now."

"Where the police can't find him," Mitchell said. "He's got to be where the police can't find him. And he's got to be kept there. Physically kept there. Otherwise—" He shook his head, spread his huge hands. "Otherwise, they'll find him, and arrest him."

"He won't go," Holloway said. "I know Elton. He won't go. He won't go away, won't run. Whatever he's done—" He broke off, momentarily closing his eyes as he searched for the strength to finish it: "Whatever he's done, he's done it for God. He believes he's God's instrument. So he won't run. And he won't refuse to answer questions, either. If anyone questions him—if they're smart enough, skillful enough—he'll tell them just that. He'll tell them everything. He'll insist on telling them everything. Believe me."

"He's God's instrument," Mitchell said. "He hears voices, and he does what they tell him. He told me that tonight."

"If he won't go away willingly, then we've got to force him to go," Gloria said. "Lloyd's right. He's got to be physically restrained if that's what it takes. And it's got to be done immediately."

Impatiently, Flournoy shook his head. "We can't force him to go to a sanatorium, though. Not unless we get a court order. Which, God knows, we don't want to get, because of the publicity."

With heavy emphasis, speaking slowly, Gloria said, "He's got to be confined. And he's got to be isolated. That's the bottom line." Impatiently, she gestured, compelling Holloway's close attention. "My God, *buy* a sanatorium. How much can it cost? Buy one in—in Europe, where the reporters will never find him."

At the thought, calculating, Flournoy looked up, his eyes sharpening.

"If one reporter finds him, though—" Holloway shook his head. "If just one found him, that's all it would take. And they're sure to ask why Elton isn't singing on Sundays."

"Tell them he's on a mission somewhere," Flournoy said impatiently. "South America, maybe. It's happened before. He was in Africa for two weeks. Remember those pictures we got—that canned footage?"

"A mission—" Holloway said it softly, reflectively—without hope. Missions ended. But madness went on forever.

"I hate to strike a crass note," Flournoy said, "but this couldn't come at a worse time. I mean, it's ironic—" Wincing as if he were in sudden pain, he sharply shook his head. "I don't know whether you were aware of it tonight, Austin, at the banquet, but at the end you had them absolutely riveted. Not at first, admittedly, which makes it so very significant. At the first, they were probably the toughest audience you've ever faced. But, by God, at the end, they were yours. They're still yours, if you can deliver what they want. And then, to have this happen . . . now . . ." Flournoy shook his head.

Deliberately, Holloway allowed a long moment of silence to pass as he stared full into Flournoy's colorless eyes. Then, precisely on the beat that would produce the provocative emphasis he intended, speaking very softly, he said, "What is it, would you say, that they want from me?"

Holding Holloway's gaze with his own, Flournoy matched the other man's quiet gravity as he said, "They want to control the way the country votes. And they think you might be able to do that for them. And if you can—" Like Holloway, he allowed a significantly timed silence to finish the thought.

Holloway remained motionless for a moment, still staring at his chief of staff. Then, rising heavily to his feet, he turned to Mitchell. "I'm going to talk to Elton. Then I'm going to my room. I'm going to my room, and I'm going to ask divine guidance."

Also rising, Mitchell nodded silently, with deep compassion.

"You'll have him watched," Holloway said. "Closely."

"Yes," Mitchell answered quietly. "He'll be watched. Around the clock."

"Good. Thank you, Lloyd."

"You're welcome."

"I want you where I can find you, Lloyd, when I need you. Do you understand?"

With infinite regret, Mitchell nodded again. "Yes," he answered. "I understand."

24

He opened the door with a passkey, entered the room without knocking, slipped the passkey into his pocket. One lamp was lit, in a far corner of the room. Slightly snoring, Elton lay on his back, his head on the pillow. As Holloway approached the bed, he looked at the bedside clock, a reproduction of a French antique. The time was almost exactly midnight.

Should he remain standing while he spoke the words?

Should he awaken his sleeping son or let him sleep?

These were important considerations, matters of extreme gravity, once-in-a-lifetime decisions.

It was established, certainly, that the subconscious controlled the thoughts, therefore controlled the man. And it had also been established that, awake or asleep, the subconscious was alive, receptive. Therefore, even though his son was asleep, the words he was about to speak would register.

The words, the matching gestures, these were his stock-in-trade, the fountainhead of his success, the source of all his wealth—his wealth, and the wealth of others. Even, potentially, the wealth of nations, if he could believe what he'd heard tonight at the banquet.

At the thought he shook his head, raised his hand to lightly touch his temple. His thoughts were wandering. And if the thoughts wandered, so also would wander the words. And the world, his world, would fly apart if confusion overtook him and the words went wrong.

He was, he realized, momentarily confused, his little secret.

So far, his little secret. Since the euphemism of his cardiac event had cast its narrow, sharp shadow across his life, these moments of secret confusion had become more frequent, more disquieting, ultimately more threatening. And now it was happening again. The circuits were overloaded. Within hours, a few short hours, he'd been lifted to the heights, then dropped down to the lowest depths. Those closest to him had first told him what he'd wanted to hear, then told him what he didn't want to hear. They'd laid out the alternatives, as always. Then, as always, they'd left him alone, to make the decision.

Once he would have turned to God, prayed for guidance. He'd told them, earlier, that he intended to pray. Had they believed him? Or did they, like him, realize that, in his sixty-third year, his partnership with God had run its course, had been terminated by mutual consent?

Somehow, somewhere, he'd lost his faith—in exchange for twenty million viewers each Sunday. Minimum.

His account with God was square.

And, long ago, he'd settled with the Devil.

So there was nothing left but the benediction he'd come to pronounce:

"Of the four of us, Elton—you, your sister, your mother, and me—only two of us have survived. Gloria and I, we're the survivors. Why Gloria and not you, I'm not sure. I think it might have had something to do with the circumstances of your birth. I'm quite sure of it, in fact. I've never talked about it, never spoken the words. But now it's time. Now the words must be spoken—" Aware that, suddenly, the strength was leaving his legs and lower body, he stepped away from the bed, fumbled for a small bedside chair. The chair was draped with Elton's clothing, neatly folded. From the first, Elton had been a neat child, an orderly child.

Still fumbling, he swept the clothing to the floor, sat down, once more touched his temple, once more closed his eyes. Was his heart beating irregularly? Would death solve everything—his death, not Elton's death? Had God reconsidered their previous articles of agreement?

It was possible. Tonight, anything was possible.

But now, reprieved, he could feel strength returning. It was necessary, therefore, to begin speaking. He owed it to Elton, to begin speaking, as soon as strength permitted.

"Gloria, you see, was a love child. Your mother was only seventeen when Gloria was born. She was seventeen, and I was thirty-one. And your mother was essentially unformed. That's important to remember. She was a child of nature when we met. But I was complete, at age thirty-one. I was the same person then that I am now. For me, nothing's changed. But your mother—" He shook his head, lifted his arm, tilted the shade of the nearby lamp to put his face in shadow. "Your mother, I'm afraid, was damaged. She wasn't damaged giving birth. It was her father, I think, that damaged her. He was a minister, you see. And when he discovered that your mother was pregnant out of wedlock, his rage was monumental. He was a vindictive man, an avenging archangel. He put his mark on both of us—me, and your mother, too. She'd been more than a daughter to him since her mother died—more than a daughter, but less than a wife, so that it was a terrible blow for your mother when he was murdered. But, ultimately, it was God's judgment, and eventually your mother accepted that. Because, you see, her father had cursed her, burdened her with guilt when he accused her of sin. So your mother was blighted in her bloom, and Gloria was born under a dark cloud of vengeance.

"However, Gloria was unmarked. From the first, she was a laughing child. But your mother couldn't laugh. She was marked forever by her father's curse. She tried to escape it. God knows, she tried. She twisted and turned, and she cried in the night beside me. But it was no use. She was lost. Forever lost.

"And then, later, when she was pregnant again, after Gloria was born, she suffered a miscarriage. And the damage begun by her father's wrath was compounded, grieviously compounded. Making it necessary, you see, for her to give birth again—to you."

As he said it, he heard his son moan, saw him stir. Yes, the words were registering, even in sleep. Elton had always loved his mother. In his own twisted, tortured way, he'd always loved her, always needed her.

"Gloria was unmarked," he said softly. "She escaped. But you were marked, Elton. Your grandfather reached out from beyond the grave and laid his curse upon you."

As his son stirred again, he once more broke off, his eyes fixed upon the face on the pillow, lying in a shaft of pale light from the window. Even in sleep, as always, the pale face was expressionless. But, beneath the sallow skin, small muscles twitched. Yes, the subconscious was listening.

"So you were born without love, Elton. Gloria was a love child, but you weren't. And—" He drew a long, deep sigh. "And that's the essence of it, I'm afraid. Love is a miracle, and you were denied it. I knew it when you were born. I knew you'd be blighted. Because, you see, by that time I no longer believed in miracles. They're just words now, Elton. Love—God—to me, they're just words. They're powerful words, as I well know. With those two words—love, and God—men like me can control the world. But before that's possible—before you can control how other men think, you've got to first realize that nothing's real, nothing is ever what it seems. Everything is a mirror image, Elton. That's the one essential truth. We live in a world of mirror images. Love isn't really love, and God really isn't God. There wouldn't be love if there wasn't loneliness. And there wouldn't be God if there wasn't fear. I finally discovered that, you see. I finally discovered that love doesn't change the world, and neither does God. It's fear that changes the world. Fear is the one great truth, the only real tool. If a man wants power—and we all do— he nourishes fear. Because hatred is what it's all about, Elton. It isn't love that drives us. It's hate. And hate and fear go together. That's obvious. So if you control them, manipulate love and hate, fine-tune them, you will control the world. But, of course, you don't use those words—never 'fear,' never 'hate.' You must always say 'love,' and 'God.' Always."

For a moment Holloway sat in silence, head bowed, his broad forehead delicately supported by long, gracefully tapered fingers.

When he began to speak again, his voice was hardly more than a whisper.

"Now you know, Elton. You know I lost my faith. It probably happened very early. We're already formed, you know, at a very tender age, and I suppose I lost whatever faith I had in God at the moment I realized what a fraud my father was. Because when I made that discovery, I also learned about hatred. I learned about hatred and love, all at once, when I was just a child. You learned the same lesson, too, when you were very young. Oh, yes, Elton—I saw you looking at me. When I couldn't see you, I could feel you. I remembered, Elton. I remembered those ancient feelings of mine, remembered enough to know how you must hate me.

"Most of us make some kind of deal with the Devil, so we aren't consumed by hatred. But you couldn't do that, Elton. You don't bend, you break. That was our secret, Elton—the only secret we ever shared. We never talked about it, of course. So both of us were keeping the same secret from each other. That's what a family does when love turns to hate. They keep their secrets—hoard them, use them like weapons. Because secrets *are* weapons, the cruelest weapons of all.

"I never told you all this, of course. Parents don't do that. They can't afford the risk. So, instead, they buy their children expensive things, and send them to expensive schools, and they hope their children will provide some ornamentation for their lives, like a well-tended lawn or an impressive car. And you did that—at least on Sundays. You still do. So now—" He drew a long, labored breath, infinitely regretful. "So now you know the secret, Elton. You know about love and you know about hate. You know that hate is the only weapon that matters. But—" Once more, he deeply sighed. "But the secret's out, Elton. The secret's out, and my enemies have the keys to the armory. And if they open the doors, lay hands on my weapons, then it's all over. Everything." Slowly, struggling against a sudden, overwhelming lassitude, he rose to his feet, moved close to the bed, stood motionless for a moment, looking down at the figure in the bed, the baby that had become a boy, the boy that had become a man . . .

     . . . the man that had become a monster.

"If you thought God was commanding you, Elton, then I hope you die still believing it. Because then it will surely be true." He let a last long moment of silence pass, then said softly, "I'll never be forgiven. Never. I want you to know that, Elton."

He stooped, kissed his son on the lips, straightened, and automatically turned to the bedside lamp, about to switch it off. But then he remembered: Elton was afraid of the dark.

25

"So what you're telling me," Hastings said, "is that he didn't touch you. Is that right?"

"Jesus," she wailed. "I already *told* you. It wasn't the young one that was bothering me. It was the old one—the big one, with the goddamn gun. *He's* the one you want. Not the other one, the young one."

"Listen," Canelli said, "we'll tell you which one we want. You just tell us what happened, how it came down. Do you think you can do that?"

Sitting on the edge of the bed, peevishly plucking at the tufted chenille bedspread, she sullenly shrugged.

"But the young one had the cord," Hastings said. "The gold cord. Is that right?"

"I already *told* you, he—"

"As often as I tell you to tell me," Hastings said quietly, "that's how many times you tell me. Otherwise, we'll haul your forty-dollar ass downtown."

"Fifty-dollar, please," she said wearily. "Not forty. Fifty."

"So —?"

She nodded. "Yeah, he had the cord. He was holding it in front of him with both hands. And I gotta say, he was pretty weird looking. Weird acting, too. But, Christ, you get used to that in this business. I mean, if it wasn't for the goddamn weirdos, we'd all be out of business, probably." She sighed, shook her head, turned to face Hastings squarely. "Listen, speaking of business, do you mind if—"

"So tell us about the cord, what happened to it?"

"Again?"

"Listen, Angie—" Hastings dropped his voice. "I'm not going to tell you again. Either you—"

Hastily, she raised both hands, palms out. "All right. Okay. Jesus—" She shook her head, plaintively exasperated. "What happened, after the big one broke in, and shoved me down on the goddamn bed, he took the cord, grabbed it out of the young one's hands. He went into the bathroom, and he must've flushed it down the toilet."

"Did you see him do it, flush it down the toilet?"

"Well, no. But I heard the toilet flush. Twice. Then he came out of the bathroom. And then they left."

"Mitch—the big one—he was the only one that went into the bathroom. He went in with the cord, and flushed the toilet twice. Then he came out, without the cord. And then they left. Is that right?"

She nodded heavily, mocking him as she said, "That's right, Lieutenant. Exactly right."

Hastings nodded thoughtfully. He looked at Canelli, who shrugged, signifying that he could think of nothing more to ask. Now Hastings withdrew a card case and pen, handed her two business cards and the pen. "Those are my cards, Angie. Write your address and phone on one of them, and give it to me. Keep the other, in case you think of anything you forgot to tell me." He watched her working with the pen, silently mouthing the words and numbers as she wrote. When she returned the pen and the card, he said, "And remember, if you even think about leaving town, it's your forty-dollar ass."

"Fifty-dollar," she muttered, reaching for her bag. "Fifty."

26

Holloway pulled the door closed, stood motionless for a moment, head bowed, leaning his full weight against the door frame. He was conscious of someone nearby: a security man, sitting at an ornamental table, eyes averted. Slowly, heavily, Holloway pushed himself erect, turned to his left, away from the security man. It was a reflex, a conditioned response, that made him stand erect and turn so that his face was averted. Because it was essential that his chosen mask of infallibility remain firmly fixed in place. If salesmen projected geniality and politicians pretended nobility, then the evangelist must cloak himself in eternal infallibility. Even though he was living through his lifetime's moment of disaster, he must keep the mask in place, playing the mummer's game.

To some men, this moment of truth came when danger threatened, or death suddenly loomed. Some faced this moment in an alleyway, some in a hospital room, some while they chased a tennis ball, or sat on the toilet, reflecting.

To him, it had come in these midnight hours, in this overdecorated hotel hallway, alone, with his tie loosened, wearing his bedroom slippers, an utter emptiness within, a desperate void of fearfulness where once there had been a fullness of faith and certainty. He could hear the sound that his slippers made on the carpeting: a slow, leaden scuffing, an old man's shuffling.

As he turned the corner of the adjacent corridor, an inexorable, apocalyptic choice confronted him, the parable of the doors.

One door—his—signaled a sad surrender to the inevitable, Christ's way, without question.

But there was another door—a second door.

Fittingly, his was the first door, requiring that he must make the choice, must go beyond his door . . .

. . . as he was doing now.

Must stand before Mitchell's door . . .

. . . as he was doing now.

Must take the talisman, the passkey, from his pocket . . .

. . . as he was doing now.

Must enter the room as silently as a murderer might . . .

. . . as he was doing now.

With the instant's touch of Holloway's hand on his shoulder, Mitchell's eyes came open, his whole body tightened. On the counterpane, his hands clenched into fists.

"Austin . . ." Mitchell blinked, sat up, reached for the bedside lamp.

"No—" Holloway raised his hand. "There's enough light from the street." As he spoke, he gestured to the view window.

"What's wrong? What's happened?"

Holloway turned away from Mitchell to look out over the San Francisco skyline, one of the world's most exciting vistas. Somewhere out there, in a refrigerated drawer, lay the body of the woman Elton had murdered. In another part of the city, policemen were making their plans. Judges were issuing search warrants, arrest warrants. Reporters were asking their questions, cameramen were searching for targets.

And, always, the enemies were waiting—the men with watchful eyes.

"Austin, are you all right?"

Still facing the cityscape, Holloway spoke slowly, softly: "I can still remember the first time we ever talked together, Lloyd. Do you remember?"

"Of course I do—in the warden's offce, it was."

"How old were you then? I've forgotten."

"I'm sixty-two now, and that was thirty-five years ago, at

least." As he spoke, Mitchell swung his thick legs over the edge of the bed and reached for his robe, draped across a nearby chair. Standing, he put on the robe, tightened the belt, turned down the collar. He decided to sit on the bed, decided to wait in silence for whatever was coming.

"More than half your life," Holloway said, "you've been with me."

"It's been the best half, Austin. You know that."

"Yes—" Gravely, Holloway turned to face the other man. "Yes, I'm sure that's true. You wouldn't say it, if it weren't true, Lloyd." He stepped to a nearby armchair, sank into it. On the bedside table, the clock read almost one o'clock. Tomorrow—Friday—would be a busy day, beginning with the news conference at eleven.

"You're the only one I can trust to tell me the truth, Lloyd—the whole truth. Gloria tells me the truth, but it's always tainted with rancor, because part of her hates me. Flournoy tells me the truth, if it suits his purposes. Otherwise, he lies. And Elton—" He shook his head. "Elton is blinded. And Marvella—" He paused, searching for the word. "Marvella suffers too much to think about what's true and what isn't true.

"So it comes down to you and me, Lloyd. It comes down to history—to all those years. All night, I've been thinking about those years. I've been thinking about myself, thirty-five years ago. I wasn't even thirty, when I heard that you might be paroled. Many times I've wondered what it was in that newspaper story that made me feel I must talk to you. It wasn't just because I needed a bodyguard. I could've hired a hundred men for a job like that."

"You needed more than a bodyguard, Austin."

"And, God, I *got* more than a bodyguard. And I got more than a friend, too. I've discovered that friendship—protestations of friendship—come pretty cheap. But when you stood between me and that crazy man with the gun, in Knoxville—" Marveling, he shook his head. Then: "You're the only one of us who really believes in God, Lloyd. You've killed human beings. You've killed before I knew you, and—God forgive us—you've killed afterward, for me. But you're the only real Christian among us, the only one who hasn't been corrupted. You know what's right—and you know what's wrong. And, most importantly—" Holloway paused, preparing himself to measure the effect of the words he'd come to say: "Most importantly, once you've determined what's right, decided what must be done, you do it. You do your duty, regardless of the consequences." Looking at the other man, he allowed another carefully calculated beat to pass as he gazed deep into Mitchell's eyes. "That's rare, Lloyd. That kind of dedication, that magnificent disregard of consequences in the service of what's right, it's very rare. Someone like you, a man who truly disdains worldly goods, disdains the trappings of the ego, of vanity, you're unique among men. That sounds over-blown, I know—highfalutin, as my father used to say. But I mean it. And you *know* I mean it. I've been preaching for so long, singing for my supper, that sometimes I don't know whether I'm simply talking, or whether I'm preaching. These lines get blurred as time goes on. But you know, Lloyd. You can recognize the truth, recognize your duty. And that's the whole point, the whole reason I'm here—because you know what's right. And you know what's wrong, too. You're my conscience."

Still sitting on the edge of the bed, his face impassive, his eyes steady on the other man's face, Mitchell made no reply. If he was aware of what must surely follow, he gave no sign.

"Sometimes," Holloway said, "I can hardly believe it, what's happened to me. Neither of my parents finished high school. Except for the Bible, I don't think my father ever read a book all the way through. My sister married a construction worker who beat her regularly. Until my father had a stroke, and the money, such as it was, quit coming in, I gave no thought to preaching. I was fifteen years old then, and my only thoughts were for girls. It was hard times, in 1937, especially in our town, with the lumber mill on short hours, and the main street half closed down. So, on Sunday, with much trepidation, I drove our Model A to the meeting place, and I eulogized my father—who I despised, really. I didn't have the faintest idea what I'd say, or how I'd say it. And I was scared. God, I've never been so scared, before or since. But I got up on that stage, like I'd seen my father do, and I put my father's Bible on the pulpit, open, like I'd seen him do. Then I grabbed that pulpit as hard as I could, and I lifted up my face to the heavens, and I closed my eyes, and I waited for a miracle.

"And it happened. How—why—I'll never know. The words came from somewhere. To this day, I don't know where they came from, or why. But when I needed them, they were there. And they're still there, thank God. Sometimes, especially the last year or two, when I walk out to that pulpit, and face those cameras, it seems to me that the words will fail me. And I suppose they will someday. I suppose it's inevitable. And when that happens—" Reflectively, he shook his head. "When that happens, if it ever does, I doubt that I'll be ready. Because I'm famous now. And I have power, too. I discovered that tonight, discovered how much power I have. And if I'm honest with myself—honest with you—then I'll admit that I'm addicted to that power. Right from the first, I was addicted, right from that first Sunday when I looked out over those faces. I can still remember that Sunday. I don't think I was conscious of what I was saying. I think I just stood there, holding to that pulpit, with my eyes cast up to heaven. I opened my mind, and opened my mouth, and hoped for a miracle, as I said. And then, when the words did come, and I ventured to look down over the congregation, I could tell they were moved. And right then, right from that very first moment, I became aware that I could control other human beings. Through words, nothing more than words, I could rouse them, make them believe what I wanted them to believe, make them do what I wanted them to do. *Words.* Not armies. Not the power of money. Just words, and ideas." As if he were still marveling at the memory of that first meeting, Holloway sat silent for a moment, head slightly bowed. Then, softly ironic, he said, "So now I'm famous. World famous. And, thanks to Herbert, I'm rich. I've got money, and I've got property. There's the Austin Holloway University, and the Temple of Light—and those two satellites up there, solely owned. Not to mention the stocks and the bonds and the other real estate. And not to mention, either, those fat cats at the banquet tonight. I've been reading upturned faces for a lot of years, now, Lloyd. And I can tell you, I can absolutely guarantee you, that those fat cats will give anything—*anything*—if we'll take them along with us. They've got the money, and they want the power—want what I've got. And, unless I'm very much mistaken, they'll pay anything, do anything, to have their way with the voters in this country."

Holloway let another moment of solemn silence lengthen. Then, speaking directly to Mitchell now, full-face, he said, "All that's on one side. Everything. And then—" He drew a deep, regretful breath. "And then there's Elton. There's Elton and his golden cord."

As the words fell between them, Mitchell realized that he was sitting straighter on the bed, unconsciously bracing himself.

"I've just come from Elton, Lloyd—just come from his room. He was sleeping—as soundly, as innocently as a baby sleeps. I sat beside his bed, and I talked to him. I don't think I've done that three times in my whole life, Lloyd—sat beside him and talked, whether or not he heard me. And I was aware of that, aware that I'd failed him. It was one of those moments when, suddenly, your life is reduced to its essentials. I could look back over fifty years as if they were no more than fifty minutes, beginning on that Sunday after my daddy's stroke. And I realized that from that first Sunday, my life was one long, elaborate illusion. I was an actor with only one part to play. I was one person when I got up onstage on Sunday, and another person during the week. I'd preach against the sins of the flesh, and the next night, in another town, I'd be in bed with a stranger. I'd preach against avarice while I schemed how to get rich. And there was the other thing, too, the thing only we know about, Lloyd. Just you and me."

"It had to be done, Austin. It *had* to be done. We both knew it, knew it had to be done."

"But you did it, Lloyd. I only talked about it. We prayed about it, side by side, on our knees. We prayed to God. It was the last time I did it, the last time I prayed to God." Shaking his head, as if to escape the sudden, searing pain of memory, he lapsed into exhausted silence. Then: "I prayed, but you did it. You lifted up your hand. You struck the blow."

"I'd do it again, Austin. You know that." Mitchell paused. Then, speaking very deliberately, he said, "I *will* do it again. If that's what you want—if that's what has to be done—then I'll do it again."

Holloway sat motionless for a moment, head low, body slack, hands listless in his lap. Then, as if he were lifting an impossible weight, he raised his head to meet the other man's calm, steady gaze. In the pale half-light from the window, Holloway's eyes were haunted; his face was shrunken on itself, suddenly an agonized death's-head.

"It has to be done, Lloyd. We both know it, know it has to be done. But this time—" Hopelessly, he shook his head, closed his eyes, felt his voice thicken with the first genuine emotion he'd experienced in many years. "This time, we can't pray."

27

"**J**esus Christ," Friedman grated, "it's Friday. In my experience, judges play golf or go to the track on Saturday. Then comes Sunday. And Holloway's show at the Cow Palace, I happen to know, goes from one o'clock to two o'clock. And then they're gone. By five o'clock Sunday, Elton could be in Los Angeles. We'll forward our stuff to Los Angeles, and the FBI will do the same. Which is to say, in plain words, that because we can't get warrants, we'll be screwed out of the bust of the decade, maybe the bust of the century, for all we know. And all because the people at City Hall think that Holloway is some kind of a saint. You want some more coffee?"

Hastings shook his head, then said, "I'm glad you mentioned City Hall. Because that's where the problem is, you know. The chief serves at the pleasure of the politicians."

"As far as I'm concerned," Friedman retorted, "they're all politicians." Glowering, he made his way to the cafeteria's coffee urn, refilled his Styrofoam cup, returned to the table. Even before he sat down, Friedman began to talk: "We've got everything but an eyewitness to the actual crime. We've got Dancer Browne, and we've got—what's her name, from last night?"

"Angie Forster."

"Yeah. And we've got Amy MacFarland's room sealed tight and guarded. Everything's covered."

"We don't have the gold cord, though."

"That's true. But if we could get his fingerprints and the clothes he wore on Tuesday, we could put him in that room. I *know* it. I *feel* it. And then there's everything the FBI's got. It might not be admissible for trial, but it sure as hell should get us warrants."

"When I think about what happened last night," Hastings said, "hammering on that goddamn door while Mitchell was destroying evidence and then hustling Elton out the back way—" He clenched his right fist, struck it lightly on the Formica tabletop. "I'm going to get Canelli, and haul Mitchell's ass down here for questioning. I'm going to lean on the bastard. *Really* lean on him."

"Why don't you wait until tomorrow?" Friedman said. "Wait and see what happens tonight. The way it appears, Elton isn't controllable. I mean, if they could keep him in the hotel, I'm sure they'd do it. So the assumption is, all they can do is follow him, protect him from himself. That's what Mitchell was doing last night. Maybe the same thing will happen tonight or tomorrow night. After all, he's been out three times in four days—Monday night, Tuesday night, and Thursday night. The second time, he got his rocks off—killed Amy MacFarland, got away clean. So then, Wednesday and Thursday, we started poking around, putting the pressure on him. You talked to him, and I'm sure they've talked to him—Gloria, and her father, or whoever. So then, instead of lying low, like any reasonable serial killer would, he goes out last night, presumably to try his luck again. He missed. He's frustrated. So maybe tonight he'll go out again and give it another shot."

"That's no reason I can't interrogate Mitchell, though. For that matter, we might be better off if we kept him locked up overnight, according to your theory. If Mitchell hadn't been there last night, maybe we'd have Elton in a cell right now."

Sipping his coffee, Friedman considered the point, then nodded. "That's a possibility, I suppose."

"So what'd you think? Should I go for it? Bring Mitchell in?"

"Why don't we see what happens tonight? Why don't we put on extra people tonight at the St. Francis? If it doesn't work out tonight, we can bring Mitchell down here tomorrow. I mean, he's not going anywhere until Sunday, we know that. Meanwhile, we can keep up the pressure for the warrants on Elton."

Without enthusiasm, Hastings shrugged. "Whatever you say. You're the strategist." He glanced at the wall clock. "Maybe I'll have some coffee after all. Want anything else?"

"Thanks, no."

28

Covertly, Benton glanced at his watch, then looked at Holloway. Simultaneously, both men nodded. Benton took a last sip of coffee, checked his French cuffs, touched the knot in his tie, buttoned his jacket, rose, and half stepped to a portable lectern that had been placed on the head table. He cleared his throat, smiled, waited for those assembled to turn toward him and fall silent. During the shifting of chairs and the businesslike riffling of notebook pages, two TV cameramen looked to their equipment while three photographers looked to their Nikons. Altogether, the audience numbered twenty-six, a few more than projected.

"My name is Charles Benton," he began. "I've been with Austin Holloway for eight years. And in those eight years I've learned that after I've made sure that the reporters have been wined and dined, the wisest thing I can do is what I'm about to do now, which is introduce my friend Austin Holloway—and then step aside." As he said it, he turned to Holloway, smiling as he gestured with a full, courtly sweep of his arm.

To a perfunctory scattering of applause, Holloway rose, stepped to the lectern, seemed to smile intimately at each of the reporters in turn.

"First," he said, "I'd like to invite each of you to our service on Sunday. Your press passes are all you need to get in, and the front row'll be reserved for the press, as always. And let me say, before I forget, that we welcome picture taking—before, during, and after, whatever's your pleasure. And now—" The famous smile widened, the famous voice dropped one warm, welcoming octave. "And now, I'm at your service, ladies and gentlemen. Please—" He raised a hand, as if to anoint them. "Please, ask anything at all. We're all friends here."

Immediately, three hands were raised. Holloway gestured to a young woman who was with one TV cameraman. She rose, raised her jaw aggressively, and spoke in a high, clear, assertive voice:

"Can you give us some idea of your history—your background? Are you a theologian, a graduate of a seminary?"

His smile was touched with conspiratorial, tolerant good humor, suggesting that they shared a playful secret, he and this competitive woman with her smug mouth and cold eyes.

"No," he answered, "I didn't go to college. I come from humble origins, I'm afraid—proud, pious origins, but humble, nonetheless. My father was a minister, you see, sprung from the soil of the Middle West, from farming folk. What he learned about religion, he learned from the Bible—from the Bible, and from God. Because my father was a simple, unsophisticated man. He believed—deeply believed—that if he listened long enough, and hard enough, he could hear God speak. He had faith, you see—a deep, abiding faith. And I submit to you that faith like that is what we lack in this day and age. So I'm proud to say that I share my father's simple faith. And that's why I've come here to San Francisco. I'm carrying a message. It's the same message my father carried, and it comes from God."

The young woman smirked. "Or so you believe."

"Yes, madam—" Gravely, Holloway inclined his silvery head. "So I believe. So I deeply, devoutly believe." He let a beat pass, watched her pantomime a supercilious disbelief as she shook her head, resumed her seat. Then he turned to a middle-aged man, gray-haired, conservatively dressed.

"I'm Dick Frankle," the man said, "from the AP. Last night, you hosted a dinner for some of the most powerful men in America, here in San Francisco. It's my understanding that the possibility of forming a third political party was discussed. Would you care to comment, sir?"

"I'm afraid I can't comment directly on what we discussed last night. However—" He paused to consider, quickly reviewing how much he intended to tell—and not tell. "However, I can tell you—I'm delighted to tell you—that we reached a remarkable degree of unanimity last night. Nothing was formally decided. No commitments were made, no committees were formed. But we agreed—unanimously agreed, I think—that America stands at the crossroads. We agree that, on the one hand, America is singularly blessed. Our wealth is immense. Our energies, even though they may be depleted by drugs, and immorality, and irresolution, are nevertheless prodigious. But—" He paused, swept the closed, indifferent faces with eyes that both challenged them and calculated the true extent of their cynical disaffection. "But we agreed, last night, that in the process of becoming the richest, most powerful nation in the world, this country has lost its way. We've turned our back on God. Consequently, we're destroying this country from within. Drug use in America is reaching epidemic proportions. Illicit sex is glorified on every magazine rack, celebrated in Hollywood movies that, in our fathers' time, would never have been made. Even television has sold out to the pornographers. Homosexuality is running rampant. And, consequently, the family—the cornerstone of every civilization since time began—is disintegrating. In California, marriages barely outnumber divorces. Now—" He lowered his voice to a harder, more worldly note: "Now, this process—this decay—isn't irreversible. True, it's far advanced, grieviously far advanced. The hour is late, and time is therefore short. Because our enemies are watching, make no mistake about that. They are watching, and they are waiting—barbarians, clamoring at the gates. However, even though time is running against us, we believe—I believe, and my guests last night believe—that it's not too late for America. We believe it's still possible to get our message through to the people in this country who really care— who really want to help."

As he bowed his head, he covertly assessed the reaction. Yes, he had their attention. And perhaps their grudging professional respect.

"Assuming that you're right about sex in the media," Frankle said, "what would you do about it? How would you control it?"

"Moral pressure," Holloway answered. "Those same people who really care—who want to help, want to vote for candidates who'll carry their standards—they're the same people who turn the TV knob to respectable programs. They'll complain to the networks, too. And, instead of paying to go to corrupt movies, they'll go to church on Sunday, and drop their five-dollar bills into the collection plate."

Nodding good-naturedly, smiling, then shaking his head in mute concession to a point well made, Frankle sat down, reached for his half-filled glass of champagne.

The next question came from a tall young man who wore no tie, and who spoke in a high, thin voice: "What about censorship, Mr. Holloway? Would that help?" He asked it wide-eyed, projecting a half-mocking innocence.

"Censorship," Holloway said, "definitely would *not* help—not, at least, at this point. However—and I'd like to be clear about this—should moral persuasion fail, then a responsible government would certainly have to act. That's self-evident."

"Was that self-evident to your friends last night?" the young man asked.

"It wasn't discussed," Holloway answered crisply. "I'm giving you my opinion. No one else's but mine."

"How do you feel about abortion?"

"I think abortion is a sin."

"The law says a woman can have an abortion if she so chooses."

"Then the law should be changed. I intend to do everything in my power to see that it *will* be changed."

"If you should run for elective office, would that be part of your platform?"

"I have no intention of running for elective office. Ever."

"Then you believe in the separation of church and state?"

Holloway let a beat pass, then spoke carefully, concisely: "As I said earlier, I believe that our country is in crisis. And in times of crisis, everyone must help."

"So you don't believe in separating church and state?"

"I didn't say that. However, it's obvious that, in times of crisis, extraordinary measures must be taken. Morally, this country is under attack. We've got to repel that attack." Brusquely turning his attention away, he pointed to a middle-aged, overweight woman who was waving a fat palm high over her head.

"So far as I know," she said, "you're the only TV evangelist who's ever come to San Francisco. Can you tell me why?"

As engagingly as he could, Holloway smiled: a wide, rich smile, especially for her. "Just because everyone gave up on San Francisco without even a fight, madam," he said, "that's no reason I should give up, too."

The ripple of laughter was polite, no more. From this group, the newspaper stories and the TV footage would be mixed at best.

Over the diminishing snickers, she said, "What do you think about gun control, Mr. Holloway? Are you for it?"

"No, madam, I'm against gun control. I'm against violence in all its forms. But I *am* for self-defense. And the truth is, the criminals in this country are armed to the teeth. In some cases, I'm told, the criminals have better weapons than the police forces they oppose. And so long as that's the case, then I think the God-fearing among us must arm themselves, too. I've never made any secret of it—I carry a gun, a Smith & Wesson .38. And whenever I get the chance, I practice with it."

Eyes widening, the plump woman sat up straighter. "On you? Do you carry it on you? Now?"

Benevolently, he shook his head. "No, madam. I carry it among my effects. But I can assure you that, at night, it's never far from my hand."

The young, aggressive woman who'd asked the first question was the only one still with her hand raised. Regretfully, Holloway acknowledged her.

"You mentioned homosexuality earlier. Do you consider homosexuality a sin, too?"

"Yes," he answered sternly. "Yes I do. I don't intend to quote to you from the Bible. But I think there's ample proof that God considers homosexuality a sin. What other reason can there be for the AIDS epidemic that's sweeping this city?"

Her retort was cold, contemptuous: "AIDS is God's revenge against homosexuals. Is that what you mean?"

"I've already said what I mean, madam. Plainly, God approves whatever benefits mankind. And if homosexuality should somehow ever become universal, then civilization would surely die out. That should be obvious."

"It's just as obvious," she said, "that unrestrained reproduction would be disastrous."

He decided to smile, to raise a placating hand in benediction. "I don't believe, madam, that this is the time or the place to discuss matters of this complexity. Especially—" He smiled out over the audience, at the same time lifting his chin to give one of the TV cameramen a better angle. "Especially since I seem to sense that some of your colleagues are beginning to think about their deadlines."

Grudgingly, the young woman surrendered the floor as Benton rose to his feet, ready to close the meeting.

29

Outside, in the hallway, they waited. Downstairs, in the lobby, they waited. On the streets, in the cities, everywhere, they waited, the unclean women and the traitorous men—all of them watching, waiting, fingering their weapons, stalking him. Even Mitchell had gone over, had joined them, offered them his weapon. Mitchell, the last of the make-believe friends, the ultimate traitor, the big man with the gentle hands who had pretended to laugh with him when he was a child. But, all the while, Mitchell had plainly been making his plans, biding his treacherous time, patiently waiting for his orders. Until finally, last night, Mitchell had betrayed himself, revealed himself an enemy.

And with Mitchell's unmasking, the whole plot had come clear. He'd always suspected the truth, and now it had been confirmed: the men, enemies of the light, traitors of God, had always used the women, the unclean women, as their lures. He'd always suspected it, always believed that, really, the men were his real enemies, the women merely the pawns, the moveable whores.

Yet it had taken him all this time, until last night, to be sure. Completely, utterly sure.

From earliest memory, for as long as God had laid the burden upon him, he'd known this moment would surely come when he stood alone, completely alone, one man facing the multitudes, defiantly. Only Christ could have known this sorrow, this burden of betrayal.

Their plan, of course, was plain, transparently simplistic, unbelievably naive. By disarming him last night, they hoped to deter him. But if Christ, surrounded by enemies—and, yes, one traitor—had refused to bend, then he, too, would surely prevail.

But it must be tonight. Now. Before they could make more plans, gather more assassins. He must rise from the chair that, for the last hour, had held him a prisoner. Then he must change his clothes, taking care that his clothes were different, always different. Tonight, he would wear a necktie. One tie, around his neck . . .

. . . and another tie, in his pocket, ready.

At the thought, he gently smiled. Because he'd known, long ago, that this moment must come, when they would seek to disarm him, for their own purposes. And, accordingly, he'd anointed this one necktie, this secret necktie, with all the properties that were required.

The foot-long length of three-quarter-inch pipe lay on the bed, heavy enough to make its own indentation in the quilted bedspread. Buttoning his vest and slipping on his jacket, Mitchell picked up the pipe, slipped it up the left sleeve of his jacket against the inside of his arm. Straightening his left arm down along his side, he was able to support the pipe in the cup of his hand, concealing it from all but the most meticulous observer. He stepped in front of the mirror, moved his left arm up and down, closely watching the telltale sag of the sleeve.

It was possible that, tonight, the police would stop him, question him. The concealed pipe might be all the excuse they needed to arrest him. The .45 automatic in its shoulder holster wouldn't endanger him. For the .45 he had a permit, a personal permit, separate from the permit he had for the .357 that he carried on duty. The pipe, though, bought two hours ago in a downtown hardware store, could spell disaster.

But the decision had already been made; the choice was no longer his.

He looked at his reflection one last time, verified that, with the arm held straight down at his side, the bulge of the pipe was hardly visible. The surgical gloves, bought in a drugstore before he bought the pipe, lay limp and lifeless on the bureau beneath the mirror. With his right hand, he slipped the gloves in a side pocket. Conscious of the pipe's awkward weight, he lifted his left arm, pushed back the cuff, looked at his wristwatch. The time was almost nine-thirty—time to take up his post.

"Why don't you go to the can?" Canelli said. "Go to the can, and get rid of it. And then go home. Christ, you look terrible, all pale, and sweating. It's stomach flu, sure as hell. It's going around, you know. My sister's whole family had it last week."

"I'll go to the can," Friedman said, rising cautiously to stand erect. "But then I'll come back, wait for a replacement."

"Whatever." Canelli waved the other detective away. "Just go to the can. You aren't going to be much good with a pants full, you know, if the suspect shows up. Besides, the lieutenant just called about fifteen minutes ago. He's on his way down, should be here any second. So what's the problem?"

"All right, I'll take a crap, then I'll come back, see what the lieutenant says." Mincingly, Friedman began walking stiff-legged across the crowded hotel lobby. Sympathetically shaking his head, Canelli settled himself more comfortably against a massive Grecian-style marble pillar, refocusing his attention on the bank of elevators.

"Going out?" Mitchell asked, stepping into the elevator to stand beside Elton. Two men and a woman, brightly talking, companionably laughing, were the only other passengers.

Eyes front, standing close to the door, Elton gave no sign that he'd heard.

"I'll walk with you," Mitchell said.

"No."

Stepping close and lowering his voice, Mitchell whispered, "Then I'll follow you. Like I did last night."

The doors slid open. Elton stepped out of the elevator, began walking in a straight line directly across the lobby to the revolving doors. Standing beside the newsstand, Canelli saw the suspect come out of the elevator, closely followed by Mitchell. Canelli stepped away from the newsstand, switched on the surveillance radio clipped to his belt, verified that, yes, the red light was glowing. He put the tiny plastic earpiece in his ear, pressed the "transmit" button, spoke into the tiny microphone concealed in the palm of his hand.

"St. Francis one." As he released the "transmit" button, Canelli looked anxiously toward the hallway that led to the men's room. How long had Friedman been gone? Two minutes? Three? It was hardly enough time to let down his pants, get himself settled on the toilet seat.

He checked the radio's volume control, checked the cord connecting the earpiece to the radio, pressed the "transmit" switch again. Across the lobby, Elton Holloway was halfway to the revolving doors, walking steadily, looking straight ahead, his eyes blank. Mitchell was a dozen paces behind, grimly determined, moving as stolidly as a beat cop grinding out his shift.

"St. Francis one. Smitty, come in. *Quick.*"

Not even static came from the walkie-talkie. Canelli looked at the north arcade, which led to the hotel's Post Street entrance. Was there time to reach Smith and Backus, stationed at Post Street? Already, the suspect had his arm raised, ready to push through the revolving doors. Somewhere in the night, Lieutenant Hastings was driving toward the hotel. He could be a block away, a mile away, a city's length away. Without a radio or a telephone, it was impossible to know.

Friedman—Smith and Backus—Hastings—none of them could help. As Canelli began moving toward the revolving door, he thumped the walkie-talkie hard with his knuckles, and was momentarily rewarded by a brief sizzle of static, followed by silence.

Ahead, the neon glow was growing, an obscene color splash against the dark sky, brighter than the stars, beckoning the sinners, guiding them, luring them, finally snaring them.

If spiders spun webs, then whores lit the neon lights.

First the lights, then the darkness.

And finally, inevitably, death.

If the lights were bright, the body was dark: the pit consuming the shaft of unclean flesh, digesting it, both of them diseased. The woman, like the spider, killed one man, consumed him, then set her snare for the next, and the next.

Until, finally, she must pay with her life.

First she was judged at the bar of celestial justice, in absentia. Then, with the sentence pronounced, absolved of earthly consequences, he was given the warrant. Thus was the Devil defeated, his minions rendered impotent.

Until last night.

Until Mitchell, the Judas traitor, had joined forces with the Devil, betraying him.

Mitchell, the companion of his earliest memories, the big man with the gentle hands, had stalked him last night, betrayed him. Just as now, the enemy unmasked, Mitchell was stalking him again, surely seeking to betray him again.

Unless . . .

As the beginning of a thought surfaced, the rhythm of his footsteps faltered. His gaze, which must be strictly focused, must be tunneled only straight ahead, was inexorably widening, as if he were about to turn his head, about to look behind.

Because, yes, he could see it now, could glimpse a small forbidden sliver of possible truth, God's secret stratagem, knowledge denied to all but the chosen, God's most trusted, most precious few.

Because, yes, even God needed them: the double agents.

Mitchell, and the other chosen few.

Therefore, he was no longer moving forward. Instead, he was standing motionless, feeling the jostling of humanity and yet not feeling them, the unclean bodies, the sinners surrounding him.

If he listened carefully, closely, he could hear the truth, God's forbidden truth, celestial secrets disguised as ordinary voices, ordinary laughter. He could listen, and even smile as, himself all-knowing, the initiate now, he turned to face the friend of his childhood, God's double agent, therefore now surely his secret ally.

Lightly, vehemently, Hastings tapped his clenched fist on the steering wheel. Both sides of Post Street were lined solidly with illegally parked cars. The sidewalks were crowded with high-spirited pedestrians, part of the city's Friday night frenzy of barhopping merriment. During three traffic light changes, he'd advanced less than half a block. The time was almost ten o'clock, the time that Elton Holloway had left the hotel, both on Tuesday night and last night. Impacted in traffic, without knowing the frequency Canelli was using, he was cut off from the surveillance operation during its most critical phase. Ahead, beyond the Powell-Post intersection, a foot patrolman was walking past a brightly lit store window. Should he leave his car on Post Street, collar the patrolman, order him to take charge of his car? Should he try for a patch-through to the desk clerk, who could call Canelli to the phone?

Or should he simply wait it out, try to relax, try to calm a stomach that was beginning to rumble ominously?

Stopping momentarily on the crowded sidewalk, Mitchell stepped into the doorway of a video arcade. Turning to face the display window, he took the surgical gloves from his pocket, surreptitiously slipped them on, then rejoined the pedestrian flow, walking briskly now, to close the distance. Earlier in the day, walking this same route, he'd picked the place where it must happen, barely a block and a half away, on Mason Street.

At the corner of Geary and Powell streets, Canelli stopped, turned, looked back to the entrance of the St. Francis, a half block behind. Beyond a long line of yellow cabs, he saw a car that looked like a dark-colored Honda turning the corner from Post Street to Powell. Was it Lieutenant Hastings's car? Could he afford to wait until he was sure, afford to gamble? Would Elton take the same route he'd taken Tuesday and Thursday, walking west on Geary to Mason, then south on Mason, deeper into the

Tenderloin? Already, Mitchell was a half block away, walking steadily. Elton, the smaller figure, had already disappeared in the Friday night crowds.

If he waited for help, Canelli risked losing both of them.

But without help, he might risk his life.

Always, it happened like this: weeks—days—hours of plodding police work compressed into a few make-or-break moments, everything reduced to a single can't-win decision.

Quickly, he stepped into the intersection, arms spread, palms wide, stopping the slow-moving traffic. Then, jumping up and down in the middle of Powell Street, facing the anonymous Honda, he waved his arms crisscrossed over his head.

The night was a madcap medley of San Francisco sounds: cable car bells clanging raucously, automobile horns bleating, doormen whistling for cabs, Friday night revelers laughing, calling to one another—all of it focused on Union Square, the city's good-time center, daytime-bright in the glare of a thousand lights. Ahead, down the Powell Street hill, two cable cars were coasting toward the turntable at Market Street. A third cable car had stopped fifty feet short of the St. Francis, waiting for the Powell–Geary intersection to clear before the gripman took another hold on the cable. Two more cable cars, filled with passengers, were coming up from the turntable.

Turning right into Powell Street, Hastings had a choice: get in the taxi line, or get behind the stopped cable car. Choosing the cable car, he guided the Honda out of the taxicab line, let it coast slowly ahead, downhill.

As the Honda came to a gentle stop, Hastings saw a familiar figure standing beside the smartly uniformed figure of the St. Francis doorman. It was Friedman, looking anxiously up and down Powell Street, plainly worried. Repeatedly, Hastings pressed the horn button, but realized that the sound would be lost in the din of traffic. He stopped the car, set the brake, put his SFPD placard on the dash, got out of the car in the middle of the street. As he trotted on an angle to the curb, slipping between two parked cabs, he heard the shrill blast of a police whistle. The sound focused Friedman's attention, and Hastings waved, catching Friedman's eye. From behind him, almost as loud as the whistle, came the predictable bellow:

"*Hey, buddy.*"

Walking to meet Friedman, Hastings half turned, beckoned the uniformed man to follow as he took out his shield case, showed the patrolman his gold badge.

"What is it?" Hastings asked Friedman. "What's happened?"

"I don't know, Lieutenant. I'm sick. Stomach cramps, bad—the flu, I guess. I was in the bathroom for maybe five minutes, on the can. When I came out, Canelli was gone. I checked with Smitty and Backus, on Post Street. But they didn't hear from Canelli."

"Has he got a radio?"

"Sure."

"Do you?"

"No."

"How do you feel? You look terrible."

"I *feel* terrible."

"You go back inside—" Hastings pointed to the lobby. "Phone in. Get two more people here, right now. Then stay by the phone—in the house detective's office, my authority. Clear?"

"Yessir."

"I'm going to take a chance, go down Geary to Mason, the way Elton went before. Got it?"

"Yessir." One hand on his stomach, Friedman turned gingerly away, began walking painfully toward the lobby doors. Hastings turned to the patrolman, holding out his arm, keys dangling from a forefinger. "Here's the keys to the Honda. Park it, lock it, give Inspector Friedman the keys. Then stand by, out here, until I come back. Tell Friedman you'll be out here."

"Yessir."

Hastings turned away, began running south on Powell Street.

Standing in the middle of the sidewalk, he turned deliberately now to face Mitchell. The big man was advancing, his squared-off face implacable, resolution bunching at the shoulders, clenched in either hand, moving the legs like round wooden posts made of muscle, a miracle, perhaps—the second of the night's revelations, this man who might not be mortal, but instead a being from the dimension beyond, flesh but not flesh, substance but not substance, God's centurion in his earthly disguise.

Yes, it was the movements of the members that was the final, substantive delineation: muscles but not muscles, the ultimate proof that Mitchell had been transformed, would therefore reveal himself.

Yet caution was essential, even though recognition had finally been achieved—as if when he was younger, so very young, Mitchell might have given him the secret, or even . . .

Even . . .

Was it possible?

Anticipating the miracles of electronics still to come, was it possible that Mitchell had been implanted with a receptor that matched his own? Their receptors could have been preprogrammed for activation now, for this time of recognition, revealing the essential secret they shared since, last night, skillfully pretending to be one of them, the infidels, Mitchell had done what he must to preserve his secret identity, conceal his true status, God's chosen emissary, his ultimate protector.

Yes, it was a masterful choice.

But, as always, the receptors knew.

Because plainly, when their flesh touched, if only for a moment, Mitchell had managed to activate the circuits within, charging the receptor beneath the skin, therefore completing the secret electronic loops.

So it was a guessing game that they must play—the same games they had always played, the boy and the man. He would guess. With his fingers touching some secret part of himself—his heart, or his temple, at first—he would guess. Silently, communicating only electronically, not verbally, he would guess.

And then, when Mitchell nodded—once, only once—he would know.

Finally, ultimately know . . .

Therefore saved.

Released, therefore, to continue unthreatened, therefore safe. Finally, eternally safe.

At the intersection of Mason and Geary, panting, stumbling, Hastings slowed to a trot, then to a walk as he stepped into the street, momentarily stopping as he tried for a better angle, scanning the sidewalks on both sides of Mason. Ahead, across from the Bayside Hotel, just as it had been parked on Tuesday night, he saw Dancer Browne's Continental. Drawing air deep into his lungs, Hastings began trotting again, dodging, sharply bumping shoulders, forcing his way through the sidewalk crowds. As he came closer to the Continental, he saw Canelli suddenly step from between two parked cars on the far side of the street, anxiously waving. Gratefully slackening his pace, Hastings waited for a break in the traffic, then crossed the street to meet Canelli, running toward him.

"Jeez, Lieutenant, am I glad to see you."

Nodding, struggling for breath, hands on hips, head low, Hastings managed to ask, "What's up? Where are they?"

"In the next block—" Canelli pointed toward Market Street. "I been tailing them, and also looking out for you, or someone. I figured you'd probably—"

"Let's go." Hastings turned, began walking as fast as exhaustion would allow. "Show me. Tell me while we walk."

"Here—" Mitchell gestured to the entryway of an all-glass storefront displaying cameras and radios. "Let's stop a minute." As he spoke he looked quickly behind them. Across the street, standing between two parked cars, looking back the way he'd come, Inspector Canelli was broadly, urgently waving. Reinforcements, Canelli's backup, had arrived. All the time—all the years, all the memories, all the pain—it had come down to this moment, this place: eternity unhinged, sanity shattered, all of it focused in this pale face before him, the child grown into a madman, this monster with nothing behind his eyes. The monster raved, but the child still mewled, words twisted into gibberish, his hands bent to implore, abjectly appealing to a god long lost:

"All this time," Elton was saying, "all these years, and I've never known. But now I see, finally I see, why they sent you."

For a moment, one last long moment, Mitchell made no reply. But sadness—regret—took time, and danger was coming closer: the two detectives, walking shoulder to shoulder now.

"Here—" He took the thin forearm in his massive hand, drawing the other man away from the display window, toward the place he'd chosen, the alleyway close by. "Here, Elton. There's something I've got to show you, something you've got to see, before we talk anymore."

"Yes—" Solemnly, the young man nodded. "Yes, I knew it— *know* it. That's what I said, what I meant, when I said that I see. We're together now, just the two of us. And nobody knows, will ever know."

"Please—quick. *Quick.*" Tightening his grip, he looked a last time backward, calculating the distance, therefore the time. If the sidewalk was brightly lit, neon glaring, the alley was dark—and, yes, deserted. Thank God, deserted.

No, God couldn't come into it, not now, not tonight. God must be blind tonight. Mercifully, charitably blind.

"Here—" A final tug, and they were alone in the darkness: the damp-smelling, garbage-reeking darkness. Momentarily alone.

He released Elton's forearm, stepped one pace back, dropped his left arm, gripped the pipe with his right hand as it fell free from the sleeve.

"Hey—" Canelli pointed. *"Hey.* Where'd they *go?"*

"Come on—" Sprinting ahead, fighting free of pedestrians, Hastings reached across his body and yanked his revolver from its spring holster. Beside him, slightly behind, Canelli was loudly swearing. Five running strides took Hastings to Ellis Street: two lanes of traffic, jammed bumper to bumper. Throwing up his left arm, he drew back from a bouncing front bumper, heard brakes protesting, tires squealing, horns blaring, drivers shouting.

"Hold it," the two detectives called in unison, bobbing, weaving, shouting obscenities. *"Police. Hold it."*

Until, finally, they were on the opposite sidewalk, wildly running, both of them already breathing hard.

As the pipe fell free from his left sleeve, Mitchell grasped it firmly with his right hand. Holding the pipe low, concealed along his right leg, invisible in the alleyway darkness, Mitchell raised his left arm, pointing back to the brightly lit street. Instantly—mercifully—Elton turned his head, following the gesture. Mitchell raised the pipe, asked for forgiveness, brought the pipe down on the narrow, unprotected head, striking squarely on center. Sighing softly, twisting, Elton fell to his knees, sighed again, toppled to his left side, his face striking the pavement. Once more the pipe flashed up, then down again, this time sinking into the crushed bone of the skull, a bloody pulp.

He dropped the pipe beside the body, knelt, ripped at the hip pocket, found the wallet. He took the money, dropped the wallet beside the pipe, straightened, thrust the money in his jacket pocket as he began walking fast down the alley, away from Mason Street. As he walked, keeping close to the buildings, in deepest shadow, he looked over his shoulder, scanning the mouth of the alley. The rectangle of light from Mason Street limned the shape of the dead body, already shapeless, strangely amorphous.

Arriving first at the alley, Hastings threw himself against a brick building front, raised the muzzle of his revolver, held his breath, listening. Then, pivoting as he crouched, legs spread wide, revolver level, he sprang forward, into the dark rectangle of the alley's mouth, darker still beyond the glare of the street.

"Jesus," he muttered seeing the body. "Jesus Christ." With Canelli behind him, covering, Hastings knelt, cocked his head, looked into the dead face, its left cheek flattened against the slime of the uneven paving bricks. In the uncertain light, the slime had a pale, silverescent sheen, a contrast to the dark, fluid crimson of the blood.

Elton Holloway. Dead.

Not Mitchell dead. But Elton.

As Canelli began to speak, Hastings sharply raised his hand as he straightened from his crouch, turned to face down the long, dark length of the alley.

"Shhh. Listen."

What was it, that soft scurry of sound? Footsteps? Rats? Imagination, abetted by a cop's sudden fear of dark, silent places?

With a working radio, they could call for backup, get lights, get the other end of the alley covered, get shotguns. Working in unison, a trained team, four men could slowly, carefully flush him out, nobody hurt—

—nobody killed.

"He's got to be here somewhere," Hastings whispered. "He didn't have time to make it to the other end."

"Yeah."

"Ready?"

"Yeah."

"Keep to the sides, out of the light."

"Right."

Moving to his left, picking his way through the nauseous litter of plastic refuse bags and raw garbage, crouched low, Hastings began silently advancing.

Standing motionless in the shadow of a doorway, he stripped off the surgical gloves, dropped them behind a dumpster, unbuttoned his jacket, drew the .45 automatic from its shoulder holster. Was there a cartridge in the chamber? To make sure, he must pull back the slide, let it slam forward, carrying a cartridge from the clip into the receiver. But the sound, in the silence of the alley, would betray him. So, gambling, he must cock the gun: two clicks, drawing the hammer through half cock to full cock.

He couldn't run. He'd never been a runner. So he must wait for them. He must take careful aim, must squeeze the trigger—and hope the gun fired.

With his back pressed hard against the steel of the door, pistol raised, ready to fire, he drew a long, deep breath. He could feel the hammering of his heart, hear the rush of blood at his temples.

But he could control it, control his body. However the heart hammered, the blood rushed, the demons raged, his mind was still clear, his hand still steady.

What had to be done was done, finally finished. They'd been created together, Elton the infant, himself already a man, both of them created by the same man.

But first, the hunted tracking the hunters, he must identify the sound of approaching footsteps, must separate that sound from the other sounds of the hostile night. He must distinguish substance from shadow, movement from stillness. He must find them, sight them over the barrel of his pistol.

Then he must kill them.

Kill them, and escape, return to the father who had just lost a son.

In the deadly silence of the alleyway, the night sounds were individualized, eerily clarified: a distant siren, the thunder of a departing jet, rock music, auto horns, someone crying, someone swearing—all of them concealing a soft shuffle of footsteps on paving stones, a rustle of clothing, the metallic scrape of a weapon: the sounds of the urban jungle, the sounds of life or death.

Across the alley, the squared-off shape of a dumpster cast a long, dark shadow. Above the dumpster, light from a second-story window fell on a building wall beside Hastings. If Mitchell was crouched beside the dumpster, and Hastings stepped into the rectangle of light . . .

The thought—the fear—had locked his knees, forced his back sharply against the rough brick wall, numbed him at his center, closed his throat, left him momentarily helpless. If he were alone, he could have gotten out of it, gone back the way he'd come, to the safety of Mason Street.

But Canelli was there, his witness.

And he was there, Canelli's witness.

So, separately, each of them trembling inside themselves, secretly afraid, they must nevertheless continue this deadly game, each fearing disgrace more than death. They must—

Across the alley, from the shadow of a doorway, pale light

glinted on moving metal: a gun barrel, tracking him. As he dropped facedown, the shots sounded. Bullets screamed, ricocheting: one shot, and another. And another. He was rolling—once, twice, bricks bruising elbows and knees: a merciful pain, better than the bullets tearing into his flesh. He was on his feet now, crouched, springing across the alley, crashing against the clanging side of the dumpster.

Safe.

"Canelli. You okay?"

"Okay, Lieutenant." The reply came from across the alley. Good. When Canelli saw him cross to this side, Canelli had crossed to the opposite side and crouched low behind a row of garbage cans, safe.

Both of them, safe.

"He's in the doorway, on this side. Ten feet up the alley."

"Right."

And now, yelling: "Give it up, Mitchell. Throw it down. You've got—"

Footsteps, clattering: slow, clumsy footsteps, running.

Exposing only his head and his revolver, Hastings looked, saw him: Mitchell, shoulders hunched, head down, legs pumping slow-motion: an old man, running, escaping.

"Hold it. Freeze."

Across the alley, with his torso showing above the garbage cans, Canelli was crouched over his gun, holding the big .357 Magnum with both hands, head low, crouching in the approved departmental stance.

"Hold it." Hastings raised his gun, fired in the air. Above him, a woman screamed, a man was shouting, loudly swearing.

As if he'd been hit, Mitchell suddenly faltered, fell heavily to the pavement.

Was he giving it up? Was he—?

"No—" Canelli yelled. *"Don't."*

But the big man in the blue business suit was on one elbow, lifting his arm, raising his hand, aiming the pistol at Canelli—

—as Canelli fired. Once. Twice.

The first shot drove Mitchell back against the pavement, his head smacking the bricks like a rotten melon.

With the second shot the big man's body bucked, as if he'd been kicked hard. Then he lay still, with only the fingers of one hand slightly twitching.

30

As Holloway checked himself in the bathroom mirror, then raised his wrist to check the time, Flournoy spoke through the open bathroom door:

"I still say you should think about this, Austin. It's too early. You should be in seclusion, not talking to reporters. Besides, you don't know what they know—what they've found out from the police."

"It'll take the police days to decide how they're going to handle this, what they're going to do. They'll be looking for guidance. That's what I intend to give them. Guidance." He turned away from the mirror, walked into the living room. Dressed in funereal dark blue, Flournoy was standing in the middle of the room. His expression was grave.

"Austin, we've got to talk."

"It's ten o'clock. We told the reporters ten o'clock."

"I think you should wait for Harlan, Austin, before you make any public statements. I really do. He's probably at the airport by now. You should wait for him."

Decisively, Holloway shook his head. "I don't want to talk to the press with a lawyer beside me. That's begging the question, a presumption of guilt. You should understand that, Herbert."

"I'm not saying you should have him beside you on camera. That's not what I'm saying. But you should talk to him, get his advice, before you go ahead with this."

"Herbert, the few times I've ever taken other people's advice on what to say, it's been disastrous. I learned long go that whatever it is we're selling, it comes from me—from deep down inside me, from my subconscious, if you will. When I keep to that—when I'm talking from deep inside, operating on instinct, that's when I'm most effective. And that's what I intend to do now downstairs. I think I know what needs to be done. I have faith that when I start speaking, the words will be there."

"I understand that, Austin. And, basically, I agree with you. But I'm saying that—"

"I know what you're saying, Herbert. But you must listen to what *I'm* saying." He paused, compelling the other man's fretful attention. "I'm saying that, for better or worse, your fortunes— and mine, too—are tied to whatever it is inside me that produces the words and the gestures and the smiles and the frowns that constitute our entire stock-in-trade. That's always been the case. It's still the case, in good times and bad. And these, certainly, are the bad times. But I'm convinced—I feel deeply—that those inner thoughts will see us through."

"Austin—" Tentatively Flournoy stepped closer, to touch the other man's sleeve. "Austin, I'm not disputing that. I'm simply saying that you've had a shock. We've all had a shock. And I'm suggesting that you should—" He broke off, searching for the phrase. "You should give yourself time, that's all."

"The reporters have been here all night, sniffing around. They've been talking to the police, too. They're going to print something, that's a certainty. I want to make sure they get it right."

Resigned, Flournoy first shook his head, then shrugged, then reluctantly nodded. "If that's what you want . . ."

"That's what I want, Herbert. I've never been more sure of anything, never seen things more clearly."

"What about Sunday? Have you thought about Sunday?"

"Of course."

"And?"

"And it will be a memorial service, of course. For Elton."

"Before I take your questions," he said, "I'd like to make a statement, if you'll allow me." Solemnly, standing erect behind the lectern, he paused, waited for their murmur of sympathetic assent to subside.

"As you all know," he began, "my wife and I—along with all our friends—have suffered a grievous loss. Our only son, Elton, died. And Lloyd Mitchell, too, died, at the same time, in the same horrible accident.

"Most of you know in general what happened. But many of you might not know the details. So, if you'll bear with me—" He paused, allowed his voice to thicken, his eyes to mist. He cleared his throat, wiped judiciously at the corner of each eye.

"It was perhaps inevitable," he said, "that Elton would die as he did last night. For months—years—myself and my wife had feared the knock that finally fell on our door last night.

"Because, you see, each of us must serve God in our own way, in our own time. I was only fifteen when God called me to his service. I was called to finish the work my father began. My call was to the pulpit. But Elton's call was different. Like Sister Teresa—like Christ himself—Elton realized that he must go out among the people. He realized that he must seek out the sinners, talk to them, lay hands on them, help them find their way to God's salvation.

"It was dark, dangerous work. My wife worried about Elton, and so did I. But we respected Elton's calling, respected his convictions. So, as all parents do, we worried in silence, knowing that we couldn't, and shouldn't, try to dissuade Elton from the way he'd chosen to serve God.

"Instead, whenever Elton went forth into the mean streets, I sent a protector along behind him—a guardian angel. That man was Lloyd Mitchell, to whom I've entrusted my life for more than thirty years. Wherever I went, whatever risks I might have taken in God's service, Lloyd was always beside me, protecting me from God's countless enemies.

"And so it was, my friends, that, last night, about ten o'clock, Elton left the safety of his hotel room and went out into the city streets, looking for souls to save. And, as always, Lloyd followed, the silent, secret protector. According to his custom, Elton went deep into the heart of the city's secret center of corruption, where women sell their bodies, and vicious men prey on the virtuous.

"And so it happened that last night, from out of the shadows, Elton was attacked. He was struck on the head, and was pulled into a darkened alleyway, where he was robbed and left to die. It happened suddenly. One second he was alive, the next second his skull was crushed, and—" Holloway broke off, fighting to control a surge of strong, real emotion. Drawing on deep reserves, he said, "—and he was dying." Another pause, to regain control. Then, with the worst behind him, concluding: "Lloyd Mitchell was following Elton, only a half block behind. But, by the time Lloyd reached Elton, it was already too late. And then, tragically, a terrible accident happened. Lloyd had drawn the pistol he always carries, and as Lloyd bent over Elton, with his pistol in his hand, two detectives—Lieutenant Frank Hastings and Inspector Joseph Canelli—arrived on the scene with their own guns drawn. To the policemen, in the darkness, it probably seemed that Lloyd was the murderer, bending over his victim to rob him. Or perhaps Lloyd thought the policemen were the murderers, returning to the scene of their crime. In any case, shots were fired—and Lloyd was killed." He broke off, drank water from a glass placed on the lectern, sadly shook his handsome head. "Of course, we do not blame the police for this terrible tragedy. We realize that they, like us, are victims." As he spoke on a falling note, concluding, he bowed his head, let the moment lengthen into a long silence, an impromptu benediction. Still with his head bowed, he listened for cues: an embarrassed clearing of throats, a shifting of chairs, a few self-conscious whispers. Having been manipulated into joining him in something like silent prayer, the irreverent members of the press were restive. Therefore, it was time to raise his head, square his shoulder, manfully say, "If you have any questions, I'll be happy to answer them."

"Will you be canceling your service tomorrow?" a woman asked.

"After much thought—much prayer—we've decided that we must go on with the service," he answered. "For one thing, it's what Elton would have wanted. Both my wife and I feel very sure about that. And, secondly, we have a duty to go on—a higher duty, to God. We are, literally, soldiers serving in the ranks, God's crusaders. Two of our members have fallen, one struck down by a sinner. But we cannot lay down our arms. When the battle—the war—is done, finally won, then we can pause to grieve. But not now."

"You're known for your opposition to gun control," a man said. "In fact, you told us at your last news conference that you always carry a gun with you. Is that true?"

"Yes, sir, that's true."

"However," the man said, "unfortunately it seems pretty clear that, as you describe one of last night's killings, it would never have happened if Lloyd Mitchell hadn't had a gun. So my question is, will your loss cause you to rethink your opposition to gun control?"

"No, sir, it will not. Just the opposite, in fact. The lesson of this tragedy is that the streets of our cities are dangerous. And until the police are better able to defend our citizens, I devoutly believe that our citizens must defend themselves."

"Would Christ have given that answer, Mr. Holloway?"

Gravely, he nodded. "Yes, sir, I believe he would have. Christ taught us to turn the other cheek. But he was speaking of turning away insults and petty abuse. With one's life at stake, facing a murderer, I believe Christ would counsel resistance in kind. But please—" He lifted an imploring hand. "Please, I don't feel that I have the strength, now, for debate."

A black woman raised her hand. "You seem to be saying that the police are at fault. Will you prosecute them?"

Gently, he shook his head. "No, madam. I'm not saying that. Not at all. I accuse no one. The police were simply doing their duty. No more. No less."

"Speaking of the police," a young man dressed in a wind-breaker said, "there have been persistent rumors that the police department—the Homicide Bureau, in fact—has had the St. Francis under surveillance since Wednesday. There've also been rumors that Homicide investigators have interviewed members of your staff. Does all that have any connection to last night's murders?"

Holloway shook his head. "I'm sorry, but I'm not aware that anything of that kind happened." Projecting a sudden deep exhaustion, he looked away from the questioner, at the same time signaling surreptitiously to Flournoy, who immediately rose to his feet.

"I think I'm going to intervene," Flournoy said. "Mr. Holloway needs rest. And Mrs. Holloway is waiting for him, in seclusion. I'd like to thank you all for coming here today. I hope we've been able to help you with background to this tragedy. I'd only like to add one thing, if I may—" For emphasis, he paused before he said, "The service we'll be presenting tomorrow will, of course, be in the nature of a memorial service for Elton Holloway." He smiled sadly. "That goes without saying, of course. But I thought someone should say it, nevertheless. Meanwhile—" He raised his hands, in farewell. "Meanwhile, good-bye. We hope to see you tomorrow, at the Cow Palace. And remember, the first two rows are always reserved for the press."

31

"**A**ccording to what you say about Lloyd Mitchell," Friedman said, "according to how you describe him, there's only one way this could've come down. Someone told him to take Elton out. And that's what he did."

"It could've been Holloway himself that gave the order," Canelli mused. "I mean—" He shook his head. "I mean, as far as I can see, the way they're set up, and everything, it's pretty much what Holloway says that goes. Like he's—you know—a god." As he spoke, he turned to Hastings, questioning the lieutenant with his eyes.

"There's no way we can know, though," Hastings said. "Holloway could be a figurehead, a cardboard man. Flournoy could be pulling the strings. Or Gloria. We just don't know."

"The question is," Friedman said, "what do we do now? What're our options?"

"By five o'clock tomorrow," Hastings said, "they'll all be back in Los Angeles. And there's not a goddamn thing we can do about it, not without warrants. We've got two bodies, and that's it."

"It could be worse," Canelli offered. "After all, there won't be any more hookers killed. At least not by Elton. Mitchell took care of that for us."

Friedman slapped a pudgy hand on his desktop, hard. "I know Holloway put that pipe in Mitchell's hand. I *know* it. And I just plain can't stand the idea of that unctuous, blasphemous bastard getting on an airplane and leaving town. I mean, I *hate* it."

"Jeez, Lieutenant," Canelli said, turning his attention to Friedman. "Jeez, I can't ever remember seeing you so riled up, I don't think."

Friedman studied the other man for a moment before he said, "That's very interesting, Canelli. Because, come to think about it, you're probably right. In this job, you get used to almost anything if you last long enough—everything but the smells, anyhow. But, personally, I always have trouble adjusting to the fact that people can get away with murder. And the fact is, a couple of times the past year or two, we've had fat cats get away with murder in this city. Literally, get away with murder—just because they're rich and famous. Or, anyhow, rich. And it bothers me. It bothers me a lot."

"Maybe you should've been a social worker," Hastings said. "A do-gooder."

"Very funny." Moodily, Friedman began unwrapping a cigar, searching his pockets for matches.

"So what's the plan?" Hastings said.

Friedman lit the cigar, threw the smoking match into his wastebasket, then pointed to the afternoon paper, open on his desk. "According to the *Sentinel*, Holloway is going ahead with the show tomorrow. I don't know about the two of you, but I intend to be there. And afterward, I intend to talk to Austin Holloway. With or without a warrant, I intend to talk to him, let him know I'll be thinking about him—a lot. I want him to start worrying, looking behind him."

"But—" Hesitantly, Canelli cleared his throat. "But they're having their service at the Cow Palace, Lieutenant. And the Cow Palace isn't in San Francisco. It's in Daly City."

"That'll be our little secret, Canelli. However, since you raise the point, and since a low profile is called for here, you're excused." As he spoke, Friedman turned to Hastings. "Well? What do you say? Tomorrow?"

Smiling, Hastings rose to his feet. "It's a date."

32

Five years ago, when they'd taken The Hour to Cincinnati for a week, there'd been a fire in the Bel Air house. Ever since, wherever she went, she carried the small leather photograph album with her. The album was worn, the leather cracked, the pages dog-eared. It had been her daddy's album; he'd kept it in a dresser drawer, beneath his shirts. When she'd been a little girl, she'd sometimes ventured into her daddy's room and taken the album from beneath the shirts. She took the album to her daddy's bed, where the light from the room's single window was good. Very carefully, she would turn the pages—heavy, awkward pages, weighed with the magic of photographs, some of them dimmed with age, pictures of relatives in period clothing, some of them people she'd never seen. But she'd learned their names from her father; she'd memorized their stories. With the album open in her lap, the faces and the stories called to her from across the years: Uncle Fletcher, who'd gone to Alaska to pan for gold; Aunt Ludie, who had never married, and who never seemed to smile; a cousin named Ned, wearing a cowboy hat and chaps, mounted on a horse, looking sternly at the camera.

Of all her daddy's possessions, she'd only kept his watch, and his Bible, and the photograph album. The album had been half filled with pictures when her father had died. Even now, more than thirty years later, the album wasn't full.

Had Austin ever seen the album?

Did he ever go through her things, like she'd gone through her daddy's things, so long ago?

If he'd done it, gone through her things, would he have told her? Would he have wondered why she'd only included pictures of the children, never pictures of him?

Would he have asked her? Would he have cared enough to ask her?

If he had asked her, what would she have answered? How could she have explained that, since the album was really her daddy's, and since her daddy had hated Austin, it would have been wrong for her to—

At the door, a knock sounded. It was five o'clock, then. Five o'clock exactly, time for her bottle.

As she'd taken Elton his bottle of milk, always on time, so Susan, too, was on time. Always. The milk sustained life, the vodka destroyed life. Babies were born, grew into children, who grew into adults—who finally died.

Some died, some were killed. Murdered.

At first, for the first few months of life, the bones of the skull were fragile, unknit. Even the slightest blow could—

Again, Susan's knock. Still softly, still discreetly. But now subtly more insistent. Because, certainly, Susan was concerned for her, worried about her. They were all worried about her. Their voices had softened. Their eyes had changed, dark with sadness, with sympathy.

"Come in, Susan."

Carrying the embroidered satchel with the bottle inside, Susan Gaines opened the door, came gravely into the room, quietly closed the door. Today, for their ritual ceremony, Susan was dressed in black. Her face was somber.

"How are you feeling, Mrs. Holloway?"

"I feel lost," she answered. "I feel very lost, very alone."

"Yes—" Susan was nodding. "Is there anything I can do, anything I can get you, besides—" She raised the satchel.

"Where's Austin, do you know?"

"He's with Mr. Flournoy. At least he was, a few minutes ago."

"What about Gloria? Where's Gloria?"

"She's in her suite, with her children. She's left word that she doesn't want to be disturbed. I mean—" She frowned. "I mean, she doesn't want just anyone to disturb them. I'm sure she'd like to see you, though."

"Do you know where—?" In confusion, she broke off. *Do you know where Elton is?* she wanted to say. But she couldn't say it, not like that, not as if she were asking which hotel room he was in. Because she wanted to know where his body was, where they'd taken him. But she couldn't say it, couldn't say "body" out loud, not to Susan.

Expectantly, Susan stood waiting. Then, as the silence between them lengthened, Susan moved a half step toward the bar. "Shall I—? Would you—?"

"First," Marvella said, "I wish you'd see Gloria. Tell her I'd like to talk to her. Now. Here. Ask her please."

"Then you don't—" Tentatively, Susan raised the satchel again. "You don't want—?"

"Just put it on the bar, there, for now. Don't open it, though. Not now."

"Yes—" To conceal her obvious surprise, Susan Gaines turned away, walked to the bar.

Another knocking, three short, decisive raps of knuckles on wood, unmistakably Gloria. Even now, saddened though she certainly was, Gloria would be assertive, firm, assured.

Gloria had gotten it all, inherited the best, from both of them. Five years later, when Elton was born, the unwanted child of a love long lost, the blood had gone sour, the genes had been corrupted. The baby had grown into a silent, tortured stranger.

"Come in, Gloria."

Gloria, too, was dressed in mourning: a dark blue dress with a small, formal white collar, a dress that a nun could have worn. Were there reporters watching—savages, lurking in the shadows?

"How are you, Mother?" As she asked the question, Gloria's eyes slid involuntarily to the bar. The unopened bottle of vodka stood where Susan had placed it fifteen minutes before. Between Gloria's eyes, a small crease of puzzlement showed.

A line of colorless liquid inside a bottle . . .

For years, for more than half a lifetime, they'd looked at it, looked silently away—looked at her, looked silently away.

But now Gloria's eyes lingered on the bottle, lingered on her. Still silently. Always silently.

"Are you okay?" Gloria came to her, sat beside her on a small love seat, touched her hand. As she looked down at their hands, still touching, she realized that she, too, was dressed in mourning. It was a change, a significant break in her normal routine. Always, at five o'clock, dressed in a flowing hostess gown, hair coiffed, makeup meticulously drawn, she had awaited Susan's discreet knock. The costume had always been part of the ritual. Just as, on Sundays, in front of the cameras, her dress was—

"Mother?" As she said it, Gloria was squeezing her hand. Just as she'd squeezed Gloria's hand when Gloria had been a child and her attention had wandered.

"Yes—" Wearily, she knew, she returned the pressure.

"Are you all right?"

For a moment she didn't reply. As she sat in silence, she realized that she, too, was staring at the bottle of vodka.

Was the bottle still her friend?

Or her enemy now?

She must speak, must ask the question: "Where is he, Gloria? Where's Elton?"

"He's at a funeral home, Mother. Paly's Funeral Home."

"Have you seen him?"

"No, not at—" Gloria broke off, drew a short, agonized breath. "Not at the funeral home."

"You saw him at the morgue."

"I—I had to identify him, this morning."

"I want to see him."

"Mother, I—" Reaching out to grasp her other hand, holding both her hands now, Gloria was looking at her intently, her face anxiously drawn. "I don't think you should see him so soon. I really don't."

"I'd like you to go with me, Gloria. But if you won't, I'll go alone. I don't want to see him with someone else, with strangers. I want to see him with you. Just with you."

"Let me talk to Dad. Maybe he can—"

"No." Doggedly, vehemently, she shook her head. Repeating: "*No.*"

For a last long, silent moment they sat facing each other, hands clasped, eyes locked. Then, slowly, plainly reluctant, Gloria nodded. "All right. I'll phone down for a car."

Consternation twisted the man's primly pursed mouth, pinched at his nostrils, chilled his eyes.

"The, ah, deceased isn't really ready yet for viewing. We were told—we spoke to Mr. Flournoy, and we agreed—that nine o'clock this evening would be time enough."

Gloria turned to Marvella, took her elbow, guided her to an elaborately carved chair placed beside an elaborately carved table. The air was oppressive, heavy with the cloying fragrance of funereal flowers. A dirge was playing on the speaker system.

When Marvella was seated, Gloria turned abruptly, beckoned for the man in the dark gray double-breasted suit to follow her as she walked into the hallway, out of earshot. She turned, spoke softly, intently:

"What's your name again?"

"Sigler. William Sigler."

"Are you the manager here?"

"Yes, ma'am, I am."

"Do you know who I am, who my mother is?"

"Yes, ma'am, I do." He was a tall man, expert at the dolorous role he played. But now, plainly, he was losing his place in the script, running out of lines.

"Have you started to work on my brother's body?"

"Well, ah, yes, ma'am, we have. But it's only six-thirty. And Mr. Flournoy and I agreed that—"

"What I want you to do," she said, "is get him ready for my mother to look at. I saw him at the morgue. I know the condition of his body. And I understand that—" She broke off, bit her lip. "I understand that his head is—damaged. But I want you to get

him ready for my mother to look at. Now. Right now. He doesn't
have to be in a casket, and he doesn't have to be dressed. You can
drape him, like they did at the morgue. You can drape something
over his head, his skull. And you can—"

"Yes, ma'am. I understand what you're saying. But my
problem is, you see, that we'll be delayed. And I promised Mr.
Flournoy that—"

She stepped close, spoke in a low, furious voice: "Mr.
Flournoy works for my father. He's an employee. Do you
understand that, Mr. Sigler? Do you understand what I'm telling
you?"

"I—ah—"

"The only promise you have to worry about is the promise I
made my mother. Do you also understand *that*, Mr. Sigler?"

Slowly, sadly, he nodded, resigned. "Yes, ma'am," he
answered. "I understand that."

"In here, ladies . . ." Sigler opened a carved oak door,
stepped aside, gestured for them to enter a small, sparsely
furnished, dimly lit room that smelled of something thick and
sweet. A long table had been placed against the far wall. The
table had been draped in black velvet. Except for the face, the
body on the table was completely covered with white sheeting.

"I'll be in the office if you need me," Sigler said, speaking to
Gloria.

"Thank you, Mr. Sigler. We appreciate this." Gloria waited
for her mother to enter the room, then closed the door. They
stood side by side for a moment. With her eyes on her son's face,
Marvella placed her purse on a nearby chair. Then she stood
motionless, hands clasped at her waist, as if she were on stage,
waiting her cue to begin singing. Finally, one slow step at a time,
she moved close, standing within a few feet of the body.

Until now, she'd never seen it: the similarity between her
daddy's face and her son's face. The shape of the forehead and the
line of the jaw were the same. And their noses were similar, too,
long and flat.

But their eyes had been different. And the eyes were the

windows of the soul, someone had written. Her daddy's eyes had been lively; her son's eyes had been lusterless—dead, before they died.

Standing before her daddy's coffin, staring at the dead face profiled against billows of white satin, she'd felt as empty as she felt now, just as helpless, just as lost.

Both of them, murdered. Both of them with their skulls crushed, lying in their own blood—her father on the path that led across the fields to town, her son lying in an alleyway, a stranger in a strange city.

Standing before her father's casket, dry eyed, she'd felt her life lurch, begin to fall away.

Now, looking down at her son, his body shrouded, she could feel her life ending. Finally, mercifully ending, leaving only the final riddle of death to be solved.

"It was Mitchell," she said. "I know it was Mitchell."

Standing in the shadows, a witness as well as a victim, Gloria tried to speak, tried to deny it.

33

Standing in the corridor across from the elevators, the security man came to attention as the elevator stopped, the doors opened, and Gloria and Marvella stepped out. Nodding to the security man, Gloria moved with her mother to the door of Marvella's room.

"I want to spend some time with the children, Mother, then put them to bed. Are you all right?"

Marvella nodded. "Yes, Gloria. Thank you."

"I'll tell Susan to sit with you. Are you ready for tomorrow, for The Hour? Is your dress ready? A dark dress?"

"Susan's got it ready. She always does, you know. She's very efficient. Always very efficient." She spoke in a low, uninflected voice. Her eyes were far away.

"After I've put the children to bed I'll look in on you. Shall I?" As she spoke, Gloria tried Marvella's door. The knob turned; the door swung partially open.

"Where's Austin?" Marvella asked. "Do you know?"

"He's with Herbert, I think, in the conference room. Harlan Collins is with them."

"The lawyer?"

Gloria nodded. "Yes."

"But it's too late for lawyers—too late for everything."

Facing Marvella, Gloria looked intently into her mother's eyes. Should she call the doctor who'd been summoned from Los Angeles, her father's personal doctor? Should she demand that her mother be sedated? Or would she sedate herself with vodka, as she did every night? Gloria touched her mother on the forearm, ventured a smile, pushed the door open wider. "Let's go inside, Mother. I'll call Susan. You should lie down, rest. I think I'll call Dr. Piernan."

As she entered her sitting room, Marvella shook her head, sighed, sank onto the chaise longue, put her handbag on the floor. "No, don't call the doctor. I don't need a doctor."

"Then I'll call Susan." Still with her eyes on her mother's face, searching for clues, she moved to the phone. "What's her room number?

"I don't want Susan, Gloria." As she said it, she allowed her eyes to close, allowed her head to sink back against the chaise. "I don't want to see anyone but Austin."

"I'll tell him, then. I'll tell him you want to see him."

"No—" Slowly, as if the movement caused her pain, Marvella shook her head. "No, don't tell him."

"Mother, I—I hate to leave you. But the children, they're upset. I've got to see how they are."

"I'm all right, Gloria. Now that I've seen Elton, I'll be all right. Thank you for going with me. It was hard for you, I know." She spoke without opening her eyes, still lying motionless. In exhausted repose, with sunken eyes and mouth gone slack, the musculature of her face had shrunken on the bones beneath: a death's-head, its beauty distended by despair.

"I'll come back after I've put the children to bed."

"Yes . . ."

For a moment Gloria stood in silence beside the chaise. Then she bent over her mother, kissed her lightly on the forehead. The acknowledgment was a soft, sleepy sigh, nothing more. Gloria straightened, stood irresolutely for a moment before she went to the door. With her hand on the knob, she looked at the bar. The bottle of vodka was still unopened, its seal intact, its clear liquid reflecting the mirrored surfaces of the small bar. In the quiet room, the bottle was the third presence, the ultimate enigma.

As the door clicked closed, Marvella opened her eyes. Her gaze was on the bar, on the bottle.

Four steps, and a twist of the top, to break the seal. The ice cubes were in the tiny refrigerator, together with the tonic water and the limes. Or, if she chose, she could eliminate the tonic, and instead pour the vodka over the ice, and add a dash of bitters. She would return to the chaise, stretch out, lift the crystal glass to her lips, take the first swallow. Instantly, with that first swallow, the world beyond the room would begin to soften. The pain of the past would subside; only pleasurable memories would remain, suffusing her, bearing her back to those days of sunlight, those nights of limpid expectation, of forbidden ecstasy. Until finally sensation ceased, setting her free.

But what of the body beneath the shroud?

What of her father's body, long ago returned to dust?

What of their shattered skulls? Could vodka liberate her from the phantasms that followed upon these images, these terrible, terrible memories?

They were dead, the two of them. Liberated, finally free, all sensation ceased, all torture stilled. *Praise the Lord*, Austin would intone tomorrow. And the echoes would come back: *Praise the Lord*.

They were free, but she was still enslaved, still his prisoner. Until now, her nightly bottle of vodka had been enough to numb the pain.

Until now, but no longer.

If only death had liberated her father, and only death had liberated her son, then only death would liberate her, finally set her free, really free.

Amen.

Outside, in the corridor, one of the security men looked at her expectantly. His eyes were sympathetically solicitous, his voice soft: "Can I help you, Mrs. Holloway?"

"Yes. I've got to get into my husband's suite, to get some things. He's not there. Do you have a passkey?"

"I—ah—" Consternation shadowed his eyes, puckered his forehead. She knew what he was thinking, could calculate his dilemma. He needed Mitchell's approval to open Austin's door, even to her. And Mitchell was dead.

"*Do* you have a key?"

Slowly, reluctantly, he nodded. She nodded in return, then began walking toward her husband's door. Behind her, the security man's footsteps obediently followed. She heard the jingle of his keys, coming free from his pocket.

Would he be blamed for what would happen, this nice young man with the sympathetic eyes, whose name she could never remember? She hoped not.

Yes, it was there, as deadly as a snake: a blue-steeled snake, concealed beneath the socks and underwear. God, how she hated them, feared the guns they kept, both her father and her husband.

Until now, she'd hated them. Until this very moment, when the cold steel pressed to her belly beneath her blouse produced an obscenely erotic thrill, a long-forgotten rush of forbidden excitement.

34

"**W**hat we should do tonight," Ann said, "is go out for dinner and then see a movie." Seated beside Hastings on their living room sofa, she leaned forward, took a copy of the *Sentinel* from the coffee table, opened it to the entertainment section. "You have no idea how much good it'll do you, to see a movie."

Hastings sighed, then nodded. "Fine." He kept his gaze straight ahead, focused somewhere just beyond the room's far wall. With the newspaper on her lap, Ann let a long moment of silence pass as she looked at him.

"And over dinner," she said finally, "you should tell me about it. Just this once. I know how you feel about bringing worries home from the office. But rules are meant to be broken. It's a cliché, but it's true. We should—"

In the hallway, the phone rang.

"Shall I get it?" she asked.

Sighing again, Hastings rose, shaking his head. She watched him as he walked into the hallway. From the first, the first time they went out together for an Italian dinner in North Beach, she'd always liked to watch him move: gracefully, economically, confidently, quietly purposeful. And the movements, she'd later discovered, summarized the man. He was a quiet, purposeful man, more self-confident than most men his age and status, even though his early life had been difficult. Sometimes they talked about it: the ones he'd won, the ones he'd lost. "Some of us get blindsided," he'd once said. "I guess that's what happened to me when I was a teenager."

In the hallway, she heard him quietly talking on the phone. From the sound of his voice, from its cadence, she knew he was talking to Friedman.

Blindsided . . .

"When you think about it," her father had once remarked, "you can sum up most people's lives in a hundred words or less, just like you were entering a boxtop contest."

And Frank had once said something similar, telling her about his own life. He'd always been big for his age, and well coordinated. And that, he'd said, pretty much summed him up. Because athletics—football, especially—had been his whole life. Until one Sunday afternoon in Detroit when a defensive tackle had clipped him. The other team had been penalized—and he'd gone to the hospital with a ruined knee.

He'd grown up in the "middle of the middle class." His father had been a small-time real-estate broker who ran off with his "girl Friday." Frank had been fourteen, and had just made the freshman football team at San Francisco's Washington High. He'd come home from practice to find his mother sitting at the kitchen table, crying, clutching the note his father had left propped on the refrigerator.

The week after Frank had been elected captain of the varsity football team, his father and his "girl Friday" had been killed in west Texas. It had been a one-car accident, in the wee hours. His father had been drunk, and had been three payments behind on the five-year-old Packard he'd been driving. When he heard about the accident, Frank had gone to his room, locked the door, and tried to cry.

When he'd told Ann about it, she'd heard his voice thicken, seen his eyes glistening. And somehow she'd known that he'd never told anyone about it, about trying to cry when he'd heard his father had been killed.

From the hallway, she heard his voice rising. Invariably, at some point in any conversation with Pete Friedman, his voice rose, an expression of that particular level of exasperation with which he expressed his essential fondess for Friedman. Women hugged each other. Men punched each other on the arm. Pete teased Frank, who obligingly bristled.

From high school, he'd gone to Stanford, on a football scholarship. For Frank, the amiable clichés of the campus football hero hadn't come true. His yardage-gained statistics were impressive, but he'd never been at ease among the sons and daughters of the rich, probably because he hadn't been at ease with himself. His mother, during those years, had sold better dresses at Sears. And Frank had always—

In the hallway, the sound of his voice had ceased; the phone rattled in its cradle. As he came into the living room, he was smiling: a small, quizzical smile.

"If you think I'm suffering because of this Holloway thing," he said, "you should talk to Pete. I've been working with him for twelve years. And I've never seen him so upset."

"Upset? *Pete?*"

"Hard to believe, I know." The smile widened and warmed as he sat beside her, moved closer. With their thighs touching, she felt a sexual quickening. And—yes—he felt it, too. His left arm was around her shoulders, drawing her to him. She turned, looked at him, smiled, then kissed him: a thoughtful, contented, companionable kiss. Answering, his mouth was open, inviting, exploring. His breathing was faster now. His right hand came to the small of her back, urging her body into full contact with his, both of them twisted on the couch. This was the beginning of the jokes passion could play: this straining together, half on the couch and half off, reclining but not reclining, both of them aroused: two awkward, inarticulate teenagers, making out on the living room sofa.

So, together, they drew back, smiling into each other's eyes, both of them breathing deeply.

"Where're the kids?" he asked.

"Dan's out on a date. And Billy's with his father for the weekend."

"Then what would you think about me taking you into the bedroom?"

"No dinner? No movie?"

"The late show, maybe."

"Hmmm . . ."

Lying on his back, staring up at the bedroom ceiling, Hastings drew a deep, drowsy breath. At ten o'clock on a warm September evening, with Ann sleeping contentedly beside him, the world was better than it had been only a few hours ago. Whatever else sex accomplished, the simple act of orgasm was a quick, effective means of reducing tensions, inducing sleep, putting the day into better perspective.

Sex, someone had once said, was much like money: when you didn't have enough, you thought about it all the time. But when you were married the problem diminished, ideally disappeared. Like tonight. A touch of their thighs, a kiss, and they were on their way to the bedroom, amiably stumbling as they held each other close, giggling.

Married . . .

That's how he thought of it, that they were married. Did Ann, too, think of them that way? They'd never talked about it, might never talk about it. Each of them had been divorced. Each of them had two children, his in Detroit, hers here, living with her. Each of them had been deeply wounded by divorce. They'd never talked about that, either. Not in so many words. But each knew that the other wasn't ready to marry again.

They'd met a little less than two years ago. On their second date, after dinner at a Russian restaurant on Clement Street, she'd invited him in for a drink. They'd gone to bed that night, made love in the same bed they shared now. Billy and Dan, her two sons, had been visiting their grandparents. He'd stayed all night, and she'd made him breakfast the next morning. The rest had been a love story: a calm, comfortable love story that sometimes seemed too good to be true.

Then he'd made the mistake of turning his back on a spaced-out cultist who'd been standing within reach of two ceremonial Mayan spears crossed on the wall. The skull fracture had put Hastings in the hospital for ten days. Ann had picked him up at the hospital and taken him here, to her flat, to convalesce. Two months later, he'd given up his apartment.

He yawned, settled himself more comfortably, turned on his side to face Ann. She was lying on her back, mouth slightly open, profiled against the pale light from the window. Her fine-spun tawny blonde hair lay across her cheek, diffusing the perfection of her profile. Gently, he touched her at the temple, drawing the hair back from her face. When she stirred, he smiled.

35

With Holloway inside the first limousine, Flournoy stood on the sidewalk, looking back at the other two limos drawn up in front of the St. Francis. Marvella and the grandchildren were already inside the second limo, finally settled. Now Gloria was striding briskly across the sidewalk, getting into the car, pulling the door smartly closed. The third limo, carrying the security men, the program director, and Pastor Bob, The Hour's longtime featured soloist, was ready to go. Flournoy nodded to the two security men standing watchfully on the sidewalk, and got into the limousine beside Holloway. One of the security men stepped quickly forward, closed the door, then slapped the car's roof twice. As the limousine moved away from the curb, Flournoy checked his watch. The time was exactly eleven A.M., two hours to air time.

Flournoy settled heavily into the limo's leather seat, glanced at the window dividing the passenger compartment from the driver, checked the switch on the small microphone.

"I've talked to Harlan," Flournoy said, half turned in his seat to face Holloway, "and he agrees with me, absolutely. So after the service, you and Marvella are going directly to the airport. It's all arranged. You'll be going in a chartered airplane. Hennessy will be going with you. He's got all the details, and your light luggage. The point is, day after tomorrow, there's a coroner's inquest. And Harlan thinks it'd be better if you're not here in San Francisco, in part because you could be subpoenaed. He also thinks it'd be better if you, ah, avoid the reporters. I think so, too. Definitely."

Sitting with his head resting against the cushions, eyes closed, Holloway made no response. His head moved loosely, surrendered to the gentle motion of the limousine. The flesh of his face was waxen, sagging in loose folds beneath his jowls.

Only minutes before, projecting his public persona for the news cameramen waiting for him in the hotel lobby, Holloway had been masterful: the strong, saddened patriarch, majestically bearing his burden, an inspiration to lesser men. That was the myth, those few minutes on camera. This, Flournoy realized, was reality: this tired, slack man, suddenly grown old.

"Austin?"

Still with his eyes closed, Holloway nodded. "Yes. Fine. Whatever Harlan says."

Relieved, Flournoy settled himself more comfortably. The ride to the Cow Palace would take about twenty minutes. It was valuable time, the two of them alone, able to speak freely, confidentially, concisely:

"I'll come down to Los Angeles tomorrow, if I can possibly do it," Flournoy said. "Gloria will handle all the funeral arrangements. She'll come down to Los Angeles with the—" He hesitated. "With the bodies."

"Yes . . ."

"Did Mitchell have any relatives, do you know?"

"No close relatives," Holloway answered. "There was just an older brother. But he died several years ago."

"We don't want them buried with the same ceremony," Flournoy said. "That wouldn't be appropriate."

"No, it wouldn't. You're right. But Mitchell's ceremony must be first-class. Absolutely first-class. And I plan to speak."

"Will you speak at Elton's service?"

"No, not at Elton's. That's not done, I don't think."

Approvingly, Flournoy nodded. "You're right."

"I'll speak for Elton today."

"Yes . . ." Flournoy cleared his throat, touched the knot of his tie, glanced again at the glass partition. Then: "I—ah—I'm concerned about Marvella, Austin. She's not acting normally."

"She's had a shock. We've all had a shock." As he spoke, Holloway opened his eyes, sat up straighter, looked at the other man.

"But that's the point. I mean—" Flournoy hesitated, choosing his words. "I mean, let's face it, Marvella's been drinking for years. It—it's part of her daily routine. But last night, according to Susan, she didn't drink a drop. And she went to see—" Once more he hesitated, this time delicately, regretfully. "She went to see Elton, at the mortuary. Without consulting anyone except Gloria. And today, this morning, she seems to be off in her own world. She's not connecting."

"Susan will take care of her. And Gloria, too. They'll take care of her."

Flournoy nodded. "I understand that. And you're right, of course. She *has* had a shock. But I was thinking about today, about The Hour. Maybe you should tell her not to appear today. The people will understand. It could even be a plus, when you think about it."

"She wants to appear, though. She told Gloria that she particularly wants to appear, to sing."

"Have you talked to Marvella yourself?"

Holloway nodded. "I spoke to her last night, late. And this morning, too."

"And?"

"She'll be all right, Herbert. Trust me."

Seated side by side on the two jump seats, their favorite places, the two children faced Marvella and Gloria.

"How long does it take to go to heaven?" James asked. "If Elton and Mitchell started on Friday night, then how long would it take them to get there?"

"Not long," Gloria answered. "It just takes a little while."

"But how *long*? Fifteen minutes?"

"I suppose so," Gloria answered. "I suppose it'd take about fifteen minutes."

"I miss Mitchell more than I miss Elton," Carole said. "Elton never played with us, even if he was our uncle. But Mitchell played with us sometimes."

"Once he let me hold his gun. And I pulled the trigger, too." As he spoke, James raised a thumb and straightened forefinger, aimed out the window. "Pow. Pow pow pow." With each shot, he jerked his arm upward, simulating a pistol's recoil.

"James, please . . ." Gloria shook her head. "Don't do that. Not now." As she spoke, she turned to look at Marvella, who was staring steadily out the window, her eyes fixed on the western profile of the city: Twin Peaks, with countless houses and small apartment buildings clinging precariously to the lower slopes, and greenery tracing the topmost ridges against a clear blue sky.

"It's a beautiful city," Marvella said. "It's magic, really. Pure magic." Her voice was dreamily soft. Her eyes were fixed on some far distant vista, bemused, lost in time past or time future. "You should live here, Gloria, you and the children. You'd like it here. I know you would."

"We've got to live in Los Angeles, though. Because of The Hour."

"The Hour . . ." Still gazing pensively out the side window, Marvella gently shook her head. "It's more important than we are, Gloria. Soon it'll be more important than James and Carole. Maybe it's more important than they are already." She turned to face the children, looking at each of them in turn. "You shouldn't be here, in this big car, all dressed up. You shouldn't be onstage, singing. You don't even know what the hymns mean, most of them. Do you?"

Frowning, the two children exchanged puzzled looks. Gloria was about to speak when Marvella said, "You should be out playing with friends. It's a nice, sunny day. You should be playing."

"Mother, they—"

Ignoring the gentle interruption, her eyes unfocused now, Marvella said, "It was the same with me. My father was a preacher, you know. And Austin's father, too. He was a preacher. So I know what it's like, how it feels, not to be like other children. And your mother, too—she knows how it feels. Except that, by the time your mother was your age, her father was famous—or, anyhow, getting famous. That was in the fifties, when television was just starting out. Austin had been on radio, you see—and when he got a chance at television, he took it. And that's when he changed, when he started to change. Or maybe . . ." Frowning, she shook her head, puzzled by a sudden thought. "Or maybe he didn't change. Maybe he was always the way he was, and I just never saw it, until the money started to come in. Because that's all he cared about, then—the money. He was possessed by it, all that money. But now it's something more, besides the money. Now it's the power he's got over people. He'll do anything to keep that power. Anything at all . . ." Her voice faded as her eyes wandered again to the window. In the silence, Gloria saw her children look at each other, then turn to look at their grandmother, solemnly studying her.

"He sold his soul to the Devil," Marvella said. "He made a pact with the Devil. And we're part of it, too—we're all part of it. Because he sold our souls, too, along with his." She broke off, numbly shook her head, struggled to find the words she needed to finish the thought: "And that's why Elton died Friday night." As she spoke, she moved closer to the door, away from the others. Shoulders hunched, head bowed, forehead pressed forlornly against the window, she was withdrawing from them. In her lap she held her purse. She held the purse with both hands, clutching it close, as a child clutches a long-favored possession, for security.

"Let's sit down in front," Friedman said, pointing. "The only empty seats're in the first two rows."

"They're reserved." Hastings pointed to a small PRESS ONLY sign.

Mock-dolefully, Friedman shook his head. "There're badge flashers in this business, and there're non-badge-flashers. And you're just about the most dedicated non-badge-flasher I ever knew, honest to God." Impatiently, he gestured Hastings into the second row, with three empty seats close by. Shaking his head and raising a protesting hand, a tall young man in a blue blazer was coming down the aisle toward them. Friedman waited for the usher to come close before he surreptitiously produced his badge.

"Police," he said. "City police. We're working with your security people."

"But—" Worriedly, the clean-cut young usher shook his head. "But this is the press section."

"Exactly. That's where we're supposed to be sitting." He turned his back on the usher, and followed Hastings, who was already seated, eyes front, ignoring Friedman. As Friedman sat down beside him, Hastings said sotto voce, "'City police'?"

"I couldn't very well have said 'San Francisco,' could I? And if I'd said 'Daly City,' why, that would've been a lie."

"Good thinking."

"Thanks."

Twisting in his seat, Hastings scanned the audience, all of them seated in the first tier of seats, facing a stage that had been erected close to the front row. A blue curtain divided the cavernous Cow Palace down the center, with the stage backed against the curtain. High above the stage, lights and loudspeakers hung from the enormous curved steel girders that made the Cow Palace one of the largest clear-span buildings in the world. The stage was draped in rich golden cloth, iridescent in the amber glow of floodlights. Except for a plain wooden pulpit and a set of risers for the choir, the stage was deserted. Between the stage and the front row of seats, separated by a steel railing, music stands and empty chairs were arranged in a semicircle around a large organ. Like the draperies, the organ was an iridescent gold.

"There must be twenty thousand people here," Hastings said. "And they're still coming in."

"I keep telling you, TV evangelism is big business."

"Will they pass collection plates, do you think?"

Friedman shrugged. "If they do, it'll probably be just for appearance. The real money comes from the telephone number they run at the bottom of the TV screen."

"So what's the plan?"

"We're going to talk to Holloway. One way or the other, after he finishes, we're going to talk to him."

"We're going to sweat a confession from him. In Daly City. Is that why we're here?"

"We're here," Friedman answered, "because, as Canelli observed, Holloway rings all my bells. And that was before his tame gorilla killed his crazy son, the mass murderer."

"Serial murderer," Hastings corrected automatically.

"You're pretty blasé about all this, considering that it was you Mitchell was shooting at."

"He missed."

"You're getting to an age when you should start to think about staying out of dark alleys," Friedman said. "That's what the chain of command is all about, you know. We devise the strategy, and the rank-and-filers take the risks. We get paid for— Ah." He interrupted himself as a richly robed man rounded the corner of the stage and made his way gravely toward the organ, his head bowed over clasped hands, moving one slow, measured step at a time. "Ah—the show's about to begin."

"Okay, folks, everyone ready?" As he'd done so often before, the assistant director grinned at them: a genial coach, guiding them through these last few seconds before they fixed their smiles in place and stepped through the parted curtains into the heart-racing glare of the spotlights, with the pale ovals of countless anonymous faces upturned in the half-light beyond.

This was the mummer's moment of magic, this addictive rush of anxious anticipation, waiting protected in the backstage semidarkness for the final cue that would send them out to face their performer's fate.

On the other side of the curtain, the last strains of "Nearer My God to Thee" were rising, holding, finally fading to silence. The applause began, rose, crested, held—and finally trickled down to silence. Now Holloway was speaking, softly at first, gathering the audience to him, working them gently, lovingly, expertly. At the curtain, with his hand resting lightly on the fold beside the parting, the assistant director stood poised, ready. His face had gone blank now, his attention centered on the small earphone that connected him to the control booth suspended high above them, on the far side of the curtain.

But now, with the cue coming up, the assistant director's automatic, sustaining smile flickered, suddenly faded. Anxiously, he stepped close to Marvella, urgently whispering, "You've got your purse, Mrs. Holloway. Give it to me. I'll keep it for you."

Slowly, gently, she shook her head. "No. I want it with me today." As she spoke, dreamily decisive, Holloway's voice was falling on cadence, concluding. Their cue was only moments away.

"But—" The assistant director looked at Marvella, looked down at the purse, looked appealingly at Gloria. She shrugged, turned away. Now the assistant director looked anxiously at the curtain. Then, peevishly resigned, he stepped to the curtain, nodded to a watchfully waiting stagehand. The two men grasped the heavy curtain, drew it aside. Onstage, at the pulpit, precisely on cue, Holloway turned to face them as they came through the parted curtain: first Marvella, then Gloria, finally the two children. Following Marvella with his eyes as she walked to the spot the director had marked in rehearsal, Holloway raised his arms wide, in loving salute. He was smiling: a patriarch's sad, grieving smile, consummately projected. A long, sympathetic round of applause had swept the audience as the curtains parted. But then, as he held the pose, still facing his family, still solemnly smiling upon them, waiting for the applause to die, Holloway realized that his smile-for-the-cameras was jeopardized by an involuntary frown as he saw the purse Marvella carried, clutched close in both hands.

She's not acting normally, Flournoy had said.

As always, Flournoy had been right. Ominously right. Because her face was rigid, a stranger's face, staring at him with a stranger's eyes.

But, with the applause fading, he must turn to face the audience, a helpless victim of the performer's imperative to constantly fill a void. As always, he would make a short speech, followed by the introduction of the "Holloway family hymn." Backed up by the choir, the family would sing as the cameras came in close on their faces, especially the children's faces, as they stood holding to their mother's hands, earnestly singing. Then, with the hymn finished, the choir would file offstage. After a few loving words from Holloway, usually followed by a fond caress for each of the children, the family would follow the choir, leaving Holloway to deliver the day's sermon.

Today, facing the audience, Holloway allowed a long moment of silence to lengthen to its outermost limits as he looked out over the thousands of faces, most of them upturned: the faithful, patiently waiting—and the unfaithful, too, also waiting.

"Most of you," he began, "are familiar with the format of this weekly service. Most of you, thanks be to the Lord—" He raised his eyes to near camera level, smoothly transitioning from the in-house audience to the TV audience. "—most of you invite us regularly into your homes on Sundays so that we can worship together, giving thanks for this wonder of television, God's own miracle, that enables us to spend this precious hour together each week.

"Most of you, as I say, are familiar with our routine, with our way of doing things. We've become predictable—comfortingly, reassuringly predictable, the way members of a family, one vast God-fearing family, become predictable to one another. Oh, yes—" Tolerantly smiling, he nodded. "Oh, yes, some will say, I suppose, that it's dull, knowing what's about to be said, knowing exactly what comes next. But I don't think it's dull, my friends. I think it's wonderful, being that close. I think—I'm sure, absolutely sure—that God meant us to live like this, in close communion with one another. I think God wants us—commands us—to live like that. However—" He broke off, lowered his eyes to the pulpit, sadly shook his silvery head.

"However, as it does in all families, there sometimes come breaks in these routines, in these reassuring rhythms of life. And that's what happened just this last week, to our family—" As he spoke, he turned toward his wife and daughter and grandchildren, all of them standing at their designated places, ten feet from him. The children, he saw, were beginning to fidget. But Gloria was controlling them, her hands knuckle-white. As always, he could count on Gloria.

"And if I may—" He turned again toward the cameras. "If I may, I'd like to tell you what happened to us—what tragedy befell our family on Friday night. It—it won't be easy, telling you. I may stumble. But if you'll bear with me—if you'll pray with me to find the words—I'd like to tell you what happened on Friday night."

Once more standing with his eyes lowered, gripping the lectern with both hands, as if for support, he could sense a welling up of sympathy from beyond the glare of the footlights. He'd been right about this—about the wisdom of coming to this audience, in this city, with this sermon. Because, in spite of themselves, despite all their degenerate sophistication, they were with him, these San Franciscans. Today—now—here—their hearts were with him.

He raised his eyes, let the silence lengthen as he looked out over the audience. When he finally spoke, he allowed his voice to thicken, allowed his eyes to mist, suggesting tears.

"Every family has its mavericks, its stubborn, willful sons. And Elton was the maverick in our family. He wanted his own ministry, distinct from my ministry—just as I wanted my ministry, distinct from my father's. That's human nature, part of every son's rite of passage. In the nature of things, the old among us must give way to the young.

"And so it was that Elton established his own ministry. He established it among the poor, and the downtrodden, and the disheartened. He went out among them, sought out the misfits and outcasts, followed them down their mean streets and dark, dangerous alleyways, doing his best to help them, pray with them, save them for Christ. While the rest of us remained at our ease, safe and secure, doing God's work, Elton was risking his life, night after night, seeking out sin at its source, praying with the robbers and the rapists and, yes, even the prostitutes among us, doing his eternal best to save them.

"And so it was, dear friends, that Elton was walking the dark, dangerous streets of the district San Franciscans call the Tenderloin, on Friday night. We'll—'' He broke off, dropped his eyes, cleared his throat, blinked—then raised his head heavily, to look full into the camera. "We'll never know what happened, really happened, Friday night. There'll never be proof, not the kind of proof that would convince a judge or a jury. And yet I know precisely what happened. I know that, while Elton was at work, imploring some poor, benighted sinner to take Christ for his saviour, another sinner attacked Elton, and killed him, and took the few dollars Elton carried with him. And so—'' Struggling for control, he broke off. Then, huskily: "And so, that anonymous sinner took Elton from us, Friday night.

"And so this service, today, is dedicated to Elton. And I hope you'll join with me in prayer for the soul of one dearly beloved servant of Christ, who died as he lived, saving souls for God.'' He closed his eyes, bowed his head, dropped his voice to its lowest, most solemn register as he began the prayer.

"Jesus Christ,'' Friedman muttered, both outraged and awed, "Talk about chutzpah. Talk about the ultimate blasphemy. Talk about the goddamn big lie, this guy's—''

"*Shhh.*'' Uneasily, Hastings ignored a hostile stare from the woman seated on his right.

"What 'shhh'? Jesus, it's your hide this guy could nail to the barn. Your hide and Canelli's hide. He gets down to Los Angeles, he's going to call another press conference. He's going to accuse you guys, sure as hell, of killing Mitchell without cause. This time next week, you could be up on charges. Both of you.''

Watching Holloway finish the prayer, caught up in spite of himself by the sonorous phrases, Hastings made no reply.

In the control booth suspended high above the audience, Flournoy flicked the switch that silenced his microphone. Softly, incredulously, he spoke to the director, who sat intently before the three camera monitors. The director's fingers hovered delicately above the toggles that cut between the three live cameras.

"He's doing it,'' Flournoy said. "He's never been better.

Never.'' Marveling, he shook his head. "Incredible. Really incredible.''

"And now—" Holloway turned to face his family. "Now—without Elton—my family will observe the most meaningful part of this hour we spend with you, joining together to sing today's featured hymn. Because of the tragedy that's touched our lives, they've chosen "Come to the Church in the Wildwood," which was Elton's favorite hymn from the time he was just a—'' He broke off, blinked, cleared his throat, finally finished: "—just a little boy.''

As the organ led into the hymn and the overhead microphones began lowering on their cords before them, Gloria squeezed her children's hands, then released them, signifying that, in moments, the cameras would be on them, and they must begin singing with her. But, with the organ introduction almost completed and the microphones fully lowered, Gloria saw sudden puzzlement register on her father's face. Following the disapproving direction of his gaze, she saw her mother stepping forward, leaving her mark, moving toward the pulpit. As Marvella advanced, one slow, stiff, dreamwalker's step at a time, Holloway's puzzled expression changed to vexation, then to mild alarm. With his back to the cameras, urgently, he looked to Gloria for some sign, some explanation. In moments, the organ introduction would be finished, and they must begin singing. But now Marvella was within arm's length of the lectern. With her eyes on the audience, she was smiling slightly, ethereally, the way she always smiled just before she began singing. Mindful that one of the three cameras could see him as he turned to face her, Holloway extended both hands, as if to welcome her to stand beside him at the pulpit. Marvella put her handbag on the pulpit beside Holloway's Bible and reached for the microphone, bending the flexible shaft to suit her height. Moving one step aside, Holloway looked at the organist, covertly shook his head. Smoothly, the organist softened his sound, allowed the strains of "Come to the Church in the Wildwood" to slowly fade into silence. Looking out across the audience with empty eyes, Marvella timidly cleared her throat, nervously licked her lips.

Pushing his lightweight Lucite headset down around his neck, Flournoy leaned intently forward. Frowning, he glanced at the three monitors. Of course, the red light glowed beneath the monitor that focused on Holloway and Marvella, standing at the lectern. Simultaneously, Flournoy and the director exchanged wary, puzzled glances before both men returned their eyes to the monitors. Nervously, the director advanced the volume control as Marvella's voice began coming over the loudspeaker.

"There are about five hundred people," Marvella said, "who work for my husband. That's how many people it takes to put on The Hour, and do the direct mailings, and then handle the other mail, and all those checks. And there's the Temple of Light, too, in Los Angeles. It takes a lot of people just to clean it, and change the light bulbs. And all that's not even counting the college. That's another few hundred people right there, in the college.

"But when I first met my husband, there was just one person working for him—not really working for him, even, because a lot of the time Austin didn't have enough money to pay him, or have anything for him to do, not really. But they were together, Austin and Lloyd—Lloyd Mitchell, his name was. And they were bound together, he and Austin, bound fast together. Because when Lloyd was a young man, and just married, he found his wife with another man. And he killed them. Both of them, right in the bedroom. He slaughtered them, some said, like cattle. And then he went to the sheriff, and surrendered himself. And he went to prison. For years, he was in prison."

"What the hell?" Flournoy muttered. "What's she *doing*?"

"But then," Marvella was saying, "they let him out of prison, paroled to Austin, as long as his behavior was good. So Lloyd became the first person that Austin ever owned. He—"

"*Marvella*—" Angrily, involuntarily, Holloway stepped quickly toward her. But then he heard the single word "Marvella" echo and reecho, and he realized the microphone was still live. And beside the camera lenses, tiny red lights still glowed. Desperately, he stepped back, looked at Gloria, who still stood motionless, holding her children tightly by their hands. Gloria's expression was blank, utterly blank. She couldn't help him—or wouldn't help him. Now he turned toward the part in the curtain, where the assistant director should be showing himself—the assistant director, Flournoy, someone should be there, someone to assume command, someone to come onstage, take Marvella by the arm, lead her gently, firmly away, let him recover the microphone and the cameras. Then, with a single gesture, a single sad, sympathetic phrase, he could suggest that the loss of her child had deranged Marvella, made her—

"Austin came to the town where my daddy preached," she was saying, still staring blankly straight ahead, out over the audience, "and Austin made a deal with my daddy, to share the church, share expenses, he said. My daddy never liked Austin, never trusted him, really. But Daddy needed the money, so he did it, made the deal. And for a while, it worked fine. Because, even then, Austin was a good preacher—" For the first time, she took her eyes from the audience, turned to Holloway, stood silently staring at him. Her face was still expressionless, her eyes still utterly empty.

"Maybe it'll be okay," the director was saying. "It could be okay. It could play."

"A *good* preacher," she repeated, still facing Holloway. She spoke very softly, her voice hardly more than a whisper. But she was close enough to the microphone, Holloway knew, for her words to be broadcast, nationwide, over more than two hundred TV affiliates, live.

Live.

Meeting her eyes, he tried to smile. His expression, he knew, must be charitable, must be loving. Because this was the mother of the son he was eulogizing. Until the cameras went blind and the microphone at the pulpit went dead, he must keep his eyes fixed kindly, lovingly upon his wife, must keep the smile in place. Covertly, he glanced at the tiny red light still glowing beside the camera. Meaning that, taking a calculated risk, Flournoy had decided to let the show run, let the camera roll. Because there was a chance—a good percentage chance, probably—that her monologue, poignantly portraying a mother's grief, would play, live, the way a sermon could never play. And Flournoy was a percentage player.

But Flournoy didn't know what he knew—what he and Mitchell, only the two of them, knew.

"I suppose," she was saying, finally turning back to face the audience, "that I fell in love with him, with Austin, because he was so much like his daddy. I've thought about it a good deal, these last two days, and that's what I've decided. I was only sixteen when Austin came to town. But I was an old sixteen, and the boys in town didn't interest me anymore. I was ready for a man. And Austin was ready, too—ready for me, just like I was ready for him."

"From the expression on Holloway's face," Friedman whispered, "it doesn't look like this is in the script."

"He's trying to look sad," Hastings whispered. "But he's looking sick instead."

"Hallelujah."

". . . saw each other in town, at his hotel. So, of course, everyone in town knew, or at least suspected—which is the same as knowing in that town. But I didn't care. I was in love, really in love, for the first time. And, besides, Austin had promised to take me with him when he left town.

"But then my daddy found out. And he came to Austin's hotel room, and he found us in bed together."

"Jesus *Christ*." Flournoy gestured furiously. "Cut the mike at the pulpit. Keep the camera on them, but cut the sound."

Instantly, the loudspeaker in the control booth went dead.

"Get the choir singing. *Quick.*"

Obeying, the director spoke into his microphone. Onstage, the curtain flicked. Pastor Bob's eyes moved to the parted curtain. Then Pastor Bob turned to the choir, said something, raised his hand.

"Come in on Austin's face," Flournoy snapped. "His expression, it's good. Hold on it, with the choir singing."

"Right." On the control console, toggles were flicked, tiny lights came on and off.

"And Daddy went crazy. He just went crazy. It was like his sermons on hellfire and damnation, everything he ever preached, had all come together. It was at night, I remember, a Thursday night. And he stood before us, and called down the wrath of God on us, and damned us for all eternity. And then he said he was going to take me home, and lay his belt to me, and then lock me in a closet. And then he was going to go to the sheriff, he said, and swear out a complaint against Austin for rape. And on Sunday, from the pulpit, he would do it again, damn Austin for eternity. And he would damn me, too, for a fallen woman.

"And that's what he did. He took me home, dragged me home, really, like he did when I was little, and he was going to whip me. He dragged me home, and he made me lean over the dining room table, just like he always used to do, and he whipped me. And between every stroke, he'd call up to God, and recite from the Bible, too—whichever verse fitted. And then he locked me in the hall closet, just like he said he would, and he set off to find the sheriff. I don't know why he didn't phone. Maybe that wouldn't've been appropriate, he didn't think, for something so serious. But, anyhow, I heard him leave the house. And I remember thinking that he'd gone insane, really crazy."

"Look at the press section," Flournoy grated. "They can *hear* her. They're hearing every word, every goddamn word."

"And then, because I'd cried so much, and hurt so bad, I pushed the shoes out of the way on the floor of the closet, and I went to sleep. And the next thing I knew, I was awake, and trying to understand where I was, and what'd happened, and who was calling to me, calling out my name, like they were scared for me. And then I realized that it was the sheriff that was calling for me. So I hollered back, and they let me out. It was still dark outside— it was in the wee hours. And—" Her voice fell, hushed by the pain of distant recall. Gripping the pulpit with both hands, looking squarely at the nearest of the three cameras, she spoke softly, without inflection. "And they told me that my daddy was dead, that he'd been killed while he was walking to town, along the path that led through the fields. He'd been hit in the head—hit in the head and robbed. And right away, I knew what had happened. So I went to Austin, the first chance that I got, and I told him that I knew Mitchell had killed my daddy. Of course, Austin never let on, never admitted that I was right. But he didn't deny it, either. He just never answered me, and never talked about it, ever again. And I was pregnant, even though I didn't know it then, and so Austin married me. I don't think he would've done it, married me, if it hadn't been that I was pregnant. Because I could see, just looking in his eyes, that he was already tired of me. But maybe he was thinking about what I'd said, about how my daddy died. Maybe he was worried about what I'd say if he left me."

As the choir began to sing, loud in the speaker, the director turned to face Flournoy. "Let's cut away from Holloway. He sees the red light on the camera, but he doesn't know the sound's off. There're no lights to show whether the sound's off. He's getting uptight."

"Of course he knows the sound's off. The fucking choir's singing," Flournoy flared.

"But—"

"And his expression's okay. Still okay. He looks like he's taking her confession, for Christ's sake."

"But—"

"Give it a few more seconds," Flournoy ordered. "Then cut to the choir. I'll tell you when."

* * *

"So we got married. We left town, and we got married, up in Chicago. And it was just about then that Austin started in radio, and then later in TV. And before any of us really knew what was happening, Austin was famous. There's five years' difference between Gloria and Elton. But by the time Elton was born, Austin was famous, or at least getting famous. And I was glad for him, too. Even though we'd grown apart, and never saw much of each other, except sometimes when he'd come to me in the dark, into my bed, I was glad for him. And, of course, all that time, I tried not to think about my daddy, and about how he died. And I tried not to think about Elton, either. Because Elton—" She drew a deep, measured breath and dropped her eyes to the pulpit, to the purse she now held with both hands. Almost inaudibly, still with her eyes lowered, staring at the purse, she said, "Elton was never really right. Even when he was little, just a little child, he was always a stranger. Sometimes, to myself, I'd call him my little stranger, and I'd pray that he'd be all right. I—" She shook her head, tightened her fingers on the purse. "I didn't think I had a right to ask God for more than that, because of why my father died, how he wouldn't've died except for me, except for what I did when I was sixteen with Austin.

"But that prayer was never answered, because Elton was never normal. I can say that now. I've got to say it now. That's why I'm here, what I'm going to do . . ." As she spoke, she turned to face her husband, still standing a few feet away. His face, she saw, was pale as death. And his mouth was twisted into a death's-head smile. Did he seem to be shrinking inside his clothes, shriveling to the size of an ordinary man?

"Look at Holloway," Friedman whispered. "He's *green*."
Sitting far forward in his chair, his eyes intently fixed on Marvella's face, Hastings made no reply.

"Cut," Flournoy hissed. *"Cut to the choir."*
* * *

"The truth is," Marvella was saying, still facing her husband, "that Elton was insane. He was always insane, probably. But when he got close to twenty, he got worse, much worse. And it had to do with—with sex. It started when Elton would begin by preaching to prostitutes on the streets, or wherever, then end up shouting at them and beating them. Once he was badly beaten himself by one of their pimps. We thought Elton would lose an eye that time. And I remember thinking, then, that maybe he'd stop, because of the beating. And he did stop, too. At least we— we thought he'd stopped. But then the—the prostitutes started to die. They were strangled. At first I—I didn't believe that it was Elton. I still can't believe it was Elton, even though I know, really, that he did it, killed those women. But the police never came, never asked about Elton, about the killings. Not until—"

She broke off, took her eyes from the sickly spectacle of her husband's face, looked reflectively down at the purse. As if they were a stranger's fingers, part of a stranger's hand, she saw her fingers working at the clasp, opening the purse. And now her voice, too, was a stranger's:

"Not until just this last Wednesday," she was saying, "did the police come. And then, the next day, Lloyd started following Elton, wherever he went—"

—as the fingers closed around the cold steel of Austin's revolver—

"—just like Lloyd followed my daddy, all those years ago—"

—as, yes, the revolver was free of the purse, coming up to chest level—

"Christ!" On his feet, Hastings drew his revolver, raised the weapon. Shouting, *"Hold it,"* as the sights steadied, lined up on Marvella's chest. *"Hold it!"*

Beside him, above the sudden frenzy of hysterical voices Friedman was shouting, "Wait, Frank. *Wait. Don't."*

Conscious of the scene's slow-motion momentum, aware that he was helpless, an actor rooted to the stage, Holloway saw the revolver—yes, his own revolver—moving inexorably toward him, immobilizing him, impaling him, draining him of everything but fear. As it moved, the muzzle grew larger, as someone had once said it would, aimed directly at him now, with Marvella's face behind the gun. And behind Marvella's head, just to the left, he saw the camera lens. Finally, the red light had gone out—too late. More than two hundred affiliates, all of them witnesses . . .

. . . all of it consumed in a flash of blinding brightness. Gone.

Seeing the pistol drop to the floor of the stage beside the pulpit, murmuring something that could have been a prayer of thanks, Hastings lowered his revolver, unfired.